By Andrea Stewart

The Drowning Empire

The Bone Shard Daughter
The Bone Shard Emperor
The Bone Shard War

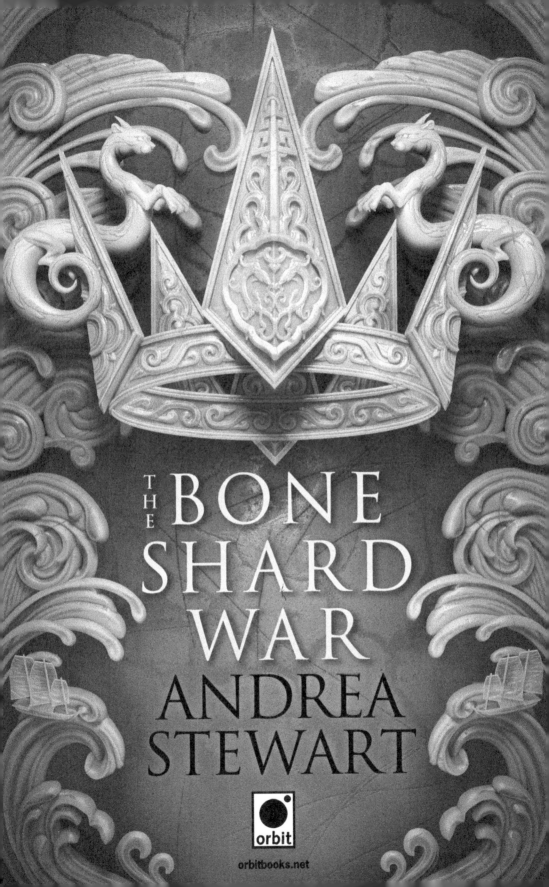

THE BONE SHARD WAR

ANDREA STEWART

orbit

orbitbooks.net

ORBIT

First published in Great Britain in 2023 by Orbit

Copyright © 2023 by Andrea Stewart

The moral right of the author has been asserted.

*All characters and events in this publication, other than those
clearly in the public domain, are fictitious and any resemblance
to real persons, living or dead, is purely coincidental.*

Map illustration by Charis Loke

A CIP catalogue record for this book
is available from the British Library.

Hardback 978-0-356-51503-8
C format 978-0-356-51502-1

Typeset in Fournier by M Rules
Printed and bound in Great Britain by Clays Ltd, Elcograf, S.p.A.

Papers used by Orbit are from well-managed forests
and other responsible sources.

Orbit
An imprint of
Little, Brown Book Group
Carmelite House
50 Victoria Embankment
London EC4Y 0DZ

An Hachette UK Company
www.hachette.co.uk

www.orbitbooks.net

*For my brother, Kavin, who is always
encouraging me to dream bigger*

THE PHOENIX EMPIRE IN THE SUKAI DYNASTY

RIYA

DEERHEAD

MONKEY'S TAIL

I

Nisong

Gaelung Island

Nisong was used to death. She was even used to having death follow her from place to place, content as a pup on the heels of its master. But she hadn't counted on it coming for her throat.

"I told you they'd be after me," Ragan hissed.

She clutched his arm, pulling him close so she could whisper into his ear. "Quiet." Lozhi crouched on her other side in the ruins, a soft whine in his throat.

Ragan shrugged off her hand. "Take it *out*. You wanted to wait? Fine. The time is now."

She wanted to walk away and to keep walking until she had no idea where she was or where he was, no matter how hard she'd worked to find him after the battle at Gaelung. Several months of scraping by, of avoiding discovery, of frenzied searching in the midst of grief. She'd tracked him to a drinking hall, though it had taken her a moment to recognize him. He'd smelled of sour sweat, his once-shorn hair grown over his ears. He hadn't been wearing the monk's robes anymore; he'd traded those in for farmer's clothes – all in brown and faded white, with a straw hat to hide his face. It had taken a long time for them to come to an understanding. He'd fought her every step of the way, convinced he didn't need to rely on anyone, least of all a construct. But she was the only one other than Lin who could remove the shard from his body and she dangled this knowledge like a fishing lure, teasing and pulling away, waiting for him to finally bite.

Not that she'd removed it yet. There had been a few times she'd considered doing so, but each time she'd stopped. This was the only lever she held over him.

His breath warmed her ear. "You've left it in me for two years now. If you don't take it out, we'll both die here."

Nisong clenched her teeth until she felt they might crack. He just needed to stop *talking*. For a moment, he was blessedly silent and then she heard it again – the soft brush of bodies slithering through underbrush. If it had been raining, she wouldn't have heard that first cracking twig. They'd have sat in their little campsite in the Alanga ruins, the sky slowly going dark, blissfully unaware of the people sneaking up on them, arguing until their throats were slit. Admittedly, she'd at first dismissed his insistence that someone was hunting down the Alanga. When they'd heard of the tenth Alanga death, he'd begged and pleaded. "They'll come for me next," he'd said, drunk, tears in his eyes, his hands held out to her. "Do you want to be responsible? How can I defend myself if I cannot kill those who would kill me?"

By then, she'd had to readjust her viewpoints. Someone *was* assassinating Alanga. She just wasn't sure who. Still, she resisted removing the shard that Lin had placed into Ragan's body. She knew by now how quickly he could turn from kindness to anger if she didn't give him what he wanted. Nisong could still feel his fingers around her throat as he'd threatened her after that first time, trying to force her to do what he'd asked. She'd only laughed; he couldn't do anything more than apply light pressure to her neck. His intention was always to kill, never to injure – in this way he was so predictable. The command Lin had placed in him always stopped him.

Lozhi pressed against her side and Nisong stroked the beast's cheek absentmindedly. Better if the creature could calm down enough to help them. He'd grown to the size of a pony and looked quite intimidating now, but he still cowered around men. He still cowered around Ragan.

She needed to think. Her other hand found the cudgel at her belt. Ragan would be useless in a fight; he'd never learned to temper his emotions. He'd just want to kill these would-be assassins and then he wouldn't be able to do the least bit of harm. But he could do things other than fight them. She checked the ruins around them, the small fire they'd built flickering with every gust of wind, the water gathered in between broken tiles. Everywhere, the jungle seemed to encroach on crumbling ruins. She could use this terrain to their advantage. They both could.

"We won't die here if you listen to me. We keep our backs to this corner. Don't bother trying to use your sword. There, there and there." She pointed to places where the ruins were broken, where a little pressure would make them crumble. "Lozhi and I will push them toward these areas. Don't watch the fighting. When I ask you to, shake the earth." She held out a hand. "Give me Lozhi's shards."

He glared at her. She glared back.

For a moment she thought he might refuse. He only let her have them when he knew exactly what she would do with them, when he could supervise her closely. Because if Lin had used a shard from her ossalen's horns to subdue him, how much more could Nisong do if given the chance? But then he reached for his belt, untied the pouch and handed it to her.

Bones clicked against one another as it settled into her palm. Only a few left. Her engraving tool was in her sash pocket. She tied the pouch to her belt but didn't have time to say anything else.

The assassins chose that moment to materialize out of the brush, dressed in dark clothing, only their blades glinting by firelight. Nisong pulled her cudgel loose and went to meet them. Lozhi didn't follow at her side, but she could feel his presence at her back. Distantly, her mind cataloged and assessed. Even when she'd had to acknowledge that Alanga were being killed, she'd thought it the work of disgruntled and angry citizens. No matter what Lin did to try and integrate these new Alanga into society, old prejudices died hard. Her predecessors had spent years painting the Alanga as the enemy and themselves as the saviors. That sort of thing didn't change overnight. Or even in the span of two years. But now, seeing these assassins, she had to acknowledge they weren't just townsfolk. These were professionals. Five of them.

Which meant she was in a good deal of trouble.

She feinted as the first one approached, letting herself appear small, weak. When he darted in with his blade to take advantage, she slammed her cudgel into the side of his head. He crumpled. Four left, and none of those would fall for the same trick. They slowed, circling like hungry wolves. Their faces were not covered, but they might as well have been. Each of their expressions was a mask of grim determination, showing neither pity nor fear.

Lozhi whimpered behind her. Three of the remaining assassins were men.

For the first time in a long time, Nisong felt a quaver of fear in her heart. She'd been subsisting with Ragan – unable to fully trust him but also unable to make much progress in her goals.

There had been small victories. They'd worked with the Ioph Carn for a couple of jobs, bringing in enough money to live comfortably for nearly a year. And she'd had a few chances to experiment with Lozhi's shards, building smaller, simpler constructs. Each of his shed horns only allowed for twenty shards – so with forty in total, she couldn't build an army. But she'd built two little spies – neither of which were currently here.

Taking back the Empire? Making Lin and all those close to her suffer? It seemed a laughable goal now, though she burned for it. She *needed* it. She *would* survive because this was the only thing that would make the deaths of her friends worth something.

Nisong's gaze darted about as she tried to keep track of all four assassins. She didn't feel the warmth of Lozhi's presence at her back anymore, and she'd stepped beyond the protection of the partially caved-in roof. The oppressive early-evening air settled over her shoulders, the humidity smothering as a wet cloth at her nose and mouth. Dimly, she registered a mosquito whining past her ear.

All four of the assassins darted in at once.

She swung her cudgel wildly, forcing two of them back. One of them missed as he sliced at her side, but she felt a sting across her calf, a shock, and knew the last one had found her mark. A trickle of warmth, but not a rush, which meant it couldn't be that deep. She gritted her teeth and pushed forward. If she could just get two of them beneath that wall ... She'd still have to hope it fell in their direction, but she'd have hope.

"Now!" she called out.

The ground trembled beneath their feet. Nisong, who had been expecting it, nearly lost her footing. Tiles cracked; stones tumbled. She held her breath as the wall she'd urged the assassins toward crumbled and fell.

It fell away from them, carved stones and plaster tumbling

down the slope, disappearing into the long grass. Nisong backed away but then whirled, remembering she'd left two more behind her. They'd closed in, cutting her off from the guttering fire. Beyond them she could see Ragan, obediently facing the wall. Lozhi had stopped as she'd advanced, his belly low to the ground, ears flat against his head, his gray eyes wide.

"Did that do it?" Ragan called to her.

She heard footsteps rushing in behind her. She pivoted again, knowing that it would only open her up to attack by the other assassins. She met the two in front of her with her cudgel raised. At least she'd die fighting. At least she'd die cursing the names of everyone who'd wronged her. For Shell, for Frond, for Leaf and for Coral.

A gray furry shape rushed in front of her, nearly knocking her off her feet. Lozhi snapped at the two assassins, seizing one by the arm and tossing him into the underbrush. He seized the leg of the next one, teeth sinking deep. The man screamed, slashing at Lozhi's face. The beast ignored the blows. Nisong knew from experience that he'd quickly heal from any cuts. "Leave!" he cried out. "Leave alone!" He stalked toward a third assassin who'd come to help his fellows.

For a moment, she couldn't move. Nisong knew that ossalen could speak, but it was the most she'd ever heard Lozhi say. She'd come to think of him as a silent companion, one who said more with his gaze than with his mouth. The sound of steel being drawn came from behind her. She glanced over her shoulder.

The remaining two assassins advanced on Ragan. She cursed her foolishness — of course they were after him. If they killed him, she'd be back where she'd started. No friends, no one to help her. Alone. She hastily pulled the shards from her pouch, carving commands onto them. And then she rushed toward their backs.

One of them turned to face her, but the other one didn't.

Nisong calmed her breathing, forced herself into the concentrated, meditative state and then pushed her hand toward the woman's torso. Her knuckles cracked against a hard leather breastplate. For a moment, all she could do was curl her hurt hand at her chest, the edges of the shard digging into her palm. It should have *worked*. Sometimes she'd been too distracted, too hasty, and she hadn't been able to use the bone shard magic.

She'd only ever tried Lozhi's shards on Alanga, not on mortals. Did it not work the same way for them? Was this weakness only unique to the Alanga?

There wasn't time to examine hypotheses. Her cudgel felt heavy in her hand as she swung it, trying to keep the two assassins at bay. The woman sliced back at her while the remaining man lifted his blade over Ragan's back. Nisong blocked him with her cudgel, barely in time. "Behind you!" she called to Ragan. He whipped about, drawing his sword in one smooth movement. He caught the assassin's sword and then kicked out, fast and hard. The man tumbled.

The woman Nisong was fighting drew her blade back, circling and then lashing out again. She was used to the thick of battle against semi-skilled opponents. Not assassins, trained to take out opponents one-on-one. She dodged to the side and felt her injured leg give out as she stepped on a fallen stone. The assassin's blade glinted above her.

Ragan came to her rescue this time, his sword flashing between her and the assassin. Briefly, his gaze met hers. "We have to trust one another or we'll both die." And then he stood in front of her, sword lifted to meet the assassin's. She glanced down the slope and saw Lozhi, bloodied, three more assassins materializing from the bushes to surround him. They'd brought backup.

Part of her raged – how could he ask her to trust him? He'd tried to kill her once, no matter how ineffectually. Another part of her acknowledged that he'd given her the shards, that it had been two years, that unleashing Ragan was a chance she had to take if she wanted to make any progress toward Imperial.

She took a half-step forward and put one hand on his shoulder, another between his shoulder-blades. "Stay as still as possible," she whispered into his ear. "Focus only on defending yourself and me; don't think about striking back."

His muscles tensed as the assassin attacked. It was difficult not to pay attention to what was going on beyond the wall of Ragan's back, but she knew him well enough by now. He wouldn't be able to hold his temper for long. As soon as he thought about killing them, he wouldn't even be able to lift his blade. She needed to be quick.

Nisong breathed in deep, closed her eyes and pushed her hand into Ragan's body.

This time, the body yielded beneath her fingertips, clothing and bones gone insubstantial. It was like dragging her fingers beneath the surface of a warm pond, with a little more pressure and a little less give. His body jerked around her hand as he blocked the assassins' blows; she felt the tremor of his bones and flesh as his muscles tensed, as he called on the power that Lozhi's bond had given him. From somewhere, she heard the sound of rushing water. The humidity she'd felt only a moment before dried up. And then she found it: a sharp-edged brightness within him, a shade warmer than the rest.

He will kill you, Coral's voice whispered in her mind. *In the end, he will kill you.*

She ignored it, wrapped her fingers around the shard and pulled it free.

The change was quick, as stark as a room with all the lamps blown out. Even the assassins must have sensed it. They hesitated. The sky grew dark as full night, the guttering fire the only illumination. Ragan stepped forward with a confidence he hadn't borne only a moment ago. "Don't go," he said, his voice soft. "Not yet."

The woman attacked first. He slid past her swing and gutted her smoothly and calmly as he might have a fish. At the same time, he brought the water down.

He must have been gathering it while he'd still had the shard within him. It looked like an ocean's worth of water dumping from the skies. Lozhi let out a little cry of delight as he bounded around his disoriented attackers, biting legs, arms and torsos. Most of the water fell to the ground, but some of it hovered in spheres around the heads of the assassins. Nisong watched, dread choking her as the assassins clawed at their faces, as they gurgled uselessly, as they tried to shake the water loose. And Ragan stood there, his hands lifted, black hair wet and sodden about his face, his expression cold and murderous.

No regret, no mercy in that one.

One by one, they fell, until the ruins were silent once more. Ragan turned to face her and she wondered if this was how past mortals felt when they'd displeased an Alanga. She swallowed past the ache in her throat. "You still need me," she managed.

Lozhi padded back up the slope, winding first around her and then returning to Ragan's side where he sat, ears flicking back and forth.

Ragan lifted a hand and she waited for the sphere of water she knew was coming. She didn't have it in her to fight back, not when he was so much stronger than she was. She'd only look foolish and that wasn't how she wanted to die. She'd face her death head-on, as she'd faced everything since she'd first awoken from the mind-fog.

But he only pointed past her, his stony expression breaking into a grim smile. Relief swelled within her, washing away the tightness in her throat and making her legs weak. It took her a moment to see where he was pointing. Past the treetops, in the distance, the lamps of Gaelung's palace glittered like fireflies. "There. That is where we're going next."

He strode up to her, her heart beating in time with his steps. He held out his hand. "Give me the shards." There was a hardness in his voice and a glint in his eye she didn't like. He'd enjoyed killing those assassins. She might have been accustomed to death following in her footsteps, but Ragan treated it like a trusted friend. All he needed was an excuse.

She untied the pouch and let it drop into his palm. "You have a plan?" she said, and was pleased that her voice didn't tremble. She needed to maintain control.

He hadn't drawn back his hand. "The other one too."

Only once he spoke did she feel the point of it digging into her palm. The shard she'd taken from his chest. Nisong opened her fingers over his hand and it joined the pouch. She couldn't seem to calm her heartbeat, her mind racing through all the implications of what she'd done.

He closed his fingers around all of the shards. And then his face relaxed, as though he hadn't just drowned all those assassins, as though he hadn't stood over her, his expression begging her to give him a reason to do the same to her. "Of course I have a plan." He gazed out over the treetops toward the palace. "We're going to go on a little tour, you and I. We're going to remind them all what it's like to live with Alanga."

2

Lin

Imperial Island

Lin Sukai. 1522–1525. I watched the flames lick up the side of the ripped piece of paper I'd taken with me from the census book, turning the corner from brown to black and then to ash. I should have burned the thing years ago, should have hidden my origins better, but it was a part of my past – a reminder of who I was and where I'd come from.

I was Lin. I was Emperor. I was Alanga. The savior of Gaelung. That could be the whole of my story. My mind could be record enough of where I'd actually come from: grown from parts in the pool beneath the palace, stuffed with the memories of my father's dead wife and set to wander the palace in search of keys. I needed to have my wits about me for this; I needed to be unshakable in my knowledge of who I was now.

Above me, heavy footfalls creaked, claws scraped against the deck and the ship listed to one side. Thrana had insisted on coming along, and really, there was nothing I could have done to stop her. She was larger than a war horse now, and could swim nearly as quickly as a ship burning witstone. She didn't fit in my cabin anymore, though not for lack of trying. She'd become used to curling up next to my bed in the palace, her head resting on my mattress. My hand resting on her head.

I dropped the paper to the bottom of the lantern, letting it burn out. Something about the color of it, the way it shriveled, reminded me of the box.

Two years ago, the palace guards had found the box at the gates, labeled with my name, though no one could tell me who'd placed it there or when. One of my maidservants had insisted on being the one to open it in case the box was trapped with blades or poisons. But there hadn't been either.

Instead, there'd only been a note – *So you have something to burn* – and beneath that, a leathery piece of skin. I felt it all over again, the jolt to my ribs, the sensation of the world going still around me, the weightlessness of my mind. And then the crushing, crippling pain. Shutting the box hadn't made its contents any less real. Because inked into that piece of skin had been a rabbit tattoo.

Jovis had promised he'd return to me. In his own small way, he'd kept that promise.

Grief and anger poured over me, sluicing like the storm water outside. I let it drench me, let it fill me to the brim. And then, slowly, it drained away, leaving me exhausted and helpless. It had been two years, and still I woke hoping that it hadn't been real. I wished I could rid myself of that hope so I could stop realizing all over again that it had indeed happened, that Jovis was gone. That I'd wandered so far now into this branching reality that even the remembered scent of him had become hazy, indistinct. I couldn't quite recall the exquisite way our bodies had fit together, the feel of his hands in my hair. Had he told me he loved me or had that only been a dream?

And there was the anger. He'd lied to me, only admitting that he'd been spying on me for the Shardless Few once he'd been caught. I'd never had a chance to shout at him again for the lies, to hear him apologize once more, to feel the tightness in my chest easing with each repetition and response until I found my way to healing and forgiveness. I would have forgiven him had I only been given the chance. I wasn't sure I could forgive myself. I shouldn't have let him go after Mephi alone, to face Kaphra with only his steel staff and his magic and no one at his side. But I was an Emperor. I had obligations. Numeen, Thrana, Bayan... Jovis. I supposed sometimes death was being rushed from a play mid-scene, and never getting to know the rest of it. Regret was a feeling I had to live with. There was too much still to be done.

A knock sounded at my cabin door. I swallowed my sorrows and checked inside the lantern. There was no trace of the burnt page – only ashes and embers. "Yes?"

"We're ready to disembark," one of my guard's voices said through the wood.

"I'll be right out." Quickly, I swung my oilskin cloak over my finery, ensuring my boots were snug and my white-bladed sword fastened tightly at my side. I'd remove it before any formal talks, but I wanted Iloh and his people to remember who they were dealing with. I'd not just brought an army to Gaelung to meet the constructs; I'd fought in that battle. I was not a person sitting on a throne, ruling from afar; I was invested in the safety of my people and I would defend them by whatever means I had at my disposal.

Even if it meant stopping a governor from mining his own island into the bedamned sea.

The downpour had not abated by the time I made my way above-deck. It was a wonder my cabin was dry at all. Thrana appeared at my side. "Good fishing weather!" she said, shaking off the rain. Her spiraling horns branched twice now, the black surfaces slick and gleaming. I couldn't tell if she'd been back in the water recently, or if it was just the rain that had drenched her.

My guards fell in behind me. One of them gestured to the hold, where several boxes of witstone lay. "Should we bring the witstone up to the palace?" I still remembered, years ago, stealing a handful of witstone from one of my father's stores. Back then, the supply had seemed limitless – enough to fill entire rooms. But the more we used, the less we had, and at some point everyone would run out – fostering isolation. And the Ioph Carn kept harrying my ships, stealing and smuggling what witstone they could, exacerbating the problem. But "low" was not "empty" and it was still a problem for another day. Iloh was a problem for today.

"No, not yet." I'd had time to form plans on the way to Riya. The winds had fortunately been favorable, the trip quick. We hadn't flown the Imperial flag. He wouldn't know I was coming and I preferred it that way. The man had been a thorn in my side ever since I'd put a moratorium on witstone mining. Now that thorn had turned into a dagger poised to plunge into my heart. "It's quicker if I go alone. Follow after me with the witstone."

Before my guards could protest, I mounted Thrana and urged her to the gangplank. It bent beneath her weight so sharply I thought it might crack. But then we were onto the docks, people moving out of our way, exclaiming at Thrana's appearance. Alanga had been returning to the Empire, but none of their ossalen were quite Thrana's size yet. She maneuvered through the late-morning crowd with a gracefulness that seemed impossible given her bulk. I felt her shoulders roll beneath me and loosened my hips to maintain my center of balance. The main street of Riya's capital city rose from the docks in a gentle slope. Some of the stone lanterns lining the street were still lit, their light doing little to cut through the gloom. People stumbled out of the door of a drinking hall near the docks, smoke wisping after them into the rain. A whiff of fresh steamed bread reached me, only to be whisked away in a puff of wind in the next moment. Even the rain couldn't completely drown out the smell of fish and rotting seaweed.

It faded the farther up the hill we climbed. I felt the way Thrana drew everyone's gazes, heard the whispers we left in our wake. The palace walls rose before us, the tops lined with blue tiles. The gates were open, guards standing on either side, a few servants moving in and out. I slid from Thrana's back while she was still moving, water splashing beneath my boots, my momentum carrying me forward and toward the gates. With a quick flick of my hand, I removed the hood of my cloak.

"I am here to see Iloh."

The guards stared at me. No one said a word.

"Well? Will you let me pass or will you refuse the Emperor an audience with her governor?"

That got them moving. I'd put them in a difficult position – should they send someone to Iloh and make the Emperor wait? – but I couldn't be sorry for it. One of the guards slipped away to tell Iloh, and another moved to the side to give me larger passage. Yet another put up her hand as if to stop me and then thought better of it. I felt Thrana's hot breath on the back of my neck and strode confidently into the courtyard.

Men and women rushed out of our way as I followed the guard I'd presumed had gone to tell Iloh. It wasn't until we reached the entrance hall that he noticed me following him. He blanched, stopped, shifted from foot to foot, opened his mouth, shut it and then turned to resume his path.

"Is he in his study?" I called after him as I dogged his steps. "His bedchambers?"

He was in his dining hall. As soon as I saw where the guard

was headed, I overtook him and placed my hand on the door-knob. He drew his hand away before he committed the grave offense of touching me without my permission. My father had been known to execute people for that.

"Eminence," the guard finally ventured, "if you'd only sent word—"

I stared him down and he backed away, hands raised as though afraid I might attack him. Or maybe he was afraid Thrana would. I felt her looming behind me, a constant presence. From behind the door I heard muffled voices. "And what of everyone else? If we secede and no one else follows? She still has an army."

"And Alangan magic," someone else added.

I flung the door open.

Iloh sat at the table, several men and women sitting with him. He hadn't changed much in the past two years, his straight black hair tied back, his beard neatly trimmed. The lines of his face might have been deeper but it also might have been a trick of the light. Bright and calculating eyes fixed on mine, and though I registered surprise there, he quickly hid it. He sat on his cushion with the upright ease of someone who knew how to appear relaxed in even the most tense of situations. I recognized a couple of those near him – governors of islands near Riya – and the others I did not. But I had the sense from the richness of their clothes and their immaculately groomed hairstyles that they were powerful and important.

So. The rumors were true. He'd not just been hounding me to allow witstone mining again; he'd roped other governors into his schemes. If even Riya seceded, however, the Empire would fracture.

It took them a moment to register who I was and what I was doing there. Everyone else was not quite so stoic as Iloh. Faces paled, gazes darting to both the sword at my side and Thrana's large head over my shoulder. And then they rose, all of them bowing. I caught several hands trembling and felt some measure of satisfaction. They *should* be afraid, fomenting rebellion against the Emperor. Thrana sat on her haunches as I walked further into the room. "Eminence," they all murmured.

I returned their bows with a tilt of my head.

Deliberately, I unstrapped my sword, made my way to the table and sat upon an empty cushion. Everyone else sat as well, the tension lifting only marginally. I wasn't here to serve as executioner.

"You didn't tell me you were visiting," Iloh said, his voice as smooth and deep as the Endless Sea on a windless day.

Then again, I wasn't here to befriend anyone either. "Don't think I haven't noticed the rumors, the unrest, the resentment — all wafting from Riya like the stink of a days' old fish." I set my sword on the table but did not remove my hands from it. My neighbors on either side of me leaned slightly away. The day was not overly warm, but I caught the bead of sweat on the face of the woman to my left. "And now I find you *conspiring* against me."

Iloh waved a dismissive hand. "We were discussing, not conspiring. You happened upon a private conversation, not one that is meant to be taken seriously."

"And yet all of these governors have traveled here to be in this room. No matter what you may think of me, I am not naive, Iloh." I wanted to rebuke him more severely; I wanted to draw my sword and make him tremble before me — but I still needed Riya's support. "Tell me exactly what it is you want."

We both knew but I wanted him to say it. I wanted to make him defend his foolish decisions in front of the other governors — so that I might defend mine.

Iloh sighed, as though he knew exactly what I was thinking.

"We need you to lift the ban on witstone mining. While Imperial may have its own stores to bridge this gap, other islands are beginning to suffer. It's taking too long for goods to get from one place to another. No islands have sunk since Luangon. It's time for the mines to reopen."

No doubt he had a vested interest in this policy changing, given that Riya had the largest mines of all the islands. "No islands have sunk *because* of this policy."

Iloh scoffed. "Surely a small bit of mining won't sink us."

"We cannot know that," I said. I glanced about the table, and only two of the governors dared to meet my gaze. Finally, I let go of the sword, tried to temper the sharpness in my voice. I'd reminded them of who I was. Now it was time to remind them why I'd enacted the ban in the first place. "The ban is temporary. I have the smartest people at the Scholars' Academy on Hualin Or working on the problem. As soon as we have more information or a solution that allows us to use less witstone, I promise things will return to normal."

"The way you promised me to help develop Pulan's mine?" Iloh spat back.

Oh, he would dig and worry at that broken promise like a dog licking at the very last marrow in a bone. I wanted to shout back that it was not my fault, but knew that would only make me seem a child. He'd successfully made me seem the fool before. I'd not let him do that to me again. "As your Emperor, I have to keep the best interests of all citizens at the forefront of my mind. It's not in my nature to break promises, but new information warrants new strategies."

"And how is that strategy working out for us? For the Empire?" Iloh gestured broadly. I watched those around him nod, given courage by his boldness. "You are an Alanga. We all know this now. You worked miracles at the Battle of Gaelung.

And yet you cannot solve this one thing? Are we really supposed to believe this is beyond your power? It's been two years!"

Two years of scraping by, of calculating how little witstone we could use, of trying my best to distribute caro nuts equitably. And all the while, grieving the man I'd just come to love, whom I still didn't know exactly how to forgive. Iloh couldn't know what it had cost me. I didn't think he would have cared if he had. "So you think I'm doing this on purpose?"

His lip curled. "Your father often played such games with his governors."

Before I could stop myself, I was on my feet, my ears ringing, hands lifted to the stormy skies. The rainwater obeyed my commands, sliding in between the cracks of the shutters, coalescing on the floor into larger and larger droplets – until we were surrounded by a moat of water, knee deep. It roiled, tendrils of it lashing out and making the people sitting at the table jump. Iloh's face paled, his hands curling into fists so tight that his knuckles whitened.

I heard the shuffle of feet behind me and knew I'd unsettled my guards too.

"Don't think this will frighten me into keeping my silence," Iloh said, though his lips trembled. "Riya will secede if it doesn't get what it needs."

And there it was – the threat I'd been fearing ever since I'd taken the throne. He'd break this Empire apart and sink his own island, all to satisfy his coffers. "Riya will *not*," I said. The water surged.

He let out a hollow laugh. "And what will you do to stop me? Murder me?"

Thrana's nose touched my elbow and that was all it took. I'd worked so hard to differentiate myself from my father, to ensure that my rule would be different. Shiyen would have threatened

Iloh with the same fate the man's mother had met – death by the shard sickness. He would have sent his constructs to watch Iloh's every move, to loom over those he cared about.

I wasn't Shiyen. And much as I didn't want to admit it, I needed Iloh. Carefully, I lowered my hands, directed the water back between the shutters and into the storm outside. There had to be things I could offer him, ways I could make him understand. "I'd like to speak to Iloh alone." I kept my voice soft as I sank back onto my cushion.

They fled from the room as though I'd shouted.

And then it was just me and Thrana and Iloh, the sound of rain dripping down gutters filtering in from outside. We regarded one another in silence. I could see his pulse quicken at his throat, the way his chest rose and fell rapidly. He was not as at ease as he wished to appear. I'd frightened him. I wasn't sure whether to feel satisfied or irritated with myself. My father had often let his temper rule him. I couldn't allow myself to do the same. I'd come here intending to intimidate him only a little, just enough so that he'd take me seriously.

I wouldn't murder him. I wouldn't threaten him. I folded my hands in my lap, arranging my skirts. "Witstone is the problem."

"Yes," he responded. He let out a soft huff of breath, though it didn't have the venom behind it that his earlier scoffing did. "Obviously."

"We still have stores of witstone in the palace. I've been holding it in reserve, but if you're truly that desperate . . .?"

Iloh shifted in his seat and I could see the struggle on his face. He was desperate but didn't want to admit that he was. "Eminence," he said finally, "it's not just my impatience; it is my people's impatience. Trade has slowed, and with it the flow of goods and money. Luangon was two years ago. We can reopen mining and set quotas. We can be careful."

"I understand your position. And I *am* sorry about Pulan; I didn't—"

He cut a hand through the air, his expression dark. "I don't wish to speak of it."

We lapsed back into silence. A soft knock sounded and a servant entered with tea.

"Give me time. We're close to a solution and I don't wish to risk any more islands sinking. I've brought a small box of witstone with me as a gesture of goodwill, though if we can come to an agreement, I'll send you more. It's all I can spare, but I do want to help." The servant set the teapot between us and left two cups next to it. She bowed and left the room.

"And what am I supposed to do about everyone else? That takes care of Riya for a time, but what about them?"

"This isn't a matter of life or death."

"It is for those with bog cough, waiting for caro nut oil."

I wanted to dash my teacup to the ground in frustration. Someone always had to suffer, no matter what decisions I made. "And you care about every individual on each of these islands?"

He tilted his head and gave a little shrug. "All I'm saying is that it isn't enough. You dictate the use of our lands and Riya wonders if you truly are doing what's in our best interests. Give me a reason not to break this Empire, Eminence. By my reckoning, it's already broken."

Iloh was an opportunist; he wasn't a philanthropist. I had to make this his problem, not just mine. And then, as my hand drifted to Thrana's head to stroke the soft fur behind her ears, I knew what I could offer him. My mind went again to the box, the piece of skin inside, the withering of my dreams. I'd once hoped that when Jovis found his way back to me, we could build a life together. An Emperor and her Captain of the Imperial Guard – not the most advantageous of arrangements, but we could have made it work. I would have *found* a way to make it work.

I needed to keep this Empire together – at all costs. Even if the cost was to myself. I couldn't be Jovis, chasing his dead wife across the Endless Sea. There were people who relied on me. I let the grief rise in me, let it pass through me.

At some point, I had to let go. I just hadn't thought it would be today.

"Be my consort," I said. "Take a place at my side. Together, we can decide what's best for Riya. And for everyone else."

His black eyes widened slightly, his back straightening. Something changed in the way he regarded me and I felt myself being sized up in an entirely different way. I wanted to shrink from his gaze; it was as palpable as the skittering of insect legs against my skin. But I was the one in power here. So I sat still and returned his stare. Iloh was a bit older than me, but that wasn't unheard of in these sorts of arrangements. And he wasn't bad to look at. He was no Jovis, with his graceful brow and long-fingered hands. But then, I was no great beauty either. He was the governor of Riya and the leader of a coalition looking to either unseat me or to break up the Empire. I needed him on my side. That was enough.

He gave a slight nod as though deciding I satisficed. "And in return?"

"You help me keep this Empire together. You help me keep the islands united." I left unsaid the threat we all faced. The Alanga were returning. And beyond that, there'd been skirmishes between citizens and Alanga – fights that bred more distrust. A fractured Empire invited predation, and given everything I'd learned about Dione and Ragan, I would not make the mistake of thinking all Alanga wanted peace.

"We make the announcement soon," he said briskly. "I'll

keep the other governors in line. If you give me that witstone, I can dole it out, give them something to hang on to as I urge them to wait."

Now that I'd made the decision, I wished I could take it back. I'd always known, somewhere in the back of my mind, that I'd need to choose a consort or at least to choose an heir.

"Yes," I said, rising to my feet. "And once you've sorted things, you'll move to the palace. You'll have to choose a steward you can trust to watch over Riya."

He rose as well, approached me hesitantly. I did not step away. He smelled of green tea and the hint of smoke. His presence was wholly different than Jovis's, and it wasn't just that he was shorter. "I know you're not making me this offer out of any great love of me."

I felt the ghost of a smile touch my lips. "Was it the sweeping, romantic proposal that tipped you off?"

He laughed and took my hands. His skin felt papery beneath my palms, his hands thick. I closed my eyes briefly, wishing it was Jovis. Wishing I could feel his lips against my skin one last time. I cut that feeling free, let it drift away with the wind and the rainwater. This was here and now. I could not go back.

I felt the brush of lips against my cheek, the roughness of stubble. His voice sounded in my ear. "If we don't kill one another, I'll count our arrangement a success."

There was a part of me, the larger part, that wanted to pull away from him, to shout, to demand that he obey – that screamed at me not to do this. But Jovis was gone and the Empire needed this, so I merely smiled. "Keep your word, Iloh, that's all I ask." He'd broken it once before – although to be fair, I'd broken mine first. "I'll leave one of my constructs with you – use it to send word to me if there is anything urgent."

A swift knock at the door and then it opened before either of us could respond. I whirled, annoyed and surprised.

One of Iloh's guards stood there, a box in her hands. "Eminence," she said. She held the box stiffly, farther away from her body than seemed comfortable, given its size. "This came for you." She set the box on the table and stepped away.

If Iloh was to be my consort — and I still wanted to run from the thought — then he would be privy to nearly everything. I went to the box and opened it. It felt as though the floor were dropping out from beneath me, my mind floating behind. Somewhere I was aware of my heart beating in a rising crescendo.

Urame's severed head was in the box, smelling strongly of brine and rot. The last I'd seen her we'd been saying our good-byes in her palace study, repair work going on around us as her workers rebuilt broken walls and gates. She'd survived the Battle of Gaelung. And now, two years later, she was dead. I didn't need to ask who'd killed her. One word was carved into her forehead, the flesh red and gaping as the mouths of baby birds.

Ragan.

3

Jovis

In the Endless Sea, south of Riya

I'd always thought that being a ghost would mean haunting all those who'd wronged me. Frightening the man who'd once spat at me as a boy, rearranging the clothes of the teacher at the Navigators' Academy who'd made me sit in the back of the class. A bit spiteful, perhaps, but I imagined it might make me feel alive, if only for a moment. Instead, I found myself standing at the prow of a ship, fingers tracing the messy scar on my wrist, wishing again that things had played out differently. Lin was alive and I was a ghost. I'd grown a small, short beard to mask my features, and I now had another scar across one cheek. As far as most people knew, Jovis was dead. I felt dead, cut free from a life I could no longer return to. I flattered myself sometimes by thinking how Lin must miss me. But no matter how she felt, I couldn't deny that I missed her, that I missed the man I'd been then, conflicted but in love, full of hope.

But those were morose and brooding thoughts, better suited to a world-weary hero than to me. The ship in front of us was burning witstone, but so were we. And I'd made sure I had a damned fast ship. You had to, when you were carrying black market goods and raiding Imperial boats. "Ready yourselves," I called to my crew. "They'll be armed to the teeth, with plenty of Imperial guards to back them up. It won't be an easy fight."

Someone – I wasn't sure who – let out a brief snort. Everyone began their preparations to board. Archers pulled strings from oilskin packets, fitted them to their bows. Others checked their swords and daggers, tightened the buckles on their armor. I paid them little mind; they'd been through this sort of exercise enough times. Each time I said it wouldn't be an easy fight, and each time, my Alangan gifts proved that pronouncement wrong. I wasn't sure if I was making a joke or just hoping that this time I'd be proved right.

The mines might have been shut down, but witstone was a valuable commodity, and valuable commodities were still traded. Which meant they could be stolen and smuggled and sold illegally.

I pulled my steel staff from where it was fastened on my back, feeling the crosshatching of the grip beneath my fingers, drawing my hood over my head. Ready to fight those I'd once protected. I could see the faces of the people on the Imperial ship as they ran back and forth across the deck, could hear the shouts of their captain carried on the wind. The air between the ships seemed filled with white witstone smoke, swirling about the sails like a mist. The smell – like burnt marrow – didn't make me sick the way it did Mephi, but I now found it extremely unpleasant. It roiled my belly, left me with a faint, lingering queasiness for hours afterward.

My crew fired their first volley at the other ship. I ducked behind the rail as they returned fire. Arrows *thunked* into the deck and a tremor started in my bones.

The shouting grew louder. The battle waging around us felt like the burgeoning storm cloud above, dark and ominous. One of my crew near me went down, an arrow wedged into her shoulder, her face twisted in pain. I waited until I heard the knock of the ship's prow against the side of the Imperial ship. And then I sprang to my feet and leapt aboard, a chill wind biting at my cheeks.

I'd raided trading ships before, but this wasn't a trading ship. It was an Imperial caravel, with all the trappings of Imperial. Uniformed soldiers strode across the deck before me; I saw one leveling her bow at me out of the corner of my eye. I'd once fought Imperial soldiers, had stolen children from their Tithing Festival. And then I'd joined Imperial as the Captain of Guard. Now I'd gone so far round the bend I was back where I'd begun, my feet unsure of the path I'd taken.

The deck rocked gently beneath me. A silence descended on my mind, blocking out thoughts of Lin, of my time with her, of my time on Imperial. I was here, on a ship, and I had witstone to find. That was all that mattered.

I ducked, feeling the buzz of the arrow where my neck had been. And then I lifted my staff to meet the first of the soldiers.

I'd lived so much of my life on the Endless Sea, feeling its motion beneath me, comforting as a mother's arms rocking me to sleep. I moved with the swell of the waves, using the rolling of the deck to add force to my blows, to slip away from blades that would otherwise find my flesh. I'd not been formally trained before, but I'd trained with some of the Empire's best fighters in the past two years, not using my Alanga talents and holding back some of my strength.

I'd received a different kind of beating at their hands. But I couldn't complain too much. Not when the staff now felt like a part of me, an extension of my arm that moved with the same precision as my fingertips. Soldiers fell away as I fought, unable to hold their own against my blows. I felt one sword graze the skin of my back, but the wound healed as I retaliated. They circled me, trying to find openings.

"Don't make me do this," I said to them. I nodded to the south. "There's a small isle that way — if you're a good swimmer, you can make it. This route is well traveled. Someone will pick you up."

One of the soldiers gave me an incredulous look. "Don't make you do what? Die?"

The others laughed.

"Don't make me hurt you," I said. "I really don't want to do this, I promise you."

But they didn't listen. They never listen. They rushed in, blades leading the way.

I didn't fight to kill. The men and women I fought would awake with heads aching or would fall against the mast, bones broken, unable to rise to fight me again. A chance — they'd have a chance. My gaze found the hatch leading into the hold. I made my way toward it, batting away a soldier the way someone might a fly.

"*Alanga*," I heard someone behind me mutter. And then someone else shouted the word. I gritted my teeth as I pulled open the hatch and slid down the ladder. There would be a shift in the way they fought against me. More cautious but also more angry. More hateful.

For all that the people of the Empire had once praised me as their hero, I now knew what it felt to be an Alanga who was *not* the Emperor or a folk hero. These two were acceptable; the rest were treated with unease and distrust. In this case, I really couldn't blame them. I *was* attacking their ship.

Footsteps sounded above me. The rest of my crew would

be boarding now, engaging with the soldiers still able to fight, giving me time to search for the witstone. Lamps shone dimly from the walls, barely illuminating the floor beneath my feet. The hold in the ship was small, not meant to carry much cargo. Somehow I knew it wouldn't be so simple, but I turned the place over anyways, feeling like a common thief as I emptied boxes and rifled through crates.

If Lin was sending the witstone to Riya from her personal stores, she would have overseen this operation herself. She knew trading ships were being raided for witstone, so this time she'd chosen an Imperial caravel. But she wouldn't have counted on that being enough cover. Lin was a woman of layers – a sharp, exacting exterior, a tender heart, a hidden identity she'd not revealed to anyone but me . . .

I was getting distracted. The longer I took, the more Imperial soldiers would die.

I'd once smuggled items in a hidden compartment of my ship. I pried at the floorboards, searching for any that felt a bit loose. But that had been the way *I* had hidden things. Frustrated, I left the hold, my staff in hand, tapping it against the boards with every step. There was a sparse crews' quarters. I did a quick search through it and found nothing. Above, someone screamed, the sound running like a shiver down my spine. One of my crew or an Imperial soldier – I couldn't tell.

Think – I had to think.

As much as Lin tried to distance herself from her father, she was like him in many ways. The same piercing gaze, the same intelligence, the same propensity for keeping secrets. She'd hidden things behind the locked doors of her palace, the locked door of her ship's cabin, in the locked chest at the foot of her bed.

I tried the other doors and only found one locked.

I whispered an apology to Lin as I threw my shoulder against it and felt the wood creak. The door didn't budge. I felt a smile touching my lips in spite of myself. She'd had it reinforced. She knew the strength of Alanga and had wanted to plan for all contingencies, it seemed. Trying to ignore the sounds of fighting, I tapped my staff against the wall on either side of the door, listening for a hollow-sounding knock where the wood was thin. And then I swung the steel at the wall.

Wood cracked. I pulled the broken board loose and slipped sideways into the captain's cabin. It was a small, cramped space, but the bed was broad, taking up nearly half the room. I moved for it, knowing somehow that this was where she'd hidden the witstone.

The faint whiff of jasmine wafted into my nostrils as I lifted the mattress. For a moment, I was struck still.

Come back to me. Lin's arm around my neck, another around my back, fingers tracing patterns along my spine. I shivered at the remembered feel of it. I'd made her a promise, one I'd never intended to break. I was a person who kept my promises – or at least I'd thought I was.

But a ghost couldn't keep promises. A ghost could only drift through the world, carried by whispered breaths, by dreams that faded with the morning, by hopes that took too long to die. I didn't have enough substance to contain promises. And then my gaze was focusing on the space beneath the mattress, the dark hollow, the boxes of witstone that lay beneath. I took in a breath and whistled as loudly as I could. I heard shifting from above.

One of my crew members found me, barely managing to squeeze past the boards the way I had. "They're better fighters than we are," she said, breathless. "The Emperor sent her best soldiers with this shipment."

I considered. "Get some of the others and take the boxes. I'll handle the soldiers."

I emerged from below-deck to fighting. A soldier swung a sword at my head as I climbed the ladder, and I lifted my staff to block the blade. I saw the fear in the man's eyes as he looked upon my scarred cheek, my rough face. "Take a good long look," I said as I pushed my way onto the deck, annoyed that no one – *no one* – had taken my earlier advice. They were all still here, awaiting their dooms. "I might get better posters made this time."

The words barely made their way past my throat. It was a bit too close to revealing who I was. My bones hummed, the power within pressing against my skin, searching for release.

I lifted my free hand and water flowed up and over the sides of the ship, wrapping around ankles, climbing up legs, slowing movements, making people gasp and sputter as it made its way to their mouths. I'd grown in this way over the past two years as well. I couldn't come close to the destruction that Dione wreaked – not yet – but I could feel my control firming up, my abilities and concentration broadening. It probably helped that I'd had so much opportunity to practice lately.

I shoved the man I was fighting, tossing him like he was merely a fish on a line. He landed with a splash in the water I'd drawn onto the deck, coughing and sputtering. I glanced about, taking a quick count. Six of my crew left fighting above-deck against ten soldiers. Bad odds for them; easy odds for me. The water I'd brought on deck parted before me as I strode toward the fighting. I couldn't shake the ground, not on a ship, but there was plenty of water to be found in the Endless Sea.

If I wanted to, I could kill the soldiers – one after another, swiftly and efficiently, my magic lending me strength. But that wasn't what I wanted. I lifted my hand again, concentrated, drew it in a circle. The water around me moved with my thoughts, gathering into a glittering wall that surrounded the fighting, water moving within it in shimmering droplets.

"Put down your weapons," I called out. "Or I will drown you all."

I didn't have to have Lin's perception to see the fear blossoming on their faces. It swept over them clean as a wave, their hands shaking, their gazes trained on the top of my wall, expecting it to come crashing down at any moment. "The Maelstrom," someone whispered. "It's *him*."

I could drown them with little tendrils of water, but this was a far more impressive display. They stopped fighting, but no one dropped their weapon. I cast my gaze about and found their commander unconscious on the deck. No one to tell them what they should do. I tried a different tactic. They'd know what they'd been brought aboard to guard. "It's witstone," I said. "It's not a construct army. It's a good, bought and sold and traded within the Empire. You don't want to die for that."

Still, they hesitated.

A bit of truth, sprinkled in. "Lin wouldn't want you to die for that."

The soldier nearest me gave me a sharp look and I realized my mistake. *Lin*, not *the Emperor*. I'd stopped thinking of her as the Emperor in my mind, her name holding far more meaning to me.

The man was still looking at me, his sword lowered but still in his hand. "Who *are* you? I know you from somewhere."

I shook my head. "No. You don't. Drop your weapons."

This time, they obeyed, blades clattering as they fell to the deck. I let the seawater retreat, sending it back over the railing, undulating in flowing lines along the wood like serpents. My crew was carrying the boxes onto our ship. I waited until the last one was safely aboard. "I didn't want to do this," I told them. "I hope . . . I hope some of you survive."

They only stared as I backed away, as I retreated onto the deck of my ship. "Get us out of here," I told my captain. She nodded and called out orders to the crew.

I remained at the rail, one last task to complete. I lifted a hand. The Endless Sea roiled beneath us. All those people on the Imperial ship, people who were only doing what Lin had asked them to. But I couldn't leave the boat to pursue us. My bones trembled and the water rose between our ships. The crew around me tended to the sails; one readied a chunk of witstone to burn. No one paid me any heed. The wave built, water pushing gently against the other ship, testing its balance. The soldiers ran about, trying to get the sails filled again, trying to flee.

They'd not be able to get away in time. I wished they'd left the ship when I'd told them to. I wished I could stop this. But my will was weak.

It felt as though I watched through someone else's eyes as the water crashed over their ship, as it heaved at the hull, at the mast, forcing the boat past the tipping point. Wood creaked and cracked, men and women screamed, and above all of it the roaring crash of water against water. Around me, my crew carried about their business, not caring at all for the people who were about to drown.

I was still Jovis and yet – not Jovis. The Maelstrom – that's what they called me. A name that better suited me now. A wonder that the man on the Imperial caravel had been pricked by recognition at all in spite of my slip. I turned away, not wanting to watch the ship sink into the Endless Sea. The clouds above took that moment to let loose, rain pattering in big droplets across the deck, wind flinging it into my eyes. Blinking, I dashed the droplets away, retreating below-deck for my usual post-raid sulk.

I tried not to think about those men and women dragged into the endless depths.

It took three days of storm-filled sailing to reach the safe house. By the third day, the sky cleared, a rare bit of sunlight glittering across the Endless Sea. We docked mid-morning, the sun strong enough to make me feel a bit of burn at the back of my neck. Uncommon for a wet season day, but not unheard of. My crew brought the boxes of witstone above-deck, stacking them for inspection. There was no Imperial bureaucrat at this short, small pier. There was nothing on this small isle except the safe house.

Kaphra was waiting for me at the end of the dock.

He stood facing the sun, squinting, a tight-lipped smile on his face. The wind off the ocean did its best to ruffle his slicked-back hair, though it succeeded only marginally. Mephi sat next to him.

Two years might not have marked Kaphra in any noticeable way, but Mephi had grown. His head towered over Kaphra's, horns spiraling and branching twice like some cross between a deer's antlers and a gazelle's horns. His brown fur seemed even thicker than it had once been, his front paws like two massive serving plates.

Kaphra held the white-bladed sword to Mephi's throat. "Ah, Jovis. I see you've brought me that witstone. And it's good to see you in one piece."

"Kaphra," I said, nodding my head. There was a tightness in my chest, a sharp-edged feeling urging me forward. I couldn't stop my feet from moving, even had I wanted to. The gangplank bowed beneath my weight. "I wish I could say the same."

You will return to me when you have completed this job.

And then I set my foot on the dock and the command shards within me stilled.

4

Jovis

In the Endless Sea, north of Imperial

I could convince myself, in those rare moments between, that this was what I wanted – to be out in the Endless Sea with Mephi at my side. Kaphra liked to think of himself as both merciless and merciful, a dichotomy which meant that while he kept me on a tight leash, he also made sure I had time with Mephi. Or maybe it was just that Mephi was persuasively likable. I'd found that out when I'd once tried to set him free into the Endless Sea. I'd only discovered him waiting for me later, ready to continue on at my side. And I hadn't been able to say "no" to him, much as I'd thought I'd wanted to.

But we were fast approaching Imperial, and all the lies I'd told myself were crumbling. The rain was light this evening, more of a mist than anything. I blinked it from my eyelashes and tossed another scallop at Mephi. It went far too wide, dropping into the ocean beyond the ship's rail. My hands shook. Mephi's ears flattened in annoyance as he watched the morsel disappear, but then he looked to me and his brow furrowed.

"It's this place, isn't it?"

The last time I'd approached Imperial had been on a ship with Lin. We'd arrived at the docks of the capital then, but the outline of the island, the backdrop of the mountains – it all reminded me of when I'd been free. Oh, I'd still been beholden to the Shardless Few, but I hadn't been theirs the way I was Kaphra's. He would make me hurt people again. If I was a hero, as I'd once thought I was, I would walk into the Endless Sea to spare everyone the misery I would visit upon them. I took an experimental step toward the rail, wondering if a command against self-destruction was a thing written into the shards Nisong had placed inside my body.

I took another step. Maybe someone would even rescue me, take me to Lin. Mephi raised one furry eyebrow.

"What are you doing?" Philine's voice sounded from behind me. I turned to face her, hands clasped behind my back as though I'd been caught with something I shouldn't have had. She hadn't changed at all in the intervening years. I still felt if I looked away from her I'd immediately forget what she looked like.

I shrugged. "What do you think I'm doing?"

Damn Philine and her uncanny ability to be right where I never wanted her to be. It was as though her tracking relied on an ability to sniff out hope – a feeling she quickly arrived to snuff out.

She peered at me, her eyes narrowed. She didn't have the same stare Lin had, that way of peeling back my layers to glimpse the core beneath. Hers dug like the tip of a blade. I endured its sharpness. "You want *me* to tell you what I think you're doing." She glanced behind me at the seaside city. "Most likely something you ought not to be – but isn't that always the way with you?"

A hand clapped me on the shoulder, startling me. "Time to disembark soon." Kaphra's voice at my ear.

I wanted to shrug off his touch but stopped myself. Better to be compliant, easy — it was what I told myself would make it simpler to escape. Someday. But days had stretched into years, and I still hadn't found a chance. I remembered the darkness of those early days, the constant threats to Mephi's life. Throwing myself against the commands like a bird beating its broken wings at the bars of a cage. Philine using the white-bladed sword to cut the tattoo from my wrist, careful not to nick any arteries. I'd thought, back then, that I'd seen the glint of pity in her gaze. Only my imagination. Kaphra might like to think himself merciful but the Ioph Carn had no pity to spread among them.

I could see the rooftops of the Navigators' Academy as we docked at the north-eastern end of Imperial, the green tile nearly blending in with the trees as dusk fell. City denizens had begun to light lanterns; they hung from metal hooks beneath awnings and palm frond-covered alleys, lending an orange glow to the streets. "You still haven't told me what it is we're doing here. On Imperial, no less. We couldn't take a longer break?"

"Better not let you grow idle," Kaphra tossed back. "Isn't that one of Ningsu's proverbs? Something something idleness and rotting brains."

"Truly a scholar among men," I said dryly.

He only shook his head in disappointment. "Sarcasm. I believe that's one of the first signs of rotting brains. Dreadfully sorry. Well, we'll be docking soon and you can fire up your thinker."

"What need do I have of that when you do all my thinking for me?" My tone was light, and a part of me hated how easily I'd slipped into our old pattern of banter.

"So morose! Have I not rewarded you handsomely for your time with me?" He gestured to the finely woven clothes I wore, the leather bracers embossed with sea serpents. "The worst thing I've done to you is to stop you from returning to the Emperor.

And, Jovis, *please*. You are one man. She doesn't need you at her side so desperately. You're making a far bigger difference here with me." His gaze fell away from me and he studied the harbor before nodding to himself. "Simple enough task," Kaphra said. "When the sun is fully set, and the harbor is darker, set a wave upon the ships at that pier." He pointed down the docks. "Capsize them and break their masts."

The commands settled into my bones. No killing anyone this time, and the relief was a balm to my soul. I glanced over at my ossalen, who had one back foot lifted in the air and was grooming the space between his toes. He'd been cooped up with Kaphra and on this ship for too long. "I want to take Mephi with me."

Kaphra's lips pressed together. I still took some small measure of satisfaction from the fact that he had to peer upward to look me in the eye. "It's too risky."

"Come on, Kaphra." I made my tone cajoling, thinking of the times before when I'd been working for the Ioph Carn. We were familiar with one another. He was maybe ten years older than me at most — and looked younger than that — but he'd treated me like a wayward son. One he'd veered wildly from pride to disappointment in, depending on how my latest job had gone. I tried to evoke the fonder times. "What am I going to do? I can't tell anyone who I truly am. You made sure of that. And there have been other Alanga out and about." I waited only a moment before sagging my shoulders. "But I understand if you can't risk it."

If he were anyone but Kaphra, he might let me go. I could see the answer in his narrowed eyes before he opened his mouth.

"Ah, let him have some time with his beast." Philine spoke up from the rail, where she was helping one of the other Ioph Carn with the gangplank. "I'll watch over them if you like. Make sure this job gets done."

A spike of surprise ran through me, and I knew I wasn't doing a good job of hiding it. *Philine?* She was a constant, silent presence – and she certainly never stuck her neck out for anyone. Least of all me. She never could stand me, even when we'd both been working for Kaphra of our own free wills.

Kaphra let out a sigh, as though we were two children begging their father for gifts he could barely afford. "Fine. Go."

"Thank you," I said, and I meant it. I hated that I couldn't stay angry, couldn't loathe him as much as I wanted to. But a reprieve was a reprieve. The sun hadn't set yet, and that gave me a little time to wander, to feel as though I were free again.

I knew this city almost as well as I knew myself. Mephi hadn't been among people other than the Ioph Carn for two years. He jaunted at my side, drawing dark and angry looks. I felt the stares following me, whispering at the back of my neck like spiderwebs. I was accustomed to such looks, back when I'd been the first half-Poyer to attend the Navigators' Academy. But never since I'd become Jovis, the folk hero. Somewhere a little behind me was Philine, an invisible entity, as she always was. She slipped through the streets like a breeze.

No wonder Kaphra could allow me a longer leash. Everyone thought Jovis was dead, and people weren't exactly fond of Alanga in general. Who would listen to me if I asked for help? Two years, and he'd been having me steal witstone from the Empire and from its citizens. But witstone wasn't the only part of his plans. I'd overheard more than one hushed conversation with his lieutenants. I'd always known him to be simply greedy, but something had changed in him after he'd taken control of me. The power I gave him had made him more than greedy; it had made him hungry. I could see it in the haunted look in his eye, the hard-edged determination. Kaphra now wanted something more than just money.

And I was helping him to get it. I just wasn't sure how this task fit in. What would destroying a few boats accomplish?

I stopped at a street stall to buy a few cakes filled with lotus paste. I tossed one to Mephi, who swallowed it so quickly I wasn't sure he'd even had the chance to *taste* it. Another one I proffered to Philine.

She regarded me suspiciously.

"Do you think I've poisoned it? When would I have had the time to do that?"

"Now I *know* you've poisoned it."

I sighed and made as though to toss it into the gutters. She seized my wrist and pried the cake from my grasp, though she gave me a nasty look as she did so.

"You should learn to relax," I said as I bit into mine. The taste brought back memories of my time at the Navigators' Academy, of my time at the palace and Imperial City. I was so *close*. I'd promised Lin I'd return to her and she was a day's travel away, down a road that wended through the forest. I knew the way. At the same time, I was so far away. Two years, and it felt like a lifetime's worth of distance. I was peering through the glass at something I could never again touch. There was so much I needed to tell her. She needed to know about the brief alliance between Kaphra, Ragan and Nisong – the one that had been my downfall. She needed to know that Kaphra was up to something, that he wanted to remake this Empire in his own vision.

And I just desperately wanted her to know that I was alive. Endless Sea, I missed her. I missed the jasmine smell of her hair, the softness of her lips – a memory I couldn't seem to relive with a satisfactory amount of clarity – and even the stubborn set of her jaw.

Around me, men and women went about their evenings, cleaning up pots, dumping old washwater onto the street, taking refuse out. I knew, intellectually, that the world was falling apart. Witstone was scarce, bog cough was prevalent, the Shardless Few threatened war and tensions between Alanga and the citizens were rising. Yet clothes still needed to be mended, children still needed to be fed, and people still found the time and money to have a drink or two or three. Live in a crisis long enough and it just becomes normal.

Philine finished the cake and wiped the crumbs from her hands. "You seem to be enjoying your time in the city. Didn't know brooding was one of your pastimes."

I rubbed a finger at the spot where I'd furrowed my brow, cracking one eye open at her from beneath my palm. "Why *did* you volunteer to watch me and Mephi? You didn't need to."

"A horse kept in a stall all day doesn't ride well. Don't make the mistake of thinking I care."

I snorted. "I would never insult you in that way."

I might have imagined it, given the dim light of the lamps and the fading sunlight, but I thought a corner of her lip twitched upward.

Mephi rested his chin on my shoulder, the weight of his head like a barrel. "More?"

I scratched the wispy beard that had grown at his chin. "Not today, sorry."

And then the last orange of the sunset melted into the blue of night. The compulsion to complete the task Kaphra had given me tugged at the spot within my chest. Best take care of that. I wove through the streets back the way I'd come, doing my best to give a wide berth to suspicious citizens. "I don't suppose you can tell me why Kaphra wants me to destroy some ships?" I said beneath my breath.

As I'd suspected, Philine somehow heard me. "It's not my place to say."

I turned to face her, and for the first time seemed to catch her off guard. She nearly ran into me but stopped herself in time. "Endless Sea, when will it ever be your place? What are you biding your time for? Or are you actually content as you are?"

The glint of some long-buried want flashed in her gaze. Her brows lowered. "I—"

Music sprang up from the other side of the street, and my gaze whipped to the sound. A man was playing a stringed instrument, a tune I unfortunately knew. He cleared his throat and sang in a sweet and reedy voice.

> They fought the constructs, they set Gaelung
> free,
> The Emperor Lin and her consort-to-be.
> He held her in a warm embrace
> When the sun did finally show its face

More stanzas had been added to the original song, it sounded like, and was I her . . .consort-to-be in this version? I'd thought we'd been subtle about the growing attraction between us, but it seemed people could take the whispers of rumors and turn them into lyrics. I wanted to keep moving, to stay on task, but the blasted man kept singing and fool that I was – I kept listening. There was yet another stanza about clothes falling to the floor, clasped bodies, in which it sounded as though I'd performed quite admirably.

Night had fallen, yet my cheeks felt as hot as if they were baking in the sun of a dry season day.

Mephi sat on his haunches and put one big paw on my chest. He peered into my face, whiskers tickling my temple. "Are you all right? Your face is very red." He sniffed me, as though he could determine what ailment I was suffering by my scent. Endless Sea, was I *blushing?* We'd kissed in private. We'd been in *private*. And we certainly hadn't gotten to more vigorous activities. Not that I hadn't wanted to. Not that I still didn't want to. Not that I didn't think about it each time I laid in bed.

Yet there was a song that included our hypothetical coitus.

For the first time since I'd ever known her, Philine *cackled*. "Oh, he's very not all right. People suffering from his affliction have been known to do things like dig holes to bury themselves in, or to walk into the sea."

Mephi redoubled his attentions, his cold nose jamming into my eye socket. "Please don't do either of those things."

I pushed him away. "I'm fine." It seemed that Lin and I hadn't been as subtle as we'd thought we had. Too many moments alone in rooms together, too many servants and guards all watching. Whoever had written the song had written us as though we were to be married. I'd not asked to be her consort, nor had she asked me to be hers. We'd kissed *twice*.

Well, when she'd said being in a relationship with her would mean extra scrutiny, I hadn't considered this. The song continued on to my supposed death, to Lin's grief.

"It's just a song," I choked out. "People make a lot of stuff up in those. Lin didn't—"

Lin. Not *the Emperor*.

Philine gave me a very knowing look. "Well, seems as if Kaphra saved you after all. Emperors don't marry their Captains of the Imperial Guard. You'd have always been a side piece, pining for her sole attentions."

"I was never a side piece," I snarled. I stalked away, Philine's giggles following in my wake. Time to get this job done and to get back on the ship so I could put this whole incident behind me. At the docks, I veered into the forest, Mephi and Philine on my heels, and crept closer to the pier Kaphra had indicated.

I studied the ships, figuring out the best angle to bring the wave in from so it wouldn't damage other boats. Mephi's whiskers tickled my ear. "Are we doing a good?"

"We really don't do much good, not these days," I said. "I don't know why we're doing this."

Only one man remained on the pier, unloading the last of his catch. I waited until he'd taken his handcart and strolled all the way to shore, softly humming to himself. And then I let the trembling fill my bones and opened my consciousness to the water around me. I could feel the depth of the harbor, like a bowl I dipped invisible fingers into, my awareness trailing the bottom. It was easier to work with the natural flows of water, building a section of wave up from a wave that was already forming, directing it higher, faster.

Boats crashed together, tipping, one of them ripping into the pier, cracking the wood to splinters as it capsized. Then only silence and bubbling as the ships sank beneath the surface. It took a moment for anyone to react, and then there were footsteps, loud, angry voices, cries of dismay.

A group of cityfolk gathered at the docks, muttering among themselves, watching as the wrecked ships slipped into the harbor. Most of what they were saying I couldn't make out, though I could gather the gist. I'd destroyed the livelihood of several fishermen and they were not happy about it.

But I had other things to occupy my attention. Philine hovered at my back.

"We're done here," she said. "Let's go."

"We can't stay even a little longer?" I watched, only paying half attention, as a woman in the mob gestured angrily toward the city while others nodded. Voices rose, a noisy hum in the back of my mind. "Let me have a meal in the city, a little reminder of freedom?"

"Mephi draws too much attention already." I could hear the slightest bit of give in her voice.

I pressed, trying to buy time to think, to plan. "Just let me stay here a moment before we go back."

Philine sighed, but didn't say anything more.

My mind churned as the mob made its way into the city. Kaphra hadn't commanded me to return. Had one of the commands inside me been marked so that I could not cause harm to any of Kaphra's Ioph Carn? Or had he only ensured I would not harm *him*? My hand tightened around my steel staff. I heard Mephi sniffing a tree behind me as Philine shifted from foot to foot. She was an excellent fighter, perhaps better than I was. But I had Mephi and my Alanga powers at my beck and call. It had to be now, so I could buy myself enough time before Kaphra came after me. Sweat slicked my palm. If I got this wrong, I'd be punished for it.

As soon as I turned to try and attack her, I felt a rumbling.

I froze, panic spiking my heartbeat. In a flash I was back on Deerhead Island, the sun hot against the back of my neck, the air filled with dust and screams. I reached instinctively for the tree next to me to steady myself and then jerked away, fearful that it might fall on me. I couldn't think past the wild beating of my heart. It thundered in my ears, the panic making my vision dim.

Philine touched my shoulder. "Jovis. Jovis? It's over. It's not sinking."

Mephi pushed his horns beneath my hands, steadying me.

She was right. The ground had stopped moving but I thought I could still *feel* it sliding beneath my feet. Dizziness washed over me as I sucked in a breath; my vision cleared. I'd stopped breathing. No wait – I'd been breathing, just too quickly. I took in another deep breath. This wasn't how I died. Not sinking, not crushed by a falling tree, not down, down into the depths of the

Endless Sea. Philine had once spoken of her hope of my death by her hand, one last witticism on my lips, and that felt comforting in comparison. I finally calmed my heart enough to speak. "Look at that. You *do* care," I said.

This close I could see her eyes narrowed in disgust, her hand drawing away as though she'd been touching a refuse pile.

Someone screamed from the edge of the city.

"Jovis," Mephi said, his ears flicking back and forth. "It's not a quake. Not a natural one."

Alanga.

When I focused my attention that way I could hear the angry shouts, could see the mob milling around a focal point. "Philine," I said, my voice sounding far and away, "why did Kaphra want me to destroy the ships?"

Her sigh seemed to echo from the trunks of trees. "It can't hurt now, I suppose. Kaphra has you, and you give him power. He doesn't like being competed with."

The Alanga being picked off one by one . . .not by some mysterious other faction. By Kaphra. His reach was far and wide; someone powerful on nearly every island owed him something. He liked having others in debt to him. And he relished in calling in favors, especially when those favors were difficult to procure. How easy it would have been for him to send word to his associates, his debtors: *kill any Alanga you hear of.* Most Alanga were still so new to their powers – it wouldn't have always been hard. Kaphra didn't like to get his own hands dirty when he didn't have to.

The quakes, the angry mob, the ships – they all fell together in my mind. Why send in your most prized possession to assassinate some pesky Alanga when you could just have angry citizens do it for you? Just as with the witstone, the fewer Alanga out and about in the Empire, the more power Kaphra held in his grasp.

Someone was there in the city, and I'd framed them for something they didn't do.

It felt as though someone were physically tearing me in two, a burning, ripping sensation at my core. Lin needed me. I could help her hold this Empire together. Yet I'd committed a wrong here – one only I could right. Somewhere in that city was a frightened Alanga, surrounded by angry, shouting mortals, trying to keep them at bay with the only power they had.

Mephi had told me I was the person who helped, but he'd never said what I should do when more than one person needed my help.

I might have a chance here to escape. I'd made a promise to Lin. Tried never to break my word.

Yet I found myself climbing onto Mephi's back, pointing him in the direction of the city. "Hey!" Philine called after me. I didn't look back to see if she chased me. We emerged from the forest and ran for the crowd at the edge of the city streets. I chided myself even as we moved forward. Was it vanity that made me interfere? Was I so convinced I was the one who could make a difference? Even as I mocked myself I knew the core of it: I was doing this because no one else was.

And someone needed to.

We pushed our way through the crowd. I used my staff to prod people back who sprang for me. More than one carried a knife and more than one stone was lobbed at my head. But I was quick and ducked out of the way. The crowd was more than just hostile; they were bubbling with violence, a pot threatening to boil over. I found not one, but two men standing with their backs to the wall of a drinking hall, surrounded by various items that had been tossed at them: stones, dead fish, rotten vegetables, refuse, a few blades. Brothers, by the look of them, and though one had a beard and the other did not, their faces were mirror images of one another. Twins.

"Stay back!" one of them shouted, his foot lifted. Two black ossalen wound about their knees, making worried chirruping noises in the backs of their throats.

"There's a reason all the Alanga were once driven from the Empire!" someone shouted from the crowd.

I swung down from Mephi's back, my staff held tight in one hand. "These men did not destroy your boats," I called out. "They can't even move water at this phase."

For a moment, the crowd quieted, gazes focused on Mephi's bulk, my practiced stance. "Then who did? You?" shouted a man in front of me. He might have looked soft if only he'd smiled, his stature short and his belly rounded. But he held a broom in his hands, gripping it so tightly that his knuckles whitened. It wasn't really possible to stab a person with a broom handle, but this man looked as though he were willing to try.

All thoughts in my mind stuttered to a halt as I regarded the man. What was I supposed to tell them? That it had been me? I had no desire to fight a mob of powerless citizens who were only angry that some of their livelihoods had been destroyed. "Ragan," I said, and then stopped.

Everyone waited.

"There was an Alanga at the Battle of Gaelung who fought against the Emperor."

The silence broke and I could feel them slipping from my grasp as though I were an actor who'd tripped on stage.

"What, and you want us to believe you were there?"

"Who are you anyways?"

"You're just as bad as the rest of them."

A stone came flying from the darkness, striking me on the forehead. I heard the blow before I felt it. And then a sharp bite of pain before the wound began to close. A few warm drops of blood slipped into my eyebrow.

I caught the eye of the man in front of me. He'd gone still, his grip on the broom handle going slack. I couldn't hear his voice above the roar of the mob, but I saw his mouth move. *I know you.*

Years ago, a bumbling merchant, asking if I could take not just one child to hide from the Tithing Festival, but two. They were best friends, after all. Age had changed the lines of his face, though they'd changed mine too.

"Jovis," he said, and that word cut through the crowd. "You're . . . dead?"

I moved my mouth, unsure of what words to form, unsure of what would cause the shard in my chest to burn in warning. I'd been commanded not to reveal who I was, but did the command still hold if someone else revealed my identity first? I tried out a half-hearted shrug and was rewarded with only a pinprick of heat.

The mood in the crowd shifted.

"This man is a hero," the merchant said. "He saved my daughter and her friend from the Tithing Festival years ago." I'd been paid, but he didn't mention that. "He fought against the construct army at Gaelung. If he says it was not these two men, then I believe him."

How deeply can a person feel self-loathing? I wanted to walk into the Endless Sea, to bury myself in loose kelp and to wedge my feet into the sand. I wasn't a hero anymore. I'd been doing Kaphra's bidding, acquiescing without a fight, lulling him into complacence so I might have an opportunity to escape. And in the meantime, I'd hurt people who hadn't deserved it. I'd killed people.

"Wait." My voice was weak. I waved at the two men behind me, hoping they took my meaning and that they'd flee. I hoped they'd go to Imperial City – Lin would help them; I knew she would. And then I waved at the crowd, who were now closing in around me.

"The Ioph Carn killed you," a woman said, reaching for me. "That's what we were told."

"Jovis, things have been so terrible—"

"—we need your help—"

"There's no more witstone and so few caro nuts—"

Always so many people reaching, wanting, *needing*. Once, I'd not cared to be their hero. Now I wished I could be. Mephi's cold nose nudged my ear and I knew he wanted us both to do good. But we had to get away, before—

"Come here." Kaphra's voice cut through the din. I moved toward him without a second thought, my legs stiff, horror wriggling in my belly. I fought the command in the way I'd done when he'd first tested his commands on me – trying to press my will against the shard in my chest, to break it, to force it out of me. It was like trying to move a stone with my breath.

"When will you leave things alone that are not your business?" he said to me when I arrived at his side.

I swept an arm over the crowd. "This *is* my business! You made it my business when you forced me to sink those ships."

I could feel the confusion from the people around me, their uncertain expressions. I knew how strange this all must look to them – they didn't recognize Kaphra, but they thought they recognized me. They expected me to save them, to start righting all the wrongs made against them – because that's what heroes in the stories did.

Maybe I'd been a hero once, briefly. Now I was just trying to survive.

Kaphra held my gaze for a moment more before turning to the crowd. People in the windows above peered out from between shutters. "You think you can trust any of the Alanga?"

No. Not this. Better to be thought of as dead. Mephi whimpered, sensing what was coming.

"Jovis," Kaphra said, "destroy this city."

5

Lin

Imperial Island

Urame's death sent ripples throughout the Empire, the arrival of her head followed by a flurry of letters — from other island governors fearing the same fate, from various factions on Gaelung, jostling for power, from captains of Imperial trading vessels, fearing how this might affect the flow of goods beyond the already tight stores of witstone. I burned her head in the palace gardens, knowing she didn't have family who would wish for its return, but unsure whether she had friends who would wish to lay a sprig of juniper across the pyre.

It would be so easy to let this Empire fall to pieces, to turn inward, to let all the islands do as they wished when it came to witstone mining. To worry only for myself and those I cared about. But I also knew that governors would make decisions their citizens would have to live with. And the Shardless Few? There were possibly individuals in that group that still believed in their founding principles, who still believed in a Council. But Dione was their leader, and they cleaved to him first. Did he care about the citizens? He'd once helped us save Gaelung from the constructs, but after that he'd retreated, making it clear we were enemies once more. I would hold these fraying threads together even if it tore me apart.

And then there were the reports of a riot in a city on Imperial, where the Navigators' Academy was. Ikanuy had hesitantly and gently told me that people there had said they'd seen Jovis. For a moment, my heart had soared, not knowing how it could be true but not caring. But Ikanuy had described what the Alanga man had done. Instead of helping anyone or defusing the riot, he'd destroyed some of the city. It couldn't have been him. Some other Alanga, then.

Still, I wished I'd not been away at Riya. I wished I could have gone there as soon as I'd had word, to see if I could find this man for myself. Whoever he was, he was long gone by now.

I studied the translucent edge of the white-bladed sword, tapping the blade with a fingernail. Thrana's ears flicked back toward me, her gaze fixed on the courtyard outside my bedroom window. "Looking at it won't change its properties," she said, her voice a rumble. The floorboards creaked beneath her feet – each large as a dinner plate – as she shifted. She'd been the size of a pony when I'd ridden her into battle at Gaelung. Now she was the size of a horse.

I picked it up, feeling the weight of it, the bindings of the hilt pressing indentations into my palm. "I know. But I can't help but feel I'm missing something important." I flipped through the pages of Dione's journal, the paper brittle beneath my fingertips. He'd spoken of the swords' creation, of how Ylan, the first Emperor, had betrayed him, intending to use the swords to kill the Alanga.

In the past two years, I'd done everything I could to smooth the relationship between Imperial and the cloudtree monasteries, including allowing a monk out to see the tree my father had maintained. In turn, they'd haltingly, cautiously, told me a little of what some of the restricted texts in the monasteries said – the books from before the Alanga purge. The Alanga and their descendants had lived among the denizens of the Empire, but as a different class of people. The original Alanga were powerful, and bestowed favors on their descendants, some of whom had some small measure of magic. They used this favor and their magic to set themselves apart, to build fortunes, leaving everyone else behind. The ruins of the beautiful cities I'd seen, the mural in Imperial Palace – all built by the hands of ordinary citizens.

They called them Alanga ruins, but in truth, they were not. The Alanga had only lived there.

I better understood Ylan's anger at Dione now, his desperation in deceiving him. But the swords still didn't quite make sense to me. According to Dione's journal, Ylan had created seven swords. But even if there had been seven of them, how could the Sukais possibly have hunted down each and every Alanga? Each Alangan descendant? It would have taken decades and even then, some would have slipped between grasping fingers. There were always gaps.

A knock sounded, the door opening before I was ready. I seized the sword, sliding it and the scabbard into the gap between my desk drawers and the floor. My heartbeat sped up. Dione. Was he here already?

Thrana, as though sensing my mood, spoke up. "It's not him. No one's come through the front gates just yet."

A servant had peeked her head through the door, black eyes large and wet as a doe's. "Apologies, Eminence. Phalue is here to see you."

I couldn't get my heartbeat to calm again. In spite of Ragan, in spite of Iloh, the greatest threat to my Empire was the Shardless

Few. Their army had grown in the past years, and who built an army who wasn't intent on conquest? But Dione had agreed to meet me – that had to mean something. There was still a chance we could avert an all-out war, I was sure of it. "You must be new," I said, my voice a trifle sharp. "Or you'd know better than to walk in unannounced on an Emperor. Do not open the door until you hear a response."

She bowed her head, contrite.

"Send her in," I said.

Phalue's broad shoulders took up nearly the breadth of the doorway. "Eminence," she said as she entered. There was something ponderous and loud about the way she moved into the bedroom, like a draft horse fitted with a plow. The leather armor probably didn't help. It always surprised me how quickly she moved during our sparring lessons, how vast the difference was between her political self and her fighting self. One certainly seemed to fit her much better than the other.

She left the door open behind her.

"It's time I return to Nephilanu."

That was Phalue, never bothering with polite pleasantries, never attempting to gauge the mood or inclinations of the people she spoke with. I found it refreshing, especially after people like Iloh.

"Are we done with our lessons, then?" I felt competent with the blade now, though I was no master.

Phalue shook her head. "You'll have to find someone else to continue training you. You're not a bad student, Eminence, but there have been too many interruptions. And I have a wife and daughter at home."

I studied her face and saw fear in the tightened corners of her mouth, the pensive look in her eye. "You're worried the Shardless Few will attack. We've come to an understanding – I've left Khalute alone and he's not attacked the Empire."

"Khalute isn't far from Nephilanu," Phalue said. "And during the wet season it's strategically important. Dione . . .threatened us with as much."

"And hasn't followed through," I pointed out. "He's agreed to meet me. He helped us at Gaelung. It's been a long time."

"Yes," Phalue said. She let the silence hang. Perhaps she wasn't so uncomfortable with politics as I'd thought.

I liked having Phalue here in the palace – someone who'd been there at Gaelung, someone who treated me like a peer, at least when we were sparring. She'd started to feel like a friend. But then I thought of Jovis and how I would have done anything to find myself reunited with him. "I won't keep you. If you intend to return home, then by all means pack your things and return. I understand why you'd want to be there." I rose from my desk and inclined my head. "It's been an honor to be trained by you, Sai."

She grimaced a little and then put out her hand.

Bemused, I took it. She pulled me in. For the barest moment I thought she was attacking me, and my shoulders tensed. But she drew me into a quick hug, the way I'd seen soldiers do – right hands clasped, left hands patting one another's backs. My left hand hung pointlessly by my side as she patted my back and drew away. "I can't support the Empire," she said, her voice low, "but you as an individual – you're not like your father. I know what it's like to be different from your parents. Don't let anyone tell you you're not."

She cleared her throat and abruptly left, leaving the scent of cured leather in her wake. Something swelled within me, crowding out the loneliness. Not all the governors hated me, it seemed.

"He's here." Thrana's deep voice reverberated from the shutters. "He's brought others with him. Five of them in total."

Dione. The last time I'd seen him, he'd said we would always be enemies. I'd done my best to prove myself different from my forebears, to counteract my father's anti-Alanga propaganda. Perhaps it had finally been enough. I had to hope it was enough – otherwise why would he have agreed to come?

I'd instructed my soldiers to take them to the questioning room when they arrived. I didn't bother with the Imperial headdress – it wouldn't make the Shardless Few feel any more favorable toward me, and Dione especially had reason to hate the sight of it. I'd dressed simply in a black dress with curling black embroidery on the sleeves. The collar was stitched with gold phoenixes; several keys lay against my chest, subtle reminders of my lofty station.

I took one last deep breath, gestured to Thrana and we went to meet the Shardless Few. Two Imperial guards fell in behind me after I locked my bedroom door. I found the doe-eyed servant girl on my way to the questioning room. "Fetch some tea," I told her. "And for Empire's sake – wait for a response this time after knocking."

I didn't make them wait. Dione had taken the far end of the table, his five Shardless Few arrayed on either side of him. He looked exactly as I'd remembered, hair graying, beard neatly trimmed, the lines in his face no more deep than when I'd seen him last. A scar ran over his left eye, the eye itself milky and sightless. His remaining eye glowered at me. I sat opposite him, my back to the door, while Thrana curled into the corner. The Shardless Few woman in that corner could likely feel Thrana's breath on the back of her neck. Her darting eyes and stiff posture told me that, yes, she could. The other four were calm as the Endless Sea during a windless day. They might have tried to keep their expressions neutral, but I could see the contempt simmering beneath – the slight wrinkle of a nose, the tap of an impatient finger, the tilt of a head. I didn't know what Dione had been telling his people about me.

I could feel my spine stiffening, my body leaning into one

of the defensive postures Phalue had shown me. I'd seen what Dione could do when he unleashed his power. Even now, sitting across from him at this table, in *my* palace, a trickle of awe flowed into my chest, mingling with the fear. This man had been the greatest of the Alanga. He'd survived the purge, had identified what made people angry, had built a movement around it. And now he stood at the head of an army. It was hard not to respect that. I felt like a child next to him. I *was* a child next to him.

Whatever truce we'd formed was tentative. I had to be careful here if I wanted to keep it. I'd sent my soldiers to Gaelung to stabilize the island and prevent infighting over the gap left by Urame's death without an heir. Ikanuy was researching the bloodlines, trying to find a distant relative who would be a suitable replacement. It had to be someone blood-related to stave off further argument.

If Dione chose to break our truce, I'd have barely enough time to recall those soldiers, to send them south.

"I trust you had a pleasant trip," I said.

"Pleasant by the standards of a wet season. Which meant we spent the voyage drenched and rolled about in the cabin like pebbles in a jar." Dione studied me and I knew he was considering my expression, the outfit I'd chosen, the golden stitching at the collar. He knew how to play this game as well as I did. "But we did not suffer any sea serpent attacks. Or Ioph Carn attacks."

Did he know about my dwindling supply of witstone? "Yes, well, I've heard Kaphra has an Alanga in his employ now. The Maelstrom, he calls himself. I'd hate to think of the destruction that might have followed had you clashed with the man."

I was rewarded with a twitch of his lips, though I had trouble interpreting what it meant. Was he surprised by this information, or just surprised that I'd kept abreast of the rumors? "A wet season, Ioph Carn attacks, the brutal assassination of Urame . . . I suppose we must be glad there are no constructs."

The day was dimmed by rain and burgeoning clouds; could he see the pulse pounding at my throat? I'd been experimenting with Thrana's shards, deep in the cavern where my father's replica still lay asleep. He couldn't know about that. No one did except Thrana.

"Yes, we should be grateful."

His posture relaxed and he sighed. "Can we speak alone for a moment?"

"Thrana stays," I said. But I waved away my guards as the Shardless Few rose and filtered out of the room. We both knew there were things we had to speak about that our subordinates should not hear. I preferred this to the veiled sparring.

The door shut and I felt Dione studying me again. I waited him out. He wanted to speak alone? Then he could be the one to speak first.

"You didn't kill the monk at the battle," Dione said. "Ragan. I heard he carved his name into Urame's head. That will set your efforts back."

I wasn't sure if he meant my efforts to keep the Empire together or my efforts to dispel my father's anti-Alanga propaganda. I chose to think he meant the latter. I closed my eyes for a moment and shook my head, letting him see how tired I was. Vulnerability could still be a weapon. "Old prejudices die hard. I cannot set up situations in which all Alanga can save citizens from impending armies or rescue their children. I'm afraid Jovis and I are seen as exceptions. I've heard more than one person mutter that we should do what Ylan did and hunt down the Alanga altogether." It was talk I did my best to quash, but how could I stamp it out without being like my father?

Dione tapped a finger against the table. "That doesn't serve either of us."

The feel of the room shifted from a tense silence into a companionable one. This, at least, we could agree on. Neither of us wanted the Alanga slaughtered. It wasn't in either of our interests. I wanted to ask him, to plead – was I still his enemy? Could we not work together? But I held the words in.

His lips pressed together, his focus on his fingers on the table-top. "You shouldn't have let him live."

"I didn't think he deserved to die."

Dione's eyes narrowed, his gaze flicking to Thrana and then back to me. "And yet before this he spent all this time wreaking no havoc, leaving the governors alone. Tell me, did you ever find the body of the construct leader?"

We hadn't. "What does that have to do with anything?" I tried to make my tone light, confused, guileless. But I heard my words and found them laced with suspicion.

He knew.

"What you did to Ragan is an abomination. You should have killed him." He ran a hand through his hair. "Now look what you've done in your ignorance. Ragan and that construct will come for you – don't think they won't. But they'll go after others as well. You gave them the keys. Ossalen bones and commands."

I'd only brushed against the implications in my thoughts, too occupied with keeping the governors from seceding, keeping the islands from sinking, trying to understand the secrets of the past. Secrets he could have told me, had he wished. I'd hoped Ragan had paid for someone to kill Urame, that he'd just briefly found some way around the command I'd placed inside him. But Dione's question sparked new possibilities in my mind. Of *course*. We'd not found Nisong's body, though that didn't necessarily mean anything when the battlefield was as chaotic as the one at Gaelung, and so many bodies rendered unrecognizable. But if she and I were similar in any way, she would not have given up.

She'd set her sights on Imperial. She'd gone after Ragan. She'd removed his shard. And now she knew that ossalen shards could be used on Alanga.

"And what was I supposed to do? I showed him mercy. How was I to know what would happen, or even what I was doing? It's not as though anyone told me."

A slight grimace crossed Dione's lips before his expression flattened. "I would not teach a Sukai."

"Then you've only yourself to blame if you're angry." For a moment, we only glared at one another. I wondered if he felt the same tremor in his bones as I did, the raw power waiting to be seized and unleashed. "It's happened before, hasn't it?" He said nothing, and that was answer enough. I'd been trying to figure out how the swords could have been used to kill so many Alanga. Here was another puzzle piece, though I wasn't quite sure how it fit. "What else happened before the Alanga purge? What happened during it?'"

He rose and went to the window, staring out into the cloudy night sky, his hands clasped before him. A light rain was falling, dripping from the eaves.

I shifted in my chair to face his back. "Why won't you tell me? I want for us to live peaceably with the citizens of the Empire. I don't want to repeat the past. How can we do that if we do not know what it was?"

"Because there are so many who would seek to repeat it. They wouldn't see the past as a warning, but as a lesson."

A knock sounded. "Come in." A servant entered, carrying a steaming teapot and a stack of cups. He placed the tray onto the table, bowed and retreated. Not the servant I'd sent to the kitchens, and later than I'd expected. I'd have to tell Ikanuy to have a word with the new girl.

The door closed behind him and I slammed a hand on the table, frustrated. "So you would prefer we stumble through the dark with only you to guide us, shepherding us like sheep who can't see the cliff's edge. Tell me what happened. I'm not my father, nor Ylan – haven't I done enough to prove that to you? Can't we work together?"

"You are the antithesis of everything that the Shardless Few have worked for." Dione didn't look at me, his gaze still fixed outside the window. He shifted, his hands fluttering and then settling by his sides.

"And you're *not*? You're just as powerful as I am. Don't pretend you care about their Council. You're using them; you've been using them from the very beginning." I could see the shape of his plans – depose me, remove the governors, remove the power structures of the current regime. But what would he put in its place? He'd betrayed the Alanga so long ago, had been the cause of their demise. "You think you can control them this time around, don't you?"

"You don't know what I want."

The tremor inside my bones subsided, the tingle of realization running up my throat. He was still facing away from me. Not just to keep me from reading his expression. If he wasn't here to tell me what he wanted, to lay out his demands, then he was here for different reasons.

Pieces began to slide together. The flutter of his hands – not a nervous fluttering. A signal. He'd asked to speak to me alone; I'd not been the one to initiate that. And the servant girl, the new one, who'd walked in on me with the sword. How long had she been working here in the palace? How long had she been snooping around for? *How long had she been working for the Shardless Few?*

I jolted out of my seat and went to the door.

"Eminence," Dione said from behind me. The word resonated against my feeling of wrongness, that sour note growing louder.

He would never call me that, not unless he was striving to get my attention.

His Shardless Few entourage looked up at me as I stormed into the hallway.

Four of them. Not five.

"There was another of you." The words slipped past numbed lips. Thrana pushed her way through the open door to my side, sensing that something amiss.

"She went to relieve herself, Eminence," said one of the men. But the lamps were brightly lit and I caught the pounding of his pulse at his neck. Dione hadn't come here to make peace with me; he'd come here to steal from me.

The sword.

I turned to find Jovis, to tell him to apprehend Dione while I went after the sword. I caught myself halfway through that arc. He was dead. Huan, my new Captain of the Imperial Guard, was competent, but she wasn't Jovis. I wavered, unsure of which to prioritize. Dione had come all this way, had set up a meeting, had infiltrated my palace – all for the sword.

"Huan!" I called to the guard. "Apprehend these men and women. No one leaves the palace gates!"

And then I ran toward my rooms, Thrana thundering beside me. The door was shut and locked and I fumbled the key to open it. The room was dark, the lamps unlit. I went to the desk and felt beneath it with trembling hands. The space was empty, the sword gone.

"Lin. The balcony." Thrana's voice sounded in the darkness, her shoulder brushing against mine. I looked.

A woman stood there, oilskin cloak about her shoulders, frozen as though caught by my gaze. The Shardless Few woman. The one missing from Dione's entourage. She tore herself away from my stare, leaping up and seizing the edge of the roof.

I darted for her feet, shoving past the half-opened door to the balcony. But she was as quick as I was, clambering onto the roof with the agility of a monkey. Thrana was there in a heartbeat and I clambered to her shoulder, seizing the gutter and pulling myself up after the woman. I wasn't dressed for this, my dress draping all the way to my ankles. It had been some time since I'd stolen away on rooftops. My limbs seemed to remember, moving with a swiftness augmented by my Alanga magic. Tiles clicked beneath my feet as I chased the woman across the palace rooftops.

The palace was large, but there was only so much space atop it. I swerved to the side, herding her toward a corner. I knew there were no balconies beneath that corner, no place she could climb down to without hurting herself. She'd be trapped.

The woman took one swift look back at me, and then sped up. I watched, a little mystified, as she reached the edge of the roof. And jumped.

She landed on the roof of the Hall of Earthly Wisdom and kept running. I paused for a brief moment and heard Thrana's whining on the wind. It always upset her when I went somewhere she couldn't follow. This woman wasn't just Shardless Few. She was an Alanga. I took a breath and sprinted toward the edge of the roof. It didn't matter. She'd taken the sword and I needed to retrieve it.

A shock of pain went through my knees as I landed on the Hall of Earthly Wisdom. The woman was already nearing the edge of the roof, running quickly, ready to jump.

I unleashed the magic inside me. I could feel the moisture around us, filling the air, the gutters, trickling in streams through the grooves in the paving stones below us. I pulled it together into a sphere of water as big as I was, and threw it at her back. She stumbled as it hit her and then slipped, rolling down the roof as she threw out her hands, trying to stop her momentum.

I half-expected the sword to come tumbling out from below her cloak.

Wait.

The servant girl hadn't gone to the kitchens. Why would she not bring me the tea and risk blowing her cover? Unless she didn't have need of it anymore. Unless she was playing a key role in this heist.

I broke off my pursuit, sliding to the edge of the roof, dropping over the edge. My dress was ripped and muddied, my hair a tangled mess. I made for the gates with all the speed I could muster. Footsteps sounded behind me and Thrana came abreast of me. She'd made her way out the front door. I seized the fur of her shoulder, hauling myself in one smooth movement onto her back.

She stopped just short of the gates. Guards milled there, the gates half-closed.

"Has anyone left?"

The man who'd been pushing the left side closed stopped and shook his head. "Not since you gave the order."

"And before that? Did anyone leave."

I watched his brow furrow. "Just a servant. She had a handcart of worn linens she was taking to sell in the city. They do that every so often."

I wanted to bite back that I *knew* that, that I wasn't so out of touch with the inner workings of my palace, but I also knew, with certainty, that the sword was on that cart. Dione layered his plans like pastry dough; he wouldn't have had the Shardless Few woman take the sword. Too obvious. He'd made contingency plans in case I found him out.

I dismounted, pulled the chain of keys from my neck and handed them to Thrana, who took them between her teeth. "Wake him up," I said. Dione wasn't the only one with contingency plans. "Meet me in the city." I waved to the guards. "All of you, with me. Try to keep up."

The city streets still bustled with evening activity, people selling wares or cleaning out cooking pots or bringing in their dusk catch. I wove around them, the people recognizing my guards too late to give way. She wouldn't take the main street — too obvious. I remembered a walk back to the palace I'd taken over two years ago after failing to catch a spy construct. It was the first time I'd had the chance to really speak to Jovis alone. The first time I'd felt as though we had a sort of understanding with one another. The first time I'd felt that spark of attraction, though I hadn't known it at the time. We'd taken the side streets — a quick way back to the palace, though one littered with refuse.

I swerved into one of those alleys, found the path no longer littered with refuse, but with painful memories. The guards followed, though they fell behind with each turn I took.

There. Around the next corner I saw a woman with a handcart, her back to me, plaited hair bouncing against her back as she ran. She must have heard the guards pounding through the alleys; they were not subtle.

Her shoulder was thin and bony beneath my hand, but when she whirled she had a dagger clutched in her fist. "Stay back," she hissed.

I seized her wrist with one hand, elbowed her in the stomach with another. The girl went down coughing, struggling to take in a proper breath. She dropped the dagger and I kicked it away. "Where is it?"

She didn't answer.

I went to the handcart, pulling off the cover, rifling through the linens. My hand struck something cold and hard. Carefully, I drew the sword from within the sheets, looping the chain on the scabbard around one shoulder. My heartbeat calmed in increments. I had it back.

"The swords belong with me." Dione's voice sounded from behind me.

I whirled and found the blade in my hand before I could remember gripping the hilt.

He lifted a hand, as though trying to calm a frightened horse. "You don't know what it does."

"I know it kills Alanga." I lifted it, took a step toward him.

Dione took a step back, but I felt the air shifting between us, the rain gathering. I opened my awareness to the moisture around us, and tugged at the water he'd pulled to him, testing his control. It was iron-strong. But this was a wet season, and there was always more water. I pulled it to me, felt it bubbling at my feet. The wind picked up.

My guards came running around the corner, out of breath. I shifted, placing my back to the wall of one of the buildings. "How many of the Shardless Few you brought with you are Alanga?"

"Give me the sword."

Only the one, then, though I wondered if he had more waiting for him on Khalute. I'd done my best to mitigate the prejudices of the Empire, but I couldn't blame the Alanga for wanting to stay in hiding. I'd had the feeling some might try to join the Shardless Few, but I'd also hoped the Shardless Few would turn them away. They'd alway said their purpose was stopping the Tithing Festival, overthrowing the Empire, setting up a Council of peers. They'd always had the same distrust of Alanga that the general populace had. But Dione had revealed himself and now the organization seemed to be changing, shifting to accommodate new ideals.

Power always did have a way of warping those surrounding it.

Several cloaked figures entered the alleyway behind my guards. They were flanked. I was outnumbered.

A breeze stirred the back of my neck, one that did not come from Dione. I dared not look up. Thrana slipped into the alley on my right, past the servant who was still struggling to right herself. "He's here," she said in my ear.

It took a moment for everyone to realize we were not alone. Claws scraped against tiles above us, a low rumble filling the air, echoing the tremor in my bones. Dione and everyone else looked to the rooftops and I watched with satisfaction as their faces drained of blood. Before anyone even had the chance to gasp, a beast swept into the alleyway, three sets of black feathered wings blocking both light and rain. A construct with the heavy paws of a jaguar and the heavy jaw of a wolf landed next to me. His tail ended in a barbed tip; his fangs were filled with venom. I'd built him with the shards of Thrana's horns, only to be awoken during desperate times.

"This is Hao," I said, and even my guards' eyes were wide with fear. I'd named the creature after the squirrel construct that had once saved my life. "Poison still incapacitates Alanga for a time." I had Jovis to thank for that knowledge. "Maybe not as much for you, Dione, but certainly all your fresh new Alanga friends. So do we fight this out, or do you take your friends and leave?"

He stared at me, his jaw tightening, and I knew the word that rolled itself in his mind: *abomination*. His fingers curled around the hilts of his daggers, water rising up the walls of the buildings on either side of us.

"Think carefully," I said, my voice low. "I've built the beast with the quickness of striking snakes. He is just as swift as you all are." I could see him considering, his gaze flicking between me, my guards, Thrana and Hao. Two Alanga against one, but I had the construct. There was still a small ember in me, burning with the hope that we wouldn't have to fight. "You once decried the Alanga destruction wreaked upon innocent citizens, all as a result of squabbles between your brethren. This much of our history I *do* know. Is that a part you wish to repeat?" I stared into his milky eye, hoping that some part of the man who'd written the earlier section of the journal still existed.

"Fine," he said at last. He lifted his hands from the hilts of his daggers and the rain he'd gathered fell splashing to the cobblestones. He gestured to his entourage and they fell in behind him. I glanced at the spot where the servant had been and found the space empty. She must have fled when Hao had arrived.

Huan, my Captain of the Imperial Guard, made her way to my side. "I thought we were done with constructs," she said. "Eminence," she added belatedly.

"I'll explain later." How *would* I explain? "It doesn't use shards." A half-truth. "There was a servant here, pushing the handcart. Did you see her?"

Huan nodded. "She fled when your creature landed." Still a slightly accusatory tone in her voice. I'd have to smooth things over, and quickly.

"Find her. Bring her back to the palace."

I sheathed the sword, swinging it back over my shoulder. Rain pattered cold against my scalp. I should have felt relieved. I'd uncovered Dione's heist in progress. I'd recovered what he meant to steal from me. Why, then, did I still feel so uneasy?

He'd taken Khalute on his own, had built the Shardless Few, had lived for so many more years than I had. He'd given up too easily. There was another angle here.

I was on my way back to the palace, my arm around Thrana's shoulders, when Huan met up with me. She held a young woman by the elbow. The servant girl. She had a lost, hopeless look on her face, accentuated by the rain plastering the hair to her forehead.

"Was this it?" I called out to her before Huan could say anything. "Was this all he had planned?"

The girl shook her head. "You're too late."

I found my fingers tightening around Thrana's fur, my jaw clenched. "Too late for what?"

"It will have already happened; you've just not received word yet. The Shardless Few have attacked Nephilanu."

6

Ranami

Nephilanu Island

Ranami had once thought her doom would come by hunger, by sickness, by the knife of a criminal looking for an easy target, one no one would miss. She hadn't thought it would come to her as she stood atop the gates of a palace – one she was the mistress of. The smoke rising from the docks was thinner than she would have liked. Curse the dampness of a wet season. She'd already had word from another city that they'd tried to burn their docks, only to have an Alanga douse it with a wave.

They weren't prepared for this.

Oh, she and Phalue had discussed, over and over, what they would do if the Shardless Few tried to invade. On paper it had seemed a good plan. Burn the docks in all the cities; they could be rebuilt. Fire on them from land with flaming arrows. Hide the food and caro nuts to make it more difficult to maintain an occupation. The Shardless Few had a larger army than Nephilanu had defenses, and Phalue knew they couldn't count on Imperial troops. Not with the Empire spread so thin already. But when they'd found out that Gio was actually Dione, the Alanga from the stories, their plans hadn't seemed worth the paper they'd written them on. How were they to contend with such power?

In the distance, if she squinted, she thought she could see the bright spots of fiery arrows, arcing through the air. The Shardless Few were trying to make landfall.

Ayesh practically vibrated at her elbow. The girl was taller than she once was, though she'd always be small — a result of her years on the street, malnourished. Her ossalen, Shark, towered over her, mottled gray and brown fur stirring in the breeze, emerald gaze focused on the Endless Sea. "I should be down there," Ayesh said.

"You're fourteen," Ranami said, her voice clipped. She left it at that; they'd had this argument before.

Ayesh only lifted her arm, the one with the missing hand, the shield prosthetic Phalue had designed strapped tight to her wrist. Ranami had long since given up trying to get her to switch it out for something practical. Oh, Ayesh still wore the other grasping prosthetic sometimes, but she preferred the shield. Casually, the girl's hand went to the sword strapped at her side, her foot tapping.

Ranami felt a slight tremor in the ground beneath her feet. "Stop that. I know what you are, Ayesh."

"Then you know I'm worth at least twenty of their Shardless Few."

"We don't know if there are any Alanga down there."

"And if there are? They'll mow down our guards without me."

How had she gotten pulled into this fight again? For what felt like the thousandth time, she said, "You are still a child. I won't put you in the role of an adult."

Ayesh had kept her hair trimmed short, and it curled around her ears. Her jaw jutted, her black eyes catching Ranami's, refusing to look away. "If I were still on the streets, I'd be selling my body to any men and women who could pay. Tell me again I'm still a child."

Ranami felt her brows lowering, the crease between them deepening. "You're not on the streets anymore." Not for the first time, she cursed Lin for sending soldiers to Gaelung and not Nephilanu. For taking Phalue away from her. For the woman's arrogance in thinking the Shardless Few could be reasoned with. That Dione could.

It still dug away at her when she awoke in the middle of the night – that the Shardless Few had been so subverted. Once, she'd admired them and their purpose. She'd touted their values, their commitment to easing the suffering of those the Empire oppressed. Now they followed Dione, not Gio; now they called for the Emperor's head. The focus on what came after seemed to have dissipated, replaced instead with a hunger for violence, for wreaking havoc on those they saw as having inflicted pain on them. She could see the purpose in it, in getting people riled up for a fight. But a part of her wondered if even Dione had the power to keep that sort of anger under control.

People from the city shuffled past them, taking refuge within the palace walls. Only one bag of belongings per family; they hadn't the space for more. The scent of sweat mingled with the petrichor scent of drizzling rain, of wet bark. She wanted to make them move more quickly, but they'd had little enough warning as it was.

"I wish Phalue were here," Ayesh said, using the words like a lash.

Ranami closed her eyes briefly, letting them strike. "I do too, little one." She could still feel the shoulder buckle on Phalue's armor digging beneath her chin as she'd embraced her at the docks, the rough feel of Phalue's palm against her cheek, the softness of her lips.

All the anger burning in Ayesh's gaze winked out, her eyes filling with tears. "She shouldn't have gone." Ranami opened her arms and Ayesh fell into them, her head resting on Ranami's shoulder.

Did she hear shouts and screams drifting on the wind? All those guards on the beach, giving their lives in a bid to keep Nephilanu free. What would Phalue say to that? They'd made plans, but things had shifted so quickly. "She made a promise, and if you know anything about her, you know this: she keeps her word."

"I'm sorry," Ayesh said into Ranami's collar. "I just want to fight. I wish you'd let me. There are guards who are only two years older than I am."

"And you can win against them in a fight, even without your magic, I know." Ranami stroked the girl's hair. Someday, she'd have to let her go, the way she'd had to let Phalue go – waiting behind, her breath held, hoping for news. Sometimes, she wished she was a fighter too, so she could share that space with her wife and daughter, so she could stand at their sides. "Battles are ugly."

"I know what ugly is like."

Life on the streets did that to you. A merchant had cut off Ayesh's hand when she'd been caught stealing from his stall. She'd barely escaped the sinking of Unta, the other gutter orphans she'd known all dead. Over the years, the girl had told her a little of her experiences – and each time she seemed a little more exhausted, a little more relieved. It was difficult work, trudging through the mire of one's past, excavating memories, bringing them into the light where others could see their ugliness, where all the facets of them were exposed. Ranami had done this work too, but every time she thought she'd finished, a word, a smell or a sound would bring yet another terrible remembrance bubbling to the surface.

"Let's talk about this later?" Ranami whispered into her forehead.

Ayesh wriggled free and Ranami looked to the harbor. Most of the ships had dropped anchor just out of arrow's reach. Here at Nephilanu's capital they might not have an Alanga with them who was far along enough in their development to work the waves. The dinghies that had made it past the flaming arrows would be making landfall, Shardless Few pouring onto the sand. As soon as they'd seen the ships, Ranami had bid her soldiers to lay out traps between the palace and the docks, things she hoped would slow them down. But numbers were not in their favor.

It didn't seem right, to just let this happen, but she still held on to a thread of hope. Perhaps there wouldn't be so many making their way past the beach. Perhaps. Her heart felt pierced by her ribs, hanging in the cavity of her chest like a beast hung to bleed out after slaughter. She made her way down from atop the gates and into the courtyard below, Ayesh and Shark on her heels.

"I can see them," one of her guards called from the walls. "They're making their way around the barricaded main street. Our rooftop archers are ready for them."

The confidence in his voice bolstered hers. But then he spoke again.

"There's a lot of them, Sai. More than we've got."

She heard the scrape of boots against wet stone as someone came abreast of her. Tythus's widow. Her face was more lined than it had been two years ago, a streak of white hair at her forehead, mingling with the black. Her son and daughter lingered behind her, their heads now nearly to her shoulders. "Sai, we'll need to let people into your bedroom as well. There simply isn't enough space. We've laid reeds across as much of the open space of the courtyard as possible, but it's not a suitable place to sleep."

Ranami nodded. "I've lived in closer quarters. If it comes to a siege, I'm fine with sharing. Let them in, but keep everyone ready – we may have a way out."

She went to the gates and past them, her boots sinking a little into the muddied ruts left by passing carts. The palace was filling to the brim. Ranami could hear them shuffling behind her, stirring and muttering like cattle pressed together in a slaughtering pen.

Morbid thoughts. They wouldn't be slaughtered. There was still the hidden entrance in the palace walls, the one that led down the slope and into the forest. She hoped it wouldn't come to that. If they could just hold out long enough for the Empire to get here. For Phalue to get here.

A tall figure pushed his way through the crowd, a bag slung over one arm. His gaze met Ranami's and then slid away. She did her best to keep her expression neutral. Phalue's father. She supposed she couldn't deny him refuge.

"The first Shardless Few have made their way past the archers," the guard called from above.

There was the wall of fire next, and she could hear a faint roar as the guards lit the barricade. They'd thrown cooking oil onto the wood to encourage a hot, bright flame – one that would scorch anyone trying to climb it. But it wouldn't last. Not in this damp air.

Instead of slipping past her, his head lowered, Phalue's father approached Ranami. He had his daughter's same broad shoulders, though his frame was thinner, his arms like weathered driftwood. "I've received word from one of my contacts in the northernmost city. The Shardless Few have already made landfall there and are making their way here."

Phalue hadn't been pleased, two years ago, upon finding Ranami had thrown him out. Or freed him from the cellar prison. It depended on your perspective, really, though Ranami knew he'd seen her actions through the former lens. But he'd stopped drinking, had used the money they'd given him to buy up an interest in a merchant ship. And now, two years later, he owned three, all flying beneath the Imperial flag.

He'd been doing his best to insinuate himself back into palace life. Ranami still didn't trust him, no matter how much Phalue remarked on his growth, the ways he'd worked on himself in the past two years.

"I know," Ranami said. "My guards have been keeping me informed." She took the slightest bit of pleasure in the furrowing of his brow even as she scolded herself for taking joy in it. What did it matter? Let him try to assert his importance – they could use any and all help. She could disentangle his grasping fingers later. "But thank you for telling me. You've another ship that moors in Thalanga, have you not? Any word from the city to the east?"

"Nothing yet." He never used her title with her. He might pretend all he liked, but the power dynamic between them had changed once she'd let him out of his cell.

"They've taken losses but they have breached the barricade," her guard shouted down to her.

Another guard on the northern end of the walls cried out, "Another force, from the north! They're headed for the switch-backs." That would be the force that had the Alanga with them.

The people still lingering on the road crushed together, eyes wide as they pushed toward the palace gates. There wasn't enough time. She took the arm of Phalue's father, pushed him through the gates. "We'll take ten more and then we close these up tight," she told one of the guards at the gate.

Ranami turned and then realized: the looming presence of Shark was gone. She should have noticed it earlier when she'd been preoccupied with Phalue's father and he'd said no words of greeting to Ayesh. The man thought he could buy the girl with pleasant words and gifts, but orphans knew to be wary of both.

She seized the guard closest to her, her stomach roiling, a wave of nausea crashing at the back of her throat. "Ayesh – did you see where she went? She was here only a moment ago."

The woman nodded at the gates. "Back into the palace, Sai."

Relief made her weak. She had to be strong, to be firm. "There's not enough time or space for everyone inside," she called out to the crowd. "The rest of you – scatter into the forest. They'll come for the palace; they won't be occupied with searching out individual families." At least, not for a while. She could feel the fear and anger emanating from the remaining crowd, the rising tide of panic.

Phalue might have been able to ease it. But she could not.

She slipped in through the gates, leaving her guards to close them. Her gaze swept over the courtyard and found no sign of Ayesh. Shark's head would have towered over the heads of the city refugees. She felt the nausea rising again, knew she wouldn't feel whole until she set eyes upon her daughter.

But there was an army to face. Ayesh had returned inside the walls; the guard had said it was so. She repeated this assurance to herself as she climbed the steps to the palace walls.

What she saw when she reached the top made her heart clench.

Shardless Few soldiers were marching up the switchbacks. Their armor was haphazard, thrown together from various gathered pieces. They wore no uniform; the only thing marking them as one were the blue armbands each had tied about their upper arms. Yet they moved in unison, stepping with precision. Someone shouted orders from within their ranks and she searched for the source of the voice, finally finding it. Her heartbeat was a stab, each one only slightly less painful than the last. She knew that face, the gently sloping nose, the generous lips, the strong chin. He'd been going prematurely gray the last time she'd seen him; now the streaks were even more prominent, falling behind his ears like two silver waterfalls among the rocks.

Halong. They'd met when they were teenagers, had come to trust one another as they'd grown up on the streets. She'd told Phalue he was her brother. She still thought of him that way. She'd known he'd left to join the Shardless Few. She hadn't known he'd become Dione's general. Never, in all the years since they'd met, had she ever thought they'd be pitted against one another. How could she fight him?

She couldn't.

Some of the cityfolk she'd turned away had done as she'd asked and had scattered into the surrounding forest. Others had begun to pound at the gates.

And the guards she'd sent to the beach and to the city – she saw no sign of them.

"Should we fire on their army?" There was a waver in the voice of the guard next to her, though he was already moving to string his bow.

"No." Her thoughts crystallized. Now that she saw them, the sheer number of them, she knew they wouldn't be able to hold the palace. It was time for last resorts. She reached into the pouch at her belt and pulled out several small oilskin packets.

He stopped, surprised.

"There aren't enough of you. I want you to gather the rest of the guards and begin escorting the citizens out the hidden entrance. There's an Alanga with them. We won't last during a siege. Take the food stores. Split into four groups and go to the places marked on the map. There are shelters in the forest."

"And the caro nuts? If they find us, they'll search for them."

"Hidden," was all she would say. It had taken many expeditions over the years, searching for an appropriate spot to keep the caro nuts – a place only a few knew about. "Go. I'll do my best to keep them occupied. Make sure Ayesh gets out first."

He went, and the other guards followed him to the stairs. And then she was alone on the palace walls, feeling as though she were the figurehead on the front of a ship – useless, decorative, stiff and as unmoving as wood.

The last citizens gave up on the palace gates and scattered as the Shardless Few made their way up the last switchback. So many of them. They filled the path – one unbroken line from the gates to the bottom of the hill, a serpent of people, sliding up the slope.

"Ranami," Halong called from their midst. He'd drawn his sword, and its white blade caught and held the dim light.

There was a wrongness to this encounter, to this conversation. It went against the grain of the world's order, one in which he wrapped her warmly in a hug whenever they greeted one another. They did not stand on two opposite sides of a wall. "Halong," she called back.

He'd risen in Dione's esteem since she'd last known him. Back then, he'd been farming caro nuts, and though he'd helped steal some away from Phalue's father, he hadn't been as deeply involved in the machinations of the Shardless Few as it seemed he was now. He'd left for Khalute with his wife and child almost two years ago, had told Ranami that though he respected what she and Phalue were doing with Nephilanu, he had to follow his heart. What had happened to him in the interim? And then he lifted his hands and the surrounding water flowed to his command, forming ribbons that cut through the air, swirling and joining and pulling apart. The people in his army did not cast their gazes upward; they were used to such displays.

That was an answer of sorts, though it stirred her anger. Once, during an argument, Phalue had said she seemed full of hidden blades, and she felt them all rising to the surface as she bristled. He'd become Alanga. She wondered if it had happened before or after he'd left. She wondered if he'd told her the truth about his reasons for leaving.

Trust was so hard to earn and so easily broken. She shouted over the walls. "So it seems Vasuvian was right: power is like a wolf howling at night, calling others to him, forming a pack that makes the hunting of prey easier."

"You are not my prey," Halong said. "The Emperor is."

"It certainly doesn't feel that way right now." She eyed the soldiers beneath her, their hands resting on the hilts of their weapons. She felt exposed, trapped, forced to watch the city she'd come to love go up in flames, its people displaced. "So that's it, then? We're in your way?"

She caught the flush of color in his cheeks. Behind her, the citizens were being herded into the palace by one of the guards. They'd go down one floor, take a couple of turns through the hallway, to a room with a hidden door. She needed to buy them time.

"You know it's not that." Halong drew his hand back to his side and the water stayed where it was. Ranami tried not to look at the scintillating ropes of water just below her. She'd seen what Ayesh could do, pushing waves of water at practice dummies, tumbling them from their supports. He could easily wash her from the walls if he chose to.

"Then what is it that you want? How many of my guards did you slaughter on your way to the palace? And here you are, with an army at your back." She was glad it wasn't Dione, who would have swept her aside without hesitation. Then again, he was only absent because he'd been providing cover for his army to make its way to Nephilanu. How would Halong have felt if Dione had killed her? Would he have cared?

"Surrender Nephilanu to the Shardless Few, hand over your stores of food and caro nuts and give us control of your farms."

She let him stew in the silence, though she could hear quiet footsteps from behind her, and the creak of armor from the men and women below as they waited for their orders.

"Will you?" he finally said.

"I was waiting for the rest of that," Ranami said. "Because it sounded like there was a threat at the end of it." She looked pointedly at the water hovering just below her. "Is this the way the Shardless Few have learned to conduct themselves? Now that you have Alanga, you can just murder whoever stands in your way?"

"And I suppose we should just let ourselves be murdered instead? There is still an Emperor."

"She's not a tyrant."

"But the next one may be. We cannot afford to be complacent. We need to break the system if we're to experience any real and lasting change."

Ranami didn't disagree with him. But this was her home he was storming, and she knew what he would do with the caro nuts. He'd withhold them, choking off the cure that the rest of the Empire so desperately needed. He'd make them suffer so that they'd be more willing to rise up against Lin. He thought it was necessary.

Ranami wasn't so sure.

She thought of the people inside the palace, making their way to the secret door and then down the slope. She needed to buy more time – not just for them, but for herself. She had to withdraw all those hidden blades, let him believe he had a chance to end this peaceably. "Halong, you know me. You know I would never have chosen Phalue if I thought she would betray my values. She has never thrown her support behind the Emperor."

"She went to Imperial."

"To fulfill a promise. Being friendly with someone doesn't mean that you wholly agree with them and all their actions. I know what Dione would intend to do with our store of caro nuts. People will suffer."

He gave her a level look. "People will suffer if you don't hand them over."

And there it was. The threat. Ranami wished she could say she did not fear it, but she'd been through enough in her life to know that fear was a warning. She could have used Phalue's solid presence at her side, that certainty that when they were together, they were on the right path. "Let me speak with my advisers on the best course of action." She did her best to sound considered, less angry, less certain that she was right. "Please."

Halong searched her with his gaze, trying to uncover signs of deception. At last, he nodded. "I can give you that. You have until the sun sets before we take apart the gates."

Not long, but long enough. Swiftly, she made her way to the steps and back down to the courtyard. It was empty now, her people already fled. There was a part of her that wanted to keep her word. It was Halong. She never would have survived her childhood if it wasn't for him. She ached for the changes that time had wrought, wishing she'd protested more when he'd chosen to go, that she'd dug more into his reasons. But she'd taken their friendship for granted, sure it would weather anything.

One of her guards met her with her bag of things, his voice a barely audible whisper. "Most of them are out on the slopes.

There's plenty of cover but it's slow going. Only . . ." He paused, hesitated. "No one's seen Ayesh, Sai."

All the anger she'd been doing her best to suppress erupted. She dug her nails into her palms. That foolish, *foolish* girl! She knew about the hidden door. She must have taken Shark and left through it while everyone else had been busy. Where was she now? In that first year, she'd crept away from the palace so many times, uncomprehending of the fact that other people could worry about her. Sometimes she'd return days later, her jaw set, eyes defiant, certain they'd change their minds and set her back on the streets. It had taken time for her to learn to truly trust them, to become comfortable growing beneath the light of their love and attention.

But setbacks — there were always setbacks. This was just the worst possible time for one. Or had she decided to defy Ranami, to wade into the fight on her own? Would they even realize they were fighting a child before they killed her?

One thing was certain: she wasn't in the palace.

"Get me out of here." She took her bag from him — he'd be better able to fight unburdened — and slung it over her shoulder. Just the necessities, nothing more.

The guard nodded, falling into place behind her as she made her way through the palace corridors. A pang of loneliness, of heartsickness hit her. This place had become her home. So many shared memories of Phalue, Ayesh and her together. The Shardless Few would ransack the place when they broke through the gates. They'd leave nothing untouched. Even if she was able to return here it wouldn't feel the same way. It had been, for a time, a sanctuary.

She entered the small room and went to the hidden door. It was a remnant from Alanga times, the craftsmanship impeccable. When it was shut, it looked nearly seamless, blending in with the wall outside. She opened it.

From this angle, she could make out a few people hidden in

the brush, making their way downslope. But the wet season had spurred new growth, and the slope was covered in green.

"We'll go to the northernmost camp," she said as her guard closed the door behind them. It was closest to the place she and Phalue had hidden the caro nuts. "But first, I need to find Ayesh."

She slid down the slope, doing her best to find footholds in the muddy ground, holding onto the slender trunks of saplings to steady herself. She'd made her way nearly halfway down when she heard the crack of a branch breaking behind her.

Her guard had already whirled, blade held at the ready by the time Ranami was able to properly turn. The vegetation beneath her feet was slippery with moisture, the slope steep.

"I was hoping you were telling me the truth. I thought we owed one another that, at least." Halong sat astride a russet-brown ossalen just above them, soldiers flanking him. Ranami couldn't tell how many. "Dione knew about the door. He didn't enter the palace with the rioters when Phalue deposed her father. He took the back way in."

Realizations flashed through Ranami's mind, her breath quick in her throat. They must have let at least some of her people get away – they'd have had to in order to take her unawares. But they didn't need to capture everyone. Mostly, they needed *her*. She was the one holding authority over Nephilanu in Phalue's absence, the one who knew where the stores of food and caro nuts were. What methods might they use to extract this information? Dione clearly had no compunctions over the pain he caused others. How much had Halong changed, truly?

She wouldn't let them take her, not without a fight.

Halong's eyes narrowed. "Your daughter, why is she not with you?"

"I wish I knew," Ranami snapped back before she could stop herself, her irritation at Ayesh bleeding into her tone.

He let out a snort in spite of himself. "Ah, I see. She is that age . . ." For the barest moment, it was as though they were in Halong's hut again, sharing a drink, laughing over the folly of youth. The moment fled; she couldn't grasp it.

And then Ranami caught the shadow of movement in the trees beyond him, the dark gray and brown shape of Shark, nearly invisible against the brush. She started to inhale sharply, caught herself, coughed into her hand instead. *By all the old Alanga, stay where you are.* But thoughts couldn't travel through wind and air and lodge themselves in others' ears. Ayesh wanted to prove herself – what better way than by rescuing her mother?

"I surrender," Ranami said, pitching her voice so that Ayesh could hear. She stepped forward, her hands lifted. "No one else should die on my behalf." She spoke to her guard, as though he were the one her words were for. Ranami put a hand on his sword arm. "We are vastly outnumbered. And this doesn't mean the end. This doesn't mean we will accede to all their wishes. This is only a pause on the fight yet to come."

Her guard lowered his sword and Halong's soldiers moved downslope, reaching for her. She dared one last look at the trees as they bound her wrists.

Ayesh was gone.

7

Lin

Imperial Island

I had the guards bring the servant girl to the courtyard and questioned her in the rain, Hao a frightening presence at my back. There was something ominous about the setting, which I'd wanted to use to my advantage, and no matter my position, I knew that my construct — his teeth, his flashing green eyes — would buy me much more intimidation than I could ever procure on my own.

"I already know you were working for Dione," I said, rain dripping from the hood of my cloak. Even in a wet season, the weather was warm, but the lanky girl had her arms wrapped around herself, shivering — whether out of fear or a chill, I wasn't sure. "Why did he want the sword?"

The girl only shook her head. Two guards stood behind her, though neither they nor the girl paid one another any heed. All eyes focused on Hao, whose black wings spread out behind me, his barbed tail raised. He wasn't the same Hao as the spy construct I'd once befriended, but I'd fed this beast, petted him, cajoling him with kindness as well as with commands. I didn't want to repeat my father's mistakes. Constructs – even simple ones – had some small measure of autonomy.

Thrana had retreated into the palace for her morning meal, and I wasn't sure what it said about me – that I was relieved she wasn't here, that she didn't see this. I was glad, too, that Phalue was busy packing her things.

"Why did he want the sword?" I asked again, my voice a trifle louder. When she shook her head again, I shouted at her. "Why did he want the sword?" I gestured and Hao lifted his head to the sky, a roar in his throat. He took a step toward her and her gaze snapped to his mouth, the long, sharp teeth.

"It's not the teeth you should be most worried about," I said, my tone even and calm. "They're the teeth from a colossal shark and it took me a long time to procure them. Yes, their edges are serrated and they'll shred you to pieces in moments. But it's the tail that is Hao's crowning glory. Did you know that there are islands where the insect life is enormous? They feed on one another, competing to become bigger and stronger and more deadly. That stinger comes from a giant poisonous insect and it liquefies the insides of others, making it easier for them to feed. We're a bit smaller than they are, but first – I've been told – you just feel paralyzed. And then, give it several heartbeats, the fiery pain starts to—"

"He didn't tell me," the servant girl said, tears in her voice. "I had the least involvement in his plans."

"You had enough. Did he take you to Khalute? Did he train you?"

She gave a faint nod. "He trained the entire team. This was supposed to be a quick job. You weren't supposed to notice."

"Then you must have seen something, overheard something. You cannot tell me that people don't talk, not even the Shardless

Few." She hesitated and I pressed forward, sensing she was at a breaking point. Dione might have trained her, but I could tell he'd spent less time with her. "You think I don't have other constructs? Ones that can tell me what I want to know? Or would you rather die senselessly with all your nerve endings aflame?"

Hao, behind me, took a step closer.

The girl buried her head in her hands, wilting to her knees. "I was paid," she said, weeping. "Eminence, I was only doing this to help my sick mother. The price of caro nut oil has been going up as the wet season goes on, and with the shortage of witstone, prices have been even higher. Everyone knows your stores are running low."

Shame cut me – through skin and flesh to the bone beneath. It ached. I wanted to apologize, to tell her I was doing everything I could to stem the shortages, to ensure my people were cared for. Instead, I waited.

"He's been doing his own research on the swords. I don't know what they do; I only know that Dione thinks they will win him the war."

She was withholding something; I could see it in the tension she carried at the corners of her lips. I felt the thrumming in my bones and tapped a foot against the paving stones. A tremor worked its way through the ground.

The servant lifted her tear-streaked face, eyes wide. "I also saw a name," she gasped out.

"A name," I repeated.

"When Dione called me into his study to explain my role in the theft. He had stacks of books on his desk and there was a sheet of paper with names on it, underneath the heading 'the first seven'. I only saw the first name under that heading. Tianlu of Khalute. That's all. That's all I have."

"Can you write it for me?" I didn't know how many Tianlus

had lived on Khalute then, back when the reign of the first Emperor had begun. I needed to know how the name was written, to see the family mark.

She nodded.

I hesitated, and then spoke to her softly. "Tell my guards here your mother's name. I'll get her some caro nut oil, even if it has to come from my own personal stash."

Hope filled her eyes.

"I cannot let you go, but I've not held up my end of the bargain between a leader and her people. I'm doing my best." It eased the ache of guilt from my bones.

Thrana found me walking through the palace hallways, the paper with Tianlu's name written on it in my hand. I'd had the servant locked in a room for further questioning, though I'd asked that the guards attend to her needs.

Thrana sidled up to me, her shoulder brushing mine. She barely fit inside the corridors now, her horned head nearly at the rafters. I'd have to move her into one of the halls at some point or build a shelter for her in the courtyard. The larger she grew, the more I wondered how the ossalen were not depicted with the Alanga in all the old paintings and carvings. They were certainly hard to miss.

"The library?" Thrana asked.

"Yes. And then to my experiments."

Though I'd kept the library with the bone shard books locked, I'd left the larger library on the main floor unlocked. I'd taken Imperial's most recent census book to my room, but the others were shelved in neat rows by the library entrance. They stretched back for hundreds of years — the older ones had been copied once or twice.

My father, however, hadn't bothered with that task. As I sifted through the volumes, more than one binding came apart in my hands, dust rising into the air. The windows with their large awnings let in shadowed light, forcing me to squint at the words. I found Tianlu's name in the first of Khalute's records, then traced his children's records, and his children's children. I found myself seizing a piece of parchment, tearing it into strips and marking pages I knew I needed to refer back to.

I followed the genealogies of the eldest children – those who would stand to inherit. There was one dead end, and I traced the line of the relative who would have received the most precious belongings of the dead.

Thrana watched me, offering a helpful observation once or twice, pulling records out and putting them away. "You haven't eaten," she told me.

I held up a hand to quiet her, flipping the pages of one of Anau's census books, searching . . .and finding. I stabbed at the page. "Tianlu's most direct descendant is on Anau. She might have one of the swords." I marked the page with a torn piece of paper, just in case. "I need to go there. If I find the sword and gather two of them, that means two fewer in Dione's possession."

"And what of everything else?" Thrana said.

I set the book back onto the shelf. "I can't lift the ban on witstone mining. No one will die if they receive goods a little later than they're expecting. Except caro nuts. And Dione has a blockade on our largest provider."

Thrana squeezed through the door after me and we made our way to the shard room. This, the shard magic library, and my bedroom were the only doors I now kept habitually locked. I ran my hand along the chain around my neck, pressing a palm to the cold keys hanging from it. It was so different from the heavy chain my father had worn, keys for every room strung along it, clinking together as he limped through the palace hallways.

I took the lamp from next to the lintel and lit it as the door closed behind us. Never enough time, nor enough resources. A fourth and fifth key lay within my sash pocket. I pulled them out and went to the cloudtree door. Jovis had wanted me to stop using bone shard magic. But Jovis was dead and I had an Empire to save.

Thrana and I crept through the old mining tunnels where the palace abutted the mountains. I'd explored them in the past two years, chalk marking the walls where I'd written instructions to myself. The tunnel on the left at the fork led to the cavern with the pool and my father's old workstation. The tunnel to the right led to Ilith's chambers. There was another smaller tunnel leading from Ilith's chambers. I'd squeezed my way along it a short distance once, the way tangled with the taproot from the cloud juniper above. And then I'd decided, finally, that my father hadn't hidden anything down there.

Someday, when I had the time, I'd make a spy construct and send it that way, just to be sure.

When I had the time.

I unlocked the door set into the tunnel on the left, making my way down to the cavern with the pool. The first time I'd been here the place had felt foreign, strange. I'd found Thrana in the water and we'd both climbed toward the light. Now, the sight of the sparking stalactites felt familiar and warm. The workstation that had once been my father's was now mine, and I didn't murder citizens to rebuild a person from my past.

I touched Thrana's shoulder after I lit the lamps, after I made my way to the metal table. "Are you sure?" I asked her for what felt like the thousandth time.

She gave me a long look. "Lin, the shards you've taken from my horns are not even a part of me anymore. They are yours. I've given them to you."

Still, I couldn't help but hold her chin in my hands, feel the warm *whuff* of her breath on my face before I let her go. It had been years now and she seemed well and hale. And we'd puzzled this out together. She was right – her shed horns weren't a part of her anymore. Was this one of the things that had been purged during the Alanga massacre? The knowledge of this power, this magic? My father's magic seemed a grotesque imitation in comparison, a parody of the life and giving that was a part of Thrana's. What, then, had the old Alanga used the shards for?

A tattered book sat on the side of the table and I thumbed through it. The book of Alanga tales that I'd once caught Bayan reading, so very long ago. The remembered feel of his hand in mine made my gaze flutter to the pool. The body my father had intended to inhabit still lay in it – not dead and not alive. There were times I was tempted to try and bring Bayan back from the dead.

If I'd had a drop of Jovis's blood, I wondered if I would have thrown all caution aside just to see him smile at me once more. But I was not my father's daughter – I was *not*.

There was a mention in one of the pages, a tale of Arrimus and Dione, of an Alangan artifact Arrimus had given to her great-grandson. One that made a giant wave. He never used it in the story, and much as I raked through other stories, I found no other mentions of such an artifact.

Alangan artifacts didn't just warn of other Alanga. People had always speculated on magical artifacts being weapons of great power, but this was the sort of thing mentioned in the same breath as a tale about someone swimming to the underside of an island, or the tales a fisherman told of people with fins and gills living in the deep reaches of the Endless Sea. Nonsense.

My notes lay scattered next to the book. I'd set the Empire's best scholars at the Scholars' Academy to researching both the artifacts and ways to make our ships faster. I'd sent them the piece of the fountain I'd found two years earlier to study. They had more resources and time, I knew, but I couldn't help but to worry at both problems.

The cloudtree monks had only been able to verify that there had been artifacts used as weapons. "They did not write down how they made them," they'd written in their letters. "Even the restricted texts do not say. Our understanding is that there were few new actual Alanga, and each was taken under the wing of their elders and taught how to create such artifacts. The descendants of the original Alanga were never taught this magic. So there was no reason to write it down with so few new students."

How easily things could be lost to the ravages of time! Dione would know, but it wasn't as though I could ask him.

I turned to the other books on my desk – tomes I'd found fallen behind shelves, though I suspected some he'd purposefully hidden. I wasn't even certain why. I pulled one out from the pile I'd not had the chance to read and found only an account of a man, armed to the teeth, clambering through underground caves, rainwater dripping from above, his courage flagging. The text made specific mention of the sword he carried, though did not describe it.

The account ended in the middle of a sentence, the rest of the pages blank. Thrana had settled onto the cavern floor next to the pool, her breathing calm and slow as she slept.

My gaze flicked to the shelves. A plain clay flask sat on the top shelf, its mouth stoppered. The last of my father's memories. Thrana hated when I drank them. But Thrana was asleep and I was feeling desperate. I'd sipped a little over the past two years, slipping into my father's skin as he ordered my mother's maid-servants slain, as he tended to the cloud juniper, as he created Bayan from the various parts of citizens he'd kidnapped and

murdered, as he discovered the properties of the pool by accident – a stray body part he'd let fall and had forgotten about.

My head feeling light, my limbs heavy, I went to the bookshelf
and unstoppered the flask. The metallic scent of the fluid within
swam into my nostrils. Iloh was right. The Empire was fractur-
ing. Dione was bringing back the Alanga, and if Ragan was any
indication, he wasn't taking any precautions or attempting to
limit them in any way. He would destroy us all in a vain attempt
to assuage his own guilt.

Unless I found answers.

I tipped the flask over my mouth and swallowed the last drops.

The sweet, coppery taste lingered at the back of my tongue,
the coolness of it sliding down my throat. And then the world in
front of me went white.

Colors began to bleed back into my vision. I was in a room I
recognized – my old room – though it seemed a little brighter, the
wall hangings a little less faded. A girl sat by the bed, dressed in a
silken robe painted with chrysanthemums. She had a lamp on the
floor and was flipping the pages of a book. Several other books
were stacked next to her. Black hair hung loose about her face.

"Your nursemaids were supposed to put you to bed some time
ago," I said to her. Even through the memory I could feel the
swell of affection, mingled with a vague irritation and the hint
of sadness.

The girl looked up. She was so young – three, maybe four.
"They did their job, Father," she said. Her face turned back to
the pages of her book again. "They locked the books up. They
took away the tinderbox for the lamp. I took the door off the
cupboard and had a tinderbox in my pocket from earlier. Don't
punish them."

I wandered closer and found the book she was poring over
to be a catalog of animals from the various islands. She was

skimming through the section on the creatures that lived on the Empire's southern islands. She should have been tired. We'd only arrived home that afternoon after a long trip on the Endless Sea.

"Something you saw when we were on Nephilanu?" I asked her. "Would you like to tell me about it?"

She glanced up at me. "No. I just wanted to read about animals."

"Lin, I know when you're lying to me."

With a frustrated grimace, the girl shut the book and crawled into bed. "I'm not lying. Not really. I did want to read about animals."

I sat on the bed, pulled the covers up to her chin and brushed the hair back from her forehead. "Go to sleep."

Her lips pressed together as I leaned over and picked up the lamp. I stopped, waited. She wrung her fingers together above the covers. "If I did see something on Nephilanu, and I brought it back, could I keep it as a pet?"

"Maybe." I felt my gaze flit from corner to corner in the small room, searching for whatever creature she might have brought back with her. I would have been a fool not to know the girl was lonely, especially after her mother had died. I was a poor substitute, always in conference with advisers, always poring over books and records. Always, always missing Nisong, hoping to find a way – I stopped the thought, focused on my daughter. "It depends on what it was."

She turned over beneath the covers. "Just asking." And then she let out a sigh, her breathing evening out.

I set the lamp on the desk in the corner and then began to collect the books. Servants' work, but they'd already proved inadequate once. And there was that affection, still brimming in my heart – a feeling that spilled over each time my gaze brushed over the girl. A feeling now constantly tinged with grief.

As I crouched to pick up the last book, I saw the flash of eyes from beneath the bed, reflecting the lamplight. My heartbeat quickened. I took the lamp from the desk, brought it back and looked beneath the bed. Lin had built a nest for the creature of old blankets and clothes. It curled within, its nose laid atop its rump, ears pricked as it watched me. It looked liked an otter, a kitten, a weasel. Webbed paws, nubs where horns would grow. I recoiled, scrambling back from the bed, wanting nothing more than to blow out the lantern and to forget what I'd seen. My jaw ached as I clenched my teeth.

I wanted to believe it was something – *anything* – else. But I remembered my mother passing the description down to me, forcing me to create drawings which she'd burned immediately after. Just to be sure I'd know one when I saw one.

Ossalen.

Fear and anger constricted my throat. Implications stumbled through my mind, one after another, making it difficult to breathe. I made myself face the creature, ducking back down to peer beneath the bed. "Not her," I hissed at it. It trembled at my voice. "She's clever, yes, but she's too young. She's far too young. Why her?" They weren't supposed to come back. Not yet. Not when there were so few who'd not had their shards removed. And there were no records of ossalen bonding those younger than eight. But the Shardless Few had been stealing children away from the Tithing Festival, the monasteries still existed and there were always exceptions, no matter how few.

Lin stirred at my words and I clamped my mouth shut, pressed a hand to it, bit my shaking fingers. My insides roiled as I shouted in my mind – *Not her! Not her! Not her!* Another, calmer part of me knew what I must do. What I'd been born to do. Protect the Empire. No matter the cost to others.

No matter the cost to myself.

I looked to my daughter sleeping peacefully, the only remnant left of my late wife. One last time, I smoothed the hair from her forehead, felt the warmth of her breath against my palm. My head felt light, my movements not my own.

And then I reached beneath the bed and seized the creature. I felt the soft fur around its shoulders, the way it wriggled as it tried to get free. But before it could cry out, I wrapped my fingers around its throat and squeezed. Sharp little claws scrabbled at my wrists, leaving marks, drawing blood. I didn't feel the wounds. All I could feel was the pounding pulse at my neck, in my ears, the sick working its way to my mouth, the hollow in my chest that grew and grew.

In the dark, I listened to my daughter's breathing, soft and steady as waves lapping at the shore. I listened to it slow as the creature weakened, as it stopped struggling. I listened to her breathing stop.

1522–1525. Lin Sukai.

I came back to myself in the cavern, my hands trembling. I couldn't look at them for fear I could still feel the ossalen's soft fur beneath my fingers, the pressure as I squeezed its throat. I seized the waste bucket next to the table and vomited – over and over until my stomach was empty. Even then my belly still heaved, my throat opening, as if I could remove the memory from my body by force.

I'd wondered how the original Lin had died, why she'd only lived for three years. It had been *him*. He'd murdered his own daughter, kept her death a secret. How? Had he made little girl constructs, one year after another, until he grew me? Had he simply locked the door and pretended she was still in there, alive? I didn't want to know.

There'd been a time when he'd loved his daughter, when he'd loved his wife. I hated that I now understood his coldness, his inability to ever love me or raise me as his. He'd thought he *had* to kill his own daughter. He'd been molded all his life to fear the Alanga, to do everything he could to keep them from returning.

Everything and anything.

It took me time to recover from this revelation, for my emotions and stomach to calm, for my mind to begin working again. There was still important information that I could glean from this memory. Killing an ossalen killed the person they bonded with. That meant that a person could hunt down ossalen instead of Alanga. As far as I could tell, all Thrana could do was blow a strong wind and heal quickly. She was big and strong, but she couldn't wield a sword or make the ground tremble or control the waves.

Was she more vulnerable than I was?

A faint knocking sound came from the entrance to the cavern. "Thrana," I said, "do you hear that?"

Thrana lifted her head and nodded.

We traced our way back to the shard storeroom. Here, the knocking was louder, filling the room. I pulled open the door. Ikanuy stood there, two of my guards behind her.

"Your prisoner has escaped, Eminence."

It took me a moment to process what she'd said. My prisoner? The lanky servant girl who'd broken with the threat of poison? Who'd wept at being threatened by Hao?

"She asked for tea, and when the servant arrived with it, she took down the servant and both guards. She is an Alanga."

A sense of dread settled into the pit of my stomach. "And did she flee immediately?"

Ikanuy shook her head. "No. She went to the library. And then she made it onto the roof and fled into the mountains."

My mouth went dry. She'd been a plant – someone left behind to be captured, to feed me information, to garner the information she wanted in return. The location and name of Tianlu's descendant. "Shut down the harbors. No one leaves by boat without a thorough search for the missing servant."

But if she'd left her ossalen in the foothills, she could make her way to another of Imperial's harbors, and faster than we could send messengers to stop her. Dione wouldn't have gone far. She'd tell him this information. I no longer had the leisure to send someone to check on this descendant, to ask them to come to Imperial. Dione would make his way to Anau. He'd try to get there before me. I was the only one who could face him.

"Ready a ship for me."

"Eminence?" Ikanuy's face was wan by the fading light. The servants were beginning to light the lamps and I realized the day was coming to a close.

My head swam as I tried to organize my thoughts. In spite of Thrana's admonition, I'd been so focused on my research that I'd forgotten lunch. How long had I been caught in my father's memory? "I need to gather a few items. I'll need my guards. Provision for a short journey. We leave tonight."

8

Phalue

Imperial Island

She owned too many things. That was the problem. Phalue stuffed her belongings into bags, her hands moving frantically. Clothes, trinkets she'd intended to bring back for Ayesh, a jade necklace and matching bracelet she'd bought for Ranami. She wouldn't have packed at all if they hadn't needed time to prepare her ship in the harbor.

She should have been there. That was the thing that bothered her the most. She and Ranami had made plans for what they would do if the Shardless Few tried to invade, but they hadn't updated them after Gio had been revealed to be Dione even as Alanga rose within the Empire. There had been too many other things to do. And Dione had helped against the constructs at Gaelung, hadn't he? He'd seemed to have grown complacent, comfortable with the new arrangement of an Emperor who actually cared about her people. Or at least, comfortable enough to accept her invitation to peace talks.

And so Phalue had also grown complacent, busying herself

with the day-to-day running of an island, agreeing to leave in order to train Lin in swordplay. An invasion of the Shardless Few seemed unsure, unreal, a distant island spotted through the mists. And as time passed, so did the distance seem to grow larger.

Of course he hadn't changed his plans. They should have been building their retinue of guards, fortifying the walls of the palace. Instead, they'd been reforming the laws of Nephilanu, providing homes for refugees, ensuring that farmers were treated more fairly – all things that had seemed more urgent at the time.

Now Ranami and Ayesh were alone on the island, without her – *without her* – weathering an invasion.

She gazed about the empty walls of the room she'd lived in at the Hall of Earthly Wisdom for a few months. She slung her bag over her shoulder, checking the rumpled bed, the small desk. The room seemed starker for the fact that it was not the room she shared with Ranami at Nephilanu. If she could only close her eyes and reawaken there, Ranami lying spread beneath the sheets, one arm flung, warm, over Phalue's shoulders, the crisp, clean scent of her thick in Phalue's nostrils . . .

Instead, she was half an Empire away.

Her mind played out terrible images as she strode from the room, as she made her way to the double doors of the hall. Ranami overrun by soldiers, a sword run through her chest. Ayesh bounding out atop Shark, slain easily by one of the Alanga who'd taken up with the Shardless Few. The people she loved most in the world dead and gone, the city burning, Nephilanu razed and ransacked by people who only cared about hurting the Empire without caring that it meant hurting the innocents within it.

The double doors opened just as she put her hand to the knob.

Lin stood there, Thrana behind her, sitting on her haunches and scratching an ear. "You can't go."

Phalue's hand fell, resting on the pommel of her sword, though this time she was aware she was doing it. Brooding, Ranami had said. She didn't feel like she was brooding. She felt like she was crawling out of her own skin, trying to make herself into a thing that could be carried on the wind, weightless, back to the ones she loved. "You can't make me stay. Not unless you wish to hold me prisoner."

Lin let out a sigh. "And what good would that do me? Sai, this is not about what you want and don't want – and I know you want to be with your family. But what are you hoping to accomplish?"

Phalue wanted to shove the Emperor aside, to storm past her. She didn't have time to listen to these petty words, to play these games, to make these calculations. Ranami was in danger. Ayesh was in danger.

Ranami's face swam in her mind, looking at her in consternation as she remarked on Phalue's impulsiveness. Was this impulsiveness? They'd still be readying her ship. She forced herself to calm, to remove her hand from her sword. "I mean to be there with them."

"To rescue them?"

Phalue scowled. "Don't shepherd me. If you've something to say, then say it."

Lin stepped to the side, making room for Phalue to pass. "I'm not trying to trap you here. But if you go back, you'll be playing right into Dione's hands. The Shardless Few have already attacked. It took time for word of that to arrive. Dione has lived hundreds of years. He's familiar with war tactics. He won't have just directed whoever is acting as his proxy to take the palace; he'll ensure that no one gets in or out. That means a blockade. You'll have one ship. He'll have hundreds, ringing all the way around your little island. You won't be able to make landfall without being spotted. As soon as you do—" She lifted a hand and then clenched it into a fist. "—he closes the trap. Now he doesn't just have Ranami and Ayesh, he has you. And you . . . have no leverage."

Phalue wanted to snarl at her that it wasn't true. That she'd find a way through. She held the words back, swallowed them.

The woman was right, much as Phalue didn't want her to be. "I have no leverage from here, either. Unless – recall your soldiers from Gaelung. Send them to Nephilanu."

But Lin was already shaking her head. "Gaelung has to be stabilized first. And Dione will anticipate that."

This was a pointless talk then. The least she could do was to be at her wife's side. Phalue strode past Lin. Thrana pricked her ears at her approach, watching her with bright eyes. Phalue slowed to give the beast a quick pat on the neck. She'd grown fond of her. And Thrana reminded her of Shark, who reminded her of Ayesh and Ranami.

Lin, however, chased after her, falling into step beside her. Phalue lengthened her stride, knowing that the Emperor would have to jog to keep up and not caring. "Listen," Lin said, "your wife isn't a foolish woman. It's possible she's been able to establish some sort of resistance on Nephilanu. We won't know until we wait for word. If you march straight back to the island, you'd be putting any plans she has in jeopardy."

That stalled Phalue. She skidded to a halt. "Then what would you have me do instead? You're the Emperor – surely you have a plan." She'd thought to stump Lin, but the woman only nodded. Infuriating.

"Dione came here not just as a distraction, but to steal the white-bladed sword." Lin had told her, in confidence, what the blade did – cut Alanga, burned them, made it so they couldn't heal from the wounds it inflicted. She leaned in, glancing about for listening ears. "There is more than one of these swords. They must do more than they appear to; I just don't know what or how. If he spent so much effort trying to obtain mine, they must be important."

"Or he's two steps ahead of you and knows you'll waste your efforts trying to find them."

Lin frowned. "I've considered that. But I can't afford to assume that is the case. I've corresponded with the cloudtree monks. There were seven swords made which meant seven original wielders of them. By going through the genealogies, I think I've been able to track down the possible location of one."

Of course. Her words sounded as though they made sense but this was why the woman was trying to stop her: so she could use Phalue for her own means. "And I suppose you want me to go with you to find it?"

"You're good in a fight, but it's more than that. There aren't enough people that I trust," Lin said. "And I trust you."

It warmed a spot in her chest, to hear the Emperor speak of her this way, but Phalue had also learned hard lessons about trust and flattery upon finding out that her father had been leaking information to the Shardless Few. "Don't try to manipulate me." Phalue could feel the shift in the air, the hum of power – a soft buzz she could feel but couldn't hear.

Lin's expression darkened, her hands curling into fists. "Whatever you may think of me, that is the truth."

"A truth you tell me to bend me to your will. I should never have come here."

The anger melted away, gone as quickly as though it had never been there. "Here, you have a chance. I know you must feel guilty, not being there for your wife." Her tone turned cajoling, conciliatory. She was a cat who'd unsuccessfully tried to leap a wall and was now searching for a way around it.

Phalue liked Lin – and part of that was because of her insight, her empathy, the fathers they both wished they hadn't had. But something about the woman always made Phalue feel as though she still had to have a wall in the first place. Emperors had grand visions; one person would always seem insignificant in comparison, no matter how much Lin appeared to care. Still, she felt the words echoing in her heart. "Of course I feel guilty." And there went a bit of that wall, dissolving.

"Come with me. I need your help. Surely having these swords in safe hands would help your daughter. She's an Alanga too."

Phalue touched the spot below her right ear where the shard had once been taken from her. Her feelings surrounding the Empire and the Emperor were . . .complicated. Lin, the person, she liked. Lin, the Emperor, she was unsure of. "As I've stated before, I can't support your rule. That hasn't changed. What are these swords if not just a way for you to have more power?"

Lin's face twisted in consternation even as Phalue knew that she was choosing to let her see this emotion. Still, she knew Lin would not make herself so vulnerable to just anyone. "Ah, so it comes to this. I thought we were coming to at least some sort of understanding. What else can I do to get you to trust me?"

"Eminence," Phalue said, her voice gentle, "there may be nothing you *can* do."

"Then why am I even *trying*? Why should I keep trying to hold this Empire together, to protect it from Alanga who would seek to harm its citizens?"

"And I'm glad that you are trying. But you are still Emperor."

"So you would hold a grudge against me because of my position?"

Phalue blinked. "You think it is a grudge? Eminence, you are the most powerful person in this Empire, in more ways than one. I'm a governor and still, the amount of power you hold over me and my family is frightening. Think, then, what it must be like for a commoner on the street. How can they ever trust you? How can I? You may show me a bear and say, 'This bear is a friendly bear; you don't need to carry weapons around it,' and that may even be true. But if all the last bears I met tried to maul me, why should I ever trust bears? They're so much larger and stronger than I am."

Lin pressed the heel of her hand to her forehead. "I only want what's best for everyone."

Phalue sighed, thinking of the way she'd believed everything her father had said of the caro nut farmers, of everyone's place in Nephilanu's hierarchy. "Do you even know what that is?"

Now, at last, Lin fell silent, her arguments dried up.

"I am not the Empire's lackey," Phalue said. "You can find someone else to accompany you on your expedition. Ranami and Ayesh are my priorities and I need to be there for them." She readjusted the bag on her shoulder, felt the comforting shift of the sword on her hip and made for the gates. This time, Lin did not follow.

The streets of Imperial City were slick with moisture, rainwater running down the gutters in clear streams, all the filth and garbage long since washed away. The buildings on the main road towered over her, tucking her into their shadows, the rising sun visible just over tiled rooftops and swaying palms. She checked the sky and noted the dark storm clouds on the southern horizon. She'd be in for a downpour, if not a thunderstorm. Not the best way to start this journey.

"Sai! Sai!" A few orphans had begun to follow behind her, hands cupped and held out. Even Imperial, for all its luxuries, had children living on the street. "Please – a bit of coin for food and comfort?"

One young girl swept out of an alley, striding beside her. "A storm is coming and it would be so nice to get out of the rain."

There was something of Ayesh in the girl's impish expression, her short, tousled hair and her hollow cheeks. Or at least, Ayesh when they'd first found her.

Phalue stopped and dug into her purse. A man frowned from the storefront nearest to her as he unlocked his shop. "You'll be robbed for your kindness, Sai. Now they know you've got the money."

She ignored him. She was leaving this morning. And even those who were well-equipped would hesitate to attack someone of her stature. So what if kindness included a little personal risk?

Phalue doled out the coins to the nearby orphans, pressing them into small, dirty hands, saving the last batch for the girl at her side. The girl looked up at her with dark, hopeful eyes. "Where are you going, Sai?" Her gaze trailed to the leather breastplate, the sword at Phalue's side. "Are you going to be like our Emperor? Going to fight and be a hero?"

The words stole the breath from her, left Phalue standing there, mouth open but words not finding her tongue. "I'm going to do my best," she finally said, and the girl whirled and disappeared into the alleyway.

She'd been thinking only of storming Nephilanu, of demanding her wife and daughter be handed over, unharmed. But there were more people in the Empire than just them. There was more than one way to be a hero. She pivoted and marched back the way she'd come, her footsteps feeling more forceful, more purposeful.

The guards at the gates to the palace seemed confused, but let her pass. Lin was no longer in the courtyard, but all Phalue had to do was go to the palace and follow the wet footsteps Thrana had left in her wake.

"Is her eminence expecting you?" one of Lin's Imperial guards said at the doors to the Emperor's rooms.

Phalue suppressed a snort. Perhaps she was – that seemed to

be the way Lin worked, knowing others' thoughts before they knew them themselves. "She'll want to see me." At the guard's nod, Phalue knocked on the door. "It's Phalue."

"Come in," Lin said from within her rooms.

Phalue entered, her cloak still damp from outside. She pushed back her hood. "I'll go with you," she said, "on a couple of conditions. As soon as you stabilize Gaelung, you send your troops south. I'll meet them at Nephilanu and take back my home."

Lin sat at her desk, pen raised, the end dark with ink. Thrana lay on the floor next to her, taking up nearly half the space on the floor. "And the other condition?"

"You set up a string of orphanages across the Empire. You've been focused on researching these swords, on finding other Alanga, on building your armies. These are grand goals. But the Empire is now at war with itself, and war only makes more orphans. While you've been thinking about Alanga and civilization-ending swords, children are on the streets, suffering."

Phalue could see the dismay on the Emperor's face – of course she hadn't even considered this, hadn't thought of the gutter orphans. To her they were a fact of life, a thing that had always existed and would always exist. She moved in a different hierarchy than Ranami or even Phalue did.

Lin set her pen down, smoothed the paper she'd been writing on. "I'll meet your conditions."

"We'll find that sword," Phalue said. "If it's been passed from one generation to the next, I'm sure we can convince its current owner to give it up. This is by the Emperor's will, after all."

One side of Lin's mouth twitched in an expression Phalue could only describe as concerned amusement. "You never do things by halves, do you?"

It was something Ranami had once said to her. She felt a pang. *Wait just a little longer, my love.* "No. I don't. And you didn't actually tell me – what do you intend to do with this other sword once you have it? You want me to teach you to wield a sword in each hand? If the others are like yours, they're light enough for that."

The Emperor shook her head. "I don't want it to consolidate power, no matter what you may think. You might not ever fully trust me – fine. Then trust yourself. There will be at least one Alanga at Nephilanu; Dione's added some to the Shardless Few's army. The sword kills Alanga. *You* wield it."

9

Nisong

A small isle south of Gaelung

They swept through the governor's mansion like fire through dry brush. Ragan strode down the hall in front of her, his bloodied sword held in one hand, the other directing spouts and waves of water. Every so often, he'd stamp a foot, and a section of the tile ceiling came crumbling down. Screams reverberated throughout the building.

"You could just *tell* me where your governor is," Ragan called out. Servants scattered before him, fleeing into side rooms. Rainwater still clung to his hair and clothes; he hadn't bothered with an oilskin cloak. He'd wanted them all to see him, to know him.

Lozhi walked beside her, gazing into the distance as though he could not see what lay in front of him. Perhaps he couldn't – the creature had been through enough trauma in one lifetime. She stroked the soft fur of his cheek and he didn't respond at all to her touch. She had her cudgel in one hand, though she'd barely had the chance to use it. Ragan was making plenty of headway on his own.

"With the ban on witstone mining and trade slowed, Lin is barely holding things together," he'd said to her that night in the Alanga ruins. The fire had cast his face in glowing orange, outlining the underside of his dark, wide-set eyes. "We can topple this Empire by destabilizing it only a little more. I'm going after the island governors."

"That can't be the only part of your plan," Nisong had said. She'd been afraid, but knew the only way he would respect her was if she continued to stand her ground against him. "You need other Alanga."

"The strongest of them will rise to take the islands I've left in chaos," he'd assured her. "And they will see me as their savior."

She'd left it at that back then, though she knew she needed to push the issue again. Ragan was, at best, disorganized. What he proposed was a fantasy. If he wanted to lead the Alanga, he needed to *lead* them – which meant finding others and working with them. Haphazardly killing the governors and leaving his mark on them would inspire the chaos he wanted, but it wouldn't create any order from that.

He seized a young man who was trying to get into a locked room to flee, rattling the knob so desperately that it sounded as though he might tear it loose. "Where is the governor?" Ragan snarled.

The man only gaped at him and Ragan shook him by the collar as he might a disobedient dog.

"I don't . . . I don't know!" he gasped out. "Hiding."

The former monk threw him casually at the wall, his strength hurtling the man with such force that Nisong heard the *crack* of bone. She should have reveled in this destruction – it was what she'd once wrought herself – but she only felt vaguely annoyed by it all. This was getting neither of them what they actually wanted.

Four guards marched around the corner, shoulder to shoulder, shields locked together and weapons held high.

Ragan swung an arm out to encompass them, his head swiveling to look at her. "Well, see? At least we know we're headed in the right direction." He tried to peer around them. "Is that where your governor is hiding?"

"He's a good man," one of the guards said. "He doesn't deserve to die at the hands of someone like you."

Ragan only rolled his eyes. He stamped a foot and a section of the ceiling behind the guards crumbled, filling half the hallway. They ducked forward to escape the debris, breaking their formation. Ragan didn't bother with Alanga magic this time. He only stepped forward coolly, his sword whistling through the air.

She'd forgotten the way he'd fought at the Battle of Gaelung. It had been two years – two years of him being repressed beneath the command. He'd told her he'd been a prodigy, that the monks had marveled at his skills even as they'd denied him the title of master. She'd listened to his bitter words as he'd told her of beatings, of being locked in rooms, of having food withheld – all as they tried to teach him temperance, patience and wisdom. They hadn't broken him; they'd only fueled his hate. And all the while, he'd honed his fighting skills.

A few clashes of metal against metal, the frenzied footsteps of the guards, one last cut – and it was over. Ragan's sword dripped anew, blood pooling on the tile floor. He stood with his arm outstretched, the blade an extension of his limb. "Come," he said as he drew his sword back to his side. He didn't even look back at her and Lozhi, certain they would follow.

Rain pattered in through the hole he'd opened in the roof, debris littering the floor in a pile waist-high. They had to clamber over the wet, fallen stones and slick tiles to get to the hallway beyond. Nisong pressed her lips together. He simply didn't *plan*. The one most in Ragan's way was himself — though he'd never see that. She'd have to guide him, nudge him in the right directions.

She slipped.

Ragan caught her, barely, though her foot still jolted into the tile floor a touch too hard, making her ankle ache. Sometimes, in her dreams, she didn't see herself in the palace on Imperial. Sometimes she dreamed of one of her shards failing as its originator died, of falling to pieces — all the various parts Shiyen had made her from disconnecting from one another, flesh and bone sliding away.

She had the brief impression of warmth, Ragan's face close to hers, rain dripping from his brow. There was a tiny scar beneath his left eye; she'd never noticed it before, a pale mark against brown skin, like a half-moon at dawn. Her gaze trailed up to meet his. There was something of a stern recognition there — he'd seen her looking. But beneath that, she thought she saw something softer, something yielding. And then he set her on her feet, took a step away. Lozhi filled the empty space at her side.

"There's a door around the corner." Ragan cleared his throat. "I think he's hiding in there."

He kicked it in, the lintel and mortar cracking beneath the force of the blow. Dust rose from the broken door. The governor, a middle-aged man with graying hair, crouched behind a table with a child who couldn't have been more than five. Books were scattered on the table and looked as though they were in the process of being packed into a crate that lay next to it. Ragan's sword still dripped, and he strode into the study with the air of someone who was deciding whether or not to rent a room. He picked up a vase on a side table, glanced at the glaze and then set it back down. Slowly, he made his way to the larger table and flipped through the books. The child, cradled in the governor's arms, began to cry.

Lozhi whimpered.

"What's all this?" Ragan said, gesturing to the books.

For a moment, no one answered. The rain pattered against the shutters and somewhere else in the palace, hurried footsteps sounded.

"Hm?" Ragan said, his sword lifting fractionally.

The governor ducked his head, and Nisong could see his pate beneath his thinning hair, shiny with sweat. "Just books, Sai."

Ragan barked out a laugh. "I'm no Sai. I suppose the Alanga deserve some title, though Sai is not the right one. I was a monk once; did you know that?"

The man's lip trembled. "I . . .I did not."

"So," Ragan said with mock-patience, "what were you *doing* with the books? Packing them away? Strange thing for a governor to be doing and not his servants." He flipped through another one, frowning. "These are old." He stopped at a page, pressing the book open with one spread hand, and frowned. "This mentions Alanga artifacts. What were you doing with these? Tell me quickly."

"The Emperor requested all islands send any tomes they had that mentioned Alanga artifacts to the Scholars' Academy on Hualin Or. She said they would be returned."

"Why would she do that?" Ragan furrowed his brow. "Is she trying to build a weapon?"

Nisong had already worked out the reasons. "She's trying to find a way around witstone. She hasn't lifted the ban on mining. Throw in the Ioph Carn taking all the witstone they can get their hands on and the Empire is teetering on the edge of collapse."

The governor lifted frail hands. "You don't need to kill me. I'll step down, I'll—"

Ragan slid around the edge of the table, smooth as flowing water, and cut the man's throat. The boy in his arms did nothing, eyes wide and lips trembling as blood spattered his cheeks. Nisong stepped forward, a feeling rising within her that she couldn't describe. Flashes of memories lit the space behind her eyes. Holding a baby, shining black eyes looking back at hers. Her heart filled with a joy she hadn't known before, mingled with a tender fear — that this child could never come to harm or she would fall to pieces.

"Don't," she said, her voice choked.

Ragan wiped his blade clean on the governor's sleeve, just before the body slumped to the floor. "Relax. I don't kill children. Look at him. He's too small to take over as governor, to lead this island."

The boy was all tousled hair and soft cheeks and limbs as thin and delicate as a tree's spring growth.

"Find me some flint," Ragan said to her. He swept the remaining books into the crate, tearing some of the brittle pages to lay on top. Nisong found flint in one of the desk drawers, laid next to an inkwell and some pens. She handed it to him and he struck it against his sword, casting sparks onto the books until they caught flame.

She stood at his shoulder, so close she could feel the warmth from the back of his neck. The tension around him uncoiled as he watched the books burn. There was an air of lazy satisfaction about him now, a cat who'd just finished devouring a large meal. Now was the time to nudge him in the right direction.

"How many governors do you expect to kill before the Alanga rise up to take their place?"

He waved her off as he might a fly, though the gesture held no vehemence. "As many as it takes."

She touched his shoulder and felt a minuscule flinch. Had

the monks ever touched this man with kindness, even as a boy? Something like pity and understanding welled within her, but she pressed it down. Somehow she knew that expressing that pity would only anger him. "We could *find* other Alanga. We could go to Dione," she said. "Work with the Shardless Few. They're actively trying to bring down the Emperor. So are we."

She might as well have taken a stick and poked a jaguar. He drew sharply away, straightening like a snake ready to strike. "You think I would work with Dione? You didn't see how he dismissed me at Gaelung." He seethed venom with every breath. "He doesn't want to work with me and I don't want to work with *him*."

"We could use allies," Nisong said. "Even if you kill every governor, even if you destabilize each and every island, we'd still have to get past Lin's personal guards – and then to Lin herself."

"Are you saying I can't defeat her?"

"No, that's not what I'm saying." How was this conversation already going sideways?

"If you want to work with the Shardless Few, if you think they'll give you a better chance of taking Imperial, then go join the Shardless Few. I won't stop you." He was facing her now, and she could almost feel the tremor in his bones, the magic vibrating from his skin. "Go."

She *should* go. Not to join Dione – she wasn't Alanga, and she had the feeling he didn't appreciate bone shard magic – but to leave. It had been two years and she felt no closer to becoming Emperor, to making all she'd suffered worth it. She kept hoping something more would change. There was a certain relief in thinking of leaving him, of setting off on her own, no more tightness in her chest at the thought of being *left*. She didn't move, half afraid that if she did, he'd pull his sword free and cut her throat. He wouldn't actually do it, she was sure, but she felt the fear creep up her neck, freezing her to the spot. More than that, she knew, it wasn't time to part ways, not yet. She could still use him.

He relaxed, and she let out a breath.

"That's what I thought," he said. "You'll stay." His hand grazed the side of her neck and she thought of his hand on Lozhi's head, the approving way he sometimes scratched behind his ears. "Maybe you're right," he said, not looking at her. "We do need allies. But *not* Dione."

It was a start — something she could work with.

He regarded the flickering flames. "First, though, we pay a visit to the Scholars' Academy."

"What do you know about the artifacts?"

His began to pace the length of the room. "Enough. Not enough. But if they can be used to help the Emperor, we need to stop her from discovering how to make them. She's been using her ossalen's shards to make constructs again. We can't let her have more power."

"Is that why you won't let me use Lozhi's shards to make constructs?"

He stopped pacing, his gaze sliding to meet hers and then softening. "No. You're not like her. You're different."

She found herself looking into his eyes for a little too long, trying to read whatever emotions and thoughts lay beneath the dark surface of his eyes. There was something tempting in the way he said it. She wanted to take that mantle, to drape it about her shoulders. It was the closest she'd heard to praise from him and she wanted to sink into its meaning. She was unique to him — and so much of her wanted to believe that. Sometimes she felt as though she'd come a long way from the girl she'd once been, hoping for the approval of others — her parents, her older sister and Shiyen. Sometimes she felt as though she'd only circled around, climbing a staircase that doubled over on itself, returning her to the same spot over and over again.

Lozhi shifted, his shoulder rolling into her thigh. Absentmindedly, she stroked the fur there and felt the beast sigh beneath her hand. Now that the killing had ended, he seemed to have come out of his stupor.

A sob escaped the boy sitting next to the fallen form of his father. She'd forgotten he was there. So, apparently, had Ragan. "Get out of here," Ragan snarled at him.

The boy fled, weeping.

She let the matter of Dione drop, following Ragan as he picked his way out of the mansion's ruins. He'd reacted violently, but she'd successfully introduced the idea. He'd be mulling it over each time they encountered some setback. Even the most stubborn of tortoises had gaps in their shells through which she could *press*. Ragan might be the one with the Alanga powers, but she had skills he could not compete with. She was Nisong. She'd found her way to the Emperor's side, had convinced him to teach her bone shard magic.

She'd bring Ragan to hand, and she wouldn't even need shards to do it.

10

Lin

Anau Isle

I had too much time to think on the boat over to Anau, to finally come to terms with what I'd had to offer in order to save my citizens. Iloh had agreed to my proposal. I'd have to make it official as quickly as possible to solidify our new alliance.

Jovis was gone – a fact that lodged in my throat as we dropped anchor at Anau. I'd sent one of my four bird constructs ahead to let them know I'd be arriving. A small party was waiting for us onshore. Ah, there was Jovis's mother. A Poyer man stood behind her, hands on her shoulders. Jovis's father, Jesnay. They'd come to Imperial for the burning of Jovis's tattoo – the only thing of his body we'd had. There was something of Jovis in each of them – in Jesnay's height and build, in his curling hair, in Ongren's quick smile and dark eyes.

There was another man standing next to them, an Empirean one, who'd clearly put on his finest clothes, though they were now a touch out-of-date with the latest fashions. A small retinue of three people stood behind him. Anau's governor, no doubt.

Thrana swam in the water below, diving and rolling as the crew lowered a dinghy for disembarkment. I jumped into the water and waded toward shore as soon as we were close enough, Phalue at my back. I'd brought my white-bladed sword and it hung from my belt, the scabbard tracing a trail in the ocean. A little water sloshed over the sides of my boots, leaking into the bottoms. It seeped between my toes as I stepped onto the sandy beach. I lifted a hand and pulled the moisture from everyone's clothes and from Thrana's fur as soon as we were all ashore.

The governor's eyes widened. I'd forgotten how unused most people were to such a display of power. Using my gifts had become second nature to me, a thing I barely thought about.

"We received your letter," the governor said. He was an older man, around Ongren's age, and nearly as short. He bowed hastily, as if he'd only just remembered. "It's been a long time since an Emperor has set foot on Anau. I checked the records, you know. Not since your grandmother's time."

"Thank you for having me." I inclined my head. "If you received my letter then you know I'm here to visit someone and the matter is urgent."

He exchanged glances with Ongren. She waved a hand at him. "Waiting is not going to change the information you give her."

So it seemed even governors deferred to her. No wonder she'd had no fear when she'd first met me. The governor licked his lips. "The woman you're in search of, the one you wanted to speak to . . . she's dead, Eminence. She's been dead for over a year."

There were no further descendants of Tianlu who had somehow escaped notice. No relatives, no in-laws, no one to take his things when he died. "Do you have the ledger from the sale of her estate?"

The governor gestured to one of his entourage, who handed over a heavy book. I took it from his hands and flipped to the page marked with the ribbon. "It wasn't much. No one from outside Anau came to buy anything. If you're looking for something of hers, it'll be on this list."

I could sense Phalue's impatience at my back, hear the tap of her fingernails against the hilt of her sword. There was a woman who much preferred being in a fight. The tension in this room was of a different sort. Most of the belongings the governor had sold were fishing implements: nets, poles, his boat. There were a few personal belongings. Carvings of sea-dwelling animals, furniture, a set of porcelain dishes with "rarely used" written next to it.

No swords.

I curled my fist, trying to still the hammering of my heart. I hadn't come far, at least. I hadn't wasted too much time. Someone must have taken the sword somewhere back in Tianlu's lineage, or a family member had sold it to pay for other things. The importance of an item that had passed down generation to generation could only be emphasized for so long before it lost meaning, especially in the face of base needs. How could I find it now? I traced my finger back over the ledger of items again, hoping I'd just missed it.

My finger stopped. Not on a sword, but a wooden box, which according to the ledger had a sword carved into its lid. It was something. A place to start. I drew my finger to the left, over to where they'd noted who the item was sold to. "Eina?"

Ongren scowled. "She sells scallion pancakes."

And that was a reason to dislike her? Clearly there was something deeper going on here. "Ongren, do you know where she lives? I need to speak to her."

"It's a box," Phalue said flatly. "Not a sword."

"Patience."

It wasn't the right thing to say; I knew it as soon as the words left my mouth. Phalue shifted. "It's hard to have patience when your wife is in the hands of the enemy."

Ongren, the governor, and Jesnay all exchanged glances.

I wondered, not for the first time, how wise it had been to urge Phalue to join me. Part of the reason — which I hadn't told her — was that having her land in Dione's hands would weaken my position. With Ragan killing governors, I needed to keep Nephilanu's alive. Yes, she was good in a fight, and it was true, I *did* trust her. And I needed someone I could trust after I'd found out one of my household servants had been a spy. But I also knew it would mean managing her, keeping her in check — and I had little enough energy for that these days.

I gave a backward glance to Phalue and kept my voice even. "This is a lead. We may find more with the box."

Jesnay spoke up in accented Empirean before Phalue could respond. "We know where Eina lives," he said, his voice deep and even. "We can take you to her."

I shut the book and handed it back to the governor. "Thank you," I said, inclining my head. I looked back over the Endless Sea, the horizon dotted with fishing boats. In the cove, I couldn't see the entire horizon. Dione could be on his way right now — he likely was. We had to hurry.

The path to Eina's house wasn't along any road; it was an actual path, worn bare by the tread of thousands of footsteps, but still muddy, vegetation always threatening to overrun it. It wended part of the way through the forest and then over a rocky hill. I could see the shoreline from the hill, the waves crashing over the beach, sea grasses rippling in the wind. It licked at my hair, tearing tendrils free from my braids. And then I saw a ship — larger than the fishing vessels, moving more quickly than the wind would allow. Thrana drew up next to me, making a worried sound in the back of her throat.

I touched Jesnay's arm, aware that he'd been a fisherman here on Anau, had taught Jovis to sail. "Do you know that ship?"

He squinted at the horizon. "No. Not one of ours."

My heartbeat pounded in my ears, drowning out the wind. Dione. He'd come.

We descended, our steps quick, the wind dying down as the peak of the hill sheltered us. Ahead I could see a house, a small vegetable patch next to it, clothes hanging to dry beneath an awning.

Ongren didn't wait for me. She went straight to the door and knocked. Eina took her time in answering. When she did, she opened the door only a crack. "I sold out of pancakes this morning," she said. "I took the rest of the day off. You'll have to come to the docks tomorrow morning if you want them." She stood a little taller than Ongren, average by almost every measure, though her hair was only lightly streaked with gray while her face looked older. Her mouth had a slight pucker, as though she was always in the middle of tasting something sour.

"Eina," Ongren said sharply. "You know I'm not here for your pancakes."

"Then you are here for . . .?"

Ongren gestured behind her, and I didn't need to see her face to know how satisfied it looked. "I'm here with the Emperor. She wanted to ask you some questions and I knew where you lived, so I brought her to you."

The woman's face went as white as one of the shirts hanging to dry. "You brought her *here*? She glanced at her laundry, still hanging outside her home, the chickens clucking behind their fence. And then her face turned, very slowly, from white to red.

Behind her, I saw the box on the fireplace mantel. Dione could work the wind. I'd tried a few times, but had only managed little breezes – not the hurricanes that he'd brought forth. He'd be filling his sails, propelling his ship to Anau. I pushed past both Ongren and Eina as politely as I could, hearing only a sharp, whispered exchange between the women – one I couldn't discern.

My focus was on the box.

Too small to house a sword. It rattled when I picked it up and I opened it to find an assortment of cheap jewelry. I should have asked permission, should have been more polite, but we were running out of time. I emptied it onto the table.

A soft, velvety material lined the inside the box. And that was it. I turned it over and over, searching for some hint, some clue. But it was just a box.

I felt Phalue's solid presence behind me again, knew she was waiting for me to produce some satisfactory answer – something that would make our trip to Anau worthwhile. My jaw clenched. Would she always hover behind me, a witness to my failure?

At least I hadn't gone far. At least I'd only gone to Anau. Still, I couldn't help the despair rising in my chest. I'd spent time chasing nothing. Meanwhile, the Shardless Few were blockading Nephilanu and the Ioph Carn were attacking my ships. But I couldn't shake the feeling that the swords were even more important than I was thinking they were. Yes, they could kill Alanga easier than a regular blade, but did that explain the genocide? How exactly had that been carried out? I wasn't sure. My father had kept that secret too.

My father. Secrets.

My heartbeat quickened. He'd hidden a key in a secret compartment of the chest containing the memory machine. I ran my fingers over the bottom of the box and stopped. Was it shallower than it appeared on the outside? I checked the outside of the box again. Yes, there was space . . . "A knife. Can I borrow a knife?" Everyone scrambled. Phalue placed the hilt of a knife in my hand. Carefully, my breath held, I wedged the knife into the space between the bottom of the box and the inside wall. I pried a little and pulled the blade upward.

The bottom of the box rose with it. I got my fingernails beneath it, and then my fingertips, and then the whole thing came free. There, in the bottom of the box, nestled in cloth, was a key. The bow of the key was much larger than the blade, the metal poured into a lace-like pattern. When I held it up, the light from the window shone through the empty spaces. "I'll pay you for this," I said to Eina. "And for the box as well."

"Yes, Eminence. Thank you, Eminence." She bowed her head over the table and then lifted her gaze just shy of mine. "May I ask . . .what it is you're looking for?"

"No. It's better you do not know."

I tucked the key into my sash pocket, tucked the box under one arm, went to the door and pulled it open.

Thrana crouched low by the house's entrance, her ears laid back, a growl in her throat. I followed her gaze.

The unknown ship was nearly to the cove where we'd dropped anchor. "My apologies," I called back to Ongren and Jesnay. "But I need to get back to the ship. Right away." Phalue was there again, at my shoulder. "Can you ride? At least well enough to hold on?" She gave me a grim look, but nodded. I pulled myself onto Thrana's back, helped Phalue up behind me and urged the ossalen into a run.

She carried the both of us easily, in spite of Phalue's size. Wind whipped past us, making my eyes water, the ground a green blur beneath our feet.

When we reached the beach, the strange ship was at the entrance of the cove. I bypassed the dinghy, urging Thrana into the water. Water sloshed into my boots, weighing down the skirts of my dress. I ignored the discomfort: if we were in a downpour I might get similarly soaked. I seized one of the ropes used to lower the dinghy and climbed the side of my ship. Thrana made her way to the back where we'd attached a ladder she could use to board.

I found an uneasy standoff when I pulled myself onto the deck. My four guards stood with swords drawn, watching a man who stood across from them near the prow. His ossalen sat at his knees, the beast's head coming up to the man's hip. I recognized him – one of the Shardless Few who'd come with Dione to Imperial. He was not as mature an Alanga as I was, his powers still limited to shaking the earth and some rudimentary working of water. He had no connection to the ground here.

I proffered the box to Phalue. "Take this to my cabin. Lock the door."

She took it from me, her gaze still on the Alanga.

"I can handle him," I said to her in a low voice. "Go."

She hesitated, but obeyed. Behind me, Thrana hauled herself onto deck, her massive presence causing the boat to sway. I kept my legs beneath me easily enough, as did the Alanga man.

"What do you want?" I asked him.

"The box your friend just took below-deck," he said, his arms crossed, posture relaxed.

"And you're going to fight me for it?" I gestured to the four guards behind me, my ossalen who stood with teeth bared. "You've long odds."

His lips tightened only a fraction as he looked briefly at the sword I had strapped to my belt. Had he expected to have to fight me as well? And did he know what these swords did?

"If I have to." He didn't uncross his arms, though I saw his fingers twitch.

I didn't draw my sword. We watched one another. "Why Dione?" I burst out. "Why the Shardless Few? Why not ask me for clemency? I would have granted it, would have given you a place at the palace to grow and learn – safely."

"The Shardless Few saved me from the Tithing Festival. I owe them my life."

"I would have too, if I'd been able to. But I was a child. Now I've ended the Tithing Festival. There will be more Alanga. I'm doing my best to keep you all safe."

He looked me up and down – the elaborate gown I'd not yet taken the time to dry, the braided and styled hair that had worked a little bit loose. "You have no idea what it's like out there, do you? Hirona's Net is overrun with bog cough – every other person there seems to have it. The islands there are small, not as rich as Riya or Hualin Or or Imperial."

"I can't be everywhere at once." I knew it was the wrong thing to say as soon as the response left my mouth. It was defensive, snappy, dismissive. I wanted to use words, not blades, not constructs. I calmed my temper, studying the man's face, thinking about what words would be the right ones for him. "Please help me understand. I don't want war with the Shardless Few or with Dione."

"You can't possibly ever understand." But he sounded defensive and he seemed to recognize this. He sighed, his arms uncrossing. "All the Shardless Few want is for you to step down and to put a Council in your place."

I nodded to show him I understood. "But what does Dione want?"

"The same thing."

"I don't think that's true. I think Dione only sees one way forward, and it doesn't involve a Council of mortals having power over the Alanga. Do you think he hasn't noticed the Alanga being cut down across the Empire? Do you think he doesn't feel that the past is repeating itself? He's using you; he's using all the Shardless Few." Dione could speak of a Council, but he and I both knew it was a carrot he dangled to the people who followed him – one he never intended to give them. How could he prevent the same thing from happening, prevent the Alanga from being destroyed? By setting the Alanga as the rulers again and ensuring no one betrayed them. He wanted to go back to the beginning.

But this world wasn't the same as it once was.

"You *would* try to turn me against him."

I heard Phalue's footsteps up the stairs as she joined us above-deck again. Behind me, my guards shifted. Someone cleared her throat.

I was standing on the deck of my ship, *arguing* with an Alanga who had popped up on board. One of the Shardless Few. What were the rest of his fellows doing? I wanted to believe that he hadn't attacked us because something I'd said resonated with him.

I *wanted* to believe that – but that colder, calculating part of me filtered out the emotions, the desire to be wanted and needed. This wasn't about hesitation. He was distracting me.

"Check the sides of the boat!" I shouted. "All of you!" My guards and my crew sprinted for the rails. And I went straight down the stairs, knowing that I had only two things of true value to Dione on this ship: the sword and the box with the key. I'd asked Phalue to lock the door, but the porthole . . .

I could hear Thrana squeezing her way below-deck behind me, claws grasping at wood. Her hot breath seemed to fill the tiny space as I dug for the key in my sash pocket, hands feeling as weak as in a dream. At last, I pulled it forth and turned it in the lock.

A woman stood by the porthole, her clothes dripping. She'd rifled through my things, quietly but with the ruthless efficiency of a hawk dismembering a fish. The entrails of my room lay scattered across the floor. I could tell by the way she'd disassembled everything, flipped the pages of books, that she'd been looking for something, only she hadn't been quite sure what it was.

She held the box in one hand, opened and upended. In the other hand she held the key. The clouds had briefly parted; the light from the porthole striking the bow, casting dappled light across the cabin floor. There was something familiar about the pattern of it, the interaction of the shadows with the light – the one focused pinprick of brightness.

I darted for the key.

She pulled away just as I grasped for it, though a moment too late. My fingertips grazed the bow, seizing one of the curved arches, feeling the intricate metalwork dig in as I tightened my grip. She wrenched it away from me. A *thud* sounded, my vision darkening as she clobbered me with the box.

Thrana growled from behind me, trying to fit through my cabin door.

Before I could recover, the Shardless Few woman had leapt out the porthole.

How could I have been so foolish to think I could sway one of Dione's lackeys? I'd given myself too much credit, had thought I always had points others hadn't considered.

I tried to reach for the water where she'd fallen, to see if I could bring her back onto the ship – but it was like running into a wall. Someone else had already taken control of the sea there. The tremor in my bones increased as I tried to wrest the water away from whoever had it. It was like trying to tear a piece of meat from the jaws of a wolf.

Dione.

Thrana finally pushed herself into the cabin, taking up the entire space. She huffed at the porthole, nostrils flaring.

I put my hand to her neck. "It's no use. She's gone."

Phalue appeared in the open doorway. "So now the box we came for has been taken too. You asked me to go with you to Anau to retrieve a sword. This isn't the task you promised it would be. The man above-deck – he's escaped."

Thrana sat on her haunches, her head lowered so her horns wouldn't graze the ceiling. "I'm sorry, Lin. I know you were hoping . . ."

We were so close! Dione had left the invasion of Nephilanu to one of his generals, was focusing on the swords. As was I, though I stood at a distinct disadvantage. He had an entire history at his disposal that I had no knowledge of; I only had the scattered bits of information my father had left me. Did Dione know what the key was used to unlock? Did he know where the sword was hidden?

My mind flashed to the shadows of the key on the floor of the ship, the way the sunlight had struck it. My breath caught. "Paper, I need paper."

Thrana moved to the side as I pulled open the drawers of my desk. Behind me, I heard Huan's voice, her tone tight. "Eminence, the man escaped."

"A moment," I said, taking a stick of charcoal to the paper. I sketched out the shapes I'd seen on the floor.

No wonder they'd looked familiar. Not a random play of light. A *map*. Of an isle I recognized.

Maila.

II

Jovis

Somewhere in the Endless Sea

I'd thought I was doing good, helping those two Alanga brothers. Instead, I'd only allowed myself to be caught again.

I'd brought down one building, the ground shaking beneath my feet, before Kaphra let me stop. I'd begged, I'd wept, I'd promised him anything – everything – if only he'd not hold me to destroying the entire city. Even at the first shake, they'd all run, some of them screaming in terror. I'd seen it in their eyes – I was not a hero anymore. Perhaps they'd just refuse to believe it was me. I wasn't sure what was better – them believing it was me and word getting back to Lin, or just fading into obscurity once more.

She wouldn't recognize me after these two years gone. I barely recognized myself.

I moved the cards around in my hand, studying Mephi over the tops of them. He was still dripping from the time he'd spent swimming, catching fish and leaping the waves with young sea serpents. And here I was, playing cards with my ossalen on the deck of Kaphra's ship as we docked to resupply, trying my best to just keep my head above the water. I'd tamped down despair by falling into the role, by making myself believe it. Because when I didn't, the dread came creeping back in. He'd use me to hurt people again.

I now understood that this was what Kaphra wanted: to ensure I was one of the few living Alanga left. I gritted my teeth. He wanted me to be an assassin? Fine. I could play that part and play it well. And the better I played it, the more lax Kaphra would be. I'd find another chance to escape. The problem was, I didn't know where the performance ended and reality began.

Mephi laid out his next card. A giant grouper on my spider crab.

"Ah!" I threw my cards down in disgust. "Never should have taught you this game. Am I really going to be beaten by my pet?"

He bared his teeth at me, his creaky voice smug. "I'm bigger than you. Looks like I'm smarter than you too. Who is whose pet?"

"Is that a philosophical question?"

Mephi flicked his ears back and forth, the wind catching the tufts at the ends. "Friends," he said finally, before reaching out and taking the cards in the stack.

"Always." I reached out to ruffle his ears.

He leaned into my touch, a hum in his throat. But then he opened one big brown eye. "You're looking at my cards, aren't you?"

I averted my gaze, though I'd already seen his hand. "No, never. Are you calling me a cheat?"

"And a liar."

But not a hero. I felt the grin slip from my face. How could I even smile at a time like this? How could I sit aboard this ship and play cards while everything fell to pieces around us? I should be moving, I should be fighting, I should be doing *something* to help, right now.

Mephi drew a card from the deck and then looked across at me, as though he knew exactly what I was feeling. "Jovis. This is not for ever. Be patient. We will get through this together."

A bit of the tightness in my chest eased. I watched Kaphra from the corner of my eye as he spoke to a couple of Ioph Carn who'd come to the docks to report to him. I wished I could read lips. All three of their expressions were taut, their whispered words rushed. Once in a while, someone would pass between me and them, obscuring my view for a moment. I wondered what they were reporting. Witstone gone missing? Merchants refusing to pay their dues? I frowned as I watched them. No. It had to be something bigger than that.

I had my answer a moment later, as Kaphra came straight for me. "We're going to Hualin Or," he said. "There's something there I want you to retrieve."

"Well, that's just frustratingly vague."

He didn't even fix me with a glower; he only stared out at the Endless Sea, his mouth pressed into a thin line. If I were Lin, I'd be able to pull conclusions from his expressions, from those few words he had said. The only thing I could determine was that he couldn't be this upset about something on Hualin Or he wanted me to retrieve.

"And that's all your spies told you?"

His brows drew low over his eyes and he spat out one word. "Ragan." His hands tightened into fists. "He's killed the assassins I sent after him. The man is becoming a problem."

"Didn't he and Nisong help you capture me? You're not friends?" I remembered two years ago, when I'd broken into Kaphra's safe house. I'd reached Mephi, sure that I had defeated all of Kaphra's defenses. All his lackeys, all his traps, even the two tigers Kaphra had kept in his courtyard. But when I'd reached for the lock on the door where Mephi was being imprisoned, I'd felt a hand reach for me – and then *inside* me. An echo of the cold terror I'd felt shuddered through me.

"A business transaction, nothing more. He's killed three governors so far and I don't doubt he'll go after more." He polished his fingernails on the front of his shirt. "This may surprise you, but some of the governors are under my protection. In return for other certain benefits, of course."

I put a hand to my mouth. "There are people in power who are corrupt? Shocking!"

He gave me a sly look. "Oh, they're all corrupt, Jovis. Each and every one of them. You don't sit in a seat of power like that and never look the other way when it's convenient. Me? I have the freedom to be openly so."

His words burrowed into me, wriggling larvae finding a place in my chest. I'd been doing my best to look the other way during my time with Kaphra because it was the only way I could survive. "So what is it that you want me to retrieve?" I said, turning the conversation back to safer ground.

"Some of the teachers at the Scholars' Academy found something on an expedition. A sword with a white blade. It isn't made of metal. When we reach Hualin Or, steal the white-bladed sword."

I felt the command settle into the center of my chest, the compulsion making me itch to be at Hualin Or. Kaphra's lip curled into a smirk. He knew how his commands made me feel, and he knew the discomfort would last all the way until Hualin Or. "They'll have told the Emperor. Her people will also be on their way."

"My spies tell me they have not. The Chancellor wants to verify what he has before he sends word to the Emperor."

I frowned. That wasn't the protocol. Any new discovery was to be reported to Lin right away. Part of me pretended not to care, but the rest of me had been listening to every scrap of news I could gather about Lin, about her plans, about what was happening on Imperial. So the Scholars' Academy was keeping secrets from her. How very unfortunately human of them.

Kaphra gave Mephi a cursory pat on the head as he passed him on the way back to his cabin, which Mephi endured with a clenched jaw.

"I *don't* like him," Mephi hissed to me when Kaphra was out of earshot. When I didn't answer, my ossalen circled around, pressing his shoulder to mine and settling in beside me. "You are still good," Mephi said, laying his chin on my shoulder. "Never doubt that, Jovis." It was easy for him to say when Mephi had only ever tried his best. When he had never faltered. "And I won that game."

I snorted. "By *forfeit*. It hardly counts."

A smile tugged at the corners of his mouth, showing the tips of pointy teeth. "Again, then?"

I found myself returning that smile. He always could pull me out of one of my moods. We were *together*.

But not for long.

It was storming on the morning we reached Hualin Or; the sky opened up as though some celestial being had decided to toss out all their wash water at once. Even my oilskin cloak couldn't keep me dry. Water seeped into every level of the ship until I felt as though I might as well just throw myself into the Endless Sea – I might get better sleep anyways. Three years into a wet season. Only four more to go.

They'd squeezed Mephi into the cargo hold, though he barely fit through the ship's hatches and doorways. This section was flooded, the water ankle-deep. That was where Kaphra found me, holding my beast's head, scratching his wispy beard.

"It's time, Jovis. I've arranged transportation into the mountains for you. Philine will be accompanying you. You will do whatever she asks of you."

She slid out from behind Kaphra, one hand resting easily on her dagger, as the command settled into my chest. I didn't bother asking if I could take Mephi with me. I'd raised Kaphra's suspicions on Imperial. I had to be spare with my requests, to seem content with this mockery of a life. To have what I'd never had very much of before: patience. I pressed my forehead to Mephi's, gave him one last scratch and turned to follow Philine from the hold.

"One last thing," Kaphra said as I set foot on the first stair.

I froze.

"Kill anyone who sees you take it."

The transportation Kaphra had arranged turned out to be an ox cart. It was not covered. As the cart creaked up the road and rain trickled into the space between my boots and my calves, I thought about what my mother would say if she could see me now. I'd climbed all the way to a place at the Emperor's side and now I was keeping esteemed company with sacks of rice and barrels of fish – provisions for the Scholars' Academy kitchens. Once, I'd ridden in palanquins with Lin. Now I did my best to sit on the back of my cloak to avoid wetting the seat of my pants. Not exactly bragging material for her ongoing feud with Eina. I glanced over at Philine; I'd almost forgotten she was there again. She blended in with the barrels as though she, too, were made of wood, a provision being sent to the Scholars' Academy for use in the kitchens.

I wished there was a way to send word to my parents that I was still alive. I wished there was a way to send word to Lin. It hadn't been for lack of trying. But each time I tried to write something out, the command Kaphra had given me to never reveal my identity stopped me. Each time I put pen to paper, the shard in my chest burned a warning.

The ride to the Scholars' Academy was neither long nor brief, and I had more time alone with my thoughts than I'd ever wanted. The faces of the people I'd killed in the past two years filtered through my mind. The soldiers, the civilians, the people who had fought back and the people who hadn't. *Kill anyone who sees you take it.*

I hadn't expected, when I saw the blue-tiled roofs of the Academy, for all the old feelings to come rushing back in, washing away my guilty thoughts. Although the Scholars' Academy was older than the Navigators' Academy on Imperial, they'd been built in the same style. It was nestled among the trees, a sprawling campus surrounded by a white-plastered wall. Bamboo along the road swayed with the wind, carrying with it the sounds of rustling and shouted instructions. I remembered when I'd arrived at the Navigators' Academy, barely more than a child, hope and awe swelling my heart.

They'd beaten both out of me quickly enough.

"Have you been here before?" I asked Philine.

She lifted an eyebrow as the cart juddered in and out of a hole in the road. "To the Scholars' Academy? Do I look like a scholar to you?"

"You don't look unwise."

"From what I hear, it's intelligence that is prized over wisdom in these parts."

"Fair enough." And it *was* fair, judging by the treatment I'd received at the Navigators' Academy in Imperial. The way I'd been treated there certainly hadn't felt wise, not given my scores on all their tests and the money they were spending simply having me there. But ah, there wasn't always reason to human behavior.

Surreptitiously, I leaned around the edge of the cart to check our progress. There was one cart in front of us, bringing in a small shipment of parchment and ink. I watched as one of the guards checked a wax tablet she held in her hands. My breath caught and I pulled back. "Philine – did Kaphra know the Scholars' Academy is now logging visitors?" All the Academies were well-known for allowing visitors to freely visit their grounds. All of them had public libraries. Books couldn't be removed from the campuses but they could be read.

Those who'd defended Shiyen's iron-fisted rule always pointed to this one amenity as though it were the most important thing in the world.

Philine glanced over the edge of the cart. Her brows drew fractionally lower. "No. It must be a new change. Tensions rising, and with the Alanga returning . . ."

I slipped from the cart and into the surrounding bamboo, mud squelching beneath my feet. Philine followed. We watched as the cart driver gave his name to the guards and then passed inside. Philine leaned over. "We can bluff our way past the guards."

I tapped my fingers against my staff. "No. I don't think so. I'm a good liar, and maybe you're decent enough, but we don't have a plan and we'd need to keep our stories straight." I squinted at the guards through the rain.

Philine said nothing. She was Kaphra's tracker and now his right hand; I was the one known for my sometimes foolhardy smuggling attempts. I was the planner. I tapped my chin, feeling a bit of a thrill run through me as my mind went to work. I'd once come up with elaborate stories to fool the Emperor's constructs, sending them reeling over their commands as though they might find some clue to help them with such a novel situation.

People . . . people were more difficult. But they were possible to fool nonetheless.

"Well," I said, eyeing the guards. "You're not going to like it."

"Have I ever liked your half-cooked plans? They never go as you think they will."

"But they do end up where I think they will," I said, turning a smile on her, "and isn't that what matters?"

She let out a huff of very tired-sounding breath. Rain pattered against the bamboo leaves above us, trickling in streams down the stalks. "The worst thing that happened to me was Kaphra taking control of you."

I put a hand over my heart. "I *knew* you cared. I knew it."

She didn't even blink. "Because it means I can't kill you without repercussions."

"If you *could* kill me. Don't forget that part. Now listen closely. We're going to use their own paranoia against them." I explained what I had in mind. She nodded at parts, frowned at others and stopped me at the last point. "No. That's not happening, Jovis. Kaphra's given me specific orders."

"So inflexible."

"Is this where you quote me Ningsu's proverbs regarding flexibility?"

"I'd never be so gauche."

She shook her head. "For the last time, no. You're going to have to use the power of that famed charm to get them to believe you. Make it good. Surely you're capable of that?"

I held my hands up and apart. "Fine. Do it. Quickly. Before I change my mind."

She drew two daggers from the sheaths at her sides, made a quick cut across my forehead and then stabbed me in the side. The shock of it tore the breath from my lungs. Never did get used to being stabbed – though I didn't think that was a thing a person could get used to. She met my gaze as I sucked in a deep breath, and then drew the dagger free. Did she twist that blade just a little bit, or was it my imagination?

"Better go." Her voice was low and slightly dangerous. "Before that heals."

I staggered out from the bamboo, Philine following after me. In a smooth, quick movement, she tucked an arm around my waist and slid beneath one of my shoulders. I leaned on her more heavily than was necessary and heard her grunt.

"Help!" she called out.

The guards at the gate – four of them – hesitated. And then two rushed toward us, the other two holding their posts. One of the two took my other arm. "What happened?" he said.

I groaned, closing my eyes as though in severe pain. Wait. I *was* in severe pain. Blood trickled from between my fingers, though I could feel the wound beginning to knit. "An attack. An Alanga."

Each guard except one straightened. The one who didn't peered at me, his eyes narrowed. "Where were you attacked? We just had supply shipments come in and they said nothing about an Alanga attacking anyone."

Always a skeptic. One in every crowd. "Dione's balls, man!" I hissed out a pain-filled breath, staggering one theatrical step forward. Blood trickled from the wound at my hairline. Philine and the guard on my other side stumbled with me. "You think I went and got stabbed on purpose?"

He didn't back down or look away. "How'd you survive a fight with an Alanga? And you were alone? Even with her –" He nodded in Philine's direction. "– you wouldn't stand a chance."

"The rest of my companions are dead."

"*Who* are your companions, exactly? Who are you?"

I looked at Philine. She looked back at me. I might as well have looked to a brick wall for assistance. I held up my bloody hand. "I need help. And quickly. The Alanga who attacked me – he's on his way here to lay siege to the Academy."

The man didn't budge, and I could feel his sentiment seeping into the other three, a bit of sour milk poured into the pitcher. Even the guard helping to hold me upright took a half-step away. "Who are you?" the skeptical guard asked again.

"Someone in need of assistance before he bleeds out onto this path."

The man's lips pursed, nearly hidden by his beard. He waved his companion back. "Don't let him in. There's something else going on here. Get the Academy physician. She can treat him outside the walls."

Again I looked to Philine, who again gave me nothing. "It'll be too late. You need to let me in and you need to close the gates. You'll need my help."

"Your help?" Now the guard helping to hold me stepped completely away, and all four of them raised brows at me.

"Yes." I took Philine's shoulder. "Tell them who I am."

I could hear Philine's teeth grinding together. "This wasn't part of the plan."

"It was; you just removed it. I'm putting it back in."

"You bloody bastard," she hissed at me beneath her breath. "Kaphra will have my head. And then I'll have yours."

I didn't think it prudent to point out the logical fallacy of that statement.

Philine drew away from me, though she kept one hand on my shoulder as she addressed the guards. "Surely you've heard the rumors. This is Jovis of Anau. And he is very much alive. For now."

Making a show of grimacing, I took my bloody hand from the wound in my side – it had stopped bleeding – and used it to pull back the sleeve of my left wrist to show the scar. "It's where the tattoo was cut from me. I've been in hiding."

And like fog burned off by the sun, I could see their skepticism begin to vanish. The rumors that I was alive would multiply. Lin would hear about them. Some small part of me hoped she would find a way to rescue me.

First, though, I had to steal this sword. "Let me past."

But the guards were no longer looking at me. Their gazes had gone beyond my shoulder, and I felt a creeping sense of dread. Footsteps padded behind me. The feeling crystallized into a cold spike in my spine. I whirled, my staff held high.

"Well, Jovis," said a drawling voice, "you continue to surprise. Didn't think you'd try to play the part of a hero again. How *did* you know I'd be here?"

Ragan sat astride Lozhi, with Nisong pulled up behind him.

12

Ranami

Nephilanu Island

The wet rope chafed Ranami's wrists, rain seeping beneath her oilskin cloak, sticking her dress to skin. Halong hadn't taken her immediately to their camps; he'd focused his attentions on taking the palace, on rounding up any stragglers he could find. She'd bought enough time for most of her people to escape, for which she was thankful.

Thankful, too, that Ayesh hadn't tried to save her.

Even so, this wasn't how she'd wanted this encounter to end. Ranami had hoped she'd be able to escape, to lead some sort of resistance – at least until Phalue could come back and take over.

Both things seemed foolish now. The Shardless Few had planned this too well, and if they'd put half that thought and planning into the blockade, Ranami wasn't sure when or how Phalue would be able to return. She'd once thought their relationship wouldn't survive their ideological differences, that it would inevitably end and she'd be on her own once more. She'd come to peace with that realization. But they'd found ways to bridge the gap in their understandings of one another, had grown together like the roots of two trees, and now Ranami wasn't sure how she was meant to do this all alone.

The two soldiers standing watch over her were still, gazes fixed ahead, waiting for their general to return. If Ranami had been like Phalue, it wouldn't have been a challenge to fight them, to escape, even with her hands bound. Or if she were like Ayesh, with her power over water and earth, her supernatural strength and speed.

But she was Ranami. Only Ranami.

The squelch of muddy footsteps sounded, a branch bent to the side, and Halong appeared, flanked by a few more Shardless Few. The brass pins on his armband were bright against the backdrop of the forest. "It's done," he said to his soldiers. He nodded to Ranami, not meeting her gaze. "Bring her — we go back to camp."

The woman to her right took her arm, guiding her down the slope behind Halong.

Ranami wrung the rope in her fingers, staring at the general's back, remembering how much lankier the man had been when she'd first met him, his face still boy-shaped, his legs and shoulders more bone than muscle. They hadn't trusted one another until she'd distracted a merchant who had been chasing him. He'd shared the steamed buns he'd stolen from the man; she'd shared the crabs she'd caught and then boiled on the beach, and then slowly, they'd shared their thoughts, their hopes and dreams. That one chance encounter had blossomed into a lifelong friendship. Or she'd thought it had. How quickly trust could be lost. "What do you want from me?" she said.

"The general will discuss terms back at camp," said the woman holding her arm.

Her instinct was to lash out, to hurt those who'd hurt her. To curl in on herself, showing only the blades and not the softness. Ranami breathed in, felt the rain gathered, cold, on the tip of her nose. Once, she'd thought all governors and their ilk were corrupt, hard-hearted, foolish. And then she'd met Phalue.

This woman holding her arm might not deserve her abuse. This woman might become a future ally.

Halong was not Dione. He'd once believed the same things Ranami had. She didn't have magic, or weapons, or muscle – but she had words.

"I'd rather discuss terms now," Ranami said. "You haven't murdered me, so you want something from me. Wouldn't it be better to obtain whatever terms you want from me now rather than later?"

Halong tossed a glance back at her. "It's simple: you will tell your citizens to stand down and allow the occupation, give us full access to your stores of caro nuts and production on your farms, and you will tell your daughter to hand herself in."

"Is this what the Shardless Few stand for now? You once told me that war would never be bloodless or peaceful, but that the Shardless Few would only hurt those who deserved to be hurt."

She watched his shoulders roll as he shrugged. "That was a long time ago." He paused a moment to work his way down a rock, gripping a nearby tree to hold himself steady. Ranami's captors dragged her down the same path. Her dress tore on a branch, and the man escorting her had to stop to disentangle her cloak.

She lifted her wrists, shaking them though she knew he couldn't see. "Do I deserve this hurt?"

"You married a governor."

"And our daughter? She was a gutter orphan before we adopted her. Should she have run off, refused to be adopted by a governor and her wife? Or does accepting our love make her complicit as well?" she called after him, sharpening her words, hoping they pierced.

Halong sighed and turned to her. He waved off the man and woman escorting her and then held out his hand. "May I?"

Ranami snorted. "How civilized."

"Your hands are tied. Someone has to help you down the slope. Unless you want to be carried?" She grudgingly nodded her assent and he took her arm. They took a few more steps before he spoke again. "I'm not intending to harm you."

A tightness in Ranami's chest eased. She'd heard stories of what had happened to people imprisoned by Phalue's father. Hung like fish to dry. What was the point of the imprisonment if he just meant to kill them in the end? It seemed another unnecessary cruelty.

"Not if you cooperate," he said, and that painful anxiety returned to Ranami's heart.

"Imprisonment is an injury not to the body but to the soul," she quoted.

Now it was Halong's turn to snort. "*Ningsu's Proverbs?* How rudimentary."

"Popularity doesn't make a thing less valid. On the contrary, I'd argue that the book is popular because the proverbs ring true to so many. How long do you intend to hold me?"

"Until you agree to terms."

A lie. How could they let her roam free with only her word to bind her? Dione wouldn't do such a thing and he wouldn't have instructed Halong to. They saw her as choosing Lin's side – and that had never been the case. Even so, that made her their enemy. She chewed over her thoughts, letting Halong guide her over the terrain. When the slope finally evened out, she'd finished organizing them. Birds called to one another overhead, bright chirping mingled with the cooing of doves. She pitched her voice low – she was a dove singing sweetly to attract a mate, not one of the birds that screeched for attention. "Halong – I know I broke with the Shardless Few and you may not understand why. But this is what *I* do not understand: why do the Shardless Few still follow Gio now that he's revealed himself to be Dione? He lied to everyone for years, kept his identity a secret from people who trusted him. How can you still take the orders of this man?"

"He is still Gio."

"Is he? We once both agreed that the purpose of the Shardless Few was threefold: to stop the Tithing Festival, to end the Sukai Dynasty and to establish a Council that would have the interests of the commoners at heart. But I hear Dione intends to usher in a new era – one where the Alanga live freely among us. He betrayed his brethren once and now he seeks to repair that mistake."

"And what's wrong with that?" His voice was cool, but his gaze flicked to her.

She had to be careful here. Halong was an Alanga now too. She couldn't show any prejudices against them, any of the wariness that the vast majority of the Empire's citizens held. "It is not wrong, but it's also not right. What are Dione's priorities? Does he care more about establishing a Council for the commoners, or does he care more about striking down the Sukai Dynasty and shepherding the Alanga?"

Halong pushed aside a branch and they walked in silence for a while. She hoped he was thinking over what she'd said. Eventually, they made their way onto a road – the one leading from the city. "I don't see why our goals cannot be aligned. Practically speaking, the Alanga are powerful. They can help us unseat the Emperor and to establish order as we work to found a Council."

"If you take in allies no matter their motivations, then you weaken your own cause."

His fingers tightened marginally around her arm, his jaw setting. "You're not the only one to come from the streets, Ranami. It doesn't give you moral superiority. I was there with you, huddled beneath stinking, flea-ridden blankets. I was there, being treated more like a pest than an actual human being. I spent so many years hoping that I might be adopted or taken in by a well-meaning merchant. But we shouldn't have to hope for the kindness of the rich. We need to take what we're due."

"And that's all the more reason to cast Dione aside," Ranami argued. "Or do you hope that all the Alanga that are reappearing will show kindness, will see your cause as just?"

"What does that matter? Dione and the Alanga will help us win this war. We will set up the Council. We'll have accomplished all the purposes of the Shardless Few."

They turned off the road and into a familiar part of the forest. Halong tugged her along. Somewhere out there, Ranami hoped that Ayesh had found other people who had escaped the Shardless Few. That she'd been able to make her way to one of the predetermined camps with food and fresh water and caro nuts.

"So you don't question why he hid his identity. You don't question if the Alanga will allow the Shardless Few to set up a Council to rule them as well as the common citizens. You think they want to be ruled by people who still regard them with suspicion? A Council for the commoners – where do the Alanga fall in this vision of the future?"

"The Alanga have long been persecuted." She heard the shift in his voice that told her when he said "the Alanga" what he really meant was "we". She'd stepped too far, forgetting that he was now one of them. He'd found kinship with Dione, similarities, a belonging. And that clouded his judgment. "I can't say if I were Dione I would have done any differently. When he found it was no longer in the best interests of the citizens to keep his identity hidden, he revealed himself. He took the Shardless Few to Gaelung and saved us all from the construct army. Why wouldn't I still follow him? Why wouldn't we all? He still cares about the commoners."

They emerged from the forest to a commotion of activity. Soldiers were working to clear the vegetation in front of the cliff face, hacking away at branches and grass with scythes. Some had begun to set up tents. The Shardless Few hideout might have many corridors and rooms, but there was only one way in and out that Ranami knew of. Halong led her to the crack that led to it, letting her enter first. She'd never admitted to Phalue how much she hated this part, being closed into the darkness. She'd told her wife so many things, lancing the wounds of her past, Phalue's quiet, accepting presence a balm she hadn't known she'd needed. But this – she always thought the next time she'd be less afraid, feel less unease.

Halong caught the arm of a woman as they approached the entrance. "Get everyone organized," he said in a low voice that Ranami barely made out. "We sweep the forests tomorrow morning."

"What did he say about that day, when he went to Khalute and ordered all the boats to Gaelung?" Ranami's voice echoed off the stone as Halong pushed himself through the gap. Behind her, two soldiers guarded the entrance, a lamp hanging on a hook between them.

"He said that the people needed him," Halong said, his voice tinged with admiration. He grunted as he pushed himself past a tight spot. "He said that innocent people would die if he didn't stand against the construct army, and that they shouldn't pay for the Emperor's mistakes. That they were still the citizens of the future country we would form and that he had a duty to protect them."

He led her down a corridor and then a set of stairs and she let him sit in that feeling – that admiration, that comfort of following someone he still trusted. She'd once known what that was like.

Halong put his hand to the smooth stone of the wall, his face a mask of concentration. The sound of rocks cracking against one another filled the corridor. A door appeared in the black stone. He dug his fingers into the crack and pulled it open.

The room beyond must have once been grand. A hole marked the ceiling, green-tinged light streaming in from somewhere above. Rain filtered in, running in a stream across the floor and disappearing into a stone grate set into the right side of the room. Ranami could imagine a table in the space, Alanga sitting on cushions as they ate and drank and discussed trade and business.

He placed a hand on the small of her back, encouraging but not forceful. Ranami stepped into the room, wondering if this was where she'd die, if she'd ever again get to see Phalue, or Ayesh, or even sunlight across the Endless Sea. She whirled before he could close the door. "Halong," she said, letting all the hurt and longing into her voice, suffusing his name with the memories of their younger years together. "That's not what he said to me. Dione told me that if the people of Gaelung died it would be an acceptable sacrifice. That the construct army would weaken the Emperor's rule and if these commoners suffered, then they suffered.

"I told him he was a coward. That he was volunteering others to die in his place. He may have had a change of heart, but if you think Dione cares as deeply about all the people of this Empire as you do, then you are sorely mistaken. You may not know where his priorities lie, but I do."

She stopped there, stood tall as he shut the door, as the stone sunk back into place. But for the barest moment she saw what she'd hoped to see: a glimmer of doubt in his black eyes.

She didn't rest long on this triumph. It took only a moment later for her to lose her composure completely. Fear and anxiety tangled in her chest, knotting ropes around her heart. This was the end she'd always feared – trapped in a cell, subject to torture, living out the rest of her days confined by four walls, the damp earth heavy over and around her.

Ranami checked all the obvious exits first. She tried the place in the wall where the door had been – pushing and pulling at stone until her fingertips were sore. She threw her shoulder against it and was rewarded only with the abrading of the oilskin coating on her cloak. There was no furniture in the room except for a thin mattress. She still took it and folded it, standing on it to try and reach the vines hanging from the hole in the ceiling. She managed to reach one but her grasp pulled it free – a section only as long as her forearm, useful for nothing.

The grate was next, though whatever magic kept the door shut also bound the grate to the floor. Either that or it had been carved from the floor itself, though she couldn't see how they'd also then carved the drainage tunnel and chute beneath. She could fit through that tunnel. When she knelt and tried to see into the darkness, she thought she felt the stirring of a fresh breeze at her cheeks.

Every place she could touch in the room she pressed, she kicked, she searched for cracks, for weakness. She formed and discarded a hundred plans. The walls were smooth; she had no tools; she had no weapons but her own two hands – and those had grown soft since her days on the street.

Finally, exhausted, she lay on the mattress, trying to catch her breath.

When she woke, the light coming through the ceiling had dimmed. Her heartbeat drummed in her chest. Something had awakened her. And then she heard it. A soft scraping sound.

Ranami rolled from the bed, searching again for a weapon and not finding one. Had a rat made its way into the cave? Some other wild animal?

It shouldn't matter, but she listened and heard it again, louder. This time she could tell where it was coming from. The drainage grate. Ranami crept to it, her wariness increasing with each step. It was almost certainly a rat and she wasn't afraid of rats. She'd been bedfellows with them often enough when she'd lived on the streets. But there was a creeping sense of dread in her chest, a growing nest of spiders wriggling between her ribs. Maybe it was being alone in this room, the way every sound echoed from bare walls, the oppressive sense of so much weight above her. Ranami pressed forward.

"Dione's balls!" a small voice said.

"Ayesh?" And then she was scrambling, her heart filling up, running to the grate, lacing her fingers into it.

A dirty face stared up at her from the drainage tunnel, hair plastered to her head with moisture. "Did as you asked, didn't I? I got your meaning. So I just found a safer way to rescue you."

And this was safer? The girl was trapped in a cave beneath an immovable grate. Did she even have room to turn around? She'd removed her shield prosthetic, her bare wrist raw from chafing. "Ayesh, I still don't have a way out."

"Is that so?" The girl wrapped a hand around the grate, her face taking on the same expression of concentration that Halong's had. Ranami thought she felt the slightest tremor. The stone grate moved free of the floor around it. It was nearly as long as Ayesh was, but she lifted it free with her hand, pushing it to the side. "Now look."

She clambered out of the hole and then swept an arm toward it. "There's another grate near the cliffs where it drains out. Tried to use a quake to destroy it, but then it opened."

The tunnel looked cramped and wet, but it was a way out of this prison. She could rejoin the people of Nephilanu, begin planning for a long occupation, figure out ways they could resist the takeover of the caro nut farms. Scheme on ways to break through the blockade.

She put a foot into the drainage channel, eyeing the hole.

"It gets bigger," Ayesh said.

But that wasn't what was stopping Ranami. She thought of Halong's face when she'd told him that Dione had wanted to leave the people of Gaelung to die. He might have espoused practicality, of using the power of the Alanga to get what the Shardless Few wanted, but he was still an idealist at heart. He might have been able to convince himself that Dione had his reasons had the Shardless Few not gone to Gaelung's aid. But if there was anything of that boy she'd once known left in him, she could make him understand.

And there was the information he'd let slip.

Ranami gritted her teeth. She wanted nothing more than to leave this place, to be out beneath the open sky again. But she'd known Halong; they'd shared meals together. He didn't seem capable of hurting her. She might be a fool for believing it, but she weighed her two choices – their risks and rewards.

She removed her foot from the drainage channel. "I can't go with you."

"What?" Ayesh had crossed her arms, her frown a close approximation of Phalue's. Strange, how a child who was not their actual get could remind Ranami so strongly of her wife.

"I have to stay here."

"Did they – I don't know – give you opium or something? You have to stay here? In a dark room with water running through it? Come with me." She tugged at Ranami's arm the way she'd done when she'd been smaller, and it both warmed and broke something in her. In some ways, Ayesh was right. She wasn't that young anymore, and in a time like this, Ranami needed to start letting go, lest they all suffer.

"The Shardless Few aren't just a faction – they're a group made up of so many different people. *Different* people, Ayesh. Some of them are angry enough to hear Dione's rhetoric about tearing down the Empire, and not to hear anything else. They don't care who it's coming from or that his reasons may be different than theirs. But some of them, I think, will listen to me. Out there, all I can do is delay them. Here, I think I can fight back."

"You're always telling me to be more careful."

Ranami took the girl's wrist in her hands, examining a sore where the cap went over it. She wiped away the dirt and the moisture with the skirt of her dress. "You should be. Try to keep this dry, Ayesh. And sweat will make it worse. You should use different prosthetics, not just the shield." Things she'd told the girl over and over so many times that it had the feel of ritual. There wouldn't be much time; Ranami wasn't sure when the Shardless Few would be back to interrogate her. "I have information. Go to each of the camps. Tell our people the general is sweeping the forests tomorrow morning. Tell them to stay quiet and hidden." She hesitated, not wanting to draw Ayesh too deeply into the fighting. "When you can, scout out the tunnels – quietly. They may provide us with some avenue of attack if it comes to that."

13

Phalue

Somewhere in the Endless Sea

She should have been on a ship headed back to Imperial, and then on another – bound for Nephilanu. Phalue paced the length of the deck, wishing she could walk the surface of the Endless Sea. She would have walked all the way to the blockade and she would have found a way past. If she were Alanga, she would have gone straight home, would have used her power to fight for her family, because though the odds were long, they weren't zero.

But she was not Alanga. Lin was.

"There are no ships leaving for Imperial until tomorrow," Lin had told her as she'd set the course for Maila. "You can stay here on Anau for a night and then go but, Phalue, I could still use your help. I cannot send that army south until I have this sword. Would you rather help me find it or would you rather wait on Imperial until I do?" She left unsaid what they both knew – that Phalue couldn't take back Nephilanu without that army.

She'd wanted to rail against Lin that those weren't the original terms of their agreement – but when she'd thought about it, it *was* what she'd agreed to. Back then, she'd thought it would be a simple matter. She'd always thought that way. If she decided on a thing and put the force of her will behind it, she could make it happen. So far, this was the way her life had worked. Now she found herself thwarted, her will frustrated, diverted onto a path that felt too long and too winding.

And her patience was in shorter supply than the Empire's witstone.

Thrana lay grooming herself next to Phalue at the stern, an enormous fish she'd caught laid out beside her. Phalue thought about what it had been like to be astride the beast, the powerful movement of the muscles beneath her, and felt a sharp pang of envy. She touched the soft spot behind her ear, where a shard had been taken from her. Oh, her father had wept on the day of her Tithing. He'd held her close. He'd lamented the necessity of it all.

But he was her father. He'd never missed a tithe. Not even this one.

Lin stepped onto the deck, her cloak pulled over her head. Thrana immediately rose, striding across the slippery boards to join Lin behind the sails. Lin lifted a hand, Thrana took in a breath, and they both summoned winds that jolted the ship forward. Phalue turned her face to the wind, feeling the damp air gust past her cheeks. The skies overhead were dark, clouds heavy and low.

The Emperor strode toward her. This close, Phalue could see the dark circles beneath her eyes. Lin had been filling their sails as often as possible, switching on and off with Thrana and the witstone brazier. Each time they burned witstone, Thrana had to squeeze herself below to get away from the smoke. When Lin wasn't filling the sails, Phalue saw her below-deck, poring over books. Lin pursed her lips and looked out at the horizon. "Have you seen them?"

Phalue shook her head. "Lost sight of them two days ago. You should check with your man in the crow's nest, but I doubt he'll say differently."

"We didn't lose them," Lin said. "They'll be going to Maila too. But we'll both need to stop and resupply. And there's another matter."

"The reefs."

"Yes."

They stood in silence for a while, rain misting from above.

Lin let out a breath. "We're stopping at Gaelung to resupply. I have no way of knowing if Dione can get past the reefs, if that's also knowledge that he possesses from the past. No matter how old he is, I can't imagine he knows everything about everything. I don't know how to get past the reefs, but I know who does."

And then she whirled away, holding an arm up to receive the gull construct she'd brought with her, as though she simply had more important things to do.

They arrived at Gaelung two days later, during which Phalue avoided Lin as best she could lest her temper get the better of her. Gaelung was not as she remembered.

The harbor town closest to the palace was still small, but it felt more crowded than it had before. She caught sight of soldiers in blue Imperial uniforms on the streets. Citizens kept their heads down as they went about their business.

Lin joined her as the crew tied the ship to the docks and lowered the gangplank. She was dressed in plain traveling clothes – an oilskin cloak over a brown tunic and trousers. She'd tucked her pants into her boots; the only clues she was not an ordinary citizen were the sword strapped to her waist, the squirrel construct on her shoulder and Thrana at her back.

"Do you know where to begin?" Phalue tried to keep the impatience from her voice.

Lin only leaned her head toward her squirrel construct, whispered some commands into its ear and then lowered it to the deck of the ship. The beast leapt to the docks and disappeared into the crowd. Most people didn't notice, but some of them did, and Phalue saw the way they jerked away, like horses shying from a whip.

"I don't. But I'll find out."

Phalue resisted the urge to grab Lin's arm as they walked down the docks, Thrana's heavy footsteps behind them. "There wasn't a better way to find out than sending your spy into the town? It'll scurry along rooftops and into people's homes. It's a violation."

"It's just listening."

"It's not right."

Lin stopped, forcing foot traffic to flow around her. "Sai, we are not in training anymore. You cannot speak to me like I am one of your guards."

Phalue felt her hand coming to rest on the pommel of her sword. "It's not right, Eminence."

Lin's gaze flicked down to where Phalue's hand rested and then back to her face. Her eyes narrowed.

"Ah, just a nervous habit." She removed her hand from her weapon. An angry habit, really.

After fixing Phalue with one last glare, Lin stalked to the end of the dock and onto the street.

Whiskers tickled Phalue's ear. "She wants to do the right thing," Thrana rumbled. "Be gentle with her."

Gentle? With the Emperor of the Phoenix Empire? An *Alanga*? "I need that army." She wasn't sure why she was talking back to Thrana. The beast might tell her thoughts to Lin, just as the constructs would. But she didn't have anyone else to confide in. "She's holding it from me until she gets what she wants."

"That is a story you are telling yourself."

Phalue marched after Lin, rubbing at the spot where Thrana's whiskers had tickled her ear. It wasn't a *story* – it was what was happening. First Anau, now Gaelung, and then Maila. What if they didn't find the sword on Maila? Would she be forced to chase after Lin for an eternity, begging her to send the army to Nephilanu, while Ranami and Ayesh waited in vain? How long until the general on Nephilanu decided Ranami wasn't worth whatever ransom he might get from Phalue? These were dire straits. How could she be gentle at a time like this?

She nearly ran into Lin's back when the woman stopped, her gaze fixed down a shade-covered alleyway. Phalue followed her gaze. A portrait of Urame sat beneath a small roofed structure, surrounded by a few lanterns. The late governor's black eyes shone with life, her rounded cheeks soft, belying the determination of the woman beneath. The smell of burnt juniper lingered in the air.

Urame had been newly appointed governor when they'd come to Gaelung, yet she had not hesitated to throw her support behind Lin.

"She's dead because of me," Lin said, her gaze distant and forlorn. "Do you know what that's like? She was kind to me. She was a hero to her people. And Ragan killed her because he wants to bring everything I've worked for crumbling to the ground."

A group of soldiers marching past them inclined their heads in Lin's direction, murmuring "Eminence" when she noticed them watching. Everyone gave Thrana a wide berth, though there was a magnetic feeling about them, as if they were only just resisting the temptation to reach out and stroke the beast's fur. A gutter orphan darted in front of the soldiers, disappearing into the alley opposite the one with Urame's shrine.

Lin looked to the sky, blinking away the misty rain. "Who am I meant to replace her with? She had no heirs. Ikanuy hasn't been able to find any blood relations. The only thing keeping the most powerful people on Gaelung from fighting for the palace are my soldiers. If I choose the wrong person, I set off what could become a bloody war."

Ranami still talked about a Council with her wife in their more peaceful moments, their fingers laced together as they considered their shared future. Phalue felt like the change was too big, too drastic, too distant from the reality they lived in now. But there were places they could start. "Eminence, why not let the people decide?" There. That was gentle, wasn't it? And why not? What better solution?

"Elect someone?" Lin raised a brow. "The start of that Council the Shardless Few are always talking about?"

"Put that aside for a moment. Eminence, look around you. Really *look*."

She cast her gaze about. "What am I meant to be seeing?" And then she focused on her squirrel construct, which was scurrying back along a rooftop. "Ah, that was quick."

Phalue touched her arm. "That's not what I meant." She pointed to an elderly woman who was walking down the street, coughing into a rag. To the gutter orphan who was searching the refuse for anything valuable. To the citizens who anxiously regarded the squirrel construct as it climbed down a gutter and onto the street. "Their concerns are so different from yours. They didn't grow up in a palace."

Lin wrenched her arm away, her expression twisting with anger. "You have no idea what it was *like*. I do these things because someone has to. Because we are all running out of time.

Would that I had the luxury to consider everyone's plight." She crouched and held out a hand for the spy construct. It scurried up her arm and back to her shoulder, squeaking into her ear.

Phalue's fingers curled in frustration. All the words she wanted to say became a snarled tangle in her head, a knot that only became tighter the more she tried to work it loose.

"We have a lead," Lin said, listening to her construct. "There's a man who started a stall selling carved coral just after the construct battle. He's trying to sell a boat to pay for his own shop. A boat with strangely dark wood." Her eyes lit up. "There are solutions to more than one problem here." She started down the street, listening to her construct's muttered directions.

"Is she always like this?" Phalue said to Thrana. "Just off from one thing to the next, barely listening to you?"

"She listens to *me*," Thrana said, a smug note in her voice as she followed Lin.

Another pang of intense jealousy struck Phalue as she fell into step beside the beast. She would never be an Alanga. She would never, on her own, have the power she needed to breach Nephilanu's blockade. It struck a spark of wrongness in her. It wasn't *fair*. She'd had no choice in the matter; the only choice she'd had was what to eat for her after-Festival feast. Ah, but who had a fair life? If Ranami heard her whine about something not being fair, she'd have given Phalue a look that could have neatly eviscerated her from soul to skin.

"It must be nice," she said to Thrana, her gaze on Lin's back, "to follow someone so absolutely like that. To trust them with your life and your morality."

Thrana blinked serenely back at her. The outer layer of her fur was damp from the ocean and the rain. "I knew I made the right decision when I chose her. Is it not the same way for you when you chose your wife?"

Phalue should have been used to the ossalen speaking by now, but Shark was still young and spoke in fragments. Thrana spoke with the rumbling gravitas of a philosopher. And aimed just as true. Phalue trusted Ranami with everything she had and knew, by now, that Ranami felt the same way. Ranami would know she was coming for her. That Phalue would be there to rescue her before things got bad.

If only Phalue had that same trust in herself.

They found themselves traveling down several alleyways covered in palm fronds, the rain increasing to a patter above, remnants dripping to form puddles between the cobblestones. Each turn they took seemed to mean quieter streets, fewer soldiers. "We should have brought the guards." Phalue put her hand to her pommel and this time it wasn't anger that stirred her to move.

"They would have slowed our progress." Lin lifted a hand and a thin trickle of water rose from the streets, winding behind her like a snake. "And we are not defenseless. It's no wonder he wants to buy a shop. We're far from the town center and the flow of traffic now."

They turned one more corner and found a row of stalls. Lin passed a nut up to her squirrel construct and it hopped away onto a gutter. There were a few citizens out here shopping, and Phalue eased her palm from her sword. Perhaps she'd just become too jumpy after so long at sea, tossing and turning as she dreamt of terrible things happening to her family. But then she noticed the way the men and women shopping looked at Lin and Thrana, their faces blanching, before they scurried away with their heads bowed. Vendors shuffled around their tables, hands moving quicker than was necessary. Phalue caught a flash of white. Witstone? Most likely counterfeit.

She leaned down to Lin's ear. "I don't think that what some of these vendors are selling is strictly . . . *legal*."

"I'm not here for them."

"They don't know that."

Lin waved a dismissive hand and made straight for a stall with coral carvings laid out on display. They'd been polished smooth, their bright colors reminding Phalue of what they must have looked like beneath the surface of the water when they were still alive. A few rough, untouched pieces of coral lay to either side, as though to remind shoppers of the work that went into producing each piece.

The man who stood behind the stall didn't look any different from the others. He was of middling height, black hair tied back into a bun, his angular face shaved clean. His shirt was damp – with either rain, or sweat, or both. He turned white as witstone as Lin approached, though he did a fair job of keeping his voice steady. "Eminence." He bowed and then bowed again, as though making sure he was paying the proper deference. "What brings you all the way out here?"

Lin picked up the carving of two dolphins jumping free of a wave. "Remarkable." She set it down and picked up another, a sea serpent coiling as though it rested in the shallows of an island. "My father spared no number of shards in making you."

The man opened his mouth as though to dissemble, and then darted to the side. Phalue was too slow to react, her hand still on her pommel. She reached for his collar and grasped only air, her feet faltering beneath her.

Lin, though, had been expecting this. She put out a palm and a wall of water slammed into place before the man. For a moment, he looked as though he might try to run through it – a terrible idea considering that Phalue had seen Lin use water to block the air from people's lungs – but then he turned to face them, hands held up. "I'm only trying to make a living."

"And I have full sympathies for your predicament." Lin's voice was soft.

Strange. Phalue thought that she'd just stride up to the stall and threaten him until he told her the way through Maila's reefs. She seemed to Phalue a force of nature, a hurricane that did not stop for person or beast – that *could* not stop. Yet she heard the pain beneath Lin's words, felt the truth of them.

"I don't want to be unmade," the man said, his lip trembling, his voice thick with tears. "None of us do."

Us? The splash of a footstep in a puddle sounded from behind Phalue. She whirled to find that some of the other vendors had abandoned their stalls. Weapons now filled their hands – swords and knives. They circled like wolves uncertain of their prey's strength.

There was a sense of relief in finally being able to draw her sword. Words were tricky, slippery things, and Phalue could never seem to bring them under her command. Weapons were easier. Thrana growled low in her throat, a solid presence at Phalue's side. She glanced back, checking on Lin.

"I'm not here to fight," Lin said. She kept her hands out, her sword still sheathed. "I wanted to ask you some questions. You've lived in peace among my people. I'm not here to disrupt that."

The man barked out a short, bitter laugh. "How are *we* not your people?" He put a fist to his chest. "Your father made us. He abandoned us. And now you talk about us living peacefully among everyone else as though we are things you must protect them from. What about us? Who is protecting *us?*"

"Nisong tried to start a war."

"Yes. And we're all that's left."

"I don't think we have to be in conflict. Please help me, and let me help you. We can find a way to coexist." Lin held out a hand, entreating.

But the man was a cornered dog, snarling and yelping and not wanting to be touched. "We are draining people's lives by our existence. How can we not be in conflict?" He drew a knife from within his tunic and lifted it.

As if on signal, the constructs attacked. Phalue moved into the swing of the first one, taking the blow on her sword and shoving the woman back. Four others that she could see. From the sounds behind her, there were at least two more. Why hadn't they assumed more of the constructs might still be alive? The aftermath of the Battle of Gaelung had been chaotic. They'd lost track of some of their own dead, never mind the dead of the opposing side. And with the Shardless Few thrown into the mix, it would have been easy for survivors to quietly go missing. Ragan had.

All questions she could ponder later. She ducked the swing of a man, the lower half of his face covered in a thick beard, and used the momentum to slash at another. Her blade tore through cloth but clanged against something beneath. Was he wearing plate armor beneath his clothes? She supposed the constructs did have reason to be paranoid.

She whirled to find a third construct mid-attack, two daggers in her hands. The only experience she'd had fighting this many people at once had been at Gaelung, and she'd had Tythus at her back. Phalue tried to bring her sword up. Too slowly.

Thrana seized the woman's arm between her teeth, shook her and tossed her over to the side. She crumpled into one of the stalls, various metal scraps flying. Thrana roared and then turned to a construct trying to attack Lin from behind.

The alleyway turned into a miniature maelstrom of chaos. Vaguely, Phalue was aware of cracking one of the coral sculptures beneath her feet, a palm frond falling from above as Lin used wind and water to create a stinging whirlwind. Two more stalls collapsed. All of the non-constructs had long since fled. Did the soldiers just not patrol out this far?

Phalue thrust her blade into the first construct who'd attacked her. The woman's face contorted in agony as Phalue pulled her sword free. It should have felt different, killing constructs. And it had, when they'd looked like beasts. But this just felt like killing *people*.

She swung again, cutting the throat of the bearded man. Thrana's face was bloodied by a blade to her cheek, but Phalue could see the wound closing. The beast leapt between her and another construct, crushing the man's shoulder between her teeth. He stabbed Thrana's leg and she groaned. Phalue thrust her sword into the man and knelt in one smooth movement, pulling his blade free from Thrana's leg.

"Are you well?" she asked the beast.

"Not well but not dead." Thrana's voice rang into silence and Phalue realized that the fight was over. Thrana limped over to where Lin stood over the coral carver. His angular face was pinched in pain, his hand covering a bloody wound in his side. Lin stood over him, her blade held loosely in her hand. She glanced at Phalue, wiped it clean on her tunic and sheathed it.

To Phalue's surprise, she knelt at the man's side. "I don't want to kill you. I want to buy your ship from you. I want to find a way past Maila's reefs. I want to find a way to help you live. This isn't what I wanted."

He scoffed. "We don't always get what we want."

Lin held out a hand. "You can come down." The squirrel construct scurried down a drainpipe, hopping over puddles to get to her wrist. She gestured to it. "This construct doesn't use shards from people's skulls."

"That's what you've *told* people." He coughed, pressing his hand harder to his wound.

Thrana stepped forward. "The shards are mine, freely given."

And then, for the first time, something like hope lit the man's eyes.

"Tell me how to get past the reefs." Lin pulled a piece of parchment and charcoal from her sash pocket, proffering them to the man on the ground.

He took them and drew. "Here," he said, lifting the page to Lin. "There's an alcove on the eastern side of the island. It took us a while to figure out how to get past the reefs, but there's an opening here." He pointed to a spot he'd circled on his drawing. "It's near this alcove but it's narrow. You can't take a large ship through it. My ship barely fits as it is."

"And your ship?"

"Moored at a cove south of the docks. We changed the sails but it's the same ship. Now help me."

Lin reached into a different pocket of her sash, producing sharp white pieces of bone. "This could take time. Thrana, Phalue, watch over me."

Phalue felt her heartbeat quicken. Part of her was curious to see how this bone shard magic worked, this bane of the people. But if what Lin said was true – and bone shard magic could be worked from the ossalen – what did that mean? Was this how the Sukais had discovered bone shard magic in the first place? A stunted version of what it had originally been?

She stood over the Emperor as she reached into the man's chest, her hand disappearing to the wrist. He froze.

Other than the initial shock of seeing Lin's hand enter a man's chest, it wasn't as exciting as Phalue thought it would be. She watched and waited as Lin sorted through the bone fragments, muttering to herself, sorting through her own supply.

"I don't have enough," Lin said. "I think I can combine some of his commands onto one shard, though. Hmmm . . .it's not like my father to be sloppy, but I don't understand . . ."

The rain above dimmed to a faint, periodic pattering. People gazed down the mouth of the alleyway, though none dared to enter once they saw Thrana and the bodies. People loved to gawk, but there was a certain point at which risk assessment tipped things in the other direction.

Finally, Lin finished carving the last of the shards, placing them into the man's body. She sat back on her heels.

The man slowly unfroze. "What . . .what have you done to me? No. No – this isn't right." He clawed at his chest with scarred fingers, tearing at his shirt.

Lin lifted her hands, imploring him to remain calm. "I only changed the commands you didn't need. The logic of your commands is still intact. You won't die."

"You *changed* me," he said, anguish in his voice. "I didn't ask for that. I didn't want that. I don't feel right. This isn't who I am. Do you know what it's like? Do you know what it's like to have someone just reach inside you and change who you are?"

"I hardly think these things fundamentally changed your personality," Lin said.

Phalue's mouth went dry. Death on a battlefield was one thing. This felt far worse.

"This isn't me." His fingers found his hair, pulling clumps free. He stared at a bloody fistful of the hair as though unsure of what he was seeing.

Dread formed a hollow in Phalue's belly. Before she could stop him, he was reaching for the knife discarded next to him. But he didn't thrust the blade at any of them. Instead, he drew it across his own throat. Blood welled up from the wound, spilling down his shirt.

Lin cried out, lunging forward, pressing hands to the wound at his neck. Blood spilled between her fingers. "No. Please, no, don't do this. I tried to save you. I'm sorry. If I'd done things differently, maybe I could have saved you. If I'd been stronger, more clever. I'm not . . .I'm not enough. I never have been."

And then the man was dead and Lin was sobbing as though her heart were breaking. Phalue reached a hand out and then withdrew it, unsure of what to say or do.

They had what they'd come for, but somehow — it still felt like they'd failed.

14

Jovis

Hualin Or

Telling the truth by accident – that was a first for me. I'd set out to tell a lie, to play on the paranoia of the administration at the Scholars' Academy. Instead, I was the one who'd been played, and by my own damn words, no less. The expression on Philine's face – startled, and then settling into resigned – told me that she, too, thought this was a fitting way for me to go. Fate had a way of catching up to me.

"Well," she said, "this figures."

Nisong slid from Lozhi's back and panic closed its fingers around my throat. Ragan, I could deal with. I'd dealt with him before. Even if I'd lost that fight. It was Nisong, with her shards and her commands that set sweat to rolling down my back. "Don't let her get close to me," I whispered to Philine.

Philine rolled her shoulders, placed her hands on the daggers at her belt and gave me a terse nod. All business, that one.

Behind me, I heard the guards shifting. If they knew what they were doing, they'd move to close the gates. They needed time. So

I did what I did best. I talked. Never could shut up, even when I was supposed to, so might as well use that.

"Ragan. Nisong. Yes, I was just telling them about you. Ah, and Lozhi too; I can't forget you." The beast's ears pricked at his name, his head rising a fraction higher. "They say you're defined by the company you keep but, friend, I know this isn't company you would choose of your own volition. No hard feelings?"

Lozhi only tilted his head, his eyes bright. "Hard feelings? How are feelings hard?"

I'd barely heard him speak before, and something in me was relieved to find Ragan hadn't damaged the creature as much as I thought he had. "Well, you can divide feelings into categories. Soft feelings are things like love and affection. Hard feelings are feelings like anger and hatred."

"Are you actually trying to give my ossalen a lesson on *feelings*?" Ragan pulled at the fur on Lozhi's neck, turning his head from me. The beast let out a small yelp.

"Well, you certainly haven't bothered to. Not that you'd be a very good teacher."

He let out a long sigh. "You are, quite simply, the most exhausting person I've ever met."

I inclined my head as though accepting a compliment. Behind me, I heard the creak of hinges. Only a little more time. "What are you here for, Ragan?"

"Ah!" He smiled – that same infuriating smile from when we'd first met – and pointed a finger at the sky. "I suspect the same thing you're here for. Kaphra does like his baubles, even if he doesn't know what to do with them. Look at you." The smile dissolved into a pouting frown. "This is all he could think of? Sending you off to fetch things?"

"Sometimes I kill people," I said lightly, though I didn't feel light about it in any way.

Ragan tapped his chin. "Are you implying you're here to kill me?"

I saw, out of the corner of my eye, Nisong slip through the bamboo just off the path. So he thought talking was helping him gain an advantage too. All Nisong had to do was to press some new command into my body and I might be theirs instead of Kaphra's. Much as I hated being beholden to Kaphra, being under the sway of Ragan or Nisong would be worse. Ragan especially. His cruelty didn't always have a point.

Philine shifted, moving to cover my side, placing herself between me and Nisong. Sometimes, she really wasn't half bad. Well, yes, she was working for the man I hated, but that was the only mark against her. Granted, it was a *big* mark. Oh, and that time she and her lackeys had beat me half senseless.

I was getting lost in my thoughts. I needed to focus. I gathered the trembling magic in my bones, pulling more, until I thought I could feel my teeth chattering. "I could be here to kill you. I don't think Kaphra would be unhappy about it."

"Jovis. Do you really think gates are going to stop me?" They juddered closed behind me, the scrape of wood and a *thunk* telling me they'd barred them. "Would they stop *you*?"

"No. But they'd delay me." I stamped a foot. The ground beneath me buckled, shifting in a wave of earth toward Ragan. Lozhi leapt as it reached him, clearing it and landing neatly in front of me.

But I'd already moved on to the next attack, my staff in my hands, water swirling around me. I felt the flow of air, moving it with the water, whipping it into a frenzy around me. "I'm not as untrained as when we first met."

"You're still Jovis." Ragan slid from Lozhi's back and drew his sword.

Was I? I felt utterly changed by the past two years, my mind and body warped until I no longer recognized myself. I still felt the tug beneath my breastbone. *Get the sword, get the sword, get the sword.* It pulled me in the direction of the Academy.

No. Not yet. He could command me to retrieve the sword but he'd not set a time limit on it. I set my feet.

Both Ragan and Nisong struck at the same time.

Nisong swung her cudgel for Philine, though I barely had time to register that, as Ragan lunged for my throat. I ducked back, feeling the blade nick my skin, and then pelted him with the water just as I jabbed my staff at his gut. He was quick, but so was I, and I had a longer reach. I felt the staff connect, heard the satisfying grunt as air left his lungs. It bought me a fraction of a moment to survey my surroundings.

I'd spoken truly. The gates *would* delay me. But I had to get beyond them. And while Philine looked to be holding her own, and I'd grown stronger in the interim years, there was still Lozhi to contend with. It was still three against two. We couldn't win this fight without substantial losses, and, oddly enough, I wasn't willing to throw Philine beneath that particular cart. That meant we had to retreat.

"Philine!" I called. "The bamboo. You first."

She knocked away Nisong's cudgel, looked at the bamboo that stopped just short of the Academy's walls and groaned. "You've got to be joking."

"When do I ever tell a joke?"

Oh, that one cost me. Ragan came darting back in, tossing a ball of water at my face with such force that I felt half of it go up my nose. I coughed and spluttered, barely catching his sword with mine. I blocked his next blows in quick succession, even in spite of my stinging nose and eyes. Kaphra's training had heightened my senses, had me acting on muscle memory.

I had to act quickly. Though Lozhi hovered on the edge of

battle, his tail lashing nervously, I could hear a low growl starting in his throat. I stamped a foot, sending out a quake in a semi-circle, and at the same time I brought water down from the sky in a flood. The ground beneath Nisong and Ragan turned to mud. "Now!"

Philine sheathed her daggers and in the same movement, leapt to the bamboo. She had shimmied halfway up a stalk by the time I reached it, tucked my staff onto my back, and jumped. I put all my strength into the leap, seizing the bamboo close to the top.

The stalk bent a little as Philine shimmied toward me, but not as much as I needed it to. I swung my weight, hoping to bounce it far enough so I could reach the ground. I wasn't even close.

"So this was your brilliant plan?" Philine met my gaze, her mouth in a distinctly displeased line. "Hang from a bamboo stalk like drying fish?"

"I was hoping to do a flingy-thing, you know, just toss you to the top of the wall, nice and gentle-like."

Before she could respond, I felt a sudden searing pain at my legs, a weight that almost made me lose my grip. I stared down into a pair of large gray eyes. Lozhi was clinging to my thighs, claws digging in. The beast was smaller than both Mephi and Thrana, but "smaller" was relative.

"No hard feelings?" he said, his voice plaintive even as he opened his mouth to reveal sharp white teeth.

The bamboo stalk sagged toward the ground. "Lozhi, I could never have hard feelings for you."

The creature grinned, and I let go.

I felt the bamboo whip away from my palms as I fell into the mud with Lozhi, his claws raking the rest of the way down my legs, leaving my pants fluttering in shreds and my flesh just a little way behind. I caught a glimpse of Philine, touching down on the top of the wall.

That was done; now I just had to figure out how to follow. The mud I'd been so proud of conjuring was sticking me in place now too. And though I knew my wounds would close quickly, right now they were open and bleeding and burning with all the strength of a bonfire. I staggered to my feet, conjuring a wind to cushion me and help push me away from Lozhi. I pulled my staff free again, and just in time. Ragan had left his boots in the mud and he stood between me and the gate, his sword drawn, socks spattered and squelching with each step. "Is something funny?"

"It's a little hard to take you seriously right now."

But Nisong joined his side and I quickly sobered. They were standing between me and the gates. I didn't have anyone to help launch me over them. I could try to climb them, but something told me Ragan and Nisong wouldn't just sit back and watch. And neither would Lozhi, apparently.

Ragan lifted a hand and the moisture from the mud drew into the air, coalescing into a wave to my left. The man always had lacked creativity. Make a big, intimidating wave – that was his go-to. But much as I inwardly mocked him, I wasn't quite sure what to do against it. All he had to do was knock me to the ground, knock my staff loose from my grip and Nisong would pounce. Dying was one thing. Being made into a puppet was another.

Never did want to die, not even when Kaphra had a hold of me. I was certain Ragan could make me regret living, though. And if he ever got his hands on Mephi . . .the thought nearly stopped my heart.

An arrow ripped through Ragan's shoulder.

Philine still crouched atop the wall, a bow and arrow in her hands. She looked just as surprised as Ragan did, though I wasn't sure if it was because she'd fired or because she'd hit him.

The wave next to me dissolved as Ragan's concentration slipped.

I sprinted for the gates. Someone had cracked them open, just slightly. I was thin, always had been, no matter how much of my mother's cooking I'd indulged in. Took after my father that way. I could make it.

Nisong moved to intercept me.

I had Alanga-enhanced speed, but she had a shorter distance to cover. I tried not to look at her, tried not to think about the shard of bone she had clenched in her fist. I would make it. I had to.

And then I was passing her and I felt her make a final lunge. Time seemed to slow as her hand grazed my side.

But then I was past her and slipping through the crack in the gates, my heart thudding in my ears like thunder. The guards slammed the gates shut behind me, pressing against them as they let the heavy wooden bar fall into place once more. Something thudded against the gate. Lozhi.

Philine was there, handing the bow back to the guards.

"Looked like you were surprised you took the shot," I gasped out, my legs collapsing beneath me. They were still healing, blood staining my tattered pants. Lozhi's claws had missed my boots. Small blessings.

"I *was* half-tempted to leave you to your fate," she said, her voice sharp. But a smile tugged at the corner of her lips.

For a moment, I felt the swoop of joy of a job well done and just under the wire. The camaraderie between two colleagues. And then cold reality trickled down the back of my neck like the water that trickled from my scalp. I wasn't here to save the Scholars' Academy. I was here to steal from it, and then to kill those who tried to stop me.

"The gate won't hold," I said, trying to press the thoughts from my mind. "Take me to your Chancellor. We need to prepare for an assault."

15

Jovis

Hualin Or

As the guards jumped to obey me, I could see the appeal of being Emperor. No slogging through the messiness of human interactions, no cajoling, just orders barked and obeyed. I knew what Lin would say – she'd look up at me with those ink-dark eyes, disappointment heavy in her features –"Is that what you think of me?" And then the breath would catch in my throat, my arms would snake around her waist and I wouldn't know which way was up or down because I'd be drowning.

"You're coming up with a plan, right?" Philine murmured next to me.

I cleared my throat. "Yes, of course. A good one."

I had no plan. When I'd come to the Scholars' Academy, I hadn't expected it to actually come under attack by an Alanga. But the Chancellor would know where the white-bladed sword was, and if they wanted to keep their most valuable possessions safe during this siege, they'd try to take it with them if they fled. I just had to continue this thing that was no longer quite a farce.

As two of the guards led us away from the gate, others rushed to fill the void they'd left. I counted fifteen, maybe twenty. Not enough to face down Ragan, Nisong and Lozhi. We had to hurry.

We wove past students meditating, students eating together, students testing their experiments outdoors. I remembered being on the outside of such gatherings, always in a corner, alone. Prodded and poked at but never included – no matter how much I excelled at my studies. I'd always thought if only I were smart enough, good enough, they'd have to accept me.

Always I'd been wrong.

The guards led us to a building with a long hallway. The place smelled of old wood. At the end of the hall, the guards stopped in front of a door on the right.

I pushed it open, Philine on my heels.

A face I knew looked up from a broad desk, his gray beard falling to mid-chest now instead of just past his chin, his long silver hair pulled into a bun. He was in the middle of dipping his pen into an inkwell and I could see the flat of his hand stained gray from where he'd brushed pages that were not quite dry. This was a stern face, carved from stone and weathered with time. If he was surprised to see me, he didn't show it. To my surprise, recognition sparked in his gaze. He did have an uncanny memory for faces. "Jovis," he said in a gravelly, disapproving tone, as though I were a young man of twenty again. "What in all the Endless Sea are you doing washed up here?" He wrinkled his nose. "At least you didn't bring that animal I hear you have around you all the time."

I bristled. He was *not* just an animal.

Buphan had once split his time between the Navigators' Academy and the Scholars' Academy, teaching complicated mathematics to the students at both places. I'd never liked him and I was certain the feeling was mutual. And now he was

Chancellor of the Scholars' Academy. I hadn't kept up with that shifting hierarchy.

"An Alanga is here to destroy the Academy," I said. It was easier than saying he was here to take a sword. And knowing Ragan, he'd throw in destruction as a bonus.

Buphan raised an eyebrow, wiped excess ink onto the inner rim of his inkwell and resumed writing. He flicked a couple of beads on the intricate abacus to his right, nodded and wrote some more. "And when is this destruction happening?"

"Now. Soon. As soon as he gets through the gates," I said, frustrated, feeling like I was a student again. I remembered his voice ringing through the classroom as he rapped the table with his knuckles. "Precision!"

"One Alanga," Buphan said, frowning.

"And the construct who led the construct army. In addition to his ossalen. They're not just people, and ossalen aren't just animals, Chancellor. Even just the one Alanga could crumble this place to dust if we do nothing to prepare."

Buphan held up a finger. "Quiet. I'm thinking." He turned to the abacus and began shifting beads around on it, muttering to himself. He shook his head and then looked at the guards. "Did you send anyone to inform the governor?"

They both looked at one another. "We'll try to send someone right away."

"They won't get here in time. We must evacuate."

It took me a moment to process his words. Somehow I'd expected he wouldn't believe me, that he would protest, that he would send me away. I couldn't help but recall with bitterness how he'd refused to write me a letter of recommendation, how each time I'd tried to sit in the front of the classroom he'd sent me to the back. How he'd marked me down for the slightest mistakes while praising the inferior work of others. But our positions had both changed. "Yes – the walls won't hold." They weren't very tall. Ragan wouldn't find them a barrier. "But the work you've been doing on faster ships, on using less witstone, any artifacts you've uncovered . . ."

"It will take time for us to gather our books and our calculations." Buphan's gaze fixed on mine. I didn't mention the sword and neither did he. But I had the feeling – he had it.

Oh, I still hated him. During my time at the Academy, he'd pointed out to everyone that I was half-Poyer, had stated that the Poyer had fewer islands, and thus didn't have the capacity to learn complicated calculations and navigation. That it was a great accomplishment for me to overcome my heritage and pass the entrance exams – but that he didn't expect much more of me. I realized, as I looked at him, that he didn't hate me back. He disliked me, but everything he'd done to me, everything he'd said had meant so much less to him than it had meant to me. How different things might have been had he and the other teachers treated me fairly! I might have found employment as a Navigator; I might have kept clear of the Ioph Carn. What if we'd moved away from Anau? Would Emahla even have been taken? The thought brought a fresh wave of grief. But Buphan's life hadn't hinged on his treatment of one half-Poyer student. He'd been carelessly cruel and I was the one who'd paid the price for it. In his long history of students, I was just one.

One he was now asking for help.

The students here weren't fighters. There were the guards – but they would be no match for Ragan. They'd slow him down only a little.

If they wanted to escape with their lives and their research, I'd have to cover their retreat. I'd have to risk my life for miserable people like Buphan who'd only ever been a thorn in mine. But there were students here who had nothing to do with the way students had treated me when I'd been younger. There was research that might help preserve trade and communication throughout the Empire, that might stop other islands from sinking. I wanted to be here only for that. But that spot in my chest burned and I also knew: during the chaos of an attack, people might be less likely to notice something was missing.

"I'll do what I can to hold him off," I told Buphan. "Is there a way you can go that's not on the main road?"

He nodded. "There's a small footpath through the bamboo. It's not an easy hike, but the trail goes up into the mountains and eventually winds around to the palace. We can manage with hand carts."

"You organize the escape," I said, and it felt odd to be giving my old teacher orders. "I'll head Ragan off at the gates."

Buphan moved quickly for an old man, lurching up from his desk and ringing a bell by the door. A student appeared. "We're evacuating," he told the student. "Up the trail, just as though there was a fire. But we don't wait in the mountains – we keep going. Tell the teachers to pack the research on witstone. Do it quickly; we don't have much time."

Philine and I left the office, the guards on our heels, but then I stopped. "Hold on, there's something I forgot to tell him."

I whirled before she could say anything, pushing open the door without knocking.

Buphan stood by a cupboard, the door open, a sheathed blade in his hands. I knew he'd have kept it close to him. His face was slack with surprise, his fingers light on the scabbard.

Part of me wanted to go up to him, to just wrench it from his grasp – to make him feel as powerless as he'd once made me feel. I was supposed to steal the weapon anyways; why not get a little satisfaction? But the rest of me knew what Mephi would think of that, and Endless Sea take me, I didn't want to disappoint him, not when I had a choice. I let the anger boil into nothingness. "I know what that is." I strode toward Buphan, the words coming to me quickly. Had to be confident for this part. "And I know what it does. I need it to fight Ragan. Let me use it." And then I held out a hand.

He didn't want to give it up. His hands tightened around the scabbard, his brows lowering. "Scholars died to find this blade," he said.

"All the more reason it should be in my possession and then Lin's."

"We're studying it."

"She's been studying hers for longer." I hadn't pulled away my hand. A *crack* sounded in the distance and someone screamed. "There's no time."

The scream seemed to loosen something in him, and finally he handed over the blade.

The burning in my chest subsided, but beneath it, I could feel the other part of Kaphra's command: *Kill anyone who sees you take it.* I felt the roughness of the hilt beneath my palm, the muscles of my forearm tensing. Despair welled within me. I did not like Buphan, but I did not want him to die.

Another scream sounded and one of the guards burst back into the office. "Jovis. We need your help. Now."

Without thinking, my fingers loosened on the blade's hilt and I turned to go. The command flared in my chest, sharp-edged and burning. But there was still time to complete that task. Right now, another one demanded my attention. Kaphra didn't care what happened to the Scholars' Academy – all the students, the teachers, their books and their work. I did.

I followed the guard out the door, Philine falling into step beside me. Her gaze flicked to the white-bladed sword and then to my face. She leaned in. "We have what we came for."

"No. *You* have what you came for."

Her stride lengthened as she hurried to keep pace with me. "Jovis," she hissed. I could barely hear her above the gathering din. "This is not what Kaphra ordered you to do."

"Are you going to order me to do something else? Ragan is an Alanga. You and I both know Kaphra wants other Alanga dead. Do you really think he'd want me to miss this opportunity?"

"You're not ready."

"Is that your assessment? Or his? Maybe my survival instinct isn't as well-developed as you think it is. Besides, with this sword, I have an advantage. What better time? Do you think Kaphra would want me to miss this opportunity?"

She subsided into silence after that, and I moved ahead of her, though I could feel the heat of her gaze on the back of my neck.

We exited the building to a whirlwind of activity. Students were shouting, running about, grabbing things, searching for their friends. It was barely contained chaos. I broke into a run. The gates were broken, the bar barely holding the pieces of them in place. Guards pressed against the wood, their backs to the bar, their eyes wide. As I watched, a wave built beyond the walls, a dark wall of water rising above the bamboo.

"Run!" I cried out.

It was too late. The wave crashed into the gates and poured over the top of the wall. I watched in horror as the guards at the gates were swept into that dark, swirling mass of water; I lost sight of them beneath the froth. Splinters of wood flung out in every direction, one landing neatly at my feet.

I jerked the blade free of its sheath.

I wasn't trained from a young age the way Ragan was, and I preferred the staff to a blade. But Kaphra had made me practice with a sword, and the weight of this one felt light and familiar in my hand. The water bubbled toward us, sweeping past my ankles in a cold rush. I stood at the ready, letting the tremor fill my bones, ready to unleash the magic without a moment's thought. To either side, from the corners of my vision, I saw the guards' bodies carried with the wave, slowing to a stop, like detritus washed ashore. I didn't have time to check if they were still alive.

Ragan stepped over the debris left at the gates, his sword drawn, Nisong astride Lozhi behind him. "Well," he said, his gaze focusing on the sword I held, "looks like you did my work for me."

"Is this where you tell me to hand it over and you'll let me live?"

He gave me that silly grin, a finger pointing to the sky. "But, Jovis, what if I don't want you to hand it over? What if I'd rather take it from you?" He surveyed the fleeing students, trailing loose sheets of paper, bags overflowing with books. "This is a pathetic institution. The Alanga will build something stronger. Something not filled with lies about us."

I wrapped both hands around the hilt. "Can't you just leave them alone?"

"They wouldn't leave *me* alone if they had the choice, would they? I've heard the stories from across the Empire. Alanga being mobbed by citizens, killed in their beds. Lin won't stop this conflict. She won't protect this world from its own people. She's too soft."

"What about Dione and the Shardless Few?" I tossed back.

His face twisted into a snarl. "He is a relic and the Shardless Few are mortals. It is *my* right."

Ragan had always felt he'd been denied what he deserved. Apparently some people didn't change, no matter what evidence was laid before them. I lunged to meet him. I had to hope that Philine or the guards would take on Nisong and Lozhi, that someone would cover my back. No one else could face Ragan.

His blade struck mine and I felt the hum of the impact travel through my wrist and up my arm, mingling with the tremor in my bones. I moved to the side, letting him finish his strike, hoping he'd overbalance. But he pulled back just as quickly as he'd attacked, his momentum carefully controlled. I heard grunts and a low growl from behind me. Nisong and Lozhi, engaged with the guards. If she came up behind me ... An itch started between my shoulder-blades.

Ragan took advantage of my momentary distraction, batting at my blade and lunging forward to score a strike against my cheek. "Ah, if only our blades had been switched, I might have given you another pretty little scar."

"Kaphra wants you dead." I circled, feinting, testing his defenses. He seemed to anticipate which movements of mine were feints and which were actual attacks.

"What do I care for your criminal organization?"

Mine. Yes, it was that, now. I rolled the word around in my mind, tasting the bitterness of it. And then I probed past that, thinking about the commands Kaphra had given me. He'd never commanded me not to speak of his plans. "He wants all the Alanga dead. Except me. Do you really think that all the attacks on Alanga have been random and carried out by disgruntled citizens? How long before he sends me to kill not just you but other Alanga? You put my powers into his hands."

"We needed money," Ragan said, slashing at my side. I ducked away barely in time. "And I don't like you. No loss for me."

I knew, deep down, he was insecure about his intelligence, no matter how he tried to play it off. "So of course you didn't think through the consequences. How like you. No wonder the monks never wanted to raise you to the rank of master."

His eyes narrowed, his jaw clenching so hard it shook. "Why would he care about killing us?"

"Think for just one moment. I know it's hard for you." He

took a wild swing at me and I easily sidestepped it, kicking at his knee and scoring a strike across his upper arm. He hissed in pain, nearly dropping his sword as he clutched at the wound. But he breathed heavily, straightening with difficulty and meeting my sword with his before I could press my advantage. "Fine," I said, doing my best to channel Buphan's infuriating superiority. "I'll help you. Kaphra's sole purpose is to accumulate power. Others with power threaten him. If he has me under control and most other Alanga are dead, he's the only one at the table holding a winning card."

Ragan scoffed, though I could nearly hear the gears churning in his head as I watched his anger fade into uncertainty.

I spread my arms wide. "How simple did you think your path to power would be? Did you really think there would be no one competing with you? Did you actually think the other Alanga would bow down to you and raise you as their leader for no other reason than that's what you want? You have to be smarter than that. You have to know you'd need to do more. Right now, you're not convincing anyone."

"Shut *up*!" Ragan thrust his blade toward my middle and I turned aside. He was becoming erratic. My loose tongue had gotten me into countless predicaments over the years, but it had sometimes gotten me out of them, too. I hoped this was one of the latter times.

"Think how much power Kaphra will have over you once he has this sword too. Why would anyone follow you? They'll be too afraid to reveal themselves, wondering if they'll soon feel the cut of a white blade."

"At least I won't be as pathetic as *you*," Ragan spat back. He attacked in a flurry of blows that I nearly didn't block. His blade locked with mine, his face so close I could feel the heat of his breath. "A slave to Kaphra's wishes. I don't know what's worse – people thinking you're dead, or people beginning to discover you're alive."

I thought about the crowd on Imperial, their stunned faces as their folk hero had begun to tear down the buildings around them. They'd thought I was there to save them. My heart clenched, my step faltering. His blade pressed closer to my throat. "Well," I said, trying to keep my tone light, "Alanga live longer than people. Someday he'll die and I'll be free again."

He smirked. "Oh, so you didn't hear?"

The sounds of fighting around me grew dim, Ragan's mud-flecked face the only thing I could see, his dark hair wet and lank. For one of the few times in my life, I couldn't find a clever response. "What do you mean?"

"Lin. Your Emperor. She's chosen a consort. And it isn't you."

I found my arms giving way, my hands weak. She had...what?

Ragan gave me one final push, his blade scoring a line across my throat before I staggered back. And then, in one swift movement, he'd hooked his sword beneath my guard and knocked my blade free of my grasp. I reached for my staff but it was too late. Ragan swept up the white-bladed sword.

Well, *shit*.

He held a sword in each hand and he swung them experimentally, finally deciding to sheath his original sword and tossing the white-bladed one to his dominant hand. I lifted my staff, knowing I was outmatched. I could take on Imperial soldiers; I could even take on most other Alanga. But I just wasn't as skilled a fighter as Ragan was, no matter how much training Kaphra had put me through.

At least, if I died here, I wouldn't have to do what Kaphra told me to anymore. At least Lin had moved on, found happiness with someone else. My heart twinged. No – couldn't feel anything but pain about that yet. The wound was still too fresh, newly struck. I lifted my staff, Kaphra's last command still burning in my chest, urging me to kill Buphan. I'd buy the students some time at least.

Ragan lifted the white-bladed sword and advanced.

A *thud* sounded from behind me, and then a worried chittering.

And then Ragan was abandoning his attack, the sword limp at his side. "Nisong!" he cried out, running to the construct's side. She was laid out on the ground, a hand to her head where she'd been struck.

I wasn't about to wait and find out how quickly she'd recover. Philine was facing off Lozhi with two other guards, her daggers clutched in her hands. She'd actually stayed? I'd thought she would fade into the walls of the Academy, arms crossed. "Not my business. Not my fight," she'd say. The campus was silent now, the students having fled. I had to give Buphan credit; he was efficient.

I ran for Philine and seized her arm. "We have to leave." I nodded to the guards, jerking my head in the direction Buphan had indicated when he'd talked about the footpath. They nodded and fled.

"The sword—"

"Is no good to us if we're dead. I stole it, like Kaphra asked. Not my fault someone else stole it from *me*." Without waiting for a response, I sprinted across the courtyard of the Scholars' Academy, looking for the back way out. We found the small wooden door ajar, the guards having just slipped through. We followed them up the narrow, winding path, the way nearly closed in by bamboo. I wasn't sure if Ragan would follow, or if he'd just vent his anger on the Academy itself. Knowing his temperament, I suspected the latter.

My legs burned as we climbed the path, echoing the burning in my chest. *Kill anyone who sees you take it.* I'd fulfilled the first part of Kaphra's command, but not yet the second. Buphan was ahead of us somewhere, and I felt the command take over, pressing me forward even as my knees wanted to give out.

"I think we can go a little slower," Philine said, panting. We'd left the guards behind.

"No. Not yet. My business isn't finished here."

For a while, all I could hear was her breath behind me, her labored footsteps. "Buphan."

"Yes. I have to complete the command."

We made our way around one more bend and found the last of the group. Students pushed handcarts full of books and diagrams, oilskin cloaks thrown over them to protect them from the burgeoning rain. Their shoulders and backs were damp with sweat. Buphan was there with them, pushing his own handcart. He'd stayed behind to help the last students. I wasn't sure how surprised I felt by that. People were complicated.

But I didn't have the chance to contemplate the morality of my former teacher. The command drove me forward. I felt, distantly, my hand tightening around my staff, my stride lengthening. I couldn't stop it. I watched as though through someone else's eyes as my other hand gripped Buphan's shoulder, as it forced him to the ground.

He looked up at me, his beard trembling, eyes wide. And then he stopped. "Oh, it's just you."

I'd already lifted my weapon, the end of the metal staff poised to strike. I knew how to kill a man with it, how hard to hit so that the skull cracked. He wouldn't even know it was coming; he didn't expect it. My heart shriveled in my chest, a dried husk. He'd handed me the white-bladed sword and now I would kill him for it.

Jovis, there has to be another way.

"Mephi?" I could have sworn I'd heard his voice in my head,

clear as day. I turned about but didn't spot him. I froze. He was right.

Buphan had *handed* the sword to me. *Steal the white-bladed sword*, Kaphra had said. *Kill anyone who sees you take it.*

I'd still stolen it; if Ragan hadn't taken it from me, I would have walked off the grounds with the blade in hand. I wouldn't have given it to Lin as Buphan had thought I would. But I hadn't *taken* the sword from him. He'd *given* it to me to fight Ragan.

I didn't have to kill him.

The burning in my chest eased, the command fulfilled with my changed interpretation. And with it, a strange and wild hope rose to take its place.

I was still Jovis, and I was a liar, through and through. Words were slippery, fickle things, meanings changing and altering with context and intent. All this time, I'd been trying to break the commands. But I didn't have to break them.

I only had to slide through the gaps.

16

Nisong

A small isle near Gaelung

The sword satiated Ragan in the same way that a large fish might satiate a cat. He kept it strapped to his side, his hand falling on it at random times, a faint smile gracing his face each time he touched it. Putting Jovis under Kaphra's control had been a victory to him in more than one way. It subdued Jovis, but it also left Lin thinking he was dead.

And now he'd stolen the sword from Jovis, thwarting him once more.

There had been moments she'd wanted to bring up Dione again, but it never seemed the right time. They'd not come across any other Alanga since burning the Scholars' Academy and time was frittering away. It took several days after that fight for her aching head to stop spinning, but she worried less about her bruised scalp and more about other deeper matters. She thought often about the shards inside her, about how long it might be before she began to break down, with no one except Lin knowing how to repair her. She needed to take Imperial, to build a court, to find someone she could trust to teach bone shard magic to. But she knew how Ragan would react to mention of Dione and that somehow always stopped her. She curled her fingers into Lozhi's warm fur, her gaze finding the pouch at Ragan's side, where she knew he kept the shards. If he'd only let her have them . . .

But of course he wouldn't. Not when his own freedom was on the line. He crouched by the fire, his back to her, hands spread to capture the warmth. There was a town just down the beach, but their money was quickly running out and Lozhi was getting larger. Lodgings were not a feasible option.

There would never be a perfect time. She took a step toward him, saw his head cock as he heard her footsteps. "We should join Dione. He has the resources we need to take Imperial, to set you up as the leader you want to be."

He flicked his gaze to her. "We don't need Dione. We will find other Alanga here who will join me."

"So you say." She tried to keep the sharpness from her words but she had led armies. Now she was reduced to foraging for food and camping on beaches while this man did little to improve their situation except wreak violence on others.

He was on his feet in an instant, striding to loom over her. "Do you have better ideas?" His voice crackled like an ember turning to flame. "Do you have better *options*?"

And that was the sticking point. He could threaten her, he could cajole, he could lavish her with praise and attention and it wouldn't change this one thing: she had no better options. But this idleness was getting them nowhere. "Yes." She swallowed. "Give me Lozhi's shards. I can make constructs. Lin has constructs; we should have some too."

He took her chin in his hands, eyes boring into hers. She wasn't sure what he was looking for, but she was used to scrutiny – she had so many memories of a past life spent being studied and then passed over. He spoke softly. "Push, push, push: that's all you do. No wonder you got all your friends killed."

His words cut the still-tender part of her, that part that would never forgive herself for Coral, for Leaf, for Frond, Shell, and Grass. It was a bruise that had yellowed at the edges but would always remain sore. She turned her face from him, unwilling to let him see the tears gather in her eyes. Yes, she'd let them die. She'd had loving, loyal friends. And now she had Ragan.

She deserved this.

A memory flared to life. Shiyen, smelling of smoke and sandalwood, his long fingers gripping her face, pressing, but not enough to scratch. "So this is what my advisers find for me. They said it was an advantageous match, that you were the best option. You are no great beauty."

She didn't flinch from the words; she'd heard them too many times before for them to cut her with any depth.

He must have found her reaction curious because he kept staring into her eyes. "Where is your value, then?"

"Where is *yours*?" she tossed back. "Or are you just a pretty face?"

His fingers did dig then; she felt the crescents of his nails sharp at her cheekbones. But before they could cut, he dropped his hand. "Are you insulting me?" His voice was low, dangerous.

He'd insulted her *first*. But he was the Emperor and she was only his chosen consort. They weren't even married yet. She understood then: she could push him, and he might even enjoy the challenge, but she could never push him too far. She would always have to hold back. She would always have to make herself a little bit smaller than she actually was.

But how long had she lived as a smaller version of the person she'd wanted to be? At least here, she had some room to expand.

Nisong looked to his feet, her lashes against her cheeks, though her voice was strong. "No, Eminence, I wouldn't *dare*."

He let out a small snort and she knew — she'd successfully walked the edge of this blade. But how many more blades would she encounter? Ah, her sister had been right. She'd won herself a place by Shiyen's side, but that didn't mean her troubles were ended.

And then she was back on the beach, Ragan standing over her, her chin in his hand. Odd, that flash of memory. They'd been in love, so much so that Shiyen had spent years trying to bring her back. Why did that memory leave her so uneasy?

She met Ragan's gaze and did not waver. "Another army of constructs?" he said, his voice a low rumble in his chest. "Nisong, Nisong. It failed you once and you'd like to try that route again? No," he said, his hand falling away from her face. She could still feel the heat of his fingers against her jaw, almost wishing he'd dug his fingernails in. "We do this my way."

"Your way isn't working either. Dione has gathered an army and is gathering some of the Alanga to his cause. What have we done except find one sword?" She knew he hated hearing Dione's name. He'd humiliated Ragan on the battlefield at Gaelung, breaking his attack into a thousand tiny droplets of water with a mere wave of his hand. With what appeared to be little effort. Ragan still talked about it sometimes over meals, how helpless he'd felt, searching for sympathy that Nisong felt obligated to give.

"Then I suppose we are *both* failures," Ragan growled. His fingers tightened into a fist.

Was he going to hit her? Strike her across the face? He'd never dared. If he did, she'd leave. She'd let him chase his fate whatever way he wanted to. And she would find a way to build her army. Alone. Let him strike her. Let him find his own damn way to what he wanted.

And then, from the direction of the nearby town, she heard the angry shouts of a crowd. Ragan's head whipped about. "A riot?" He snapped his fingers and Lozhi rose to his feet, reluctantly joining Ragan by his side.

Nisong dropped the fish she'd caught into a bucket and covered it. "Did someone see Lozhi?"

Ragan held up a hand to silence her. She itched with resentment but she held her tongue.

The noise grew louder, but only marginally. "They're not coming in this direction," Ragan said. He mounted Lozhi and beckoned to Nisong. "I want to see what this is about." She took his hand and he pulled her up behind him.

They dismounted at the edge of town, leaving Lozhi there, and followed the sound quickly, finding men and women gathered around the mouth of an alleyway. Some were picking up and lobbing stones from the road at someone unseen. Nisong shouldered her way through the crowd, Ragan at her back. A young woman crouched in the alley, lifting an arm to protect her face from the stones being thrown at her. She wore a fine blue dress, painted with cherry blossoms. The hem was muddied from the road, blackened in spots from the rain and refuse. An ossalen, dark as the depths of the Endless Sea, sat behind her, a whimper in her throat. A smattering of white ran across the creature's back, like stars against a night sky. A sharp rock struck the woman on her forearm, cutting a gash across her flesh. As Nisong watched, the gash began to knit itself closed.

"Get out of our town!" a woman next to Nisong cried out. "We don't want Alanga here."

The young woman spat at the crowd. "You were all perfectly happy to host me before I became Alanga. Tiger Island's first courtesan – a bit of culture for your backwater village. How many of you have I entertained? How many of you were proud to be seen in my company?" Her eyes flashed. "How many of you kissed my lips and shared my bed?" She cast her gaze across the crowd and Nisong felt a few of the people near her shift uncomfortably.

"You're not a courtesan anymore," said someone from behind Nisong. Another stone came flying out of the crowd, striking the woman on the cheek. Her face whipped to the side and the ossalen at her feet yowled.

She lifted a sleeve and wiped the blood away. "Move out of my way and I'll leave," she said. The crowd didn't move. Nisong could feel the anger in them, the fear. They didn't just want this woman to leave: they wanted to see her trampled beneath their feet, her body bruised and broken. Because how could they turn their backs on her? How could they let her leave without waking up in the middle of the night, afraid she'd returned to kill them?

The young woman lifted a foot and brought it down onto the gravel. The ground shook beneath Nisong's feet; the buildings on either side of the alley rumbled. The wound on her cheek had begun to close, but blood still stained her face. "Move," she said softly, "or I will make you move."

The crowd finally began to dissipate, fear winning over anger.

And then it came to her, how she could get what she needed from Ragan while also assuaging his need for control. She leaned over to whisper in Ragan's ear. "What if we had constructs *and* Alanga? Loyal only to you, without fear they'd turn against you or to Dione. Give me the shards."

He turned to face her, their breaths mingling. She thought he might snap at her again, accuse her of pushing her agenda. But she could see the gleam of greed and understanding in his eyes. He unhooked the pouch and handed it to her.

Her heart soared. As simple as that? The shards clicked against one another as she shifted the pouch in one hand, reaching inside to feel their cool, white surfaces, ready to be carved.

Ready to subjugate this Alanga to Ragan's will.

The young woman locked gazes with Ragan as she stalked to the mouth of the alley. "Are you going to move or will I be forced to make you?"

He smirked and opened his mouth to speak.

"There's no need to fight anyone," a deep voice said from behind them. "Step aside and let her pass, boy."

If Ragan were a cat, his tail would be a bottlebrush, all the fur on his back standing on end. Nisong turned and found Ragan facing an older man, one eye black, the other milky and marred by a scar. Dione – once known as Gio. The leader of the Shardless Few. The last of the old Alanga and the only survivor of the massacre. She almost felt like she should be bowing. By the sweaty, sick look on Ragan's face, he didn't feel the same way. "I'm not a boy," he said to Dione, and his voice held the edge of childish petulance.

Dione regarded him, crossing his arms. "Ragan, then," he said.

"I found her *first*," Ragan said.

The old man only raised his eyebrows. "That's not how recruitment works." He looked over Ragan's shoulder at the woman. "I am Dione." Water coalesced at his back, rising into a wave that surrounded him, cutting him off from the rest of the street. The crowd that had hurried to dissipate now rushed inside shops and homes, their voices raised in alarm.

Her heart pounding, Nisong pulled a handful of shards from the bag and stuffed them into her sash pocket, readjusting it so they lay in the small of her back. She couldn't wait any longer, and she couldn't trust Ragan.

Dione was still speaking to the courtesan. "As I think you've already found, the mortals of the Empire won't be kind to you. The Sukais have whispered lies and distrust into the ears of the citizenry. No matter what Lin says, she will put you in danger. She will put us all in danger. Join me. There are others who have. Help me depose her. Only when the Emperor is gone will the Alanga truly be safe."

Ragan waved an arm and a section of the Dione's wave sheared off, droplets scattering. "You can't trust him," Ragan said. "He's spent years and years *hiding*. He's spent years pretending to be one of them. I am Ragan. I was a cloudtree monk and a keeper of the ancient texts."

And then the young woman threw her head back and laughed.

Nisong could understand the sentiment. These two men, vying for her attention, much the way some of her customers must have. Nisong stepped toward the courtesan. "We all want Lin dead. We all want the Empire ended."

"Don't tell me you're an Alanga too."

Nisong shook her head. "I'm a construct."

The courtesan sucked in a breath. "An odd combination. A monk, a construct and an ages-old Alanga. You work together?"

"No," Ragan said at the same time Nisong said, "No, but we *should*."

The young woman looked to the sky as if searching for storm clouds. "I've heard that the Emperor is an Alanga. Would she truly treat her own unkindly? Why shouldn't I go, be a part of her court? Someone like me could surely do well on Imperial." Her gaze swept over them. "And where are your ossalen, if you are Alanga too?"

Ragan opened his mouth to retort, but Dione spoke over him. "Come with us, and I'll teach you. Just know that the Alanga cannot be safe as long as a Sukai sits on the Imperial throne. I should know. I was there when the first one ascended. Meet my people; hear our stories. If you are not convinced then you are free to go join Lin."

Nisong's mind raced. This was their chance. She stepped back, took Ragan's arm, tugged his head down. "We join Dione."

"What?" He pulled away, his face wrinkled in disgust.

"We join his side too."

He waved her off like she was a biting fly. "No. I won't follow his orders."

She squeezed his arm, hard. "Listen. If you do not, all we will *ever* have is you and me. You think we can compete with him or even Lin? You think Alanga will flock to *your* side? It hasn't happened yet. But you cannot join Lin's court and both you and Dione want her dead. If you truly want to have mastery of the Alanga, you will *listen*." And if he wouldn't, she would make this decision alone. She'd searched for Ragan after the battle because she'd hoped for another chance at Lin, and she'd known she needed allies. She hadn't counted on his anger, his pride, his petulance. Power did not always choose the most deserving masters.

Dione was watching them, and she felt certain he could overhear a little of what she'd hissed into Ragan's ear. But there wasn't time to go off somewhere, to have some secret conference. Ragan hesitated, his teeth grinding, feet shifting. She knew his past; he'd grumbled enough about it during their long days on the ship together. The monks who had refused to give him the status of master, who had refused to give him access to the restricted texts. They were right to deny him – he was too reckless – but how could she ever admit that?

He reached for her and seized the pouch in her hands, tying it back at his belt. He hadn't felt its heft, hadn't counted shards. The ones she'd taken seemed to dig into her spine.

Dione looked bored and annoyed, but then his gaze flicked to the sword at Ragan's belt. His expression shifted slightly.

"You're powerful," Dione said, considering. "And you have

a good deal of potential. I could use someone like you in the Shardless Few, teach you refinement in your powers."

Nisong watched Ragan's jaw unclench, his shoulders straightening. She saw the flattery war with his ingrained dislike of Dione, hoping her words would tip the balance. "Fine," he finally said, and his voice sounded diminished. "We will join the Shardless Few. Nisong and I both. We go with you."

How wonderful of him, she thought bitterly, to speak for her as well. What was she to him? A dog? Just following where he led?

Dione looked to the courtesan. "And you?"

She hitched her skirts up, stepping around the refuse in the alley, the stones that the townsfolk had lobbed at her. "Aye," she said finally. "If you will have me, I will come."

Dione had two ships with him, and they moved Lozhi and their supplies onto the deck of the larger one before they disembarked. The courtesan peered around the deck as though searching for Dione's ossalen. The ship was host to a score of Shardless Few without any particular powers. They seemed used to the presence of Alanga, or at least they'd made their peace with it.

"We have to be quick," she overheard Dione saying to the captain as the sails were hoisted. The other Shardless Few ship was preparing for departure across from them. Not an army by any means, but a sizable expedition. "She knows the location of one of the swords now, but so do we." And then his gaze met hers and his mouth pressed into a thin line.

She let her eyes slide away from his, feigning inspection of the rigging. It didn't matter – she'd find out where they were going eventually. Their goals currently aligned. Nephilanu was under Shardless Few occupation. Dione wasn't there, which meant he saw these swords as more important, and Ragan had one. He'd be reluctant to do anything to lose Ragan – not until he could find a way to get the sword away from him.

Another blade to walk, then.

Nisong found a place to set her bedroll, wedged between two crates in the hold. There was only one established sleeping berth on the ship. She didn't mind. She'd been through rougher conditions back on Maila. Just as she was settling in, Ragan came to find her. She was spreading out her blanket when she heard footsteps creak behind her.

He loomed over her, the light from a nearby porthole barely creeping into the shadows of his face. She quailed. Had he counted the shards? Had he kept better track of them than she'd thought he had? He knew. But then he opened his mouth. "You wanted to leave me back on that beach, didn't you?"

Relief flooded through her veins, mingling with anger. Life with Shell, Frond, Leaf and Coral had been tough. They'd struggled through the muck and the rain, their blood running freely as they'd fought their way to Gaelung. But at least they'd done it together. At least they'd been *united*. Dione was right to call Ragan a boy. No matter the power he held or the books he'd read, he lashed out at the people around him without taking even the barest moment to think. Nisong slammed a hand to the wooden boards and pushed herself to her feet. She wished she had her cudgel. She'd killed before. She'd enjoyed it. Ragan took a half-step back at the look in her eye and she thought, *Good.* "So what if I was going to leave? I sought you out because I thought we could be of use to one another. Instead, I find myself running about at your orders – orders that only halfway make sense. You don't plan anything farther than two days ahead. I'm not one of the cloudtree monks. Neither is Dione. Neither is that courtesan. If you want people to follow you, if you want *Alanga* to follow you, then you need to start admitting that you need other people.

"You need *me*."

He was staring at her, looking suddenly lost. "Why am I always bowing to others? Why am I always conceding?"

She tamped down her exasperation. "Because sometimes that's how you get what you want. It doesn't mean you're forever going to be in Dione's shadow."

His hand came up, gripping her face again. This time, though, his fingers were soft. "I won't be. Not for ever." She felt helpless in his grasp. She'd been so irritated by his attitude, his stubbornness that she'd forgotten that Dione was right: he *was* powerful. Reflexively, she grabbed his wrist and felt the tension there, all the strength he was holding back.

"Nisong," he said, his voice husky, "promise me you'll stay. Follow me to the end and I will give you what you want in your heart of hearts. You want to make them suffer but you also want them to worship you. You want the throne. When we take Imperial, it will be yours."

Her throat closed, her chest heavy with desire.

"There," he murmured, his fingers moving into her hair, tightening until she gasped. "Is that how I'm meant to speak to people?"

Before she could stir her tongue to speak, he lowered his face to hers. He tasted like the salty spray of the ocean, his lips soft against her mouth. She still had her fingers wrapped around his wrist. She could push him away but found she didn't want to. His oilskin cloak wrapped around both of them as she stepped into him, leaning her head back, surrendering.

Oh, Nisong, said Wailun's voice in her head, *must you always seek the sharp edges of broken men?*

She banished the voice of her long-dead sister, the voices of her past self. She wasn't just Nisong: she was Sand. And Sand hadn't felt anything like intimacy since Coral had died. She let go of his wrist, wrapping her arms around his shoulders, hands tracing the hard muscles of his back. The calluses on his palms brushed the skin of her neck as he trailed his hands down, as he moved to the buttons of her tunic. She shivered at his touch.

Irrelevant thoughts flitted through her head: did cloudtree monks sleep with one another? She thought they didn't and that was why they took in children left outside their gates. But was Ragan even a cloudtree monk anymore? How old was he, really? Wait. How old was *she*?

He broke the kiss, his breath hot against her cheek. "Tell me to stop," he said. "Tell me to leave you here alone." He waited, and Nisong found she couldn't form the words. She was tired of being alone. Instead she reached up, catching her fingertips behind his ear. She kissed him, forgetting for a moment about her missing fingers, the scars, the exhortations that she was plain, below notice. All she could feel was the pleasure of their two bodies pressed to one another.

As she dragged him down onto her bedroll, Wailun's voice wriggled free. *You will regret this.*

Nisong hoped she was wrong.

17

Nisong

Somewhere in the Endless Sea

Nisong slid between the crew like a rat – just below notice. She was known less for being the construct who'd brought an army to Gaelung and more for being Ragan's companion.

Water dripped from between the floorboards above, a few salty droplets landing in her mug. She grimaced as she lifted it to her lips in a dark corner of the mess hall. She'd sat cross-legged on the floor, feeling steadier there than at a table. They'd left their second ship trailing behind as Dione used his magic to speed this one ahead. But Lin, with both her magic and her remaining reserves of witstone, had gotten a head start to Maila.

To watch Ragan, though, one wouldn't have known it.

He sat at the center of the mess hall, spearing pieces of fish with his chopsticks, talking unselfconsciously around mouthfuls. Nisong knew him better than they did, and though he appeared nonchalant, she knew he was drinking in the attention of the Shardless Few surrounding him.

"Oh, I won't disagree with you," he said, waving a piece of fish in the air. "The Empire is rotten to its core, no matter what this new Emperor tries to do. But if you think bringing the Alanga back will right some sort of wrong, then I don't know what to tell you."

She frowned at his flippant tone. He'd won himself some goodwill during this voyage by helping Dione fill the sails, and he would spend every last coin of it if he wasn't careful. But to her surprise, a few people at the table nodded.

"Alanga are just people with more power, and some of them are just as wretched as the Emperor. Do you think they'll stand by and let the Shardless Few set up a Council? Mortals destroyed them once – *massacred* them. We may not know all the details or all the stories, but we all know that much."

"Are you forgetting that you're an Alanga?" a woman next to him asked.

Ragan lifted a finger. "Ah! Of course not. But I'm not the same as the rest of them. I know what it's like to be pressed down, to be held back from what I deserve – and isn't that what you all are fighting for? Some Alanga might be on our side – but I propose we take the rest of them and lock them up. Or find some way to control them."

A murmur of assent went through the gathered Shardless Few but someone on the fringes snorted. "You'd lock up your own kind?"

Ragan stabbed another piece of fish, his expression suddenly dark. "They're not *my kind*. If they want to live in this new world, then they need to prove their loyalty. Do you think I've not learned things in my time as a monk? Do you think I've not felt the breath of the Empire down the backs of our necks as the Emperor coveted our knowledge? As he sent wave after wave of assassins and soldiers to try and wrest it from us? If you want to build something new, something that will last, you don't pave over old buildings. You burn it all to the ground.

"How long have we had an Empire? Did the first Sukai content himself with threatening the Alanga, with trying to contain them? No. He rooted them out. He murdered them, their offspring, their associates. Should we do any less? Don't give me a weakling Council filled with bickering representatives. Give me a strong leader – one who can protect us from all threats. One who can swiftly and decisively use the power granted to him to right the wrongs wrought by the Empire."

A good many of them didn't agree, and Nisong caught their rolled eyes, their irritated expressions. But more than she'd expected regarded Ragan with admiration, absorbed his words as truth.

"And who would you propose as this leader?" a soft voice said. Dione stood in the entrance of the mess hall, leaning against the door frame, his hair wet and his arms crossed.

The circle around Ragan drew back, sensing blood in the water and not wanting to be caught in the ensuing frenzy.

"Why you, of course," Ragan said with a smile, not missing a beat.

"My place is to midwife the birth of this new world, not to lord over it," Dione said.

"And you really believe that?" Ragan's smile didn't fade, though the air in the room grew taut. "Must have been a bloodbath, the massacre of the Alanga," he continued smoothly. "How many of those were your friends? Maybe some were even family – you know, I never asked if you had children. So much about your past life we don't know. Even the restricted texts don't delve too deeply into the personal lives of the old Alanga. You must have felt guilty, since you were the one who let the wolf in among the sheep. Since you were the one who betrayed the Alanga."

Dione didn't move, his one eye fixed on Ragan. "You don't know what you're talking about."

Ragan's smile slipped only a fraction. "On the contrary, I'm a cloudtree monk. I've read the old texts, the accounts of what happened. I'm the only other one in this room who *does* know what he's talking about."

Nisong held her breath. This was too much, too soon. He needed to back down or he'd have Dione's wrath unleashed on them both. And no matter how powerful Ragan was, Dione was older, wiser, more skilled.

But then Ragan laughed and turned his back. "How silly of me. Of course you wouldn't want to rule, not with all your talk of a Council. Surely a Council would keep the mortals in check, keep the Alanga from being slaughtered again."

"Yes, if I'd have wanted to rule, I would have started by killing off all those who challenged me." Dione's voice was level and smooth, though it carried with it a reminder: he could have quashed Ragan when he'd had the chance. Instead, he'd spared him.

And Ragan knew it. Nisong could feel the hatred seething from him, the resentment that he wasn't good enough, that he'd never been good enough.

Dione looked to the gathered Shardless Few. "If you're done eating and bloviating, there's work to be completed. Lin has gotten ahead of us, but she's also heading straight for Maila. We're moving, but not quickly enough."

Men and women rose from their seats, taking empty bowls to the cook. The tension seemed to seep out in a slow hiss, though Nisong knew that this wasn't over. She could see it in the tightness of Dione's shoulders. How could she have ever thought Ragan and Dione could work together? Ragan needled Dione at every turn, trying to assert his superiority.

And each blow Dione dealt in an effort to smack him down only made Ragan angrier. It was an anger reflected in some of the Shardless Few. A Council sounded good – a lofty goal, a better one. But Nisong knew, intimately, the rage that came from being trodden upon.

Burning it all down was not an unappealing solution. Setting up a Council was slow, plodding, gentle. There'd be no venting, no catharsis. She could feel the tides within these Shardless Few shifting, and she was certain she wasn't the only one.

She slid through the dispersing crowd to find Ragan, still chewing on one last piece of fish, his expression thoughtful. He rose when he saw her, gave her a mocking bow, but followed her beckoning fingers.

It was louder just outside the mess hall, footsteps creaking above. They wouldn't be overheard.

"You tell me I can have the crown and yet you place it upon your head in the next breath," she said to him.

He waved her off as though she were a fly he couldn't be bothered to kill. "Stop. You think I want to sit around performing administrative duties? It's time to start implementing our plans."

"Dione is too—"

"Not him. The courtesan. Leave Dione – we can deal with him face to face once we have enough Alanga on our side."

They'd whispered plans to one another at night, stealing a little lamplight so that Nisong could carve commands onto shards. He'd not been so careless with the shard pouch again, doling them out to her piece by piece, watching her carve. And he knew some of the Alanga language so she could not lie to him.

But language was slippery. There were ways to still ensure he didn't have complete control. She took the loophole, knowing that someday – not today – she might need to use it. "So you'll send me against her alone?"

He reached out, taking a lock of her hair between his fingertips. "You're capable. Surely you must know that I care for you." His voice was both as velvety and harsh as smoke.

Oh, she hated him. She wrenched herself free. "You care for me the way a person cares for their spoon."

"That's a lie," he said. "You are the broth on that spoon; you are the only thing giving me nourishment. Nisong, look at yourself. Would I be treating you so if I didn't care for you?"

She was suddenly aware again of her scarred face, the two missing fingers. She held out a hand and waited as he placed the shards into it. "The palace is mine," she said. "And everything in it." She stood defiant, her chin lifted, knowing it was the way her past self had often stood when faced with a threat.

His fingers trailed down her cheek, tracing the scar, his gaze somewhere on her forehead. "Everything in it except you. You are *mine*."

She hated how his possessiveness made her feel. Wanted. Needed. Important. Nisong pushed away from him. "Just don't get yourself thrown overboard by Dione in the meantime."

"He only wants to return the Alanga to the world. He thinks the Shardless Few want equity, and to be fair, that was tempting enough for a time. But I will offer them something better."

She didn't ask him, but he continued on anyway.

"I will give them what they really want: to cause the suffering they feel has been heaped upon them all these years. To make the Empire and all those who oppose them *pay*. To lock away all the ones that they fear. Dione thinks pigs want clean, fresh water and an enriching environment. What they really want is to root around in the mud."

Nisong glanced about, worried that someone might overhear. Ragan's contempt wouldn't win him any followers. But understanding had begun to filter through her mind. The Shardless

Few had been loyal to Gio, but many were still uncertain how to feel about Dione. Ragan had been right to be reluctant to work with Dione; they were not easy partners. Instead, he reached for something more.

And she would help him achieve it.

Her gaze locked on Ragan's and she knew they were in alignment. "I'll do it. But we wait to make a move until I think we're ready."

He gave her a swift nod and then brushed his lips against hers.

She let him kiss her, unsure whether or not she wanted this aspect of their relationship. It made her weak, unsure. Was this how it had been with Shiyen? Were her memories of surety and control merely fictions she'd told herself? There was a part of her, buried deep, that knew Shiyen wasn't capable of love in the way she really wanted it, just as Ragan wasn't.

But without it, she felt adrift. No followers. No army. No one to lean on or to share a dream with.

This had to be enough.

"Ragan." Dione's voice called from above-deck. "I need you up here."

Ragan pulled away, his full lips curved in a smile. "See. He needs me." And then he swept away, and Nisong was left with the cold feel of water dripping onto her scalp.

They took the shortest route toward Maila, skipping around the coast of Gaelung and using the currents to their advantage. Most of the islands past Gaelung were smaller, more sparsely populated. The air felt different here – quieter, marginally cooler. They had to stop to resupply at a small isle, but Lin would have had to stop too. Everyone could feel it: slowly but surely, they were gaining on her. Anticipation bred a restlessness in the crew. Though they appeared at ease, Nisong felt the air simmering around her as though a storm were about to break out. Once the mid-morning meal was finished, she found her way onto the deck with Ragan and made for the rail. A slight sprinkle of rain brushed her cheeks, but it was so light as to be nearly unnoticeable.

Nisong found herself walking to Dione, his gaze on the sandy shore. It looked a little like Maila, with its stretches of empty shoreline, the cliffs overlooking the beaches.

She leaned her elbows on the rail, gazing out at the small isle – unsure of how to feel. Coral had felt like Maila was home. For the longest time, Nisong had felt it had been a prison. But looking at the reefs of this isle, the sandy beaches, the green trees swaying in the wind, she felt the tug of familiarity. How was it possible to both hate a place and to miss it?

"It reminds me of Maila," she said when Dione didn't turn to greet her. "I used to live there. I don't even know for how long. The Emperor sent all his failed constructs to Maila. During his experiments, he'd infused us with his dead wife's memories and the memories of her family. None of us met with his approval. But he didn't want to disassemble us. So he sent us to the far reaches of the Empire. He sent us there."

Dione only let out something halfway between a snort and a sigh, bowing his head as though she were an old woman who'd saddled him with a story he didn't want to hear.

"It took me a long time to break free of the commands he'd embedded inside me."

And then he did turn toward her. "So you found a new master?" She didn't follow his gaze but knew he was looking at Ragan.

She bristled, feeling her lip curl. "Oh, you think you see the way of things so easily. He needs me if he is to gain any real power in this new world. He's lived a sheltered life most of his years, and you think he knows how to make his goals a reality?"

Dione didn't seem chastised or even annoyed and she felt the gulf between them. She was a construct, filled with past memories and experiences, but it had not been so long since her creation. And he was an Alanga, his life stretching over the years, encompassing the whole of the Sukai Dynasty. He knew patience of the sort she couldn't even fathom. The look he cast upon her was neutral. "What would he say about you if I asked, I wonder."

Ragan's description of her would be even more dismissive, she knew. He expounded on her virtues in one breath, and then picked her apart in the next. His regard for her changed with his moods, with their last interactions. It was understandable, she supposed, that he should be angry with her. She was angry with *him*.

Something of Dione's calm demeanor dampened the fires of her anger. She wasn't here to fight. She wanted to remember that brief time on Maila before they'd found a way out – after they'd all come out of the mind-fog. Their interactions at first had been awkward, unpracticed. But in only a short time they'd flourished as quickly as wet season plants at the first heavy rain. Shell, with his spear and his fondness for spice. Frond had turned quickly to whittling, giving his dreams some reality. Grass had been a steadying presence, technically only as old as the rest of them, but appearing older. Leaf had always been at her side, even from the beginning. Nisong had taken leadership, and he had taken point.

And Coral. Always Nisong had underestimated her. Not physically strong, constantly afraid, but underneath all that she'd had a heart like iron.

"It must have been hard," she said, focusing on the rocky cliffs above the beaches, "losing everyone you cared about." Tears stuck involuntarily at the back of her throat as she said the words. As she thought of her own friends, now gone for ever. "Even though it's been so long." She'd watched him with the Shardless

Few, issuing commands, clapping shoulders, handing out kind words like coin.

He'd come to lead them. But he hadn't come to befriend them. He'd always set himself apart.

For a long time, he said nothing, but he also didn't leave his spot at the rail. So she waited. She could do that.

"Yes," he said finally. "Though you don't know what it was like. We fought. We bickered. And still I loved them like they were family. Even when they did terrible things. Even when mortals were caught in their arguments and they destroyed entire villages.

"It has been a long time, but you don't really know what that means. I have seen countless seasons pass, and to me they are like the whisper of waves on the shore, ceaseless and beneath notice. Sometimes ...I forget their names. Sometimes I don't even remember the way their voices sounded."

He wished he did — and that told her more than enough. Even if he'd forgotten their faces, he'd never forgotten the way it felt to lose them.

"The restricted texts in the monasteries say you betrayed them. That you were the cause of their massacre and the slaughtering of their descendants."

His lips tightened. "It's funny what people will say about a person they think is dead." And then he whirled from the rail, leaving her standing there alone, Ragan still glaring daggers at her from a distance.

She felt the vibration of Ragan's footsteps before she heard them. Lozhi got there first, his big head pressing against her hand. She stroked the fur around his ears and watched his eyes flutter.

"What did he say about me?" His dark expression told her she'd displeased him. What was he going to do? Kill her? Strike her out here in the open, in front of all the crew? He couldn't actually hurt her, not while she was still the only one between the two of them who knew how to work bone shard magic. Then why did her heart beat so fast, her stomach thick with queasiness?

"He said nothing about you. People don't always speak of you."

And that displeased him too. He seized Lozhi by one of his horns, pulling him away from Nisong. "Leave the beast alone. And Dione for that matter. Have you turned the courtesan yet?"

"Not yet."

"I gave you those shards for a reason."

"So I'm to always leap at your command? Even when the timing makes no sense?" Her words echoed off a memory, buried deep within. Had she spoken to Shiyen thus, once? The words tasted familiar, like an old recipe on the tongue.

"Nisong." His words were soft but firm. "We want the same things."

Did they? She'd thought the same of Ragan and Dione, yet putting them on the same boat had been like tossing water onto hot oil. Still, she felt her temper cooling. He would conquer Imperial, and she would get the crown. The Alanga would become his purview; the mortals would be hers. They were close now: she could feel it. The Empire was falling to pieces and Lin, instead of solidifying her alliance with Iloh and directing her army from Imperial, was chasing Alanga artifacts across the Endless Sea. "I'll do it now."

Lozhi made a soft, sad sound in the back of his throat. She reached out, pulling Ragan's fingers free of Lozhi's horn, replacing her hand on the beast's head. He leaned into her touch as she scratched the gray fur of his cheek.

Ragan let out a sigh, though she saw his fingers twitch toward Lozhi's horns. He turned away, gripping the rail tighter than necessary. "Of course you will. I didn't mean to imply you wouldn't. You know how I get sometimes."

Dissatisfied with his progress, with hers, impatient with the years of waiting, angry at everyone he saw as holding him back. Oh, she knew.

The courtesan was in a corner of the hold she'd closed off with boxes, hanging her cloak between two stacks in a makeshift curtain. She was smoking a long pipe, lounging on the mattress she'd set on some crates. Her dress pooled at the edge, the salt-stained hem brushing the floorboards. Her ossalen curled about her shoulders, head nuzzling her neck. "Most people knock," she said, smoke swirling around her face like mist.

Nisong's cheeks heated in spite of herself, the shards she'd need to use pricking her palm, sweat dampening her closed fist. Those early memories of her family came to mind, the ones in which she lurked in the shadows, envying the brightness of lavish dinners, her sister's easy elegance. It was an elegance she'd done her best to emulate when she'd been sent to the courts of other governors.

Even in this dank corner of the hold she felt out of place, somehow less. The courtesan, Alyara, had a way of always seeming she belonged somewhere.

Alyara, perhaps sensing Nisong's unease, sighed and patted the mattress next to her. "You've something to discuss with me?"

Nisong sat, doing her best to ignore the smoke. "There's a rift growing among the crew." She kept her voice soft and low.

"Ah." The courtesan's voice was crisp. "You want me to choose your side. Your lover put you up to this."

Nisong started in surprise.

The courtesan looked at her from beneath long, dark lashes, her lips curved in a slight smile. "You think you're the only one who's been trained to read faces? Oh, you run a tight ship," she said, fingers reaching out to touch Nisong's cheek, "but there will always be gaps where the water can seep in. I've watched you and your Alanga. He's easy to figure out. You . . .have been more difficult."

She blew a puff of smoke toward the porthole and it was sucked away with the wind. "You and I could have been friends, maybe, but I'll never be his. I know the type. He'll always feel the world has wronged him in some way." Her finger had trailed to Nisong's chin and she leaned in close, her breath hot against Nisong's ear. "Here's a secret: the world has wronged *all* of us in some way. There is no one on all the islands who hasn't suffered something they didn't deserve." Alyara pulled away, leaving Nisong's cheek feeling cold. She sucked in another breath of smoke, held it and turned again toward the porthole.

Nisong took her chance. One breath in, one breath out, her hand extended, moving into the courtesan's chest.

The ossalen let out an alarmed chitter, climbing down the courtesan's shirt and sinking its little teeth into Nisong's wrist. She gritted her teeth against the pain, let it pass over her as she arranged the shards inside Alyara.

She let go.

It took a moment for the woman to stir back to life, though her ossalen ran in agitated circles around her neck. She clutched at her chest, at the space where Nisong's hand had sunk within her. "What . . .what have you done?"

"Nothing you can speak of. The second command guarantees that." She took a little satisfaction in the dawning horror on the woman's face, the sudden reversal of the power dynamic between them.

The courtesan's fingers dug at her skin, as though she might be able to remove the shards by force. "So he meant what he said – about controlling Alanga. Only it's you who can do it, not him."

She gasped out the words, as though they were hard to say. A little too close to violating the second command.

Nisong rose from the mattress and drew aside the makeshift curtain. "He'll call on you when he has the need." She left the courtesan there gasping, her ossalen's angry chitters following her.

Nisong wiped the blood from her wrist onto the skirt of her dress. She'd been careful to place that first command at the top to ensure it stood above all the others.

Submit to Ragan.

18

Lin

Somewhere in the Endless Sea

It should have worked. All I could think was that it should have worked.

Instead, I'd murdered a man I'd been trying to save. It might not have been my hand on the blade, but it certainly felt that way.

Storm clouds gathered on the horizon as we sped toward Maila on one of the two ships my father had built to kidnap citizens for his experiments. It cut through the water so swiftly it might have been floating above it. I ran my hands over the rail. I'd never seen its like before. It wasn't any wood I was familiar with. Smooth and dark and with the faint, sharp smell of sap. I knew the scent, though it took me several days to place it.

Cloud juniper.

No wonder the monasteries had been reluctant to correspond with me in the beginning.

Thrana swam alongside the ship, turning and diving through the waves at the prow with all the grace of a sea serpent. She could fit on deck, though the ship swayed with her weight. I'd pared down my retinue until it was just me, Phalue, four Imperial guards, the captain, the navigator and two crew members. It was a tight fit. Everyone ceded the cabin to me, but there was barely enough space in the hold for bedrolls once we'd brought all our supplies aboard. No one said anything, but I could feel every-one's tempers fraying around me as they were forced into close quarters with people they barely knew.

Nothing could truly soothe my conscience. I slept poorly, waking up in fits and starts, staring at the ceiling and trying to fall asleep again. We burned witstone until it was gone, and even though Thrana was a good deal happier without its white smoke filling the air, I chafed at the speed we were going. Somewhere behind us – I wasn't sure where – Dione or his Shardless Few would be on another ship, following us to Maila. Every time I saw another ship on the horizon, I snapped out the spyglass and tried to determine whether it was Imperial, a fishing vessel or one of the Shardless Few's.

For the twentieth time that morning, Phalue passed my posi-tion at the prow. I reached out and seized her elbow. "Please. It's making me nervous just watching you."

She frowned, her gaze going to the ocean past the stern. "You'd be anxious too if your wife were clear on the other side of the Empire, left to face Dione's general alone."

"It will be worth it if we can find this blade, I promise you."

"The way you promised that construct you'd help him?"

Oh. That stung. I felt tears prick my eyes though I did my best to blink them back. "I know this must be hard. But this Empire needs you. If it falls, what happens to your wife?" I was pleading with her, trying to make her understand. I missed the easy banter from our days of practice, when we'd both shed the titles that weighed us down. Now we were set to the same purpose, but it was like being yoked to the same cart as an ox with very different ideas about the direction we should take to get there.

Phalue leaned against the rail, a low grumble in her throat. "When you say these things, it seems so reasonable."

"That's because it *is* reasonable."

"Yet here I am, leagues away from my family." Phalue gripped the rail. "It doesn't seem reasonable when I look at it from their perspective."

I opened my mouth to respond, still uncertain of what I should say. I couldn't blame her for her position.

"Eminence!" the captain called from his place by the wheel. His gaze was above, on the crew member in the crow's nest. The woman was signaling. "Ship on the horizon."

Phalue and I exchanged glances before we made for the back of the boat. I almost felt relieved. It was on the same trajectory we were. Two more days and we'd reach Maila. No more worrying when I'd see the Shardless Few again. They were here.

Rain pattered against the deck and the hood of my oilskin cloak, the sky above painted in blues and grays, the colors seeping into one another. Below us, the Endless Sea tossed, dark and foaming. Thrana dropped back so she could be near me. I'd once teased her for thinking she might keep up with a sailboat, but she cut through the water like a dolphin, her webbed feet more powerful than I'd given her credit for.

I peered through the spyglass and focused on the horizon, wiping away drops of water that settled on the lens. I didn't see a column of white smoke rising from the ship, no matter how many times I wiped the lens free. How was it moving so quickly then? I shifted positions, sweeping the spyglass slowly from one side to another. A figure stood beneath the sails, arms raised. I squinted and almost thought I could make out a grizzled beard, an angry face. He must have been raising hurricane winds to get his boat to move like that.

"Captain!" I called over my shoulder. "Do we have any last witstone reserves?"

"No, Eminence," he shouted back. "Not even one last crumbling rock. But there's another thing you should know."

I snapped the spyglass shut. They'd catch us before Maila. "And what is that?"

The captain pointed toward the horizon. "We're about to hit a storm. We've a couple of choices here: we go straight into it and hope to make it through, or we veer that way —" He moved his hand to the left, away from Maila. "— and hope to just catch the glancing edge."

I marched the distance to midship so we weren't shouting at one another, Phalue on my heels. "If we try to avoid the storm? How much time do we lose?"

The ship's navigator, next to him, was making some calculations on a board with a wax crayon. She tucked it away and pulled an abacus from her belt. Deft fingers moved the beads. "Depending on the winds and how long the storm lasts . . . another day. Maybe two."

I looked to Phalue but she only looked at the abacus, her lips pressed together. She had no opinion on the matter.

It was my call. I was the Emperor, after all. I closed my eyes a moment, sank into the tremor of my bones. My awareness sharpened and I could feel the rain all around us, the ocean roiling beneath us, the crest of each wave as it struck the sides of the ship. And the wind . . . ? I tugged at it, wondering how much more I could sway it to my command. I felt a little give, though not much. Ahead of us, the sky darkened, a flash of lightning illuminating the underside of looming clouds and the crests of roaring waves.

Once, Jovis had asked Ragan if he couldn't just calm the seas outside our ship. He couldn't, he'd explained. Only Dione might have that power. And here was Dione, chasing me on his own ship, trying to get to Maila before me.

He'd go into the storm.

We'd have to too.

"We go into the storm," I said to the captain and the navigator. The captain took it in his stride, but the navigator paled. "I can calm the ocean around our ship," I said, with much more confidence than I felt. "We'll make it through. What I'm worried about, though, is whether we'll make it through before they do."

I went to the side of the ship and called Thrana back to the deck. She scrambled aboard, her fur soaked but her eyes shining like two polished stones. She circled me, unable to contain her excitement. "There are fish and bright, *bright* creatures down in the depths. Water is a bit murky with the storm, so I can't see everything, but ah! The noises! There are whales up ahead in the storm, singing to each other."

"Thrana." I reached up and touched the side of her neck. She brought her head down so she could look me in the eye. "We're going into the storm. I'm going to do my best to calm the water. Can you do anything to counteract the wind?"

She shook her head, water flinging from her fur. "Can't," she said. "The best I can do is bring wind. I can't change the direction of it. But, Lin – you can."

So I'd have to do this alone. Nine lives on this ship and all of them reliant on me for survival, including my own. I hoped I wasn't making a mistake by going into the storm. I checked behind us and saw Dione's ship, looming larger. They'd not turned. And they were gaining on us. The stories said that when Alanga fought, towns and cities often drowned. I was certain that applied to ships too. A part of me hoped he'd focus on getting his ship through the storm, but the rest of me knew he'd come at me any chance he got. I'd seen the look on his face after I'd confronted him with his true identity. He thought I was a true-born Sukai, and to him, all Sukais deserved death.

"You see it?" I said to the captain.

"Yes, Eminence," he said. "They'll draw even with us just after we hit the storm, if I judge it right. And no witstone aboard. That's Alanga doing then, am I correct?"

"You are."

"Then I hope you can do more than just calm the ocean around us. I've been in a fight before, Eminence. And I've been through more storms than I'd like. But I've not been in both at the same time." And then he was striding off, barking orders to the crew, telling them to get below and to find a weapon in case we were boarded.

Phalue's presence at my side was no longer a bowstring, pulled taut, every movement a vibration in my ear. Oddly enough, she seemed more relaxed than she had before we'd seen the ship. This was something I was starting to understand about her: she preferred to be in motion, to be doing something. Leaving her to sit idle had been like putting a tiger in a cage – of course she'd been pacing back and forth. I stored the information away for later. I'd have to find something to occupy her or she'd be snapping at me each time I made some overture of conversation.

That was if we made it through this.

I had the white-bladed sword strapped to my side. It still felt odd there, even though I'd made a habit of wearing it. It was the legacy of my father's ancestor, created to subdue the Alanga. And I was an Alanga myself. "Stay aboard," I told Thrana. "I can't risk losing you."

"And I can't risk losing you," she said, lowering her gaze to meet mine. "So I'll do what *I* think is best."

Had she spoken too much to Mephi? Or was it just that she was getting older? Less my charge and more a friend with a will and a mind of her own? I patted her shoulder. "Then just . . .do your best to stay safe."

"And you as well."

The Shardless Few ship drew closer. It was only a little larger than ours, the crew running about, shouts carrying over the noise of the storm. The figure behind the sails became clear and I saw I'd been right: it was Dione. I couldn't see his eyes, but I felt the heat of his gaze even through the distance. He lifted his hands and their ship surged forward. The rain against the hood of my cloak turned from a patter into a thundering downpour. I threw off the hood, letting the water soak into my hair, trickling cold against my scalp. Better to have full visibility. I could handle getting damp.

"Thrana!" I said to her. "Send us into the storm."

She bounded behind the sails, took in a breath and blew. Wind gathered as she breathed, puffing into the sails. I grabbed for the railing as the boat rocked beneath me, surging through the choppy waves. A *crack* sounded, the sky turning, for a brief moment, a blinding white. We hit the storm front and the sky went from light gray to nearly black.

I closed my eyes and let loose the tremor in my bones, feeling it course through my body, a low note that only I could hear. I reached out to the ocean. It was like trying to calm a bucking horse while riding it. I wasn't sure what the right touch was, what would bring all these volumes of water to heel. The waves weren't just what I could see on the surface. The water moved far beneath me, only the crests visible above the surface. That was where I had to work, not up here. I gathered control of as much of the water beneath and head of the ship as I could.

"Eminence!" Phalue shouted. I cracked an eye open and saw a monster of a wave approaching. My throat tightened.

Now. I let go of the rail, trying my best to keep my feet steady, and smoothed my hands out in front of me, as though I were smoothing a sheet over a bed. I could feel the water beneath us calming, the waves diminishing like wrinkles in cloth, fading at the touch of an iron. The wave that was about to crash over the ship shrank into something that the prow barely dipped over.

To my right, I saw the Shardless Few ship drawing even with us. Dione had abandoned his spot behind the sails. I felt a small bit of satisfaction that he could not fill the sails and soothe the storm at the same time. But then I saw two other people emerge behind him; two people I recognized. Ragan and Nisong. Panic fluttered up my throat, my arms feeling suddenly weak. They were both alive and here with Dione, ready to fight against me. I'd felt enough anxiety over trying to face off against Dione. Now there were two Alanga on their ship and only one on mine.

Dione lifted a hand. A wave that had been building ahead of us grew, taller and taller.

I hadn't counted on this. Thrana, behind me, blew into the sails again. Our ship sped forward toward the wave. This was how much faith she had in me: this was a problem she thought I could take care of, so she focused on the one task I'd given her. Her confidence bolstered me. I reached out, felt the wave – so much water, all obeying Dione's command.

I tried to seize control. It was like trying to remove the stone from inside a carved tiger's mouth. The grip Dione had on it was unyielding; I couldn't seem to tear his control away. Our ships were abreast of one another now. Even through the rain I could see the triumphant expression on his face, the satisfaction as the wave bore down on us. It would clip his ship too, but he didn't seem to care.

I reached down, tried to find the base of it. The wave curled over our ship.

"Lin!" Thrana broke from her spot behind the sail, seizing me just as the water came crashing down. One paw curled around my torso. I sucked in a breath.

Cold and darkness, buffeting me from all directions. The roar of rushing water.

And then suddenly there was air again, people around me shouting. I gasped, the taste of salt on my lips. "He's too strong for me," I said. "I tried to take control and there was just nothing I could do."

Thrana's voice sounded not in my ear, but in my mind. *Lin, is it your strength that has saved you, over and over?*

I met her gaze and she nodded as though to assure me it was her. She could speak to me without opening her mouth? This was a new development and not anything I'd expected. How far did this extend? Did Dione have an ossalen he could speak to over the distances? Was that why I'd never seen his? "No," I shouted back to her over the din. "No, it hasn't been." I'd tried to stop a mudslide with my hands instead of finding a way to keep myself from being swept away by it. Another wave was forming in the distance. Phalue knelt at my side. I seized her arm. "I know the boat is rocking, but we're in range. The guards have bows, yes? Have them fire on Dione and Ragan. They can do their best to hit them, though even distracting them will be enough."

I let her go and she went to obey. I couldn't pry the water from Dione's control, that much was clear. But I had power too. Maybe not at his level of skill, but I might be able to best Ragan. I just had to keep us from being crushed until we were free of the storm. "Thrana, watch my back." There was a stillness I had to find before practicing bone shard magic. I reached for that same stillness now, seeking to bolster my concentration. I blocked out the shouts from around me, the crack of thunder, the flashes of lightning. I focused on the feel of rain drumming against my shoulders, trickling down my scalp and over my cheeks, mingling with the salt water that had drenched the rest of me. And then instead of reaching for the wave that Dione controlled, I seized the water in front of the ship and lifted it.

A wall formed ahead of us just before the wave hit. Water crashed into water in a spray of sea and salt. Lightning struck the crest of the wave, illuminating the water – a flash of bright blue-green, the silhouette of some sea creature caught in our magic – and then dark once more. The rumbling thunder layered over the roar of the waves, deafening me.

I glanced to my right and saw the first of the arrows fly toward the Shardless Few's ship. I saw Dione's hand move, saw the arrows go askew. But at least he wasn't building up another wave to crush us. Ragan dodged, his sword in hand, lacking the abilities that Dione had. Still, they had more men and women with them than I did. And Dione had more control over his Alanga magic. I had to keep moving forward, one step ahead of him, or we'd all be drowning in the Endless Sea before long.

There had to be more I could do. I reached out with my power, testing it against the waves. I could smooth the area in front of our ship; could I roughen the sea in front of theirs? I seized hold of the water in front of their ship and then scrunched my fingers as though mussing up a blanket. Their boat bucked on the choppy waters and I felt a small sense of satisfaction.

Until they returned my guards' volley. I barely had the chance to push a current of wind against them, to make them go wide. One *thunked* into the wooden floor just left of my foot. That could have been disastrous. I imagined being pinned to the deck, trying to pull the arrow free so my foot could heal. Two guards using bows. That meant two whose skills were being currently underutilized. There were too many Shardless Few on the other ship for us to even attempt boarding. We'd be outnumbered.

Unless I was able to get rid of some.

Another enormous wave hurtled toward the prow. I gathered the water in front of the ship and waited.

"Eminence!" Phalue shouted. Her sword was in her hand, though she looked about helplessly, as though uncertain what to do with it.

Now. Just as it began to curl, I lifted the water into a wall, but not a wall to block the wave. One to divert it.

The wave crashed into my wall of water. Both bodies gave way. But I'd raised the water at an angle – one that tilted toward Dione's ship. The wave sloshed to the side and over the Shardless Few's boat.

It was diminished by the time it poured over the boat, but they hadn't expected it. They hadn't had the time to brace.

"Captain – hard right into their ship. Do it now!"

The prow turned. I lifted a hand, guiding the Endless Sea beneath us, augmenting the motion of the ship. Lightning flashed just to the left of us, the crack of thunder mingling with the knock of wood against wood as our ships collided. The guards did their best to secure our ship to theirs, but the storm proved too rough. I heard their shouts of dismay as the side of the Shardless Few's ship slipped away.

There wouldn't be another opportunity. Dione knew what I was trying to do now. "Stay here," I said to Thrana. "Protect the crew. Phalue, keep Ragan off my back." She nodded, her lips pressed together in grim understanding. Her legs coiled beneath her as she prepared to follow me. I ran to the edge of the boat just as our ships were ricocheting away, and leapt.

I landed just inside their railing, thankful that I'd been climbing and jumping rooftop to rooftop for years. I rose to my feet and pulled the sword from its sheath in the same movement. It gleamed despite the darkness overhead, like lightning given solid form. I felt the retreating presence of my ship behind me, my heartbeat pounding, my mouth dry in spite of the rain. I'd seen Phalue hold off war constructs twice her size, and I'd watched her do it easily.

She'd taught me. Dione might have been powerful, but I was Lin. I was the Emperor and I was so much more. A daughter without a father, an Alanga, a friend. I would not let Dione tear the islands apart to bring back the Alanga. I would not let him set us all against one another to appease his own selfish conscience.

Phalue hit the deck behind me at a run, lifting her blade as she approached Ragan. I didn't have the chance to watch her. Two Shardless Few came at me, sliding across the moisture-slick deck. I caught the sword of one on mine, steadied myself on the rail and kicked out at the other. He went flying back. I turned my attention to the woman whose blade I'd blocked and found her trying to force her strength against mine. I looked slight, but looks here were deceiving. I easily shoved her blade to the side then used the hilt of mine to club her in the head. She went down. Others were drawing weapons, climbing down stairs or ropes, all now focused on me. An arrow *thunked* into the deck, far from anyone. Too much wind, too much rain, the sea too restless to allow for proper aim. I kept my knees soft as the boat rocked beneath me.

Dione.

He stood suddenly before me, two daggers drawn. A flash of lightning, the flash of a blade. I brought my weapon up to block and felt the impact as his dagger's edge scraped against my sword. He grimaced, the lines of his face carved with darkness. He swiped at me with his other dagger and I jumped back. "You don't deserve to be an Alanga," he sneered at me, rain dripping from his lips.

"Thrana does not agree with you," I said. I circled and feinted, watched how quickly he responded. He might have looked like an old man, but he moved with the vigor of someone my age.

"You say we can never work together — why? Wouldn't it be better to put the past behind us, to try to found a better future for both Alanga and commoners?"

"Ylan used to talk like that. But in the end, as I lay there with my eye mangled by his blade, he told me the truth. As long as the Alanga existed, the commoners would always be at risk. Oh, and he was so sorry about it too," Dione spat. "For all his talk of fairness and equity, he went out, rounded up all the Alanga and their descendants, slaughtered them and then named himself Emperor. I watched your family commit atrocities, one after the other, all to keep the Alanga from returning. And the witstone mining—"

"Yes," I shouted above the storm. "What about it?"

His lips pressed together.

"Why won't you just tell me? What are you afraid of?"

"You Sukais always knew how to twist any information to your advantage." He thrust at me with both daggers, one after another in quick succession.

I danced around his attacks, thankful for Phalue's thorough instructions. "No," I said. "You don't get to do that to me. I'm not like them."

"So you say."

"So I have *shown*." I searched his eye, trying to find some spark of humanity in its depths. His scowl only deepened. The answer came to me in pieces. "You *are* afraid. You're afraid if you tell me, I might do the right thing — and then what were all these years and years of anger and plotting for? You're afraid you've been lying to yourself." I pushed on. "I made a promise to be a better leader than my father. To be a leader who cared."

"Foolish child. Do you think that caring solves all problems? You will always look at issues through the lens of someone in power. Not just an Emperor, but now an Alanga too. What perspective do you have on the problems the common citizenry face?"

"What perspective do *you* have?" I shot back.

He came at me again, a whirlwind of blades, whipping at me like the wind and the rain. I turned his attacks aside, which only seemed to make him angrier. I should have taken advantage of his loss of concentration; I should have pushed back. But I couldn't feel his same anger. Ylan had once moved Dione to compassion, and then had betrayed him. That one betrayal had defined our history, left Dione alone and steeped in grief. "You're leader of the Shardless Few, but how can you ever be one of them? You've been *manipulating* them."

"I am keeping them *safe* from people like you!" He thrust at me again and I put all my strength into batting his blade away. He lost his grip on it and it went skittering off into the darkness.

"That's exactly how my father would talk about the Alanga. Admit it to yourself. You've been using them, sending them to die just to bring the Alanga back."

"Our goals aligned."

"For how long? When do you abandon them? Before or after this supposed Council?"

"And your way is so much better?" he scoffed, stepping back, giving me space. "Even if you are not like your father, how many generations until his blood runs true again? Will you teach your heirs the bone shard magic or will you truly leave them defenseless against people like Nisong who would use it against them?"

Difficult questions: ones I had no answer for. And then I noticed the movement of his free hand. He wasn't letting me have a breather; he wasn't listening to what I had to say. He'd been distracting me.

I turned to run and found myself facing the blue-black of a wave.

I lifted a hand, trying to sway it in a different direction. This time, I thought I felt it move, my grip on it nearly as strong as Dione's. I was stopping it from falling, my concentration holding, though barely. And then someone came hurtling out of the darkness, her hand outstretched. Nisong. I caught a glimpse of something bright and white in her hand. A shard? Instinctively, I curled away. My focus faltered.

The wave curled over me and then fell. I could feel the unnatural movement of it, carrying me back and over the ship's railing.

Into the dark of the Endless Sea itself.

19

Phalue

Somewhere in the Endless Sea

Phalue watched with a stunned sort of horror as the wave crashed over Lin and then disappeared, taking her with it. Even if Lin knew how to swim, the ocean was roiling like something alive.

But then Ragan was advancing, his white-bladed sword at the ready, blocking the way between her and Lin. "I've been training since I was a child," he shouted over the storm. "Who are you, one of her guards?"

"A governor," Phalue said. "And I've been training since I was a child as well."

He smirked, and then whipped out his sword, quick as a viper. Phalue blocked it, the ringing of their blades vibrating into her ears. He seemed momentarily taken aback, but what Phalue hadn't told him was that she'd trained both Lin and Ayesh. And Lin and Ayesh had inadvertently trained her in turn, teaching her how to respond to the speed and strength of an Alanga. She took all those lessons now and applied them, letting her sword fall away, stepping back and to the side to let him overbalance. She could not fight him the way she had fought Tythus, the way she had fought the constructs at Gaelung. Her strength was no longer an advantage. She had learned to give way in a fight when she'd never had to before.

She struck out, catching him on the calf just before he slipped away. She tried to make the hit count, but he was slippery as an algae-covered rock. He pivoted to face her, his expression grim, and she knew he wouldn't underestimate her again. Rain pounded the deck, the waves sending the ship careening back and forth in a way that made Phalue's stomach swim. But judging by Ragan's brief grimace, he didn't enjoy it either. A quick glance told her that Lin had taken out a good deal of Dione's crew, but the rest were rallying, making their way toward her and Ragan.

How long could Lin keep her head above the waves? That was assuming they hadn't tossed her below already, that she was able to find the surface again in the storm-darkened sea. Could Alanga still drown? They hadn't been getting along lately, but Phalue didn't want Lin to die. "Damn it," she cursed to herself. She swung wildly at Ragan, hoping it was enough to distract him, and then dashed for the rail. She heard a shout from behind her, felt a scrape against her back. But it didn't fell her.

The world seemed to tilt as she seized the rail and heaved herself upward.

Her foot hit the wood just as the whole ship lurched beneath a wave. She launched into the air, the space between the two ships now too large a gap to jump. And then she, too, fell into the Endless Sea.

The water closed briefly over her head, cold filling the space between her skin and her leather armor. And then she burst above the waves, gasping in a breath. She knew how to swim — every Empirean child learned when they were young — but the

calm coastal waters of Nephilanu were not the same as the churning waters of the open sea. She kicked off her boots, felt the drag
of her clothes and her armor. A wave knocked her in the back of
the head, water going straight up her nose as she submerged once
more. She coughed as she surfaced again, salt burning her nose
and throat. A tight bud of panic formed in her chest, threatening to burst into full bloom. Lightning flashed, illuminating her
ship – too far away. She'd never make it.

An enormous shape erupted from the water beside Phalue.

Her limbs froze, her heartbeat thudding against her ribs. For a
moment, she thought it must be a shark or a sea serpent or some
other creature surfacing from the inky depths. Her fingers were
still curled around her sword. She could barely keep her head
above the water; she couldn't fight at the same time.

And then the beast let out a soft chirrup and Phalue felt
weak with relief, her panic wilting away. It was Thrana, and
she gripped a mass of sodden clothes in her jaws. Not just
clothes. Lin.

Phalue seized a fistful of Thrana's fur as she passed, and the
ossalen swam through the churning water as though she were
a bird darting through the sky. The Endless Sea parted before
them, sliding against Phalue's skin as they cut toward the ship.
They reached it quickly, and with an extra burst of speed, Thrana
leapt from the water. Phalue's arm nearly jolted from its socket.
She let go of Thrana's fur, her knuckles sore, her fingers numb.
She finally sheathed her sword, promising herself to take care of
it when she had the chance. "Get us out of here!" she called to
the crew. "As fast as you can." Lin had knocked a good deal of
the other ship's crew into the water – they'd have to stop and find
them. It gave Lin's crew a moment's breathing room.

Thrana nudged at Lin's body, rolling her onto her side. The
Emperor's face was pale, hands curled as though she were asleep.

Could Alanga heal from drowning? Was that even possible? Waiting to find out didn't seem like the best idea. Phalue knelt at Lin's side, feeling for breath and a heartbeat, trying to remember what she'd been told about drowning by her mother so very long ago. The lessons had been overwritten by years of living in the palace on a hillside, lessons about fighting, Ranami's lectures about equality. She reached for Lin's face.

The Emperor coughed, water sputtering from her mouth. She rose to her hands and knees with the help of Thrana's gentle nudges, expelling what looked like an entire mug-full of ocean water. And then she took in a ragged breath. Phalue had to lean in close to hear. "I told you to stay on the ship," she said to Thrana.

"And I said I'd do what I thought was best," the ossalen said.

Another bolt of lightning struck the Endless Sea, illuminating the Shardless Few's ship only a short distance away. Phalue hated to ask something of Lin, not after she'd nearly drowned, not after the arguments they'd had. But they all needed a way out of this storm and away from Dione. They couldn't afford to take the time to regroup. "The wave that took you was not small. He may think you're dead," Phalue said. "There has to be a way to use that to your advantage. They'll be back on us as soon as they've retrieved their crew."

Lin's chest heaved. "Taking existing waves and augmenting them isn't hard, but he sees them coming and can take control."

Oh, Ranami, Phalue thought, despair pulling the strength from her limbs, *we are so far from where we started.* "Then don't let him see them coming, no matter how hard it is."

The Emperor's lips pressed together and she gave Phalue a fierce nod. For a moment, it was as though they were back in the palace courtyard, each with a sword in hand, sparring and sweating as Phalue barked out instructions.

Thrana put a paw on Lin's shoulder as she sat up. "Your strength is low."

"It'll be lower if I'm dead." She patted the top of Thrana's paw before gently removing it.

Phalue watched her rise to her feet, standing on the rocking deck, her feet firm with determination. She lifted both hands overhead.

Two vast walls of water shot into the sky on either side of the Shardless Few's ship. Lin's face was a grimace of determination, her fingers trembling. "He's trying to take control." She lifted her arms higher, her whole body trembling. Then she curled her hands one over the other, and the walls came crashing down onto Dione's ship so hard that its deck sunk nearly level with the Endless Sea before bobbing back up again. Phalue heard the crack of wood, the screams of the Shardless Few.

And then Lin collapsed.

Their ship passed the Shardless Few's. Above them, the sky lightened marginally. Thunder rumbled, but it sounded faintly behind. They were past the worst of it.

Thrana nudged at Lin's shoulder, a worried sound in the back of her throat. She'd saved them all, apparently at great cost to herself. But then, they wouldn't have needed saving if they hadn't been on this reckless journey in the first place. Still arguing with herself, Phalue reached out, took Lin's hand and wrapped it around her shoulders. She lifted the Emperor to her feet. You weren't supposed to touch the Emperor without permission, but they were in the middle of the Endless Sea, and she'd *struck* the Emperor during their training sessions.

Thrana hovered over them, her great big head nearly blocking the pattering rain. "Is she . . . ?"

Lin's feet caught beneath her. Corpses couldn't stand. "She's fine. I think she just needs rest." She took Lin to her cabin, every movement of her salt-heavy clothes chafing against her skin. Lin wasn't the only one who needed rest.

Everything felt heavy.

The next thing she knew, she was waking up in the hold, sunlight streaming through the hatch, water dripping from above. She touched her face and found it wet. Ah. So that was what woke her. That and the light. How long had it been? She moved an arm and found her clothes dry. Someone had removed the leather armor and changed her. Slightly embarrassing – no one had done that for her since she'd been a child – but it wasn't as though she'd been in any condition to help herself.

Or Lin.

Phalue sat up, throwing off the thin blanket and rolling from the pallet. Above-deck, she found the wind cutting through the air, the sails filled. The sky was overcast, but the clouds thin enough to let the sun periodically shine through. The Endless Sea glittered where the sunlight struck it, the surface now so much calmer. When she looked to the horizon, she caught a glimpse of neither storm clouds nor the Shardless Few's ship. The door to Lin's cabin was open, Thrana curled next to it, her fur ruffling in the wind. Her enormous head was blocking the doorway, her gaze fixed inside with the woebegone look of a pup whose master has forgotten to take it for a walk.

Lin was bent over the cabin's tiny desk, scrawling wildly across several sheafs of paper, muttering to herself as she worked. Her hair was tangled; it looked as though she'd just let it dry, and salt crystals clung to the harried strands. She'd put on a fresh set of clothes, but it seemed hastily done. A bowl of noodles lay at her elbow, untouched, any steam long since faded. She didn't even look up when Phalue stepped over Thrana's head. "Maila isn't large, but it's not tiny either. There are a lot of places that sword could be. But when I sketched out the map I'd seen on the key's bow, I remembered – there was a little notch in the pattern, but I can't remember exactly where it was." She pointed to the paper in front of her, the crude map she'd drawn of Maila. "It was either here, here or here. I think. We may have bought ourselves some time, but Dione will repair his ship. He'll be after us. We'll need to check each spot until we find the sword, but we also won't have a lot of time. This is why I needed you, Phalue. If you check this spot –" She pointed. "– I can check this one, and then we can meet at the last one. I don't trust anyone else to lay their hands on that sword."

Phalue leaned against the door frame, her arms crossed. She felt oddly vulnerable without her leather armor, her shoulders less broad. Or maybe it was the weakness in her limbs from the battle they'd just fought, her narrow escape from drowning. If *she* was tired, how was Lin feeling? She knew the Alanga healed quickly, but Lin had also expended a lot of her Alanga powers last night. And she looked a mess.

"You should be resting," Phalue said.

Lin shot her a sharp look. "As if you'd listen to that advice. The sooner we find that sword, the sooner we can get you off to Nephilanu with my army."

The squirrel construct sat in the corner of the room, grooming its ears with its paws. Above it, on the corner of the tiny bed, sat the gull construct. Phalue hadn't noticed it before; it had been sitting so still. It must have just returned from another island. "Word from Ranami? Is she being threatened?" she said, breathless, her heart in her throat.

"No," Lin said, and Phalue wasn't sure if she was relieved or disappointed not to hear from her wife. "From Imperial. We're out of witstone. We're almost out of caro nut oil. Even if we had it, it might take too long to get to any areas that have outbreaks. Ikanuy is doing her best to keep everyone calm, but the only thing that seems to be holding this Empire together is Iloh at this point. The governors are listening to him. They're counseling their citizens to have patience. I don't want to trust him, but he's not me – and that seems to be an advantage in some ways." Her voice was thick with bitterness. "Regardless, I need to return as soon as possible and finalize our alliance before he changes his mind. As soon as we get back to civilization, I'll have to choose a new governor for Gaelung, and my soldiers will help them get established before they withdraw. Ranami just needs to hold out until then."

Not for the first time, Phalue was grateful she'd been able to marry for love, that Nephilanu was strong enough not to need alliances backed by marriage. Oh, if she could just see Ranami one more time, she'd tell her exactly what it meant to her to have her for a wife. She'd tell her a thousand times, every day, until Ranami laughed and begged her to stop. Phalue hadn't taken Ranami's presence for granted, but out here on the Endless Sea, leagues away, she also felt she'd never appreciated her quite enough. Each thought of her made Phalue smile at the same time it made her chest ache.

"We've made good time," Lin was saying, moving on from the message she'd received from her steward. "We'll be arriving at Maila this afternoon. The storm pushed us in the right direction, at least. We weren't blown off course."

Phalue turned to go and then hesitated on the threshold. Something had shifted between them during that battle, burning away the anger she felt at Lin. She'd watched the Emperor throw everything she had at the Shardless Few, do everything she could to protect the ship and the people on it. She'd been shouting at Lin to understand her, to know the deep and abiding need she had to be there at her wife's side, to see the common people the way she did – not just as things to be protected and uplifted, but as people who had very deep and individual goals, whose needs were seldom being met. But what she hadn't realized was that she'd not done the same for Lin. She didn't truly understand the woman.

She met Thrana's gaze and the beast gave a small, encouraging nod of her head.

"Eminence—"

Lin set down her pen, her fingers going to her temples. "Please, at least when we're alone, just call me Lin. I'm sorry I threw my title in your face like that."

It seemed they'd both softened. "What are you afraid will happen if Dione captures the swords?"

Lin looked at Phalue, her hands still pressing into the sides of her face. The woman was in her mid-twenties, but she looked like she'd aged a decade, worry drawing lines across her forehead. For a moment, Phalue thought she wouldn't answer, but then she let out a sigh. "I'm afraid of the end, Phalue. Not of myself. Not even of the Empire. But of so much more. I don't know what the swords do. Dione does. Do you know how much that keeps me up at night? How I toss and turn, wishing I just *knew*? There are a thousand possibilities milling about in my mind and none of them are good. The things I see in my head before I finally fall asleep . . ." She trailed off. "If I don't do this, if I don't stop him – who will? The other Alanga are so new. Their powers are like flickering candles while Dione's is like a bonfire. At least mine is stronger. Maybe not as strong as his, but stronger than theirs. He wants to bring the Alanga back to their former glory. He won't work with me; he refuses to. What else could it mean except that he intends to destroy everything I've worked for? And now he's working with Ragan. That can't mean anything good."

"Ragan has one of the swords," Phalue said, remembering the way the lightning flashed bright white against it in the storm.

"All the more reason we need to obtain this one. All the more reason to get it into your hands."

If Phalue set aside her fear for Ranami, she could see why Lin had acted the way she had. Lin weighed the life of Ranami in one hand, as well as her relationship with Phalue, and then weighed the lives of all her citizens in the other. Not that Phalue didn't still feel some resentment. But it eased the anger that had been stirring in her belly.

"Land spotted!" the captain called from outside.

Lin got to her feet and without even thinking, Phalue offered her her arm to lean on. Together, they made their way onto the deck.

Like any governor's child, Phalue had been educated on the islands of the Empire. Maila was part of the Empire, but was the sort of place people marked on maps simply so others would know what location to avoid. It wasn't a destination for any-thing — not for fishing, not for trips of leisure, and not for trading. As far as anyone had known before — no one lived on Maila. The reefs were treacherous and kept even the most skilled sailors away. It wasn't as large as Imperial but Phalue could make out the jagged outline of twin peaks, the lush green of forests, the white of sandy beaches.

Lin unfolded a piece of parchment from her sash pocket, the bottom of it faintly spattered with blood. The captain and the navigator had both already made copies of the map the construct had drawn for them. "Can we get past the reefs?" she asked the captain as they approached. Phalue stared at the clouds past Maila, out into the open sea. She knew there were islands past the Empire, but they weren't on any of the maps her father had shown her.

"If this boat got past the reefs before we can get past them again." He was looking at his copy of the map, comparing it to the eastern edge of the island. "It's not the most precise map," he muttered.

"What happens if we hit the reefs?"

He raised an eyebrow. "Like claws through a soft belly. They'll gut us, Eminence."

There was time for a quick meal before they drew close to the island. Phalue barely tasted hers, gulping it down before marching back above-deck. Everyone on the ship went silent as they approached the reefs, as though refraining from speaking might help guide them safely to land. Thrana had leapt overboard, swimming ahead of the ship. "It's here," she called, circling an area just large enough for the prow of the ship to squeeze through. Just where the construct had said it would be.

While everyone else cheered, Phalue watched a number of complex emotions flit across Lin's face, remembering the way she'd spoken to the construct on Gaelung. "He told us the truth when he didn't need to. But you expected that," she said, trying to distract them both from the delicate passage they were about to undertake.

"Yes," Lin said, her fingers tight around the rail. "I grew up with constructs. The ones most people are familiar with – the lower-level spies, warriors and bureaucrats – they're not like the ones my father kept in his closest company. Those ones could think for themselves. They . . .had feelings. Sometimes I think even the lower-level ones do."

They floated over the reefs. Phalue glanced over the railing of the boat. She could see fish swimming in and out of the coral, crabs scuttling over the sections close to the surface, larger unidentifiable shapes moving in the depths. She opened her mouth to respond to Lin, but then held her breath as the hull scraped against something.

Like claws through a soft belly.

But then they were through and into the shallows. She thought she could hear a sigh echo through the ship as everyone let out their breaths. Thrana dived and rolled and then disappeared beneath the water in pursuit of a fish. They'd made it to Maila, and before Dione had too. "You did your best for that construct. You can't save everyone," Phalue said, hating that it was true. "No matter how hard you try." She felt things click into place in her own mind. "You can only do your best to make things better."

Lin cast her a grateful look, reaching out to briefly cover Phalue's hand with her palm. "I will always try. I promise."

Phalue wasn't on her way back to Nephilanu. She didn't have that sword or Lin's army at her back. But somehow, those words made her feel marginally better. Like somehow, they now stood on the same ground. She hadn't realized how much their conflict had been weighing on her, how her anger had soured everything else.

The captain dropped anchor in the shallows, and they took a dinghy to shore with the guards. Thrana swam up from the shallows to meet them on the beach. She shook out her fur, sand sticking to her webbed paws. The clouds parted again, sending rays of light through the ocean, illuminating it like the bright spots on a sea serpent's sides. They were setting foot on the same beach Nisong and her compatriots had fled from. Now that Phalue looked about, she could see small, subtle signs that someone else had been here. The frayed end of a rope, charred wood in what must have once been a firepit. A broken, discarded clay bowl, right where the sand was interrupted by sea grasses. They were treading on the island the leader of the construct army had once called home.

Lin cleared her throat. "We split into two groups. I'll lead one and Phalue leads the other. There may be constructs still living here, or hostile wildlife."

Phalue set off along the beach with two of the guards. She only remembered the name of one – Huan – a short woman with a stout build and deep-set eyes. The other Imperial Guard was a man with a neatly shaved mustache. They climbed to the cliffside, eventually trekking through the forest. An abandoned basket, the trails through the brush, a decaying refuse pile among the trees. They saw no one, but Phalue felt the ghostly presence of the constructs, like the fingerprints left behind on a pane of glass. Halfway through their hike, she spotted the construct village through the trees, the huts still standing, thatched roofs and abandoned cooking stations. She caught a glimpse of movement but let out a breath when a wild pig made its way out from one of the huts, followed by several spotted piglets.

She felt as though she crept through someone else's home in the dead of the night.

It was afternoon by the time they reached the spot Lin had indicated on the map. Another beach, facing out toward the open Endless Sea. Only one small blip of an isle and then nothing as far as the eye could see. There was something dizzying about the prospect. Phalue felt suddenly aware of the earth beneath her feet, aware of the shape of it, knowing that somewhere deep below the ground ended and the Endless Sea began. It made her feel unusually small, insignificant.

"Search the trees and rocks," Phalue called out. "Look for anything unusual."

Her group scattered as they obeyed. Phalue found herself kicking her feet along the line where sand met grass, her heart nearly as heavy as it had been when she'd stared down the construct army at Gaelung. There was another army to face now, and she yearned to be in the thick of it, fighting her way back to Ranami's side instead of this interminable search.

Something prickled at the back of Phalue's neck. She knew

this feeling, like someone had brushed the hair there without touching skin. Slowly, she turned around, her gaze going into the forest.

There was no one there.

She let out a breath, felt her fingers ease from around her sword's hilt. And then she saw the eyes. Green as the surrounding forest, set into a face covered in russet fur. The creature was small, only as long as Phalue's forearm. It took a hesitant step in her direction and Phalue suddenly couldn't breathe. The beast let out a little *chirrup*. Her heartbeat thundered in her ears, loud as the storm they'd just escaped.

An ossalen.

20

Lin

Maila Island

There was nothing at the first spot – no clues I could latch on to, no signs that a magical sword lay there. We spent the morning fruitlessly circling before I decided we needed to check the next location. "Phalue might be waiting for us," I noted.

But when we arrived at the last location, Phalue was nowhere to be found. It was late afternoon by the time we reached it. Another beach – this one facing out toward the open Endless Sea. Nothing about this beach appeared remarkable.

"Search the trees and the rocks," I called out. "Look for anything unusual."

My group scattered as they obeyed. And I found myself kicking my feet along the line where sand met grass, my heart heavier than it had felt since I'd stared down the construct army at Gaelung. I'd been on the move ever since then, rarely stopping to think. Always there were things to deal with. I'd once told my secrets to Jovis, but he was gone and there were few I could confide in. There would always be distance between me and the others — because of my station, my powers, my secrets. I'd told Phalue the truth, that I needed someone I could trust on this mission. But the deeper truth was that I needed someone I could feel less alone with. She told me the truth even when I didn't want to hear it; she spoke her mind. She said she could not trust me, but she trusted me enough for that.

"I found something!" one of my guards called out. I hurried to his side, though I wasn't the first one there. The other guard peered over my shoulder as I inspected his find. The gnarled trunk of a tree, and near the base, something carved into the bark. The tree had grown around the scar, making the original carving difficult to make out. But if I closed my eyes and felt the edges, I knew what it was.

A sword.

"Dig," I said. "Around the roots. We're looking for a box."

We worked in and around the tree's roots. Judging by the state of the carving in the bark, the sword had been here for a long, long time. I couldn't put my arms around the trunk if I tried. We found a good many beetles, unearthed an indignant nest of snakes, and found the buried skeleton of a wild pig. Despite the protests of my guards, I took a turn with the shovel, feeling sweat gather between my shoulder-blades. The sleep and a full meal had restored me, though my muscles still ached from the battle at sea with Dione. But it felt good to be doing things rather than standing to the side and watching.

I hit something with a clink, and it did not feel like a root. "Here," I said. They put their hands into the hole, scraping away dirt, reaching. One of my guards pulled something from the soil. An old board, half-rotted, the metallic piece of a lock attached to it. Had someone been here already? "No, that can't be it," I said. "The box must have rotted. The ground shifts. It's still here — it has to be."

I plunged my hands into the sandy soil. My fingers brushed against something. I felt a sudden shock as skin parted. Pain followed, burning bright and hot as fire. I was cradling my hand before I could recall having moved, blood dripping from my fingertips. My knees were digging into the dirt, a cool breeze lifting the hair on the back of my neck. For a moment I was absorbed in these sensations, nausea bubbling in my throat.

"Eminence." Someone was taking my hand, pouring a skin of water over the wound.

The cold water brought me back to myself. "It's there," I said. "Keep digging." The other guard kept digging while the one guard bandaged my hand, Thrana hovering over me and making little sad, worried sounds.

"It's fine. I'm fine."

They lifted a white blade from the ground. The scabbard was gone. The wrappings had rotted away, revealing the command carved into the hilt. But it was the same sort of blade as the one I'd found in my father's cavern. Triumph blazed through me. We'd done it. That was two blades of seven now, giving us a distinct advantage over Dione and his Alanga, his Shardless Few. Some of the tension in my heart eased. I glanced at the faces of my guards as I tucked the blade beneath an arm.

The trees beyond the shoreline rustled, and I tensed, my hand going to the sword at my belt.

Phalue stepped onto the beach, her expression a bit bewildered. "You found it. Good." She looked around at her surroundings as though seeing them for the first time. "We found something too." One of my guards appeared next to Phalue, holding something in her arms. Huan, my Captain of the Imperial Guard.

"I named her Bao," Huan said. As I drew closer, I saw that a small ossalen lay curled in her grasp, green eyes peering out from red-brown fur.

"What . . .what do I do with her?" She looked to me and the other guards.

Thrana leaned her head over to sniff the newcomer. She let out a sighing breath, which Bao answered with a chirrup. I reached out and gave the creature a scratch on her cheeks. "You take care of her. The magic will follow."

Our procession from the beach to the ship should have been triumphant, but when Phalue fell into line beside me, her gaze was distant, her brow furrowed. Her hand did not stray to her sword hilt, however, so whatever was bothering her didn't feel like a threat. The tension between us had eased since the last time we'd spoken, and I felt she understood my reasons for this quest a little better.

I took the blade out from beneath my arm and handed it to her. "This is for you." She hadn't asked for it, too preoccupied with whatever dwelled within her thoughts.

"Ah, of course." She took the blade from me, though she seemed unsure of what to do with it. It was as though I'd broken the surface of a calm inlet, movement suddenly visible on the ocean floor.

Ahead of us, Huan scratched the ears of her ossalen, each glimpse of her face showing pure delight. Phalue stared at the woman's back and frowned. I took an educated guess. "You wish it had been you."

She let out a sigh, though she didn't meet my gaze. "It couldn't have been me. I talked to Huan. She was one of the few orphans who wasn't tithed. Me? I was. There was never a chance. I saw the beast first, though, and for a moment I thought . . ."

The wistfulness in her voice struck me to the core and my heart ached on her behalf. I wasn't sure how I would have felt if I'd pulled Thrana from the water and then she'd fixated on one of my guards, or a servant, or someone else entirely. I let the silence stretch, let that unspoken grief breathe.

Phalue finally shook her head. "It wasn't meant for me. But it would have made returning to my family easier. I could go in with the force of my new Alanga powers; I could face down whoever Dione had put in charge there." She averted her gaze from Huan's back, looking briefly southward. "I don't know why I'm telling you this. It doesn't matter. We have the sword now; you can deal with Gaelung, and you'll send your army south with me."

"I'm sorry," I said without thinking.

She tilted her head, her brow furrowed. "What for?"

My thoughts and feelings arranged themselves, the empathetic ache in my heart still present. "I know it's not my fault." The words tumbled from my mouth in a rush. I knew if I waited too long they'd sound too formal, too studied. "But it's my father's. He continued the Tithing Festival. And I ... I benefited from that. I learned how to use bone shard magic; I never had a piece of my skull taken. Thrana is mine, yes, but she never would have been mine if my father hadn't committed atrocities. I wish I could make things right for you."

Phalue shrugged, though her shoulders seemed a little lighter at the movement. "Lin, you've dragged me across the entire Empire, away from my family, for something you say is more important than all of us. For something you say is important for our futures." Her eyebrows lifted as she considered her words. "Ah, I'm not making sense. What I mean to say is don't make things right for me – it's too late for that. Make things right for Ayesh. I could forgive you anything if you do that.

"The girl wants to fight, and she shouldn't have to. She keeps that shield on her wrist like her life depends on it   and someday it might. I don't want that for her. She should be learning to write more, she should be reading books and going out with friends. She may be an Alanga, but she shouldn't have to feel like the burdens of the Empire are hers. Stop looking at the Empire as a whole and start looking at its people. Make the world safe for my little girl so she can be a little girl. That's enough."

I swallowed past the tears that had suddenly gathered in my throat.

One of Phalue's dark eyes landed on my face, judging my expression. "Still wouldn't mean I support you. As long as you know that."

I choked out a laugh. "Fair enough."

We made good time back to the beach where we'd landed. The dinghy was still on the sands where we'd left it. Once we pushed it back out into the water, the rain began to fall again. Everyone pulled their hoods over their heads, gazes low to keep the water from falling into their eyes. The hood limited my visibility, so I wasn't the first to see it. Huan sat across from me, and I saw the look on her face first. The shock, the tension. I followed her gaze.

Two ships had appeared on the horizon, hazy through the rain. Dione's ship and another that we must not have seen during the battle.

I'd thought we'd left him behind us in the storm. I'd thought when he hadn't appeared again that he'd given up. Instead, judging by its position, it looked as though both ships had hidden behind the slope of Maila's single mountain. Dione didn't need to know how to get past the reefs; he only needed to wait until I'd done so.

As soon as my feet touched the deck, I was moving, seizing the captain by the shoulder. "We need to get back out past the reefs, and quickly. You know the right spot? I won't risk Thrana back in the water again, not with Dione so close by."

"Already on it, Eminence. As soon as we spotted their ships. What I can't account for is the magic he's using to move it. We can't sail quickly past the reefs if we want our ship to stay intact.

Once we're free of the reefs we can pick up speed, but I fear they'll be able to catch us."

We were on a ship made of cloudtree wood. My father must have chosen that wood because it was quick. Dione might have magic that could fill his sails, but I did too. I didn't need to be as good as Dione; I needed only to be good enough so that our naturally quicker ship could leave his behind. I let the tremor fill my bones, focusing on the air currents around me. I wasn't as practiced at this as I was with water.

"Can I . . .can I do something to help, Eminence?" Huan stood in front of me, Bao wrapped around her neck.

"No, not yet. Just be ready with your sword and protect your ossalen." She nodded and left me alone at the prow.

Thrana's head came to rest on my shoulder. "Try to stay calm. You've been through worse. You always think you are not up to the task."

I watched the approaching ships, my heart as cold as my father's iceboxes. "And sometimes I've been right."

"Would you have changed anything about what you did?"

I'd always tried, even when the odds hadn't looked good. "No." I supposed that was the most I could ask for. To try – to put everything I had into this, and to hope it was enough.

The reefs moved below us, dark shapes in the blue-green of the Endless Sea. The blue deepened and then we were scraping past the reefs, everyone on board holding their breaths. I marched to mid-ship, positioning myself behind the sails. Thrana stood with me, webbed feet planted, head held high.

"We're past," the captain called to me.

I focused all the magic in my bones, seized the air currents moving around us and forced them into the sails. The boat leapt forward. Someone on board let out a whoop. We skimmed across the waves like a tern floating just above the water, searching for fish. Thrana breathed white smoke and the sails filled with wind again. The white smoke emanating from her mouth smelled different from the witstone smoke – sweeter, less pungent. But it looked the same.

There was a connection there.

One I didn't have time to explore. I seized more air currents, diverting them toward our ship, pulling more and more from farther away. Would Dione follow us all the way back to Imperial? I knew he wanted these swords, and badly. And he wasn't just satisfied with one; he wanted all of them. I lost myself in the work, the feel of the wind around me.

Maila was well behind us when I faltered. The tremor in my bones slowly faded as exhaustion crept up on me. I leaned into Thrana, my knees weak, my shoulders trembling. Slowly, I loosened my hold on the air, my chest aching as though I'd run for leagues in the cold. "Are we far enough?"

Thrana sat on her haunches and looked toward the stern. "His ships are still there."

I whirled. One of Dione's ships had dropped away, but the other was still advancing, its sails full of wind. The air around us had grown still, which meant that Dione was using his magic to fill the sails. His endurance far exceeded mine. I weighed my options in my mind, calculating the advantages and disadvantages of each. If I continued using my power on the air around us, I'd grow too tired to fight or even move. If I stopped, he'd catch us. He'd probably catch us anyway. I could hope I'd reduced their numbers during our last fight. But looking about at my sparse crew, I wasn't sure it would make enough of a difference. There was a small isle ahead of us, one on which I could see a small fishing village. They'd catch us before we reached it.

A plan began to form in my mind.

I left my spot behind the sails and found the captain at the prow. "We can't outrun them. Our ship is faster, but this is Dione we're talking about. The Alanga from the stories. I simply don't have the power to match his. Not with wind."

He glanced about at our crew and I knew he saw the same thing I did. There were too few of us. I beckoned them all over; there was no point in tending to the sails now. The captain snapped his spyglass in and out, though he didn't look through it. "We can do our best to take on the Shardless Few, Eminence. They want the sword so they'll board us."

Phalue appeared at my shoulder. "We barely made it out the last time. What do you propose this time?"

I took in the ship – the tall sails, the tiny crow's nest, the narrow body of it. "We offer them a bargain. And I rest until they get here."

My crew had finished the preparations by the time the foremost of Dione's ships reached us. The other trailed behind, but not so far. He'd be tired, I hoped, and I'd taken the opportunity to sit on the deck, Thrana at my back, watching Huan in the crow's nest prepare our offering.

Dione's ship slowed until they slid abreast of us, Shardless Few ready and waiting with swords drawn.

"Hold," I told my crew as I rose to my feet, as the Shardless Few leapt aboard, their fellows securing their boat to ours with ropes and hooks. Dione stepped onto the deck of the cloudtree ship, gazing about as though the thing were both intriguing and abhorrent.

So. He knew about the cloudtrees too. Of course he did.

He strolled toward me, his daggers out, Ragan behind him, his white-bladed sword drawn. My heart thumped. A white-bladed sword. Ah, so that was why Dione was now working with Ragan. Three Shardless Few fanned out behind them.

"Stop," I said, holding my hand up. All five of them halted.

And then I pointed up toward the rigging. All gazes trailed upward.

Two swords hung from the rigging, out over the Endless Sea. In the crow's nest, Huan held a knife to a rope.

"You move one more step forward, she cuts the rope, and both my sword and the one we found on Maila sink into the depths of the Endless Sea." No one moved. The wind ruffled the hair about my ears and rustled the sails. "I wish to negotiate."

"Negotiate for what?" Dione's gaze fell upon mine and I looked back into his one good eye. I felt the weight of his many years, his power, his experience. My lifetime was a grain of sand next to his long span.

But my will was as strong as his. I could not waver here; if I did, we would all be dead. "I'll hand over both swords to you. But in return, you must let us go, you must stop occupying Nephilanu and you must acknowledge my reign."

The calm on his face shattered, his brows dropping low over his eyes. "Your demands are ridiculous. Look at your position. You're outnumbered. We have more ships than you, more fighters, more Alanga. Don't act like you're in a position of strength when you're not. Give me the swords and I'll spare your lives, no more. Surely your lives are worth that much."

I heard feet shifting behind me, knew my guards were beginning to doubt this course of action. I was their leader, and I put all the conviction I had into my words. They needed me. We needed this. I'd not dragged them all – Phalue included – halfway across the Empire for nothing. I'd not risked Nephilanu to come home empty-handed, with one fewer sword than I'd had when I'd left Imperial.

"But, Dione," I said, my voice carrying across the deck, "what are they worth to *you*?" I lifted a hand.

The swords fell.

Dione started forward before they just as quickly jerked to a stop, Huan's hands on the ropes that held them suspended.

I knew I had him then. He'd broken when the swords had started to fall, had given away his hand. "They're important to you," I said. "So I say again – let us go, stop occupying Nephilanu and acknowledge my reign as Emperor."

His lips pursed as he regarded me, the muscles in his jaw clenching and unclenching. But behind that angry facade, I could see: he desperately wanted those swords. A brief flash of terror seized me. *He would agree to these terms.* And if he did – what did that mean? What exactly did these swords do?

Before I could react, Dione was before me, his blades flashing. I barely managed to block his attack with the sword I'd borrowed from Huan. I didn't have the time or chance to signal to her to cut the ropes.

"You're a Sukai," Dione said from between his teeth. "I cannot allow a Sukai to rule."

Around me, I heard the clash of blades, shouts as the Shardless Few and Ragan engaged my guards and crew.

I attacked him as a response. He lifted his daggers to block. I barely made contact with my sword before I was whirling, striking at his legs. He grunted as he slid out of the way. I tested him again, slashing for his shoulder as soon as he moved. He blocked and I pressed my blade against his. There was give there.

I leapt back. He was tired. He'd spent much of his energy filling the sails of his ship, chasing us. I'd had the chance to rest. Thrana was right; I still had a chance.

And then he gathered himself and surged toward me.

He moved like running water, every thrust and strike smooth, flowing one into the next. I managed to block and dodge the first few before I slipped up, before I felt the cut of a blade across my arm. Warm blood mingled with cold rain. He'd had centuries to practice. What did I have but a few short months with Phalue? I was outmatched. I just couldn't stand against him. Not alone and not even with Thrana. I needed Jovis with me. I missed the way it felt to fight back-to-back with him, anticipating his movements, having him anticipate mine. One of my guards rushed over to help me.

"Don't!" I held up my left hand, the fingers still bandaged and stinging. "He'll kill you." I wouldn't use him like fodder. Still, he hesitated. It was his job to protect me. "That's an order." He turned back to Ragan and the Shardless Few.

Dione only smiled. "You know it wasn't just a story that I took Khalute single-handedly. Do you really think *you* could conquer an entire island by yourself? To me, you're fresh as a mewling lamb."

He said it to intimidate me. There was uncertainty coloring his words, a wound in him that had never healed, much the way his eye hadn't. "What Ylan did to you . . .it wasn't fair," I said. "It wasn't right."

His face twisted and he thrust at me with both his daggers. I leapt back but not quickly enough. The point of his left dagger caught the space beneath my leather jerkin. I felt blood well up, the pricking sensation of pain and parted flesh.

But the wound on my shoulder had healed. This one would too. I wouldn't win this fight with weapons. I had to use my words. Ylan was a sensitive subject for him, even after all this time. After everything he'd done, I still didn't want to use my words to cut or provoke him. All I could think about was how it must have felt to be lying there on the cold stone of his home, his eye bleeding, the wound feeling like fire and ice, not healing, knowing his friend had betrayed him. That his friend had taken a gift and would use it to kill all his kind.

But pity couldn't stay my hand. I took the opportunity to

signal to Huan. She cut the ropes. The swords fell and Dione surged forward.

They caught on the rigging, the ropes tangled, dangling the blades above the water. I followed Dione, calling after him, hoping to buy Huan more time. "It must have been lonely," I said, "all those years without friend or family."

"I had the Shardless Few," he spat back, whirling to face me again.

But he hadn't thought of them as truly his. How could he have, when he didn't believe in the future he'd painted for them? All this time, the long years, spent waiting and wanting, refusing to truly connect with the people around him – because what if they were just like Ylan? "They weren't who you wanted. You could never be honest with them about who you were, so how could they ever know you? How could anyone ever truly love you?" The words struck me at the same time they struck Dione. They were the same things I'd once told myself. His one remaining eye widened, his grip loosening on his daggers. "I want to work with you," I said. "I don't believe in any of the things my father did – not the Tithing, not the constructs, not keeping Alanga from the world. Why are we fighting at all?"

He stared at me, his gaze boring into mine. His expression calmed. Hope surged in my breast. We could do this – we could work together and find a way for Alanga and commoner to live in peace.

But then I felt the hum of magic around him.

The wind slammed into me just as I noticed, throwing me away from the rest of the fighting and against the mast. Everything hurt. I took in a breath and felt a sharp pain in my ribs. Broken. Thrana darted to my side, standing over me, protective. Slowly, I felt them begin to knit together. High above us I saw Huan

climbing toward the caught blades, a knife between her teeth, her
ossalen chittering at her shoulder like an angry auntie.

"Move," Dione said to Thrana.

She bared her teeth and growled in response

Another gust of wind hit Thrana in the side, sending her
tumbling across the deck. Before I could push myself to my feet,
Dione was standing over me, his expression as dark as the storm
clouds we'd sailed through. "You're a Sukai. I can never trust a
Sukai." He lifted his daggers and I tried to bring my sword up to
block. I wouldn't make it. I had to buy Huan time. I had to buy
myself time.

"I'm not a Sukai," I gasped out.

He froze.

"I'm one of my father's experiments." I kept talking as I felt the
thrum in my bones building. I couldn't count on Dione's mercy.
"He killed his own daughter. She was *three*. She'd bonded with
an ossalen so he killed them both. I'm just something he grew
from pieces of his citizens."

His mouth moved and nothing came out. I watched his throat
bob as he swallowed. "You're still your father's creature through
and through. He treated you like a daughter."

So. Even this secret could not save me. I scrambled backward,
my ribs aching, hoping I could find someone to help me. He followed, his daggers lifted. My guards and Phalue were fighting
Ragan and the Shardless Few. Thrana was still recovering from the
blow Dione had dealt her. I wasn't going to make it. He'd kill me.

Huan cut the rope.

The splash of the swords hitting the Endless Sea made Dione
freeze. It took a little longer for Ragan, for his Shardless Few
followers, but in the next moment, the three Shardless Few were
running for the rail.

Dione didn't move, not even as his fellows dove into the water after the swords. His expression shifted as he gazed down on me. "Those were not the white-bladed swords," he said.

Behind me, Phalue was still engaged with Ragan, doing her best to hold her own against his strength and magic. A flicker of triumph crossed Dione's face as he studied mine, peeling back the layers to see the truth beneath.

I felt myself giving way, my flat expression crumbling beneath the weight of his gaze. He would always be after me, no matter who I was, because I called myself a Sukai and I ruled the Empire. We could not work together, not in the ways I'd hoped. "No, they were not." I could only see one way out of this – one way we survived.

I reached back and beneath Phalue's cloak, seizing the blade we'd found on Maila from the spot she'd hidden it at her belt. "But this one is." I threw it, hard as I could, for the Endless Sea.

Both Ragan and Dione moved for it at the same time.

"Cut the ropes," I told my crew as soon as they'd dived into the water. Piercing pain filled my lungs with each word. I lifted a wave of water with one hand. "Take us to the island village!" I shouted at my captain. "Get us out of here."

I struggled to my feet, and then Thrana was there at my side, lending me a shoulder, limping but healing, just as I was.

"He'll get back on his ship," Phalue said from behind me, her voice dark. "We won't be able to get away from him."

"That was never the plan," I said, my voice calmer than I felt. My ribs slipped back into place, the bones knitting back together. I took in a breath without pain. Without waiting for another breath, I seized the air currents around us and pushed them toward the sails. They billowed, our ship leaping toward the island. I was tired, but I could feel I still had some fight left in me yet. Dione had to be exhausted by now, which was exactly where I needed him.

I pointed at the island as we approached, the wind whipping

at our clothes. Blood stained us both, though my wounds had healed and Phalue only appeared to have scratches. "We just have to make it to that village. We stop right before shore. The water is shallower there – I can hit them with waves that will keep them from boarding."

She frowned at me, shouting over the wind. "Why didn't you do that earlier?"

"Because Dione could have just crushed us beneath a wave."

Her gaze turned to the village clinging to the shore of the island, half nestled near the beach and half climbing the forested slopes. "You can't mean . . ."

"I know some of his history, Phalue. You have to trust me. He won't destroy the village. Once, he upbraided his fellows for destroying a village in the midst of an argument."

Phalue seized the rail, steadying herself as the boat skipped over a wave. "That was a long time ago."

"It was still within his lifetime. It's the best idea I have."

"If you're wrong . . ." She trailed off and lapsed into silence, though her grip on the rail looked tighter than necessary. Absently, she reached for the spot where the blade had been hidden and then dropped her hand as she remembered. We'd have words about that, I knew, if we lived through this.

I glanced behind us and saw the sails of Dione's ships fill. He was pushing them both toward the island, using up more of his strength. It had to run out soon – it had to. I could feel exhaustion creeping in at the edges, adrenaline keeping it at bay. I only needed to last a little longer.

I only needed to last longer than he did. And to hope that some part of him was still the man he'd been long ago.

21

Nisong

An island near Maila

Nisong watched Dione's back as he lifted his hands, as he took control of the currents of air around him, directing them toward the sails of both their ships. He was spending too much magic – she could see it in his tense shoulders, his straining hands, his knees that seemed ready to buckle. He might have been the most powerful Alanga of his age, but either his power had since diminished or Lin was nearly his match.

But there was nowhere for her to go.

"She's headed straight for the village," she mused aloud. Lozhi, sitting at her side, let out a little grunt. She wasn't sure when she'd started talking to the beast as though he were a person. He didn't always talk back, but he did usually respond in some way. She curled her fingers in the soft, dense fur below his ear and felt him lean into her touch. "Why would she go there instead of around the island? She's cornering herself."

"Maybe friends there," Lozhi said in his creaky voice.

She found herself smiling at the creature. "There now, you can speak more than just one or two words."

He bowed his head, his tail winding around his paws. "He doesn't like when I speak."

She felt an odd protective tug. Lozhi deserved a better master than Ragan – one who actually paid the poor creature some attention, who was invested in his development. "Well, you can speak to me," she said. "Don't let him tell you that you can't."

He leaned gratefully into her hip and she felt her expression slip into a frown again. Friends – Lin didn't have them, not on this remote island. But something about the word had triggered a memory. Not one from her past life, but one from her current one.

Dione.

She understood, with sudden clarity, what Lin was doing and why. She found Ragan at the prow, unconcernedly watching the approaching island.

"You're not helping," she said flatly as she came up behind him.

He shrugged. "Dione didn't ask for help. Look at that man." He turned and leaned against the rail, gesturing to the Alanga, his fierce pose, his gritted teeth. "So single-minded. All he wants is to take down Lin. As though that will bring his precious friends back."

Shardless Few milled about on the deck, hands on the hilts of their weapons, looking unsure as to whether or not they should be preparing for something.

"She's forcing him to make a choice." Nisong tugged on his cloak, trying to get him to pay attention. "This could help you. He won't do anything that would hurt that village."

Ragan shrugged her off, casting her a skeptical look. "He's invaded entire islands – what does he care for one village?"

"This is different. They're not involved in this conflict. He didn't want his fellow Alanga to keep killing innocents in the midst of their arguments. It's why he betrayed his people in the first place. He regrets that, but I think he still feels the same way about mortals caught in Alanga conflicts. Use this."

"If it makes sense to." And then he turned his gaze back to the village, leaving Nisong grinding her teeth. Lozhi gave her a questioning chirrup and her jaw unclenched a little. She scratched his big chin, feeling the beginning growth of a beard there. If only she'd been the one to bond with an ossalen. She didn't have a shard taken from her skull. It could have been her. It should have been her. Not Ragan.

Instead, she kept needing to rely on him, herding him down a path he was always reluctant to follow.

Dione finally lowered his hands and the ships slowed as they approached the island. He was breathing heavily, his fingers trembling. For the thousandth time, Nisong wondered where his ossalen was, whether he kept the beast hidden away the way Ragan had. But where would he hide a creature that large?

She could make out figures on the deck of the small, dark-wooded ship that Lin commanded – the same one Nisong had once commandeered to escape Maila. One of the figures lifted her hands.

The ocean roiled. A wave lifted from the water, rushing toward them and the other Shardless Few ship. Dione lifted a hand, meeting the wave with his own. They clashed, the water falling back into the Endless Sea and the tops of the waves dissolving into mist.

Again a wave rose, gathering speed as it approached their ships. Again, Dione neutralized it. She looked to Ragan, wondering if he was seeing the same things she was. Lin had to know Dione was tiring. She was trying to wear him down. She was counting on him only playing a defensive role with her so close to the fishing village.

Ragan waited until Dione had defended against three more waves. The ship rocked gently, the air filled with salty mist. "Sink her ship," Ragan called. "We've all seen how powerful you are. Take her down."

Though the skies were cloudy, Nisong could see the sweat beading on Dione's brow. She knew what he was thinking from their earlier conversations. Lin's ship was too close to the fishing village. If he sent a wave to capsize her, he'd almost certainly drown some of the people in the village as well. It was too close an echo to what his brethren had once done – caught up in their own arguments, willfully ignorant of the harm their conflicts caused to the mortals around them. He wanted to bring them back, to correct his own mistakes.

But he didn't want to repeat theirs.

Dione turned from the rail. "No."

Ragan hesitated and Nisong leaned over to whisper in his ear. "We can take him on. We have the support."

The set of his jaw firmed and he stepped forward. "So this is who you would have as your leader." Ragan swept an arm out. "Dione. Or should I still call you Gio? What did you tell them all? That you were raised in a poor village? That you were just like them? You let them all believe that someone like them could take Khalute single-handedly. But you're not. You're an Alanga."

He pointed to Lin's ship. "And now it seems blood calls to blood. When given a chance to crush your enemy, you hesitate."

Dione looked as though he were watching this scene play out from a distance. Nisong could see the calculations taking place in his head – how much he should react, what he should say, how truthful he should be. "I promised to topple an Empire," Dione said. "I did not promise to kill hapless villagers."

"So this grand goal, years in the making, is held up by your moral qualms? How many people have you killed on this quest?

Hundreds? Thousands? Yet you continued on." Ragan strode across the deck, speaking more to the people around them than to Dione himself. "Are we to believe that one small fishing village would stop you?" He held up a hand, pointing a finger at the sky, a knowing smile on his lips. "Lin may be a Sukai, but she is also an Alanga. And you've worked so hard to bring them back." Nisong could sense the shift in the watching crew as they listened to Ragan. The crew on the other Shardless Few had stopped working, still and silent as they strained to hear his words.

"I've worked to bring down the Empire," Dione said, his voice level. "The Alanga returning to the islands has merely been a side effect of that change. It was not intentional."

"You've lied about who you are; you expect everyone to believe that?" Ragan lifted his arms, beckoning like a storyteller calling his audience in closer. "I am a cloudtree monk. I have read the restricted texts; the only ones that survived the Alanga purge. Do you want to know what they say about Dione? Do you?"

Some of the Shardless Few shook their heads, their expressions annoyed. Ragan wasn't likable and they weren't easily swayed. But others nodded, murmuring their assent.

"He did indeed grow up in a poor village before becoming an Alanga, so that much is true. But he is the reason the Alanga are gone. He didn't just vaguely know who the first Emperor was. He was friends with him – Ylan Sukai. He gave Ylan the means to destroy the Alanga. So what do you think matters more to him – taking down the Empire or ensuring that the Alanga survive this time around? Guilt colors all his actions. He's already shown you cannot trust him."

For the first time, Dione's expression cracked, showing a measure of impatience. "And they can trust you?"

Nisong knew what Ragan would say. She held her breath – it was too soon; he'd not laid the foundation properly yet. He touched a hand to his chest. "Of course they can. I am the only one who can lead us through these changed times. I'm an Alanga – a powerful one by your own admission – and I won't hesitate to strike against our own. I will crush any who oppose me. I will make the Empire pay for what it's done to its people. I will punish those who let it happen. You think I haven't suffered at the Empire's hands, just because I was a monk? Do you know the harsh training they put us through in the monasteries? Do you know why? Emperors have long coveted our knowledge and have attacked us every chance they get." He seized some of the rigging, took a step up onto the ropes so everyone could see him. "I would see it all burn."

The rage in his voice was infectious. A cheer rose from the throats of the Shardless Few – not from all throats, but it might be enough. It was an angry, hateful sound. She felt her own fire stirring in her chest, the remembered feel of bones cracking beneath her cudgel. The satisfaction of blood spraying across her lips.

These people didn't want peace. They didn't want one bloody fight followed by a transfer of power into the people's hands. They wanted to make those who had hurt them hurt in turn. They wanted to punish the ones who hadn't stopped it. How many here had lost friends or family to the Tithing Festival, to the slow draining of their lives from shards? How many had felt the heel of the Empire's boot upon their necks as they toiled to meet their rulers' unreasonable demands? They couldn't overthrow the Emperor and then make peace with the governors and their families. Of course, of course – it didn't make sense, did it?

Ragan might not be able to make friends, but he was good at stirring resentment into a simmering boil.

He lifted an arm and the Endless Sea surged, a wave rising past the railing. Dione's expression was as dark as the roiling water as he cut a hand through the air. The water didn't dissolve back into the sea, but it didn't rise any higher, either. She could see the struggle on each of their faces as they tried to wrest control from the other.

And then Ragan's wave leapt free, bearing down on Lin's ship and the village beyond.

Dione lifted a hand and another wave rose. They crashed together and subsided back into the ocean. Ocean spray hit Nisong's cheeks. Every part of her felt tense, drawn taut. A furry head nudged its way beneath her hand and her heartbeat slowed. Lozhi. He made a distressed sound in the back of his throat and she found herself kneeling automatically by his side, taking his cheeks between her palms. Ragan often seemed to forget he had an ossalen at all. She wondered again where Dione's was, what the creature was feeling, right now.

"You're pathetic." Ragan stalked toward Dione, and some of the Shardless Few left their posts, hands on weapons, surrounding Dione protectively. "You would let her go." Lin's ship was already rounding the point of the island, the sails filled with wind.

"I would not needlessly kill innocent citizens," Dione said, his one eye glaring at Ragan, his arms crossed. "There will be more chances. She can't run for ever."

"Or there might not be. She might run into the safety of her army and where will you be then?"

They locked gazes, and Nisong felt a strange vibration in the air, like the low hum of cicadas.

"Get off my ship," Dione said. "Now."

"Then Alyara is coming with me," Ragan said, his gaze still on Dione. A flutter of surprise crossed Dione's face as the courtesan crossed the deck to stand next to Ragan. Only Nisong noticed the set of her jaw, the way her ossalen let out a worried coo in the back of her throat.

"Aye, me as well," another of the Shardless Few said, defiant.

Others stepped forward as well, pledging their support to Ragan. He was a bonfire being fed dry bits of kindling. With each new person who joined his mutiny, he grew more and more incandescent. For a moment, she glimpsed the Ragan that could have been, had he left his bitterness behind. Aglow, powerful, the air around him vibrating. But, like a flame, he would never be truly satisfied and that darkness would creep back in. She knew this now. And she knew her role. Until they took Imperial, she was his support, the guiding hand that protected that flame.

She let go of Lozhi, moving across the deck to slide between Ragan and Dione. She felt the force of their gazes hit her, caught as she was in the crossfire. It felt strange to be here; she'd never before been one to make peace. But she had larger goals, and battling Dione wouldn't do anything but weaken them. Nisong turned to Dione. "Let us go."

He'd closed up his face again, his expression as stony as a cliff face. And then he tilted his head, his gaze going through her, as though he were listening to some far away song. "A third of the supplies," he said finally. "And the other ship. If you no longer want to be part of the Shardless Few, I won't stop you."

Things moved quickly after that. Ragan hadn't split off all the Shardless Few, but he'd swayed enough of them to his side. Nisong moved with the flow of them, caught in a tide she wasn't fully a part of, letting the others carry her along. A little dazed, unsure of how she felt about being this one step closer to Imperial. To the throne. That night, Ragan found the corner of the hold she'd set up her bedroll in, a half-shuttered lamp in his hand. They'd yielded the captain's cabin to him; he must have declined.

"You see," he said, sliding in beside her as though he'd been invited, "I've done what you asked."

It should have satisfied her, but all she could feel was unease.

He'd allowed himself to be nudged in the right direction; he was taking her advice. What more did she want? "Give me the shards. Let me make constructs. Why do you need to hold on to them?"

He eyed her, his gaze distrustful. "I'll give them to you as I see fit, one at a time, when they're needed."

She hated this, the way he made her feel, like she was a leashed animal. She wanted to strike at him but wasn't sure how, not when she'd already come this far, when she'd tied her fate to his.

What was done was done. His mouth pressed beneath her ear and she shivered. Memories rose, bubbles coming to the surface of her consciousness. Arguments, harsh words, exhortations that he was the Emperor and she the consort. Shiyen used to kiss her in that exact spot when she was upset. He'd laugh at the way it undid her, at the way she'd angrily declare that she hated him, even though they both knew it wasn't true. And then she'd apologize and he'd say he'd known she hadn't meant it, and they'd continue on as they had — even though she'd ached to hear an apology in return.

But there had been love too, so much of it.

Hadn't there been?

She ran her hands beneath Ragan's tunic, felt his breath grow quick as she traced wide circles across the muscles of his back. He leaned his head into her shoulder. He was not immune to her, much as he liked to pretend he was. She might have been plain, but she knew now she was compelling in other ways. He was drawn to her sharpness, her pride, her anger — as she was drawn to his.

Nisong seized his chin the way he'd once seized hers — as though she were ready to make him pay for what he'd done. He let the lamp go and it settled onto the floor next to her bedroll. The light illuminated him from below, highlighting the beat of his pulse at his throat. She made him wait before she pressed her lips against his. And then they were two as the two waves crashing into one another, dissolving into one Endless Sea.

Afterward, he tangled his fingers in her hair, his other hand stroking the scars on her cheek. They lay across from one another, gazes locked. If Shiyen were alive now, would she go back to him? She still wondered, sometimes, about the offer Lin had made, about the man she claimed her father had grown beneath the palace. She said she did this for her fallen friends, and she did, but there was still a part of her that yearned to see the past undone, to know what it was like to truly be Nisong.

"Now that this is done, where will we go?" The boat shifted around them, the waves passing beneath them in a gentle rocking motion. They were going somewhere. He must have already set a course.

"First to Riya to see if I can make another ally. And to find more Alanga we can turn. But that won't be the only stop," he said. "I'm not a fool; I know one ship isn't enough to take Imperial, even if I do have the sword. Even if we find more Alanga."

"So you will go south."

The flame of the lamp reflected in the black of his irises, turning them to fire. "We will. And then I will make my way past the blockade and claim the Shardless Few's army as mine."

22

Jovis

Somewhere in the Endless Sea

Kaphra was not pleased. He railed at me, face red, hands flailing. "I gave you a command! You should have fulfilled it or died trying."

I crouched on the deck, my hand pressed to my chest, doing my best imitation of agony. Really believing it – that was the trick. So I thought about the only time Kaphra had given me a command I couldn't fulfill. He'd wanted to test the limits of his power and had commanded me to turn water into stone. Oh, I'd tried. I'd had to. And he'd laughed at my pathetic attempts, watching the water run through my fists as the burning pain inside me only increased. Was this what constructs felt? Or did they not feel anything at all – just going about and obeying their commands without any thoughts of their own?

Regardless, I groaned. "*Please*," I whispered. "You're killing me."

Mephi stood behind Kaphra and he quirked his head slightly

to the side. A voice sounded in my head. *You're laying it on a little thick.* This time I was certain it was him.

Neat trick, I tried back.

Pay attention, Mephi said. *Or you'll clue him in.*

I heaved out a breath, bringing my face closer to the salt-soaked boards. Through the curtain of my hair, I glanced at Philine. She stood next to Mephi, her face blank. I might have been a magnificent liar, but there was a woman who could win every game of cards if she brought that face to the table. She'd seen me lower my staff. She'd seen me reach out to Buphan to help him up. I hadn't been sure how much she knew of what Kaphra had told me to do until we'd been walking silently back toward the harbor.

"You've learned to carry pain better than the last time Kaphra gave you a command you didn't fulfill," she'd said, her tone neutral.

I gave her a sidelong look, doing my best to conceal the panicked kick of my heartbeat with a charming smile. "Careful – you almost sound like you care."

Philine merely pressed her lips together and brushed a bit of moisture from the front of her vest. She let out a sigh. "I would have hoped one of the commands they put into you was 'you are not funny stop trying to be funny' but I suppose that was too much to hope for." Her gaze met mine. "Then again, who would have known if it would have worked?"

"Words are slippery," I said. "'You are not funny' is a lie, not a command."

"Someday, when you're bleeding out on the ground, your last words will be some terrible witticism, and the last thing you'll feel is regret."

"Ah, now you're sounding like my mother."

"A wise woman."

We fell into silence. I fidgeted as we strode down the path and cleared my throat. Never could stand a silence. "Philine, I—"

She'd held up her hand. "Don't. Don't tell me anything. We are not friends, Jovis."

But when I'd clutched at my chest, leaning on my staff, making every step labored, she'd given me an approving, knowing look. "Ah," I said, "there's the pain kicking in now."

Philine's loyalty had always looked from the outside to be firm, unwavering, no matter the tasks Kaphra set her to. But now I could see – she didn't just always keep her game face on; she held her cards so tight I'd wager no one had ever even gotten a glimpse of them. What a lonely life.

I stared at the grain of the wood beneath my fingertips, the faint smell of simmering fat rising from the kitchen below. My mouth watered. Wasn't supposed to be thinking about food. Was just supposed to be thinking of how to stop the pain. I readjusted my expression before I looked up again.

"Foolish of me," Kaphra was saying, every word bright with rage, "to think you could complete this simple task."

I bit back a retort – that I'd completed nearly every task he'd ever asked of me – and put all my effort into making my eyes look pained and sad. "I did my best," I gasped out, bowing my head once more. If I looked too long into his eyes, I'd let something slip. I hated him. I didn't know how well I could lie about that.

Kaphra circled around me. I tensed, expecting a kick. He liked to remind me of my place once in a while. Instead, I saw his booted feet return to their spot in front of me. "I'll find some way for you to redeem yourself." A pause. One booted foot tapped the deck. "You don't need to steal the white-bladed sword for me anymore."

I collapsed, breathing heavily. A light rain misted my cheeks as I rolled onto my back, my eyes closed. I opened them to find

Kaphra standing over me, a hint of satisfaction in his gaze. I grimaced and rolled back onto my knees. "What is it that you want me to do now, Kaphra? Are you going to give me some new impossible task?"

He regarded me for a long time. "Yes. And until I figure out what that will be, we have witstone leads to hunt down. Your pet can stay in the hold for now."

The words stole my breath, set cold fingers of dread curling around my heart. "Kaphra, wait. You can't. He needs fresh air. He needs to move about."

He drew the white-bladed sword and handed it to Philine. "Put him in the hold. No visits."

Mephi turned wide eyes on me. "Jovis—"

But they were already putting their hands on his horns, on his shoulders, guiding him toward the hatch. Philine held the sword to Mephi's neck.

"Please!" I called after Kaphra, begging in truth now. "I'll do anything."

"What I wanted you to do was to steal the sword. Don't say you'll do anything when you *can't*."

Kaphra existed in two modes: overly friendly and cold as ice. As the days passed and as we chased after rumors of witstone supplies on the Endless Sea, I experienced the second of those modes. The man ignored me unless it was to utter a command. I was no longer his cherished pet; I was one who had disobeyed, who had proved himself unreliable. I hated that I felt cast out.

What I hated more was how Mephi felt.

Will he let me out soon, do you think? his voice would say in my head every few days, each time sounding more sad and more wistful.

Soon, I responded – even though I couldn't know for sure. Lies were better for the soul than truth sometimes. I needed to get him out. But I knew if I hounded Kaphra about it, he'd only keep Mephi in the hold for longer.

Finally, after we'd raided the third ship, taking its witstone for our own, Kaphra approached me, his mood lighter. I'd played a pivotal role, taking on most of the crew with my staff as the Ioph Carn sat back and watched, sparing their people any injury. Kaphra clapped a hand to my shoulder. "I've found a job for you. There's a cloudtree monastery on Riya. My spies tell me that two of the monks there have bonded ossalen and are Alanga. Find them. Kill them."

The command settled into my chest. I wasn't sure how to get around those commands, not yet. But I'd find a way. I had to be careful about this next part – Kaphra didn't want me to die, not truly. He wanted me beaten down, obedient. I needed Mephi with me when we disembarked. But if it was my idea, he wouldn't allow it. "I didn't have enough back-up," I told him. "If I had, I could have taken the sword."

Kaphra hated excuses. I'd never given them before, so we'd gotten along. He pivoted to face me. "You failed. That's the short of it."

"Send some of your men and women with me. Give me people I can command." He wouldn't want that. Put his pet Alanga in charge of people? Never. "I'll find and kill these Alanga, but I need help. You know they have the cloudtree bark and berries. It makes them as strong as I am."

"You're not attacking them in force; you're sneaking in."

"I'm not trained as an assassin. I'm a liar, not a silent killer."

Kaphra tapped his chin, his irritated expression melting away. "You are that, aren't you?" His gaze slid to Philine, who was idly fishing at the rail.

She stiffened as his gaze locked on her. "Kaphra, you can't—"

"I'll let Mephi out, but he's not going with you. Not this time,"

Kaphra said. "But you have a point. We don't need a back way in. Tell them who you are. Tell them you're there on behalf of the Emperor, that she has a message for them. It'll be easy enough to get in that way. She's been doing her best to ease relations with the monasteries. They'll feel obligated to hear you out."

I felt the blood drain from my face. The thought of using Lin's name in such a way made me queasy. What would she think of me when word finally made its way back to her? I'd have ruined what she'd worked so hard for. Still, this was the only way I could see myself getting free. I needed Mephi with me when I attempted to break the commands. I could no sooner leave him behind than I could cut my heart out and walk away from it. "You've kept my identity a secret for so long; wouldn't—"

"Philine goes with you."

And then he was gone again, his back brooking no argument. Philine reeled in her line, her movements swift and jerky. She pulled up an empty hook. "Well," she said, "haven't you dragged me into enough dangerous situations for one lifetime?"

"But we work so well together." The words fell from my mouth before I could stop them. I was still reeling, trying to figure out where I'd gone wrong.

Philine gave me a glare that could cut glass and then stalked after Kaphra, doubtless to ask him to reconsider.

A shout sounded from below, and then a thundering of paws against wood. Mephi burst from the hold, his mouth open in a toothy grin. He looked worse for wear – his fur worn in spots where he'd been forced to crouch in the small space, the skin bare where sores had formed and then healed over.

I threw my arms around his neck, burying my face in his fur, relieved that he was out of confinement.

We will find a way to get free together, Mephi cooed in my mind. His big head nudged its way beneath my hand and I found myself absentmindedly scratching the base of his horns, the panic in my chest easing somewhat.

Kaphra didn't reconsider. That wasn't his way. On the way to Riya, I ran into him every chance I got, waiting for him to issue commands. I knew now that commands could be subverted. They were fallible. Each command he gave me I turned over in my mind, finding ways around them. "Be quiet" – for how long? He might have meant only a moment. "Shut up" – shut up what? The portholes? "Please just stop talking" – well that one was phrased as a request, not an order.

I obeyed each time, but kept in the back of my mind how I might get around the commands. Each time the solution seemed to come faster to me. It gave me hope, but I knew it was not the same as facing commands in the midst of a job, while I was stressed out or under attack. And I'd have to do this job; I couldn't find a way around it. The only way to get back to Mephi was to complete it. Even if I managed to get past Kaphra's commands, he'd have the chance to shout more after me as I tried to escape.

Philine already knew I didn't always have to obey. She hadn't told Kaphra, though I wasn't sure why. Perhaps she was only waiting for the right moment.

We arrived at Riya to a torrent of rain. It gathered on the deck, running off the sides of the boat with each gentle swell of the waves. Everything smelled like wet wood and clothes that hadn't had the opportunity to dry for days. The mess hall was the only respite, and water dripped periodically from above, adding an unwelcome flavor to food and drink. Mephi spent most of his time in the water, but Kaphra called him back onto the boat and into the hold before we docked. I held his big head in my hands before he followed Kaphra below, the white-bladed sword strapped like a warning to Kaphra's side. "I'll be back as soon as possible," I told Mephi. Being parted from him like this, over and over, hurt each time.

"I will be fine, Jovis." And then he disappeared below-deck.

Riya was just as I remembered it, the streets clean and lined with stone lanterns. It was a far cry from the dirt and gravel roads I had grown up with on Anau. I'd come here with Lin long ago, and I retraced the steps we'd taken as she'd angrily marched up the road to Iloh's palace. There was an ass if I'd ever seen one. Lin had eventually won him over, even if he'd flipped sides when it had suited him.

"You're reminiscing, aren't you?" Philine didn't look at me, her voice flat as she stepped around the puddles in the streets. We hugged the edges of the buildings, covered mostly by roof and storefront overhangs.

"No."

She let out a sigh as though she'd known I would lie. "The monastery is a hike into the mountains. It's one of the oldest cloudtree monasteries, and they carved steps into the slopes. So the climb isn't anything too technical, but it is a long way. There's a road a little way past the palace that turns into a path." She shifted the pack on her back. "Let's not waste time."

"I won't argue with that." In spite of my words, it was difficult not to think about the time I'd spent with Lin here before we'd trusted one another. I wished I could go back, do things differently. I might have ended up in the same spot, but at least Lin and I might have had more time. I dodged someone who was coughing into her hands, wary. With caro nut supply from Nephilanu cut off, bog cough had been spreading. I wasn't sure if my newly magicked constitution allowed me to get bog cough, but I wasn't really interested in finding out.

I stepped on the discarded case of a firecracker in the gutter and frowned. My gaze rose, finding the remnants of red cloth streamers hanging from the rooftops. I hadn't noticed them before. Had they had a celebration here recently? What for? The Empire was fraying into pieces. People were getting sick. Witstone was scarce, the Ioph Carn gaining more power.

I touched the elbow of an older woman passing me with a basket of vegetables and fish beneath her arm. "Auntie, was there a party here?" I nudged the firecrackers. "What is there to celebrate?"

She patted my forearm. "You're not from here, are you? The Emperor has chosen a consort, haven't you heard?"

"I've been at sea," I said weakly. Somehow I'd hoped that Ragan's taunt hadn't been true, that he'd only said it to get me to lower my guard.

Philine had turned and was tapping her foot impatiently into a puddle.

I ignored her. "Who?" It felt like the words were coming from someone else's lips.

The woman gave me an odd look. "Our governor Iloh, of course. Why else would we celebrate? If he's in her favor, we'll get the best of what Imperial has to offer."

I was gripping her arm. I let go, reeling back, as though that old woman had been the only thing keeping me grounded. And then a hot, angry feeling flooded me, setting my shriveled heart to pumping again. *Iloh?* "Are they married yet?" I called after the woman, but she'd already walked away, the pattering of rain above drowning out my voice. She didn't spare me a backward glance, though a few people near us turned to look at me.

"What are you doing?" Philine hissed, seizing my sleeve. She dragged me away from the spot, pulling me up the main street. "The Emperor is no longer your concern."

"You know, saying that over and over doesn't make it more true. I could say that you're terrible with those knives but we all know that won't make a difference in the way you fight." I couldn't stop the images flashing through my mind – of Iloh with his hands on Lin, his lips. I wanted to shove them away even as I knew it was my thoughts creating them. How could she choose *him*? I made a quick, fruitless comparison in my mind. I knew I was tall, charming, good-looking enough to get away with things I shouldn't have. But I was half-Poyer. I talked too much. I was a man of no consequence except the titles Lin had bestowed on me. Iloh was the governor of an island – a powerful one. He was older than I was, but he wasn't *old*. He had the faintest flecks of silver in his hair last I'd checked, but few wrinkles. Did women care about that? He was solidly built, shorter than I was. "Is Iloh handsome?" The words seemed to come straight from my heart, bypassing my brain. "I mean, do you think he is?"

Philine let out the most aggrieved sigh I'd ever heard – and that was saying a lot given how often I'd heard her sighing lately. "Is this really a conversation we need to be having?"

"You said it was a long way. Would you prefer to talk about the weather?"

I watched her shoulders roll. "I can't really say whether or not he's handsome. I suppose so? I've heard others say he is."

If my chest was now a furnace, her words added several logs of fuel. I would *kill* him before he laid a hand on Lin. My anger turned suddenly to despair, quickly as though doused in a bucket of cold water. She'd chosen him, not the other way around. I might very much feel as though Lin were still my concern, but the world had moved on without me. I'd let it do so once before, except this time, it hadn't been my choice. "She can't actually mean to marry him. She can't love him. She *hates* him." Philine dodged a merchant's cart carrying cabbages and I followed blindly. "He's fickle. He's too ambitious. He won't support her in the way that she deserves."

Philine whirled, her black braid whipping her cheek. "For once in your life, keep your inside thoughts *inside*." We stared at one another for a moment. I opened my mouth. She lifted a warning finger. And then she looked beyond me, her eyes widening.

Something struck me in the back so hard it almost knocked the wind from me. My pack jolted, my staff falling from my fingers. All thoughts of Lin and Iloh fled as my mind tried to make sense of what was happening. Was I being attacked? Why?

"Found you!" Mephi said. He wedged his head beneath my arm so that I had my hand thrown over his neck. I ruffled the fur there, still too startled for a response. He was supposed to be on the ship, under guard of Kaphra himself. Under guard of the white-bladed sword. I lifted my hand away and found it red with blood.

"Mephi—" I was examining him from head to toe, my motions frantic, my fingers parting the thick fur to find evidence of injury.

"Only a small scratch," Mephi said, his voice calm. He stood still as I checked his neck. "It will heal with a scar but – oh, Jovis! – it was *worth* it. Kaphra was very surprised. It was extremely funny. His face was like this—" Mephi let his jaw fall open, his eyes wide, his massive tongue hanging out between his teeth. And then he scrunched up his expression like a person trying to keep the splash of a wave from his eyes. He spread his feet. "I blew a *wind*. A big one." Mephi pranced in place, drawing the gaze of passers-by. I thought I saw someone peering down from a window above us. Alanga had been returning to the Empire, but most ossalen were still smaller than he was. It was part of the reason Kaphra mostly kept him out of sight when we docked.

"Kaphra won't like this," Philine said. "He explicitly told you that your beast was not to go with us."

I looked ahead, finally finding something to distract me from the thought of Lin in another man's arms. *Iloh's* arms, no less. "He'll be helpful and it's not as though he'll obey me if I tell him to go back. Which way do we turn after the palace? Left?"

"Yes, but—"

"Having Mephi will make this task easier. Kaphra can punish us when we get back," I said.

She squinted at me as though trying to see a fish through the glare of the sun off the water. "Whatever punishment he comes up with will be worse than anything you've suffered so far. What is *wrong* with you?"

"A great many things," I replied lightly. "I could list them if you like."

"I'd like you to murder me first. It would be a less torturous way to go." The edge of danger had gone out of her voice as we fell into the familiar grooves of the banter between us. But then her jaw firmed up. "He can't come with us. You know that."

I put a hand to Mephi's neck, trying to think of some way to slide around her command, of some way to convince her. If I had him here with me, I might finally find a way to be free of Kaphra. *Free.*

Something caught the corner of my eye, instinct making me duck behind a building. Both Mephi and Philine followed.

"What? What is it?" Philine whispered.

It took me a moment to process what I'd seen. "Ragan," I said. "He's *here*."

23

Ranami

Nephilanu Island

Ranami sipped the tea, regarding her old friend from over the rim. The tea itself was now lukewarm; she'd spent so much time talking. Odd, how quickly one could get used to the comforts of wealth and privilege. Tea instead of murky water would have been a wild luxury when she'd been living on the streets. And she'd never have been able to have it hot. Not without a fire – which always attracted the attention of guards and other, bigger street dwellers.

The corner of Halong's lip twitched as though he knew what she was thinking. "Yes, well, it was hot when I made it."

"The general of the Shardless Few army – making tea for a prisoner?" She sipped again. The tea itself was high quality, probably from her own personal stores in the palace.

For a moment she'd forgotten she was a prisoner – here among the Shardless Few in the main cavern, the low murmur of their chatter a comfortable background noise, their blue armbands blending into one continuous line, the bonfire flickering in the center of the room. It had taken time for him to trust her outside the locked room, but she was not a fighter and not an Alanga. What threat did she pose? So he'd eventually begun bringing her out for meals.

The twitch in Halong's lip faded. They'd once been as close as siblings – closer, even. They'd come to rely on one another when they'd both lived on the streets, sharing food, defending each other from larger children. She'd seen more orphans than she cared to admit get sick and die, or disappear. But together, Halong and she had made it through. She owed him her life, and he owed her his. She'd thought that they'd be that close for ever. Maybe she'd taken that for granted.

For the thousandth time, Ranami wondered if this rift in their friendship was her fault. Yes, he'd gotten in deep with Dione and had fully bought into his false rhetoric, but Ranami had also focused wholly on her relationship with Phalue and on parenting Ayesh. She should have been to see him and his family more; she should have checked in. Maybe he wouldn't have obeyed Dione's order to attack Nephilanu then. Maybe they would have remained close. Maybe he wouldn't feel now like a dangerous stranger instead of a friend.

He'd listened to Dione, but he'd also been surrounded by others who believed what Dione had to say. She could have provided not just a dissenting voice, but another person he could trust. Now she looked into his dark eyes, studied the crisp brown and yellow jacket he wore, the sword belted to his side – and she wondered how much she knew him anymore.

Whether she'd ever actually known him at all.

"Eat," he said, waving at the bowl of curried noodles and fish. "Unless you'd rather forgo it to preach your nonsense at me."

She wanted to protest – it wasn't nonsense – but also knew from experience that the harder she pressed, the harder he pressed back. She wasn't sure how to upset this equilibrium, or if it was even possible at all. Still, she had to try. Not just for her people. For Halong, for all the people who followed him. She'd been careful to pitch her voice loudly enough so that those near them could hear, but not so loudly that Halong would accuse her of causing trouble.

"It doesn't bother you that you've been lied to?" she said, picking up the bowl and digging in with the pair of chopsticks speared into the center of the meal. The sides of the bowl were still warm.

He shrugged, his gaze going to the walls of the cave. "Dione did what he had to. Would all of us have followed him if he'd said from the beginning that he was Dione? That he was an ancient Alanga? No. We wouldn't have trusted him. But he's built the Shardless Few now; he's taken Khalute and is looking to take the Empire. He's earned our trust."

Ranami watched his face but saw only the strength of conviction in the lines of his jaw. "I didn't know it was possible to build trust on a bed of lies." She couldn't keep the sharpness from her tone. It was the wrong thing to say, and she knew it as soon as the words left her mouth. But wasn't she entitled to these feelings? He'd *betrayed* her, had taken her island and tried to take her daughter. All in the service of a man who'd lied.

Halong's jaw tightened. "And what is trust meant to be built on except actions and not words? You say you want better for the islands, yet you live in a palace with a governor, ruling from on high as though you were born to it."

Is *that* what fueled his anger? She wished he could no longer hurt her, but beneath her defiance, beneath the sharpness, there was a hungry orphan girl – starved for both food and love – who still cared about what he thought. "Is that all you see when you look at me? What about the reforms we've enacted, the

orphanage we've built? These are actions. Do they mean nothing to you?'"

"So you throw us trinkets and demand we be satisfied." He
sighed before she could retort, rubbing at his forehead. "The
truth is, Ranami, you've lost perspective. You've lost your way."

Trinkets? What did he want? Just war? *He* was the one who'd
lost his way. But she bit her tongue, afraid that what she might
say would just push him further away. She remembered her
arguments with Phalue, the way that nothing had really gotten
through to her except seeing the truth for herself. Sharp edges
had helped her to survive on the streets, but she wasn't on the
streets anymore. She'd made the same mistake with Ayesh; she
had to handle this differently. "Phalue is a good woman," Ranami
said. Somehow it was easier to be gentle when she spoke of her
wife. "She means well, and she's been proving her intentions.
The people of Nephilanu love her. Halong – what are you asking
for?" She ate while he thought, grateful that he was at least feeding her well.

"We have to break the system. You should be on *our* side.
After everything we've been through together . . . It's not enough
to have one ruler who is good. How long will that last? This is
what I mean when I say trinkets – I'm not trying to belittle what
Phalue has done. I'm trying to show you – these are short-term
changes. Or they could be."

"I understand." And she did. "The people still don't
have control."

"Exactly," he said, lifting a hand in the air and leaning back
on his cushion. "Phalue isn't the solution."

Ranami scooped up the last bit of noodles and then set the
bowl down in front of her, letting him rest on this moment of
triumph, this feeling that he had *gotten through to her*. "But she
isn't the problem, is she?"

Halong rose, gesturing for her to follow him. "She's part of it. She's part of the system we need to break." But he sounded less sure.

She stood. "If you were in her position, if you had that power, wouldn't you use it to do what you could?"

His step hesitated for only a moment before he continued walking, trusting her to follow. She caught the gaze of one of the nearby Shardless Few, who then turned away, pretending not to have heard her. Ranami knew what could happen once he'd locked her up again. He might sit down with the rest of his Shardless Few next to the bright light of a fire. He might speak to them, tossing her ideas out to them like eggs meant to be broken. And they'd crush them, just like he asked. After, he'd eat his bowl of noodles and lay his head down to sleep, comfortable again with all that he'd wrought.

She'd watched Phalue make enough rationalizations to understand how these things worked.

He said nothing else as he led her back to the room, using his Alanga powers to lock the stone door behind him.

The grate at the end of her room moved, stone scraping against stone. Ayesh poked her head out, followed by Shark. "What were you doing? Talking again? Talk talk talk," Ayesh muttered to herself. "So much talking." She pulled herself out of the drain, her clothes damp.

"Talking can change minds."

Ayesh only rolled her eyes. "I know that's what you'd rather I do. Sit in a locked room and just talk myself to death."

"It *would* keep you safe," Ranami said lightly. She held out her arms and was gratified when Ayesh, grumbling, still came to her for a hug. It had taken a long time for the girl to accept any physical affection. Touch wasn't usually a gentle thing when you were on the streets.

She held Ayesh at arm's length afterward, examining her dirt-stained clothes. "Are you cold? Have you been eating well?"

Ayesh pivoted out of her grip. "I've been sleeping in leaf piles and eating bugs." She sighed. "Yes, I'm being well taken care of. I'm in a hut in the woods with one of your guards. She still makes me do lessons and read books, which I'm sure you're happy to hear. It's dry and we all have plenty of blankets. They have the hidden food stores and there's fresh fish from the Endless Sea. I'm not starving. And I'm wet right now, but it's warm outside. I'm not cold."

"It's easier to catch the bog cough when you're cold," Ranami said. Ayesh's expression immediately shifted in a way that Ranami didn't like.

"What's going on in the camps? Ayesh, tell me."

"Bog cough," Ayesh said. Behind her, Shark wandered through the room, sniffing the spot where Ranami's bowl had once been. She nudged the blankets around into a nest, curled up on the mattress and tucked her nose beneath her tail. "It's not just the camps. It's in the city too."

They'd hidden their store of caro nuts in order to keep it out of the hands of the Shardless Few. Now Ranami found herself in the same position she'd once excoriated Dione for. She was withholding the nuts to stop him from wielding the supply like a cudgel, bringing the Empire to its knees. But by doing so, she was harming the very people she wanted to help. And could Alanga get bog cough? She didn't want to find out.

There had to be a third way. "The cave system. You've explored it?" Ranami asked. "Is there a place to hide things?"

Ayesh pursed her lips. "There's a larger cave, down deep. It's not hard to get to." She judged Ranami's frame and Ranami knew she was taking in her fuller figure, her wider hips. "The passages aren't too narrow. Even you would fit. Why?"

This wasn't the way Ranami had wanted things to go. It was already making her nervous having Ayesh come and visit her in this Shardless Few hideout. And asking her to map the caves had been yet another risk. She'd be asking Ayesh to help her do something even more dangerous. All she really wanted was for Ayesh to be safe, to get an education, to grow and thrive without having to fight and scrape for everything the way she had.

But that wasn't the world they lived in. Not yet.

Ranami clutched the front of her dress, as though she could dig her fingers into her chest to soothe the ache beneath. "I have to ask your help."

Immediately, Ayesh was nearly humming with energy. Ranami thought she could feel the girl's bones trembling. Shark lifted her head from the mattress, ears pricked. "We help?"

"Yes," Ranami said, reaching over to scratch the creature's ears. "I can't risk Halong or his army finding the location we've hidden the nuts. Only a few people know about it. But if we hide a small supply here in the caves, it would make it easier to trickle them out to the city and the camps without getting caught." If they did get caught, they'd only lose the supply hidden in the caves, and not the entire stock. It was a compromise between the two extreme choices.

"Got it," Ayesh said. She'd left her sword behind, but her hand went to the dagger she still had strapped to her belt, looking so very much like Phalue when she got a thought in her head she wouldn't be dissuaded from. Shark, knowing her companion's mind, rose from her spot on the mattress, circling around to stand at Ayesh's back. Ranami gave the beast a firm look. Sometimes it was like parenting *two* children, not just one.

"But you're not going alone. I'm going with you."

She had to strip the outer layer of her dress in order to avoid getting it dirty. Halong had enough questions for her; there was no reason to add another. Shark scrambled down the hole first, and then Ayesh, and then Ranami handed down one of the lanterns Halong had left to her.

"Oh. So that's what it looks like down here." Ayesh's voice echoed up and into the chamber.

"Have you only been finding your way around by feel?" The thought made Ranami even more anxious. She'd assumed Ayesh had always brought a lantern she just left in a wider tunnel before coming to see Ranami. The stone closed in as she slipped after Ayesh and just that momentary darkness made her heartbeat spike. She'd gotten used to slipping through the narrow crack into the Shardless Few hideout. But then, she'd always known it was a very temporary thing.

"Sort of?" Ayesh lifted the lantern as Ranami joined her in the small, damp space below the drain. A pool of water gathered on the floor but then trickled out and down a tunnel behind Ayesh. That tunnel was tall enough that Ranami could nearly walk unbent in it. "I use my hands, but also I can sort of *feel* the stone and dirt around me when I have the magic going through my bones. So I always know where I am."

Ranami took Ayesh's arm. "I told you to use string. You didn't use string?"

Ayesh shrugged her off as though she were completely unaware of the stress she was causing. "Didn't need it. Besides, it's not that far to the forest from here. But we have to be quiet." She led Ranami down the tunnel and she did her best to move her feet as silently as Ayesh did. Around a bend, Ayesh shuttered the lamp. Ranami almost asked why until she saw the light filtering in from above.

Another drain. From above, Ranami could hear muted voices. She held up a hand, asking Ayesh to stop. Shark was already past the drain, and she stopped, her ears pricked, her head tilted.

Ranami crept closer to the light, her heart pounding. As she grew closer, she could make out what the people above were saying.

"He's too soft on her," one woman muttered. "I know they were once friends, but Dione will get impatient. He had one job: take control of Nephilanu and take the supply of caro nuts."

"We've blockaded the island." A man's voice responded. Ranami didn't recognize either of them. "The nuts won't be getting out either way."

"But we still don't have them under our control. It's only a matter of time before someone attempts a smuggling run. The governor's daughter is an Alanga. We don't have her either. She might be able to get them out. He needs to start using more pressure."

"What? Torture? That's not our way."

"Not our way." The woman scoffed. "Are you a babe newly off your mother's breast? Think about what's at stake here. If Halong won't do it, someone else will. She may have once been one of us, but she decided to become a governor's wife instead of going to Khalute. I've no sympathy for her."

"You need Alanga powers to open the deep doors. He's the only one who can get into the room."

"Is that so?" There was something in the woman's tone that said she didn't agree with the man's assessment.

Ranami could feel the prickle of sweat in the small of her back in spite of the cool air in the drainage cave. Ayesh and Halong might have been the only ones who had been able to get into her prison, but there was the hole that let in the sunlight. Someone could fit through it. It was nearly covered in vegetation, but she could see the hint of sky through the leaves. If someone searched for it . . .

She took Ayesh's arm and hurried past the grate. She'd heard enough. She'd thought she would have time to convince Halong, to bring him around to her point of view. But it seemed the Shardless Few were not a monolith. She couldn't tell Halong what she'd overheard without giving herself away.

How much was she willing to risk in order to try and change his mind?

Two more turns through the tunnels and Ranami could smell fresh air. The water at their feet had long since disappeared down a separate chute and the way was now dry. Ayesh shuttered the lamp as they approached a knee-high tunnel. "Through here." By the musky smell, it had been used as a den for animals. Ranami held her breath as they crawled through, and then they were out into a part of the forest Ranami was unfamiliar with. It was beginning to get dark. They'd have to hurry.

Once she'd oriented herself, they made their way to the closest hidden stash of caro nuts. "Keep your eyes, ears and nose on the lookout for anyone following us," she told Shark.

Shark, for her part, took this job as seriously as any of Phalue's guards. Her mottled pattern hid her well in Nephilanu's forests, and she slipped through the trees, stopping every so often to sniff the air. It took them time to find the buried stash, to uncover it, remove a box and cover it again.

By the time they made it back to the tunnel, they were following Shark's lead, her eyes better accustomed to seeing in the dark. It was more difficult going back through with the box of caro nuts. Ranami had to push it ahead of her, wincing at the scraping sound it made, the way it caught on outcroppings of rock.

Ayesh led them down a different fork this time, one that descended into the earth. It was cooler down here, so quiet that Ranami could hear her own heartbeat, mingling with the constant *drip* of water filtering through the stone. Though Ayesh hadn't unshuttered the lamp, a dim bit of light filtered from between the slats, catching glittering veins of stone. Ranami thought she caught a glimpse of the white chalkiness of witstone.

She felt the tunnel open up and Ayesh lifted the lamp shutters, revealing a vast cavern. Stalactites hung from the ceiling, nearly meeting in the air in some places with stalagmites. Still, there was plenty of space free of obstacles. A pool of water stretched nearly from one side of the cavern to the other, the dark water two steps from Ranami's feet.

"Here," Ayesh said. "Keep them here. I'll bring some to the camps and the city." Her voice echoed from the walls, soft but almost too loud in the silence.

Ranami shifted the box in her grip. Something snagged on the skin of her palm. Pain lanced up her arm and she hissed.

"What happened?" Both Ayesh and Shark were there in an instant. Shark sniffed the blood that slowly trickled from Ranami's hand and down her arm.

She must have pulled a nail loose when she'd been hauling the box through the tunnels. "It's nothing. It's fine. Just a cut from a loose nail." Ranami took a step to the water, set the box down, and knelt.

Ayesh sucked in a breath. "Wait—"

But Ranami was already plunging her hand into the pool. The cooling sensation took her off guard for a moment. Something about it didn't feel like water. She wriggled her fingers experimentally. Ranami had grown up by the Endless Sea, had lived off its bounty more than once when food on the streets had been scarce. She knew the feel of water against her fingertips. This felt . . . different.

Ranami pulled her hand out.

"Shark told me not to go in the water," Ayesh finished, her voice nearly a whisper.

"It's just water. There's nothing to be frightened—" Her

words died on her lips as she opened her hand and found the skin of her palm unblemished. She turned her hand over and back, searching for a sign of the cut. Nothing, only a small smear of blood on the part of her arm she hadn't submerged. She *had* cut herself. Something was wrong. Very wrong. "Ayesh," she said, her voice sounding distant even to herself, "did Shark say why?"

Shark only whimpered. "No. Just don't think it is safe for you. Smells strange."

A cold sense of dread had wrapped its fingers around the back of her neck, and as much as she tried to shake the feeling, she found she couldn't. Silly of her. She'd had a cut. The pool had somehow healed it. Why should she feel so odd? "Look." She showed her hand to Ayesh, trying to sound soothing. "Something in the water healed it. Whatever it is, it's not bad."

Ayesh only gave her a skeptical look.

Oh, this was foolish. They both knew magic existed. Ranami might not have been wholly comfortable with it, but she wasn't an Alanga. She needed to focus on her own predicament and the predicament of Nephilanu's people. This was something for scholars to look into, not her. She'd just avoid the pool from now on.

They made their way back to Ranami's room and embraced below the grate. Ayesh wriggled free, as she always did, and pushed the lantern back into Ranami's hands. And then, silently, she ventured back into the darkness with Shark. It wasn't until Ranami was clambering back into her prison, thinking how far her relationship with Ayesh had come, that the yawning black space in her memories suddenly loomed.

She could not remember the day she had met her daughter.

Ranami set the grate back into place, and it was all she could do to keep breathing. She hadn't simply forgotten. The space in her memories wasn't hazy or indistinct; it was blank, as though that day hadn't existed, even though she knew it did. She had the disorienting feeling of having begun a walk only to mysteriously end up at her destination having only taken a few steps.

"So you were never actually trapped here."

Ranami whirled, the lamp still in her hand.

Halong sat on one of the cushions, the white-bladed sword laid across his lap.

24

Jovis

Riya Island

Ragan looked better than when I'd seen him last – sleeker, better-fed, more relaxed and more confident. Nisong wasn't at his side and neither was Lozhi. In their place, however, was an entourage of men and women, all armed to the hilt. His white-bladed sword was strapped to his side, his fingers touching it every so often as though he were reminding himself it was still there.

They weren't Ioph Carn. Mercenaries?

What in all the known islands was Ragan doing here? It felt like a cruel twist of fate, that I'd run into him again after he'd beaten me so soundly on Hualin Or. But both Kaphra and Ragan wanted power and it seemed I would keep colliding with Ragan until one of us died.

Philine's hand touched my arm and I started. I'd almost forgotten she was there. "We have a task." Her voice was firm, her face even more so.

I pulled my arm away. "I have to follow him. And you can't send Mephi back. Not if Ragan's here."

Mephi gave a questioning rumble, deep in his chest. I lifted an arm, guiding him behind a merchant's stall. If Ragan looked back, he'd spot Mephi, and he'd be a dead giveaway on my location.

Philine's eyes narrowed. "Fine. Mephi stays, but you know what Kaphra commanded. You're not here to chase errant Alanga. You're here to kill the Alanga in the monastery. That's all."

I sighed. "Is this how you climbed the ranks of the Ioph Carn from tracker to Kaphra's right hand? By following orders to the letter?"

"In a word, yes."

I might not have been able to think my way around Kaphra's commands yet, but I knew how to make my words slippery as a fish, to make them leap from the grasp of my listener, until I was the one who was making my audience dance rather than the other way around. My eyes darted between Ragan's quickly vanishing back and Philine's face. "Why did Kaphra send me here?"

"To kill the Alanga in the monastery."

Dione's balls, the woman was unflappable. "No. Those were just his orders, not his reasoning. He sent me here to prove myself after I'd failed to kill Ragan. I need to follow him, find out what he's up to, figure out if I can catch him in a moment of weakness." My feet were moving before I'd finished talking.

Philine hurried to catch up, her stride matching mine. "You're talking nonsense. Kaphra was clear in his orders."

If I were a cat my ears would have been flat against my head. "Was he?" Ragan and his fellows disappeared around a corner. I ducked a low-hanging palm frond and peered around the bend. "We're close to where the path to the monastery begins. Just wait there with Mephi. You know I'll come back for him. You know I won't leave him with you."

"No." Philine stopped in her tracks. "Jovis, stop."

My feet stopped moving, refusing to obey my commands. My heart was beating wildly, still unsure exactly how I felt about spotting Ragan – excited? Frightened? Angry? Either way, I couldn't bear to be rooted to this spot, to watch him disappear into the crowd. I had to know what he had planned.

Philine had her arms crossed, regarding Mephi and me with suspicion. "Mephi could very well just bowl me over and run off to you and we both know it. If he could get past Kaphra with his sword, what's to stop him from attacking me?"

"Philine, *please*. Think beyond Kaphra's desires and being in a position to take over from him – just this once. You have to know that Ragan has things planned for this Empire. If you *must* be selfish, think about how that might affect your leadership of the Ioph Carn. I have to find out what he's doing here."

She didn't uncross her arms. "You're not a hero, Jovis."

She could not have felled me more effectively with a blade. The frantic beating of my heart pounded in my ears, my breath stilling. I was not. I was Kaphra's weapon, his pet. I carried out his wishes. I hurt people. The songs people sang were about a different Jovis, one who'd fallen into the right thing to do, who'd had to be nudged by Mephi.

I was a villain. I just hadn't admitted it yet to myself.

My gaze turned back to the street. Ragan had disappeared. Mephi hovered at my side, his muscles tense, unsure of what direction to go.

"I'm not a hero either," Philine said, her voice flat. "I'm just trying to get by. Now, come on. You're following me to the monastery."

My feet moved of their own accord, falling into step behind Philine. "Mephi," I said, my voice breaking, "I'm sorry." He'd always expected more of me. Had always hoped for more.

His furry cheek pressed briefly to mine. "No. Don't apologize. You will always be the one who helped me."

One good deed washed away by the hundreds of terrible ones I'd undertaken in the past.

No.

I'd let the world pass me by before, caught up in my grief for Emahla. This was different, yes, and I had less choice in the matter, but the world was still going on without me. I had to press upon it. If my good deed could be washed away by the terrible ones, then it had to work the other way. I could still wash away the terrible ones.

I had Mephi with me. I had to try, before I became the person that Kaphra had always wanted me to be.

Something in my mind shifted. "I've followed you far enough. To the monastery, yes?" I stopped, patted the building to my left. "This looks like the monastery to me." A passer-by gave me an odd look but continued on his way.

She turned, incredulity washing over her face — the most expression I'd seen on it in two years. "That's a bakery."

"It's a monastery. Can't you tell?" I could lie like the best of them, and the only reason I could do so was because first I had to lie to myself. If I believed it first, then so would the person I was lying to. And oh, how good I'd gotten at lying to myself over the years. To me, it was a monastery and there was nothing she could say that could sway me.

"You will follow me until I tell you not to."

My feet moved again before I stopped them. I put a hand to my ear. "Did you say something? 'Stop'? Very well." Oh, I believed it. The streets weren't quiet. It was entirely possible she'd said something beneath her breath that I'd almost missed. Almost.

She would not hold me. She could not. I was not a construct, a thing made of parts and then infused with someone else's life. I was my own.

She marched over to me, her face coming close to mine. "You will complete Kaphra's commands," she said. "You can't avoid them."

Alas, in this respect, she was right. I could still feel them burning in my chest. And no matter how glibly I'd stepped around Philine's commands, I still wasn't sure how to lie myself around Kaphra's. "Yes," I said finally. "But he didn't say I needed to do it now." The burning eased a little. "And there's something I need to take care of first."

She put her face in her palm, rubbing at her forehead as though this much expression in such a short time had made her skin ache. "Fine. Follow him. Find out what he's doing here. But, Jovis, if you're not at the path to the monastery by nightfall . . ." She trailed off, unsure of what sort of threat to level. "Just know that I'm putting my neck out for you. If you've still got one hero's bone left in your body, you won't leave me out to dry."

I scratched Mephi's ears. "I'll come back. Be nice to Philine. No eating her."

Philine opened her mouth, but before she could say anything else, I slipped away into the crowded street.

Ragan had made some headway while I'd been occupied with Philine, but I slid my way through the throngs, peering down side streets and into open doorways until I found him. I nearly missed him in the smokiness of the drinking hall, the haze obscuring half the room. But he was sitting back in his chair, his feet resting on a crossbar beneath the table, looking relaxed and as though these people belonged to him. Indeed, they leaned forward, hanging on his every word.

It had been a long time since I'd last seen Ragan; still, this change in fortune surprised me. The last time I'd seen him, he and Nisong had been alone, no one to support their cause. Were these five people with him the only ones or did he have more waiting with Nisong and Lozhi somewhere?

I paid a nearby merchant for a wide-brimmed hat, tucked it firmly on my head, and stepped into the drinking hall. I hung my cloak on one of the hooks near the entrance, and then, after some reluctance, left my staff there with it. Better to look completely unassuming.

The drinking hall was halfway full at this time of day, a few patrons still celebrating the impending union of Lin and Iloh, by the sounds of it, and others only in for a quick meal. I nudged my way past the table that Ragan sat at, turning away from it, keeping only in Ragan's peripheral vision, making my way slowly to the counter while affecting a limp.

"The trap is set," Ragan said, blowing smoke from the side of his mouth. "Iloh sent her a missive threatening to dissolve their alliance unless they seal it now."

One of his fellows lifted a mug, speaking in a low voice from behind it. "Soon?"

"Within the next few days."

"And he agreed to this?" said one of the women. "He's already in a good position as consort."

Ragan leaned in, his voice low. "Why be in a good position if you can be in a better one?"

I stopped, feigning a sudden ache in my knee, trying to listen over the raucous sounds of laughter from the two tables down.

His voice grew even lower, and I had to risk leaning in to hear. "I told him my plans and how the Shardless Few are in need of stronger leadership. Is it better to be consort to the Emperor or to have witstone mining reopened? Everyone is suffering for it. Especially Iloh. When Lin is gone, I won't do anything to restrict mining. I'll be too busy keeping the Alanga in line."

They laughed at his bravado, his sly smile. My blood ran cold. These weren't mercenaries. They were the Shardless Few and they weren't following Dione anymore. They were following Ragan. In the time I'd been chasing after witstone for Kaphra, something had gone terribly, horribly wrong.

They'd set a trap. For Lin. She would be coming here.

And I was here on a completely different course, unable to warn her, unable to do anything to help. Kill the Alanga in the monastery. That was all I was here to do. Desperation clawed a hollow in my chest, set my throat to burning. Was this what I'd been reduced to? With no way to even help the people I loved? Even as I thought – I *had* to find a way – the shards inside me pricked, reminding me of the commands Kaphra had set me to.

I was a small dog, straining at the leash in the hand of a man who barely noticed me tugging.

The woman nearest to me turned, her gaze fixing on mine. I'd lingered a moment too long, caught by the terrible dilemma I'd wandered into. "Hey, mind your own business, won't you?" Her eyes narrowed. "Are you *listening* to us, old man?" And then she realized, suddenly, that I was not an injured old man – but a younger one. Her gaze went to my leg which I'd put my full weight on as I'd leaned in to listen.

Her hand went to her sword, and I ducked my head beneath the brim of my hat – too late.

"Jovis," Ragan said, a dangerous note in his voice. In a brief moment, he was standing, the white-bladed sword drawn. The drinking hall fell into immediate silence.

I met his gaze involuntarily, reacting to the sound of my name. I opened my mouth to make some sort of retort, some clever response, and found I had nothing. No sharp words. Not even my staff in my hands. I'd thought I could be discreet and had been caught by my own hubris.

The corner of his mouth quirked. "It'll be a delight to show her your head before I kill her too. For her to know, briefly, that you were alive when she'd thought you were gone."

The woman nearest to me thrust out her blade and everything fell into chaos. I leapt to the side, easily avoiding her knife and in the same movement, seized an empty chair. I threw it, with all my might, at the table the Shardless Few were sitting at. Glass and wood shattered, the men and women leaping back, covering faces to shield their eyes.

I ran.

"You can't stop this," Ragan called after me. I heard his rapid footsteps behind me as I seized my staff, leaving the cloak on the hook by the door.

I was out in the rainy streets, puddles splashing beneath my feet, the occasional spatter of rain cold against my scalp. I didn't need to look behind me to know Ragan was pursuing. I *felt* when he seized the water around us, when he shaped it to his commands.

Without even thinking, I seized the air currents, pulled them to me, and pushed them as hard as I could behind me.

Water sprayed in a fine mist at the back of my neck, shouts sounding as passers-by were shoved off their feet by the sudden wind. I didn't look back to see if I'd caught Ragan or his Shardless Few.

His Shardless Few? What in all the old Alanga had happened? What had he *done*? And they seemed perfectly happy to think of him as their leader, as someone who would, in his words, "keep the Alanga in line". What had Dione done to lose them? I'd thought Gio could weather any change, so strong was his followers' belief in him, but it seemed his revealing himself as one of the old Alanga was a change too far. Had Ragan played on old prejudices, while somehow remaining immune to them himself?

Angry people would believe anything.

No time to examine this change of circumstances in any depth. I ducked around a sharp corner, making my way toward the street Philine and I had been on. At the same time, I focused my concentration on the breezes around me, seizing air currents, pushing some behind me and pulling others into a wind at my back, speeding me along.

I dared a glance back as I turned onto the street where Philine would be waiting for me and was spurred on by Ragan, nearly on my heels. He didn't slip through the crowd the way I did. He sent a wave of water before him, sweeping hapless passers-by off their feet, stepping over them as though they were merely refuse a thoughtless person had left behind. The Shardless Few were behind him, though not far enough that they were out of sight.

I saw Mephi's spiraling horns ahead of me first, and then Philine. And judging by their expressions, they'd seen evidence of my arrival far before they saw me.

"Go!" I shouted to them. "Go, go!"

Philine paled, Mephi's brows rose and then they both turned and ran up the path toward the monastery. I followed, keeping the wind at our backs and against our pursuers.

I caught up to Philine, and she was none too happy to see me. "Jovis, you little *shit*!" Her brows looked about to dive straight into her eyes. "I give you leave to do this one thing, and you bring an Alanga and the Shardless Few down about my ears? I wish Kaphra had sent someone else — *anyone else* — with you. Endless Sea take me, I'm a fool."

"I'm hardly little. And I didn't give you much choice in the matter. It's not your fault." She opened her mouth to retort, but I talked over her. "Less talking, more climbing," I huffed out.

The stairs to the monastery had been carved years ago, and used infrequently. I wasn't sure how often the monks maintained the path, but rocks had come loose, rain cascading down these makeshift gutters. It was damned slippery, and uneven to boot.

Philine had to struggle to keep up with me, my Alanga-enhanced strength giving me a distinct advantage. Yet she still gathered enough breath to gasp out. "I wish I'd never met you."

"That makes two of us."

Water hit my back, slamming the breath from me. I watched it wash over Mephi and Philine before it took me down. Steps cracked against my ribs as I fell, sliding back the way we'd come. I nearly lost my grip on my staff.

I rolled onto my back, jutting out my heels to stop the momentum. I hit the trunk of a tree, the impact shuddering up my leg, all the way to my aching shoulders.

Ragan and his Shardless Few were fast approaching, Ragan's hands up to gather more water to his command. I glanced back up the slope and saw Mephi, bedraggled but getting his feet beneath him.

I didn't see Philine.

As I pushed myself back to my feet, I heard a grunt to my right. A hand gripped the edge of the stairs, the mountain dropping off to a sheer cliff beyond. My stomach flipped with a sense of vertigo as I realized how far up we were, how far Philine had to fall.

I was close. I could try to help her. Mephi was too far away. But if I did, Ragan would catch me.

And why should I help Philine? She'd been instrumental in keeping me under Kaphra's thumb. Her ambition had made us enemies. She'd never betray Kaphra, not while he dangled the promise of eventual Ioph Carn leadership in front of her. I didn't understand her reasons, but did I have to understand when our goals were so opposed? When her ambition had helped force me into servitude?

If I let her fall, I could be free – of both Ragan and Kaphra. I could seek refuge at the monastery. I could find a way back to Lin.

My heart ached, but even as I thought it, my feet were moving for the cliffside.

Wasn't a hero. I'd proved that enough in the past two years. But I wasn't a villain either. Mephi was right when he'd said I was the one who helped. I wasn't Kaphra. I wasn't ruthless and heartless.

And despite Philine's stone-cold demeanor, neither was she.

I seized Philine's wrist and felt her grasp at mine, lifting my other hand to gather both wind and rain. I thrust them at Ragan and his lackeys with hurricane force at the same time I pulled Philine to safety.

She didn't thank me, didn't embrace me, limp with gratitude. She gave me a stiff nod, but from her, that was enough.

Ragan swiped a hand to the side, blunting my attack enough to keep from being thrown from the mountain. He ran for me, drawing the white-bladed sword.

"Ride Mephi," I told Philine before bringing my staff to bear. They were too close. If I ran now, he'd thrust that blade into my back. "He'll carry you up faster. Ask the monks for help."

She looked for a moment like she would protest, but then her fingers uncurled from my wrist and she was gone.

Ragan's blade clashed against my staff, the force of the blow vibrating through my bones. Rain plastered my hair to my forehead and neck, running down my chest in rivulets.

"Why do I keep running into you?" he said, though he didn't sound entirely displeased. "How loose a leash does Kaphra keep you on?" His gaze went over my shoulder. "And isn't that woman Kaphra's lieutenant? Why save her?"

"She commanded me to, of course." I shoved him down a step, aware of the cliff rising on one side of us and dropping on the other, the treacherous steps. Dangerous ground for a fight. One of his Shardless Few edged into the space between Ragan and the cliff, his sword drawn. There wasn't enough space for three abreast.

Ragan barked out a laugh. "You're such a liar, and a soft-hearted one to boot. How did you ever make a living as a smuggler without stopping to help every mouse wandering into the tracks of a wagon? Do you think these good deeds can erase what you've done?"

The screams and cries of innocent soldiers as I crushed them with my magic, as I sent them, at Kaphra's behest, to drown in the Endless Sea. There was a way around the commands. I knew that now. And somehow, the hope only sharpened my guilt. There was a way around the commands and I'd not tried hard enough to figure it out sooner. I'd let myself be subsumed; I'd let my body be used as a weapon.

I'd given up. And I wasn't sure how to forgive myself for that. I wasn't sure if I even deserved it.

Ragan's next blows were quick. I blocked the first two and the third seared a cut across my shin. I drew in a breath, held it, trying to think past the pain. The burning of the cut seemed to meld with the burning in my chest — two flames of the same candle, a mirrored pain.

The Shardless Few man took advantage of my faltering, thrusting at me with his sword. Weakly, I turned his blade aside. I couldn't take on Ragan alone, much less him and the rest of his Shardless Few entourage. My bones trembled, the magic building within them. I remembered one of the first times I'd used that magic, the way I'd nearly brought a drinking hall down about my ears.

The cliff face.

The rocks here were loose, the rain making the dirt into mud.

All it would take was a nudge, and I could shatter the mountainside. But nature was unpredictable. I was as like to bury myself as my enemies.

Ragan advanced again and I retreated, favoring my injured leg. His Shardless Few followed, weapons drawn, ready to fall on me like a pack of hungry dogs. Ragan let out a derisive snort. "You've been following after Lin like a lovesick puppy ever since I met you. Is that why you sought me out? Does it bother you that she's marrying Iloh? Does it bother you that he will inherit the Empire when she's dead?"

It certainly *did*, and I didn't need to verify that to him. "So you'd rather have Iloh on the throne? What about one of your precious Alanga? What about you?"

He shook his head. "No one was going to rule this Empire as it used to be. Not me, not Lin, not Iloh," he said in a low voice. "It was broken before she came to the throne and it will stay broken. The Ioph Carn are carving their piece out. So is Iloh. So will I."

I tapped my foot, just a little, testing the ground. The tremor traveled in the direction I wanted it to, the earth shifting slightly beneath me. I needed just a little space. I lifted my foot, found the step behind me. I tightened my hands around my staff though I knew it wasn't a weapon that could save me now.

Only words could do that, and my tongue was a fair bit sharper than any blade.

"No matter what you carve from this Empire, no matter who you hurt, no matter how much you take for yourself, you will never be worthy. Not of being a master, not of Alanga power, not of being a leader. They will never follow you for who you are, only for what they think you might do for them and only out of fear."

Something in his expression crumpled, some glimpse of the boy he'd once been, desperate to please his masters. So desperate to have the power he felt he'd been denied that he'd murdered everyone in his monastery and had forced his ossalen to bond with him. Maybe there was a different path for Ragan, where someone had been kinder to him, where he'd accepted his station, where he'd waited to see if Lozhi would bond with him of his own will. But that was not the path he'd been set upon.

He might have claimed he did not have some secret pain, but if there was one thing I'd learned, it was that everyone had a secret pain. Everyone had a soft spot that could be *pressed*.

I took three swift steps back, the tremor in my bones to a fevered pitch, and then brought my foot down on the stair, hard.

The cliffside *cracked*.

And then water and rocks and mud were raining down on me and Ragan. Something struck my forehead, blacking my vision briefly and making my head swim. I turned and ran, warm blood mingling with the rain on my cheeks.

I didn't bother to see if my rockslide had buried Ragan or the Shardless Few. Either it had or it hadn't, and I was in bad shape if it hadn't. All I could do was concentrate on putting one foot in front of the other, keeping the wind at my back, buoying me up and forward.

"Jovis!" Ragan shouted from behind me. I clenched my teeth, forcing my legs to move more quickly. The man just wouldn't *die*, no matter what I did.

The gates of the monastery rose before me. Philine and Mephi were there, Philine pounding on the doors.

We were caught. If the monks wouldn't let us in, we'd be backed up against the gates, with Ragan and the Shardless Few on the other side. How easy it would be for them to crush us, for Ragan to bring his superior strength and skill to bear against mine.

I slammed against the doors next to Philine, adding my fists to hers. "I'm here on behalf of the Emperor! My name is Jovis and I am her former Captain of Imperial Guard!"

No one cracked the door open. No one shouted back.

"It's no use," Philine gasped out, rainwater running down her face. The hood of her cloak had been blown back during her flight up the mountainside. "I've been shouting the Emperor's name over and over and they don't give a damn."

Footsteps sounded from behind me, a chill wind pricking at the back of my neck.

"Ragan," Mephi said. "He was once one of them."

I put a hand on his neck. "Worth a try." I raised my voice. "Ragan is out here, and he's trying to kill us! He was once one of your apprentices. You taught him how to fight. He stole your restricted texts. You need to help us. He—"

The door cracked open. I made as though to slip past, but was met by line after line of monks. They pushed past me, crowding the terrace outside the gates. They didn't heed the rain and it fell on their shaved heads, catching in their eyelashes. I caught a sharp, woody smell from their dark green robes as they brushed past.

Cloud juniper.

I finally dared to turn and saw Ragan standing at the top of the stairs, his Shardless Few behind him. They were one fewer than they'd been, muddy and ragged, but not as damaged as I'd hoped.

"Ragan," said the woman at the head of the monks. She wore a golden sash – she must have been one of the masters. "Turn back. These people are now under our protection."

Every monk drew their swords in unison. The sound rang out, echoing from the mountains. I could nearly feel the power radiating off them, a strange hum in the air that made it slightly warmer.

Ragan pointed his white-bladed sword at me, his face dark with anger. "No. That one is mine."

The woman's calm voice cut through the rain like a knife. "You will have to go through us to claim him."

Ragan paced, his teeth bared, like a cat searching for an opening in a bird's cage. The men and women behind him shifted nervously. He had to know he was outnumbered. And he'd be tired after our fight, after that rock slide, after whatever he'd done to keep the mountain from falling out beneath him. "I've killed more monks than you have here against me."

"Through trickery, deception and the breaking of trust. Turn back."

He took three steps toward her. For a moment I thought he would attack, but then he spat at her feet. "Fine." He hefted the sword, waving it like a threat. "But don't think you won't pay for this. That all of you won't pay for this."

And then he turned and took his Shardless Few back down the steps.

The monks sheathed their swords and their leader turned to me.

"What did he mean?" I said, an anxious, knotted feeling in my chest. We'd escaped, but I didn't feel safe. I reached for Mephi, though the feel of his fur beneath my fingertips brought me no comfort.

"Come inside," the woman said, gesturing to the gates. "And tell me how he got that sword. We don't have much time."

25

Lin

Somewhere in the Endless Sea

I only slept out of a bone-deep weariness, an overwhelming relief that we'd escaped with our lives. But despair also laid heavy in my limbs once the adrenaline had worn away: we'd traveled half the Empire to retrieve one of the white-bladed swords, and we'd lost it. The whole trip had been meaningless.

I could hear footsteps creaking across the deck outside my cabin, and I knew they were Phalue's. I folded and unfolded the letter I'd received from Gaelung just before we'd hit the storm, before we'd gotten to Maila.

Yeshan, my general, had written in her neat, precise hand that the army had stabilized Gaelung. They'd had to ruthlessly put down one violent faction loosely tied to the Shardless Few — who'd wanted to install their own ruler in Gaelung's palace. Instead, Yeshan had put the dock master of Gaelung's largest harbor in charge at Ikanuy's urging.

I felt so removed from these decisions – half an Empire away.

On the one hand, it reassured me that they'd made a good choice without me; on the other hand, it made me feel unnecessary. The dock master had administrative experience, and he'd already done much to hear out complaints and suggestions, and had implemented a couple of ideas of his own. The people of Gaelung had begun to warm to him.

Which meant the bulk of my army was now free to take back Nephilanu. But without the white-bladed sword.

How would Phalue fare without it?

Another pass of booted footsteps outside my door. This time, they halted, a sharp knock sounding. I folded the letter back up, smoothing it against the surface of my desk. "Yes?"

The door opened and Phalue had to duck to enter my cabin. Thrana lay in a small patch of sun beyond her on the deck, fur ruffling in the ocean breeze. Her ears flicked toward us as Phalue spoke.

"We need to talk and you've been avoiding me."

"A bit difficult on a ship this small."

"And yet you've managed." Phalue left the door open, glancing about for a place to sit and finding nowhere but the bed. She chose to stand instead. "I've fulfilled our part of the bargain. I helped you obtain the white-bladed sword. Now give me your army and I will retake Nephilanu."

"The sword is in Dione's possession. And Ragan has another. That's two they have now. If I gather some Imperial ships, we can go after them. You have to see that they're important. They could change the course of this war."

The light from the open door cast all the stray hairs around Phalue's head in gold, highlighted the scratches on the pauldrons of her armor. "Then you admit we're at war with the Shardless Few. During a war, it's not wise to leave a valuable part of your Empire occupied. What's more important here? The health and welfare of your people, or swords that may or may not give you an advantage over your enemy?"

"They *do* give us an advantage."

Phalue's temper snapped. She swept an arm out, nearly hitting the wall. "But you don't know what they do! Meanwhile, my island is under the occupation of the Shardless Few. The supply of caro nuts you have from Imperial will be running out. Look around you, Lin. Unless those swords can cure the bog cough and fill our sails like witstone, they're not going to make things better for everyone. I have done *everything* you've asked of me. I've trained you how to wield that sword; I've accompanied you on this mad quest. You want to follow Dione to the ends of the earth while your Empire falls apart and your people die? Fine. But you do it *without* me."

"I can't spare the soldiers." My cheeks heated. How dare she? We hadn't completed this task. It was still undone. I was trying to *save* lives from Dione and his Shardless Few. "There's too much unrest. Once I marry Iloh and secure the governors who follow him then—"

"Do you hear yourself? Always an excuse, always one more thing to be done. First Anau, then Maila, now chasing Dione and Ragan across the Endless Sea. Give me what you promised. That's what friends do."

Her words hit me in that place of self-loathing, the part of me that suspected I would never be better than my father, no matter how hard I tried. And then her last words filtered through my mind. "We're . . . friends?"

Phalue's shoulders slumped. She rubbed a hand over her face. "Maybe Ranami is right – I throw myself into everything, including arguments, without judging circumstances first. Yes, well, I thought we were friends. Or something like it. You have strange ways of showing that you care, but isn't that why you asked me to come along? You have enough skilled guards, you have enough servants and people willing to do whatever you ask. You needed someone who would always tell you the truth."

I'd known it myself but didn't know that she'd known it too. I trusted Phalue. I still did. Tears gathered in my throat, thickening my voice. "What you said about the orphans, what you said about the bog cough – it's all true. I don't always have the best impulses, I don't always see clearly. My father still raised me. I need you."

Phalue crossed her arms, letting out a huff of breath as her gaze traced the ceiling. "I know. But Ranami and Ayesh need me too. So does Nephilanu."

A flutter of wings sounded and then a tern construct flitted past Phalue and into my cabin. It landed on the bed, flicking its wings once before settling. "Took time to find you," it said in its creaky voice.

My breath caught in my throat and I dashed the tears that had been forming at my eyes. Strange, to feel self-conscious in front of a beast I'd created. But it was the one I'd left with Iloh. "Iloh has a message for me?"

It blinked once, twice, and then spoke in an approximation of Iloh's voice. "I've kept the governors from leaving the Empire and you need to keep your part of the bargain. Marry me and appoint me as your consort officially. Our witstone has nearly run out. I do not think I'll be able to keep the peace without further assurances."

My fingers twitched and I wished the message were a letter I could crush between them. Always too many things to keep track of; always too many things that needed my attention.

I had to admit the thing that I'd been loath to face: I wasn't holding the Empire together. Not anymore. No matter what I tried to do, it was falling apart.

All I could do was to salvage what I could. To save the lives I could. Phalue was right – I did not know what the swords did, and until I knew for sure, there were more immediate problems to handle.

I bowed my head, feeling the weight of defeat. I turned to my desk, dipped my pen in ink and began writing on a fresh sheet of paper. "Gaelung is stabilized," I told her. "I cannot spare the whole army, but I can spare enough to launch an assault on Nephilanu. Take this letter to Yeshan." I took the wax, held it to the lamp, and let it drip onto the folded page. I pressed the Phoenix seal into it before it could cool. "Take back your island. Make sure the caro nuts get distributed evenly throughout the Empire and I'll ensure that Ikanuy pays you for them."

I had to let the swords go. Let Dione continue on his quest to obtain more of them. If I wanted to be a leader of my people, I had to concern myself with my people and not just with winning this war. I took a deep breath in and then let it out, willing my fear, my desire, to leave with it.

I handed the letter to Phalue. "I'll drop you at the next island with a harbor and give you money enough to book a fast ship to Gaelung."

26

Jovis

Riya Island

Two of the monks there have bonded ossalen and are Alanga. Find them. Kill them. The words repeated in my head as we entered the courtyard of the monastery. I was trying to hold too many things in my thoughts at once. But Mephi was with me, which meant I still had a chance to escape. I still could find a way to ditch Philine, to subvert Kaphra's commands and to flee.

So simple. A real stroll on the beach, this.

No. I'd done enough giving in to despair. I'd done enough moping, letting Kaphra use me as his tool. I would find a way. I *would*.

The monk with the golden sash fell into step beside me. "We should have known he'd go after the swords. We thought they were hidden — so well that no one would find them. Curse the ingenuity of mankind."

"The Scholars' Academy found it first," I told her. "Ragan took it from them."

She gestured to a path that led to a small building on the left before walking down it herself. I turned onto it, Mephi at my side, water squelching in my boots. My staff clicked against the gravel as we walked. "I have a message from the Emperor," I said, remembering my original ploy.

"Yes, we heard you shouting from behind the walls. Jovis, is it?" She turned her head to look me up and down as she led us to the building. "Is it really you? You're supposed to be dead."

I showed her the scar on my wrist. It wasn't revealing who I was if she already knew. "Not dead. Just delayed."

"Anyone could have a scar on their wrist."

"And have an ossalen?"

"Alanga are more common than they once were." She opened the door; on the inside, the building was lit with lanterns, high-lighting old paintings on the ceiling and worn wooden boards. Mephi barely fit through the door, his branching horns catching at the top. He had to duck down and to the side to make it inside.

"So you don't believe me," I said as I followed the monk. Philine stepped on my foot, hard. I sucked in a breath, catching her warning gaze. Was I talking too much?

"It's not that I don't believe who you are." The monk led us to basins of water with washcloths in front of them. "Please refresh yourselves. It's that I don't believe your intentions. The Emperor has always sent us written missives. If you truly are Jovis, why would she send you away from her side just as you were discovered alive? You were her Captain of Imperial Guard. You should be with her."

"It's to do with the swords," I said, my mouth running one step ahead of my mind. The monks knew about the swords – they'd kept the only surviving books from the Alangan period. The woman had already turned for the door.

"We can speak on it when you've had the chance to rest a moment."

They had to have some idea where the swords were. "She knows you have one," I said, taking a gamble.

The woman stopped for a moment before continuing to the door without another word. I'd hit my mark true and we both knew it.

As soon as she shut the door, Philine turned on me. "What are you doing? You're about as convincing as a child – even when you're telling the truth."

I looked down at my disheveled appearance, my torn and rain-soaked clothes, the mud spattered up and down both my shirt and pants. The high-collared shirt *had* been white at one point. "I've just been chased up a mountain by a power-hungry Alanga who has *somehow* convinced Shardless Few to work with him and who really wants to kill me. I'm not at my best."

She huffed before picking up one of the cloths and dipping it into the basin. She wiped dirt and grime from her face and then let out a long sigh. Mephi, behind me, began vigorously grooming the mud from between his paws.

"You've been trouble since you first arrived; Kaphra only keeps you around because he's not the one left to deal with it. *I* am."

I grabbed another cloth and rubbed it over my wet hair, doing my best to dry it. Kaphra had let me grow it out a little before this trip, and the curls stuck out in every direction in spite of each attempt I made to tame it with my fingers. I gave up, focusing on the sweat and rain still dripping beneath the collar of my shirt. I scratched at my beard; it was a bit overgrown. "Why do you follow him? Why does anyone? He's mean; he's petty; he sets his Ioph Carn against one another to prove their loyalty."

She ignored me for a moment, taking the chance to pull the tie free of her tangled hair and to re-tie it. "He still rewards skill and hard work. No one took me in after both my parents died of shard sickness. I learned to fend for myself. I could have turned to petty thievery or I could have turned to organized crime. I had no other choices." She gave her face one last wipe and then, satisfied, dropped the cloth back on the table before turning on me. "Which would *you* have made? The Ioph Carn were harsh, but they put clothes on my back and food in my belly, and gave me a place to lie my head at night that I could call my own. At least with the one I had found something of a family, somewhere I could belong. You? You've always had someone, Jovis."

I opened my mouth to protest – I'd been lonely too – but shut it. She was right. I'd never truly been cut off from society. Even when I'd been haunting the Endless Sea, searching for Emahla, I'd still known my parents were waiting for me back on Anau. But her past didn't justify doing the bidding of a man like Kaphra. "Don't tell me it's all about belonging. You've climbed the Ioph Carn ladder of your own accord. Is this the price you're willing to pay for power? You'll follow whatever mad scheme he puts forth until he finally retires and lets you be the leader of the Ioph Carn?"

She stopped, her jaw set, her fists clenched. "You have no idea what I've been through. You have no idea of my plans. You will *never* understand someone like me."

"Fine." I cast the cloth I'd used to wipe my face and chest onto the table. I still looked a mess, but I at least felt marginally more like myself. "Maybe I won't ever understand you. But I understand Kaphra. It doesn't matter how good you are, how capable, how many promises he makes you. The Ioph Carn like you. The men and women on that ship – they seek your approval. That doesn't make Kaphra respect you; it makes him see you as a threat. He will never let you lead, Philine. I've seen the way he grasps at power. He will never give it up willingly. And if you were *half* as smart as you think you are, you'd see it too."

Her eyes narrowed. "Punch yourself in the mouth."

My hand was up and striking my own face before I could think of a way to stop it.

"Clever as you think you are," she said as my head was still spinning, "you're the one under my command, not the other way around. You're the one who let yourself be trapped. You're the one doing Kaphra's bidding, no matter what he asks of you."

I rubbed at my sore face. Mephi strode between us, making a worried sound in the back of his throat. Disloyal beast. If Philine were anyone else, he'd have taken a bite out of them for hurting me. But he liked Philine. He liked Dione too. Never understood why. One of the great unsolved mysteries of the world. I focused on the floor, trying to clear the fuzziness from my mind. A few trails of ants crept across the boards, scouting for food. The haze in my vision slowly cleared and the ants resolved into one trail.

"That's just the point, Philine," I said, letting my hand fall. "I *have* to do what he says. You're choosing to."

Her jaw set, her hands falling to her knives. My staff was strapped to my back, but I opened my fingers, knowing it was within easy reach.

The door burst open.

The monk who'd led us to the building stood there flanked by two others. She held a white-bladed sword in her hand. The two monks flanking her were young, nearly girls instead of women. Ossalen stood at their sides, knee-high, one dun-colored and the other black. The shards in my chest flared, urging me to take my staff in hand, to finish what Kaphra had commanded.

Mephi chirruped a greeting to the little ossalen and they chirped back – as though we were all meeting for a meal and not as though we were about to engage in combat.

My staff was in my hand. I hadn't remembered pulling it free. This was bad. This was very bad. I'd been so caught up arguing

with Philine that I hadn't been doing what I should have been —
which was to think of a way around Kaphra's commands. And
now they pushed me forward, my feet moving in quick, delib-
erate steps.

"You may be Jovis," the lead monk said, "but you are *not* here
on behalf of the Emperor. What are you truly here for?"

If only they hadn't walked into this room. I couldn't pretend
I didn't see the very two Alanga Kaphra had tasked me with
murdering when they were standing in front of me. The command to find them had lifted, but the one that urged me to kill
them had not.

In answer, I lifted my staff and attacked.

The two Alanga might have been young, but they'd been
monastery-trained. They lifted their hands in unison and water
flowed into the room. One ducked to the side, catching the blow
I'd intended for her head with her palm, her grip as implacable
as though I'd struck a tree. Her fingers wrapped around my staff.

Water lashed at my back like a whip, stinging my skin. It
couldn't distract me, though, not when Kaphra's commands
forced me into movement. I brought my foot down on the floorboards and the building trembled, the whips of water shattering
into suspended droplets.

The master monk strode through the shattered droplets, her
sword gleaming in the dim light from the windows. "You can't
win this. Put down your weapon. Surrender."

I pulled at my staff, trying to free it from the Alanga's grip.
Her jaw tensed as she held steady. "I would if I could," I said
through gritted teeth. With one last, hard tug, the Alanga top-
pled and my staff came free.

I caught a glimpse of Philine behind me and Mephi, holding
down one ossalen with each paw, speaking in a low voice to each
as though scolding errant puppies. I'd had to have known neither

of them would join this fight. Mephi because he had no taste for hurting innocents, and Philine because she'd just as happily watch me die. At least then she'd be free of me.

Something in the monk's expression shifted, the fire in her gaze dimming. "What do you mean?"

I caught the other Alanga in the gut with my staff, swinging it about to stop the first one from flinging a sphere of water into my face. She sprang back onto her hands, letting the water fall but kicking my staff wide. It left me open for the other two women to attack. Fists pummeled my ribs as the white-bladed sword sank into my thigh.

Fire laced through my veins, but the command was stronger, my bones trembling with unleashed magic. In one swift move, I gathered the air currents around me and then cast them out. A hurricane-force wind blasted from my hand, sending all three monks tumbling. I darted toward one of the Alanga on the ground, my staff lifted.

Her fearful expression caught my gaze, and for a moment I was thrown back to all those times I'd killed, all the people I'd slain on Kaphra's behalf. I wasn't a hero. I was a monster. And here I was, again doing a monstrous thing. A part of me wanted to settle into it, to take on that other persona, the one that did Kaphra's bidding with a smile on his face – it would be easier.

The trail of ants was still there in spite of wind and rain, right next to her head. I tore my gaze from hers and focused on them, trying not to think about what I was doing. Trying to separate myself.

Jovis. Mephi's voice brought me back to myself, ringing in my head like a bell. *You are still you.*

Kill them. That was the command Kaphra had given me.

My staff came down. And then the answer came to me.

I diverted my weapon's path at the last moment, smashing

two of the ants in the trail with the end of the staff. Kill *them*. He hadn't specified exactly who. The burning command eased and for one blissful moment, I felt free.

The white-bladed sword came to rest at the side of my neck. "Tell me why I shouldn't kill you."

I dropped my staff and it thudded onto the wooden floor. In a flash, Mephi was there, a growl low in his throat. "This wasn't his fault," he said. The other two ossalen, cowed, stood behind him, heads low and tails between their legs.

The monk regarded Mephi, gave him a slight inclination of her head. "All respect to you, little one – that's why I'm giving him a chance to explain." Her gaze flicked back to me.

I tapped my chest. "I can't—" My mouth moved, words refusing to come out.

"He was trapped with bone shard magic," Mephi said, looking proud at being able to contribute. "Sometimes he's able to get around it. Kaphra of the Ioph Carn has been commanding him. He kept me imprisoned as collateral."

The monk looked between Mephi and me. "I was not aware that shards could be used that way. We kept the old records, but even those don't detail everything, and much of the Alangan artifacts and magic were lost, replaced by your Emperor's magic."

Her sword still at my neck, she took a step closer and lifted a hand, raising an eyebrow at me. "May I?"

I nodded, and she pressed cool fingers over my chest. My shirt was still damp with rain, still a bit muddy, though she didn't seem to notice. The woman took one deep breath in, and then out, and for the barest moment, I thought I felt her fingertips sink *into* my flesh.

She drew back, her gaze meeting mine.

I swallowed. "Can you . . .can you take them out?"

"I cannot work bone shard magic the way your Emperor can,

or the way the leader of the construct army could. I'm afraid someone who can will have to remove the shards. But I can feel them. It seems you speak the truth." She sheathed her sword.

I leaned down slowly, my palms out, as I picked up my staff and strapped it to my back. "I was told to find and kill any Alanga here. Kaphra has had control over me. He didn't want any competition."

The monk's eyes narrowed. She whipped her head toward the two Alanga. "You've strayed outside the walls, haven't you?"

They glanced at one another, before one blurted, "No!" at the same time the other blurted, "Yes! We're sorry!"

The monk sighed. "Half rations for three days. Report to the Hall of Longevity for cane lashings, twenty strokes each. No speaking for five days."

I raised an eyebrow. A harsher punishment than even my mother would have visited upon me. One she might have threatened me with, but never followed through on. The two Alanga bowed and then left, their ossalen bounding behind them.

"To you it may seem cruel," the monk said, "but discipline must be tight in a society as isolated as ours. Not every acolyte makes it through the training. Although many of our initiates are not tithed, we keep them away from the water. We never intended to create Alanga. It is not our place in the world."

And now they'd created three. If this was the repressive life Ragan had been assigned to, I could understand a little of why he'd gone astray. Damn this monk for making me feel a little bit sorry for *him*. "You won't be able to keep them in the monastery for ever."

"As they've clearly shown me," she said, her voice crisp. "But that is not your problem." She nodded in Philine's direction. "And what is her role in all of this?"

Hope blossomed in my breast, unfolding with every breath I

took. I could leave Philine here. All I would have to do was to say that she was with Kaphra, and let the monks do with her as they willed. If they punished their acolytes so harshly, they would at least imprison her.

Maybe even execute her.

For a moment, I sat with the idea. I didn't owe Philine anything. She'd obeyed Kaphra's orders; she'd kept me locked away; she'd kept Mephi locked away. So what if I'd saved her life on the mountainside? A snap decision, one I didn't have to repeat. She could have let me go then. But she hadn't. She'd continued to drive me toward Kaphra's goals.

How many chances did I have to give her? How many chances did she deserve? She'd shown me over and over that she was content to let me rot.

Ah, but no, that wasn't entirely true. She could have told Kaphra that I was able to get around his commands. She could have betrayed me back on Hualin Or – what seemed a lifetime ago. Instead, she'd let me carry on, testing the limits of this magic.

Anger flared inside me. So what if she'd done this one thing? Did that make up for the rest? Did I have to keep owing her until the end of time?

I opened my mouth to tell the monk the truth. And then I caught a brief glimpse of Philine's expression, somewhere between panicked and resigned.

There was something in her that had guided her right once. It could guide her again.

"She's a friend," I said, the words tasting strange on my tongue. But it was a lie, and it fell easily enough from my mouth. "She accompanied me because I asked her to. She didn't know what Kaphra set me to do."

The monk nodded, apparently satisfied. "The sword stays

here. The monastery is one of the few safe places for it. And the one Ragan has . . ." Her mouth tightened and she shook her head. "He may not know what they do, but at some point he may discover the truth. He will rain destruction on us all. You must take it from him."

"Me?"

"We are not to stray too far from our trees," she said. "It is the second precept. We protect the cloud junipers and they, in turn, protect us. We cannot count on that protection if we leave."

I'd known their religion made them recluses, but I hadn't counted on it meaning they would set me to a task they could more easily accomplish themselves. "I still have the shards in me – how am I supposed to take Ragan's sword? And in case you haven't noticed, we don't exactly heal from those wounds." I gestured to my injured thigh, the wound still weeping a little blood. "He's got several distinct advantages on me. And what exactly does that sword do?"

Her lips pressed together. "We cannot afford for that information to get back to the Ioph Carn." She pointed to the door. "You should go."

She was right – if what Ragan said was true, Lin was coming here, to Riya, and Iloh was going to ambush her. I'd escaped Kaphra's commands. I still had Philine to deal with.

We were ushered from the grounds of the monastery as quickly as we'd been ushered in – outsiders who'd only been granted a short reprieve because of Ragan's attack. Faintly, as we left, I heard the sound of canes striking flesh, the hollow sound as they hit ribs beneath, the grunts of pain, nearly suppressed. When I'd been a child, I'd romanticized the notion of the monasteries – places where people could leave their children to be free of the Empire's control.

But it seemed they only traded one sort of control for another.

They did not pay the tithe with a shard from their skull, but they still paid a tithe with their bodies.

Mephi crowded next to me as they shut the gates behind us, leaving us again in the rain. I was very quickly soaked, feeling as though I'd gained very little at all. Philine was silent, refusing to meet my gaze.

"A thank you might be in order," I said once the monastery walls were out of view. "I could have left you there."

She shouldered past me, sullen. "Does it ever occur to you that maybe you don't need to fill a silence?"

"Why is she angry?" Mephi said. "Is it because you won't let her think?"

I mean, Mephi had a point — I knew I had a tendency to talk at times when I should remain silent, but talking helped me think through things. It didn't always occur to me that silence did the same for others. "What does she have to think about?"

Philine whirled, rain running into her eyes. "What do I have to think about? How can you be this *stupid* sometimes? You've proved to me you can get out from beneath my commands, and Kaphra's. You have Mephi and I have no white-bladed sword. You're not going to let me take you back to Kaphra. What the *hell* am I supposed to do?"

"Come with us," Mephi said, as though it were the most natural thing in the world.

I shrugged. It wasn't a terrible idea. "Why not? You don't have to go back to the Ioph Carn. What's keeping you with them?"

"What's keeping me with them? What about years of dedication and working toward one goal? What about all the money I have tied up in their accounts? What about the people who are expecting me to come back? What do you think I'll do if I go with you? Help save the Empire?"

My stomach flipped and then sank. I wasn't a hero. But Lin — I could save her. I could try to do that much. I owed her that much. "Save the Emperor. Let's start with that."

She only shook her head. "This isn't my fight."

We don't have much time, Mephi's voice said in my head. Philine didn't bother trying command me as I clambered aboard Mephi's back. But before I could go, she sighed and seized my ankle.

"There's something you should know."

I froze, not liking the tone of apprehension in her voice. "You're going to tell me something I won't like, aren't you?"

She sighed. "Yes. One of the commands in your chest — it's specifically to stop you from going back to Lin. She's the only one who can remove the commands so Kaphra wanted to be sure. It won't let you approach her. It won't let you tell her who you are. If you save her, you'll have to do it without her ever knowing you were there."

27

Lin

Riya

We approached the island flying the Imperial flag. I'd sent word ahead by the tern construct, and this time a palanquin was waiting for me, decked out in red and gold paper streamers that were quickly disintegrating in a light spattering of rain. By the look of the skies, the rain would stop soon. An auspicious day for a wedding. The most suitable clothing I'd been able to find once I'd realized Iloh's intentions was a heavy robe with a simple phoenix embroidered on the back. Damned Iloh – I should have known he wouldn't be satisfied with only a promise. I should have just married him back when I'd offered him the position of consort and gotten the whole thing out of the way.

But the weddings of Emperors were meant to be grand affairs – more for the people than anyone else.

All the Emperors before me had married for politics. I couldn't have expected anything differently. Only, I'd hoped for something different, once. And hope was a clinging, grasping thing, an ember that refused to be extinguished no matter how much sand I heaped atop of it.

I climbed into the palanquin with Huan, her ossalen curling about her neck, dark brown nose at Huan's ear. Her russet fur was striking against the deep blue uniform jacket. I'd given Huan the phoenix medallion to wear, though her uniform was a bit tattered — not truly fit for a wedding — well, times were hard. Most people would be looking at her ossalen or the symbol of her status anyway. My Captain of Imperial Guard. I still remembered the day I'd placed the pendant around Jovis's neck, so certain of my actions. So certain that I was helping both him and myself.

But it was Iloh who would be sharing my bed tonight. I shouldn't have to steel myself against the thought. He was a good-looking man, experienced by his own admission. Most likely sterile — though that was an issue we could tackle later.

What mattered now was keeping the Empire together, uniting the various dissatisfied factions against the Shardless Few. Firming up our position with the Alanga that were appearing — which Huan at my side could help with.

There was a path through, I could see it.

And the swords?

The palanquin lurched beneath us as the bearers rose, began climbing the gently-sloped hill. I peeked out the curtain to see people crowding the streets, following us, eager for a break in not only the clouds but in the hardship that seemed to have its claws in us all.

I still had one sword strapped to my side, though it felt heavier than it had before. Even dressed in my finery as I was, ready to face down my wedding day, I wanted it with me. I was a wartime Emperor. I'd sent Phalue to the south with my army to engage the Shardless Few. I had to start admitting it to myself.

"Eminence," Huan said as the palanquin swayed, "may I speak freely?" Outside, I could hear people cheering.

"Please do. Please always do." I still missed Jovis's straightforward feedback, as much as it had sometimes infuriated me.

"You seem apprehensive."

I sighed, and then words were tumbling from my mouth before I could stop them. "This whole expedition has been a mess from the very beginning. I set out to find the swords," I gestured to the blade strapped to my side, "and I found one but lost it again. So I am back where I began, with only dead people left in my wake."

She scratched the cheeks of her ossalen. "I can't say I'm back where I began, nor would I necessarily want to be," she said softly. "And you saved our lives by throwing that sword away. I'm not the person you should be looking to for comfort if you want someone to say your mistakes are not so bad, but neither are you a complete loss, Eminence. Let's get this wedding done, secure the Empire and go home."

I hadn't thought about how my words might strike Huan, who had gone from a guard to an Alanga, still likely bewildered by this change in circumstances. "You're right. I'm sorry – I think I spend too much time dwelling on my failures. It's hard not to." And then I shut my mouth because she'd not asked to be my confidant. "Are you from Imperial, then?"

She nodded as she leaned back against the palanquin cushion. The faint smells of hot oil and pan-fried fish wafted in through the curtains. The crowd outside buzzed with excitement, a low and persistent hum. "Born and raised, in Imperial City even. Oh, I tried to get away from home, but I only got as far as the other side of the island, and for just the two years it took to learn how to fight, before finding my way back." She took in a breath as though she could smell it. "No other place like it. My nieces and nephew will be missing me."

"Family on Imperial too?"

Huan flashed me a quick smile. "Just a sister. She'd be a better fighter than I am, but she decided to sew and mend sails instead. Has a whole shop set up near the docks now, with a good number of workers." I could hear the pride in her voice. She sighed. "I hope things can go back to the way they were. Not with the Tithing, but with everything else." Even as she said it, she stroked her ossalen's chest.

There was no going back. The Empire was changed; the world was changed. How could we help but to change with it? What would her sister say when she found out Huan was an Alanga? Would she be angry, sad, happy? Would she let her son and daughters still see Huan? And even if it were possible, life before still meant my father ruling with his iron-fisted ways. I understood: these things took time to process, to understand the implications, to truly know deep in one's bones that things had irrevocably changed, that one's vision of the past didn't even match reality. I didn't voice my thoughts – because why would I so rudely awaken her from such a dream?

It was the sort of dream I wanted to fall into. But I couldn't afford to – not even for one moment.

Iloh would be my consort. And then I would go back to Imperial, awaiting word on the battle at Nephilanu. I would throw the weight of my intellect into helping the surviving scholars from Hualin Or, delving into the mysteries of witstone and the sinking islands.

I had to change, and that meant marrying Iloh and being satisfied with it. I opened the curtain to find a throng of cheering people. I smiled and waved to them, doing my best to put on the appearance of someone happy with her fate. They cheered all the louder. We wouldn't be getting married inside the palace walls; there wasn't enough room for the crowds there. Instead,

Iloh had set up the ceremony in the clearing outside Riya's witstone mines.

I couldn't miss the pointed reminder he was giving me.

I caught a glimpse of Thrana next to the palanquin, half the people near her shying away and half reaching out as though wanting to touch her. My three other guards pushed their hands back, voices low in warning. Thrana's ears flicked between alert and flattening against her head. She wasn't Mephi, who would have pranced and tilted his head at the crowd. The guards pushed back hands more for the safety of their bearers than for Thrana's comfort. She'd mellowed in the years, but could still be snappish.

The mines were a little way out of the city. We lost some of the crowd halfway there, though it seemed some people had made the trek out to the mines when they'd seen my ship on the horizon. Trees had been cleared near the entrance of the mines, leaving a flat, green space that had been decorated with flowers and hanging lanterns.

Iloh was waiting there with his guards, the clouds breaking to provide a moment of sunshine. Huan left the palanquin first, holding out a hand to help me out as I ducked my head. I had to admit: Iloh looked handsome. The faint gray in his hair had come in at streaks at his temples, and one in the center of his neatly trimmed beard. He was short, but then so was I, though where I was thin and wiry, he was broad-shouldered.

He approached, took my hands and kissed my cheek, his beard tickling my face.

"I'm glad you were able to make it so quickly," he said. He'd kept his grip on my hands, his fingers colder than mine.

"Your letter was most convincing."

"Please forgive me if it seemed pushy."

"Do I have a choice? In forgiving you?" I said smoothly.

"Lin." He brought my hands together, placing one atop and

one below. Slowly, his skin warmed to mine. His expression was serious as he looked into my eyes. "I was only reflecting the pressure I was feeling. From the other governors, from my people. Witstone supplies are dwindling for everyone. Rumors say that caro nut oil has run out. They all deserve a stable government, a promise that things will be different going forward. You needed to follow through on that promise, no matter how important you thought your expedition was."

No matter how important I *thought* it was. I wondered if he'd phrased it that way just to get under my skin. I let it pass. I didn't want to be this angry. We needed to work together and I needed to concede more, much as I didn't want to.

I sighed, my gaze going to Iloh's vacant mines, the entrance partially overgrown. "Fine. We'll reopen some witstone mining. Not here – your mines are too extensive – but I'll allow some of the newer ones to open again, with strict quotas. It will buy us some time and some goodwill. And if we're fighting the Shardless Few, we'll need it. We still have money reserved in the Imperial treasury. Until we have some production running again, we don't have a choice except to buy back some of our witstone from the Ioph Carn." I'd resolved to put pride aside for necessity. And if Iloh was to be my consort, we'd at least need to share business dealings. "Now let's get this over with so we can both move on to more important things."

Iloh's guards held back the crowd, giving us space for the ceremony. After, there would be a procession through the streets, where we'd throw specially made cakes and coins to the crowd.

I said the words, feeling numb, proclaiming to all before me that Iloh was my consort, that I was taking him to stand by my side, that our children would be my heirs and that he was second to me in all things.

Thrana and Huan stood to my right; Iloh's sister and one of

his guards stood to his left. Out of the corner of my eye, I saw Thrana's ears go back, her tail thrashing.

Something isn't right. Her voice was a low murmur in my mind, thick with apprehension. *The forest around us is silent.*

Iloh was speaking now, his fingers tightly laced around mine. I barely listened to the words. Instead, I found my gaze focusing on the forest.

I thought he'd brought me here to make a point, but now I wondered if he'd brought me here for other reasons. It was more isolated here, preparations for anything sinister might go unnoticed, especially since the mines had been closed.

A shout rose from one of my guards. And then the others all looked upward in the same direction. I followed their gazes.

A man pushed his way through the people gathered at the road. His hands were lifted, a giant wave of water building in front of him.

For a moment, our gazes met. My heart jolted because I knew that face. Even with the scar, the beard, the added lines, the dark expression — I knew his face.

The wave crashed down.

28

Jovis

Riya Island

Philine's parting words followed me as Mephi and I made our way back into the city. I couldn't approach Lin, couldn't tell her who I was. My original plan to find her and tell her she was heading into a trap dissolved into pieces. I had to find another way to stop Ragan and Iloh and this sham of a wedding.

The rain had stopped by the time we made it to the bottom of the mountainside, the day a fair bit brighter. Nearly sunny in spots.

"What do you think those commands say specifically?" I said to Mephi. "How close am I allowed to get? Will they force me to hide from her, or can I just not seek her out?" I touched a hand to my chest, rubbing the spot where I still remembered the feel of Nisong's hand entering my body – a strange, tingling feeling. Cold and sharp, as though I were being pierced with a blade and not blunted flesh. I wished I could somehow sense what was written on them. I wished I had Lin's power, and could find a way to reach inside myself and remove them.

"Will speculating help?" Mephi said, fixing me with one large brown eye. "Or is it just making you nervous?"

I'd removed my staff from my back and I was tapping it with one fingernail. I slid from Mephi's back before we reached the main road and sighed. "I suppose I'll have to figure this out as I go."

"As you've always done." He sounded measured, more calm than I was. A strange pang hit me. He was growing up.

"As I've always done," I repeated. "It's usually worked out, hasn't it?"

"In a manner of speaking," Mephi said wryly. "We are, after all, in our current predicament."

And the Empire falling apart around us. I gestured for him to follow me and we turned a corner onto the main street. It was crowded, people packed on either side, holding red paper streamers. Children laughing, carrying straw baskets they'd use to try and catch the coins tossed by the happy couple.

She was *here*.

Surely they'd wait before the wedding? There'd be time for her to rest from her travel, to prepare herself? Even as I thought it, I knew it wasn't true. The crowds on the street told me it wasn't true. And Iloh – he'd want to seal the marriage quickly to ensure his place at Lin's side. To solidify his power over the Empire.

"Where is the ceremony taking place?" I asked someone, pulling at their arm.

"The old mines," the man said without even looking at me.

We slipped through the crowd as quickly as possible, issuing smooth apologies as irritated people were displaced. More than one curious glance followed us, and more than one angry and resentful one did. With Mephi at my side, it was clear I was Alanga. By Mephi's size, anyone could see I was one of the first.

Alanga might be less unusual than they'd once been, but they were still unusual.

A palanquin was coming up the street, the curtain thrown open. I saw her face and the rest of the world seemed to diminish only to her and my fast-beating heart.

Two years. I'd not seen her in two years. In some ways, she didn't look any different. The same wide-set eyes, the same stern mouth and pointed chin. But even through the distance, and in spite of her smile, I could see the ways the years had worn on her. The stress she carried in the tightness at the corners of her eyes, the line that had developed between her brows, as though she'd spent long hours curved over some book or parchment, trying to discern its meaning. I wanted to cup her face in my hands, smooth away those worries with my thumbs, kiss the space between her brows and tell her I was here.

I was stepping forward before I could stop myself.

It was like running into a wall. I halted mid-step, my foot refusing to move forward any farther. The person next to me grunted as I stumbled into him. He shot me an irritated glare.

"Sorry," I said reflexively, my attention still taken by the palanquin. Thrana followed behind, children pointing in awe at her, tugging at their parents' hands as though they hadn't already noticed. She was larger than Mephi, larger than an ox, her horns thrice-branching now and seeming to brush the sky. Lin's guards pushed reaching hands back, keeping her from being touched.

I wasn't close enough to shout over the noise of the crowd, I wasn't close enough to wave and catch her attention. And there were other commands in my chest probably preventing me from doing any of that. Intentions, though – those were tricky, wily things. I could lie to myself about my intentions. There had to be a way . . .

But the palanquin was moving into the forest, the guards and

Thrana following, the road there too narrow for me to get close without being noticed.

Too slow, Jovis.

I darted after the palanquin, mingling with the crowd that had decided to follow the Emperor into the jungle. There weren't enough of Iloh's guards with the palanquin to throw up much suspicion, and no Shardless Few that I could see, which meant they'd laid a trap at the mines themselves. It would be easy to hide some men and women in the trees, to stow some away inside the mines. Iloh was thorough, I had to give him that. Which meant he'd wait until the ceremony was complete before he had her killed. How easy it would be for him to claim that an errant Alanga had done the deed, that he'd had nothing to do with it. He'd have Ragan to contend with after that, but Iloh was a schemer. He'd know that even with Ragan running about he'd still be in a better position than the one he'd been in as governor, and Ragan had likely made him some promises. Ragan was a problem for his future self. The position of Emperor had always passed to the Emperor's heir and not the consort, but if Lin didn't have an heir, he'd be as good as Emperor when she was dead. Their interests aligned, for the moment.

Some of the crowd dropped away as we hiked further into the forest, content to wait for the procession to return. Others still continued onward.

I couldn't get close to her. I couldn't let her know I was there. Those couldn't be my goals. But I could stop this ceremony and this ambush. I could make that my goal and perhaps slide through the gaps in the commands.

I heard puddles splash behind me as Mephi followed.

Mephi, I said to him, a sudden doubt filling my heart. *What if she* wants *to marry him? What if she loves him? What if I'm just interrupting a happy ceremony and Ragan was lying about Iloh's plans?*

Jovis, he said with the loudest mental sigh I'd ever heard, *don't be a fool.*

I hung toward the back of the crowd as we reached the mines, unable to get any closer. Dimly, I heard Iloh's and Lin's voices, barely audible over the blood pounding in my ears. The forest around us was quiet – no birds singing, no calling monkeys.

I squinted and peered over the heads of the people in front of me, trying to catch a glimpse of what was happening. Lin and Iloh, hands clasped, Thrana and Iloh's guards arrayed around them.

A flicker of movement at the mouth of the mines caught my eye. Someone was emerging from behind the overgrown brush. A glint of a drawn blade.

Without thinking, I stepped forward, lifting my hands, bringing all the recent rainwater to bear. The people around me drew back, though I barely heard their alarmed murmurs. My focus had to be absolute. I couldn't think about Lin.

This was only about Ragan and Iloh and the ambush.

I shoved the wave toward the entrance of the mines, unheeding of Lin and Iloh in the wave's path. People fled out of the way, shouting.

"I knew you'd follow me back here," a voice said from my right.

Ragan emerged from the jungle, white-bladed sword in hand. Lozhi wasn't with him and neither was Nisong, for which I was glad. I didn't want to hurt his ossalen – not when I knew the poor creature hadn't bonded with Ragan out of any real choice. And Nisong . . .she was the one I truly feared. She was the one who could take away my will.

Ragan was stronger than me, and a better fighter, but I was used to being the scrappy one. I was used to winning only by the skin of my teeth.

Still, I couldn't help glancing at the white-bladed sword, licking my lips, trying to quell the tight feeling in my chest. I wasn't sure what was worse – the pain I felt when it cut me, or the anticipation of that pain.

He took a deep breath in before stepping out onto the wall, as though he could smell something of my magic in the air. "You could hide like a mouse in the monastery, but you'd never let your precious Lin walk into this trap alone." In one smooth movement, he flipped his grip on his sword and brought it to bear. "Two mice in my trap now."

A couple of Shardless Few emerged from the forest next to Ragan, brushing past the fleeing crowd. Mephi let out a rumbling growl from behind me.

Help the commoners get out of the way of the fighting. I don't want to hurt any innocent people. I can handle these three. With a disgruntled sound in the back of his throat, Mephi turned to obey.

Ragan and the Shardless Few attacked at the same time.

I lashed out with my staff, whirling in time to deflect both Ragan's sword and the man's next to him. I brought my foot down swiftly, letting the tremor inside me leak into the stones beneath me, all the way into the ground.

The ground shook. Some of the fleeing city folk screamed.

Before the Shardless Few to my right could recover his footing, I swung my staff out, sending him tumbling into the brush.

Wind and water spattered my cheek – Lin's doing if I was right – but I didn't have the chance to see how she fared. The other Shardless Few had circled around behind me, and Ragan was still before me. He'd reached into his pouch and, judging by the way his jaw was moving, was crushing a cloudtree berry between his teeth. He couldn't have had that many left now, but clearly he'd saved some for this encounter.

Now I wasn't just facing off an Alanga who was a better fighter than I was; I was facing off against an *enhanced* Alanga. He struck with dizzying speed, his blade flashing quick as lightning. I caught a feint just a moment too late, and his blade found its way through my guard, digging a little into my side before I struck it away.

The pain sent me down on one knee. The sword of the Shardless Few behind me whooshed through the air where my neck had just been. A stroke of good fortune.

"Luck is clouds and mist," my mother was fond of saying. "They may look solid but they won't hold your weight."

I had to rely on more than luck if I wanted to live through this. Ignoring the burning pain, I crouched and swept a leg out behind me, toppling the Shardless Few flanking me. She collapsed into a tree. I leapt back to my feet, wincing as the burning pain stuck a lance in my ribs, and stepped out of the arc of Ragan's strike. I had to lean back to avoid it completely, nearly tripping over the woman's body.

I stepped over her, seized her shoulder and lifted her like a shield.

Ragan's next strike caught her instead, sinking deep into her arm and catching bone. She screamed. I let her fall, gasping, as Ragan sought to dislodge his sword, doing my best to ignore the sick feeling in my belly. It was something I would have done as Kaphra's slave, and I'd done it again, unthinking. Before, when I'd been a hero, I'd done my best not to permanently injure anyone. I wasn't under his control, so what was I now? I had to survive this, that's all it was.

I darted down the path toward the mines, trying to see how I could use my surroundings to my advantage.

"Every time I'm close to success, you're here doing your best to thwart me," Ragan said, striding after me. I could barely hear him over the din of the fighting by the mines. "Why is that? Do you just yearn to be punished?"

"You didn't make out so well last time," I said.

"I'd won our battle," he said. "It was Dione who stopped me, not you."

"Ragan," I said, exhausted, "why are you like this? Do you really think you'll get the Shardless Few to follow you? Do you really think you'll get the Alanga to? What's the point?"

He scoffed at me, as though I were too foolish to see what was right in front of my face. "Everyone clings to the past. Lin thinks she can rule this Empire as Emperor. Dione thinks he can restore the Alanga to their former glory without repeating the same mistakes. And the monasteries think they can continue to live life apart from the rest of us and to stay out of conflict even as some of their apprentices become Alanga. And you –" He looked me up and down, his lip curled. "– you think you can be the Jovis you once were. But I know what you've done. I know you're not the hero of the people. You're the Maelstrom. You're ruthless. You take no prisoners."

"That wasn't me. That was Kaphra." But my words sounded more confident than I felt.

Ragan took another step forward. "Please. You always could have chosen death instead. You could have found a way. Instead, you chose to survive. A coward."

The same words I'd said to myself, over and over.

I'm coming back, Mephi's voice said in my head. *You need help.*

Mephi, don't . . . But I couldn't put my heart into the protest. I needed him, because I was faltering, falling into ways that weren't my own but that felt as well-worn as the boots on my feet. The wound in my side still burned.

I wanted to find Lin, but the shards inside me twinged each time I moved even fractionally toward her. I had to defeat Ragan or he'd find a way to kill her. Or Iloh would.

"Me?" Ragan focused on the sword he held. "I am the only

one who looks to the future, who knows how things must change. I am not a coward. I do things with purpose, not just to survive. I'll do what it takes and I won't hesitate. The Shardless Few will follow me. The Alanga will follow me. They won't have a choice."

He attacked me again and I slipped. He was right: I was a coward. I could feel it in my bones – the tremor in them weaker, my hands not as steady, my feet like two blocks of wood beneath me. I brought my staff up to block, the shock of the blow running up my arms. He pressed the sword down and my feet gave way.

Just before Ragan's blade could reach my shoulder, Mephi charged to my side, white smoke drifting from his mouth and nostrils, a storm force gale emerging from his maw. I gave a last, desperate shove. Ragan, blown back by Mephi's summoned wind, cursed as I threw him off.

And then Mephi seized me by the back of my jacket, threw me aboard his back and ran.

No shame in running when a fight's got the better of you. There was shame in moral cowardice, in failing to live up to my own standards – yes. But I've never been ashamed of running. Spent half my life running from fights in a ship that was built for running.

This time, though ... Lin was back there, and she needed my help.

Jovis, Mephi's voice said in my mind. *Giving up is not always wrong. You're not as strong as Ragan and we don't have enough help.*

Tears filled my throat and I found I couldn't argue with him, fear and exhaustion filling my veins. We fled, and this time, I couldn't stop the shame.

29

Lin

Riya Island

Jovis.

Fighting raged around me and I did my best to hold my own. I didn't know what to make of it, how to feel. He wasn't just alive. He was here. Why hadn't he found some way to let me know? Had he been a prisoner? He'd come here to my wedding and he'd thrown a wave down upon my head. Was it a misguided jealousy? Or had he truly been trying to kill me?

I'd caught a glimpse of Ragan before I'd retreated, my robe soaking wet. Were they working together? It had been two years. He'd said he loved me, but two years could turn love into something else. It could change a person.

It had clearly changed Jovis.

My heart felt twisted into knots and then crushed as I tried my best to imagine Jovis in a different role: as my enemy. I still had to know: why? What had happened to him?

Iloh's hand was still tight in mine as I led him into the mines, away from the chaos at the entrance. I needed a chance to regroup, to assess whether Ragan was here to kill me or to kill Iloh too. Knowing him, he was here to kill both of us. "Are you all right?" he called to me. "Are you hurt?"

"No," I said. "Just tossed about." The robe about my shoulders was even heavier than it had been before, dragging wet trails behind me.

I stopped when the lighting grew too dim to continue. I went to a nearby lamp and found it still stocked with oil. I lit it with the attached tinderbox. The flame flared to life and then settled, flickering with my breath before I shut the glass pane.

Iloh leaned against the cave wall, breathing heavily.

"Are you hurt?" I said finally, shivering. My hair trailed in wet tendrils down my neck. I still had the white-bladed sword strapped to my side.

"No," Iloh said. "But we should wait until my guards have taken care of that Alanga before we do anything else." He pushed away from the wall and took my hands. "This isn't the wedding day I had planned."

"You called me from halfway across the Empire to come here and marry you in a rushed ceremony, threatening me with the uprising of my governors," I said tartly. "Did you think to mollify me with a celebration and fancy food? Was that your plan?"

"Lin . . ." He lifted one of my hands to his lips and pressed his mouth against my palm. The warmth of it sent a shock running through me, made me draw in my breath involuntarily. "What if I told you I couldn't wait a moment longer to be your consort?"

"I'd say you were a liar." The words left my mouth before I'd finished thinking them.

He barked out a laugh. "Fair."

I pulled my hand from his grasp. "We have never gotten along. I cannot imagine your feelings have changed so quickly. You want me because having me gives you more power. Ragan is here, but the other Alanga is Jovis. I need to know what he's doing here, why he's fighting against me. I'm going back out there." I marched toward the entrance.

His fingers caught my arm, not roughly but firmly. "That's not the Emperor's purview. Let our guards handle it." Something flashed in his dark eyes, and it wasn't desire. It was more akin to desperation.

It was like feeling the tumblers in my father's locks click into place. Iloh wasn't in any danger from Ragan. Of course he wasn't. He was a survivor and an opportunist. He would have seen that Ragan was going after the governors. What would he have done had he had the chance to speak to Ragan? He would have struck a bargain with him in the most advantageous way possible – sparing his life and lining his pockets.

He must have seen the realization on my face. Iloh's hand, which had been caressing my arm, seized the front of my robe, pulling it tight around my upper arms and locking them against my body. I hadn't seen what he was doing with his other hand, but it emerged from behind him, a dagger clutched tight in his fingers. If I'd been less prepared, I might have been caught off guard. Instead, I tore away from him with all the strength that I had. The tip of the dagger caught the robe. A moment's resistance before the cloth ripped and I was free.

I let the robe fall from my shoulders and drew my sword. Goosebumps trailed up my bare arms. "You had everything to do with this. You pulled me into a trap."

Iloh glanced at the walls of the mines as though searching for something that might help him. And then, as quickly as he'd pulled free the dagger, he swept his arms out, his palms up, the dagger falling from his fingertips and clattering to the ground. He seemed to have lost only a little of his composure. "Have mercy on your consort, Eminence."

I let out a disbelieving snort. "You just tried to *kill* me. Treasonous actions are an easy enough reason to dissolve our partnership."

"Ah, but think of the reasons we should keep it. The guards I have here when matched against the number you have with you. The Alanga I have on my side."

My heart twinged. Was he confirming that Jovis had indeed somehow turned against me, or was he merely using my ignorance to his advantage? "You're threatening me," I said flatly. "Again."

"You must see things from my point of view." He said it as though we were having a relaxed conversation in a garden, a cup of wine swirling in his hand. "You bargained in bad faith with me. I lost not only our island's primary source of income, but the woman I loved. I can never forgive you for that."

I felt my bones tremble, felt my awareness of the surrounding moisture sharpen. At my beckoning, water trickled in from behind me, tracing lines along the tunnel's walls. "*Not* what you want to be saying when I'm the one with the weapons and you are without. Fine. You cannot forgive me."

"That doesn't mean I don't think we can come to terms," Iloh said quickly.

Trust Iloh to try and negotiate terms when he'd just tried to kill me. But Riya had no stated heir. It was richer than Gaelung was. Iloh had blood relations, though I didn't see them settling their inheritance peaceably. I'd just sent Phalue to Nephilanu with my troops. I couldn't afford another destabilized island – not one this large. I still needed Riya.

And Iloh knew it.

"I already promised to reopen the mines with restrictions."

"The mines on other islands, not on Riya."

The clash of blade against blade echoed faintly down the

mineshaft. Were we truly negotiating in the middle of a battle? They needed my help. But if I didn't get Iloh's buy-in, I'd have only my guards to face against Iloh's guards, two Alanga and their followers. Long odds. "I'll allow you twenty per cent of your usual take."

"Fifty."

"Thirty-five and you can take it or I'll kill you and name your sister governor by Imperial decree."

"You wouldn't. She doesn't think favorably of you. You'll want someone you know won't work behind your back."

I drew the water I'd gathered into a wall behind me. "Try me."

He lifted his hands. "Fine. Thirty-five. I'll back down."

"As soon as this war is over, I'm dissolving our partnership, and you'll make it known this was a mutual decision."

He nodded. "Fair."

Relief washed over me. Iloh could be bargained with. Iloh could be bought. But Ragan had come here with murderous intent, and I wasn't sure he could be dissuaded. "And will Ragan back down? Jovis?"

"I don't command either of them."

Which didn't answer the question that had embedded like a fishhook in my heart: was Jovis against me? I couldn't ask more questions without giving away what I knew and what I didn't know. And there was a simple way to find out. "We're both going back out there, and you will tell Ragan that whatever bargain you've made is broken."

30

Nisong

Riya Island

Ragan had gone after Lin himself — it was the only conclusion she could come to after the Emperor's ship had docked, she'd disembarked to a cheering crowd and still Ragan had not returned. Nisong curled her fingers into the gray fur of Lozhi's shoulder as she waited.

The beast grumbled a little and leaned into her palm. Nisong shut the porthole, returning to pacing the length of the hold.

Alyara sat in a corner with two other Alanga, smoking her pipe. Nisong had found them here on Riya and had quickly brought them under her control. Several constructs lay docile next to them — amalgamations of fearsome beasts Nisong had directed Ragan's Shardless Few to kill. It was tedious, this rebuilding, but if Ragan could break away a sizable portion of the Shardless Few on Nephilanu, then they'd have enough of a force to take Imperial.

Depending on what Dione decided to do. Ragan didn't really

believe Dione would help Lin, no matter what Ragan had told the Shardless Few who followed him.

Nisong wasn't so sure. He'd helped her once before at Gaelung.

Lozhi followed after Nisong as she paced, though he had to duck to keep his horns from catching on the ceiling. Ragan had taken some Shardless Few with him, but Nisong was convinced they weren't enough. Did he not trust her? Did he no longer want her at his side?

He'd watched her with a wary gaze as she'd stitched the constructs together, as she'd brought back the other two Alanga with shards now embedded in their chests. She knew what he was thinking – that she could try to do the same thing to him. He'd taken back the bag of shards and she'd held her breath as he'd counted them.

But whatever count he'd had in his head he must have taken later on, after she'd palmed some of the shards and had hidden them. It had taken a long time to calm the wild beating of her heart after that.

The Alanga and the constructs watched her, none of the Alanga daring to speak. She didn't command them, but she'd placed the shards in their bodies and they feared her. She still had her failsafe: the shards she'd taken from Ragan. In those moments when he was occupied, she'd carved them with a command that could subvert his, that could bring the constructs and the Alanga under her command.

She touched her sash. He was gone. Was this her chance? Take control, overthrow the Shardless Few remaining on this ship and flee with Lozhi? But she still yearned for what Ragan had promised her.

The throne.

So she waited, and she paced, hoping that Ragan hadn't somehow thrown all their plans into disarray.

Lozhi had stopped following her. She turned to see what had caught his attention. His ears pricked, his head swinging toward the city. "Ragan. He's calling me."

She went to him, touched the beast's cheek. "You don't have to go. Stay."

His body trembled beneath her touch, his eyes closing. She could tell he wanted to stay, that he didn't want to obey Ragan. Sometimes she thought his attachment to her greater than his attachment to Ragan. The beast never did speak to Ragan the way he spoke to Nisong. But then his eyes opened. "No. Have to go. He needs me."

Lozhi slipped away from her grasp, climbing the stairs out of the hold.

Alyara laughed from the corner, the sound sharp and bitter. "Even if you weren't a construct, that beast would never bond with you."

Nisong lifted her chin, unwilling to let the courtesan see the hurt in her gaze. "If Ragan were dead, he might." There it was, the secret hope, spoken aloud.

The woman raised an eyebrow. "Oh, is that what you're thinking? Careful, little one. He already thinks you're a danger to him, no matter that he takes you to his bed."

Nisong's cheeks burned in spite of herself. Why should she be embarrassed or ashamed? He wasn't using her; it was the other way around. Wasn't it? "Lozhi didn't have a choice when he bonded with Ragan."

Alyara blew out a cloud of smoke. The Alanga next to her waved it away, irritable. "We are all bonded to Ragan in one way or another now, thanks to you. But I suppose Dione didn't tell you. That makes sense – he wouldn't have. No point, really."

"Tell me what?"

"Killing an ossalen kills the Alanga, but it doesn't work the other way around. The ossalen live through the deaths of their companions."

"Which would leave Lozhi alive. Which would leave him free." It felt odd, putting words to this wild hope of hers that she hadn't even known she'd let grow. It felt dangerous.

"No. Ossalen only bond once, and never again." Alyara took another drag from her pipe, released the smoke. "Dione's lived through the age of the greatest Alanga and in all his years, he says it has never happened." Her gaze focused on Nisong's. "Lozhi will never be yours."

31

Lin

Riya Island

Jovis was nowhere to be seen when we emerged from the mines. I kept Iloh in front of me, my sword still drawn, and hadn't allowed him to pick up his dagger again. I was never leaving myself quite so vulnerable in his presence again.

Ragan was standing on the mountainside, flinging water and shaking the earth to loosen boulders beneath him. My guards and Iloh's fought. Only the presence of Thrana – huge, her teeth and claws flashing – kept my four guards from being completely overwhelmed.

"Call off your guards," I said to Iloh.

"Hold!" he called out. His guards backed off and so did mine, glancing to me, their weapons still lifted and at the ready. But there were others with Ragan – people I didn't recognize.

"Call off Ragan, if you can."

He cleared his throat, but Ragan slid from the mountainside and spoke first, his voice echoing from the rocks. "Iloh – I should have expected that you'd turn. You're a slippery thing, aren't you? Changing with not just with the tides, but with every shift in the water. Whatever she's offered you, you know I'll do better. She can't have offered to open the mines with no restrictions."

I heard Iloh swallow in the ensuing silence. So that was what Ragan had promised him. Help him kill me and he'd let Iloh reopen his mines without restrictions. "She also offered to spare my life."

Ragan lifted two waves on either side of him, striding toward us as an arrow flew toward him and sank into the churning water. "I offered to spare your life too."

I took a step toward Iloh in case he needed to be reminded: I was closer to him and I was holding a sword. I knew he'd make the decision that was more likely to immediately spare his life.

"Our bargain is broken," Iloh said. "Leave, or I'll be forced to kill you."

"As if you *could* kill me."

We both directed our guards at once. "Take him out," I cried just as Iloh shouted, "Kill him!"

But Ragan had been ready. He pushed both waves toward the guards with dizzying speed, the force of wind behind them, making the water stinging and blinding. Most of them fell to the ground. Only two remained standing – Huan and one of Iloh's. Thrana ran to meet me, flowing over the ground with the grace of a fish in the water.

Ragan went straight for Huan, as I seized Thrana and pulled myself onto her back. Together, we charged toward him. He gathered another wave, ready to attack the guards again. I wouldn't make it to him in time. I reached out and then, with a thought, I seized control of the water from Ragan.

He looked as surprised as I felt. I'd been fighting Dione, over and over, as he pursued me to Maila and back. I'd matched my will against his and had lost, each and every time. But I'd become stronger. His power was just so great that mine always felt insignificant next to his. Not so insignificant when measured against Ragan's.

My moment of triumph was short-lived. He stalked toward me as I slid from Thrana's back, his white-bladed sword in his grasp. The guards around us closed on him hesitantly. There were at least twenty of them. There were enough of us.

Ragan attacked.

He'd learned how to fight at his monastery, and the endless days of practice showed in the surety of his gait, the smoothness of his strikes. He moved from one stance into another with the grace of a dancer, the white-bladed sword flashing like the wings of a bird. Two guards were dead before I could act. I pulled more water from the surrounding air, from the mountainsides, building a wave as tall as a palace. And then I pushed it at him with as much force as I could manage before he could attack me. Thrana followed the wave, a growl in her throat.

I didn't have the chance to see if I'd knocked Ragan over. I whirled just in time to catch one of Ragan's followers, his sword pressing down toward me.

And then Huan was there, batting the man aside. Another of my guards stepped into place at my side. I'd almost forgotten I wasn't facing Ragan alone.

I turned to Ragan again. Thrana was darting back, out of reach of his sword, ducking below his swing to snap at his knees. But Ragan was too quick for her — she couldn't land a bite. His face was a mask of stony concentration as he kept her at bay. And then I noticed how her sides heaved, how labored her breathing was. I reached for the tremor in my bones and felt only a faint hum.

Thrana?

Her gaze slid briefly to mine. *I'm sorry, Lin. I've been holding it off. I thought I could—*

She collapsed.

"Thrana!" I screamed. Desperate, I sheathed my sword and pulled out my engraving tool and a shard of Thrana's bone, dashing toward Ragan, hoping to hold him off. I'd learned from Phalue but I couldn't hold my own against him in a fight of blades, and I think we both knew it. I held up the shard as though it were a fire I could wave in the face of a predator.

He merely laughed, swinging the blade about and tightening his grip. "Really, Lin? How long until I get Nisong to remove whatever new command you press into me?"

"I won't let you hurt her."

Ragan gave a little shrug. "That's not really up to you."

The guards around Ragan closed in. I could see him watching them out of the corner of his eye. Before I could shout a warning, he lashed out. Another guard down. He moved through them as though he were merely weaving through and cutting stalks of bamboo. They swayed to avoid him, unsuccessfully.

Blood mingled with the water, seeping into the ground.

Behind me, one of my guards was fighting off the last of Ragan's followers. I knelt at Thrana's side. She was alive, her heartbeat steady and strong beneath my hand. Another hibernation cycle.

A breeze brushed my cheek as Huan rushed past me, her ossalen still curled about her neck. I reached out to stop her, but my fingers grasped only the empty air left in her wake. Ragan was too quick, too skilled. We had to coordinate our attacks.

But I remembered how I'd felt when my magic had first manifested. I'd leapt from the palace walls to the rooftops of Imperial City without a second thought. It made a person feel they could do anything.

Ragan had that power too. She had to know that.

He parried her headlong attack and she stepped in to keep from overbalancing, too close. With a vicious grin, Ragan brought the heel of his boot down on her toes. I felt a slight tremor as he pushed his magic through her foot and into the surrounding ground, shattering her bones.

Huan groaned, putting all her weight on her other foot, trying to jump out of reach.

. He reached out for her neck and caught her.

Before I could even gasp, he'd wrenched the white-bladed sword across Huan's throat. As he let her fall to the ground, Huan caught my gaze, her eyes wide and startled. I watched her die as her ossalen did, her mouth open in surprise, the light in her gaze winking out. She fell like a puppet whose strings had been cut. Her ossalen shrieked, the cry piercing both my ears and my heart.

Ragan didn't pivot to face the rest of the guards; he seized the little beast and snapped its neck. Then he fell to his knees, using the sword to awkwardly gut the ossalen. Fingers trembling, he pulled at the bones inside. A look of triumph passed over his face as he pulled some of the ribs free, his hands red with blood. But then his expression turned quickly to consternation. Something was happening to the bones he'd collected. Were they . . . melting? He let them fall to the ground. And then a strange look came over his face, a dawning comprehension. He lifted his sword, gazing upon it as though seeing it for the first time.

Ragan whirled in the same movement that he rose to his feet, blocking a guard's attack.

"Ragan!" I called to him. "You are outnumbered."

He only smirked at me before turning his attention to Iloh. "Think carefully, Iloh. If you do this," he said, "if you do not keep your end of the bargain, I will kill you and everyone on this island. Every last one."

Iloh scoffed. "You're speaking nonsense. You're just a child playing at being a god."

Lozhi burst from the forest. Ragan pulled himself aboard the beast and they leapt over the guards as they tried to surround him. He went straight for the mouth of the mines and disappeared inside.

The guards hovered outside, unsure of what to do. "There's no need," Iloh said. There's only one way out."

I should have said something, should have told them to pursue. But I was transfixed by Huan and her dead ossalen, its body opened upon the paving stones.

"Eminence?" one of my guards asked as I approached Huan's body. "Are you well?"

How could I ever be well again? Another Captain of my Imperial Guard, gone. I crouched by her body, closing her eyes which were still wide with shock. She'd only just begun to explore her powers, had only just started to teach her ossalen to speak. And now they were both dead. It was such a waste – in a way I couldn't quite explain.

My gaze fell on the bones Ragan had pulled from the dead ossalen's body. Had he wanted more shards? I reached for the ribs. They didn't feel like bone beneath my fingers. They were brittle, hard. When I rolled them in my palm, they crumbled, leaving a powdery white substance on my fingertips.

32

Lin

Riya Island

Slowly, we gathered our dead, and Iloh sent someone back to the city for wagons – for the bodies and for Thrana. The rest of the guards waited by the entrance to the mines, waiting for Ragan to emerge.

Thrana was alive, but it would take everyone here to move her onto that wagon. I needed to get back to Imperial, to ready myself for the war to come. Iloh had the temerity to offer me the oilskin cloak from one of his guards, but I waved him off. I had no magic; I could not pull the moisture from my body as I would have before. Still, I felt accepting any kindness from the man would be an indignity. All I wanted was for this to be over, for us to go our separate ways.

I wished I could have killed him.

It might have disappointed Thrana, but she was caught in a hibernation cycle. She didn't even have to know. I sighed, letting my gaze slide from his departing back, letting my hand loosen on the hilt of my sword.

I'd have to name a new Captain of my Imperial Guard – but it could wait until we'd burned Huan's body with her ossalen's. It could wait until we'd returned to Imperial.

I heard a shout from the road and a few wagons emerged from the forest, pulled by oxen. One was larger than the rest – just big enough to carry Thrana. I stood and went to help them with the bodies. I couldn't help with Thrana – without my magic I wasn't strong enough – but I could do this.

Iloh, of course, stood off to the side, overseeing the work even as I glared at him. He wasn't the type to dirty his own hands.

I rubbed my fingers together again for what felt like the thousandth time, caught by the feel of the disintegrating bone between my fingertips. I'd spent so much time and mental energy trying to find out what the swords did, trying to find a way around using witstone, trying to defeat Dione – I hadn't spent any time delving into the mystery of the ossalen. I leaned down and lifted the feet of one of the guards' bodies, helping a man heft it onto the cart.

Next to me, several men hefted Thrana onto another cart using a cloth sling, their muscles straining, grunting as they finally managed to lift her high enough. She didn't seem to notice the disruption at all, her head limp, her eyes closed, her breathing steady.

There was something familiar about that powdery feel.

I wasn't sure what had caused Huan's ossalen's bones to become brittle like that – was it her death, or her ossalen's death? If someone killed me, what would happen to the shards in her shed horns? She'd given me her shards to use willingly, and perhaps that had something to do with it.

I moved back from the cart, all the bodies loaded now, and touched my thumb to my forefinger, a faint trace of white still there. Ragan hadn't emerged from the mines yet. How long did he intend to stay down there, hiding? Why hadn't he run off in some other direction?

And then a memory surfaced – my own. Me, in my father's storeroom at the palace, watching a spy construct watch me as I swiped a piece of witstone. The feel of it in my hand – cold, heavy, *powdery and white.*

I staggered to the side of Thrana's wagon, suddenly dizzy, the air like knives in my lungs. Reaching out, I put a hand on her thick fur, parted it to the skin. I was only half-aware of what I was doing, knowing instinctively that the answers were here, in front of me, but unsure of how I knew it. She was warm to the touch – she'd be growing again, changing. The fine dander that always seemed to cling to her skin, the faint earthy smell were still there, but now, when I peered closer, I thought I saw a sheen of green.

How big would she grow? It was a question I'd asked myself over and over. And now I knew. She'd grow large – immeasurably so.

"By all the Alanga, old and new," I whispered. I knew where Dione's ossalen was now. I knew what had happened to the ossalen of all the old Alanga. They were still *here*. Beneath our very noses.

Beneath our feet.

And Ragan was carrying a sword that hurt Alanga and ossalen both, that did not allow them to heal from their wounds. He'd gone into the mineshaft *on purpose*. I swept my gaze frantically across the men and women around me, all of them unaware that our doom was coming. "Iloh!" I shouted his name. "Iloh!"

"I'm right here."

I whirled to find him standing behind me, arms crossed, looking faintly annoyed. He had no right to any emotion other than gratitude that I'd spared his life. But I didn't have time or room for spiteful feelings. Not now.

"We need to send all our guards into that mineshaft right now. We need to find Ragan before it's too late. He—" I stopped, my tongue frozen. How could I even explain my cascading reasoning? I didn't have the time or patience to explain that our islands migrated not because they were on some sort of scaffolding, but because that scaffolding was bones. Because our islands were alive. "He knows how to sink islands. Too much mining will do that, yes, but the sword he has – it's a weapon that kills. It kills islands."

Iloh held up his hands, his eyes as narrowed as though he were a cat about to engage in a fight. "Calm down. What are you trying to say?"

I bristled. He did *not* just tell me to calm down, not when all the lives of his citizens were at risk. "He can do it. What he threatened. He can sink Riya – that's all you need to know right now. If he gets deep enough into that mineshaft, he'll take out this entire island. We need to send our guards to stop him." I felt the hilt of the sword at my side. "*I* need to stop him. Send someone to your palace. Get everyone ready to evacuate. Now."

His face paled a little, but he tilted his head. "Are you *sure*?"

"You and I do not like each other, but have you *ever* known me to spout madness? Have at least that much respect for me."

We stared at one another, his gaze searching mine. Nearby, one of my guards had stopped to listen to our conversation, hovering anxiously at my shoulder.

Iloh finally nodded and turned to his guards, some of whom had been getting ready to follow the wagons back to the city. The rest were still waiting at the cave entrance, postures relaxed. "All of you! We need to follow Ragan into the mines. Bring him out – dead or alive, it doesn't matter to me."

They moved to obey and I nodded to my closest guard. "Us too." We made for the cave entrance, Iloh hanging behind us.

My heartbeat thudded in my ears. I had no magic. Thrana was asleep on the wagon. I had no idea which direction Ragan had gone, which turns they'd taken.

But we had to try.

And then the ground below my feet shook. At first, I wasn't sure if I'd felt anything at all or if my imagination was only playing tricks on me. The second shake hit just as I reached the mine entrance – a small one, but more noticeable. One of the Imperial Guards in front of me put a hand to the wall to steady herself.

Jovis had told me a little of what had happened on Deerhead. The way the shakes had been small at first and then had magnified. The way the harbor had sunk, first a little, and then more, until the entire island was sinking. The way the buildings had collapsed, people still inside. The way he sometimes thought about the people who must have been alive and trapped as the Endless Sea rose higher and higher, cutting off breath and then life.

The fear that spread through my chest was dizzying, making every sensation too sharp. I reached back, seizing Iloh's shoulder, the feel of the mud-spattered cloth beneath my fingers a thing I knew I would remember until I died. The pattern burned into my eyes and into my memories as the terrible realization struck. "It's too late."

Before he could direct his guards, I raised my voice.

I was Lin. I was the Emperor. This was a moment of extreme crisis and I could not shrink away no matter how much I wished to. "Riya will sink," I called out to them. "Leave the bodies. Take the oxen back to the city. Warn the people to evacuate. My guards will come with me. We take Thrana back to the ship. Now."

"Wait." Iloh grabbed my wrist before I could let him go. "What about me?"

"Go with your guards. Find a ship. Live, if you can." All

the careful calculus I'd done, sparing Iloh's life – none of it mattered now. We were animals fleeing a burning building. I ran to the wagon with Thrana, my guards following, leaving Iloh behind.

How long before the next quake? How long until one struck that would not stop until the island slipped into the Endless Sea? If I'd had my power, if Thrana had been awake, I might have taken the risk, I might have waited for Ragan and Nisong to emerge so I could confront them. But in my state, they'd cut me down. Better to live.

"Do any of you know how to drive oxen?" Two of my guards raised their hands. I pointed to one of them. "Then drive. The rest of you, into the wagon."

So many fewer than I'd started out with. Only three. The wagon sagged beneath our combined weight, creaking forward as my guard lifted the reins. I could tell the oxen were spooked, their eyes wide and rolling. Around us, people moved in a panic, tossing bodies off the wagons or unhitching the oxen to ride them back into the city.

We were too far inland, too far from shore.

"Eminence," one of my guards said, "we should leave her. There's not enough time and we'd go faster."

My gaze snapped to his. "I am *not* leaving her. I will never leave her. You're welcome to abandon me and your oaths, but I will die before I leave Thrana to drown."

They all fell silent after that, the sound of the wheels rattling over the road filling the air. No birds sang. No animals called. It was as though the forest around us was holding its breath, waiting to see what would happen next.

We were nearly back to the city when the next quake struck. It was a shuddering movement, the shiver of a dying animal trying to still draw breath. The trembling stopped, but my guards all looked at one another over Thrana's prone body, their eyes wide, sweat beading on their foreheads.

We've been mining the bones of your fellows, I thought, though I knew Thrana wouldn't answer. *What have we done? What have my* ancestors *done?* How hadn't I made the connection before – the white smoke Thrana blew and the white smoke that rose from burning witstone?

And the cloudtrees, their taproots finding the chalky core of the islands' bones, drawing that power into their bark and berries. The way my bones trembled when I held my Alanga powers, when I drew on that magic.

These weren't separate types of magic.

They were all bone magic.

Ylan must have realized it. All the discussions he'd had with Dione, all their arguments. Had he ever had an intention behind befriending Dione beyond duplicity and betrayal? He'd found out how to make bone shard magic work for those who were not Alanga. How proud he must have been, how hopeful for a better and brighter future ...

We finally reached the edge of the city. The other guards had gotten there before us and people flooded into the streets, belongings stuffed beneath arms and into handcarts, children carried or pulled by the wrists. Shouting, screaming, sobbing – a cacophony of fear and misery. They crowded the ox cart, traffic to the harbor slowing to a standstill.

We weren't going to make it.

33

Jovis

Riya Island

I wasn't sure how long we ran for or how far. When Mephi finally slowed, I opened my eyes to see the greenery of the forest, the leaves still beaded with moisture from the last rain. The wind blew a salty breeze into my face; we were somewhere near shore, but from the quiet – not near civilization.

I'd left Lin to deal with Ragan and Nisong and Iloh alone. A part of me knew she didn't need me. She'd lived two years without me. She had her guards. She had Thrana. But the rest of me yearned to be at her side, to be telling her all the things I'd kept stored up for two years, to apologize for not somehow being stronger or smarter. Lin would have found a way out from Kaphra's grasp sooner. She wouldn't have stopped trying.

She wouldn't have given up.

I slid from Mephi's back and hiked toward the ridge line, where the trees grew thin. Branches and brambles caught at my boots, but I kicked past them. Mephi's soft footsteps followed behind me. The forest opened up, brush changing to grass.

I felt like I could breathe again with the Endless Sea in sight. I'd grown up on Anau, had lived on Imperial, but the Endless Sea was the place I felt most comfortable. The ridge I stood on overlooked a small fishing village, and the sight of the ships in the harbor and at sea filled me with a buoyant feeling, one that diminished the shame. I still had the shards inside me, but I was away from Kaphra and Philine and Nisong – anyone who might command me.

There were plans to be made, thinking to be done on how to find my way back to Lin, but for now, I leaned against a tree, took in the sight of the light breaking through the cloud cover and glittering against the waves. Birds dipped low over the water, searching for food. People in the village below mended nets or sails on the shore, or gutted fish by their houses and fed the offal to cats and dogs.

It was like seeing the past I'd come from, and I yearned sometimes to still return to – even as I knew I would chafe at the boundaries. I touched the pouch at my side. I never had much money, just enough for me to feel some independence, but never enough that Kaphra thought I had too much. The first step was to regroup and then to head back to the mines. I'd have to find a sideways way to get to her, all the while figuring out how I might get around the commands within me.

If she'd survived the encounter with Ragan.

No, that was guilt and shame talking. She was still alive. I'd disrupted the ambush – that had to be enough. Still, I had to go back. I did my best to catch my breath, to quell the fear that made my fingers shake.

The earth below me trembled.

It was a small quake, nothing that most people would concern themselves with. Indeed, the people down in the village only glanced down at the ground for a moment before continuing their work. A few didn't seem to register it at all.

But ever since Deerhead, even the slightest tremor set me on edge, made me sweat as though I were beneath that dry-season sun again, the earth sinking beneath my feet as dust filled my nostrils. Mephi appeared at my side, his shoulder nudging mine. "Bad memories?"

I reached up to scratch his ear and forced a smile past the fear. "Good ones too." I'd found Mephi at the sinking of Deerhead – the only decent thing to come of such a vast tragedy. "We need to go back. I can't just keep running, Mephi."

He scratched his other ear, one eye closing. "You could."

"She might still be in trouble. She might need my help." I pulled myself onto Mephi's back.

He didn't move.

"Mephi, we have to *go*."

"Jovis," he said, his voice slow and patient, "you must know that I do not want you to die. That I do not want you to be imprisoned again. That *I* do not want to be imprisoned again. We are finally together again and I don't want that to change."

I leaned into his neck and sighed, my fingers curling into his fur. "I know. I'll always do my best to protect you. But I made that promise to her too." I'd made that promise to everyone once, when I hadn't really known what it meant. I'd taken the oath to be a servant to the people, and Lin had slipped the medallion over my neck, and I hadn't been sure then whether it was an honor or a burden.

Both.

"Lin is capable." His feet remained planted.

"And I need her to take the shards out of me. From a practical standpoint, we need to go back."

His ears flicked back and then flattened. "Always using words, Jovis. Always using them to make terrible sense." His ears flicked up. "We could keep going. We could go away and never see

Kaphra or Nisong or Ragan again. We would be safe. We would be together." His wistful words wedged a crack in my heart, widening it to a painful degree.

"You told me I was the one who helped."

He shook his head and then sighed. "It was easier then. It just keeps getting harder and I don't know if I'm as strong as you."

"I'm not strong. But I need to do this. Help me."

"Ah, fine. We will try." He bounded forward. The forest whipped by us.

And then, when I could see the outline of mountains above the treeline, I heard a rumble. *Mephi, is that . . .?*

Another quake, yes. He redoubled his speed and I pressed close to his neck.

Two in so close a time. One might be an aftershock to the other. I'd even heard of three quakes taking place in one day. But that was a rarity. Something had gone wrong, terribly wrong, and I'd not been there to stop it.

We burst into the clearing where the mine was, finding it empty of everything except a few scattered bodies. Lin was gone. Ragan and Nisong and Iloh, gone. A quick scan told me that none of the scattered bodies were Lin's. They'd left in a hurry — so quickly that no one had taken any care with the bodies.

An eerie stillness filled the air. No birds sang; no squirrels chattered; no monkeys called to one another across treetops.

"The island—"

I didn't need to say anything else. Riya was large, but that hadn't saved Deerhead. Lin would have fled toward the city and the docks, where she had a ship.

Mephi's sides were heaving, but he turned back the way we'd come. "We have to get to the Endless Sea and on a ship. Now. The fishing village is closer than the city."

I knew he was right, but I was back where I started: leaving

Lin to her fate as I did my best to survive. I railed against it even
as I nodded and turned my face to the trees, my heart thudding
painfully in my chest. We were back to the cliff overlooking the
village in moments. Just as we started down the path leading
from the ridge line, another quake struck.

I counted in my head, the way I'd done on Deerhead, as Mephi
picked his way down the path, stones and dirt trembling beneath
his feet. I passed a count of ten and still the quake continued. Had
Ragan done something? Had Iloh? Either way Riya, one of the
jewels of the Empire, was doomed.

There was no way for me to comprehend the vastness of this
disaster; instead, I focused on what was immediately in front of me.
The village, the people there, their boats. Some had already gone to
the shoreline at the second quake, pushing off from shore and doing
their best to put distance between them and the island. I arrived to
shouts and crowded streets as people rushed from their homes with
the belongings they thought they could not live without.

A few people glanced at Mephi, but most didn't stare – not
when they had larger things to worry about. Animals had begun
to emerge from the forest – boars and rodents and even a jaguar.
They all made for the ocean.

We followed them, just another two animals in the crowd.
The air smelled of sweat and yesterday's rain. It was a choking
scent, one that left me feeling like I never quite drew enough
breath. We were halfway to the water when the strength of the
quake redoubled, the beach dipping partway into the Endless
Sea. Screams erupted around us. A creak and a groan and two
buildings began to collapse.

Mephi wove his way through the crowd, finding gaps where
I thought there were none. The beach sand jittered beneath us,
his feet sinking deeper as he struggled toward the Endless Sea. A
few more labored steps and we were on the wet, packed sand, the

Endless Sea stretched out before us. Men, women and children crowded onto boats, shouting threats and pleas at one another – there would not be enough space.

Can we swim? I asked Mephi.

His ears were flat against his head. *We may have to. There aren't enough boats and everyone is panicking. I don't know if we can get far enough away. Jovis, there are so many people . . .*

The voice in my head was thick with despair. *I know*, I told him, doing my best to put what comfort into the words I could. Once, I'd been content with saving just one. Now, with the power of an Alanga in my veins and the wrongs I'd done as Kaphra's slave – I wished I could save them all. Mephi leapt ahead of a herd of fleeing antelope and into the churning sea. I held my breath, tucked my hands into the depths of his fur and leaned into him as he dove beneath the surf.

For a moment, I thought I'd lose my grip on him. There was something strange and still about the world beneath the surface of the water. The shouts and screams became muted, water swirling in my ears, the tremor of the island a thing I could only feel vaguely. Mephi surged upward again and my body slammed into his as we broke the surface.

Noise returned at once, as did the smells of dust and smoke. Seawater clung to my clothes, dragging at the tattered edges of my sleeves. In the clear waters around me, I could see fish darting every which way, searching for cover as their home was filled inexplicably with the churning limbs of people and animals. I urged Mephi forward, flailing at the water as though that might help us go faster. The day was cooler, the clouds heavier, yet that day on Deerhead filled my mind.

I was going to die. We were all going to die. Maybe I was supposed to die that day on Deerhead and this was the world's way of correcting matters.

Breathe, Jovis.

Mephi's words jolted me back to myself, to my tight throat, my tight-fisted hands clutched around his fur, the buzzing in my mind as my vision darkened at the edges. I'd stopped breathing – I'd stopped being *able* to breathe, my lungs constricted with fear.

I tried to pull in a deep breath, felt it wheeze past my chest.

Mephi paddled steadily away with powerful strokes even as I heard the earth *crack* behind us, even as screams and sobs filled the air, blending together into one helpless wail. Ships surged past us, parting the water and throwing a wake over us. Something rumbled, a vast trembling I could feel in my teeth.

Again.

This time the breath came easier; my vision began to clarify as the terrifying images from Deerhead faded. I was here now, and I would do what I'd always done: I'd make the best of things. I settled onto Mephi's back, trying to remember the things Emahla had once taught me about swimming. Make my body an arrow, stop flailing, decrease the surface area the water could resist. My staff shifted awkwardly against my ear as I did my best to make us faster. Mephi did the bulk of the work, his webbed paws pulling us through the water, his tail steadily swishing behind us.

But I was slowing us down.

Mephi, we won't make it, I said to him in my mind. *At least, not together.*

His ears flattened against his head and he paddled harder. I could feel his heart beneath the hand I had curled around his neck, beating quickly, his chest heaving as he breathed.

You have to leave me, I told him. I'd seen him keep pace with the ship before, diving in and out of the water, graceful as the sea serpents he'd befriended.

Mephi's voice swept through my mind, steady and certain as

my father steering a ship through stormy waters. *I will* never *leave you.*

I wasn't sure whether to weep with relief or frustration. We'd both drown if he didn't. I knew that if I let go, he'd grasp me in his claws or his mouth and we'd be even slower. I'd die more peacefully knowing he'd make it out alive.

I risked a glance back and saw that one of Riya's mountains had collapsed, dust rising into the air, a brown plume against the blue-gray clouds.

"Hey! Hey, you need help?"

It took me a moment to register the voice. I could barely hear her above the din, but that wasn't what startled me. She didn't speak in Empirean, but in Poyer — a language I'd not heard in a long time. I swiveled my head to see a woman on a fishing boat nearby, her hand cupped by her mouth. Black, curling hair, woven with gray, whipped in the wind. She repeated herself.

I pulled from the depths of my memories — all those times spent playing cards at the drinking hall with my father's Poyer friends. I'd never spoken it as well as my brother Onyu had. "Yes. Please!" I called back. The words felt rusty on my tongue, my pronunciation clumsy.

"I can't take your mount." She beckoned to me. Mephi swam for the boat

"That is fine. He is better — faster — without me." I swam free of Mephi as I got close to her ship and she tossed me a rope before going back to her sails. I dragged myself aboard, careful to pull the rope up after me. We were clear of the cove and into the open ocean now, wind making the waves choppy. Only some animals had made it out this far, and other ships, overflowing with people. When I looked back to the island, I could see crowds gathered on the shore, some taking their chances by trying to swim for it. I closed my eyes briefly, the enormity of it overwhelming me.

There would be so many — whole families. Grandparents who could not walk without a cane. Children just learning to run. Babies still at the breast. I couldn't comprehend it.

Mephi dove as soon as he saw me aboard, flowing through the water as though he were born to it. I sagged with a small modicum of relief — we had a chance.

"Vashno," the woman called to me.

I blinked, not understanding. "I'm sorry, my Poyer—"

"That's my name," she cut in. "Do you sail?"

I took her meaning easily enough. She was much younger than my father, but there was something familiar in her mannerisms — the bluntness, the few words, the underlying kindness. I pushed myself to my feet and went to help with the sails. We had a favorable wind carrying us away from the island. I pitied those on other parts of Riya, who might not be so fortunate.

I couldn't stop the island from sinking, but the feel of the ropes in my hands, the steady, mindless work — this I could do. I could suddenly fill my lungs again, the tightness in my throat not gone but easing.

The water juddered as Riya slipped lower into the sea, the village I'd just left disappearing, the crumbling buildings vanishing beneath the water's surface. I caught a brief flash of intense grief across Vashno's face, her hands pausing a moment before continuing her work. She was watching her world upend. I knew the feeling, though Deerhead had not been my home. When you watched an entire island be destroyed, dry land no longer felt safe. It was an awareness I now carried even though I tried to forget.

Another mountain collapsed, Riya sinking faster now. The only slim hope I had out of this situation was that Ragan and Nisong were still there, going down with the island.

I cast my gaze to ships around me. There were many in front

of us of all sizes, launched with haste from various harbors. In the distance, I thought I saw the Imperial flag and hoped it was Lin's ship. But when I looked toward Riya, there were even more ships behind.

I felt a tremor in my bones, and this time, it was not the sinking island that caused it. Magic filled me, sharpening my awareness of the Endless Sea around me. So much water, just waiting for me to command it. I wasn't sure how much I could do to help. I wasn't the person I once was, bold and brash as you please, a lanky young man telling a group of Ioph Carn to back down lest I hurt them. I was older, and worn, and broken in places I'd thought I would always be whole.

But I could try.

"Can you handle this alone a moment?" I called in broken Poyer to Vashno. "There's something I need to do."

I didn't wait for her response. I plunged my awareness into the water around me. I had the brief impression of Mephi, gliding through the water – a bright, joyful presence – and then I was gathering the water from deeper down, feeling the strange presence of larger animals I did not know, boulders in the flow of a river.

I'd never been as skilled with water as Lin or even Ragan, so it took me an enormous effort to pull in the amount I needed, to grasp it with my will. And then I pushed it. It was like putting my back to a mountain and expecting it to move.

I could feel the strain of it on my mind, my bones trembling. I could feel it in my jaw, in my skull. My eyes, my skin began to hurt. I had the brief imagery of my bones bursting from my body, rendering me into a puddle of bony shards and bits of flesh.

But then, ever so slowly, I felt the water start to shift. I pushed it with all my might toward the island, below all those ships that were struggling to make it to the open ocean. I could feel droplets of it, streams of it, flowing away from my grasp. Sweat beaded on my forehead, my heightened awareness making each drop almost painful, splitting my focus.

Before I could lose my grasp entirely, I lifted the water into an enormous wave at the shoreline, pulling it toward me. It carried the ships with it, rushing them away from Riya.

I collapsed onto the deck, letting go. My bones no longer trembled but my limbs did, my fingers did, my lips did. Dimly, I heard startled shouts from around me.

Jovis? Jovis! Can you still hear me? I felt it — you did too much. You —

I rolled onto my back, Mephi's voice fading from my mind as I gazed up at the sky. The boat rocked as the wave hit it, as another ship knocked against ours. Time ceased to have meaning as I did my best to breathe, to recover. I tried, once, to roll onto my knees but fell back. The chaos of the world around me faded to something distant — a dream of another life. More rumbling, more screaming, the splash of waves against the wooden hull of the boat. I couldn't move, wrung out as an old wash-rag.

I wasn't sure how much time passed before I saw Vashno's worried face above mine. Her brows drew together, forming a deep crease on her forehead. "Friend, are you well?" She put a hand out to help me up, which I tried to grasp but failed.

"Did we make it?" I could feel the presence of Mephi in my mind — he was there, next to the ship. I turned my head toward the island and only saw the rail of the fishing boat. I looked back to Vashno and realized I'd spoken Empirean. I gasped, trying to get enough air before I tried again in Poyer.

She pressed her lips together. "Yes. Many did not." She reached out to me and, this time, I managed to grasp her hand. "The wave. You?"

I managed only a nod. She looked out over the Endless Sea,

toward where Riya must have once been. Now there was only a swirling, churning darkness as far as the eye could see. "I had friends on Riya. Family. Ancient Ones protect them."

A shadow passed over us. Vashno turned before I could, her breath drawing in sharply. When I managed to look, I could see why. A ship loomed over our small fishing boat, dropping ropes onto our deck. I knew that ship. I knew every seam on those boards.

A man leaned over the rail, a crooked grin on his face. "Well, don't I have heaven's own luck."

Kaphra.

34

Lin

Riya Island

There had to be a way out, a way off the island. But we had to get to the docks, and they were below us. Every side street I saw was just as packed with people who thought they might avoid the crush of the main street.

If it were just me . . . But Thrana was in the cart and there was no way I was leaving her behind. One of my guards touched my elbow. "We'll try to make a path through," he said. He gestured to the other one and the two of them pushed through the crowd, shouting things that were unintelligible over the noise.

I had no magic, and by the way my guards were forced to put their shoulders into the work, my status wasn't doing much either. We were all rats on a sinking ship, and among rats, there are no Emperors. I'd never before – not even when facing my father – felt so low, so powerless, so bereft of control. Slowly, we began to push forward and through the crowded streets, the wagon wheels rattling against the cobblestones.

All I could think of as I retreated into the confines of the covered wagon, as I placed a hand on Thrana's warm neck, was escaping. Living. Surviving. I squeezed my eyes shut, feeling my quickened heartbeat and breathing, but unable to hear them. I could feel a vibration in my jaw – though I was unsure if it was from the swell of the people around us, the rattle of the wagon, or a tremor from deep below. All I wanted was to go back in time, to stop Ragan from entering the mine.

This was my fault. I should have figured all of this out sooner. I'd been so focused on the swords, on the witstone, on Iloh, that I'd forgotten to put together the pieces that had been in front of me all along. Thrana's continual growth and the way I'd found her in the cavern pool, Dione's relentless pursuit of the swords and his lack of visible ossalen, the sinking of the islands – it all pointed to the fact that the ossalen *were* the islands, and that they could be killed. Whether that be through excessive mining of their bones or crawling into their depths and slaying them deliberately.

And Ragan – he was willing to kill the population of an entire island just to have his way. I'd failed not just the people of Riya, but all the people of the Empire. I'd brought ruin upon Numeen and his family and now I'd brought it upon so many more. If there were a cave I could crawl into, a place I could hide from the madness around me, I would have. I would have gone down with the island, the cool water of the Endless Sea finally soothing the heat of my shame.

I opened my eyes, letting that feeling of failure pass over and through me. If I didn't stop Ragan, who would? Dione? He was working with him. Jovis? I didn't know his loyalties or why he'd never come back. I needed to live through this or more islands would sink. More people would die.

The wagon had stalled, our progress halted as people pressed in from all sides. This time, when I felt the tremor, I knew it wouldn't stop, not until the island had sunk.

There was only one thing I could do, Thrana forgive me.

I pulled myself up next to the driver. The oxen were rolling their eyes, one bellowing as people pressed against his flanks. I reached out and seized the shoulder of the guard who had directed the other to make a path. We were all penned in so close that I could feel the heat of many bodies brush against my cheeks, the smells of sweat mingling with the faint fresh air from the harbor. We were near.

"Draw your swords," I told him.

He startled, his wide-eyed gaze meeting mine. "And do what?"

I steeled myself. "Whatever you need to. Get us to the docks."

His jaw took on a grim set as he nodded and reached for the hilt of his sword. I retreated into the confines of the wagon, too cowardly to face what was about to happen, sickness swirling in my stomach. I'd avoided looking at the people around us – the ones who might not make it. The ones we'd be pushing past so *we* might make it.

People began to scream. I couldn't be sure if it was my guards' work or just the shaking below us, rattling my teeth. The smell of vomit wafted through the canvas cover of the wagon.

"It's sinking!" someone screamed. The cry was taken up by others, turning into one endless wail. I hoped they were wrong. We were moving forward now. Any sinking would bring the water level up the gently sloping street – and while I and my guards could swim, Thrana could not. The wagon might float, but I imagined all the people around us, clawing for purchase... The sound of the wheels changed abruptly, a measure of the rattling dying down.

We'd made it to the docks.

I dared to look out the front of the wagon again. People were climbing onto ships; many were already out into the harbor. The harbor itself was crowded with bodies, people trying to swim from the island in one last desperate attempt to escape.

The guard I'd ordered to get us to the docks appeared in front of me, his sword in hand. I tried not to focus on the blood that stained the blade. "We're here, Eminence. Your ship."

The sailors aboard were fending off locals with knives and blades.

My guards moved quickly, unhooking the oxen, pulling the cart up the sagging gangplank and onto the ship. I jumped from it and onto the deck as soon as we reached it, helping them pull the gangplank up behind us. With all my guards aboard, people were already leaping onto the retracting gangplank, trying to climb their way onto our ship. A woman held her child aloft. "Please, Eminence!"

We need an Emperor who cares about us.

Numeen's words filtered into my mind – from what felt like a lifetime ago. My heart felt as though it were being torn to pieces. I *did* care. But we were running out of time. We could take a few more passengers but there was no way to choose, no way to filter them that wouldn't take more time than we had.

"Bring the people on the gangplank aboard," I told my guards. I turned to the captain, his lips so pale that they blended into the rest of his face. "We leave. Now. We need to get as much distance as possible."

The water lurched, the boat rocking. The docks creaked and then shattered as the shoreline sank. Stones cracked, the grand buildings of Riya's capital city beginning to shudder and fall.

And then the people on the gangplank were aboard, the sails were filling. I barely heard the murmured thanks of the citizens we'd picked up, my mind focused half on the island and half on the bloody crane Numeen's daughter had once folded, below on my desk. I'd made a promise to myself, to the family I'd failed to protect from my father. I watched as the mountains of Riya cracked and crumbled, the screams of its citizens now distant voices on the wind.

I wasn't sure whether I'd broken it or not.

35

Jovis

Somewhere in the Endless Sea

I screamed in impotent protest as the Ioph Carn cut Vashno's
throat, as Kaphra issued command after command before
I could think of how to wiggle around them. I was climbing
the rope; I was on the deck of his ship; I was looking down at
Vashno's body, rocking gently on her fishing boat, blood spreading in a pool beneath her.

She'd helped me when she hadn't had to and I'd gotten her
killed. She should have let me drown. She should have let me be
sucked into the island's wake, my useless body swirling into the
depths of the Endless Sea. At least she'd still be alive.

"I should have known you'd find a way around the commands
eventually," Kaphra was saying, his voice smug with self-
satisfaction. "I thought I'd lost you, or that you'd gone down
with the island. I should have known you'd make it out."

I heaved out a breath, noting that the Ioph Carn around
Kaphra didn't seem to feel the same sense of victory. I caught
more than one set of hands trembling. I met Kaphra's gaze,

wishing I could cut a hole in him with it. "Riya just sank. An entire island and its people have drowned in the Endless Sea."

"And Riya had the largest witstone mine," Kaphra said. He gave a little shrug. "It's not my fault that it sank. Does it benefit the Ioph Carn? Yes. Does it benefit me? Also yes. So I won't say I'm glad but I won't pretend to be sad either."

He was standing so close to me. I wanted to wring his neck. Instead, I darted for the knife at his side, jerking it free of its sheath. For an instant, I caught the fear of death in his gaze. But then I was holding the knife up to my own throat. It was the first thing I thought to do.

He would make me into a weapon again. He would force me to kill people like Vashno, people whose only crime was helping people Kaphra didn't want to be helped. I couldn't let that happen. I'd had so many chances to end my life, to stop myself from being used in this way. But I'd wanted to live.

My sweat-slick fingers tightened on the hilt as the blade parted my skin, as I felt warm blood trickle down my neck. The wound healed almost as quickly as I'd created it. I should pull it quick, be done with it. Surely I couldn't heal fast enough to halt the massive loss of blood. Instead, I found myself frozen in much the way I'd been when I'd faced off against Nisong.

Kaphra held up a hand as if to forestall me, but then a commotion from behind him made him turn. Several of the Ioph Carn were gathered at the stern, pulling something over the rail.

I should do it. Now.

They hauled something large and furry and growling up in a net. Mephi.

My hand went slack. Kaphra, as though sensing my mental state, strode casually over to my ossalen, drew his white-bladed sword and held the point to Mephi's eye. "Drop the knife, Jovis."

I wasn't sure whether it was the command or the sword held

so close to Mephi that made me do it. I didn't even try to resist. One moment I was holding the knife to my throat, the next it was clattering on the deck. My chest felt hollow, as deep and dark as the Endless Sea.

"Take him below," Kaphra said to his men. "Throw him in the cell opposite her. Mephi stays with me. Jovis, you will stay inside that cell until I tell you otherwise. And if you don't —" He cocked his head to the side. "— Mephi dies."

Hands seized me and I let them take the staff from my back. I let them guide me below-deck to a small, dark hallway and two gated cells. It smelled of piss and hay and saltwater. A figure curled in the corner of the other cell, the light so dim I couldn't make them out. *Throw him in the cell opposite* her.

The two Ioph Carn guiding me opened the cell, deposited me inside and locked it behind me. One gave a lingering glance to the lump in the corner of the other cell. "Should we sneak her some more bread maybe?" he whispered to the other.

The other one beckoned him back down the hallway, brows drawn low. "The last one caught doing that was whipped. Come on. Best leave them be."

When their footsteps had faded, the lump in the corner looked up.

She was dirty, an empty socket where one eye should have been — the wound fresh and still weeping pus. The opposite ear was gone too, a filthy bandage atop it, woven into lank black hair.

It took me a moment to recognize her — I'd never seen her in such a state, nor with her hair down. Always to me she had been sleek, professional, nearly infallible. "Philine?" I said, just to be sure.

She gave a soft snort. "Ah, it's that bad, is it?"

"Well, no, I mean . . .other than the missing eye and the ear, you're nigh presentable." I kept my voice light. At the same time,

I was screaming inside. Trapped. And across from a cell with the only person in the Ioph Carn who'd shown me any kindness. I wanted to shake the bars, to demand to see Mephi.

I probed the edges of the command Kaphra had given to me. I could get around it. The whole ship felt like a cell to me. The whole world did – as long as these shards were inside me. But where would that get me? Mephi was still under Kaphra's sword, he had command of me and I . . . I was exhausted as a newborn lamb. I slid to the floor, finally admitting I could barely keep my feet beneath me.

"Sleep, Jovis," Philine said, her voice gentle. "Nothing will change before you wake."

Oddly enough, I believed her. I let my eyes close, exhaustion washing over me, my heartbeat finally slowing as I gave in.

I awoke to the gentle rocking of waves beneath me, panic spiking my heart for a moment until I remembered where I was and what had happened. The outpouring of so much power all at once must have drained me more than I'd realized. Because how else could I have slept knowing that Riya had sunk too? How had the screaming voices of the dying not kept me tossing and turning? And Mephi – he was still under Kaphra's care.

I pushed myself into a sitting position, wiping away the pieces of straw that had stuck to my face, my tongue stuck to the roof of my mouth. I licked my lips and tasted salt. My clothes were still damp and stiff with seawater and I shivered as I slowly came to.

A piece of steamed bread lay on a plate in front of me next to a cup of water. I downed both with alacrity. I hadn't even heard anyone descend below-deck. How long had I been out for?

"They say you made an enormous wave," Philine said from her cell. Her plate was already empty, sitting next to her. "They say you pushed hundreds of ships away from the sinking island and saved thousands of lives."

"And I got Vashno killed."

"Who?"

I wiped my mouth and then grimaced at the salt still sticking to my hand. "A Poyer woman who saved me from drowning."

Philine put out her two hands as though they were a scale, one hand lifted much higher than the other. She raised an eyebrow.

"I can't think of people that way," I spat. "She should have let me drown."

"What, so you could avoid saving all those people?"

"So I could avoid being Kaphra's dog again." I'd had the knife pressed to my throat. I'd almost done it. Why hadn't I?

She shook her head, her hair shadowing the half of her face with the missing eye. "There's nothing wrong in wanting to survive."

"Isn't there?" I drew my knees up, laid my elbows across them. "And what about you? Is that why you came back? Didn't work out so well for you."

"I knew there would be punishment," Philine said, her voice level. "But this is all that I know. This is all that I have."

"You could have learned to know something else."

Her one eye crinkled at the corner as she gave me a bitter smile. "Too old for that. And there are people here who rely on me."

I turned her words over in my head, trying to understand what kept her here among the Ioph Carn. I remembered the man who'd wanted to sneak her more extra bread. She had allies here. A family.

Yet Kaphra ruled over them all.

"I made my choices," she said, staring at the wall. "He'll let me out when he needs me again. And he'll need me again."

I rose to my feet, going to the gate, examining the lock. I tested the bars, letting the magic flow through my bones, enhancing my strength. They were rusted but they didn't budge. I ran my hands over the gate. There was only one flickering lamp down the hallway from us and it provided very little light. Still, I could feel the rough surfaces, the rust flaking against my palms.

"He'll be ready for you," Philine said as she watched me. "He already knows he may not be able to hold you. He'll have Mephi."

"So . . .what? I should just give up?" I felt the hinges. They were thick and cold and damp with seawater that had trickled down from above. When I rubbed my fingers together, I felt the grit of decaying metal. Philine might not have been able to escape, but I had gifts she did not.

"That's not what I said. But Dione's balls, Jovis, think this through before you rush off into danger again. Whatever happened at that monastery was the most ill-thought-out plan I have ever—"

I gave the door a strong, swift kick. The hinges gave way, the gate cracking open. Someone might have heard that. I wouldn't have much time. The metallic scent of rust filled the air. Philine coughed.

I strode out of my cell. I wished I could feel satisfied, but all I felt was a grim determination, guilt and anger. "I'm going to ask you another time," I said to Philine. "Come with me."

She looked at me as though she couldn't believe what she was hearing. "You could just leave me here. There's nothing stopping you from doing that."

"I could," I admitted. "But I won't. Not if you don't want me to."

She pressed her lips together but then nodded, pushing herself to her feet. "Get me out of here."

I kicked in the hinges on her gate and helped her out of her cell.

Two Ioph Carn came thundering down the steps from above. The same two men who'd brought me down here. For a moment they stood in the light of the lamp, swords held high. They should have attacked us, they should have tried to herd us back into our cells. Instead, they hesitated.

Philine stepped in front of me. "It's time," she said, a hand lifted. "Kaphra is no longer leader of the Ioph Carn. I am."

They looked to one another, one of them shrugged and then the other drew a dagger from his belt and pressed the hilt of it into Philine's hand. Her fingers closed around it and she cast a glance back at me. "Time for a little mutiny."

I hurried to catch up to her, feeling a little bit lost. "Could you have just . . .done that at any moment?"

Her one eye found mine. "No. I'm taking a risk. But one that needs to be taken." A hint of amusement – so small I would have missed it had I not known her – glinted in her gaze. "Taking a page out of your book, it seems. Can I count on you?"

I followed her as they climbed the stairs toward the deck. "If it weren't for you, I wouldn't have had a chance at escaping Kaphra at all."

She screwed up her face as though she'd tasted something terrible. "Don't do that pathetic emotional thing. Just . . .watch my back."

And then we were bursting above-deck, the two men leading the way, Philine and me right behind them. It took a moment for any reaction. Everyone just froze in their places: Kaphra speaking to a man and a woman at the stern, one Ioph Carn climbing down from the crow's nest, two tending the sails and three others playing cards beneath a tarp.

Philine sucked in a deep breath and bellowed with surprising strength. I was used to her being on the edges of my vision – a thing seen but not really seen. This was a different side of her. "Choose your side. Either you're with Kaphra, or you're with me. You all know me. You all know what I would be like as your leader." Her lip curled. "And you well know what Kaphra is like."

One of the men with us seized my staff from where it had been hung just above the stairs and tossed it to me. I took it and set the end firmly against the deck, a tremor rising in my bones. I wasn't sure if they could see it, but by the looks on their faces, the other Ioph Carn could sense something of it in my stance.

Each Ioph Carn eyed the others, wondering which way they'd turn. Everyone except Kaphra. He turned away from the Ioph Carn he'd been speaking to with the confidence of a man who knows no one would dare stab him in the back. "Mephi is chained below," he said, "with that sword to his throat. One word from me and he dies."

I tightened my grip on my staff. "That's assuming you can get word to him."

Everyone moved all at once.

I pulled water from the Endless Sea, keeping my spot by the stairs, my gaze darting from one end of the ship to the other. For a moment, all I could make out was chaos. I wasn't sure who was on what side. Blades clashed, some with certainty, some with hesitation. And then Philine strode toward Kaphra, and the fighting filtered into sides – those helping her and those trying to hinder her.

I sent a wave crashing toward Kaphra, hoping to throw him overboard. But my strength hadn't fully returned and it merely made him temporarily lose his footing. "Jovis," he called to me. "Stop Philine!"

My feet were moving toward her before I could fully register his words, my staff lifting. With effort, I stopped myself. Stop Philine from doing what? From making poor jokes at Kaphra's expense? That was easy. She didn't make jokes. Done.

Of the eight Ioph Carn, five had leapt to defend Kaphra, while the other three had joined Philine and the two jailers.

"Go!" Philine shouted to me. "Free Mephi and take care of the people below-deck. We can handle this."

I didn't hesitate. She'd asked me to watch her back, but the odds seemed even now, and with Kaphra shouting orders at me I might prove a liability. Below-deck, I wouldn't be able to hear him. I turned and dashed down the stairs.

A woman was coming up the stairs at the same time and I nearly ran into her. I lifted my staff, holding her off. "Kaphra or Philine?"

One eyebrow slightly raised before her face settled into understanding. "Philine."

I let her pass and continued down the stairs. Mephi would be in the hold with any cargo Kaphra was transporting.

Someone tried to ambush me as soon as I stepped into the empty-seeming mess hall. I caught the flash of a knife, a grim expression. I snapped up my staff, striking him in the side of the head, whirling it around to catch the back of him knee. He went down with a groan, unconscious. I could see the ladder down to the hold just beyond the mess hall. From above, footsteps creaked as the fighting wore on.

I might have trouble helping Philine with Kaphra there to command me, but Mephi would have no such difficulty. When I looked into the hole, all I could see was a damp, dimly lit space, crates obscuring my view. I slid down the ladder into the hold, keeping my staff in hand and landing light enough so I wouldn't be heard.

Chains clinked from somewhere in the corner, behind a stack of crates. *Jovis?*

Yes, but keep quiet. I'm coming to you.

The woman with me has the sword but she smells sweaty. I think she's scared. I've been talking to her. She has two younger sisters she sends money to.

I don't care if she rescues orphans on her downtime. She's not good; she's holding a sword to your throat.

She's not bad, either.

I crept closer. *Is anyone truly bad?*

Kaphra, maybe.

I snorted and then realized too late that while our conversation was in my head, my snort had not been. Footsteps scuffed and chains rattled. I turned the corner into a lamplit area lined with hay. Mephi lay in the hay, chains wrapped around his body – even his horns – and secured to rings on the floor and wall. He was bound so tightly he could barely move.

How dare Kaphra? How dare *anyone*? I stepped forward, heat flooding my chest, climbing up my throat. The woman standing next to Mephi held firm, the sword tight to his throat.

"Don't come any closer," she said and she sounded serious. Her skin was marked with pocks on one cheek, her jaw set in determination, her black hair short and away from her eyes. The hilts of throwing daggers were visible on her vest, the sheaths sewn into her clothing. She didn't look like a person who sent money to her sisters; she looked like one of the Ioph Carn – a hardened criminal.

This *is who you don't want me to kill?*

You'd understand if you got to know her, Mephi said defensively. *She didn't feel she had any choice except to join the Ioph Carn.*

As I'd once felt. And Mephi knew it too. I could still hear the sound of shouts from above and wondered if any others had joined the fray.

One of her hands tightened around one of Mephi's horns, pulling his big head to the side, exposing more of his throat. The white blade gleamed in the lamplight. "I've been instructed to kill him if you try to free him."

I opened the hand on my staff except for my thumb holding it against my palm, lifted my other hand next to it. "Was it Kaphra who told you to?"

She didn't answer me. Of course it was Kaphra. "The crew is mutinying," I said, aware that the fight was still happening and that I needed to move quickly. "You may not be under Kaphra's command for long."

The woman only clenched her jaw and held steady. I wanted to scream in frustration. We were *so close*. I'd escaped Kaphra once and now, after being captured by him again, I was on the brink of ensuring he was never a problem for me ever again. There would still be Ragan and Nisong, but *this* – this would be enough for now.

She blinked, and I caught the subtle tremble of her lower lip. "I have to do this. It's my job. It's all I have." A desperate tone marred her voice. A drop of crimson marked the light brown fur of Mephi's throat.

She is a person, Jovis. Not just a criminal. We are not just what one person sees us as.

I felt caught, my muscles tense, my awareness of the moisture and the air currents surrounding us sharp. I could use them before she could do anything. I could hurt her. *I can't risk you. I can't. I'm too afraid.* Too afraid to die. Too afraid to lose Mephi. These things had held me back from doing what I knew was right for so long.

When Mephi spoke again, it was with a hint of his old sass. *You can forgive yourself for being human, you know.*

And just like that, I felt the anger leaking out of me, flowing away. I'd been in this woman's place before, doing work for Kaphra. In those days I'd never killed, but I'd stolen, I'd lied, I'd smuggled. I'd told myself I was only hurting the Empire, but I'd hurt others too. I wasn't better than her.

I lowered my staff, holding my hands out and keeping my

voice soft. "It doesn't have to be. There is a you that hurts Mephi, that bleeds him out because Kaphra told you to. There is another you who hands over the sword, who takes up weapons against Kaphra and fights for better leadership. I know what it's like to be at this sort of crossroads. Which you do you want to be?" From far above, I could hear the muted sounds of fighting – shouts and clashing metal.

The tremble in her lip was no longer subtle. "No one has ever helped me. I've had to help myself."

I extended my free hand. "Well, I'm here now. And I'll fight at your side if you'll let me."

For a moment – one terrible moment – I thought both Mephi and I had judged her wrongly. That she'd cut his throat anyways. My heart lurched, my head going light.

And then her jaw firmed up, she nodded and turned the sword to me, hilt-first. I took it in my free hand, the feather lightness of it strange when contrasted with my staff. The three of us surged up the stairs together, first one set, and then another and into the light.

The fighting was in full swing by the time we arrived, the deck in chaos. Someone had climbed to the crow's nest and was firing arrows – I couldn't tell if they were on our side or on Kaphra's. I couldn't see Philine amid the chaos, though one side appeared to be faltering and I had a feeling it wasn't Kaphra's.

"Jovis!" Philine's voice rose above the din. I exchanged a quick glance with Mephi.

"Go. Help her. I'll keep Kaphra away so he can't command you. I'll be fine."

Reluctantly, I tore myself away. I had to remember that I had the white-bladed sword now, and Mephi was no longer the little creature who could curl around my neck. He was bigger and stronger than three tigers put together. There was a part of me that would always want and need to protect him, and another that took comfort in his newfound strength.

I ran to Philine's side, fastening the staff to my back in favor of the sword. I didn't trust the blade; it didn't feel quite right in my hands. But at least, if it were in my hands, I'd know exactly where it was. From behind me, something large splashed into the water.

Had Mephi leapt into the sea? No time to contemplate why. Philine was struggling to hold off two of Kaphra's lackeys, a man fallen at her side, clutching a bleeding wound beneath his ribs.

I stepped into the gap. Philine was skilled with her blades but I was quicker. The tremor filled my bones, along with a terrifying joy. When I glanced about and was finally able to take stock, our odds didn't look good. I was still weak, recovering, the magic in me a trickle compared to its regular flood. But I was fighting with friends at my back, and if I died here at least I would die free.

Lin. The small bit of regret tickled the back of my mind. Well. If she thought me a villain, she wasn't too far from wrong.

I blocked the blow of the woman on the left, countering quickly before she could recover and taking the opening to kick her kneecap hard. She went down, though I knew it wouldn't be for long. I could feel myself slowing already, the tremor in my bones fading to a low hum.

The man Philine had felled with a wound beneath his ribs rallied, surging back to his feet, one hand to the bloody cut, the other clutching his sword. He lunged for me and I found myself faltering, one of my legs giving way. A quick flash of triumph crossed his face.

And then I heard scrabbling claws against the sides of the ship. Many, many claws.

Everyone on the boat went silent and still for a moment, apprehension filling the air.

Sea serpents the size of large dogs burst onto the deck. It

was like unleashing a bagful of wet, angry cats into a crowded
market. They ran in every which direction, tearing apart
sacks and barrels in search of food. Mephi appeared back on
deck and began making an odd, keening sound, the pitch
constantly changing. All the serpents stopped to listen and,
just as the Ioph Carn gathered themselves, they attacked
Kaphra's lackeys.

I took the moment of distraction to slide away from my oppo-
nent's uplifted sword. A sea serpent lurched between us and
struck out, grasping his leg within its teeth. He screamed.

I tried to rise to my feet and found my legs wouldn't obey. In
front of me, Mephi was advancing, slow and easy, toward the
prow of the ship, the only betrayal of his mood the lashing of
his tail. "Kaphra," he said, and his voice rang out over the deck.
Everywhere I looked, sea serpents had pinned Ioph Carn. The
ones who'd sided with Philine were straightening, still wary,
their weapons drawn. Only Philine tucked her daggers back
into her belt.

Kaphra was the only one of his people still standing, back-
ing toward the prow as Mephi approached. "Jovis," he called
out weakly.

"Don't," Mephi said and the word sounded like a command.
He planted his feet as though he were a stone lion, defending his
palace. I'd never been so fiercely proud of him. The wind ruffled
his fur, showing the thin white scars left on him by Kaphra's
sword. I found my fingers tightening around the hilt, wanting
to visit the same pain on Kaphra.

Even from my place on the deck, even through the spots in
my vision, I could see the sheen of sweat on his brow, his once
slicked-back hair now uneven. The rings on his fingers glittered in the light as he clutched at the collar of his shirt. "You
can't . . . you won't kill me."

"I don't have to," Mephi responded. He let out one last, melancholy call.

The sea serpents left the Ioph Carn and swarmed toward the prow. They carried Kaphra with them into the ocean.

I tried to stand again and collapsed.

36

Jovis

Somewhere in the Endless Sea

I awoke to the feel of Mephi's stiff, bristly whiskers against my cheek, an ocean breeze ruffling my hair. "That's not as cute as it used to be," I managed, and then groaned. I felt like I'd just recovered from a long illness, my strength only slowly flooding back into my bones. I opened my eyes to a canvas tarp fluttering above me and frowned.

This wasn't where I'd fallen.

And then I noticed the thin mattress I'd been laid on, the blanket that had been draped over me. I scrambled to push myself up, my elbows trembling beneath my weight.

"You expended too much energy. Again," Mephi said. He placed a paw on my chest as though to push me back down.

I lifted it away from me, impatient, and knocked the spoon out of a bowl of broth which had been lying next to me. As I stared at it, fractured memories came back. Thin and salty liquid, trickling warmly down my throat as I swallowed. Someone had fed me. Someone had *had to* feed me.

How long had I been out?

Throwing aside the blanket, I ducked beneath the tarp and swayed to my feet. Mephi was there to catch me, his disapproving expression reminding me of nothing so much as my mother. I was still on the deck, the sun behind the clouds, the time of day indeterminate.

"He wanted to be near you."

I whirled to see Philine, sitting on a barrel and sharpening one of her daggers. She shrugged. "He doesn't fit well below-deck so we found a place above-deck for you." Her gaze flicked to mine, her missing eye still bandaged but the area around it looking much less angry. "Seven days," she said in answer to the question I'd not yet asked.

Seven days? I found myself clutching Mephi harder, and he let out a low, uncomfortable rumble. I let him go and did my best not to sway. "I need to get to Imperial. I need to—"

Philine held up a hand to forestall me. "We're a week south of where Riya used to be. And burning the last of the witstone Kaphra had aboard too."

I ran some quick calculations in my head. We wouldn't be anywhere close to Imperial. "You should have dropped me off somewhere closer."

Philine sighed. "Yes, I regularly launch unconscious men onto beaches, abandoning them to the seabirds. You weren't in any condition to be dropped off. Besides, I've things I need to do. Kaphra is gone, but some of his loyalists may try to take control of the Ioph Carn. I need to get back to his safe house at the southernmost point of Hirona's Net and to establish myself. Slow down and *think* for just a moment, Jovis. Haven't I done enough for you?"

I rubbed at my brow. She had. "Lin—"

She sighed again, louder, cutting me off. "Always chasing a

woman, aren't you? She's the Emperor. She's an Alanga. She has an army at her back. And you think that she *needs* you."

A flush crept up the back of my neck. Was she right? Was I falling back into old patterns, focusing so sharply on one person that I missed everything else? "It's not just about her; it's about the war."

She gave me a long, skeptical look.

"Either way, I can't go with you." Getting to Imperial would take me a long time without witstone, and Philine was right: I'd asked too much of her. She was burning the last of the witstone aboard to secure the Ioph Carn. Only the wealthier islands would have any of the mineral left. I pictured the map of the Empire in my head. "Drop me at Nephilanu. It's just a minor detour for you. They'll have witstone and I can find a ship to take me to Imperial."

"It's blockaded," she said flatly.

I threw my arms out to the sides. "And I'm the Empire's best smuggler."

"*Were.*"

"I've not heard anyone else claiming the title."

She crossed her arms. "Nephilanu is unstable at best right now. I've been told the Emperor's army is on its way, and if you don't make it out beforehand, you'll be in the middle of a battlefield."

I shrugged. "Are you my mother or are you the new leader of the Ioph Carn?"

"If I were your mother, I would have drowned you at the first word out of your mouth." She waved a dismissive hand at me before I could respond. "Fine. It's your life."

"You *do* sound like my mother."

She stalked off with a scowl, shouting orders to the Ioph Carn to slightly change our course.

I draped an arm over Mephi's neck. "She likes me, doesn't she?"

Mephi tilted his head at me. "I think it's the only reason she hasn't killed you yet."

I scratched around the base of his horns and he made a pleased little sound in the back of his throat. "I wish I'd been able to stop Kaphra from taking your shards." I understood a little now why Dione had been so angry at the way Ylan had utilized the bone he'd been given.

His ears flattened. "Not your fault. Besides — I didn't give them to him. He can't use them. And he doesn't know how."

I wondered what the Alanga of the past had used their shards for — whether they'd created constructs too, or if they'd been used to create artifacts other than the swords that hurt ossalen.

By the time we'd arrived at Nephilanu, I'd eaten my way through the galley and had thankfully recovered most of my former strength. The first thing I saw were the green slopes of the island. The second thing I saw were the ships anchored at regular intervals around the coast. Some were closer together and some spaced farther apart, and most were fishing ships not built for war.

But they'd have Shardless Few on them trained by Dione. And spyglasses. "Give me one of your rowboats. That's all I'll need. Drop me off here. The water is calm and Mephi can always help stabilize the boat if things get choppy."

Philine's gaze fell to the sword I'd strapped to my belt. "I take it you're bringing that with you."

It was Kaphra's. By all rights, it should be hers now. But knowing what it did, I felt responsible for it. "It hurts ossalen and Alanga. I want to keep it close."

She nodded. And then she extended her hand. "I'll wish you the best of luck."

I looked at her hand, my head cocked to the side. "Really? You're offering me your hand? Voluntarily?"

Philine rolled her eye but then, to my surprise, seized my hand
and drew me into a hug. "You gave me the courage to do this,"
she whispered into my ear. Just as quickly, it was over, and she
was running her hands over her leathers as though I were capable
of wrinkling them. The glare she shot me afterward with her
one eye told me in no unclear terms: this moment was to be kept
to myself or she'd use all her old tracking skills to find me and
make me regret it.

They lowered the rowboat with me in it to the Endless Sea,
Mephi diving in behind. It was late afternoon, so I'd have some
time to wait — which was just as well. If we could see the ships
in the blockade, they could see us too. I wanted Philine's ship on
the horizon by the time I attempted my approach.

Mephi swam about the boat as we waited, as Philine's ship sailed
away. Here, on the Endless Sea, the air smelling of a coming rain,
I felt an enormous sense of relief. Off the side of the boat, in the
clear blue waters, I saw dark shapes moving far beneath, schools of
shimmering fish breaking the blue between me and them.

Nisong and Ragan were still out there, but for now, even with
a blockade between me and my goal, I was at peace. There were
so many things I needed to do: find witstone on Nephilanu, make
my way to Imperial, somehow let my mother and father know I
was still alive. But for now, there was nothing I could do except
wait. I sat in the moment, the pain of everything that had happened in the past two years mingling with the relief at being free
of it. I let my boat rock on the waves, the oars knocking against
the sides as the sky slowly darkened.

Mephi popped up on one side of the boat just as the sun peeked
out from behind the clouds, casting everything in pink and
orange. A light drizzle touched my cheeks.

"Jovis," he said, his voice serious. "Someone is coming. Ships.
Many of them. From the north."

Philine hadn't left me a spyglass, so I squinted into the distance. "How do you know?"

He flicked an ear. "I have friends."

Mephi was right. Sails appeared on the horizon. First only one, and then many more. Well. This changed the equation. Now I was caught between a blockade and an approaching army, just as Philine had warned. And I wasn't exactly on good terms with Lin at the moment. I racked my brain, trying to think of stories I could tell, lies I could spin. They would reach me before it grew dark so I only had two choices: take my chances with the blockade while it was still light, or take my chances with the army.

I'd take my chances with the blockade. I started rowing, aiming for a part of the island that was less inhabited and thus less guarded. With luck, I'd make it past the blockade before anyone could stop me. There was too much light, and they'd still see me, but I'd be hard to spot until it was too late.

I fell into the rhythm of rowing, the oars creaking as I stroked and the gentle lap as I dipped them into the water again. Mephi popped his head above the water again, blowing some free of his whiskers. "They're overtaking us, Jovis."

When I looked up from the stern of the boat I found the Imperial ships much closer than I would have liked. I glanced over my shoulder and found the shores of Nephilanu still much farther than I would have liked. Perhaps I wasn't as recovered as I wanted to think I was.

I redoubled my efforts, letting the tremor fill my bones, letting the strength of the magic flow into my arms and shoulders. I lost myself in the motion. Dimly, I was aware of Mephi diving beneath the water.

"Hey! Down there!"

I looked up, surprised to somehow be in the shadow on an Imperial warship, the sides sloping up and away from me like cliff faces. I was even more surprised when I saw who had spoken. I'd seen her only a couple of times before, and briefly, but there was no mistaking the woman.

Phalue, the governor of Nephilanu, wife to Ranami.

37

Ranami

Nephilanu Island

Ranami wasn't sure which had taken the words from her more: her missing memory or the appearance of Halong here in her prison, waiting for her. She couldn't think of anything to say. No pleading, no reasoning, no lies. She swiped her tongue over her lips, her mind turning uselessly. She couldn't feel the lamp in her hand or the ground beneath her feet.

Halong rose, the tip of the white-bladed sword nearly touching the stone floor as he strode toward her. "Were you just here to spy on me? Are you taking information back to all your loyal followers? I thought you were better than that." His gaze flicked to the grate. "And we checked this room several times. It was secure."

"Apparently not." There was a bit of the old sharpness in her voice, and for a moment, Ranami felt like herself. But the missing memory . . .it felt like she wasn't just missing a memory. She was missing a piece of what made her *her*. A part of her mind just kept going over that blank spot, the way she had once tongued a loose tooth, unable to stop.

Halong seized her arm in a rough grip. They'd had their disagreements over the years, but he'd never handled her roughly and she'd always treated him with kindness. This sudden shift, even more abrupt and violent than him taking her prisoner, made her heartbeat spike with fear, white spots clouding her vision.

She wasn't here. She wasn't living this life.

Except she was. She was being led from her prison by the man she'd once called her brother, the sword Halong held a clear threat. How had they gone so wrong? All she could feel was the rapid breath in her nostrils, the coolness of the air entering her lungs.

"Halong—"

"Unless you're telling me where the caro nuts are hidden, don't waste your breath." He led her through the corridors, lanterns spaced at intervals so wide that she felt nearly swallowed by darkness before she saw another glimpse of light. They climbed the stairs at the end of the hall and the faint sounds of voices became louder, more distinct.

People filled the main cavern of the Shardless Few hideout, the cooking fire in the center at a roaring height, three large pots bubbling over it as soldiers lined up to receive a meal or to stack used dishes by the washtub.

The conversation died down as Halong marched her from one end of the cavern to the other. Finally, he released her, pushing her in front of a group of rough-looking men and women. "Fine. We do it your way. Do what it takes to get the location of the nuts."

They took her eagerly, one of the men seizing her wrists in one hand, wrenching her shoulders back painfully. She was still in her shift, her dress abandoned in her prison. Ranami had never been quite so aware how little flesh the garment covered.

"Shurai." Halong pointed to a woman who'd just finished her

bowl of soup. "Take a group of five soldiers down to the prisoner's room. The door is open. There's a loose grate in there. Check beneath it for a way out from the caves."

Shurai gestured in turn to five soldiers and jerked her head toward the entrance of the cavern. They left, marching after her. Ranami hoped Ayesh was long gone by now. The girl was quick, and Shark even quicker.

And then all she could see was the woman in front of her, a knife drawn, the point glinting by firelight. It seemed everyone in the room around them held their breath – whether anticipating or dreading violence, Ranami wasn't sure.

For one desperate moment, Ranami hoped for Phalue, wishing she'd come bursting in, ready to defend her wife from any harm. She wished for it so hard she was almost certain it would happen.

She wasn't sure when in her life she'd shifted from hoping for nothing to dreaming of miracles, but she suspected it coincided with her love for Phalue. The woman couldn't help but inspire dreams, even in gutter orphans.

But dreams were fleeting, insubstantial. The knife in front of her was all too real.

No one was coming to save her.

She felt as though she were floating outside her body, waiting for the coming pain to ground her once more. Waiting for the touch of the blade against her skin.

"I'll start with things that will heal, but then I'll move on to things that won't," the woman said. She had the hard-edged look of someone who had seen too many people she loved die and who was no longer attached to anyone. The only thing she cared about now was a cause – because she could cling to that until the end of her days.

Ranami tried to catch Halong's gaze. It brushed against hers, the light touch of flower petals against fingertips. *Please*, Ranami thought. *Please don't do this*. But then he was looking away, turning his back.

The knife touched the soft flesh of her upper arm and Ranami felt the skin there part.

A woman approached Halong, speaking in short, clipped phrases. She could barely hear the words beyond the white-hot pain of the knife cutting into her flesh.

"General. Someone has left something for us at the hideout's entrance. Caro nuts. A small sack of them. Enough to help with our sick soldiers. We've got her cornered but we need your help."

Without a word, Halong strode toward Ranami, took her by her uninjured arm and followed after the soldier. "Please," Ranami said again, "we were only trying to help. She's just a child." He didn't look at her, didn't say anything, and that more than anything made Ranami's breath rasp in her throat. He'd rescued her from her torturers, but she wasn't headed into anything better. What she'd feared all along had happened: her daughter had been caught. And she'd been caught trying to *help* the Shardless Few. Everything about the situation struck Ranami as wrong, grating against her senses, making everything appear at once too bright, too loud, too painful.

They squeezed through the gap together, Ranami between the soldier and Halong, unable to do anything except to keep moving. The lantern the soldier carried cast light into the narrow opening, illuminating the rocky walls of the entrance. Underneath it all, Halong had to still be the man she knew, even past the years they'd spent apart, didn't he? He had a wife, children. He had to understand.

"She's an Alanga," the soldier said, lifting her lamp overhead and trudging through the underbrush. "Just as you said. She's young, but someone's trained her. We haven't been able to get close."

Ranami didn't try to wrench her arm free of Halong's grasp. Even if she were able to escape, she'd only go straight to where they were headed – where Ayesh was trapped by the Shardless Few. Raised voices sounded ahead. Lanterns lit the cliff face and the forest, swinging about like fireflies as soldiers moved. Moisture clung to the grasses and bushes they passed, soaking into the front of Ranami's shift, making her shiver.

She forgot her discomfort when she saw Ayesh and Shark.

They were backed up against the cliff face, Ayesh with her lantern discarded, her shield strapped to one arm and sword held in the other. Shark crouched in front of her, ears laid back and teeth bared. Even from this distance, Ranami could see the whites of their eyes.

Halong handed her off to one of his soldiers and stepped toward Ayesh, drawing his white-bladed sword.

"Don't!" Ranami cried out. Was this what he would do? Threaten her daughter and force her to give up the location of the caro nuts? Force her to give over Nephilanu to Dione? "She came here to help you!"

"Surrender," Halong said to Ayesh. "We have your mother. Come quietly and she won't be hurt. And neither will you."

"You're threatening a *child*," Ranami cried out at Halong's back. "She's fourteen."

He didn't turn to look at her. "I was younger when I was an orphan on my own." Had he forgotten that Ayesh had been a gutter orphan too? That Ranami had? He'd made enemies of them in his mind without stopping to think about what they had in common.

Desperation was a wild animal clawing up her throat. "Ayesh. Ayesh! Don't fight. They won't hurt you. Just go with them. It's not worth your life."

But Ayesh was Ayesh – headstrong, fierce, yearning to prove

herself. Halong stepped closer, lifting a hand and gathering the moisture from the plants around them. Leaves shifted as though in a breeze as water droplets coalesced at Halong's command. His ossalen came bounding out of the woods, skidding to a halt next to his master. He was bigger than Shark, stronger.

A low tremor traveled through the ground beneath Ranami's feet. Ayesh's answer – she was ready to unleash her magic too.

Ranami pulled at her captor's hands, kicking at him, screaming. All she'd wanted was to make the world safe for her daughter and now her daughter was here, being forced to fight. "There are other ways," she gasped out.

Finally, this seemed to get through to Ayesh. She straightened from her fighting stance and slowly sheathed her sword. "I need you to promise you won't hurt me or my mother. I'll go with you." She lifted her hand and the wrist with the shield strapped to it. Ayesh's voice trembled and she looked at Halong with wide eyes. Shark subsided at her side, tail and head low. Her lips covered her teeth, a quiet whine emanating from her throat. They'd gone in one moment from fierce, feral creatures to ones who looked as though they only wanted a bit of food and a warm bed to sleep in.

Ranami sagged in her captor's grip, feeling as though she'd run from the harbor to the palace and back. Her pulse throbbed at her neck, her vision swimming.

"We won't hurt you," Halong said. He didn't sheathe his sword, but Ranami saw his posture relax, the grip on the hilt looser than it once was. With his free hand, he gestured to his men and women, urging them to stay back. "I didn't mean to scare you. Come now. I have children too."

Ayesh bit her lip, her eyes widening as Halong approached and Ranami felt as though her heart had been plunged into ice. She knew that look. She'd been treated to it one too many times – each time Ayesh had been caught doing something she wasn't supposed to. It was meant to be disarming, would turn in a flash to a grin when Ranami at last took pity on her and issued a less harsh consequence than she'd first intended.

"Ayesh—!"

She was too late. She was not an Alanga, not a fighter, not a governor – only a woman who wanted to protect the people she loved but didn't have the means.

Ayesh plunged the sharpened end of the shield toward Halong's ribs. He blocked her reflexively, knocking aside the shield, but in his surprise, couldn't stop his momentum.

The white-bladed sword cut deep into Ayesh's side.

38

Ranami

Nephilanu Island

The scream that tore loose from Ranami's throat didn't feel like her own. It felt like a distant thing even as her throat was raw with it. In her mind, she was trapped in the moment where Halong's blade entered Ayesh's body. Halong looked just as shocked as Ayesh was — her face pale and tight with pain, her arms gone suddenly limp, blood soaking into the side of her tunic, dripping. Even across the distance, in the silence Ranami could hear it pattering onto the leaves of the plants beneath her.

She was too small. She was too young.

Ayesh didn't breathe, only staggered backward as Halong lifted the blade free. And then he dropped to the girl's side, hand going to the wound, pressing against the seeping blood.

"Let me go!" The hands holding Ranami didn't relent. She turned her head far enough to meet the eye of the man holding her — young, strong, black hair framing a solemn face. Human. From somewhere deep within her, she found the right words to say. "That's my *child*. She's just a girl. You joined the Shardless Few to overthrow an Empire. You're supposed to *help*."

Hesitation and doubt made fingers slippery. She wrenched free from her captor's grasp and stumbled to her daughter's side. No one else tried to stop her. Shark circled above Ayesh, reaching down to lay her nose against Ayesh's cheek, sniffing the wound but not daring to get close to it. A low keening sound came from the beast – one Ranami had never heard before.

"It *burns*," Ayesh choked out, her hands curled into claws. "Like fire. Make it stop."

She'd seen Ayesh shrug off wounds that would have felled the strongest of Phalue's guards. The girl had once fallen onto a nail and then, wincing only a little, drawn it out of her palm. The hole had closed behind and she'd lifted her hand to Ranami's horrified and astonished gaze. "It's fine."

But she wasn't healing, as much as Ranami stared at the wound and willed it so. Even as she watched, blood seeped from between Halong's fingers. She wouldn't expect Ayesh to shrug off such a blow, but she didn't expect the girl to look so pale either, so lost in her own pain she no longer seemed to see the world around her.

Ranami was reaching for Halong, her hands weak and useless. It was like trying to grasp a bird with blades of grass, her fingers sliding away from his shoulder. "Halong. Halong, you have to let me help her. You can't let her die."

"We have physicians. The wound isn't too deep. She'll survive." He was talking to himself. It was as though she wasn't even there. He tore a strip of cloth from the bottom of his shirt, tying it tight around Ayesh's wound. The girl didn't even grunt, her gaze glassy, her mouth open in shallow pants. When Ranami took her hand, Ayesh didn't respond.

"You don't even know what that sword *does*, do you?" The wound might not have been fatal by most standards, but Ayesh's reaction was strange and so was Shark's. The white blade nearly glowed by the light of the lanterns, the blood spattered on its edge dark. "She's supposed to be healing. Something's not right. She always heals." Dione had put cracks into her idealism, but now it shattered. They claimed they were going to help people, but they'd let a child bleed out on the ground because they wanted to control Nephilanu and the caro nuts. "What are *physicians* going to do for a magical wound?" Her voice went thick with tears. "You used to give your last piece of bread to the smaller orphans on the street. Who *are* you? You're not the Halong I knew."

Halong waved to one of his soldiers. "Take her back to the room. We'll do all we can for her." But it might not be enough. He glanced at Ranami, and for a moment he looked like the old Halong. "I never meant for this to happen, you have to know that."

A hand took her arm. So she was to wait in that prison of a room, hoping for word on whether or not her daughter was still alive? Wait. The grate was still open.

The cave.

She pulled at the soldier's grip. "Halong – there's a pool in the cave systems." She knew she sounded mad, like she was babbling nonsense, but she couldn't stop herself. Ayesh was silent and she was almost never this silent. "It healed a wound on my hand. Let me take her there." How long would it take for the Shardless Few physician to get here? It was taking too long. And how skilled was their physician?

He held up a hand to stop the soldier from pulling her away. "A magical pool," he said flatly.

She let out a huff of breath and nearly couldn't breathe another back in. "You throw around water and air, you shake the earth beneath our feet, you have a magical *sword* and a magical pool is somehow beyond belief?" He hesitated and she didn't relent.

"If you ever valued our friendship, if you cared about me at all, you'll help her. She grew up like us. She's . . .just like us." Ranami didn't know what else to say; her words had run out, her mouth dry and useless. All she'd had were words.

Halong's dark gaze met hers and she wasn't sure what he was thinking. There'd been a time when she would have known exactly the thoughts that lurked behind his eyes, the concerns, the worries. He was a wall to her now, opaque and unyielding.

And then he crouched lower, slid his arms below Ayesh's body and stood. "Let her go," he said to the soldier. "We'll take her to this pool."

The soldier released Ranami and she didn't waste any time, taking the lantern from his other hand and striding back toward the Shardless Few hideout, Halong and the two ossalen on her heels. For once she was glad of her stature, her lack of fighting ability, her lack of magic. For once she was glad she was not intimidating. He hadn't felt the need to have soldiers accompany them – soldiers that would have inevitably slowed them down.

Her words had been enough.

It took her a little time to find the tunnel she and Ayesh had exited from. It looked different by night – more foreboding. But she tamped down her fear, crouched and crawled through to the caves. She had to turn to help Halong with Ayesh, but the girl was still small and soon they were standing again, Halong's head nearly touching the rocky ceiling.

Shark slipped past her. "This is the way," the ossalen said. Ranami set her hand upon the creature's shoulder, giving her a small, grateful pat. She hadn't been sure she'd remember how to get back to the pool. She didn't have Ayesh's natural sense for the tunnels, her awareness of the earth and stone around her.

The cave with the pool was just as strange as she remembered it, the stone walls glittering, a vein of witstone running through the ceiling. The air was cooler down here, making the skin on the back of her neck prickle.

Halong set Ayesh down next to the pool. She was still breathing shallowly, her eyes closed. The wound had not healed.

There were so many things Ranami didn't know — would her daughter heal normally from this wound? What did the sword do? What did the *pool* do? Had it really taken a memory of hers, or had that been just a blank her own mind had formed?

Blood had seeped through Halong's makeshift bandage. The cut might not have punctured vital organs, but Ayesh was still losing too much blood. Ranami made a snap decision. "Help me."

Halong moved without hesitation, and together they lowered Ayesh into the pool. Shark whined behind her, her big gray head coming to rest on Ranami's shoulder. Ranami held her daughter's head in her lap, the rest of the girl's body submerged. Blood from the bandage trickled into the water, fogging it with pink.

"I wouldn't have let her die," Halong said, his voice echoing from the cave walls. "You have to know, I might have locked you away, but I would have done everything for her — the same as I would have done for my own children."

"Would you threaten your own children?" Ranami bit back. She ran a hand over Ayesh's forehead, smoothing the hair away from her face. Ayesh preferred to keep it short, but it had grown a bit shaggy in the time Nephilanu had been occupied. Her skin was beaded with sweat. Ranami almost dipped her hand into the pool to cool the girl's face, but stopped. She still wasn't exactly sure what it did.

"You have to understand—" Halong began.

"Do I?" She met his gaze. "You say you're doing this for the greater good, but how many tyrants have used that to justify the pain they've visited on innocents?"

"I had to weigh the fortunes of many against the friendship we shared. And Ranami, you're on the other side now. How could I still treat you like my friend?"

"How foolish," Ranami said, though her voice was soft and without venom. "We want the same things for the people of this Empire yet we are on different sides. Think what we could do if we actually worked together. If we set aside what we think makes a person virtuous – whether they are Shardless Few or governors." Before he could offer some rejoinder, she went on. "Oh, I understand. You say governors are corrupt and selfish and you're not wrong. You're not. But Phalue took power because she saw no other way to make the difference she wanted to. She could lead us, Halong. If you'd let her."

He didn't break his gaze from hers, but she saw something soften behind his eyes. The wall – crumbling, dissolving. "I've missed you, Ranami. I've missed you so much. But you never wrote. You never tried to contact me, to ask me why I left."

"I know." She reached out, laid a hand over his. "I'm not saying I'm right, because I've made a lot of mistakes. And that was one of them. I got caught up in everything on Nephilanu, the wider view. Everything else seemed less important. But you're *important*, Halong. Not just because of what you've become or who you are now. But because of who you are to me. You're my past. You're my brother. I looked only to the future and I lost sight of that."

He didn't pull away from her. "Maybe . . .there's a third way. Something we can work on together."

Tears pricked Ranami's eyes. This was all she'd wanted from the beginning – to have her brother back, to know he wasn't so changed that he'd stopped listening to her altogether. She opened her mouth to respond.

Ayesh gasped. Her arms flailed in the water, filling the cavern with the sound of splashing. "What happened? Where am I?

What——?" Her gaze bounced from Ranami to Halong, to Shark. "You lot look miserable. Did someone die?"

The wound at her side no longer seeped red into the water. Ranami pulled Ayesh from the pool, running her hands over the girl's face, her hair, untying the bandage and examining the unmarred flesh beneath. Ayesh finally seized Ranami's fingers. "Please, I'm not a goat for sale. What are you doing?"

Ranami and Halong exchanged glances. "A magical pool," Halong said. "For now, let's keep the location between the three of us."

The two ossalen grunted, one after another, their expressions a mirror.

"The five of us," Halong corrected, the ghost of a smile on his lips.

"But really, what happened?"

The edges of Ranami's elation were blunted, anxiety trickling into the gaps. "You don't remember?"

Ayesh frowned. "The last thing I remember was *you*." Her eyes narrowed as she looked at Halong. "You took my mother prisoner. I hid. Are we . . .friends now?"

The breath turned cold in Ranami's lungs, as though she'd swallowed a lungful of ice. Ayesh had lost nearly a third of a year, her memories of that time wiped clean. So Ranami hadn't imagined it. The pool healed, but it also sucked away memories — and apparently in no organized manner. Ranami had lost a memory from years ago and Ayesh had lost her most recent ones.

She told herself to be grateful. Ayesh still knew who Ranami was. There was a lot to catch her up on, but they wouldn't be rebuilding their relationship. It had been hard enough the first time for the two of them.

They took the way back to Ranami's prison, the grate still

loose. All of them were filthy, their clothes wet, covered with dirt and blood. For a moment, she thought about asking for a bath, but then she heard voices emanating from behind the door. Raised voices. All her senses sharpened. She hadn't survived all those years on the streets without developing a nose for impending danger.

"Something's happened," she said as she pulled Halong and Ayesh out in turn. The ossalen scrambled out behind them, Halong's barely fitting through the hole.

They followed Halong out the door, the commotion growing louder the higher they climbed the stairs. They arrived into the main cavern to chaos.

A man stood in the center of the cavern by the fire. He'd pulled a chair over so he could set himself higher, drawing everyone's eye. He'd dressed himself like a cross between a governor and a soldier, rich silks beneath scaled armor, a helmet held beneath one arm, a sword strapped to his side. His hair fell into his eyes, giving him a moody, brooding look. He held himself with the taut energy of a cat about to pounce, its tail lashing. Shardless Few Ranami didn't recognize stood around him like an honor guard. To his right, so close they touched, a woman leaned against the chair, a gray ossalen at her side. Her face was pockmarked and scarred, her clothes plain.

Ranami's gaze was drawn back to the man as he spoke. Some people in the cavern grumbled, but others, like her, could not seem to tear their eyes away. His voice carried. "I know how much you all admire Dione. I know because I did too. How could I not? I was lost when I found out I was an Alanga, adrift among people who hated me. And he is the oldest Alanga still living, the only survivor of the Empire's purge.

"But he didn't care about me. He doesn't care about you. All he cares about is bringing back a past that is long dead. He had the chance to strike the Emperor down – talk to the Shardless Few with me; they'll tell you – but when it came down to it, he *couldn't* do it. Do you know why? Because she is an Alanga."

Now there were angry mutterings. Ranami felt the mood in the cavern shift.

"Let me through." Halong pushed in front of Ranami, the crowd parting before him. He marched toward the fire. "Who are you? I'll ask you to get down from there and to state your business to me. Privately."

"You can ask," the man said, a sly grin on his face.

Ranami saw the position Halong was being put into. He didn't know this man's position or rank among the Shardless Few. He had a contingency of them with him and they'd known where the hideout was. If he pressed the issue, he might start a fight among his own Shardless Few. His job as a general was to set his army to one unified task.

Before Halong could reassess, the man spoke again. "I am Ragan. I joined Dione to help him hunt down the Emperor and valuable Alanga artifacts. But we broke away when his resolve failed. When we found out what he truly wanted." He looked Halong up and down, took note of the ossalen that followed him, his gaze lingering on the sword at Halong's side. It was as obviously measuring a gaze as Ranami had ever seen. "He's soft on Alanga, on his fellows. I am not. Not only will I crush the Empire, but I will ensure the Alanga are kept in line."

Ranami pulled Ayesh in close to her, the people around her, even the ones she'd spoken to genially around the fire, over a meal, all suddenly feeling unsafe. She knew what Ragan was doing. With one subtle verbal nudge, he'd placed the mortals on one side, the Alanga on the other. He was playing up the years of prejudice, of distrust. So many stories, poisoning the minds of the Empire against an enemy they all feared would return. When all along the enemy was not an outside force but had actually lived among them.

And where had he placed himself? As the one Alanga who was different, who was on their side. It was a potent message.

Halong had reached the chair. He had to crane his neck back to meet Ragan's eyes. He couldn't demand Ragan step down or grab him without appearing foolish – but this didn't look much better. "Dione left me in charge of this army," Halong said. "I am his general and awaiting his orders. He never wrote to me of you, never told me your rank. As far as I'm concerned, you're a usurper."

Ragan snorted. "A usurper." He drew out the word. "Isn't that what we all are? Or what the Emperor would call us? The Shardless Few is an army for the people, organized by the people. So let them decide."

"There is nothing to be decided."

"Isn't there?" Their gazes locked. Both their hands drifted toward their swords.

Ranami found herself stepping forward, unable to stop her momentum. All she knew was that if these two Alanga clashed, the rest of them would suffer. Including Ayesh, whom she'd only just been afraid of losing. She was not Phalue. She was not a warrior. But she found the well of her words had not run completely dry.

"You would listen to this man?" Ranami felt her voice fill the silence, ringing with a strength she hadn't known she'd possessed. "Yes, what he says may have some truth. Dione may have his own motives and reasons behind his actions. But at least you knew him, at least he has shown through his actions that he cares about the Empire's people – even bringing the Shardless Few to help repel the construct army from Gaelung." She used Ragan's words, the arguments he'd given her, and molded them to a new purpose. If he felt this way, then so did others among the Shardless Few. "He promises to keep the Alanga in line. But look – your leader is an Alanga, your general is an Alanga, my own daughter is an Alanga. How many of you will find people that you love and care about are Alanga as well, if they aren't already? Will he imprison all those that he feels aren't loyal? Be careful who you give power to. Be careful who you choose to follow."

She could see the shifting feelings around her, like currents of the Endless Sea, eddies and tides. But unlike the Endless Sea, these shifts were things she could control, that she could nudge with the right words. The anger around her was cooling, tempering.

"Yes, do." Ragan crossed his arms. "How long has Dione promised an end to the Empire? Yes, he helped repel the construct army, but he delayed the plans of the Shardless Few. How long have we waited to see the Imperial Palace in rubble, to know that a Sukai will never rule us again? We need to crush that regime so thoroughly that it is as dust beneath our feet."

Cheers broke out. And just like that, Ranami felt the currents being torn away from her, the anger in the people around her fanned to greater heights.

Ragan drew his sword, ignoring Halong completely. With a shock, Ranami realized its blade was as white as the one Halong had. Another artifact. Another magical sword. "Tell your fellows: Ragan has come to lead the army back to Imperial – with or without Dione's approval." He smirked, pointing a finger into the air, his sword held in a casual grip. "Ah, just a quaint turn of phrase. What was I thinking? *Without* his approval, obviously." His expression darkened. "We will fight. We will do whatever it takes, no hesitation. We will take back what is *ours*."

Ranami raised her voice. "No one should own this Empire! It

belongs to everyone, not just the Shardless Few." But the people around her were cheering, her words lost in the commotion.

Everything seemed to move too quickly after that. Men and women gathering their things, taking supplies, following Ragan in such great numbers that there was nothing Halong could do to stop them unless he wanted to start a battle right here.

Ranami found him when the room had cleared, when all those who had decided to leave had gone. There were still a good many Shardless Few left in the cavern, but she wasn't sure how many outside this space had decided to stay. They mulled about like survivors of a storm, unsure of what to do first to mitigate the damage.

Halong sat staring into the fire, his shoulders rounded. He heard her approaching before she could say anything. "You did your best," he said. "No one could have done better than that. And it was more than the Shardless Few deserved after what we've done to your family and to your island. I didn't think any of them would follow Ragan, but maybe the Shardless Few aren't what they once were. I should have listened to you."

She placed a hand on his shoulder, and he placed a weathered hand atop hers. She felt some of that old connection to him, some of that old friendship – if only it hadn't come this late. Now they might all suffer the consequences.

They all retreated to lick their own wounds after that, though Halong didn't order her or Ayesh locked away, and over the following days, Ranami began to mingle more with the remaining Shardless Few – speaking to them, hearing their stories, their hopes and dreams. In turn, she told them about Phalue, encouraging them to listen to the people of Nephilanu. Halong and she didn't speak on the caro nuts or the fate of the island's people, their repaired friendship still too fragile. But Ranami knew she'd have to address these things soon.

The message came twelve days after Ragan had left with a little over half the Shardless Few, taking just as many ships with them. The blockade was now a spotty thing, like a fence blown to pieces in a storm. Ranami wasn't sure exactly when the message had arrived, but when she sat down to eat breakfast with Halong by the fire, Ayesh and Shark at her side, he spoke up.

"Dione sent a missive – he wants me to take the army to Imperial. He thinks it's weak enough now, that it will give way during an attack."

She froze with the spoon halfway to her mouth. "Does he know? Over half his army left with Ragan."

"I've sent word, but it won't have reached him yet."

Ranami ate a few contemplative mouthfuls of the rice porridge, chunks of fish and scallions mixed into the broth. "What will you do?"

Halong let out a long sigh. Ayesh's gaze traveled back and forth between them. With no memory of the fight that had left her wounded, she wasn't wary of the man at all. Shark, though, never let Halong within arm's reach of her fur. "I'm not sure." He stirred his porridge, watching it swirl as though the movement of the pieces within could give him insight to the future. "There are too many pitfalls on every road I choose. Nephilanu is not as secure as Dione thinks it is. If I take what's left of our army to Imperial, will that mean the Shardless Few fighting against themselves? But Dione wants Imperial to fall and so does Ragan – does that mean we just join Ragan to accomplish this goal?" He let go of his spoon and set down the bowl, though it was still half full. His ossalen lowered his head to rub his cheek against Halong's shoulder. He scratched the beast's shoulder absentmindedly. "I need to talk to some of my captains." He rose.

A woman came rushing toward them, followed by a murmuring group of soldiers. "General," the woman said, stopping in front of him. "There's been a development. Imperial ships are approaching Nephilanu. We think it's the army."

39

Lin

Somewhere in the Endless Sea

I'd thought we'd escaped, but without witstone we were still too slow. The falling mountains of Riya created great waves that I could do nothing to stop. In a chance accident, one boulder had flown toward our ship, cracking the mast and crushing one of the sailors, taking out a chunk of the deck as well.

I stared down at my meal of plain grilled fish, vowing to never eat another fish if we ever made it home. Panicked refugees had ransacked some of our food stores, spilling some and leaving some to spoil. Even seasonings were sparse, but we still had a bit of fuel for the mess's stove, and the Endless Sea was bountiful. We might not starve, but we'd need to make landfall before we all fell ill from a lack of variety in our diets.

A faint breeze brushed past my cheeks as I ate, the silence around us even more unsettling than the chaos of Riya's sinking. Once in a while, I heard a sob on the wind, the gentle knock of wood against wood as scraps of wreckage drifted through the stranded ships around us.

Ours was not the only one that had been damaged. We drifted on the currents together, a miniature city of broken boats, all wary of one another. The undamaged ships hadn't stayed behind to help, and I couldn't blame them; I'd not stayed behind to help refugees off the sinking island. How could I ask for more than I'd given?

Still, I couldn't stop from pacing the prow of the ship, my body leaning toward Imperial, wishing that my will alone could somehow move us forward.

I heard footsteps behind me and knew they were the captain's. "How long?"

He sighed. "Eminence, there's no way to know. We're at the whims of the Endless Sea now."

"It's been *weeks*. Armies are moving. Ragan is moving." I waved a hand at the surrounding ships. "And all of us are stuck." Not only that, but I knew not all the ships out there were as large as ours. They'd run out of food soon if they hadn't already. A darker part of me, still caught in the moments refugees had tried to swarm my ship, thought they might turn their sights to the Emperor's boat, to its stores. That was what people did, wasn't it, in times of desperation? Turned on one another in order to survive.

It's what I'd done.

"Unless your powers can repair a ship's mast, we're not sailing out of here, and we're not equipped with oars. I'm sorry, Eminence. I've done everything I can."

I closed my eyes, forcing myself to eat another bite of the fish on my plate. "I know you have. It's just...the fate of this Empire is uncertain. There are things happening I can't control. And not only can I not control them, but I cannot *react* to them. I'm an Emperor and I can't even use my powers right now and I'm just *useless*."

The captain shifted behind me, clearing his throat uncomfortably.

I shouldn't be saying these things to him – but who else could I confide in? Jovis was gone, he was different; Ikanuy was at Imperial, doing her best to run the island; even Huan was dead. Thrana was still lying beneath a tarp on the deck, her breathing long and deep.

"Eminence, there are still things that you can do. There are still people you can help." I didn't respond, lost in contemplation and despair. "Ah, forgive me, I'm speaking out of turn. Please forget I said anything." And then I heard his footsteps scuffling away in hasty retreat.

Out in the flotilla, I watched two people on a fishing boat idly play a game of cards; on another, a man was patching a hole with spare lumber from floating wreckage. On yet another, a woman paddled toward a stranded boat, handing a basket of food to the man and child aboard.

I placed my hand over the folded crane in my sash pocket, remembering a time when Numeen had looked past the spoiled facade of the heir to the Empire and had invited her to dinner. I'd been so focused then on the injustices I'd felt I'd faced at my father's hands. On what I could do better if only he'd let me.

Oh, Phalue was right about me, and the realization stung more than I'd thought it would. These people out there weren't harassing their captains. They were managing with the hand they'd been dealt. Once the initial panic had died down, they were helping one another, doing their best to survive until the currents treated us favorably. And here I was, on a ship larger than many of the others, with a plate full of fish in front of me, thinking about its flavor. Leaning against the prow and trying to will us into moving more quickly. I wasn't listening to the captain or to the people around me – too focused on what I saw as greater problems.

I needed to do better, to protect these people and provide for them, to take everyone's voices into counsel, even when it irked me to hear what they had to say. Even when I thought their problems were smaller. These problems were not small, not to them. I found one of my surviving guards and took her arm. "We still have a dinghy aboard, yes?"

She nodded.

"I need you to row out to the other ships here. Find out who is running out of food. Find out if anyone needs blankets or water. We have plenty of water left and our rainwater collection capacity is greater than everyone else's. Write everything down and bring back the notes. We'll figure out how best to distribute things from there."

Something brightened in the guard's expression – I wasn't sure if it was just being given something to do or if it was because she felt like she was able to help. I found another of my guards and instructed him to catalog our supplies and to recruit a few others to help him organize what we had below-deck. Everyone began moving, and for a moment, it was almost as though we had a working ship again – the bustle and activity aboard cutting into the surrounding silence.

We found several ships running low on water, and some running low on food. A few needed tarps or blankets. I ran calculations, figuring out what we could spare, and how much. And then I sent the guards and sailors back out to distribute what we had.

I'd become so caught up in this that I almost didn't notice when Thrana began to stir. But she let out a rumbling breath and my heart leapt. She hadn't made a sound before this – nothing except her low and steady breathing. I left the guards and sailors to their work and went to her side, placing a hand on her shoulder. "I'm here," I said. One ear flicked toward me.

And then she began to change. The last hibernations she'd gone through, the changes were small, subtle. This time, her horns fell away, clattering to the deck, leaving the nubs of freshly growing horns in their wake. Her fur grew coarser, more green, her body seeming to swell with each breath. The beard at her chin had grown longer, the lighter fur there bright as corn silk. An eye opened, the iris rolling until her gaze met mine. "Help me," she said. "Help me get to the water."

She staggered to her feet and I let her lean on me, my magic-enhanced strength returning. The bustle around us paused, swallowed by silence once more as everyone turned to stare. The idle card game on the nearby fishing boat had halted, both participants open-mouthed.

Thrana stretched when we reached the rail and I felt the ship sag toward one size beneath her weight. I might have been short, but the top of my head only barely reached her belly now, her chin so far away it felt like the top of a tree.

She half-fell, half-slid into the water with a sigh. Our ship rocked with the absence of her bulk, dipping and then bouncing higher. The sigh Thrana let out vibrated in the air. I felt it deep in my bones, as though I'd uttered it myself. She dove beneath the surface.

For a moment I panicked. Was that it? Had I raised her to an age where she no longer needed or wanted me? Was this what had happened to Dione's ossalen? He'd simply become unnecessary?

Lin, Thrana's voice said in my head. *I could never leave you.*

Someday you will become an island. I couldn't stop the sadness from seeping into my tone.

And when I grow that large I will still be there for you. The world is small when we can speak like this. Her great big head surfaced and she let out a huff of misty breath. *There is an island south of here with a city large enough to have the trees and supplies needed for repairs. And ships you can hire to make your way home.*

And how will we get there? I said. *We have no mast, no sails. Only the current.*

Yes, the current. Are you an Alanga, or are you a helpless child?

My bones thrummed in response, the magic flooding my veins, and I would have cursed myself for my foolishness had I not been so overjoyed to have this feeling back. I held the magic, reaching out into the water with my senses. I could feel the currents brushing against my mind, cool and deep. They stretched farther than I could feel, but I didn't need to shift everything.

Just a touch. Just here. It would take more magic than I'd ever expended to move more than just our ship, but I felt the well of it, deeper than it had ever been before. This could be done. I could do it. And I would not leave all these people behind – not the way I'd left so many on Riya.

I'd still have to reckon with that failure. But this was not the time.

I shouted out from the railing, hoping my voice would carry in the silence. "I'm taking us to an island south of here, where we can resupply and repair our ships. The currents will shift. Don't be afraid."

And then I reached into the Endless Sea beneath us and began to do what I could to set things right.

40

Phalue

Nephilanu Island

Of all the things she'd expected upon arriving at Nephilanu, Phalue hadn't expected *this*. A bedraggled-looking Jovis stood across from her on the deck, his ossalen, Mephi, just behind him. It had been two years, yet he looked as though he'd aged seven. A crease had formed between his brows, his face more worn and weathered than it had once been. Alanga could live for a very long time, yet Jovis looked as though he were already approaching middle age.

"So the rumors were true," Phalue mused.

He looked down at himself. "That I was dead?"

She snorted. "That you were alive, you fool."

He grinned, though there was something about the expression that didn't truly look carefree. It was as though he were trying something on — the old Jovis — to see how it fit.

It didn't. His expression sobered. "It's been …a long two years. I was captured by Kaphra. He didn't kill me, though I wished many times I were dead. He found a way to control me instead. He made me do things. Terrible things." He shook his head, as though he wasn't sure why he was confessing all of this to her. "But I'm free now." He paused, as though listening to a voice he couldn't hear. "Mostly."

That wasn't reassuring. Phalue found her fingers on the hilt of the white-bladed sword. She made an effort to remove her hand from her weapon. This was momentous news. She'd have to send word to Lin. "What are you doing at Nephilanu?"

"I need to get to Imperial. This was the closest island that might have some witstone. We need to hurry. Ragan, he—" Jovis licked his lips, his eyes going glassy. Phalue had seen that look before. She'd seen it on her soldiers after the battle at Gaelung as they relived what had happened, as the trauma of their experiences finally caught up with them and they ceased to function.

This, she could understand. She'd gone through some of it herself. Her heart softened – or perhaps it had always been soft. She stepped forward, put a hand on Jovis's shoulder. The contact seemed to jolt him back to himself. "Tell me what Ragan did. What are you afraid of?"

"Riya," Jovis said. "It's gone."

Phalue scoffed, because Riya was enormous. It couldn't just be gone. He wasn't serious. One of Jovis's poorly-thought-out jokes. Lin had told her enough of Jovis in their time together that Phalue thought she knew him.

Only it wasn't a joke. No trace of a smile touched his lips. Just a tremble, as though he were only barely holding himself together. "Gone?" Phalue heard herself repeat the word, though she knew what he meant. Sank beneath the sea – like Deerhead, Unta and Luangon before it. Four islands of the Empire, crumbling into the Endless Sea.

For the first time, she realized there were others standing near them, listening in, their work paused as they tried to parse what Jovis had said. From a quick glance around, she could see pale faces, open mouths, trembling hands. She should have spoken to him privately before addressing the rest of the army. Now they'd spread the news among themselves and without a unifying message, she wasn't sure what they'd say.

Panic could spread like a spark thrown into dry tinder.

"I think Ragan might have done it," Jovis said. "I don't know how. But if he can sink islands, I don't know what he'll do next. I need to get to Imperial and to help in whatever way I can. And I need Lin's help. She's the only one who can make sure I'm not controlled again. She's the only one who can really help me."

Controlled? He needed more than the Emperor's help, Phalue was sure of it. He needed rest, a bath, a clean bed, a good meal and the comfort of friends. The first ones, at least, she could provide. The last . . .would have to wait.

"I'm here to take back Nephilanu from the Shardless Few," Phalue said. It seemed almost a petty thing now in the face of Riya's destruction. But Ranami was still important, and so was Ayesh, and so were the caro nuts the Empire so desperately needed. Bog cough had started to spread among the ships, though she and Yeshan had done their best to quarantine the affected soldiers.

Jovis looked about at the ships, at the thinned blockade around Nephilanu, his gaze a little glassy. "It's all falling apart, isn't it?"

Despair stole over her like a thief, taking what hope she'd been cultivating. She wasn't sure what she would do after she'd taken back Nephilanu. They'd distribute the caro nuts, certainly. They'd try to get things back to some semblance of normal, because what would normal even mean anymore? They were dyeing the sails of a broken ship, denying that anything had changed. But the Empire had fractured.

Nephilanu was what she cared about the most – her people, her wife, her daughter. That was what she was here for. She'd taken the most circuitous route but she was here now, an army at her back.

She couldn't hesitate.

"Nephilanu won't fall apart. Nephilanu won't sink into the sea." She turned to look for Yeshan and found the general at her shoulder. "Their blockade is spotty – we can tear through those ships easily and make landfall by night. If we don't give them time to respond, I'd wager we can have this battle done by morning."

Yeshan looked as though she were half-listening, her gaze on the island and the blockade, a line forming between her brows. "This isn't what my scouts have told me to expect. Something's changed. There should be more ships."

"Why is that a problem? It makes things easier for us."

The boards on deck creaked as Jovis shifted from side to side. "It could be a trap."

Phalue sighed. She'd only just brought him aboard and now he was already offering his opinion. The more time they wasted talking this out, the more time the Shardless Few would have to prepare. "You were just about to attempt to run headlong past that blockade before I stopped you. And now you're concerned it's a trap?"

"Well, I wasn't about to *attempt* it," he said with a fair bit of smugness in his tone.

Phalue felt her temper ratchet up a notch. "It's not dark, we weren't even looking for strays and we picked you up. And yet you think you were going to get past a blockade?"

"I would have helped," Mephi chimed in.

She was getting sidetracked. "That's not the point. The point is: their defenses are lower right now and we may lose that advantage if we wait. And there's at least one Alanga in their army. If we can't take him by surprise, he could decimate our troops." She looked to Yeshan again. "Can we do it? A night-time assault?"

Yeshan pursed her lips. "Yes. I would advise against it, though, at least until we know more. We can send a scout to their ships, offer terms. That's what I would advise – buy us some time to examine the situation and give them the chance to surrender. I've learned to trust my instincts, and something isn't right here. But I do think your strategy would work, and in the end, the decision is yours. If they've diverted their ships to some other cause, then by waiting, we would give them time to prepare, as you've said. Lin trusted you with her army and so must I."

Ranami was there on the island and so was Ayesh. The last she'd heard, Ranami had been taken prisoner. She'd traveled across the Empire and she couldn't wait any longer.

"We attack now."

Yeshan nodded and turned to send word out to the rest of the ships.

In the next moment, Phalue was flanked by Mephi on one side and Jovis on the other. "Lin directed you to take the army here?" Jovis asked.

"She trusted me with it, so maybe you should too." She heard the defensive tone in her voice, but couldn't help it.

Wind ruffled Jovis's curling hair as he looked to Nephilanu, his expression troubled. "She doesn't trust easily. Or she didn't."

"She still doesn't. But we've spent a lot of time together. I've traveled across the Empire with her, have taught her how to use that blade she carries." She heard shouts from the starboard side of ship, the fluttering of communication flags as the soldiers spread word that they were to attack the Shardless Few's fleet.

"You have an entire army at your back," Jovis said.

"Much power," Mephi added.

Jovis reached up to scratch his ossalen's cheek. "Yes. Just be careful in how you're using it."

Phalue felt her face flush, irritation creeping up her spine. She'd been doing the bidding of Lin from the beginning of this. Now it was time to do what she felt was right – no more caution, no more waiting. "And will you help us fight or will you just stay on the sidelines?"

Mephi and Jovis exchanged glances again, and Phalue had the odd feeling of being on the outside of a conversation – one she couldn't hear.

"We'll wait," Jovis said. "Don't think we aren't on your side – but I've killed too many people these past two years that I wished I hadn't. I need ..." He swallowed, his mouth working as though trying to form the right words. "I need to be sure."

Before she could ask anything else of him, he turned and walked away, the conversation clearly over. Stubborn man. Did he really think he could remain neutral while aboard an Imperial ship? For a moment, she'd thought it a stroke of luck that they'd picked up Jovis, that he was still alive – a sign that they were meant to be victorious in this battle. She wanted to call after him, to chase him down, to force him to make a decision *now*. They could use his help – couldn't he see that? This wasn't the time for a crisis of conscience.

Ranami's face slid into her memories, her head pillowed on her long black hair, bedsheets draped from one shoulder, the light from the window beyond kissing her brown skin with gold. In moments like these, she became deliciously soft, languid as a cat after a meal – no hint of the gutter orphan that always lay beneath. Her fingers brushed Phalue's cheek, touching her as though she were a precious thing. "For a long time, I knew – I *knew* – that we were never going to work. I'm so glad you took the time to see what was going on around you. I'm so glad you came along with me for all this, that we were able to make our peace with one another. I don't know how I would have weathered the heartbreak, and I'd been through enough of it." Her full lips had parted, looking eminently kissable. So Phalue had obliged, sliding across the mattress to cup Ranami's head in one of her hands, using the other to draw her closer, pressing their bodies to one another.

Ranami let out a sigh as Phalue kissed her, but then pulled away, her eyes still closed, her expression dreamy. "Are you listening to me?"

"Hmmm." Phalue nuzzled the space between Ranami's neck and shoulder. "Always."

Ranami cracked an eye open. "Always headlong into one thing without slowing to listen, you mean."

"I did that once," Phalue said, her voice a low rumble. "Isn't that enough?" She nipped the skin of Ranami's neck and the woman gasped, her body arching toward Phalue's.

All Phalue wanted was to return to that moment, when they'd found some quiet together. Before everything had gone sideways. The sails above her were now filled with wind, the surface of the Endless Sea choppy and dark as the sun set. She heard shouts from the Shardless Few ships as they prepared for an attack. Five that she could see between the Imperial fleet and landfall. There were others, off to either side, but they might not make it in time to help the fight.

She had a fleet of fifty Imperial ships with her. They'd crush the Shardless Few. Archers began to line up at the prow of the ship, stringing their bows, quivers at their sides. Other soldiers lined up on deck, armor gleaming by the last light of day. She should have felt triumphant, hopeful. Instead, she felt a drizzle of anxiety settling over her, a thin sheen she couldn't quite shake.

Perhaps it was only pre-battle jitters. Unless there was an Alanga aboard one of those ships, it would be a rout. Perhaps all she had to do was to get through the beginning of this fight, let the adrenaline take over – the way it had when she'd fought at Gaelung.

Soon they were close enough that Phalue could see men and women on the Shardless Few ships, frantically waving their fellows on the distant ships to join them. The archers nocked their arrows and on Yeshan's command, let them fly.

Since the beginning of this entire misadventure, she'd been launching herself toward two goals: take back Nephilanu, keep Ranami and Ayesh safe. She'd railed against Lin's desire to chase down the white-bladed swords, her ponderous thought process concerned with islands and Empires. But when Phalue actually paused to consider what would have happened had she gone straight to Nephilanu, she couldn't say that Lin would have been wrong.

She would have been captured. She would have been with Ranami and Ayesh, but unable to help them, no matter what she told herself. She'd stopped and listened then, and no matter how frustrating the aftermath had been – she had earned the orphans of Imperial an orphanage, and had brought an army to bear on Nephilanu.

Phalue peered at the ships, squinting, noting that they weren't yet firing back. Why weren't they firing back? She thought she saw someone on the prow of one of the ships . . .waving? Yeshan and Jovis were right. There was something else going on here.

"Dione's balls," she muttered to herself under her breath. "Stop!" she called out, marching toward where Yeshan stood at the prow. "Hold fire!"

The general gestured and all the archers at the prow lowered their bows. The flag-bearer waved a white and black flag at the other ships. It took a little time for the message to be repeated, but then they were silent in the water, skimming toward the Shardless Few ships, weapons ready but not in use.

Phalue took the arm of a nearby sailor. "Get a rowboat ready. I'm going over to talk to them."

Some of the tension at the corners of Yeshan's eyes eased, and she nodded.

A voice spoke up from her elbow. "I'm going with you." Jovis stood there, his curling black hair combed – doubtless with his fingers – into some semblance of neatness. He'd rolled back the sleeves of his tunic, exposing the scar where his tattoo had been. The white-bladed sword was strapped to his side, the steel staff in his hand. If she'd doubted his identity before, she wouldn't have now.

"And me," said Mephi. Jovis ruffled the fur at the creature's forehead with a slight smile, as though that were a foregone conclusion. "I'll swim," he added quickly, when Phalue eyed his bulk.

She could have argued with them – she was the one in charge here, not Jovis – but she had to admit that having an Alanga at her back gave her more than a little sense of security. She gave them both a curt nod and went to where the boat was being readied.

The sun had set by the time they rowed out toward the Shardless Few ships, a white flag raised high, lit by a lantern. She'd had the ship fly a peace flag as well, just so they couldn't miss it. There was still a part of her that churned with impatience, that wanted to fight someone, something, *anything*, just to feel like she was doing something. But she found she could tamp that part of her down, could bring it to heel and bid it to wait. It gave her mind space to work.

The Shardless Few ships her scouts had seen wouldn't have

just disappeared. They'd gone somewhere. Whether that was to lie in wait on the other side of the island or to another island altogether. There were possibilities here she needed to consider, because she couldn't rely on the Shardless Few to tell her the truth. They could have obtained the caro nuts and were shipping them out to other islands – ones that had agreed to support them. They could have felt their place here was secure and moved to conquer other lands. They could be waiting to ambush her fleet still, sacrificing these few ships in an effort to lull them all into complacency.

Spots of light appeared on the Shardless Few ships – lanterns being lit, casting the sails and wood in a warm orange hue.

"Phalue? Phalue!"

She knew that voice. Her gaze was searching the deck of the Shardless Few ship, bouncing wildly from one side to the next as she tried to pin down the source. And then Phalue saw her – clothes muddied and worn, long black hair loose and flicking at her cheeks. Older now, but as beautiful as the day they'd met.

She forgot about Jovis, about the sailors rowing the boat; she moved to the rope ladder Ranami threw down to them.

"Sai, one of us should go first . . ."

But Phalue was already climbing, her heart soaring a little higher than her body, her feet moving more quickly than she'd thought possible. Ranami was safe. She was *here*. Oh, by the Endless Sea, Phalue had almost accidentally gotten her killed.

And then she was on deck and Ranami was in her arms. Phalue pressed her mouth to her wife's hair, breathing in deep, the warmth of her as precious as a fire on a cold night. She barely heard Ranami's voice over the thunder of her own heart. "I came out to the blockade as soon as I heard Imperial ships had been spotted, but I didn't think . . ." Ranami's arms tightened around

Phalue, her shoulders shaking with silent tears. "You made it. You made it back."

Phalue kissed Ranami's forehead, her cheeks, her nose, her lips — each touch feeling both impossible and familiar. "I'm home."

41

Ranami

Nephilanu Island

When the Imperial ships had begun to fire on them, Ranami had cursed beneath her breath. She knew Phalue – she knew that her wife would tear stone walls apart with her bare hands to get back to her family, to keep them safe. No matter that Ranami could very well take care of herself, and Ayesh as well. Phalue was fiercely protective of the ones she loved, holding them all beneath the same shield. Those that threatened this protection were liable to feel the cut of a blade.

Or those she perceived threatened it.

The Shardless Few around Ranami eyed Phalue warily as they made their way to the their hideout – glances that slid and hopped away like frightened sparrows at the first sign of detection. Phalue, for her part, seemed not to notice, her arm slung around Ranami's shoulders, squeezing every so often as though to be sure Ranami was there, that she was real.

"We'll have to find a way to distribute the caro nuts," Phalue was saying, the lantern she held in her other hand highlighting the scratches on her armor. "The ships the Shardless Few still have here will help – but we need to get in touch with Lin, get her to send Imperial trading ships. We can't be crippled by bog cough now, not with Ragan on the move and an army at his back."

She spoke as though she were in charge, though Ranami shouldn't have been surprised. Phalue had long been governor of Nephilanu and she was back here on her own island. The Shardless Few were without Dione, their forces scattered. To Phalue, they were just another resource to be used.

In spite of everything Ranami had told the Shardless Few about Phalue, she felt like she was wading through a miasma of distrust, every sidelong glance at Phalue another mire to get stuck in. Maybe this was her own fault. Had she built up Phalue too highly? How could she not, when she thought the world of her? But she had perhaps been too careful to omit her wife's flaws, and the woman had never been one of the Shardless Few.

"Halong is still in charge of the remainder of the Shardless Few army," Ranami said, hoping her wife would take the hint.

A crease formed between Phalue's brows. "Of course. I'll run it by him."

But not ask for his approval, Ranami noted. Phalue squeezed her shoulder again, sparing Ranami a tender glance. "I'll be diplomatic, don't worry."

"I didn't say—"

"You didn't have to." Phalue leaned over, kissing Ranami's forehead. "I know I'm rash, I act before looking or thinking – but sometimes I feel if I don't, I'll never move in the right direction at all. I know. I'll give Halong his due and I'll make peace with these Shardless Few, if they'll let me. What matters most to me is that no one hurt you and that Ayesh is safe."

Well, there was the wound they'd given her when trying to extract information, and Ayesh's encounter with Halong – but neither thing felt prudent to mention right now. In spite of Phalue's reassurances that she had changed, Ranami couldn't help but imagine her marching into the Shardless Few hideout, demanding the heads of anyone who'd dared laid a finger on her family. If they were to try and heal this rift, they needed to move forward without retribution.

And they *needed* to heal this rift. Ragan was not Dione. He'd burn the whole world if it didn't respond the way he wanted to. There was no reasoning with him, no turning his path or shaming him into helping. Ranami knew because she'd once felt the same way. But she'd learned to come to terms with her anger, to use it as a shield instead of a weapon.

Ragan had not.

Lin had her Imperial army, but she was facing Ragan's faction of Shardless Few and Dione's. There had to be a way to peace without tearing the islands of the Empire apart. Phalue had once bridged the gap for the people of Nephilanu. She could do it for the Empire, too.

Halong met them on the path when they were close to the hideout. He'd been on a different ship than Ranami. "Phalue," he said when he approached, his soldiers at his back. "Sai," he added belatedly. There was no more respect in his gaze than when he'd first met Phalue in his hut on the edge of the caro nut farms.

"He looked at me like I was a sleek, fat goat," Phalue had told Ranami later. "One that couldn't run, whose horns had been blunted. I'm not pampered, Ranami." Except she was – and Ranami could sense her annoyance that she couldn't change this part of her past.

Phalue stiffened beneath his regard, her arm coming away from Ranami's shoulders, leaving the space there feeling cold. Goosebumps trailed up Ranami's arm, and she wasn't sure if it was the absence of heat or her own apprehension.

"You've been caring for my wife and child, I've been told," Phalue said. "I appreciate that they're both well and unharmed."

Halong's gaze flicked to Ranami and then back to Phalue. He fell into step beside her as they made for the cliffs. Ranami held her breath. It was a pleasant enough start. There'd been a time when Phalue would have run roughshod over the entire conversation – but time tempered even the most reckless, it seemed.

"Ranami is an old friend," Halong said. "But I won't pretend that this was a diplomatic mission. We're at war. We came here to take Nephilanu for the Shardless Few, to put pressure on the Emperor to step down."

"But there are larger issues now," Phalue broke in. "Riya is gone."

Ranami hadn't realized she'd stopped – that everyone within hearing distance had stopped – until others began asking why they were no longer moving. Riya was one of the largest islands in the Empire and the biggest exporter of witstone. Without Riya, where would all those refugees live? Without Riya, how would the gears of trade in the Empire keep turning? Each island gone meant an immeasurable loss. Even now, refugees from Unta were still being integrated into Nephilanu's structure – a branch grafted onto a tree where it didn't quite fit.

"I think Ragan sunk it."

Ranami whirled to find Jovis and Mephi at her back, his expression stern. He was not the Jovis she remembered meeting, so long ago – driven to find his wife, agonizing between that and helping the people who needed him. It wasn't just the beard and the scar across one cheek. There was something sterner in his face, something colder.

"I don't know exactly how," Jovis continued before anyone else could speak up. "And I don't know if he had anything to do with the other islands sinking. But if he's headed to Imperial and he does not get what he wants, he will sink it too. And the next island. And the next. Ragan would rather rule over an Empire of one island that follows him than an Empire of many that resists."

Phalue took Halong's arm, guiding him as they continued to walk, and the rest of the Shardless Few followed, murmuring in alarmed tones in their wake. Ranami crept closer so she could hear their hushed conversation. "I came here to rescue my wife and child. If you have no intent of harming them, and my army is larger than yours, then I am the one with the advantages here. But I'd rather we work collaboratively. We *should* be working collaboratively to help our people."

Halong gave her a reluctant nod.

"So this is who you'd have us follow," a voice murmured by her ear. She stopped before the hideout entrance. An older Shardless Few woman touched her elbow and Ranami recalled having dinner next to her by the fire one of the nights Halong had relented and let her out to join the rest of them. "A woman who ordered her fleet to attack us."

Ranami opened her mouth to respond, to defend Phalue, but couldn't find the words. The woman was right. If she gave them the choice between Dione and Phalue, who among the Shardless Few would choose Phalue? Even now, she was using her position and her advantage to press Halong to help her. Phalue wanted to place them all on the same side, but the Shardless Few might not ever see it that way. She couldn't change her past.

Ranami's gaze flicked to Halong's back as he disappeared into the crack that led to the hideout. And Halong? He was a military leader, not a political one.

Ranami had always stepped back, letting others lead. Even when she'd been on the streets, she'd deferred to Halong – the older and presumably wiser of the two of them. Then she'd deferred to Dione, and to Phalue's leadership as governor.

Phalue had constantly told her that she saw her wife as an equal, but Ranami had never felt comfortable assuming more than a periphery, advisory role.

She was too damaged to be someone whom others looked up to or followed. She was too sharp-edged, too liable to snap. The one moment she'd had where she'd almost convinced the deserters to stay instead of follow Ragan was only that: a moment. It wasn't who she knew herself to be.

But she'd changed for Ayesh, had learned to mother for the sake of an orphan who'd grown up on the streets like she had. She'd learned to put her suspicion aside, to make herself vulnerable so that Ayesh could make herself vulnerable in turn.

Could she do the same for the Shardless Few?

Troubled, she patted the woman's hand reassuringly and followed Halong into the cave. It took them time to regroup, to gather in the cavern with the fires. Someone had started several pots of a spiced soup, the sizzle of frying fish and the scent of ginger making Ranami's mouth water.

Ayesh and Shark weren't in the cavern yet – she'd relegated them to the room below until she'd returned, afraid that her gamble for peaceable contact wouldn't work and they'd find themselves mired in fighting with the Imperial ships.

A stroke of luck that Phalue had been aboard.

She let her gaze linger on the faces around her as Phalue and Halong argued. It was a peaceable argument, but a disagreement nonetheless. She heard Phalue's tone go from pleading, to firm, to cajoling. There was none of the shouting, none of the impassioned anger she knew Phalue was capable of. Something had shifted in her during their time apart.

And something had shifted in Ranami too. As she looked at the faces of the Shardless Few, she recognized herself in them. The hurt orphan who wanted something better for everyone else, the one who'd taken each cut and hadn't healed them over but had used them to make her soul sharp. If she was damaged, then so were they.

"You cannot ask me to give over control of the remaining Shardless Few fleet to you. Dione has ordered me to take them to Imperial, not to distribute caro nuts," Halong was saying. They sat on some cushions close to the fire.

"We can do both."

"We," Halong said flatly.

This was going nowhere quickly. Ranami could read the signs. They might have wanted the same things in the end, but Halong and Phalue were too fundamentally different to agree, no matter how hard Phalue was trying.

She made a choice.

"We go to Imperial," Ranami cut in. Both of them looked up at her as though surprised she was there, surprised she could speak.

She lifted her voice over the crackling fire, over the murmuring conversations. And to her shock, everyone quieted to listen. "We stand at the edge of a precipice. The Empire is at war with itself, the Alanga have returned and they live among us and the very ground beneath our feet is uncertain. These are dark times."

Every eye in the room had focused on her, food in bowls forgotten. She felt the power in it. She felt the trust in it. And she knew, surely as she knew she would protect Ayesh with her life, that she would do everything in her power not to shatter that trust.

It had to be enough.

"But we have all been through dark times and have survived. We saw injustices visited upon us; we suffered beneath the weight of those above us; we existed in the cracks of society, yearning for a way to claw our way out." The "we" she used felt more certain than Phalue's. It felt true.

"And now we have a way out. But the way is twisting and turning and less certain than we thought it was. We could, like your brethren, accept Ragan's path and visit destruction and death on our oppressors — caring not for the damage we wreak on others on the way. Or we could accept Dione's — one that comes with caveats and hidden costs.

"Or we can take the hard path. We can dig our nails into this Empire and pick out the rot while leaving the rest unharmed. It won't be easy and it won't be quick, and it will cost us, I won't lie about that. Sometimes it will feel as though we've taken the wrong path. Yes, we need to distribute the caro nuts, but we also need to stop Ragan, and if that means that we ally with those in Lin's camp who mean us no harm, then so be it. The first thing we must do is ensure that we have a safe place to live before we can figure out what that place should look like.

"I asked you before to put your trust in my wife — and she does deserve it. I didn't lie about that. She has done everything I've asked of her and more. But we don't always get what we deserve, and sometimes, that's no one's fault. If I cannot ask you to trust her, can I ask that you trust me? I've lived among you — as a Shardless Few and as a prisoner. I've suffered the same indignities you have. Follow me and I won't have any hidden agendas, any goals other than this: to put power in the hands of the people whom power affects. I will do everything I can to finish what the Shardless Few set out to do: to establish rule of the Empire by a Council of its people."

Her words rang through the cavern, echoing from the walls. For a long while, no one said anything.

And then Halong cleared his throat, rising to face her. "I've made my share of mistakes, for which I can only hope you'll one day forgive me. But this, I think, won't be one of them. I would follow you, Ranami. To the depths of the Endless Sea and back."

A roar of assent rose from the other Shardless Few.

42

Lin

Imperial Island

We arrived too late. I should have known that no amount of hope could make a ship sail faster or slower, could halt the progression of time. Yet I'd let that hope grow, twining tendrils around my heart, buoying it. Time had seemed to have no meaning while we'd been floating at sea; surely it had ceased to have meaning for the rest of the world.

I smelled the smoke on the winds before I saw it.

Imperial was burning.

Flickers of flame still licked at some of the rooftops in the city, bright spots in the heavy smoke. I barely recognized the main street running from the palace to the docks; buildings had collapsed, obscuring the cobblestones. The worst was I wasn't even sure whose doing this was: Dione's or Ragan's. I'd made two powerful enemies, each of them vying to destroy me first.

Each caring little for the ones destroyed on their way to me.

I wasn't even aware I'd folded to the deck, my knees against the wood, until my guard's hand touched my shoulder.

"I'm fine," I said, though it wasn't true. My heart was burning with that city, turned to blackened ash. I waved him off. "I'm fine." I felt Thrana's presence brush against my mind. *Lin? I'm sorry.*

If she was sorry, I was sorrier still. Imperial was my home – no matter the wandering I'd done, no matter the terrible memories I held of an overbearing father, a cold palace. There were so many more, brighter memories. Dinner with Numeen's family, the scent of the blacksmith's forge when I'd first made my way into the city, the long walk back to the palace with Jovis, finding Thrana in the caves my father had locked away.

And it wasn't just my home that had been destroyed, but the home of all the people I'd promised to protect – first and foremost, even above the rest of the Empire.

There were the Imperial guard and a small contingent of soldiers I'd left behind, but I'd always counted on being *there* if Imperial was ever attacked, on lending my considerable strength to its defense. Instead, I'd been trapped in the wake of Riya's destruction, helpless to assist in any way.

I couldn't go back to a time when Imperial City was whole. I wanted to wallow in this despair, to let the tears fall freely, uncaring of who saw. But that wouldn't help anyone. I had to keep moving forward.

I lifted the spyglass to my eye again, steeling myself against the sights I knew I would see. It was worse on a second inspection – the bodies I hadn't seen before now visible as bloody lumps on the streets. The unfamiliar troops gathered by the docks. I moved the spyglass slowly upward, away from the docks and toward the palace.

Smoke obscured the view, but I could make out green-tiled rooftops, still whole. And when I lowered my view a little, I caught a glimpse of the gate.

Closed.

Imperial Palace was still standing. We still had forces within its walls, keeping the invaders at bay.

My knees went weak but this time I kept my footing. I thanked my past self for repairing the walls, for reinforcing the gates. My father had let the world around him fall into disrepair, and it had been a first step toward setting things right.

If the palace had held, then we still had a chance. But first I needed to find a way inside. I glanced back at my crew — the Imperial guards I had left, the sailors, the weary-faced captain. Fewer than I'd left Imperial with.

The guard who'd directed our escape from Riya stood at my elbow. He eyed my expression. "Eminence? You have a plan."

"The palace isn't taken. There must still be forces behind its walls. If they've been able to hold against Alanga, then my presence will only strengthen them." My fingers closed around the hilt of the sword at my belt.

"And our presence?" the guard said lightly.

"Would slow me down," I said.

"Our duty—"

"Is to protect the Emperor," I cut in. "But that duty was written when Emperors were only mortal and though sharp of mind, their bodies needed protecting."

"Alanga are not invincible, Eminence." The man's voice was not reproachful, though it was approaching such.

"No, they are not. But the best way to get into the palace is by stealth — which means going through the mountains. If we try to get through the gates, we risk a breach of the walls. If I take you with me through the mountains, then I might not get there in time. I can take Thrana. She can climb quicker than any of us. She won't be noticed if we keep beneath the tree line and we approach from the north."

"And the rest of us are to sit idly on the ship while you undertake this dangerous mission?" He raised a brow.

I shook my head. "Get word out that this is happening. Tell the other islands not to come to our aid but to shore up their defenses. Help any refugees you find. And this is what's most important: have them protect the entrances to their mines. It's how Ragan sunk Riya. We can't lose any more islands." I wanted to protect Imperial the most, but Imperial wasn't the whole of the Empire. Every island we lost was a detriment to us all.

I had the sailors prepare the only rowboat, my heart pounding as they lowered me to the Endless Sea. Thrana swam up to meet me. Her new horns had begun to grow in, though it wasn't this that I noticed first. She'd grown even more in the time since her hibernation, her head now nearly as long as I was tall.

She took the rope I'd tied to the prow in her teeth and swam toward Imperial. It felt odd for a moment, being alone in the boat, no guards at my back, no maidservants to tend to me. I'd grown more used to these things in the past few years than I'd cared to admit.

But I'd begun this whole journey alone, with my father and Bayan both too distant for me to think of them as friends. Somehow, approaching Imperial with only Thrana at my side felt a bit like coming back to the beginning.

We skirted past the city, and I used a little of my power to lift the water in front of us so prying eyes would miss our passage. The smell of smoke grew stronger the closer we grew to the island, and soon I could hear distant shouting and screaming – the grief and confusion of those who had lost everything.

I clenched my fingers around my thighs, caught between rage and sadness. Hadn't the Empire suffered enough losses without purposefully burning some of it to the ground?

We made it aground quickly, just after it had begun to rain.

Thrana shook out her coat, though she needn't have bothered. I clambered aboard her back and we disappeared into the forest east of Imperial City. Among the green, wet leaves, with the rain washing away the smoke, it was easy to forget the devastation we'd just witnessed.

I worried for those left in the palace. How many people had they been able to take in behind the walls before they'd had to close the gates? How was Ikanuy handling things? My remaining guards? Were they safe? How much of a defensive force had we managed to retain?

It took Thrana and me until noon to make it up into the mountains by the palace. Jagged stone rose into the misty air like the fingertips of giants. She navigated the cliffs like a gecko clambering across a wall, her claws finding purchase in even the steepest slopes. I clung to her fur for dear life, though she assured me, over and over, that she would not let me fall.

We finally broke through the tree cover, the brush turning to scrub and determined saplings. Though fog obscured the view, I could still see the smoking remains of buildings in the city. Whatever attack had happened, they'd granted a reprieve. Likely they'd delivered terms to the palace and were waiting for a response.

Which meant this was almost certainly Dione and not Ragan.

I directed Thrana to the walled terrace where the cloudtree grew, and she slid into the enclosure like a cat into a bowl. I unclenched my sore fingers from her fur, the damp wood smell of the cloud juniper bark filling the air.

"Can you get to the courtyard on your own?" I asked Thrana, holding her chin in my hands, stroking the curling beard that grew there.

She gave me a derisive snort, as though it were the silliest question in the world. "Lin, I am not a horse. The terrain cannot break me." And then, as though to prove her point, she was clambering back over the wall and into the mountains, leaving me on the terrace, the rain seeping into my clothes. I patted the trunk of the tree as though it were an old friend, plucked a few ripened berries from the branches to tuck into my sash and began the trek down the stairs to the palace proper.

I was met with silence as I opened the door. The palace wasn't empty; I could feel that indefinable presence that meant there were others nearby, but it was as though everyone was holding their breaths, waiting for the next disaster.

Everything seemed at once familiar and strange, the smell of my home flooding my nostrils — all musty old wood and damp stone and the faint scent of sandalwood, still lingering from my father's reign. I'd taken the scents for granted when I'd lived here; now they rushed over me, making me ache with nostalgia and memories. Bayan, Hao and, yes, even my father. I could not go back to those times. I could not start this all over, searching for better paths.

I wasn't sure there were any.

I met no servants on my way to Ikanuy's study, though the farther into the palace I walked, the louder the faint sound of preparation work in the kitchens grew. Ikanuy was exactly where I'd expected to find her, hunched over her desk, her cheek in her hand, papers and ledgers stacked neatly around her and an unfolded letter in the other hand.

Her hair had been iron-gray when I'd first hired her, a faint web of wrinkles marking her mouth and forehead. The lines there had deepened, her hair fading into white. Guilt pricked at me as I closed the door behind me. I'd left her with a heavy charge. I'd had my justifications, but Phalue was right: I'd dealt with loftier goals and had left the minutiae to others, thinking them unimportant. They weren't.

Ikanuy started at the *click* of the door shutting, the letter fluttering from her fingertips. The hand on her cheek left a pink impression across her skin; she must have been sitting that way for some time.

"You're back." She didn't sound as though she quite believed her own words. "Oh, Eminence, you're *back*." This time she sounded more sure, color flooding her face to redden the other cheek. Ikanuy shot to her feet, gathering papers from around her, hesitating before picking up the letter again. "We tried to hold the city. We tried so hard." She was clutching the papers too tightly, her knuckles white, the papers crinkling in her fingers.

She suddenly noticed what she was doing and let out a gasp, and then a sob.

I was at her side without thinking, a hand at her arm to support her, another at her back. "It's not your fault, Ikanuy. It's not. I should have been here. I tried too – but it wasn't enough. If it's anyone's fault, it's mine." I let her cry, her shoulders shaking, feeling more wretched than I'd felt even watching the city burn from the ship. It had still been a distant thing then, and now I felt the full brunt of it up close. "Your family—"

"Safe," she said, wiping her eyes with one shaking hand. "We were able to get them and many others inside the walls before the city was attacked. Some of our guards thought we could hold the city, but I knew better. I've seen what Alanga can do. Still, there were those that didn't leave their homes, or didn't gather their belongings fast enough. Eminence, it's been terrible. We could hear them screaming from the courtyard. They didn't ask for peace before burning the city."

"Ikanuy, I'm so sorry. This should never have been your job. I only meant you to be an administrator, not a defender of this city." Is this what I would have done with Numeen had he lived? Pushed him to the very point of breaking because I needed him?

"I did my best."

"I know."

Finally, her breathing evened out, the sobs quieting, the tears drying. "Here. This came this afternoon." She pushed the letter into my hands. "It's from Dione."

So that was his army at my doorstep.

The missive was short and to the point.

Surrender the palace. The Emperor must abdicate her position and face execution when she returns. Fail to meet these terms and we will raze the rest of Imperial and take the palace by force. You have until tomorrow evening to respond.

Dione, the last of the old Alanga

43

Jovis

Imperial Island

It had been a turn of events I hadn't quite expected. Ranami, now the leader of these remaining Shardless Few? Oh, she'd have to answer to Dione for that, and I didn't think any number of pretty speeches would turn him from his path, no matter how well that had worked on the rest of them.

But maybe I was wrong. I'd been wrong before, after all. On the occasion.

I rubbed at my chest, caught myself doing it and lowered my hand back to my side. Sometimes when I woke in the early hours of the morning, I thought I could *feel* the shards within me, digging their way toward my heart. Only my imagination. But, as my mother had often noted, I had a prolific imagination.

Rain pattered onto the deck and the hood of the oilskin cloak I'd pilfered from the army's supplies. I scratched the stubble on my chin. I'd shaved the beard, and my hair was starting to grow out again. I might not have felt like my old self, but I was starting to look it. We'd be at Imperial soon. Ranami and Phalue had hidden some stores of witstone with their caro nuts, and the Imperial army and the Shardless Few had burned the rest of it to make all haste here.

I hoped we weren't too late.

Mephi lay on the deck next to me, dismantling the head of a fish that was nearly as large as he was. He gave me a bloody grin. "Almost back home," he said. His ears pricked. "Steamed buns? From the street vendors? Or maybe sticky sesame balls. Yes. I would like those too."

He might have attained a certain gravitas as he'd grown, his beard now as long as any old man's, but when it came to food, Mephi was still just a pup at heart. I'd not thought of Imperial as my home, but I supposed for Mephi, it had been the place we'd stayed the longest.

"Anything and everything you want. But first——"

Words dried in my mouth as we rounded an outcropping and caught our first glimpse of Imperial City. I'd known Ragan was on his way, and Dione too, but I'd thought Dione would have waited for the rest of his army. I'd thought Ragan would have waited for Dione. They both wanted the same thing: to depose Lin.

But why would anyone wait? Without the army, Imperial had been left with meager defenses. There hadn't been the need for more forces.

Someone had razed the city.

Blackened husks now stood where buildings had once been. The streets were half-covered, obscured by rubble. Any fires had long since been put out by the rain, only a faint haze of smoke visible – the last remnants of warmth from somewhere deep within the city. Imperial City had once been a bustling port, streets bursting with color and light, people moving from place to place with only the haste those in a city could manage. Now it was gray and listless and lifeless.

Mephi would not get his steamed buns or his sticky sesame balls.

Phalue was in front of me at the prow, Halong and Ranami next to her, and they passed a spyglass between them, detachedly noting the things they were seeing. "Shardless Few soldiers patrolling the streets," Halong said. "Not sure whose command they're under."

"If there were bodies, they've cleared them." Phalue's voice was grim.

"The palace is holding, though." Ranami pointed through the haze to the buildings nestled into the mountains, the jade-green tiles of its rooftops a bright spot of color above the gray. "It doesn't look like they've attacked it, which means this is probably the work of Dione. Can we talk some sense into him? Have him hold off his attack until we deal with Ragan? We're facing the possibility of three armies fighting one another."

"I won't make the Shardless Few fight against their own," Halong said, his jaw clenched.

I leapt up the steps to the prow, coming up behind them and slinging my arms around both Halong and Ranami's necks. Halong glared at me. Ranami pushed my arm away without preamble. "Listen," I said, "that's still three armies – Dione's, Ragan's and Lin's. We made it this far without killing one another."

Phalue gave me a wry look before her expression firmed and she nodded. "He's right. None of us except Ragan are spoiling for a fight. We can still try to deescalate this situation. We can still find a peaceable solution."

"Can you meet Dione?" Ranami asked Halong. "He might listen to you. I've taken control of some of his Shardless Few. He may not want to listen to me."

He gave her a swift nod.

"I can speak to Lin," I said, maybe a tad too quickly. They all turned to look at me.

"There are soldiers between you and the palace. How do you propose getting there?" Halong said, an eyebrow raised.

I felt something of my old self flooding into my veins, as though I'd removed a tourniquet. "You've Shardless Few here on board, and those soldiers on the streets are Shardless Few. Lend me a small phalanx. Let me spin a few lies if we get confronted. It's nothing I haven't done before."

Boards creaked behind me and the gazes of all three of the people in front of me lifted to somewhere above my head.

"Yes, well, things might have changed since then," Ranami said, her voice dry.

I looked up to find Mephi looming over me, some unidentifiable piece of gore hanging from one tooth. He swiped his tongue over his mouth, though that did little to clean up his appearance.

"He could stay here?"

A growl started low in Mephi's throat. "No. We stay *together*. I do not leave you *ever again*."

Trust me, a smuggler – my entire profession predicated on stealth – to somehow end up with a creature who would grow to a few times my size and who would insist on being at my side at all times. I closed my eyes briefly, knowing that if my mother were here she'd have her arms crossed, a knowing look on her face that would very much say, "Serves you right for becoming a smuggler in the first place, you foolish boy."

So I found myself mounted on a cloaked Mephi, a phalanx of Shardless Few at my back, clambering onto shore a little west of the Imperial City docks, hoping we hadn't been spotted. The Shardless Few with me pulled the rowboat into the trees, covering it with brush.

"You're not a very convincing horse," I told Mephi.

His tail lashed. "Tell them I'm an ox."

"Hopefully we don't get close enough for anyone to ask me anything."

"I'm your beast of burden and I've caught a cold." He gave an experimental few coughs. "See? You had to cover me up to keep me warm."

"Mephi, I can't use that. That's a terrible lie."

"Haven't had as much practice as you." He gave one last swish of his tail before tucking it beneath the cloak. It looked as though I wasn't riding a horse or an ox but a lump. An extremely suspicious-looking lump.

But it was the only thing we could come up with on short notice.

We made our way to the city streets – or at least, what was left of them. It at once felt more and less crowded than it once had. Broken tiles and charred boards covered the cobblestones and we had to pick our way through them. At the same time, collapsed buildings meant we had more line of sight than we would have when the city had been whole. I startled once to realize we were making our way through an alleyway that had once been behind a drinking hall. Both the drinking hall and the building abutting it were gone, charred to ashes.

Luck had carried me a good ways in my life, pleasant as a favorable wind. But luck, just like the wind, still ran out. We were halfway to the palace when we encountered a patrol.

"Hold!" called out the captain, lifting her hand high enough so we could see. They were all on foot – of course they were. We'd not seen anyone on horseback through the spyglass. It was the first failure of this plan.

But there were many, many more fail points. I cleared my throat, preparing to prop up this leaning house of lies with whatever popped into my head. "Ah! Good to see a friendly face out here," I called out to her.

I dug my heels into Mephi's sides and he started toward the patrol, doing his best imitation of a horse's gait. We halted a street away, a pile of rubble between us and the other patrol.

"Everything is fine in this quarter," I called out to the Shardless Few captain. I put as much authority and certainty into my voice as I dared. The armband around my upper arm felt at once too tight and too loose. I remembered the last time I'd pretended to be a soldier – back on Deerhead. That hadn't gone well either. "Haven't found any more strays."

But every new opportunity is an opportunity for things to go right, isn't it?

"Except your horse," the captain said. "We didn't bring horses."

"Oh, this old beast?" I patted the cloak over Mephi's neck as he made a tiny, disgruntled noise in the back of his throat.

Old?

Play along, I said back to him.

"Found him in some burned-out stables. Still standing there as though he had no idea there was an outside world he could run off to. Horses, eh?"

Mephi coughed.

"Smoke inhalation," I said, patting his neck again. I drew my hand back, clenching my fingers into a fist. I needed to stop doing that. It was a nervous tell if I ever saw one. "He's, uhhh...sick."

"We don't get to keep anything we find, including animals," the captain said. Her frown was as clear as if she'd been standing right in front of me. "Everything gets taken back to camp and handed in."

"Of course. Was just headed there."

She nodded, her gaze still not wavering. Dione's balls, if only we'd gotten here sooner – while things had still been chaotic and unsure. We'd come at the worst time, right at the quiet after battle, when everyone was taking stock of what had happened, when they had the time to contemplate any-thing unusual.

Her gaze finally broke from mine and she waved to her fellows. "Carry on, then."

A gust of wind blew, ruffling the cloaks we'd so carefully laid across Mephi's body, exposing one of his branching horns.

The captain stopped. For a moment, we just stared at one another.

"He's . . .*really* sick," I managed.

And then she was charging over the rubble toward us, her Shardless Few soldiers in her wake. "Help! To me! An attack!" she shouted, her voice carrying into the silent, gray city.

"Go," I gasped out to the Shardless Few with me. "To the palace." They ran, several nearly tripping over debris. I brought up the rear with Mephi. I had to put distance between us and those soldiers. Without thinking, I gathered the rain from the air, forming a wave which I pushed at our pursuers.

"Alanga!" a few of them cried out.

Well, if they thought us only a ragtag band of survivors before, they knew differently now. We were halfway to the palace, which meant there was still time for us to be cut off by another patrol.

The captain of the Shardless Few seemed to know this, too, shouting every so often about an attack and that she needed aid. Sweat mingled with rainwater as it trickled down the back of my neck. The city smelled of ashes and smoke, flashes of memory hitting me with each corner we turned. Here was the place I used to get fried fish balls from; there was the place I used to buy a packet of dumplings for Mephi and me to share; and up ahead was the drinking hall I'd gone to when I'd been a student at the Navigators' Academy. All of it – gone.

And Shardless Few quick on our heels. It was a nightmarish landscape, one I couldn't wake from.

The palace walls rose ahead of us, painted red but licked black in spots. The gates were charred but closed. Out of the corner of my eye, I saw movement. Another patrol, heading over to cut us off.

I threw off the hood of my cloak and tore the hood from Mephi's head.

"Open the gates and quickly! I'm here to help!" The gates remained closed. If someone was watching us, I didn't see them.

"It's Jovis!" one of the soldiers with me called out. "He's alive."

The Shardless Few converged. We pressed against the gates and I slid from Mephi's back, pulling free my steel staff. "Now would be a good time to open those gates," I called out. The tremor filled my bones; I stayed light on my feet, waiting.

They attacked.

I knew they didn't have to win – they only had to hold out until more Shardless Few arrived. And they seemed to know this too, darting in and away like minnows feeding from the surface of a pond. Each time I tried to use my magic, they fell away, and though I could make the ground shake I was wary of shaking it too much with the walls at our backs. I didn't want to bring down the palace's defenses. It was like having a large, heavy sword but only being able to wield it in a tiny space. Even the waves I sent lashing after them were cramped, splashing uselessly into the rubble of the city.

A mote of color appeared in the edge of my vision. Another group of Shardless Few, marching on us. A spike of fear almost paralyzed my hands mid-swing as I fought off two soldiers. Was Ragan here? Was Nisong? I couldn't fight them again, couldn't become a tool, my will subsumed.

And then a creak sounded from behind me. The gate, opening a crack. "Through the gate!" I called to my phalanx. They slid through the gap as I held off our attackers, Mephi's growls from beside me lending me strength.

"Mephi, go." I stamped a foot, sending a tremor toward the attackers, setting them a little off balance – enough to get a few blows in with my staff.

His ears flattened against his head, the cloaks we'd used to cover him now in tatters. "Not without *you*." Before I could react, he'd seized my shoulder in his mouth and was dragging me back toward the gate. The Shardless Few pressed forward.

Even as we made it through the crack, they pushed against the gates, trying to open them further. My heartbeat pounded in my ears, my face hot, horror closing around my throat. Would they finally breach them and take the palace? And would it be my fault?

I leaned into the gates with the Imperial guards who'd let us in, with my phalanx of Shardless Few, with Mephi. We shoved against the wood, slick with rain, our feet slipping against the cobblestones. Shouts and grunts arose from the other side as they pushed back.

"Together," I gasped out. "One . . . two . . . *three*!" We all put our weight into it and I, my Alanga-enhanced strength. One last glimpse of the city beyond and then the gate was closed, the Imperial guards barring it shut.

I sagged against the wood.

"Is it really you?" One of the guards was leaning over me, peering at my face as though it were a portrait she was studying. "Jovis?"

I lifted up my right hand and pulled the sleeve back to reveal the scar where the tattoo had been. "See for yourself." The shards within me prickled but did not burn.

"Lin will want to speak to you right away."

Yes, she would. Dread swelled within me as I felt the sharp burn of the shards within me – this time, not a dream or an imagining. I needed to find a way to explain. A way to get around the commands and to get close to her. An idea simmered in the back of my mind. I'd come this far, hadn't I? And there were ways around – there always were.

I peered back at the woman and felt like I was reaching into a murky cistern to pluck loose a coin. I knew that face. "Denala, is it?" She blinked but nodded. So that was why I'd been let in. Someone had finally recognized me from my days as the Captain of the Imperial Guard.

"Before you fetch Lin, there are a few things I need you to do."

44

Lin

Imperial Island

He was *here*. I didn't need this right now on top of everything else — the army at my doorstep, Dione's ultimatum, the possibility of Ragan and Nisong out there somewhere. But I couldn't turn him away, not without knowing what had happened to him these past two years, why he'd attacked me during that ambush, and why he was here now.

And if I was honest with myself, there was still a part of me that hoped there *was* a reasonable explanation for everything. We'd been apart longer than we'd known one another, but I missed his steady presence, his terrible jokes, his advice. And beyond that, I could have used his help. We'd had the chance to take stock of the situation, to count the troops marching through the streets of Imperial, and we were in dire straits.

I followed my guard through the hallways of the palace, lifting the hood of my cloak before I made my way into the courtyard. Rain fell in sheets, darkening the morning sky to a muddled gray. Thrana sat near the palace entrance, an assortment of food from the kitchen between her paws, uncaring that it was all getting damp, very quickly. The broad, empty expanse of the courtyard had been filled with makeshift shelters. Some had set up fires and cooking stations, and were helping to feed everyone who'd escaped the destruction of Imperial City. Many looked to Thrana with awe and uncertainty. I couldn't blame them – she was the largest ossalen I'd ever seen. Mephi was next to her, the size of a war horse now, but still dwarfed by her presence. She was parceling off some of the food she'd been given to him while he nipped at her paws and made a general nuisance of himself.

Mephi hadn't changed much, it seemed. Now to tend to his master.

My guard led me to the Hall of Everlasting Peace. There were people sheltering inside as well, and they bowed their heads as we passed. But the second floor of the hall was empty and dark. She stopped in front of a small door – a modest guest room. "He's inside," she said. She hesitated, as though she were about to say something else, and then just stepped back. "I'll be waiting here in case you need me."

"I won't need you. Please return to your duties."

I slipped inside the room. For a moment, I stood at the entrance, waiting as my eyes adjusted to the dimness of the interior. There was one window, but with the overcast sky, it didn't let in much light. No one had lit any lamps.

I fumbled for the tinderbox at the lintel.

"Don't." Jovis's voice emanated from the room. "I'm afraid that if you do, I'll be able to see you through the cloth and have to admit that it's you."

I opened my mouth, but he spoke over me. "Don't say anything either. I'd know your voice." He sighed. "I'd know it anywhere."

Finally, I could see him, sitting in a chair in the middle of the room. As I drew closer, my cloak brushing against the floor, I noticed something else. He wasn't just sitting in the chair. He was tied to it. And blindfolded.

"I haven't been myself," Jovis said, and then he let out a bitter laugh. "Oh, that's a mild way of putting it. The short of it is – Kaphra made a bargain with Nisong and Ragan. They ambushed me when I went to rescue Mephi. They placed shards *inside* me. And then Kaphra made me do whatever he asked, holding Mephi's life over my head in case I put up too much of a fight. He had one of the white-bladed swords."

I had nothing to lean on, though I felt suddenly dizzy, my heartbeat racing. Of course. Why hadn't I thought of that? When he hadn't come back, when I'd received his tattoo in a box, I'd assumed he was dead. And when I'd seen him on Riya, I hadn't healed as much as I'd thought I'd had from his previous betrayal. I'd just assumed he was betraying me again. I could have searched for him.

I hadn't. So much wasted time. So much unnecessary suffering – his and the suffering of the people he'd hurt.

The light from the window outlined Jovis's form. He trembled, caught in some terrible memory. "I did eventually find ways around the commands, though it takes all the skill I've built up from lying over the years – to others, to myself and to you." His voice was soft, though it filled the room. "There are shards inside me that tell me I cannot get close to Lin, that I cannot approach her. So you are not her."

"I understand," I said. He winced at the sound of my voice, as though the shards inside him were causing him pain, though he could not move away. I took the last step toward him and knelt in front of the chair. Slowly, I placed a hand on his chest. I could feel the warmth of his skin from beneath his tunic. He was here. He was real. "But *I* can approach you. I can get close to you."

"Kaphra is dead, and I took his sword, but I need to be free," Jovis choked out. "Really, completely free. I know I don't deserve to ask anything of you, not after everything I've done. But . . .please."

I moved his collar to one side, noting the scar at his chest, a remnant of his time with Kaphra. He'd fought — of course he had, the fool. Wounds from the white-bladed swords might eventually heal, but they always scarred. "This won't hurt. But it will feel strange." I took a breath, feeling it enter my lungs, diving into the mental state necessary for bone shard magic. And then, ever so gently, I pressed my hand into Jovis's flesh.

It turned insubstantial beneath my touch, warmth surrounding my hand as it entered him. A short, quick gasp from Jovis and then nothing but silence and stillness. The shards Nisong had placed inside him felt like sharp, hot spots, bright to my fingers. I traced a fingertip along their edges, knowing as soon as I did so that these were ossalen shards. Ragan's ossalen, Lozhi. I should have known those two would find one another, falling into one another's wounds, trying to fill the hollows they each keenly felt, unaware that this was what they were doing.

But a person can't heal another using their own flesh and blood.

I gathered the shards in my hand, tugging each one loose, like plucking ripened fruit. When I finally removed my hand, stuffed full of these shards, Jovis's breath left him a rush. He sagged in the chair as though he'd just run a great distance, sweat beading on his forehead.

"It's done?"

I didn't answer, instead piling the shards off to the side and working the knot on the rope wound at his left wrist. I pulled it free, the fibers rubbing against the wooden armrest. Deliberately, I took his hand, noting the new calluses, the roughness of his palms. I turned it over, tracing the lines in his palm before I gently pushed up his shirtsleeve.

A mottled white scar lay there, in the exact shape of the tattoo I'd received in the box. I wasn't sure what I was feeling as my fingers moved over his skin, over the hills and valleys of the puckered flesh. It felt like a dream, the warmth of him an intangible thing that could fade with the light.

With an odd detachment, I noted the way the goosebumps prickled his arm, the way his chest rose and fell, the blindfold obscuring his eyes from mine.

I wasn't sure I was ready to meet them.

"This one –" I traced the raised ridges of the scar. "– the one on your cheek, and the one on your chest. How many more?"

"Lin," he said, and stopped, his voice choked. "Lin," he said again, as though the taste of my name on his tongue was a thing sweeter than any honey, "it's been two years. I . . .I lost count."

"I want to see."

He swallowed and then nodded.

I knelt before him and reached for the cloth buttons of his tunic, unfastening them with one hand, still holding his left wrist in the other. He didn't ask me to remove the blindfold, nor did he break my grip to take it off himself. Maybe he felt the same thing I did – that he could fade at any moment if I pushed things too far, too fast. That this was a dream we needed to stay steeped in, lest waking washed it away.

In the dim light, the scars on his torso were still visible – stark white lines against tanned skin. His breath stirred against my hair as I let go of his wrist and traced each one, measuring their lengths. "Too many." The muscles of his stomach tensed and relaxed with each brush of my fingertips. I still couldn't look at his face. Unsure of what to say, and afraid he might push me away, I leaned in and pressed my cheek to his chest. His heartbeat was strong and quick beneath my ear, though the rest of him was still as he'd been when I'd removed the shards.

I cleared my throat. "I never should have given up on you. I shouldn't have let myself believe you were dead. I could have searched for you. I could have put together the pieces when I heard there was an Alanga helping Kaphra. I should have known it was you." I spoke all my regrets into the darkness, feeling them swallowed.

"You were trying to hold an Empire together."

"All the same, I am sorry. I am so terribly sorry."

"I know." He released his grip on the armrest, brushing his hand over my hair. I relaxed at his touch, my body sagging into his. How like Jovis – to forgive so quickly, so easily.

My breath melded with his, our chests rising and falling together. I drew away, daring to look up at his face, his hand still cupped at the back of my neck. Had I forgiven him? We'd not had enough time after the Battle of Gaelung except for a few stolen kisses, whispered words, and then he'd been gone. I'd thought he'd not kept his promise to return to me when I'd received his tattoo in a box – at once hurt, angry and filled with inconsolable grief.

But in spite of everything, he had come back. He'd fought his way through command shards, through Kaphra, through the streets of Imperial. He'd been forced apart from Mephi, made to use his powers to hurt and kill. My sweet, grumpy Jovis, with the tender heart he rarely let show. How long since he'd been touched with any kindness? With any love? I couldn't know that he still felt as he had when he'd left me. I wasn't even sure what I felt. There was something fragile about the way he touched me, even now with the shards removed. But he didn't push me away.

My gaze still focused on his face, I dared to turn mine toward him. I pressed my lips to the scar by his collarbone. I watched as he took in a breath and held it, his hand limp against my neck. He said nothing, his body tense beneath mine.

So I moved lower, kissing the next scar, and then next, as though this could heal these imperfections. I stared at the long one at the bottom of his ribs, my hands grasping his hips. I leaned in to lay my lips against it and then his fingers were tightening in my hair, a soft, mewling sound escaping his mouth.

Heat filled my belly, my hands becoming greedy things, wanting to touch every part of him, to possess him as completely as I could. How could I have been unsure of what I felt? I *knew*. He was not Kaphra's.

He was *mine*.

I scraped my teeth against his skin, feeling the bone beneath, feeling him shiver. My heart felt as though it were being drawn from me, kicking at my ribs as if trying to find a way out. The chair rocked as Jovis worked his other hand free, as he wrapped it around me, pressing me tightly to him. I laughed at this miniature escape. "I should have known you had a way out, no matter how it appeared."

He tugged at my hair and then I was rising to my feet, kneeling and straddling him on the chair, the wood creaking beneath our combined weight. I worked my hands from his chest to his neck, my lips finally meeting his. It felt for a moment as though we were still in that room at Gaelung, the battle finally passed. I wanted to live in that moment, to never have parted from him. So many things had happened since then – things I wanted to wish away. He pulled back and I felt the coldness of the space between us. The years. The uncertainty.

Quietly, he touched the collar of my robe, pushing it away from my neck, his fingers making their way beneath the cloth to my shoulders. He leaned forward and his lips brushed against my ear, his breath ragged. Stubble scraped against the soft skin of my neck and I shuddered. "Tell me you want me to stop."

"No." My voice, husky and filled with desire, didn't sound like my own.

I heard the smile in his voice. "Always so contrary, Eminence." His lips and tongue pressed hot into the hollow just behind my ear and I lost all coherent thought. I was tugging away his shirt, helping him unfasten my sash, my fingers trembling. A tremor of magic filled my chest, my hands steadied and Jovis laughed, the vibration of the sound mingling with the magic within him. Two thrumming hearts and thrumming bones, all in an odd harmony with one another.

Before I could second-guess myself, I reached up to tear the blindfold from his face. His dark gaze met mine. My belly lurched. I could barely see his eyes in the dimness of the room but I felt the heat of his regard, the wanting, the spark of hope that he'd locked away but that had never quite died.

"Be with me," I whispered. "Please."

He reached a hand to my face, tucking a stray strand of hair back behind my ear. And then he leaned in, kissing my forehead, my eyelids, my cheeks, my mouth. When he spoke against my lips, his voice soft, it was as though it were the last breath of a drowning man. "Always."

45

Jovis

Imperial Island

I woke with a start, somehow knowing I never should have fallen asleep. Lin's palm was warm against my bare chest and she murmured some soft, soothing sound that didn't quite form a word. I placed my hand over hers, marveling at how natural it felt, how right.

Dim, stormy light still filtered in through the closed shutters, so the day hadn't yet waned.

There was still an army at Imperial City's doorstep. Three armies, to be exact. And I'd been in bed with the Emperor. I moved again and felt a rope still attached to my left ankle. I wasn't sure when we'd made our way from the chair to the bed, but I remembered with a startling clarity that she'd wrapped her legs around my waist and that I'd carried her to the bed, our lips and bodies still locked together.

I turned my face toward her.

She was watching me, fully awake, her gaze serious and piercing. Not quite the way I'd imagined this would go. In my imaginings, we'd lazed about in bed afterward, the sun filtering in through the window, the faint chirps of birds whispering in upon the air along with the scent of steaming bread. Instead, it was dark, slightly cold and very gray. And nothing about Lin said "lazy", even *if* she was lying in bed next to me, unclothed. "I would have woken you if it got too late," she said.

"You didn't sleep."

She shook her head and stretched her arms and I couldn't help but trace the lines of her body with my gaze, wanting nothing more than to pull her into my arms again and to forget what we faced. She gave me a wry, somewhat sad smile. "I wanted to. But I can't – not right now. There are too many things to do, too many things we need to prepare."

"You have an army awaiting you. I came here with the Shardless Few, with Ranami and Phalue. The occupation of Nephilanu is ended. The Imperial troops are under Yeshan's command and are yours, but I don't know where Ranami's Shardless Few will fall. They follow her, but who knows what they will do with Dione now in the mix? Ragan broke off a contingent of the Shardless Few, and judging by the number of them on Imperial, Ragan is here."

Lin reached out a hand, tracing my forehead with one finger, her gaze on my hairline. "Dione is here as well, and they aren't fighting each other so I have to assume they've joined forces. They had a quarrel at some point, though it seems they've settled it for now. Both want to bring me down, so I suppose their purposes are now aligned. But there's a wedge there we might be able to use."

"Even so, there are more of them than there are of us."

"We have me. And you." She slithered across the sheets to wrap an arm around my waist, her fingers settling warm against my lower back.

Panic flashed through me. I knew what she expected of me.

She knew what I was capable of. Why wouldn't I then go on to help her defend Imperial? I'd done well enough in front of the walls, faced by the Shardless Few soldiers.

But I knew as soon as I saw Nisong or Ragan, I'd fall apart.

Carefully, I removed her hand from my waist, sliding from bed and picking my clothes up from the floor. I felt Lin's gaze on me, though I couldn't see her expression. "What is it?"

I pulled on my pants and then found my tunic, shrugging it back on. I turned to face her as I buttoned it back up again. I was such a coward – I wished to be blindfolded again so that I wouldn't have to meet her eyes. "I can't. I can't help you the way you want me to."

Her hair was slightly mussed, no anger marring her expression, no disappointment, only a slight puzzlement. She sat up, her head tilted to the side, the sheets slipping from her shoulders. Unselfconsciously, she rose, finding her robes pooled on the floor by the chair. She stepped into them, giving me a moment's reprieve from her regard. But then she was looking at me again. She touched my arm as I finished buttoning up my tunic, her fingers soft as her gaze. "What happened to you?"

I would freeze, the way I'd frozen on Riya. If I couldn't find it within me to run, they'd catch me. Nisong would put those shards inside me and I'd be caught. "You don't want me on your side, Lin. You don't want me on that battlefield."

"You think I don't want you there, or you don't want to be there?"

I squeezed my eyes shut and then took her hand and gently removed it from my arm. "Both. Neither. I don't know. Lin, I've done terrible things. I'm not who I was before. I'm not a hero. I'm not who you need me to be, who everyone needs me to be." I leaned down, picked up my steel staff and strapped it to my back. I hesitated for a moment before lifting the white-bladed sword from the floor. Lin's was there too, the hilt a match to mine. Her gaze followed it as I belted it on, and though she didn't comment on it, I could tell she wanted to.

And then we were both standing in the quiet of the room, fully dressed, the soft patter of rain at the shutters, a murmuring of voices from the people gathered downstairs and in the court-yard – punctuated every so often by a cough. She'd left the shards that had been inside me piled on the floor, as if uncertain what to do with them. It seemed strange that only moments before we'd been in bed together, our fingers and our bodies entwined.

I'd let this all happen and I hadn't even told her what I'd done. Who I was now. "I'm sorry – I should have explained everything to you before you . . . before we—"

This time, her voice was not soft. "I don't regret it." Her chin tilted up in that way I was so familiar with. Her lip trembled a moment before firming up again. "Do you?"

I took the two steps to close the gap between us, cradling her face in my hands. I'd spent two years wishing to see her again, afraid that the memories of her would fade until I could do nothing but live in the present – to be Kaphra's tool and nothing more. I'd lied to her, I'd deceived her, but in the end, she'd believed in me. I'd needed that belief. She'd helped me cling to some of my identity, to some of my hope, during my time with Kaphra, though she didn't know it.

But I hadn't been able to cling to all of it. No matter how closely I'd held the memories of my time before Kaphra, his commands had begun to creep outside of the shards and into the rest of me. I felt sullied by the things he'd made me do, even more so by the things he hadn't strictly commanded me to do, but I'd known would please him.

I'd done it to survive, to find a way through, with both Mephi and me intact – physically, at least. Could that be forgiven? I couldn't even forgive myself.

But this I could not lie about. "I don't regret it, even if I think I should."

She relaxed into my touch, her cheek resting in my palm, her eyelids fluttering briefly closed.

I swallowed, gathering the shreds of my courage. "I won't deceive you – not again, not about anything. You should know the things I've done, and not just the stories. Yes, Kaphra forced me to be the arbiter of his justice. But, Lin, he didn't force me to do *everything*. For a time, he had to command me to do everything, and he punished me for it. And the worst was – he also punished Mephi. After a while, I gave in. I couldn't take it anymore. And that's the part I'll never forget. That's one of the reasons I can't help. He's gone, but Ragan and Nisong aren't." I stopped, my throat tight. My hands were shaking. I let them fall from Lin's face, my breath coming too quickly.

She took my hands, the steadiness in her gaze and voice lending me some strength. "Tell me. Please."

So I did.

46

Lin

Imperial Island

I let Jovis talk, absorbing his tale with both sympathy and horror. Some part of me knew I had to keep moving to get our defenses shored up and ready for an attack, but I also *needed* Jovis. Ragan and Dione were against us, both powerful Alanga. I had more confidence in my abilities than I once had, and some of those in the army had become Alanga in the past two years – but they were still early on and unused to their powers.

And there was the matter of Nisong, who could use shards to create constructs and to coerce Alanga.

So I listened. Not just because I needed Jovis, but because it was what Jovis needed right then. After everything he'd been through, he was owed that much. I listened as he told me about the early days when he'd struggled against the commands, when he'd let some witstone escape his grasp because Kaphra hadn't explicitly commanded him to stop it from sinking. He told me how Kaphra had punished him, scoring his flesh with the white-bladed sword until his entire body burned and he begged him to put an end to it. How Kaphra had stopped, but had then turned the sword on Mephi, making Jovis watch.

He'd paced himself after that, trying to make his small defiances worth it. And then, after a few more times of being caught, he'd given up on small defiances altogether. He'd started to work toward pleasing Kaphra, telling himself he was doing it to make Kaphra complacent – even as he felt the stirrings of gratitude whenever Kaphra praised his performances. Even as he fell into bantering with him as though they were friends.

Lies could become truth, he explained to me. Because you had to believe the very good ones.

And this was where he'd faltered. He'd become someone else to survive, and now he wasn't sure which was truly him: the folk hero the people had praised, or the Maelstrom and Kaphra's right-hand man?

I wrapped my arms around him as he sobbed. My father had taught me the right words to say so I could manipulate people into doing what I wanted. There were things I could say that would goad him, that would shame him into helping us. And I could justify all of it – what was one man's feelings when weighed against an Empire?

Maybe I was as weak as my father had once thought. Maybe I wasn't an appropriate successor, or an appropriate would-be replacement wife. Maybe I would always be a little broken, a little flawed.

But that didn't mean that exercising cruelty would make me whole. I'd still have to reckon with that cruelty when the fighting was done. Jovis's sobs quieted and he sagged into my shoulder. "You have to ready the defenses," he said finally, drawing back and wiping a hand across his eyes. "I've taken too much of your time."

I tugged at his sleeve. "I won't ask you to fight, but walk with me, please?"

He followed me from the room. My guard was still at the door.

Her gaze flicked to us and then away and back again. I felt my cheeks heat as I thought about what she might have heard, standing outside the door. Strange, how one could still be embarrassed with so many larger things at stake.

I straightened, knowing I'd not been able to put my hair as neatly back into place as it had been when I'd entered the room. "Have we received word from Yeshan? Jovis tells me she is waiting with our army just beyond the docks."

"Ikanuy is in conference with the rest of the Imperial guards. At the palace. In the dining hall. No messengers have been able to get through to us."

But I had a couple of constructs. I could get through. I hurried down the stairs and out into the rain, Jovis at my side and my guard at my back. "I've been trying to hold this Empire together," I told him as we walked toward the palace together. I dodged a woman holding a basket of herbs and she ducked her head when she saw who I was, her voice a low murmur of apology. Others moved out of my way, clearing a path. "It's taken everything I have. It's why I agreed to take Iloh as my consort – it felt like the only way to stitch the broken pieces back together."

Something in his posture relaxed a little. "So you never loved him."

I gave him a *look*. "Jovis, please, I thought you knew me better than that."

Tentatively, he let his hand rest on the small of my back. "It had been two years. I wouldn't have begrudged you finding someone else. People move on. Life keeps pushing forward."

"But Iloh?" I shook my head. "I didn't know what else to do. I still don't. But I would give my life and my happiness to save this Empire."

By the time we reached the stairs of the palace, both Mephi and Thrana had finished their meals and lay huddled beneath the overhang, napping together – one indistinguishable pile of brown, black and white fluff, two sets of horns jutting out of this mound. Now, when I looked at Thrana, I didn't just see an animal, I saw the curves of mountains in the ridges of her spine. I saw trees and forests in the faint greening of her fur. And I saw witstone in her bones.

Jovis fell silent as we climbed the stairs, as the guard at the door opened it for us, as we slipped inside, stepping past busy servants and city refugees. Half of them still dripped with rain from outside; the other half huddled next to walls, having carved out spots they could call their own.

I went first to the shard room, where my constructs ate and slept. Hao was there, taking up the bulk of the space, sleeping in a corner. I went to a swallow construct and stroked its head. "Hello, little one, I've a message for you." It couldn't carry much, but it was small and swift. It could make it past the Shardless Few, as long as Nisong didn't spot it for what it was. She'd have her own constructs to counteract mine. "Go to the ship in the harbor flying the largest phoenix flag. Tell them your message is for Yeshan. Tell her to attack as soon as the sun sets. Go."

It chirped and then darted out the open door, winging its way toward an open window.

"The rest of you – go to the gates and await my command." My menagerie, now dwindled to five constructs, rose and made their way to the door. Hao had to squeeze through one body part at a time, his shoulders shaking dust loose from the lintel as he pushed past it.

"Dione gave me until evening to abdicate." I dared a glance at Jovis as we made our way to the dining hall. "Otherwise he attacks the palace with full force."

Jovis's hand found mine and he cleared his throat. "You say you would put your life and your happiness on the line to save this Empire."

"I would." The boards of the hallway creaked in a familiar way beneath my feet, reminding me of all the times I'd crept past servants and constructs when I'd been younger.

"The people of this Empire are one thing — I understand that you want to keep them safe. I understand that you would die for them. But the Empire? That's something different. Lin . . .is the Empire worth all of that to you?"

I stopped in my tracks, confused. Surely he couldn't mean for me to just let it fall apart? What about stability? What about the islands' reliance on one another? We'd stood together for so long, united beneath an Emperor. Strong. It was what my father had always told me: we needed the islands' combined forces in order to face the return of the Alanga.

But my father was dead. And the Alanga *had* returned — this was something I'd not prevented; I'd helped it along by stopping the Tithing Festival. But still, the Empire protected its people.

Didn't it?

Ikanuy emerged from the dining hall before I could enter, her face flushed, gray-white hair plaited and bound neatly in place but for two uncharacteristically wild strands floating at her cheeks. From beyond her, I heard the guards stirring, and beyond that, a faint roar.

"Eminence, I hope you've been doing something helpful in the time you've been unreachable." There was a hint of reproach in her voice — one I'd never heard before. I felt suddenly like a child, scolded for classroom inattention.

The roar increased in volume and a *bang* sounded in the distance, making me jump. Screams rose from the courtyard. "I sent word to Yeshan," I said, torn between defensiveness and apprehension. "I told her to attack at nightfall."

"She'll be too late," Ikanuy said. "The Shardless Few didn't wait for word from us. They're at the gates."

47

Phalue

Imperial Island

Phalue wished she could spend an eternity tracing her fingers along the lines of Ranami's shoulders, her ribs, her breasts and hips. They'd been parted for so long that everything felt new again, wondrous, her desire for Ranami's presence a thirst that couldn't be quenched.

Not that she *preferred* things this way. But she would take her delights where she could, with war on the horizon. No one could ever accuse Phalue of being impassive, immovable. She was a flickering flame, licking at anything that remotely resembled fuel, refusing to be contained.

The wind shifted and goosebumps lifted on the back of Ranami's neck as her hair swayed with the breeze. "Will your Shardless Few fight with us?" Phalue asked.

Ranami sighed. "I can't ask them to fight against their own. They said they'll follow me but, Phalue – I don't know what to do." They stood on the deck of Yeshan's ship. Ranami had claimed it was because the ship had more space for them, but

Phalue wondered if it wasn't because she didn't know what to do with this new responsibility.

"They said they'll follow you. That means they're charging you with making the decisions. They may not want to fight against their own, but what about Ragan? All he wants is to hurt and subjugate those who oppose him. Surely your Shardless Few oppose that?"

"Don't call them *mine*." Ranami waved her off.

"We're running out of time, love. Trust yourself. I trust you. So do they." Phalue brushed her fingers against Ranami's jaw, tilting her wife's head toward her for a kiss. Ranami sighed against her mouth – though the sound was more exasperated than desirous.

"I'm right here you know," Ayesh said from next to them. "Still waiting." Shark stood with her chin on Ayesh's shoulder, giving Phalue and Ranami the same tired look as her companion.

Phalue pressed her lips to Ranami's neck and drew away, the faint smile on her wife's lips more than counterbalancing the scowl on Ayesh's. Around them, men and women prepared, their bodies drawn as taut as bowstrings as they checked their weapons again, grasped at the buckles on their armor, readjusting pointlessly. They'd just received word from a swallow that they were to attack at nightfall.

A swallow.

Phalue had grown used to magic in the years she'd parented Ayesh. But there was something about bone shard magic that still felt foreign and unwelcome to her – like finding a centipede laid out among one's dinner dishes. The constructs were odd, uncanny things that made her spine prickle.

She turned from her wife, pulling her sword free from its sheath. "Just a quick sparring session, that's all. I don't want to tire myself too much. Not with a battle on the horizon. Only to limber up and then we're done."

"Are you saying that fighting little me would tire you out?" Ayesh clucked her tongue as though she were the elder of the two of them.

Phalue snorted. "You can't bait me, child. We both know that little you is more than you seem."

The girl tightened the straps on her shield prosthetic before drawing her sword, making her way to an empty part of the deck and assuming a fighting stance. "Which is why I'm joining the fight when it starts."

Phalue halted her opening swing halfway through. Ayesh batted the sword aside, a fierce grin on her face. She whirled, countering the aborted attack with two swift jabs. Phalue was big, but faster than she looked. She moved out of the way of both, but just barely.

She lifted her sword and her free hand in surrender. "Hold on. Stop. You are *not* going into this fight." Phalue had studied the terrain — Imperial City would have been treacherous in the best of times, the buildings easily hiding ambushes or archers. Half of them had now burnt to the ground, but half was still enough to hide Shardless Few, and the rubble had made the streets difficult to traverse. This was not the Battle of Gaelung, where they had stood on the high ground, a wall at their backs. They'd be laying siege to a city on a slope, working their way from the bottom to the top, trying to defend palace walls that lay in front of them. And there was the rain, running unchecked through the streets like miniature rivers, the gutters blocked.

They weren't ideal conditions.

Not that she'd send Ayesh into a fight with ideal conditions. The girl was *fourteen*, a fact she seemed to keep forgetting. Army recruits had to be fifteen at the youngest, and those were only allowed to train until they reached their majority at sixteen.

"There are Alanga in those armies," Ayesh said, her sword still lifted, her feet still planted in a fighting stance. "How many do we have with us? Not many, unless you count Ranami's follow- ers — and it's clear she's not sure whether they should count at all. They may sit this battle out, or at worst, some may decide they're better off at Dione's side after all. They're unreliable at best. If we remove those Shardless Few, the ones in the city outnumber us.

"Dione is the strongest of the old Alanga. Ragan has had longer to train than most others — and that's monastery training. It's going to come down to the Alanga. You can't afford not to have me in this fight."

Phalue had lowered her sword, but her daughter, it seemed, was still fighting. "This isn't an argument or a debate."

"You think you can stop me?"

Phalue found herself grinding her teeth. Perhaps Ayesh still *could* bait her. "I'll lock you in the deepest hold we've got and take away your shield."

It was like poking a tiny resting snake. In an instant, the girl had roused, hissing and spitting. "You wouldn't. Ask Ranami — I helped her. We'd still be locked in a cave if it weren't for me. Bog cough would be running rampant on Nephilanu. You'd be trying to negotiate for our release or you'd be in the thick of Nephilanu's forests, trying to fight the Shardless Few."

Phalue pressed a hand to her forehead as if she could forestall the headache her daughter was giving her. Ayesh wasn't wrong. They'd needed her. How could she explain this to Ayesh in a way she would understand? Slowly, trying to give herself time to think, Phalue sheathed her sword. She met the girl's gaze, studying her face which already looked so much older than when they'd first found her. Ayesh's cheeks had filled in and then leaned out again with age, her brows thicker, her limbs longer. She'd never have the build of either Ranami or Phalue; she'd always look like something of a sapling – whip-thin, flexible, strong.

"You can't fight in this battle," Phalue said, keeping her voice steady but gentle. She held up a hand when Ayesh opened her mouth to protest. To her surprise, her daughter quieted. "It's not because I don't think you're ready, or that you're not good enough. I'm asking you not to fight because you deserve better from all of us. I know you yearn to prove yourself. I know your years on the streets have taught you that you need to be tough to survive. But that's not what you need. What you need is the chance to be a child. That's what I want for you."

"And what about what *I* want for myself?" But Ayesh had eased from her fighting position, and the words sounded less certain.

"How can you know what you want for yourself if you never give yourself the chance to explore beyond survival?"

The girl frowned, considering.

"We've got movement!" someone shouted from above. Phalue craned her neck to see a soldier in the crow's nest, a looking glass to his eye. Yeshan was on deck in an instant, holding out a hand. One of her soldiers placed a spyglass into her palm and she leapt the steps two at a time to the prow. She snapped it out, searching the shore for what the man in the crow's nest had spotted.

She collapsed the spyglass after only a moment, her lips pressed together. And then she leaned to Ranami, saying something in hushed tones that Phalue couldn't discern. Ranami squared her shoulders.

This didn't look good. "Think about that," Phalue said to Ayesh. She followed Yeshan to the prow.

"They're battering the gates," Yeshan was explaining to Ranami. "I don't know what changed; according to the letter I received, they were to wait until nightfall for Lin to respond to them."

"I know what happened," Ranami said, her fingers tight around the rail. "Ragan. He doesn't keep his word, and no matter what alliance he and Dione have formed, Ragan will never see himself as subject to Dione's rules. Or the rules of combat, for that matter. And there are enough foolish Shardless Few to follow him. Alanga, too."

Yeshan raised her hand, made a sharp gesture to the captain waiting at her elbow. "Raise the anchors and ready the archers. We make for the harbor." Her gaze flicked back to Ranami. "If you've not made a decision yet, now's the time. Mine is clear: I go to help the Emperor."

Ranami's chin firmed. "The Shardless Few will fight against Ragan and his followers. We'll help you."

And then everything and everyone on the ship was moving, a blur of colors and faces. Yeshan had kept her soldiers tightly disciplined; within moments, they were lined up on deck, preparing the rowboats for launch.

Phalue found Ayesh standing among them, Shark at her side, looking a little lost. "Get below," she told her daughter. "To our cabin. Lock the door. And don't come out unless I come for you. Shark too. We may come under fire."

Ayesh disappeared into the crush, her face pale, Shark on her heels. Phalue checked her armor one last time, setting her sights on shore. A hand touched her shoulder. "You're going to fight with the rest of them?"

"They'll need all the help they can get. I sent Ayesh and Shark to our cabin. You should wait there with them."

Ranami seized her around the neck, pulling her head down until their foreheads touched. "Why is it that every time we get a moment's peace, I feel you being dragged away from me again? Why can't we just live on Nephilanu, and worry only about our island?"

Phalue pressed her lips to Ranami's hairline. "You've done it now, haven't you? Taking on the Shardless Few. I always knew you were meant for more than just being my wife, Ranami. Even when I first met you, you set me back on my heels as though I was a commoner and not a governor's daughter. I thought *I* was stubborn. You could move mountains with your will alone, and I love you for it." She wrapped her arms around Ranami's waist, wishing she didn't have to let go. Her fierce, sharp, beautiful Ranami – who had been taken prisoner by an army and then had brought it to heel. "You hear me? I love you for it."

"Being your wife was enough for me."

Phalue drew back. "Was it, though?"

Ranami looked out at the shoreline. "Wanting more has always felt ...dangerous. It still does. Stay safe and come back to us. That's all I can hope for at the moment."

Phalue tucked the hair behind Ranami's ear one last time, kissed her lips, then went to join Yeshan by the boats. Yeshan was dressed in full-scale armor, her graying hair pulled into a tight tail, her face grim. "Once we take the docks, we regroup. I don't want anyone going for the main forces of their armies until all of us are ashore. They've Alanga with them and they'll overwhelm any smaller groups. I'll send word to the Emperor and we'll do our best to coordinate our attacks."

Phalue touched Yeshan's shoulder once she was done speaking. "I'm going ashore with the rest of them."

Yeshan looked at her, taking in her height, her broad shoulders, the sword belted competently at her side. "You'll go with the second wave and you'll take commands from the captain I assign you to."

Phalue nodded her assent. "Whatever you think is best."

Yeshan pointed her to a phalanx near the back of the ship and then turned away, leaving to direct the soldiers with the communication flags at the stern of the ship. Phalue took in a breath as she made her way to the phalanx she'd been assigned to, briefly introducing herself to the captain there before falling into line with the rest of them. This was the worst part: the waiting before a fight. All she wanted was to be in the battle, her blood rushing through her ears, *doing* something.

She watched the first wave of rowboats as they disembarked, and then moved to help the soldiers in her phalanx with theirs.

"Phalue!" Ranami's voice sounded from behind her. She was pushing her way through the soldiers, her face panicked. "I can't find Ayesh. Or Shark. You sent them to the cabin?"

A thousand curses crossed Phalue's mind, all of them bursting against her skull, never making their way to her lips. "I did."

"She's not there."

Phalue turned her gaze to the first wave of soldiers heading to Imperial's shoreline. If Ayesh was out there, she couldn't spot her. And damn it – Ayesh was probably out there. She knew how stubborn the girl could be. Ranami followed Phalue's gaze.

"That stupid, *foolish* child. This is my fault. I never should have let her help on Nephilanu. Now she's got it into her thick skull that this is the only thing she's good at. And Phalue, she's good at it, but she's not *that* good. Ragan is out there. And Dione. She's fourteen and she thinks she can pit her powers against theirs?"

The rowboat swung free of the ship and Phalue climbed inside, reaching a hand out to touch her wife's. The sailors stood taut at the ropes, ready to lower the boat into the water. "I'll find her. I swear it to you – if it's the last thing I do. I would fight five armies to keep her safe."

"And Ayesh would fight five armies to keep herself from being safe," Ranami said, a trace of bitterness in her tone.

"Well then." Phalue let Ranami's hand fall from her grasp as the boat was lowered into the water. She could hear shouts from the first wave as they were bombarded with arrows and they returned fire. Her heartbeat was a steady thing in her chest now that the fighting was closer. Politics, diplomacy, measured words – she was still learning these things. This, she knew. "We'll just have to see exactly which of us is the more headstrong."

48

Jovis

Imperial Island

I'd told Lin I couldn't fight. At the same time, what was I to do? Wait inside the walls like the old or infirm? I wasn't either. Feeling more than a little lost, and swept along a current, I followed Lin as she shouted orders, as she accepted a leather chest plate from her guards along with bracers. She looked like a warrior-Emperor, ready to take on both a court of hostile rivals and an army.

I wished it were the former and not the latter we were facing.

Both Mephi and Thrana were alert when we exited the palace. Without hesitating, Lin went to Thrana and climbed up the leg she proffered, settling into the dip between her shoulders and her neck.

A *bang* sounded again from the direction of the gates, followed by shouts. Several of Lin's guards were clearing a path between the palace and the gates, urging the city refugees into the gardens and the buildings, telling them to lie low and to stay safe.

Lin drew her sword, and even in the rain it seemed to reflect light – gleaming beneath the clouds. Her gaze found mine. Mephi curled protectively around my back, his tail coming to rest at my feet. The warmth of his breath stirred the hair at the top of my head.

"I wish I could give you more time," Lin said. "I wish I could give you all the time in the world. But we've run out. I have to ask for your help; not for me, but for everyone else. I know you don't think you're a hero. I know you've done terrible things. But, Jovis, you were trying to survive. It's what anyone else might have done and it's not something to be ashamed of. You can't always think yourself stronger and better than the rest of us."

My throat tightened. "Isn't that what a hero is? Someone who is stronger and better?" I meant it to come out lightly, as a joke, but my words thudded to the ground along with my heart.

"Help us," she said simply, before urging Thrana toward the gates. She lifted her hand, the rain above her stopping, swirling around her, coalescing at her command.

She *looked* like a hero. I glanced down at myself – my clothes clean but a bit ragged. I wriggled a toe in one of my boots and felt the rain beginning to seep through the leather. I looked like something that had been washed ashore in the latest storm.

My bones thrummed, reminding me of what I was.

"Ah, damn it." I had more of a chance against the encroaching army than any of the unarmed city folk, more even than the other Imperial guards. Mephi was already in front of me, crouching so I could climb onto his back. He knew my mind better than anyone.

And then we were following after Lin, the rain splashing beneath Mephi's paws. I pulled the moisture from below us, from the gutters, adding the water to Lin's. Briefly, I felt the brush of my will against hers – not the battle I'd felt with Ragan, but something like the joining of hands, fingers intertwining. Her shoulders straightened, as though she was taking strength from my presence.

I could feel the fear around me dissipate too, as the refugees saw their Emperor and another Alanga head toward the gates astride their ossalen. We must have made a fearsome sight, all weapons and teeth and claws and flashing eyes.

Fear still crept into the corners of my heart, but I felt if I could keep this momentum, if I could just not *think* about what had happened to me, what had been done – I could fight this battle.

For Lin. For the people of the Empire.

Thrana and Lin pulled to a stop just in front of the gates. The guards were pressed against them, trying to bolster them, as the army on the other side battered the wood.

Lin turned back, tossing me something small and dark. I caught it, just barely. "For strength," she said. When I opened my palm, I saw a cloud juniper berry plucked fresh from the tree, a waxy white coating still clouding its surface.

"Let them come," she said. She took control of the water I'd melded with hers and built a wave as tall as the walls.

I popped the berry into my mouth just as her guards obeyed and the Shardless Few army hit the gates. Wood cracked, giving way. A sharp, acrid taste flooded across my tongue and then the army was flooding inside. The thrumming of my bones seemed to increase fivefold, traveling down my jawbone and rattling my teeth. Kaphra had given me cloud juniper berries and tea to take before battles he'd thought would be particularly difficult. I'd gone through the motions, detaching myself as much from my actions as I could.

Now, though, I felt fully present, and the power bolstered me. I would follow Lin anywhere.

Mephi surged beneath me and I seized the air currents around us, winding them around me like so many lengths of rope, ready to be cast out at my command.

Lin hit the advancing army with the full force of the wave she'd gathered. The barest of shouts rose from those in the front lines before the water swept over them. Men and women tumbled in the froth and Lin followed, Thrana leaping into the spray.

We were close behind. As the Shardless Few army struggled to get to their feet, I lashed out with wind, pelting them with hurricane-force gales. A roar rose from behind me as Lin's guards, emboldened, waded into the fray.

It was a bold beginning to the fight, but they still outnumbered us, and we weren't the only Alanga on the battlefield. Yeshan would use this opportunity to land her troops, but the terrain was trickier than it had once been, and it would take them time to flank Dione's and Ragan's forces.

We just needed to hold out until then.

I laid about with my staff, Lin at the edge of my vision, the blade of her sword bloodied, her expression grim. And still the Shardless Few came. So many angry citizens, and I wasn't sure which ones had been taken in by Ragan's rhetoric and only wanted to wreak havoc, and which ones genuinely thought they were fighting for a better, more equitable society.

Or was there no longer any difference?

Mephi kicked out at a man with one of his back legs just as I parried a blow on the other side, sending a woman flying. I could take on twenty well-armed soldiers in this state and barely break a sweat. I'd taken enough cloud juniper berry in the past two years to know that even as this power felt limitless, it would quickly come to an end, leaving me momentarily breathless and weak.

A shadow passed over my face as we pressed into the arch of the gates, stemming the tide. Lin had opened the gates before they could break, which meant if we could push the Shardless

Few back far enough, if we could discourage them, we could close the gates again and gain a short reprieve.

Short was all we needed.

Screams and shouts and the clash of steel against steel sounded around me. Everything was wet with blood, rain and mud. Water flowed from the gutters and toward Lin's outstretched hand, her sword held high in the other. Soldiers pushed toward her and I sent currents of wind flying about her, buffeting them, keeping her ensconced in a protected space. Under the influence of the cloud juniper, I could hold that magic and keep my arms moving, my focus easily split into two locations.

Too easy. Years as a smuggler had taught me to know the calm before a storm, and this moment had that same feel – quiet, anticipatory, a breath held before being exhaled in a *whoosh*. Every hair on my arms stood on end, prickling against my damp tunic.

A mental presence slammed into mine. It felt almost physical, like being hit broadside by an ox in the middle of a stampede. Suddenly, I was battling for control of the air currents I'd seized and swiftly losing. I felt them torn from me one by one even as I grasped to hold onto them.

Dione.

He came striding forth from the wreckage of the city, wind whipping at his clothes, his grizzled face as cold as the Imperial mountains, his brow carved by glaciers. The rain never touched him, flung away as soon as it ventured close.

I was too startled to feel fear. Was this how his old brethren had seen him? Not as a man but as a force of nature – never to be wholly contained? How had I ever seen him as just an old man leading a faction of people with futile goals? I'd been so naive, pushing back against his ideals, brushing aside his warnings. Back then, the Empire had seemed unbreakable, a hawk being dive-bombed by crows, the rebellion a worrisome annoyance that would pass. And when Lin had taken the throne, I'd thought the Shardless Few a thing of the past.

But the Alanga had returned and so had Dione.

I tried to take back control of the wind, and it was like trying to break stone with my bare hands, my nails scrabbling uselessly against an unyielding surface. I watched in horror as he took the air currents I'd used to protect Lin and turned them inward, against her.

She didn't make a sound as she was flung from Thrana's back. I tugged at Mephi's fur, turning him toward her without thinking. I couldn't lose her now – not *now* when I'd already lost too much, when I'd finally returned to her side. I'd spent half a lifetime chasing women I'd loved across the Empire, being parted from them, losing them and losing myself. She had taken cloud juniper berry; she could heal quickly; she was always stronger than I thought she was.

Jovis, we should stay, Mephi said in my mind. *Lin said to stay behind her.* I knew these things, yet I couldn't help the wild thrumming of my heart, the way my knees pressed into Mephi's sides, urging him forward.

I should have stayed put; I should have stayed in formation. But, as my mother had often said, "should" was a word I'd only ever used to describe regret. I'd always had to learn the hard way.

I just needed to know if she was hurt – and then I could return to my place, I could keep fighting. But Dione hadn't just been making a grand entrance onto the battlefield. He'd been serving as a distraction, keeping the attention of me and Lin's guards on him.

Two people stepped out from behind ruined buildings and into the main street, between me and where Lin lay on the ground. Ragan and Nisong, mere steps away. Water and wind caught me in the chest before I could brace myself, and it carried me into

the air and off Mephi's back. I landed on a broken door, feeling
the wind go out of my lungs just as the cloud juniper berry ran its
course. Lin was already pushing herself back to her feet, Thrana
standing over her protectively. If I'd stayed back, I might not
have been caught in this sort of trap.

But a face swam over mine. I caught the slight smile first, and
then the pockmarked cheeks. And then fear spiked through me.

Nisong, her hand outstretched. Nisong, with Lozhi at her side.
Nisong, with shards gleaming white between her fingertips.

I didn't remember scrambling to my feet. I didn't remember
running. But I did remember my breath growing louder in my
ears as the sounds of fighting grew quieter. I remembered the
feel of uneven ground beneath my feet, the way each stumble
seemed to last an eternity because this could be *it* – this could be
the moment I felt the coldness of Nisong's hand enter my back,
the moment I froze, helpless to do anything but watch and wait
as she rearranged my will to suit hers.

I ran, because I was not a hero.

I was a coward. And I was afraid.

49

Nisong

Imperial Island

She'd almost had him. There had been a brief moment when she'd reached her hand out and she'd thought she caught the brush of cloth against her fingertips. She hadn't counted on him running, leaving Mephi behind in a panic, his feet quicker than hers.

Lozhi had followed her, bounding over the rubble as though the broken buildings were merely rocks at a cliffside – obstacles he was familiar with. She'd had to admit she'd lost him early on. Her feet weren't powered by Alanga magic. Or fear. Only a desire to win this battle and to finally do what she'd once promised her friends she would: take the palace.

It was the only promise she felt mattered now, after she'd broken so many.

Nisong slowed to a stop, breathing heavily, the sharp edges of the shards digging into her palm. They'd taken their time getting to Imperial, stopping at a few more islands to coerce more Alanga and to build more constructs. And when they'd arrived, Nisong had convinced Ragan not to attack Dione, no matter that he had so few Shardless Few left. He could kill Dione when the fighting was done. But for now, they could use Dione and his magic.

She'd not been able to convince Ragan to wait until nightfall to attack.

She tucked the shards back into the pouch at her belt. There were other Alanga she could coerce, other things she could do to help win this fight. Ragan, though, would shout at her. He would berate her, perhaps even strike her. "I did my part, and you couldn't manage yours," he'd sneer, his hand at his sword, knowing that the implied threat would make her flinch. "I set everything up for you." It wouldn't matter that they were in the midst of a battle, he'd take out his anger on her.

Jovis didn't matter. If Lin could remove his shards, she could do it again.

Lozhi sidled up to her, encouraging her to lean on his soft shoulder. She did for a moment, the feel of his fur somehow calming even in the chaos. Ahead of her, the Shardless Few pressed forward, taking back the headway they'd lost during Lin's initial charge. Behind her, she knew Lin's army and even some of the Shardless Few were landing, making their way from the docks. They'd left some reserves there, but had put the bulk of their forces at the front. Timing was everything. If they could get through the gates, if they could take the palace, they'd be in the defensible position and not crushed between two opposing forces.

Lozhi crouched as though he knew her thoughts and she took the invitation for what it was, clambering aboard his back. She'd not been astride Lozhi without Ragan before, but somehow it felt right. Together, they rushed back to the battle, the ossalen springing over obstacles as nimbly as a squirrel. Her constructs were engaged in the fighting, monstrous teeth and claws tearing into the opposing force. The air smelled of ash, rain and the hollow, coppery scent of spilled entrails.

She pulled her cudgel free and pushed into the thick of it, feeling the swell of anger around her. Ragan had whipped his Shardless Few into a frenzy before this fight, telling them that the Alanga would seek to kill them all, that Lin wouldn't stop them, that Lin cared nothing for the people beneath her. It didn't matter what he spewed – whether they were lies or truth – the people following him eagerly swallowed both.

Her cudgel slammed into the head of one of Lin's guards, his sword falling from his hand as he crumpled. *For Shell. For Leaf, for Grass, for Coral.* The words sat heavy in her chest, a stack of fuel that refused to light. She killed another guard. It could have been one of the men that had – however indirectly – caused Coral's death. She felt a flicker of warmth and tried to stoke that higher.

But then it no longer mattered. They were past the arch and pushing into the palace courtyard.

"Retreat!" Lin called. "Protect the civilians. Retreat!"

It was like a dam giving way. The pressure dissipated as Lin's forces fled, pursued by the Shardless Few. They'd made it in time. Now all they had to do was to shut the gates.

The palace was theirs. It was *theirs*.

She slid from Lozhi's back as Shardless Few passed her, as they ran into buildings to look for resistance. "You should go back to your master," Nisong said to the ossalen even as she pressed a hand toward his soft, downy undercoat. "He'll be angry that you left."

"Always angry," Lozhi cooed in a soft voice she could barely hear. His tail flicked between his legs, his head ducking down.

Strange how she'd become so entwined with Ragan, yet she rarely felt safe with him. And when she did, there were little reminders, little digs that told her she wasn't truly safe. "I know." She scratched the area around his horns, where she knew he most liked being touched. She'd rarely seen Ragan touch the beast with any kindness.

He leaned his head into her shoulder, one blue eye meeting hers. "Want to stay with you."

She was struck by a sudden possessiveness, a fierce protective feeling she barely recognized. It had been so long since she'd last had this sense of camaraderie, this mutual respect.

Coral. Coral — whom she'd promised she would keep safe. Coral — whom she'd called on at last for help and had ultimately failed. Coral — who'd lain in her arms. Who'd died.

She had to remain vigilant. The fighting wasn't over. What had happened to Coral had been a mistake.

No — what she'd *allowed* to happen to Coral had been a mistake. It had been wholly her fault. Not Lin's, nor the fault of the army she'd fought against. She'd sent her closest friend into danger deliberately. And then they'd lost the battle and Coral had lost her life.

"I'll protect you," Nisong whispered to Lozhi, not sure if he could hear her over the din. They were the same words she'd spoken to Coral, but this time, she put the full force of her will behind them. "I pledge my life on it. I pledge everything.

"I won't let what happened to Coral happen to you. I promise."

50

Lin

Imperial Island

Somewhere in the fighting I'd lost Jovis. We'd started as an organized, purposeful group. But even as I sent my few constructs to fight against Nisong's, I knew we were fighting a losing battle. We'd needed to hold them back from the gates and we'd failed.

I was bruised, battered, bleeding from a few wounds – none of which seemed bad and were healing quickly. But I'd faced up against Dione once more and once more had been found wanting. Oh, I could make excuses. Ragan was here too, and trying to fight against both was like being caught between two angry dogs. But no matter what my excuses were, they didn't change what was happening.

I reached down and seized the tunic of a passing guard. "Get everyone to the palace and moving toward the mountains. As we discussed beforehand. Go."

She nodded and turned, doing her best to guide the panicked people toward the palace.

"Form up!" I shouted at my remaining guards. There wouldn't be time to search for Jovis, to wait for Yeshan's army. All I could do was to cover the retreat of my citizens and hope to minimize the loss of life. We spread across the courtyard, blocking the advancing Shardless Few as best we could. I could feel my strength flagging, my will shredded beneath Dione and Ragan's onslaughts.

I gathered a wave and sent it toward them, trying to speed it with wind. Someone — either Ragan or Dione — seized control of both water and air before they could reach the Shardless Few. The wave scattered into shimmering droplets, falling harmlessly to the ground.

My guards stood firm, but it was like trying to stop the wind with your fingers. The Shardless Few swarmed past our thinned lines, overtaking my guards, rushing at the city refugees who lagged behind. I couldn't watch both them and the army in front of me. But I could hear screams from behind me as the helpless citizens of my city were caught, as they were slaughtered.

My heart felt squeezed by a giant fist, each beat pulsing painfully in my chest. My eyes burned as I swung my sword at the advancing army, as Thrana clamped her teeth around the arm of a man and shook him savagely. I was one person and, even as I did my best to stop them, I could feel the gazes of my guards travel toward me and the line breaking as they hesitated.

Their first duty was and always had been to me — even if I told them otherwise.

The Empire had never protected its people, no matter how much it professed to. It had suppressed the truth of the Alanga, had forced everyone to undertake the dangerous Tithing Festival, had profited off the trade of witstone even as it slowly destroyed the islands, had always ensured a healthy supply of caro nuts for Imperial while doing nothing to ensure the fairness of distribution elsewhere.

I'd been trying, since the beginning, to uphold a corrupt system. To change it when its inner workings were already rotten. I couldn't be everywhere at once. I couldn't force change, even as I put my will behind it, even as I threatened, cajoled and bargained with men like Iloh. The Empire had propped up men like him, and I had been trying to work within the system to meet my goals.

I was not enough. Not for my father, not for this Empire, and certainly not for the Empire's people.

"Stop!" My throat was parched, my voice quiet, lost within the surrounding din. But I was stubborn, and no matter how Dione and Ragan attacked me, my will had the same wiry strength as my body. I threw up another wall of water, putting everything I had left into my voice. "Stop! I want to discuss terms!"

The words echoed from the walls, from the walls of the empty buildings. I sheathed my sword, holding up my hands in a gesture of surrender. "Constructs, stop fighting."

It took time for everyone to stop, to put away their weapons. Agonizing moments in which I could hear the cries of the refugees behind me, knowing they were still being hurt while I sat astride Thrana, waiting with no weapon at hand. It took everything I had not to pull my sword free again, to fight.

I was used to fighting.

I was less used to giving up.

My guards took my lead, putting down their weapons, letting the Shardless Few round them up like so many sheep. I railed against this outcome even as I knew it was necessary. From beneath the arch of the gateway, four figures strode toward me. Dione on the one side, Ragan next to him, and Nisong and Lozhi beside him. Both Dione and Ragan were dressed humbly – Ragan in a simple dark green that evoked his old monk's robes, and Dione in unadorned grays and browns. I knew it wasn't out of any true need to eschew fashion for either of them, but to appeal to the humble people following them. Only Nisong wore finery – a blood-red robe embroidered in gold around the buttons, tattered at the hem. I felt the subtle press of either Ragan's or Dione's mind against mine, waiting for me to try any Alanga magic. I didn't. All four of them walked in step as though they were of one mind.

But they weren't. A plan began to coalesce in my thoughts. A half-witted, haphazard plan, but it was all that I had. The Shardless Few shut and barred the gates behind them, sealing us off from the city. From Yeshan's soldiers.

"Leave the citizens be," Dione ordered his soldiers as he approached. His men and women lifted their hands from the refugees. "They were only caught in the middle of this fight."

"So generous of you," I spat out, unable to help myself. "Now that you have the advantage, they're free to go."

"My quarrel wasn't with them."

"Yet you had no compunctions about using them to pressure me into surrender. It didn't bother you to burn their homes and their businesses and to cut their throats just to get what you wanted."

Ragan came abreast of Thrana, and before I could react, he'd seized my leather breastplate and had pulled me from her back. His other hand tangled in my hair. The heat of his breath gusted against my ear. "I look forward to making you serve us. We still have plenty of shards left, you know."

Thrana growled but I lifted a hand to forestall any attack from her. Ragan's fingers tightened possessively in my hair, as though I were a prize he'd won from this battle.

I pushed down the panic that welled within me. I'd seen what such servitude had done to Jovis, had heard the tales of what Kaphra had made him do. How much worse would Ragan's commands be? I could only imagine – but my imagination was florid enough to paint terrible pictures. I lifted my gaze to meet Dione's through the curtain of my hair. "Who is in charge here? You or Ragan? I surrendered to discuss terms, not to be enslaved. I can call down the rest of my constructs if you wish. I can fight to the death." I let the magic flow through my bones, tapped a foot to the ground and felt it tremble a little beneath me.

I had no constructs in reserve, but if this was to work, I needed to make them *listen*. I needed to make Dione listen, most of all. He'd still come to Gaelung's aid after everything. After the massacre of his people, after the suppression of their knowledge, after all the years of loneliness and the subsequent years of planning – he'd found some spark of humanity buried beneath the ash.

And in the end, we were not too dissimilar. I was not my father, though I'd been more like him than I'd wanted to admit. I'd also clung to power, convinced that I was the only one who could change things, who could protect the people of the Empire. We'd had different methods, different underlying philosophies, but the pride – oh, that was the same.

Dione and Ragan exchanged long, heated glances. Finally, Ragan released his grip on my hair. I straightened, Thrana's warmth at my back a steadying presence. "Help rebuild Imperial City. Let these people back into their homes – the ones that are still standing. Use the money in the palace to pay recompense for the deaths you've caused. In return, I'll do as you've asked. I'll abdicate in favor of the Shardless Few. All you have to do is what you've promised: set up a Council ruled by the people of the Empire."

Dione scowled, the skin around his milky eye puckering. "Where's the trick? No matter what you've said you are, I know you. You *are* a Sukai and the Sukais don't give up. They're terrible. They're relentless."

He'd made a monster of me, of my father, of everyone who had come before me. And I couldn't deny that to some, we must look like monsters – some of us more than others. But seeing us as monsters meant he couldn't understand us.

He couldn't understand *me*.

"I'm not giving up in the way you think," I said, my voice ringing out into the courtyard. I blinked rain from my eyes, feeling it finally soak into my scalp. "My goal has always been to be a better Emperor than my father. If that means leaving the throne and helping to usher in a new era, then so be it. Do as you promised, Dione. Set up your Council. Make sure the Empire is ruled justly. This is what you've always wanted, isn't it?"

I knew that Dione wasn't a monster, and I could see by the way his lips tightened, the way his brows lifted, that I'd thrown him off-kilter. This was what he'd professed to want, and maybe he even believed it. But I knew, deep down, that what he really wanted was to change the past. To seek vengeance on the Sukais for what they'd done to the Alanga.

But there was no changing the past, and the Sukais had died out with my father, much as Dione didn't wish to believe it. He needed me to focus his anger on, his determination, his righteousness.

And I'd taken that away.

He cleared his throat, a man tossed about in a storm, trying to regain his bearings. "I accept your surrender."

No one cheered. They should have cheered; they should have rejoiced that this fight had – at long last – come to an end.

"You think this is over?" Ragan seized my hair again, his sword lifted in his other hand.

Dione drew his daggers. "Ragan, stand down. This is not what we agreed upon."

"Oh, I know what we agreed on. You said we'd work together to defeat the Emperor, to take the palace. And I said I'd let you command my faction until that was done. Well? I've kept my part of the bargain." He turned to the gathered Shardless Few. I still had my sword, tucked into its scabbard, but I let him drag me, knowing it wasn't the time or place to fight back. This quarrel no longer included me except as a thing caught between between Dione and Ragan.

And I hoped I'd judged Dione right.

"You think this ends here?" Ragan shouted. The pattering of the rain against tile rooftops and cobblestones was a dull, background sound. He lifted his sword and it gleamed. "You think if we let this Emperor live that she'll fade quietly away in some prison? You saw the way the people of this city cowered behind the palace walls. They didn't come asking us for succor. They fled to *her*. They asked *her* for protection. If we would make this world over new, then we must make it *new*. That means wiping the slate clean. Fully clean."

"Ragan," Dione barked out sharply. He'd seemed to have regained some of his balance, and now he stalked toward the former monk, the water at his feet stirring and rising a little into the air as he moved. "I'll have no more innocent deaths on my name. You will stop this – now."

Ragan's fingers disentangled from my hair as he turned to face Dione fully, both hands wrapping around the hilt of his sword. Nisong stepped forward, Lozhi on her heels. She gave me a warning look, though I made no move for my sword.

"Is this what you wanted?" I asked her, waving one hand toward the destruction wrought on the city. "Does this make anything better for you or the constructs you once professed to protect? Or are you now only Ragan's creature through and through, without thought or want for yourself?"

Her lips tightened though she said nothing in reply, her gaze flicking to Ragan and Dione before landing back on me.

Ragan was ignoring Dione, speaking around him to the Shardless Few army. "Did we come here to be meek and complacent, or did we come here to be strong?" I felt the stirring of the crowd, a bonfire exposed to the wind. They crackled in spite of the rain. I held my breath, for the first time afraid that I hadn't misjudged Dione but that I'd misjudged his influence. Indeed, as Ragan spoke and Dione blocked him, the man looked like nothing so much as a scolding parent, trying to settle his wayward son. Ragan looked young, powerful, sure of himself. And the words he spoke were resonating. "We cannot rest until we eliminate all sources of future sedition. Set up a Council –" Ragan scoffed. "– yes, only to see it struck down before we see another dry season. Do you kill one cockroach when you want to get rid of pests? No. You go into the nest. You kill each and every one."

"The Emperor has surrendered," Dione called over his shoulder. "The fight is done."

But with his back turned, he couldn't see the expressions on the faces of the Shardless Few, he couldn't feel the growing heat of their anger. He expected his words to be obeyed, to be listened to. I might have spoken to Dione's underlying humanity, but Ragan spoke to the underlying monster in them all. The one that wanted blood at all costs. The one that wanted to make the other side *pay*.

"We go to the palace. We nip this infestation at its root!" Ragan shouted.

And, Endless Seas, they cheered then. A pounding started at the gates, but it was too late. We were trapped inside the palace walls with an angry mob.

I drew my sword. Nisong took another step forward, her cudgel raised. Lozhi growled, Thrana answering him. She was nearly twice his size, and I knew I was a better fighter than

Nisong. But I couldn't waste time fighting her when my people needed my help.

"Let me pass," I said to her.

"I still have constructs who will fight for me," Nisong responded, her brows lowered.

I judged the set of her jaw, the stance that said she was ready to fight, her fingers that were wrapped around her weapon a shade too tightly.

She stood on a precipice of uncertainty, trying so hard to look certain, but betrayed by the subtle shifts of her expression, the way she stood so closely to Lozhi – a beast that should have been Ragan's but seemed committed to her. She was a construct, but there was humanity in her too.

"You deserve better than this," I said, my voice soft. She stood firm but I could feel her reeling from the words, caught off balance and off guard. "You always have."

And then I pulled myself aboard Thrana and turned her toward the palace, knowing that she would let me go.

And she did.

51

Nisong

Imperial Island

He gave her the palace, as he'd promised. "It's yours," he said as he strode over to her, taking Lozhi possessively by one of his horns. "As we agreed." The Shardless Few marched past him toward the massive building, weapons drawn, as Dione ineffectually tried to gather them, to keep them in one place. Too many had given in to Ragan's rhetoric, and those who hadn't were likely being swept along with the crowd.

Ragan went to mount Lozhi, but she put a hand on his arm. "No," she said, putting all the will she could muster behind the word. "He stays with me."

He looked as though he were about to protest, but to her surprise, he shrugged. Perhaps victory had made him magnanimous. "Fine. I'll find you later."

And then he was gone, moving with the Shardless Few, shouting and spurring them on.

She followed slowly, feeling lost. Some Shardless Few had stayed to man the gates, though there was little organization to them, no structure. The pounding of Lin's army echoed behind her as she made her way, numb, to the palace.

Ragan's Shardless Few had run, weapons at the ready. The distance from the gates to the palace was not as small as she'd once remembered – though in her previous life she'd been carried by palanquin, not forced to walk on foot. By the time she and Lozhi reached the doors, they had been thrown open, one of the great bronze hinges damaged, one door hanging askew.

The entrance hall was empty.

She felt like a ghost as she climbed the stairs, as she passed the mural of the Alanga – one whom she now recognized as a much younger Dione. Someone had taken a knife to the plaster on their way in, scoring a deep line from one end to the other, bits of bright paint littering the wooden floor and smeared by subsequent footsteps.

There was a door into the mountains, she remembered. It was one of the first secrets Shiyen had shown her after she'd taught herself bone shard magic. At first he'd been forbidding and stern, but she'd noticed the way his hand had lingered on her arm, the way his gaze had softened as she'd stumbled on the stairs to the cloud juniper courtyard. He'd set what he'd thought was an impossible task, and when she'd done it, the awe and wonder had festered in him, seeping into the cracks of his arrogance. He'd grown strangely shy of her.

And she'd taken advantage of that to its fullest, pressing on the balance of power between them, tipping it to equality.

The way she'd done with Ragan. No. The way he'd done with her.

Lozhi nudged his soft muzzle beneath her hand. "Bad memories?" he asked. His voice echoed in the entryway. There were many places to hide past that courtyard, in the wilderness. Lin must have taken her people into the mountains, and Ragan had followed. Still, she could hear distant footsteps and scraping noises, like people in the carcass of some giant, dead animal, pulling away the last of the meat.

"Not bad. Just memories," Nisong said. She walked through the hallways of the palace, feeling more like a ghost than a person. Here was where she'd kissed Shiyen for the first time. There, in the bedroom, was where they'd made plans with one another, their bodies pressed together. She'd felt in control, powerful.

But the only power she'd ever had was what he'd given to her.

Her footsteps creaked against the boards and she put out a hand to run against the wall, the feel of the wood both familiar and strange. The smell of smoke from the city below mingled with the faintest scent of sandalwood. She'd imagined walking these halls with her friends, as she reclaimed what she'd always felt was hers and that others were always denying her. Power, a place of belonging.

She'd thought Shiyen had given her that. She'd thought Ragan had.

Now, alone except for Lozhi, she felt hollowed out – an old stump that fire had burned through, long ago. Most of the doors had been broken by Ragan's soldiers, and she followed in their wake, opening rooms that felt just as ghostly as she did.

She was looking for something, she knew; she just wasn't sure what.

Nisong knew she'd found it when she opened the door to the old shard storeroom. She didn't close the door after her, the light from the hallway filtering into the space, lingering on the empty drawers and the cobwebs trailing from the ceiling.

In the back corner of the room was a door with the cloud juniper embossed in its surface. She went to it. Someone had rammed it open, though it looked as though they'd peeked beyond the door and not taken any further steps. The tunnel led down into darkness.

Back when she'd been mistress of this palace, the only thing that had lain down there had been Ilith's lair. She'd been newly built, a triumph of bone shard magic. But time had passed since then, and Nisong knew Shiyen had conducted other experiments since the original Nisong had died.

She took the lamp from next to the door, lighting it with the tinderbox on the lintel. Lozhi stayed always at her side, a silent gray shadow. As soon as she stepped into the tunnel, she felt the air change. It was cooler in here, the sound from the palace behind her becoming muffled and indistinct. It was like being blanketed in stone – above and below.

There were signs that things had once lived here. Old piles of scat, scratches on the walls. Constructs or animals – Nisong wasn't sure.

She reached a fork in the tunnel and stopped. Lozhi took several steps beyond her, down the left fork. And then he stopped and looked back at her. "Keep going?"

"Yes."

There was a door at the end of the left fork, bricks surrounding it and wedging it into the opening. When she tried the handle, it was locked. "Lozhi?"

That was all she had to say. Sometimes she thought the creature knew her mind better than she did. He threw his shoulder against the door. It creaked. Two more times and the wood cracked at the hinges. He sniffed at the opening, the sound echoing from the stone.

She was able to use the handle of her cudgel to wedge the rest of it free. The tunnel descended further beyond the door. There was a part of her that felt she should have been apprehensive; instead, she only felt drawn forward as though by some invisible force, a certainty building in her that what she was looking for lay at the end of this tunnel.

A cave lay at the bottom, stone glittering by the light of her lamp. Stalactites and stalagmites were scattered throughout, and water dripped into a pool that covered half the cavern. Next to the pool was a workstation – tables set up alongside chests and bookshelves, papers and metal tools scattered across surfaces.

Yes, this was where she wanted to be.

Nisong approached the pool, the dripping water seeming to fill the entirety of her senses. She lifted the lamp when she reached the edge, though she needn't have. The man was lying close to shore, submerged just below the surface. The light caught the planes of sharp cheekbones, the full lips, a brow that seemed calmer in rest than it ever had when she'd seen him awake. He was unclothed, his body fading into the yellow-orange darkness of the water.

Shiyen.

Lin had told her the truth. He'd grown a replica of himself in the water, and for some reason, Lin had left him be. She'd never again held her possession of him over Nisong's head, had never tried again to tempt her with him. Perhaps she'd realized that if it hadn't moved Nisong to surrender once, it wouldn't again.

Yet she'd kept this body – her attachment to it beyond Nisong's understanding. Or maybe it was nothing emotional, only the reluctance to discard a thing that had been so carefully made.

She knelt, setting the lamp to the side. Conflicting feelings roiled within her. She'd come to love Shiyen, yet he'd abandoned every iteration he'd made of her, sending the constructs to Maila. Too attached to destroy them and not attached enough to truly nurture them, to have the patience to see if more memories would surface. He'd worked in relentless desperation, a poet wadding up scrap after scrap of used parchment.

She'd been one of those used scraps of parchment, discarded and forgotten. The memories of her past self clashed with the memories of her current one. Shiyen's hands on her bare shoulders, moving with a gentle touch to the soft skin of her neck. Shiyen looking upon her with contempt when she'd arrived. Shiyen cupping her face in his hands and telling her she was the most precious thing in the world to him. Shiyen's anger when she insisted he share his secrets with her, the curl of his lip as he declared her unworthy. The stinging pain of that pronouncement even as she'd lifted her chin, fighting back tears, telling him he was wrong.

She'd always fought back; she'd always thought herself strong. In her memories, she'd proved herself to him and he'd fallen for her. It was the love story she'd written in her mind. But she was coming to realize that memories were fickle things, shifting with the light and the angle.

Now she saw the ways they'd twined together were not always that of two hands pressed against one another, but sometimes the choking of vines around the trunks of trees. He'd still looked at her in that calculating way after she'd learned bone shard magic, and she'd chased after his approval again and again. He'd still found ways to dig at her, to make her work harder.

She reached into the water, watched her skin glow pale beneath its surface. Carefully, she took a lock of his hair between her fingertips. There were no limits to what she could do if she put the force of her will and her mind behind it. If she wanted to, she could untangle the mysteries of the memory machine. She could find a way to bring him back, and not just his body.

She had the palace; why should she not have Shiyen by her side once more? Even now, as she remembered the ways he'd hurt her, she also remembered that feeling of invincibility when they were together, the soaring triumph each time he gazed at her with tenderness. She had done *that*.

Lozhi's chin settled on her shoulder, and the aching in her chest eased. Her friends were gone, but Shiyen was not. Not completely.

Her teeth set and she put both hands into the water, hooking her fingers beneath his armpits. And then she dragged the upper half of his body onto the cold cavern floor, her grunts echoing from the walls. She let his head rest in her lap, wet hair soaking the front of her tunic. Memories sparked as she traced her fingertips along his jaw, her heart and stomach tumbling over one another, falling toward an inevitable end.

His eyes opened. For a moment, they just stared at one another. There was no spark of recognition, no life behind those eyes. Shiyen's replica was an empty vessel, waiting to be filled. And then he sucked in a shuddering breath, his chest moving.

Firmly, deliberately, she moved her hands from his jaw to his mouth and nose. And then she pressed them shut.

He didn't fight back. Shiyen would have fought back. Always they'd been as two waves crashing against one another, clashing until he'd inevitably overpowered her. And though she hadn't felt it a defeat, not back then, she'd let herself be subsumed, drowning beneath the weight of him. Oh, she'd risen back up each and every time, and had told herself because of that he hadn't crushed her, not really.

But he'd never given her a chance to breathe.

She was as close to Nisong as Shiyen had ever been able to get, but she was not her. She'd followed in her footsteps; she'd cherished her memories; she'd made the same mistakes. Not anymore.

The past was gone. Dione couldn't bring it back, much as he wanted to. And that was a future she didn't want for herself — caught in the memories of a dead world and a dead woman, never moving forward no matter how things changed around her. Her family had been cruel to her, and so had Shiyen. She'd climbed her way through society, looking for an opening where she belonged, competing with the rest of the nobility. But for a while, when she'd awakened on Maila, she'd had true friends. And she'd let them down.

She'd found Ragan. And maybe he did love her, as he'd said. Maybe he did care. But it wasn't in the way she needed.

Shiyen's black eyes stared into hers, his skin flushing and then washing out. He blinked.

"I love you," Sand said to the replica. Memories were slippery things, but feelings were true – always. Her lips were wet, the salt of her tears against her tongue. She leaned over, pressing a kiss against his hairline, leaning her forehead against his, feeling his muscles tense and then finally relax.

She lifted her hands. The replica didn't move.

"Sorry," Lozhi said, his tail winding around her waist. "Very sorry."

Her knees ached as she gently pushed the body's head from her lap, as she rose to her feet, echoing the pain in her chest. There was nothing she could do to make the past right. She couldn't bring back Shell, Frond, Grass, Leaf or Coral.

But she could still make a difference here and now. She patted Lozhi's side reassuringly. He swung his head around, his whiskers tickling her cheeks as he sniffed at her tears.

"Come with me?" Sand asked. "There's something I need to do."

His ears flicked. "Always."

52

Lin

Imperial Island

We fled into the mountains. I'd had to break the wall surrounding the cloud juniper – not that it mattered; Ragan and his people would figure out where we'd gone without such an obvious sign. But every bit of damage done to the place I'd called home for so long – first the city, then the palace grounds and now the palace itself – raked sharp fingernails over my heart. The survivors were fewer than I'd thought there would be, and all I could do was hope that there were others, hiding in the palace, in the rubble and the surrounding forests.

The mountains of Imperial were not easily navigated, steep, rocky slopes punctuated by trees and brush clinging to the cliff sides. It was slow going, though Thrana urged the most vulnerable refugees onto her back, ferrying them from our path and to our hiding spot in batches. I brought up the rear of the party, glancing back into the sparse brush every so often to see if we were being followed.

No sign of Jovis. I had to only hope that he'd found some-where safe, that Mephi was with him.

There was a flat space, ensconced by trees, high in the moun-tains – a miniature valley. If we were careful and quiet, we might avoid detection there, for at least long enough as it took Yeshan to break through the palace walls.

Every step of the way, I wasn't aiming for victory; I was only keeping one step ahead of a massacre.

Fog laced my eyelashes with moisture. I blinked, feeling the coldness against my cheeks. It was hiding us well even as I could hear shouts from the palace, voices whose words I couldn't make out, as Ragan searched for a way to us. There were too many of us not to leave small signs of our passing.

Thrana returned once more, moving over the rocks with the ease of a falcon in the air. "Almost there," she whispered to me. Even that whisper felt too loud in the still air, every sound seeming to echo from the mountains. The birds and wildlife had fallen silent, sensing this incursion into their homes, anticipat-ing violence.

The crack of a falling rock sounded just behind me.

I urged the refugees forward with hand gestures, signaling to my guards to close in around them. My bones thrummed, though the feeling was weaker than I was used to. I'd expended much of my energy during the battle, certain that it had been our last stand. I should have planned for worse.

I couldn't see anything behind me. There was no wind, the vegetation still. A passing animal? And then I caught a glimpse of movement.

A gray shape climbed the slope just below us, someone cling-ing to its back. I recognized the beast first. Lozhi. Fear and panic clawed their way up my throat, my hand going for my sword. "Thrana, get them out of here. They've found us."

She obeyed, wrapping her length around the remaining refugees and guards, taking the slowest of them on her back, urging the rest of them to move quicker up the slope.

I drew my sword. Perhaps this was my last stand. Here, in the mountains of Imperial. I could see the rooftops of the palace over the trees and brush, pine needles half-obscuring the courtyard. It felt fitting, at least. Dramatic.

Lozhi grew closer, but his rider didn't draw a sword in response, didn't gather wind and water, didn't dismount to shake the earth loose from the mountaintops. I squinted through the fog as they grew closer, my mouth dry.

Not Ragan.

Who else would be astride Lozhi's back? And then I remembered that Nisong was the only one who'd worn red. Why would she come here alone? And with Ragan's ossalen?

I didn't lower my blade.

They stopped two body lengths away, a short drop away from me. I peered over the edge. "What do you want?"

Nisong looked up at me, and something about her face had changed in the short time we'd been apart. Small, subtle changes – her brow carried not quite so low, her mouth less tense, her gaze more open. I caught what looked like the salty tracks of tears against her cheeks.

"I have information for you," she said. "No one else is with me. They're still searching for you in the wrong direction. But I know the areas surrounding the palace. I knew where you'd be going. It's the only place you can hide for long."

"Is that a threat?" My fingers tightened around the sword. It wouldn't hurt Nisong any more than a regular blade, but it would burn and scar Lozhi.

"I have information," she said again.

I only looked back at her, bewildered. Did she bring terms?

Had Dione and Ragan settled their differences again? How could I trust such an unsteady alliance?

She cleared her throat and spread her hands, her palms upward. "I know how to stop Ragan's constructs and how to release the Alanga with him. I'm here to turn the tide."

At last I understood. She wasn't here on anyone's behalf. She was here for herself. And she was changing sides. I checked the slope as I held a hand up to Thrana. She stopped. "Can you get up here yourself?"

"I don't need help." She put a hand to Lozhi's neck and he surged up the slope. And then she was next to me, dismounting, her unbound hair smelling faintly of smoke and ash. I should have felt alarmed. She was taller than I was, Ragan's ossalen at her back – each tooth as long as my hand. But he didn't feel like Ragan's creature right now. He felt like hers.

Nisong didn't even look at the refugees; her gaze focused on me. All the same, I could feel them at my back, recoiling. "When I wrote the commands for the constructs and for the Alanga, I included a failsafe."

"Does Ragan know it?"

"No." For the first time since she'd appeared on the slope, she looked uncertain. She licked her lips. "I was . . .afraid of him. I didn't want him to have all the power over them. So I took back what power I could. I hid some of Lozhi's shards and carved new commands onto them." She reached into her sash pocket and pulled out a small, velvet pouch. "He made me go over every command I was using with him, and he had some familiarity with the Alangan language, so I had to make these."

I didn't take it. "Why?" I shouldn't have been asking questions. I should have taken it, should have gone straight back down the slope to confront Ragan. But though I'd sensed there was more to Nisong beyond the anger, the memories, I hadn't expected this.

She looked to Lozhi and then back to me. "Because he'd rather destroy everything than lose. Because he doesn't care who he hurts on the way. I can't . . .I can't be like that anymore. I need more than that." Her voice firmed up. "I deserve more than that."

There were so many things I wanted to say to her – that I was sorry for what my father had done to her, that it didn't absolve her of the pain she'd caused, that this would only begin to make up for what she'd done. But there wasn't time. I took the pouch and shook a few of the shards out, studying them.

Esun anoun us yenao vata eshas. Obey only the one who places this. I frowned. "Won't that contradict whatever command you placed that makes them obey Ragan? I'd have to find that shard and remove it."

Nisong was shaking her head before I'd even finished speaking. "I made sure the language I used was slippery enough that you only have to use this shard to countermand the other. The one I already placed says *Lentan un Ragan*."

I turned one of Lozhi's shards over in my palm, marveling at the puzzle and the solution she'd created. One Ragan wouldn't be the wiser to until his constructs and Alanga stopped heeding his commands. "Submit to Ragan."

"The wording pleased him," Nisong said, her chin tilted up in the exact way mine did, and I had the brief, dizzying impression that I'd looked into a mirror. "They'll still have to give way to him, and they cannot fight him directly as a result, but the language doesn't quite contradict. When that is the only command placed within them and he orders them about, they do as he says. But when we add in this new shard, it changes the meaning of the shard already in place. It shifts it out of the way and moves it down the hierarchy."

"You've tested this?"

She hesitated. "I haven't had the chance. But it's all I have." She turned to mount Lozhi.

"No," I said.

She stopped in her tracks, her spine going stiff. "No?"

"You and I are the only ones who can work bone shard magic. I need your help. Come with me. Please." It was the last word she turned her head on, and maybe it was because she had heard it so seldom. I pressed further, not sure if I was pushing too hard or not hard enough. "I know it's easier to run, to take Lozhi and hope that Ragan never finds you. But if you help me, we can put an end to this decisively. You won't have to worry about being chased. My army is at the gates. We can do this together, Nisong."

She pulled herself up onto Lozhi. That was it, then. I'd pushed too hard. I was in a better position than I'd been before, but still, if I faltered there would be no one left to hold the constructs and the Alanga back.

And then Nisong let out a long breath, swung Lozhi around and held out her hand. For a moment, I only stared at her outstretched fingers, unsure of her intentions. And then she wiggled her fingertips, her eyes flashing.

"Give me half of them. We'll do this. Together. And call me Sand."

53

Jovis

Imperial Island

The world spun around me as I ran, never able to quite get enough breath. I could feel my throat tighten, hear the wheezing of air past that narrow passage, my vision covered in spots. My mouth and ears felt stuffed with wool, the surrounding cacophony dimmed. Gray – all gray. Gray skies, gray ashen ground.

I wasn't sure how long I ran for, or in what direction. All I knew was that I needed somewhere away, somewhere quiet, somewhere I could feel finally *safe*.

Someone was saying my name, over and over. *Jovis, Jovis, Jovis ...*

"Jovis!" Mephi leapt in front of me, rising into a sitting position, his front paws catching me. Something in my brain clicked off. I was engulfed in sweet, earthy-scented fur, the hairs tickling my nose with each breath. His chest and belly were dry and delightfully soft. Paws wrapped around my shoulders and back and there was something so utterly warm and comforting about being held in such a way.

Sound returned in increments, the tightness in my chest loosening.

"I'm here," Mephi said. "Breathe."

I finally relaxed, my limbs going limp. He let me stand on my own two feet again slowly, staying close until I could step away without swaying. We stood in the shadow of a building that was still standing, though blackened char marked the windows and half of the roof had collapsed. In the distance, I could hear the pounding of an army at the palace gates. Yeshan's army. I licked my lips, my throat dry. "Were we followed?"

"No."

Where was I? I didn't recognize this city anymore, not after what Ragan and Dione had done to it. It was like peeling the flesh of an animal away and leaving only pieces of the skeleton behind. I couldn't parse it. "Nisong. Ragan." I could breathe again but my heartbeat was still thudding in my chest.

"Behind the palace walls." Mephi descended to all fours again, shaking his head. A faint sheen of rain sprayed from his fur.

Behind the walls that would soon be broken open. Behind the palace walls with Lin and the refugees.

I took a step toward the street and stopped as surely as though I'd run into a wall. If I wanted to help Lin and the people of this city, I'd have to face Nisong. It hadn't felt so terrible a thing when I'd still held the commands within me, but freedom had made me fearful. How would I feel if she pressed more commands into me? If I couldn't think of ways around those commands before she forced me to hurt and kill my friends?

To hurt and kill Lin?

I was shaking again even though it wasn't cold. I couldn't seem to stop trembling. Once, I'd felt invincible with the Alanga power running through my veins. Now, when my bones trembled, it came with a sick feeling – a reminder of all the things I'd done with it at Kaphra's bidding.

I took another step forward. All I needed was momentum, one more step, and then another, and quicker and quicker, until I was in the midst of Yeshan's army, clamoring to get past the gate. To fight for this island, this city, its people.

Lin had said they needed me. I tried another step. It was like wading through quicksand – an agony of effort that felt unsustainable.

Never thought this was how I'd end things when I'd been in the thick of it with Kaphra – spend two years pining after Lin, searching for a way back to her, only to then abandon her in the midst of a battle. And I'd thought I had a good imagination.

But no matter how hard I tried to force the pieces of myself back together, I could feel the edges of each seam, brittle and ready to give way at more than the most gentle of touches. I'd thought Lin's presence could heal me – and for a short time, it had. I'd been able to put everything aside, to live in that moment. But no moment lasts for ever.

"I can't do it," I finally admitted aloud. I couldn't be the folk hero, the man who'd saved children from the Tithing Festival. The harshness of the world had eroded that veneer, that face I'd worn for such a short time. Beneath everything, beneath it all, I was Jovis – liar and coward. The person I feared I'd always been. Unable to save Emahla from her fate, no matter how hard I'd tried. And now, unable to save Lin. Unable to save Imperial or the people of the Empire. Unable to even take one step forward.

Mephi pressed his shoulder gently to mine, a silent support, never wavering.

A figure flashed past the mouth of the alleyway, closely followed by a gray-striped ossalen the size of a small pony. I frowned. I knew that ossalen and I knew that girl. Ayesh.

What in all the Endless Sea was she doing here in the midst of a fallen city, making her way toward the palace gates? Where were her *parents*?

I was at the mouth of the alleyway before I'd finished the thought, the distraction putting my feet into motion again. "Hey!" I called out.

The girl whirled around, shield raised and sword brandished in her hand. Oh, she carried both well enough, but I was much too far away for them to be of use. It was that reflexive action that told me what I needed to know: no matter the bravado on her face, she was frightened.

Somehow, that made my fear feel a little less real. "Ayesh," I said. "It's Jovis."

Her eyes narrowed. "I know who you are."

"Then you know there's no reason to raise a blade against me."

She didn't lower it. "It's dangerous here."

"So it is." I tapped my foot, my staff held loosely in my hands. "Which begs the question: what are *you* doing here?"

She snorted and turned to go, as though she didn't have time to answer such ridiculous questions. But Mephi knew my mind as well as I did. He bounded forward, sliding into her path, blocking the street. The girl stopped and looked back at me.

"Tell him to move."

I lifted a hand from my staff in a helpless gesture. "You have an ossalen. Do you think he *listens* to me? He knows as well as I do that a child shouldn't be in the middle of a battle." I knew as soon as I said the words it was the wrong thing to say. What fourteen-year-old wants to be referred to as a child? I certainly hadn't.

Ayesh was no different. "I'm an *Alanga*." She drew herself up to her full height which was – and I knew better than to point this out too – quite short.

"An Alanga child," I corrected. Ah, careful. Now I was baiting her. This wouldn't help anyone. I continued on before she could fire back another angry rejoinder. "Come now. Your parents must be worried. You're not old enough to fight."

"I was old enough to be left on the streets and to survive." She was like a cat in a corner, hissing and spitting. "And I may not have all my Alanga powers yet, but I'm not an unskilled fighter. Ragan is behind those palace walls. Someone needs to fight him. Someone needs to stop him."

"Yes." I set the end of my staff down on the street, sent a slight tremor out to emphasize the word. "I will."

Her head cocked. "You were hiding in the alleyway."

Had she *seen* that? "I was preparing." Always could get my lies past nearly anyone. Anyone except those like Ranami – people who had needed to grow up suspicious of everyone and everything in order to survive.

Ayesh took after her. The girl scoffed. "What do you think happens to me if he wins? He goes on and on about controlling the Alanga, about bringing them into line. I'll *never* be brought into line, no matter what he or that construct with him does to me. So I have a choice: die now, fighting, or die later, crushed beneath his heel."

I saw the look in her eye and knew what it meant only a moment too late. She'd seized the fur of Shark's shoulder and hauled herself aboard – at the same time water coalesced around her from the surrounding streets before hurling with full force at the broken wall to her left. Shark was leaping before it had begun to fall, darting past Mephi and into the opening it left behind. Mephi reached out his paws but caught only the last bit of Shark's tail before it slipped from his grip.

"Dione's balls!" I swore. She was quick and she was power-ful – I had to give her that. But she was stupid. She wasn't a match for Ragan. I was.

I was mounted on Mephi before I realized what I was doing. And then I froze, sweat beading cold at the back of my neck. Where Ragan was, Nisong would be as well.

How had I moved so easily through the world before? How had I thrown myself at the Empire, the thought of my beheading a distant thing? Now I knew there were things so much worse than death. I'd seen the depths of myself, understood that I was never as strong as I'd thought I was. I would make terrible compromises just to survive, justifying the awful things I was forced to do because I wasn't ready to die yet.

For a brief time, I'd thought myself a hero. Kaphra had shown me that I was not.

I was sitting here atop Mephi, my staff in clammy fingers, watching Shark and Ayesh move determinedly toward the gates. My fear warred with the tired frustration of an adult watching an adolescent do something extremely ill-advised even after being told such a thing *was* ill-advised. And I couldn't just sit back and watch.

I was not a hero, but maybe – I could still do heroic things.

I pressed my knees into Mephi's sides and he responded. I could feel his satisfaction in each sure step. He would have supported me to the very end, no matter what I'd decided to do – but this felt *right* to him. And damn it, it felt right to me.

Maybe no one was a hero. Maybe I'd gotten it wrong from the beginning. Maybe there were only heroic moments and decisions and we all had to keep choosing those as best we could. When we could.

I felt the brittleness in my heart firm up, the edges still there, still tangible, but a thing I could live with. "All right," I said. "Let's go kill a villain and save a child."

Mephi's throat rumbled. "A very good."

54

Ranami

Imperial Island

For a little while, Ranami did as Phalue had asked. She stayed in the cabin, listening to the shouts from the island, the rumbles, trying to guess what each sound could mean. Yeshan was gone; Halong and the Shardless Few who'd decided to follow her, gone; Phalue and Ayesh, gone.

There were still sailors aboard, but for the most part, she felt alone, as though she were trapped beneath the earth in the stone room Halong had put her into. Before Ayesh had shown her the way out.

Everyone she cared about was on Imperial. The fate of the world she loved and the people she loved was being decided without her. She sat on the bed, aware that she'd been pacing, and tried to force herself to be still. "Phalue needs to know you are *safe*." Her voice filled the quiet, cloistered space.

She wasn't a fighter. She wasn't prepared in any way for a battlefield. What use would she be out there, with her tongue and her mind her only weapons?

More use than she'd be here.

Dione was still out there with *his* Shardless Few. She might not be able to reason with Ragan, but she could perhaps do something to sway Dione, to sway the people with him to their side. She'd done it before. Her jaw set, she pushed up from the bed and went for the door. She was oddly surprised to find it unlocked, though she shouldn't have been. No one was keeping her here except her own promises. *I'm sorry, Phalue. I couldn't stay behind.*

It took only a little convincing to commandeer one of the last remaining rowboats and two sailors to row her to shore. She'd been with Phalue for long enough to know that power was an illusion, but one that could be wielded with a strong enough belief in its cutting edge.

Yeshan had left a small contingent of soldiers at the docks. Shardless Few, to Ranami's relief. She recognized several of their faces. And they recognized her. They straightened as she stood up in the rocking boat, as she climbed onto the wooden docks. The few archers who'd drawn their bows lowered them.

"Sai," said the captain of the phalanx, the blue armband around his right arm marked with a simple brass pin, "what are you doing ashore?"

She didn't correct his usage of the honorific; there wasn't time to get into the pleasantries of etiquette – not when their armies were battering down the palace gates. The rain was beginning to abate, but she could smell a storm brewing on the winds. She had the odd sense that the dryness in the air was unnatural, spurred by magic pulling it from its place in the sky and forming it into weapons. This many Alanga in one place – it could spell disaster for them all.

All this talk of stories and history, and they were repeating it – actors on a stage putting on a slightly different rendition of the same play, night after night.

She had to find a way to change things.

"I need to find Dione." She studied the captain. "Louyan, is it? We argued about the utility of higher farmer stipends, didn't we?"

Red crept up his neck beneath his collar. He nodded, his expression surprised. "Yes, we did. It was – well, it wasn't that long ago, but it feels like it." He licked his lips. He was young, even younger than Ranami was, and she felt the weight of each of her years more than someone else might. Most of them had been hard, hard years. She felt him cede to her – her authority, her age, her experience. She'd swayed him in that argument, she remembered.

"I need you to take me to Dione. Yeshan might have set you to keep watch at the docks, but this is a greater need. I can't do this alone. I need your help."

"Dione has allied with Ragan again," Louyan said, though his voice was hesitant.

"They broke with one another before. They can again. I have to try. And quickly."

He didn't put forth any further protests, gathering his soldiers and forming them up as an escort. And then they picked their way through the ruins of the city together.

Burned-out buildings smelled faintly of char and wet wood and smoke. Broken tiles littered the streets and they were forced to take more than one turn to avoid those that had been completely blocked by rubble. Once, they had to make their way around the bloodied body of an elderly woman. The soldiers to Ranami's left shifted, trying to block her view of the body. It gave her the odd urge to laugh. She'd grown up a gutter orphan – did they think she'd never seen a dead body before? But she was a governor's wife now, and with that came certain changes in perception.

A thudding sounded in the direction of the palace, rhythmic

and loud, like the beating of a giant heart. They were battering the gates. Ranami increased her pace, urging the soldiers around her to move more quickly. She needed to be there when the gates broke, to find Dione before the courtyard was overrun with soldiers.

They spilled onto the main street in front of the gates at the very back of the army – Yeshan's troops and Halong's ordered in neat rows, not quite mingling. Halong was bringing up the rear of the army, mounted on his ossalen, his head visible above the crowd.

Ranami pushed her way past her escort and into the soldiers who glanced at her, confused – unsure of what to make of a civilian in their midst. "Halong!" She waved him down.

It took several tries before he could pinpoint the source of her voice, before he spotted her. His Shardless Few parted before him as he rode toward her. "Ranami." A frown creased a line between his brows. "You shouldn't be here. Phalue told you to stay on the ship. You're not a fighter. You have no armor, no weapons."

And no Alanga magic. Yes, she knew.

"I need to get to Dione. As soon as the gates come down."

His gaze sharpened as he looked into her eyes, as though he were piercing into her past, their past, sifting through their lives together. And then he nodded, as surely as he had when they'd been children on the streets together, always behind her no matter what. "Get up behind me and hold on. I'll get you there."

She did as she was prompted, his strong grip lifting her as she climbed. The creature beneath her was warm, his outer fur wet but dry beneath it. She felt the ossalen's muscles tense as she wrapped her arms around Halong's waist.

They surged toward the front of the army.

There was a clear space in front of the gates, soldiers holding either side of a giant battering ram, preparing themselves for another run. Several cobblestones had come loose, puddles forming in the empty spaces they'd left behind, footsteps tracking mud and ash.

Yeshan was on the ground by the gates, directing her men and women. "Thought you were bringing up the rear," she called to Halong. And then she spotted Ranami on the ossalen's back behind him. An eyebrow lifted.

"I need to talk to Dione," Ranami called back.

Yeshan's gaze flicked toward the razed city. "A little late for talk, isn't it?" She gestured her soldiers forward, though she didn't command Halong to fall back.

"It's never too late for talk," Ranami said. She couldn't be sure whether or not Yeshan had heard her. The battering ram hit the gates again, the shudder of impact a thing she could feel in her teeth. At the same time, a *crack* sounded. Splinters flew from the wood, flakes of paint floating into the air.

An opening appeared – large enough for two people abreast.

Yeshan pressed her lips together as her soldiers cheered, as they drew their weapons. She held up a hand, forestalling them and then nodded to Halong.

It was all he needed. They moved to the gap, Halong pulling free a white cloth from the bag at his side, handing it down to his ossalen so the creature could take it in his mouth. Ranami held her breath as they squeezed through.

No arrows felled them, no blades pierced their flesh. No shouts of fear or triumph. The courtyard was filled with only a slight murmuring, rain misting about them like fog.

Dione's army stood in disarray, standing in the courtyard like abandoned statues – still and silent. A few of them had reached for weapons but seemed uncertain of whether they should draw them.

"Where is Dione?" Ranami said. "We're here to negotiate, not to fight."

One of the soldiers pointed wordlessly to her right, and several others followed her gesture. Ranami looked in the direction they pointed.

Dione was sitting on the steps of the hall closest to the gates, his head cradled in his hands. There was something in his posture that made him look less the Alanga of legend and more the Gio Ranami had once known – mortal and unassuming. He wore an oilskin cloak but he'd thrown off the hood, laying his head bare to the rain. She slid from the ossalen's back. "Let me go alone," she said to Halong.

She stepped toward the greatest of the Alanga – alone, unarmed, no magic or strength to call upon. Only her wits. And her compassion.

He looked up when she climbed the first step. If he'd been crying, she couldn't tell; everything was damp. He'd taken off his eye patch and held it between the fingers of his left hand – a hand he ran through his hair in a tired way. "I lost control. Lin did as I asked." Confusion tinged his voice. "She abdicated her throne. She told me to start a Council. I thought that I would do that if she gave in – I *believed* I would. But when the choice finally came, I wasn't sure what to do. And Ragan took them before I could decide. Everyone who was willing to listen. They don't want a Council. They only want vengeance and death."

He stared at the men and women below, waiting for his direction. "And I realized that was all that I'd wanted too, all along, no matter what I'd said to myself. Khalute – he'd stopped speaking to me. For years. So many. He'd only started again recently. Not when I'd taken him back from the Empire, but when I'd saved Gaelung. *That* was what broke his silence."

Ranami sat down next to him, aware that they didn't have time. But she knew if she pushed too hard, too fast, she'd lose him. So she waited, tamping down her impatience and anxiety as best as she could. The Ranami of two years ago would have snapped at him, would have tried to bring him to task. But helping Ayesh to lance the wounds of her past, helping her feel safe and loved, hadn't just changed Ayesh; it had tempered Ranami. She'd come from the kiln of the streets white-hot and furious, strong, but now she'd cooled to a temperature that was touchable. As she expected, he spoke again.

"Ragan took half my army to the palace. He's after Lin and the rule of this Empire, and I don't have the conviction to stop him.

"I'm not who I thought I was."

She didn't reach out to touch him, didn't face him, only stared out in the same direction he did. "You still started a movement that swept the Empire. In the end, you still saved Gaelung from the constructs."

His jaw clenched. "But my motivations haven't been pure, much as I tried to convince myself that they were. I don't care about what happens after, even though I thought I did. The Alanga are back, but it's not my world anymore." He looked at her then, both his black eye and his milky one darting over her face. "It's yours." He sighed. "You really believe all this, don't you? About starting a Council, about changing the way this Empire is run. About putting the needs of the people first. Even if that meant supporting an Emperor you didn't believe in to save the citizens of Gaelung."

Something in her heart broke away, a hawk freed from its jesses, soaring ever upward. "More than anything. We need change – real change. I've done what I can on Nephilanu and with Phalue, but there's so much more that's needed." She heard the conviction in her voice and she knew this was what she was meant for. She knew it in the way she'd known Phalue would be hers for ever on the day they'd been married, when they'd both spoken their vows.

"Then take them. They're yours," he said, gesturing to the Shardless Few soldiers.

He stood and she, a little bewildered, followed.

"Most of you probably know Ranami," he said, his voice raised. "If not from her work within the Shardless Few, then from her work as the wife of Nephilanu's governor.

"She is the one who convinced me to take you to Gaelung, to save the people there. I wish I could say I'd done it of my own volition. But Ranami is the one who tore me from my apathy. If there is anyone you should be following, it is her – not me."

It wasn't enough for him to just hand them over as though they were a dog, searching for a new master. They needed direction. They needed hope. Ranami spoke to the listless army. "Right now, Ragan is attacking the people of Imperial, chasing them down and slaughtering them. He wants Lin dead. He wants to take her place. No matter what he calls himself, he still seeks to set himself up as something of an Emperor – whether that's over us mortals, or over the Alanga.

"The Empire does not belong to Lin. But it also does not belong to *him*." She felt the shift in the crowd, the straightening of their spines, the taking in of bracing breaths. "It belongs to *us*. We are the ones who've toiled, unseen, building the pieces that make this world work. We deserve a say in how it's run. Lin has agreed to abdicate." She pointed to the gates. "The Imperial army is there, ready to fight Ragan. Shardless Few are there, ready to fight Ragan. Are you ready to fight Ragan and take back what is rightfully ours?"

It wasn't quite the cheer she'd experienced in the cavern of the Shardless Few hideout – but then, they weren't in an enclosed space and everyone had already fought for one long and exhausting day. What mattered was that they followed her. And she knew, from the looks on their faces, that she had them.

"Open the gates," she said, gesturing to the soldiers closest to the walls. "Let's show Ragan that we don't need to be Alanga to be strong."

55

Lin

Imperial Island

It was easier to go back down the mountain path than up it. Sand rode astride Lozhi next to me, her head barely reaching my waist now that I was riding Thrana. Odd that such a large creature could move so quickly and so silently.

We ran into the first of Ragan's constructs halfway down the mountain. A bear with the sturdy legs of a mountain goat, scouting up the path. In an instant, Lozhi had darted down the cliff and then behind the creature, Sand clinging to his back.

I took one of the shards in one hand, my sword in the other, legs squeezed tight around Thrana's neck. I needn't have worried; her neck stayed steady as her shoulders heaved, as she ran toward the construct.

It let out a harsh bray, its breath stinking of old blood. I could see the whites of its eyes, the saliva strung between its teeth. I settled my mind and thrust my hand toward its body. The creature's head snapped around, trying to catch my fingers. My heartbeat kicked up a notch, fear spiking down my spine. But then Thrana had closed her jaws around the construct's head – gently, enough to hold it in place.

I took a moment to calm myself before I pushed the shard past the shaggy fur and past flesh and bone. The construct froze as I placed the shard at the top of the stack I found. I removed my hand.

"It'll work," Sand reassured me, as though she could read the doubt in my mind.

"Go," I said to the beast. "Go back down this path and attack Ragan's army."

It turned, hooves clicking against the rocks. Lozhi moved to the side as it passed him, and both Sand and I watched the creature pick its way back toward its former master.

She cast me a smug look – one I recognized from my own face. It would never stop feeling uncanny, like looking at myself in a pool disturbed by a ripple. I shook my head, as though admonishing a student. "Don't get ahead of yourself. That's one. There are many, many more."

"Then we'd best hurry before he realizes we're coming."

Our ossalen carried us ahead of the construct, their speed and agility dizzying each time I dared to look down the mountain slopes. Every so often, I caught flashing glimpses of the palace, of the courtyard. One flash and it was filled with soldiers. Another and it was empty.

I wasn't sure what was happening down there, but I couldn't dwell on it. I needed all my focus if we were to win this fight.

And then I could see him through the branches, the white-bladed sword held tightly in one hand, the end bloodied. Shardless Few followed him, weapons out, faces grim and angry. I spotted several Alanga in the group, a couple riding astride their ossalen though most ossalen weren't large enough and walked next to their companions. Another curled around its master's neck, black tail draped over one of the woman's shoulders. Constructs wove between the Shardless Few, some of them large and lumbering, the army around them giving them space.

"There are more left than I expected," I whispered to Sand as we considered the approaching horde. "I suppose you did your work well."

"We took shards from other ossalen," she said, not meeting my eyes. She shook her head. "We don't have time for plans and there are only two of us. Once Ragan catches wind of what we're doing, he's going to do whatever he can to stop us."

"I'll worry about Ragan," I said, my fingers tightening around the shards she'd given me. "Just turn as many constructs as you can." Without another word, I urged Thrana toward the army.

It could have been a trap; Sand could have hung back and let me plunge into this battle alone. But I could feel her following behind me, Lozhi's footsteps barely audible. I'd broken away from what my father had intended for me; I fully believed that she could too.

We climbed the slopes above the path, weaving through the brush. And then quickly, viciously, we dropped into their midst. Shouts of alarm rose up around me, but I paid them no mind. Thrana lashed out with teeth and claws, sending Ragan's people screaming down the cliff, half of them bloodied from her attacks. She shifted, allowing me to safely slide from her back in the small clearing she'd created.

A construct, part giant ape and part jaguar lumbered toward me on its knuckles. I ducked beneath its swinging fist, slicing its wrist with my sword. It howled and I used its distraction to dart the two steps necessary to reach its chest.

I thrust my hand inside. Memories flickered in my mind – the fight against my father what seemed like a lifetime ago. I'd won that battle; I'd win this one too.

I let the construct go. "Attack Ragan's army," I told it. Without waiting to see what it would do, I whirled to look for the next one and found myself face-to-face with the Alanga woman I'd seen earlier, the black ossalen at her feet.

She didn't look like a fighter – all slender elegance and soft, white fingers. But those fingers were held aloft.

A wave of water came crashing down on me before I could stop it. I tightened my fingers around the shards, knowing that if I lost them, I'd lose this fight. Their edges dug into my palm. Thrana braced me as I stumbled, keeping me from being swept over the cliff. She moved away as soon as I gained my footing, trumpeting a challenge to the army around us.

The constructs were simple. The Alanga were not. I wished I could examine her motivations, to ask her if she truly followed Ragan or if she'd been coerced. But I didn't have the time.

I seized control of the wave she'd tried to wash me away with. It was simpler than I'd thought it would be – not the colossal struggle it had been against Dione. Her face went blank with shock. I swirled the water around us, creating a barrier to give myself a moment to work. "I'm sorry," I said before I pushed my hand into her chest.

I'd thought it might feel differently than it did with constructs. But there was the same tingle of surface pressure and then warmth as my fingers floated within her. I found the hierarchy of shards and placed mine at the top.

And then my world went red with pain.

I should have felt the disruption in my wall of water, the control being partially wrested away. But I'd been caught in the concentration I'd needed to perform bone shard magic. I wasn't sure how I found the wherewithal to remove my hand, but it was in front of me, my fingers curling around empty air.

There was a blade protruding from my shoulder. A white one, stained red with my blood.

"I thought I'd have to chase you to the ends of Imperial," Ragan said from behind me. I caught a glimpse of Thrana, caught in a fight with two enormous constructs. She couldn't come to my aid, not now. And Sand? Darting about on the hillside with Lozhi, searching out more constructs and Alanga that could be turned.

I had to face this alone, fiery pain blazing down my arm and torso, pinpricks climbing up the back of my neck. I tried to breathe past it. And then I jerked forward, pulling free of the blade.

I wasn't sure what was worse – the pain of the sword entering my body or the pain of leaving. I gasped involuntarily, wanting to clutch at the wound, but unable to with both hands occupied. I couldn't drop the sword *or* the shards. It took all my willpower to straighten, to square my shoulders. I whirled to face him. "Lucky you, then. I've come to kill you."

Something like amusement flickered across his eyes. His lips curved slightly as he pointed upward. "Ah! You'll have to do much better than this. You have no *army* here, Lin."

"Then I'll just have to take yours."

I called over my shoulder to the Alanga behind me. "Attack Ragan's army."

"With pleasure," she said, her voice dark. The earth trembled beneath my feet as she sent a shockwave toward the Shardless Few behind her.

Ragan frowned and then looked past me. I couldn't be sure what he looked at but I knew what he'd find: Sand atop Lozhi, turning his constructs to her will. Confusion flicked across his face, then anger and then a coldness that chilled me in spite of the fire running through my veins. "I see," he said. "So this is what it's come to. The one closest to me has betrayed me." I couldn't tell if the hurt in his voice was genuine or feigned.

I tucked the shards into my sash pocket, gripped the end of my sleeve and tore it up the seam. Quickly, I wound it about the gash in my shoulder and tucked it in place, hoping to stop the bleeding. It wouldn't heal the way the rest of my wounds would. My injured arm ached with every movement, but I lifted my sword. Ragan waited for me to finish before he lifted his. And then he attacked.

At first, I thought I would inevitably fall beneath his sword. I was still drained from my use of the cloudtree berry, from the fighting in the courtyard. But though his first attacks were quick and vicious, he soon slowed and I realized – he was tired too. I hadn't been the only one caught in battle.

I turned aside his blade yet again, countering with a whip-quick slash at his midsection. He jumped back, just barely. "Someone has been training you." He laughed. "Emperor over all of this, the world falling apart around you, and you took some time away to learn swordplay. You could have been researching witstone. You could have been negotiating with your governors. Instead, you do this. I hope it was worth it." He tested my guard, feinting once, twice, before attacking in truth.

I caught his blade on mine, white flashing on white as they slid down to meet at the hilts, each of us trying to press the other toward the cliff. He had the height advantage on me, but we were matched in magical strength. "I learned about witstone," I said. "I know what it is. Bones of matured ossalen, gone brittle after the deaths of their bonded companions. Take a little, and the island survives. Take too much, and the island dies. We've been mining ourselves into the Endless Sea."

Ragan gave a little shrug, grunting as he pushed a foot forward, rocks sliding beneath his back foot. "As long as we don't mine the islands we live on. We can afford to lose some of them."

His admission almost took the breath from me. Could he, growing up cloistered in a monastery, not understand the scale of the deaths this would cause? The lives he would disrupt if he let witstone mining continue? Or did he just not care as long as those deaths were distant from him?

"Everything has a cost." His lip curled. "Or did you think you could find a way to keep trade the way it is for *free*?"

My bones trembled – with both anger and magic. I slammed a foot into the ground, shaking loose the rocks beneath his back foot. He stumbled and I slashed at his forearm before he could fully get out of the way. He hissed as my blade cut a thin line of red across his flesh.

"And you are, of course, fine with letting everyone else pay that price."

He recovered and lifted a hand. I felt the brush of wind against my cheek, teasing at my hair. "Someone has to pay it. And it won't be me."

I reached out, trying to pull the air currents from his grasp. Too late, too weak an effort. A wall of air slammed into me, pushing me over the cliff. A moment of stomach-churning realization, a swoop and then I fell.

Thrana was there in an instant, claws grasping the stone, her head stopping me mid-fall. She thrust her nose upward, helping me climb back to the path. *Thank you*, I said to her.

I heard no words from her, just felt a rush of warmth and adoration, comforting as a mother's touch.

Chaos reigned around us. The rain had stopped, though mist still shrouded the peaks, making it difficult to see too far in either direction. There was no way for the army to effectively gather on the narrow mountain path. Sand and Lozhi were doing their work well. Constructs tore at one another and at the Shardless Few. Bodies spilled over the cliff like water spitting from an over-boiled pot. A few people clutched at roots or rocks, trying to make their way back to safety.

Ragan, thinking I'd fallen to my death, had already moved on. I could see his back faintly through the fog, his sword shining as though it had caught the sun. "Lozhi!" he shouted. "Come here!"

A gray shape came lumbering out of the mists, Sand clinging to his back. He stopped several paces short of Ragan, his tail between his legs. Sand was whispering something to the creature, her hands at his neck.

"You are mine, not hers," Ragan shouted at the beast. "Our bond compels you! Come here."

Whatever Sand was saying, it was the same thing, over and over — a rhythm to it, her fingers moving in soothing motions in his fur.

I crept closer, my sword lifted, ears attentive for any sign of impending attack. All I heard was Thrana scrambling back up the slope, covering my back with a growl in her throat.

Lozhi stepped backward, tail still tucked low. Quietly, I took one of the shards Sand had given me from my sash pocket.

Ragan pointed to the sky, his shoulders heaving, then brought that finger down toward the ground. "Come *here*."

Lozhi's ears flicked toward Ragan and then back to Sand. She closed her eyes, leaned her head against his fur, her lips still moving. The beast trembled. He lifted one front foot. I held my breath. I only needed one more moment.

And then Lozhi brought his foot back down again. "*NO!*" he cried out. "I will *not*."

I'd never heard Lozhi speak so vehemently. Apparently, neither had Ragan. His hand went limp, sword held loosely.

Now. I leapt forward, my hand outstretched, my mind going to the calm space I needed for bone shard magic.

It was from that calm space that I observed the twitch of Ragan's chin. I'd made a mistake — somewhere, somehow. He whirled just before my fingers could touch him and caught my wrist.

For a moment, we just stared at one another. And then I caught a roar in the distance from far down below. From the palace courtyard.

Between the rocks, between the trees, I saw a crowd of people rushing toward the palace. My heart soared. I bared my teeth at him. "They're coming for you. My army. The rest of the Shardless Few." I couldn't have known it for sure, but something in my bones told me it was true.

He almost looked, and I slashed at his head. He brought up his sword blocking me, his hand still wrapped around my wrist. This time, when he pushed, I could feel my strength giving way, the wound in my shoulder blazing anew. The white blade crept closer to my face, shining as a great white spear in my vision. "And they'll find their Emperor dead."

Thrana cried out from behind me, but she was far — too far to help. She would try. I knew she would try.

The blade touched my forehead, the cut a line of white-hot pain. I sucked in a breath, trying not to let it consume me, trying to focus instead on bringing my blade to bear. The bone shard tumbled from my grasp.

I could feel my sweat-slicked fingers slipping, my strength fading. At least they would defeat Ragan's army. At least they'd take him down. If all I'd wanted was to protect my people, then I'd done that much.

I let hope flicker out, the space in my heart filling with a dark and depthless peace.

Jovis. My only regret.

The blade sank deeper.

And then Sand was there, her arms wrapped around Ragan's torso, a knife held tight to his throat as she pulled him away from

me. "No," she said fiercely into his ear, Lozhi standing behind
her. "You don't get to do this. Not without facing me." Her blade
dug into his neck, blood spilling into his collar.

But Sand was not a trained fighter. She had anger and strength
and a brawling way with her cudgel. Ragan had spent his life
training. He was an Alanga.

He stomped on her foot, and I felt the ground tremble with
his magic. She gasped and I knew that he'd broken bones. In an
instant, he'd twisted away from her grasp.

I tried to bring my sword up, to feel that tremor in my bones,
to do *something*. But all I could do was take an ineffectual step
forward, pushing a hand to the wound that had begun to bleed
again, my head pounding, the shard I'd intended for Ragan now
lost somewhere in the rocks.

He plunged his sword into Sand's belly. "You *made* me do
this," he hissed. "This is *your* fault."

Lozhi leapt on him from behind, seizing Ragan's arm between
his teeth. Ragan looked to his ossalen, his gaze filled with muted
surprise. He didn't flinch at the teeth digging into his flesh. The
wound on his neck had already begun to heal. "You picked her?
Her." He jerked the sword free of Sand's body, holding the blade
to Lozhi's neck. "Let go, or this ends badly for both of us."

Lozhi spoke, muffled, between his teeth. "You will die."

"And you will lose your bond, becoming dull and brittle,
growing until you're an island wandering the Endless Sea, people
picking away at your bones."

Thrana was suddenly there beside me, then moving past, lips
pulled back from her teeth, her chest rumbling so loudly I could
feel it in the ground beneath my feet. Swords and claws still
flashed on the path on either side of us. "Let him go," she said.
"It's over, Ragan. The rest of the Shardless Few and Lin's army
vastly outnumber you. Dione is with them. You cannot win."

I brandished my sword and together we closed in on him, pushing him back toward the cliff.

He bared his teeth right back at Thrana. And then, to my surprise, he let Lozhi go. Before I could react, he'd stepped over the cliff of his own volition. A shape surged from beneath the cliff, darting down the path before I could stop it.

A bear and giant sloth construct, ram's horns curling from its head, with Ragan clinging to its back.

He wasn't running. He wasn't going to face the encroaching army. I knew exactly where he was going. Swearing, I pulled myself onto Thrana, leaving Lozhi to nudge at Sand's body. She was still breathing – tight, shallow gasps. I didn't have time to tend to her. Not now. Not with the balance of Imperial at stake.

He was going to sink us – just like Riya.

56

Jovis

Imperial

Always children getting me into trouble, pulling me along paths I'd labeled as too dangerous. Perhaps this was the revenge my mother had once had in mind for me when she'd scowled at me as a teenager and wished as much trouble upon me as I'd brought upon her.

Shark was smaller than Mephi, still young in the scheme of things, but she was as quick as her companion, darting through narrow spaces that we couldn't fit through, forcing us to slow down, to go around. Each time, I felt sweat gathering in the small of my back, heat rising up my neck. I wasn't sure if I was more frustrated, frightened or angry. All I *knew* was that I needed to stop this small, stubborn adolescent from doing something that she would intensely regret.

I remembered what it was like to be that age, to think there was nothing out there that could possibly do me harm, while simultaneously believing I was at peace with dying. All bravado that never held out.

The gates were open when we reached them, the wood cracked, hinges askew. Only then did Ayesh and Shark slow down.

The space in front of the walls was empty. So was the courtyard. Blood and broken arrows marred the stones, but the place was deserted. Whatever battle might be taking place, it had moved to another location.

Ayesh and Shark turned about in a circle in the courtyard, Shark's ears flicking back and forth, Ayesh's expression bewildered. She held both shield and sword aloft as though ready to fight someone – anyone.

Mephi and I slowed to a walk as we passed beneath the shadow of the arch. The rain had finally stopped. I tucked my staff onto my back again. Didn't look like I'd be needing it, and the relief I felt was cut through with shame. "Have you had enough yet? Ready to go home?" I cursed myself as soon as the words had left my mouth. I did *not* know how to talk to children.

She whipped her head about, fixing me with a scowl that could have cracked boulders. How did the young have the *energy* for such extremes of passion? "I'll be ready to go home when this war is over."

Shark's ears pricked and I heard the same thing she did: clashes of metal and shouts, coming from the mountains behind the palace.

Well, shit. "I'm sorry, I didn't mean—"

But it was too late. She was charging ahead, leaving Mephi and me scrambling to chase them again. We dashed through the courtyard, bounding up the stairs to the palace doors. They hung open like the maw of some dead animal, the throat beyond dark and foreboding.

Signs of fighting marred the entrance hall. Blood spattered on a wall, a broken railing, bodies I couldn't stop to even glance at. There's a smell to death – a coppery, musty, hollow scent – and this place was filled with it. The teak pillars in the entrance hall, defaced by blades and gore, felt like the bones of a long-dead whale.

Shark was already at the top of the stairs, darting past the mural. She'd have to slow down at some point to find the way to the battle — wouldn't she? The palace was large. Surely she couldn't just get lucky.

But my luck was never good and the luck of others seemed to always outmaneuver mine.

I nearly caught her at a door that lay ajar to the outside, at the back of the palace, Shark's ears pricked, one front foot picked up. Ayesh was frozen in place on her ossalen's back, her sword sheathed but shield arm raised.

Mephi and I stopped several paces away — no point in scaring her off. "Are you ready to talk sense now?"

But she wouldn't even look at me. Her gaze was fixed on the space beyond, her short hair ruffling in the wind, the wooden floor beneath Shark's feet damp with rain.

A sense of foreboding crept up the back of my neck. I reached — not for my staff — but for the white-bladed sword. Mephi stepped forward.

Ayesh's hand went suddenly to the hilt of her sword, her eyes widening. She lifted her shield arm.

A wave crashed into both her and Shark, flooding the hallway with water. I couldn't see them past the foaming wave. Mephi dug in his claws, pushing against the current. It washed into my boots, licking at my knees.

We leapt another, smaller wave, the water nearly up to Mephi's chest. And then my bones trembled and I remembered that we didn't have to just dodge these attacks. I reached out and felt an iron will gripping the water, calling it back through the door, gathering it for another attack.

Ayesh had been thrown from Shark's back and swept down the hallway, her sword still in its scabbard. She was pushing herself to her feet. Shark was running back for her.

"Ragan!" I called out, though my tongue felt like ice. "Would you really fight a child? Wait, of *course* you would. Forgive me for wasting your time with useless questions. So how *are* things between you and Dione? Are you friends now? Didn't he make a fool of you back on Gaelung?" It had taken a little time, but my tongue was warmed up now. "Ah, of course. He flicked away your magic like he was flicking a bug from his shoulder. Are you better at it now? The magic?"

Ragan rode through the doorway on a construct with massive sloth claws, sword held aloft, his face darker than the depths of the Endless Sea. "You think you are *so* funny, don't you?"

I slid from Mephi's back, though he refused to move behind me. "I amuse myself, yes, and that's enough for me." I checked behind him and was ashamed at the relief I felt when I saw neither Nisong nor Lozhi there. He was alone. "Lost your actual friends, did you?"

He only snorted, pointing toward the sky. "Ah, the man without friends tries to make me feel bad for my lack of them."

Ayesh circled around behind him, Shark at her side. I shot her a glare and she shot me one right back. She could certainly match me for sheer stubbornness, it seemed. I was going to have to knock that girl over the head and drag her kicking and screaming from this fight.

Tend to Ayesh, I told Mephi as Ragan stalked toward me.

I won't leave you.

I'm not asking you to leave me; I'm asking you to make sure she doesn't get herself killed, because her ossalen certainly isn't doing that.

But then it was too late – Ragan was darting in, the wind at his back. I moved to counter, my heart pounding in my chest. His blade bounced off mine and then he was gone.

I whirled, my mind blank, the tremor in my bones humming, nowhere to go. Had he just . . . *fled* from me? That wasn't in character. I'd always known Ragan as tempestuous, easy to taunt, filled with a roiling anger at injustices he'd felt were done to him — so much anger that he justified everything he'd done and still saw himself as a victim of circumstances.

He wouldn't run.

Which meant he had other goals.

Thrana's head squeezed through the door that led into the mountains, and then she managed her shoulders, and then she was through, Lin clinging to her shoulders.

She glanced at both me and Ayesh as though she had a lot of questions but didn't quite have time for us. "Which way?"

I pointed down the hall.

She swore. Without saying anything further to either of us, she and Mephi took off in the direction I'd pointed.

Ayesh and I exchanged glances and she shrugged — all wide-eyed innocence. I couldn't chase after Lin and stop Ayesh at the same time. I climbed back aboard Mephi's back just as I saw Ayesh do the same with Shark. "You —" I pointed at her. "— stay *here*."

She only gave me that same innocent gaze but I didn't have time to see if she would actually obey. Mephi's muscles tightened and we thundered down the hallway after Thrana, her bulk creaking against the wooden floorboards.

Ragan urged his construct headlong through the door, the ram's horns on its head crashing into the wood, sending it splintering in all directions. Thrana stopped short at the doorway, a growl low in her throat, and Lin slid from her back. "He's going down into the depths of this island," she said as Thrana tried to force her bulk through the narrow doorway. "And then he's going to plunge that sword into Imperial's innards."

"He's going to command Imperial to die."

For a moment, I could only stare. "He would do that?"

Lin went to the door frame, striking the edge with the hilt of her sword, the wood beneath cracking. "He sunk Riya. I was there."

Aye, I'd been as well, but I hadn't known it had sunk because of Ragan. I'd suspected, but confirmation of it made my heart quail. He'd sunk Riya; he'd killed all those people. And then I was shaking myself, darting to her side, helping her break the frame so Thrana could squeeze her shoulders through. That didn't matter right now. What mattered was stopping Ragan from sinking Imperial.

Lin kept her sword in hand, following her ossalen into the room. I crouched so that Mephi and I could fit through the door, and though he ducked his head and shrunk his shoulders, he almost scraped me off at the knees.

Before either Lin or I could react, Shark was darting past both us and our ossalen, Ayesh low on her back. Children, foolish children, would be the death of me I was sure of it. I rushed past Lin and Thrana, Mephi on my heels.

"Jovis!" Lin called after me. I didn't have the time to stop. That idiot girl would be going to face Ragan and his construct alone. Her ossalen was with her, but they weren't a match for Ragan's power. I wasn't sure that *I* was. All I knew was that as surely as my mother had done her best to protect me from my own stupidity when I was younger, I needed to protect this girl.

Nisong was not here, and though I feared Ragan might have somehow picked the knowledge of bone shard magic from her, what else could I do? The fear I'd felt before hadn't returned yet, and if I stopped, I was afraid it might catch up to me. My feet carried me inexorably forward, through the second door in the darkened room, down into a rough-hewn tunnel. We'd moved from the palace into the mountainside.

The light behind us faded, enshrouding us in darkness. I put a hand to the stone wall, trying to feel my way forward. Ahead of us, I could hear the padding of Shark's footsteps, getting farther and farther away. I tried to pick up my pace and only found myself ricocheting off the wall, bright blots in my vision, my nose sore.

Imperial was once an ossalen, Mephi said, his whiskers tickling my neck. His cold nose touched my cheek. *You should know the shape of it.*

Of *course*. I let the tremor fill my bones, reached out my awareness into the stone, and suddenly felt the earth around me. I'd always just used this awareness to move it, to shape it to my will. But now I could sense the edges of the tunnel, where air met stone.

It took me a few more stumbling steps before I understood how to use this new sensory information, but then I was running again. Ahead, the tunnel branched into two forks. I listened down both and chose the right one. If only Mephi weren't quite so large, I could hop on his back and we could catch up with Ayesh. There was no darting about here, no twists and turns she could use to her advantage.

The cavern opened up. It smelled musty in here, like a closet filled with moth-bitten clothes. I took two steps forward before I encountered the first web.

It stuck to my foot, and then to my hand when I tried to free myself. I heard a low whine up ahead, scrabbling as an animal tried to free itself.

"Shark? Ayesh?"

A low grunt and then Ayesh's voice. "There's a tunnel over here. It's small. He went down it. Him and his construct."

The scrape of metal against stone, another grunt. "We have to stop him."

"There is no *we* here, Ayesh. *You* need to get back to Ranami and Phalue."

She didn't respond to me, but I heard her footsteps. She'd freed herself. I pulled my sword out, using it to cut away the webbing at my boot. *Mephi—*

His fur brushed my hand as he passed me on his way to the tunnel. *Already on it.*

He was at the tunnel entrance by the time I caught up with him. I could hear his breathing as he sniffed the air. A faint light emanated from below. *Ragan is down there. She's right.*

"Jovis!" Lin's voice, from behind me, echoing through the chamber.

I swore. The tunnel was small, the sides scraping at my shoulders in spots. It was a tight squeeze for Mephi. I moved as quickly as possible, my breathing echoing from the walls. It felt like breathing in a closet. The light ahead grew a little brighter. The tunnel opened up into a cavern, able to fit five people abreast.

I heard the clash of metal against metal, and I gritted my teeth. Why hadn't she just turned *back*?

Around a bend in the tunnel, the light increased and I caught sight of both Ayesh and Ragan, locked in a fight. A lantern hung from the makeshift saddle on the construct's back, shadows shifting each time it moved. For a moment, I stopped.

I'd not seen Ayesh fight before. For some reason, I'd expected her to fight like her mother, Phalue – all powerful swings and squared shoulders. I don't know why I'd expected that. She didn't have Phalue's height. She darted in and out like a sparrow, graceful and quick. Even Ragan seemed put off balance by her.

There was a small part of me that acknowledged that yes, she was good, which gave her a grudging amount of admiration. I darted in, hoping to get there before her luck ran out. But then she faltered, grimacing as he struck her shield arm, her foot slipping back. Shark lunged at him, but Ragan's construct met the ossalen with teeth and claws.

Ragan sliced at the girl. Surprisingly, she got her feet under her quicker than I thought she would and she slid to the side only a little too late. The white-bladed sword caught her arm.

I heard the sharp intake of breath, loud in the small space, heard her feet faltering.

And then I was there, my sword lifted, white blade clashing against white blade. The sound rang through the tunnel. Shark had thrown off the construct and now Mephi was circling next to me, trying to find an opening past Shark. The light dimmed as their bulk blocked the lantern. Behind Ragan, the tunnel narrowed again. I couldn't see how far it went into the darkness.

"Always putting yourself in places you don't belong," Ragan said.

"I'm a smuggler. That's what smugglers do." Sweat gathered at my brow as I strained against him, my bones trembling. I was taller than him, but he was the better fighter and he must have taken cloudtree berries, or drunk some of the tea, or both.

His grimace turned triumphant as he lifted a foot and brought it down, hard.

The cavern shook, dust and several small stones falling from above us. I still remembered the way Lin had once scolded me for using such magic in the depths of these caves, concerned I might bring the earth down on top of us.

Ragan had no such cares.

I shoved away from him, retreating a step. "You'll kill us all." Mephi snarled to my left, finding an opening and ducking toward the construct.

Ragan spat to the side. "But I'll kill you too. And the girl, and both your ossalen." His gaze went past me. "And her, too."

Should have kept my eyes on him. Should have just kept fighting. But I couldn't help my reflexive glance back, the pull to look into her eyes. Once Emahla's eyes, now Lin's.

And then I felt the sword slice into my side and I leapt away. The pain of it was as though I'd been run through. Before I could gather myself, the cavern was shaking again and Ragan was darting to the narrow tunnel behind him, calling to his construct. "Cave it in!"

The construct snapped back once at Mephi and Shark before following its master. Mephi swiped out with one big paw, too late, catching only fur on the end of its tail. As soon as Ragan had squeezed into the tunnel, the construct began to dig its claws into the surrounding earth and stone.

"No!" Ayesh ran after him, her sword still in hand. I'd nearly dropped my sword, my veins on fire. I could only watch, helpless, as the girl squeezed through the narrowing gap and past the construct. He'd commanded it to cave in the tunnel – not to defend it.

Words were tricky like that.

But she was just one girl, and even as Shark rushed to follow, I knew she wouldn't fit through the opening. Lin's footsteps sounded behind me but she was still too far away.

I wasn't.

There was no thought to it, only movement. By the time I made it to the tunnel, the opening was one I had to crouch through. I shoved loose rocks out of the way, wriggling past a tight spot, my wound still bright with pain.

But I could be as stubborn as Ayesh sometimes, my body still moving even when my courage gave out. I was through, coughing, dust filling the air, my face so close to the construct's belly that I nearly landed in its fur. The damned thing was still digging at the ceiling, would keep going until it had fulfilled its master's request. Rocks threatened to land atop my head, and I ducked beneath the construct to avoid them. Ragan had taken the lamp with him. Ayesh was already gone.

I stabbed the creature below the ribs, making sure to get the blade in nice and deep, to wrench it out. The construct slumped, a low moan in its throat, its claws going limp.

Only then did I lean against the wall, putting a hand to my side. Blood dripped from the wound Ragan had given me, soaking my shirt. Oh, it *hurt*. But I'd been through this over and over with Kaphra. It didn't make the pain any easier, but I'd figured out how to live with the feeling, to let it wash over me like the waves of the Endless Sea.

"Jovis." Lin's voice, at the mouth of the tunnel.

I turned and sheathed my sword. The opening was now only just large enough for me to press my face to. She'd brought a lamp, and the beam of light from beyond caught the dust in golden specks. Mephi's snout appeared next to her cheek, his nose sniffing at the mouth of the tunnel.

Somewhere behind me, Ayesh was chasing Ragan into the darkness. Ragan, with his white-bladed sword, ready to plunge it into the depths of Imperial. To kill us all. Ayesh was good, but she couldn't match Ragan.

I huffed out a breath, seeing the shape of things. Done a lot of wrong during my time with Kaphra. Always, *always* too frightened to put my life on the line, to make that sacrifice. Lin told me that I'd done what I'd had to. That I'd survived. But I knew, deep down, I'd weighed my life against the lives of the people I'd hurt and not knowing them had made it easier to sway me toward survival. And I couldn't risk Mephi. I *couldn't*. Maybe Lin was right and there was no shame in it. Maybe I'd done what anyone else would have done.

But Imperial was a living, thriving island, its Alanga companion now long dead. There was no one to protect the life of this former ossalen, no one to protect the lives of everyone living on it. No one except Ayesh.

And I couldn't let her do it alone.

"I have to go," I said, my whisper echoing through the gap in the stones. Both Lin and Mephi looked so close, yet so terribly far away.

"You're hurt," Lin said, her voice quick and soft. "We can find a way through; we can move the stones—"

"Ah, don't make this harder than it is," I said, curling my fingers around a rock, wishing it were her hand I was touching. My heart was a brittle thing, ready to shatter at a breath. I felt the warmth of blood trickling through the fingertips of my other hand.

She swallowed, nodded. Ah, she was stronger in some ways than I'd ever be.

"Jovis, *no!*" And then Mephi's face was taking up the whole of the gap. "You said we would stay together. No matter what. You *promised!*"

Crushed, like glass beneath a boot. There'd be no repairing me. "Aye, I did. I'm sorry, old friend, but you've been right about me from the very beginning. I am the one who helps."

"No! Not this time!" I heard rocks crack and shift as he threw himself against the rubble, the opening narrowing farther. He stopped, gasping. "You do not need to help! Not this time. *Please.*"

For only the second time in my life, I turned my back on Mephi, though this time it took every bit of willpower I had. He was more than a pet or a friend: he was a companion whose soul was inextricably entwined with mine. He'd brought me back to living, to life, when I'd become consumed with the dead and trapped in the past. There were no words that could convey what he meant to me, so I didn't try. He knew. It was a quiet understanding that lay between us, that each of us could not live without the other. It was true for me, but it wasn't quite true for him. If I died, he'd continue on. And that gave me a measure of comfort.

"Take care of Lin and Thrana." And then I was running down the tunnel, my breath ragged, pain burning up and down my body, Mephi's screams following me.

Down, down, into the bowels of the island, my feet moving as though I'd walked this path before in another life, another time. My head swam, turning the darkness into shapes and colors I knew weren't actually there.

I heard them fighting before I saw them. Blade against blade, grunts, hurried footsteps, the faint rumble of earth and splash of water. Light glowed ahead and the tunnel opened up again into a larger cavern.

Immediately, I saw what was happening. There was a break in the stone behind Ayesh, a soft patch of dirt on the ground. Ragan was circling, his teeth gritted, trying to get to it.

The girl was breathing heavily, her shield lifted, blood trickling from several small wounds. She was holding him back, but just barely.

I straightened past the pain in my side, new strength flowing into my veins. If she would fight until the very last, then so would I. "*Now* will you go back to your parents?" I called across the distance.

Both combatants looked to me.

I lifted my hand from the wound, my fingers red and sticky. I drew my white-bladed sword with the other hand. Ragan had tossed the lamp aside. Its light caught the two swords and *gleamed*. Ayesh's jaw set, but I cast her a glare that my mother would have been proud of. "Yes, you're very good," I told her. "And you're strong. And you're brave. But Ranami and Phalue *need* you."

Doubt and understanding flickered in her gaze. All these years and I'd finally learned how to talk to children. Now, at the end.

I pointed my sword at Ragan. "I can handle him, but only if I'm not worried about protecting you."

Ragan snorted, then backed away from Ayesh, beckoning to me. "Yes, let's see how well you *handle* me." His gaze flicked to the wound. Was it *still* bleeding? He readjusted his grip on his sword, and I felt the tremor of magic through the ground as he reached out.

Here, in the heart of the island, everything felt odd, amplified. I extended my awareness and caught the water he was gathering before he could fully coalesce it. It hung in droplets behind him as he strode toward me, teeth bared. I judged the distance between him and the soft spot in the ground, sliding to the side to put myself between it and him. And Ayesh, finally, *blessedly*, moved out of the way, wincing as she put a hand to one of her wounds.

"Go back up the tunnel. Help Lin and Mephi get through." This time, I knew she would obey. I set my feet into the stone, felt warmth seeping through the soles of my boots.

Ragan attacked.

I barely brought my sword up to block in time and already he was whirling into another movement, almost faster than my eyes could follow. I could only deflect his blade, giving ground to avoid yet another strike. Had he somehow gotten better in the time since we'd last fought? There was something both brutal and elegant in his movements, a grace I couldn't quite match. I was Jovis, smuggler and liar. I threw chairs at people when I had no other weapons at hand.

There were no chairs here, only two blades, two sets of feet and hands. No ossalen.

I could feel the rise and fall of his breath in this space and felt my breathing fall into time with his. There was something intimate about this fight, something so very personal. I knew I had to move with him, so I did, flowing around his next slash at my neck, moving from that dodge into an attack that he somehow sensed, his sword clashing against mine. Would I have fallen into the same endless cycle of anger and destruction if I'd had his life? I liked to think I wouldn't have. But then, I'd had loving parents, and I'd also never thought I would have let Kaphra's fingers dig into my soul.

There was a part of me that understood him – denied the close, loving relationship he craved, he'd tried to force one on his ossalen. He'd equated power with love, he'd felt the adulation of his Shardless Few followers and he'd thought that was enough. And now, when he was about to lose it all, he couldn't bear the thought of letting everyone live. He would have their love or he would have their destruction.

He gritted his teeth, and the droplets behind him wrenched from my grasp, coalescing. I tried to take advantage of his split attention, feinting to the side and then thrusting at his middle. But he met each blow as if he'd known they were coming.

I couldn't talk my way out of this. And I could talk my way out of near anything. But Ragan was inexorable as a tsunami, a force that had gathered too much momentum to stop.

So I fought harder than I ever had before, focusing on each breath, each movement, ignoring the bouts of pain from the wound in my side, the tickle of blood trickling past my hip and down my leg. He lashed at me with the water he'd gathered, splashing it in my eyes, sending it in waves at my feet. I didn't dare shake the earth, but I battled with Ragan for control of the

surrounding water, sometimes wresting it from him, and sometimes failing to before he attacked. I scored a hit on his left arm,
and then another on his right leg. His face was drawn with pain. I
could almost feel the burning sensation in his veins, could almost
feel sorry for him. I gathered the water from his grasp and sent
it with full force at his torso.

It crashed into him and he stumbled, his sword nearly falling
from his grasp.

I was pushing him back. I was *winning*.

And then he took two shaking steps forward, his hand went
to his belt and I caught the glimpse of bone between his fingers.

I froze.

All the fear I'd distracted myself from came rushing back,
overwhelming me. I'd pushed it aside for a time, convinced that
I'd conquered it. But I'd only hidden it from view. He'd take
control of me. He'd make me do worse than Kaphra. It was over.

It took me a moment to feel the coldness of the blade in my
belly. Not a hand at my chest, forcing a command into me,
but a sword.

"I thought so," Ragan said. Perhaps he understood *me* as well.
He showed me what lay between his fingers – not a shard of bone,
but a piece of cloudtree bark. He flicked it away.

Caught. By the same sort of trick I'd once used. Fitting.

For a while I could only stand there, shocked, trying to
grasp what had happened, that the sword in my belly was all
too real. The blaze of pain that finally erupted sent me gasping to my knees, the stone warm beneath me. Ragan followed
me to the ground, twisting the blade, sending fresh waves
of agony through me. I didn't even feel the other gash in my
side. That was one way to stop the pain from a wound. Get a
bigger wound.

Always joking at inappropriate time, my mother's voice said in my head. My father's face appeared in my mind, shaking his head in disappointed agreement. And then he'd lift his eyes to the sky and whisper something about hoping how the world would teach me to mind my tongue before it was too late. A Poyer thing – putting wishes out into the world as though the world could grant them.

The beat of the island pulsed beneath my knees in time with each fresh wave of pain. I'd thought I was alone, but I wasn't. And I wasn't just Empirean: I was Poyer too. I was both.

Perhaps my father was right and the world *could* grant wishes. I pressed a palm to the stone. Any moment now, Ragan would get tired of gloating. He'd pull the blade free; he'd go to the patch of soft dirt; he'd sink Imperial.

I let the tremor fill my bones – a weak, muted trembling, but one that was still there. I reached my awareness down, down, down into the dark heat of the island's core, searching.

And finding.

Imperial was not awake, not in the way that Mephi was. And I did not have the same connection. But I could sense it stirring beneath me. *Help me. Please.*

No words, only a soft acknowledgment, and then my bones were shaking hard enough to rattle my teeth. Strength was flooding into me, more than I'd ever felt before. I surged upward, bringing my sword to bear.

I didn't go for his belly. I went straight for his head.

I thought I caught a moment's surprise across his face – a startled, sad expression, as though he'd always known this was how things would end.

My blade separated his head cleanly from his neck. It was falling. I was falling. Someone was shouting my name and it was echoing. Or was that just more than one person?

Hands pressed at the wound in my belly. A little of the pain dissipated as the sword was pulled free. Lin's face, briefly, her cheeks wet with tears. I opened my mouth, but couldn't speak.

Whiskers tickled my face and I found myself reaching out, grasping, one last time, the warmth of Mephi's fur. Remembering sunlit afternoons napping together on the deck of my boat, his breath smelling faintly of fish.

And then even that was gone.

57

Lin

Imperial Island

He was still breathing by the time we carried him out of the cave and into the palace hallways. The sounds of the battle had faded and I knew that we'd won. Ragan's faction was no match against the reunited Shardless Few and the Imperial army combined.

I cradled Jovis's head between my hands as Ayesh and Shark rushed off to find someone – anyone – who might be able to help. Mephi lay on the ground next to Jovis, the warmth of his fur against my thigh. Thrana paced behind me, a whine in her throat.

A hand fell on my shoulder.

For a moment I started, before remembering that Thrana was there and she'd not let me come to harm. I looked up.

It was Ranami. Her dress was torn and dirty at the hem, spattered with blood. Her hair, usually smooth and shining as a waterfall by moonlight, was in disarray, wild as storm clouds about her face. Still, there was something regal and triumphant in her carriage, something that hadn't been there before.

Men and women hovered behind Thrana, giving her wide berth. Several carried injured comrades beneath their arms.

"It's over," Ranami said.

I stroked Jovis's cheek with my thumb, feeling the skin growing colder. "Yes. But I need a physician." I didn't sound like myself. My voice was thick, distant.

Ranami's gaze went to the wounds on his torso before resting again on my face. "Eminence – *Lin* – I don't think a physician can help him."

He was dying. I knew it in my bones, in my heart, but I couldn't quite wrap my head around it. We'd come so far, had been through so much. I'd thought him dead once already; I'd mourned his loss once.

I couldn't do it again. "No."

Ranami licked her lips and then knelt beside me, taking my free hand between hers. She'd always been like a feral cat in my mind – beautiful but dangerous. To feel this warmth from her was . . .odd. Odd but welcome. I leaned toward her like a flower toward the sun.

"In Nephilanu, there was a pool beneath the ground. In a system of caves below the surface. It . . .healed Ayesh. There might be something like that here, though I fear we would be too late."

Hope spiked through my heart. The pool where I'd found Thrana. The womb of the island. Father had grown me in it; he'd grown himself in it. It made *sense* that it could heal wounds, even wounds given by white-bladed swords. "Yes. There's one here. Mephi, Thrana, help me. It's just back that way; we can get him there in time."

Ranami grabbed my arm as I rose and moved to lift Jovis from the ground. She brought her lips close to my ear. "You should know, there are costs."

"I'll pay them."

"You wouldn't be the one paying them." I drew back, looked into her eyes. She nodded at Jovis. "*He* would be. The pool . . . takes memories as it heals."

The memory machine. It all clicked together in my mind. The water might heal Jovis's wounds but it leached memories from flesh and blood. "I have to try."

I couldn't stop to think, not while his breathing grew shallow and his face grew pale. Ranami nodded. She helped me load Jovis onto Mephi's back. She looked at her soldiers, at the man standing at their head. "Tend to the wounded. I'll return shortly."

She followed Mephi and me back into the shard storeroom, stopping to grab a lamp. And then we went through the cloud juniper doors, down into the depths of the tunnels, past the shattered door that led to what had once been my father's workshop.

Someone had pulled the replica of my father from the water, and by the finger marks around the mouth, had asphyxiated him.

But I couldn't care about that, not now.

I pulled Jovis from Mephi's back, my magic lending me strength. He wasn't breathing anymore, his skin sallow, the blood no longer trickling from his wound. Quickly as I could, I slid him into the pool, letting only his head rest above the water.

"Please," I whispered. I bent over Jovis's face, pressing my forehead to his. The skin there was cold to the touch, reminding me of nothing so much as the corpses I'd carved to make constructs – dead, inert flesh. I closed my eyes, putting all my will into wishing this would work. I'd lost Numeen and his family. I'd lost Bayan. I'd lost Jovis.

My eyes burned with tears, my throat so tight that I couldn't speak. I couldn't do this all over again. Not now. If I moved now, I'd crumble in on myself, my heart a sinkhole that the rest of me was falling into. I clenched my jaw, waiting for something – *anything*.

His chest rose.

I let out a choked sob and put my fingers to his neck. There, fluttering so faintly I could barely feel it, was a pulse. Under my touch, it grew stronger. It felt like the life was flooding back into me, surely as it flooded back into Jovis. I didn't know what memories he'd lost, or how many of them. I could worry about that later.

I wasn't sure how long I sat there, my feet curled beneath me, slowly going numb. Ranami was moving around my workstation, gathering flasks of water from the pool, placing them into a crate. She caught my gaze. "For those willing to pay the price. I can't let them die, not if they want to live."

Mephi had lain by the water's edge, reaching his head out every so often to sniff the water over Jovis's body. He let out a soft sigh before tucking his chin to his chest and crossing his paws over one another. "He's alive," Mephi said. Not that he would be all right, but that he was alive. "Lin," he said, "Thrana is waiting for you above. Everyone is waiting for you. I can take care of Jovis. You've done all you can."

Reluctant, aching, I rose to my feet. I felt I'd wept a lifetime of tears, their salty tracks tracing grooves into my cheeks. I was bruised, battered, injured – but it was my heart that hurt the most. All I wanted was to sit here until I *knew* exactly the price Jovis had paid for this miracle. But Mephi was right. There was nothing I could do here *except* wait.

I nodded to Ranami. "Come with me." It came out of my mouth more of a request than an order, and I remembered then that I'd abdicated in front of Dione. It hadn't been formally done. Not yet. But I knew I couldn't continue being Emperor. That something had irrevocably changed during the battle and now I was a usurper in my own home.

Thrana was indeed waiting for me outside the cloud juniper doors. She stood patiently as I threw my arms around her neck. She settled her chin over my shoulder, her beard tickling the back of my neck. "We go to help?" she said.

"Yes." I pulled myself up onto her back and then leaned over and offered my hand to Ranami.

She took it silently, the crate of flasks tucked under one arm.

Together, we went back into the hallway and then slowly made our way up the mountain to where the fighting had been the thickest. There weren't many who took the offer of the healing water, most hoping to heal on their own, over time. But there were some who were in danger of losing limbs, or eyes, and they nodded at our warning they would lose some memories. "Which ones?" they always asked. But neither Ranami nor I could provide an answer.

Frightened and weary cityfolk picked their way past us, no longer needing to hide. When we were halfway up the path, I saw Lozhi.

He was still at Sand's side, curled up around her as though he could somehow keep her warm. It hurt my heart to see. He'd lost his Alanga companion. He'd grow to be an island, but his bones would be brittle enough to be mined. But he didn't seem to care about that. About Ragan. Instead, he stayed at the side of a woman he could not bond with. A dead woman.

But when I slid from Thrana's back to tend to Lozhi, I saw her mouth open, the smallest breath escaping.

She was still alive.

There was one who stubbornly clung to life despite the odds. If nothing else, my father had given her Nisong's will — an iron will — one that could not be dissuaded or tamed. It was a terrible shame she'd put it to the use that she had.

I should just let her die. She'd done enough harm in her

lifetime. And it had been years now – sooner or later, one of the people whose shards she carried inside her would begin to feel ill. Sooner or later, one of them would die, whether by shard sickness or by accident. And then Sand would slowly fall into disrepair.

It was the fate of all constructs.

Unless –

My hand went to the pouch at my side, to where I'd kept some of Thrana's shards. I had more, hidden away on my ship.

I made a choice.

58

Sand

Imperial Island

Chrysanthemums. They were the first thing she saw — golden blooms across a white background, wild as a lion's mane. They rippled with each of her breaths. Not real chrysanthemums. Painted ones. On cloth.

"She's awake."

Lozhi's voice. Something in her relaxed. He was still here, next to her. The sheet was pulled away and then she was looking into Lin's eyes.

Sand licked her lips. The last thing she remembered was bleeding out on the ground with Lozhi next to her, the battle raging around them. She'd made her peace with death. No matter what she'd done to help Lin, to help Imperial stay afloat, it was no less than she deserved. "I'm still alive." Her voice felt rusty with disuse. How long had she been out for? And *how* was she still alive?

"Yes." Lin frowned and lifted the sheet, checking the spot where the wound had once been.

"Is it bad?"

"It's healed. Or, rather, I sewed it shut and the shards did the rest." She let the sheet fall back down.

Sand blinked against the light streaming in through the window and tried to sit up. Her elbows sunk into a mattress. She was in a room of the palace, Lozhi sitting on the other side of the bed. Her stomach rumbled. Without even asking, Lin handed her a bowl of broth. "Your body has been through a lot, regardless. I've tried before to replace the shards in a construct with ossalen shards. It didn't go well. But this time, I went more slowly and carefully. I made sure to replicate the commands *exactly*. With . . . some minor changes."

Sand touched her chest. She was dressed in a plain shift, the white fabric soft to the touch. Did anything feel different? She wasn't sure. And then she noticed: the scars she'd once had were gone. She lifted the bowl to her lips, slightly troubled. The salty, fishy broth slid down her throat.

"I took out any reference to obedience, any compulsions. You may not have been aware of these because there may not have been anything to trigger them in the past two years. But the short of it is you're free. Completely. And Ragan is dead."

The day outside was clear, a cool breeze drifting in from the window, ruffling her hair. Outside, she could hear the sawing of wood, shouts and the hammering of nails. Imperial was rebuilding. This was never a future she'd imagined for herself. It was one that felt odd for her to be existing in. She shouldn't *be* existing in it. "Why did you save me? I was dying. You could have left me there."

"I could have."

She sipped from the broth again as Lin kept her silence. There was something delightful about just the feel of cloth against her skin, the scent of the ocean on the wind. Things she'd rarely taken the time to appreciate before. Lozhi rested his head on the mattress next to her and she reached out to scratch the soft, downy fur behind his ears and around the base of his horns.

He was here, and somehow that made everything better and brighter. She'd kept her promise. She'd made sure Lozhi was safe. He'd never have to worry about Ragan again. She hadn't let him down the way she had all of her constructs. The way she had with Coral.

Lin finally cleared her throat. "I considered it: leaving you. It would have made Lozhi sad, but I've spent my life disappointing others. And you've done so much harm to this Empire and its people. But you did some good in the end. And I could feel that something fundamental in you had changed."

Sand closed her eyes, took one last sip of broth and set it on the table next to Lin. "Thank you." It was an odd feeling, this gratitude. She pressed a hand to her chest again.

"Thrana's shards," Lin said. "They won't fade, not the way the others would have. An island lives a good, long time, and there's life enough in them to share. And you shouldn't thank me."

At that, Sand looked up again. It was odd and uncanny, looking into Lin's eyes – those eyes which didn't resemble hers but which held that spark of recognition. In another lifetime, perhaps their places might have been switched, and she would have been the one in the palace.

Lin sighed at the question in Sand's eyes, her gaze going to the window, to the city beyond. "I didn't do you a favor, saving you. Dying ...dying is simple. You remove your thread from the tapestry and everyone else is weaving in and out, trying to fix the damage you've done. I'm not sending you back out into a kind, forgiving world, do you understand that?"

She thought she understood. "No one trusts me."

"No. They don't. You can't run from your face, and there are many who know who you are. Maybe you can run far enough that you won't be recognized. Maybe you can start over somewhere where no one knows your name. But eventually, someone will find you out. Living isn't simple. I've woven you back into the tapestry. You *can* hide, digging your thread somewhere into the back. Or you can help us all fix the damage you've done."

Sand scratched Lozhi's chin, a cold trickle of despair running through her heart. "I can never fix everything, even if I wanted to. I have done . . . so many terrible things. Not just to people I didn't know, but to people I cared about."

Lin shrugged, and Sand saw an echo of Shiyen in her. "Perhaps you can't. And even if you do, you cannot expect forgiveness or even hope for it. People have a right to their anger. They have reason for their distrust." Her voice softened. She reached out – though only to touch the bedspread and not Sand herself. "But Lozhi trusts you. And that, for me, was enough."

The ossalen leaned his head into Sand's lap, letting out a soft sigh. For a brief moment, the hollows of her heart filled, a flood of relief and joy. She took his chin in his hands, gazing into his soft gray eyes.

"Yes. It can be enough for me, too."

59

Jovis

Imperial Island

The world was too bright. It filtered red through my eyelids as I registered several things at once. I was in a bed. I was hungry. I was . . .

I didn't know.

Sharp panic ripped its way up my throat. In a flash, I was tearing sheets from my body, leaping to my feet, reaching, reaching toward my back for – what?

There was nothing there anyways, only a loose shirt meeting my grasping fingers. I wasn't sure what I'd expected.

Something warm tickled my bare feet. Fur.

There was an enormous creature curled next to the bed, bigger than a war horse, than a bear, than – I ran out of comparisons. Antlered horns sprung from its head, its fur gently ruffling with the wind from the open window. A stray beam of sunlight peeked out from behind a cloud briefly before disappearing once more.

I had been sleeping during the day. Why?

The creature stirred. One enormous brown eye cracked

open. "Jovis." It blinked. "*Jovis.*" And then it was on its feet, its whiskers tickling my cheeks, black nose snuffling as it smelled me. "You're *alive*. You're awake! Ah, you've missed so much!"

Jovis. Was that me? My name?

I slid to the side, away from the creature's searching gaze. Somehow I didn't feel any surprise that it spoke, but I didn't *know* this beast.

The pricked ears drooped. "Jovis, you died. I felt it. The bond we had is broken. Dione says that in all the years he's been alive – and that's a looong time – an ossalen has never re-bonded." His ears pricked again, his posture straightening. His horns nearly touched the ceiling. "But I still love you. We can still be together, just like you promised."

I put a hand to my temple. Too much information. Too much at once. I'd . . . died? Ossalen? Bonds? Dione? None of it made sense to me. The creature took a step toward me but I held up a forestalling hand. "I don't know you. I'm sorry, I don't."

It was like watching a flower wilt. I'd never seen a creature look so dejected. Or had I? I frowned, my head aching.

"But Jovis, I—"

The door opened and a woman swept into the room. She was dressed smartly – in a blue silken tunic and black pants tucked into leather boots. Her hair was bound halfway up, white porcelain flowers pinned at the top. There was nothing remarkable about her face, but I found my gaze drawn to her eyes nonetheless. Eyes that filled with tears upon seeing me.

"I wasn't sure if you'd wake up." She started to rush toward me but stopped when she saw the creature's posture. "Mephi?"

"He doesn't remember me," the creature called Mephi said. "Not even my name."

The woman slowed but still approached, her gaze locked on mine. "Do you remember me?"

I felt like a man who opens a box expecting a treasure only to find emptiness. There were no memories to rifle through, to sort into neat piles as I searched for the ones that had her face. I wished I could remember, but there was nothing to grasp – only a vague sense that I'd lost or misplaced something very important. "No."

It's a terrible thing – disappointing two others in so short a time for reasons I couldn't quite understand. There was a part of me that knew this wasn't my fault – how could it be? – but I still wished it wasn't so.

Wishes, wishes – there was a saying about wishes on the tip of my mind . . .an old woman's voice . . .

It escaped my grasp, a fish fleeing into deeper waters.

The woman turned to the beast, placing a comforting hand on his nose. "He was too far gone. I shouldn't have risked the waters. It took his memories. All of them. I'm so sorry, Mephi."

Mephi shook his head. "No. Don't be. I didn't want him to die either."

She looked to me again, tears slipping down her cheeks. "But he's gone, isn't he?"

I squeezed my eyes shut, searching that empty space again, wondering if there wasn't a false bottom I hadn't found yet. "I don't know. I just don't. I don't know *anything*. Please can I have a moment? Longer than that? And food. If it's not too much to ask."

The woman placed a hand to her breast. "My name is Lin. I'll have someone see to your needs. Come on, Mephi. Let him have his rest."

"No." Mephi had set his jaw in much the way an obstinate child would. "I stay *here*. I stay with him."

"He doesn't remember. He doesn't understand."

I sat back down on the bed, feeling suddenly weak.

"It doesn't matter – what if he remembers and I'm not *here*?" His voice was plaintive. "I promised him. He broke his promise but I won't break mine."

"Mephi—"

"No, it's fine. He can stay." Did I have a soft spot for talking creatures? How many soft spots did I have? "As long as he keeps quiet."

The ghost of a smile touched Lin's lips. "Clearly you don't remember him at all, or you wouldn't say that." And then her expression dropped. She turned to go. "I'll have someone bring up food. For both of you. But you should rest."

"Wait," I called after her. I licked my lips, unsure if I wanted to know the answer to my question. "How did I die?"

She touched the doorknob, her shoulders slumping. She glanced back at me and again I was caught by something in her gaze. "You died doing something heroic. Something I think you didn't know you were capable of. And you—" Her voice broke. She took in a deep, shaking breath before trying again. "And you deserve so much better than this. I love you. I . . . *loved* you."

And then she was gone.

60

Lin

Imperial Island

The formal proclamation was easy enough to write. It felt like the truth, flowing from some divine source directly onto the page.

I, Lin Sukai of the Sukai Dynasty, do hereby abdicate in favor of Ranami of Nephilanu, so that she may lead the Empire in setting up a Council of leaders, one from each island . . .

Ranami seemed more hesitant than I did. She paced from one side of my study to the other as my hand flowed across the parchment, her hands clasped behind her back. "I'm not ready," she said. "It's an entire Empire. It's in shambles. There are refugees everywhere, searching for new homes."

I lifted my hand briefly just so I could meet her eyes. "No one is ready for this. At least you *know* you aren't. And you have Phalue to help you. You've dealt with refugees before, and well, from what I've heard. They're now thriving on Nephilanu and have added to its economic growth."

"That was Unta. This is *Riya*, which was quite a bit larger. So many broken families. So many broken people. And Imperial is still rebuilding. What if I make mistakes?"

Calmly, I resumed writing again. "You *will* make mistakes, so make your peace with that now. And, Ranami, this is only temporary. Do you believe in the idea of a Council, in letting everyone have their say?"

"I do, but—"

"Then you have to see this through."

Dione, sitting in the corner, let out a soft grumble.

I finished the last strokes of a sentence and let my gaze flick to him. "Did you have something to add to this conversation?"

He shifted in his seat, his arms crossed. "It's not my place. Not anymore. My place is with the Alanga – teaching them. And teaching you."

"Artifacts."

"Yes," he said. "It's the best I have to offer this new Empire. Some of the old knowledge. It's what I once taught to Ylan, and what he used to create bone shard magic. Artifacts are much ...gentler in some ways. And they could help bridge the gap when it comes to witstone."

Trade had slowed to a standstill. Everyone was trying to find ways to deal with sluggish travel between the islands – everything from better preservation methods to diversifying local economies. I finished the proclamation, hesitating a moment before signing my name.

I'd spent so long trying to become Emperor. And then trying to be the best Emperor possible. And now I was ready to just give that all up? I let out a *whoosh* of breath and then signed quickly before I could second-guess things. It was hard to let go of power. My father had taught me that. His family had twisted themselves into knots to hold onto it, my father going so far as to kill his own daughter.

It wasn't a dynasty I wanted to perpetuate. That era was over. Let someone else try to make a better world. The Sukai way certainly hadn't worked.

And neither had mine.

I handed the proclamation to Ranami to sign and nodded to Dione. "I added a bit in there about you dissolving the Shardless Few, about how there's no longer a need for them. You'll need to sign too."

He snorted and shook his head ruefully. "I'm not sure this will work."

I shrugged. "It might not."

Ranami's warm fingers touched mine as she took the pen, and the weight of it in her hand seemed to return some of her poise to her. She was again the woman I'd seen during the battle, the one who had led me down into the caves – fierce, stern, but somehow also kind and generous. If there was anyone who could navigate their way to a fair and equitable Council, it was her.

Dione's chair scraped as he stood up, took the pen from Ranami's proffered fingers and signed it as well.

I fanned the page to dry the ink. "We'll keep this copy here. But I'll ask Ikanuy to have some scribes copy it – one for each island – and then we'll send it out."

"So that's it then," Dione said. "The Sukai Dynasty is ended."

I gave him a long look. "You and I both know it ended before this."

He waved a hand. "I never cared about your parentage, not really. Back then you were still a symbol of what I hated, and I still needed to be the one to crush you."

Ranami gave me a questioning look.

"It's a long story, not one that I care to tell at the moment. Perhaps someday. Suffice to say, my father kept many secrets. Far too many."

"He was a complicated man," Ranami said, her tone neutral.

"*Complicated*, yes," Dione said. "But a tyrant nonetheless. And now he's dead. And so is Ragan. And so are many, many other people."

My mind turned to Jovis, as it had so often these past days – no matter how hard I tried to distract myself. At night, all I could think about was the feel of his skin against mine, the smile on his lips as he kissed me. I'd had him back for so *short* a time. Though I'd seen him about the palace, the courtyard and the city with Mephi, I hadn't dared approach him, my heart too fragile.

He'd started carrying his staff again, and had strapped the white-bladed sword to his side. It gave me hope, but then, hope had failed me before. It was agony to wait, but I'd promised him space. I'd promised him time. I would give it to him, no matter what it cost myself.

A knock sounded at the door. Before I could answer, Jovis peeked his head inside.

How very like him. My heart jumped in my chest, running away from me before I could catch and place it firmly in its place. It was far too late for that.

"Can I have a moment?" he said.

"We'd just finished," I said. I beckoned to Ikanuy in the hall beyond him. She slipped by and plucked the proclamation from my hands.

Dione looked from me, to Jovis, and then back to me again. "Any further business we have can be concluded later." He raised an eyebrow at Ranami. "You?"

"I need to get back to Phalue and Ayesh," she said. "And to make plans. There's a lot to be done before everyone receives the proclamations. It will take time for word to get out without witstone, but that's not time I want to waste."

They strode from the room and Jovis stood to the side to let them pass. When they'd left, he closed the door behind him with a soft *click*.

My heartbeat ricocheted against my ribs, threatening to gallop to the ends of the Empire. The last time we'd been alone—

I didn't let myself finish the thought. I couldn't think of that, couldn't think of the safety I'd felt in his arms, even on the eve of battle. The relief at having him back again. The hope I'd let grow that there could be something *more* once everything was said and done.

The setting sun caught his dark curls, settling into the freckles spotting his cheeks. "Lin—" He stopped, as though there were something odd about the feel of my name on his tongue. He took a step toward me. "I'm not who you thought I was."

A tight laugh escaped my lips before I could stop it. "You've said that to me so many times before." You. Jovis. The man I'd loved and lost once already.

Hope was a weed that grew wild and unchecked, choking out all other emotions.

He didn't smile. "That was before-Jovis who'd said that to you. I don't know what he was thinking because, Lin – that's not who I am anymore." His gaze found the floor. "Mephi has been telling me, but they sound like someone else's memories. They don't feel like mine, even if they are. I thought to leave in the middle of the night but I realized that would be cruel, given what I was to you before." And then the corners of his lips curved, ever so slightly. "Yes, Mephi told me about that too, and I think he delighted most in the embarrassing bits." The faint smile faded. "But I can't stay here, not with everyone waiting and *expecting* things from me. They all seem to know me better than myself. And that's not a comfortable place to be in. I have to go. I have to figure out who I am now, and I can't do that here – where everyone already seems to have that figured out for me."

Tearing hope up by the roots ripped a bit of my heart with it too. I firmed up my lip, lifting my chin. "I understand." I thought I was the only one who might. I'd woken up without any memory of myself either, living under the expectation I'd somehow remember a person I was meant to be.

I couldn't do that to Jovis, no matter how gently. Not to him.

He took the last few steps to me and then reached out and touched my cheek, his expression slightly lost, as though he were surprised by his own daring. "Mephi said that you would." His thumb wiped a tear that had fallen from my eye. I wished I could sear this moment in my memory, make it last for ever.

And then he leaned over and softly kissed my forehead. "Be well, Lin." That slight hitch on my name, as though he couldn't quite help himself. It wormed its way into the raw, broken pieces of my heart.

It was the last thing he said to me before I watched him disappear out my door.

61

Ranami

Imperial Island

The first thing Ranami did in her new role was to open the gates of the palace walls, and keep them open. The buildings and gardens belonged to the people of the city, she proclaimed. And besides that, people needed places to sleep and to live temporarily until they could rebuild the shattered remains of Imperial City.

The next was to invite likely candidates for the Council to Imperial. She'd had to rely on every network she had access to, gleaning names of those who were respected and well-liked in their communities, who didn't live in lofty palaces without a care for what happened to everyone else.

She smoothed the front of her turmeric-yellow dress as she stood in front of the palace, waiting for their final guests to appear. She'd caught a glimpse as they'd passed the gates, but people crowded the courtyard and all she could see of this final delegation was the tops of their heads. The candidates had arrived over a series of three days, and these were the last of them.

Phalue leaned over to whisper in her ear. "More fuel for the fire?"

She couldn't help the laughter that threatened to bubble up her throat. Only two days the previous delegates had been here and she could still hear their arguments ringing in her ears. Whether it was prudent to *completely* stop the mining and sale of witstone. How were they supposed to ensure that everyone had a chance to choose their leaders? And what if there were people who didn't want to choose or didn't care? Who would be in charge of the Imperial army? All of them?

Ranami rubbed reflexively at her forehead, feeling the headache that had been in the background surfacing again. "Sometimes, Phalue, you know *exactly* the wrong thing to say."

The woman only kissed her cheek. "But you very nearly laughed."

Ranami reached out, twining her fingers with her wife's. "Yes, well, it's a strange situation we find ourselves in. First, we reformed Nephilanu. Now, the entire Empire? I didn't think anything would happen this fast."

True, the entire process was an enormous headache, and she wasn't sure whether these people would agree on *anything*, but they quieted when she spoke, they listened to her and Phalue had proved surprisingly even-handed in bridging the gap between parties and getting them to understand one another.

Even if they didn't quite see eye to eye.

They'd get there eventually. She hoped. She lifted Phalue's hand to her mouth, slowly kissing the scarred back of it. "But in the end, there's no one I'd rather do this with."

A bit of heat lit in Phalue's gaze, her lips slightly parting as she tugged on Ranami's hand, bringing her in closer.

On Ranami's other side, Ayesh let out a sigh. "You should

stop kissing before they get here." Shark sat next to her, horns spiraling toward the sky.

"Fair enough," Phalue said, her eyes crinkling at the corners. Ah, Ranami could never get enough of that smile. She was sure, in the years to come, they'd be parted again as they both worked to make this Empire whole again. So for now, she would bask in the warmth of it, storing away these memories like baubles to be brought out and admired on special occasions.

Ranami tousled the girl's short hair. "But we'll only stop kissing if you agree to attend lessons later today. Books, Ayesh. Not fighting or Alanga magic."

The girl only frowned for a moment before nodding. Her stormy expression seemed more for show than anything else. "Fine." Something had changed in her that day Ragan had almost sunk Imperial. She wasn't exactly ...compliant, but Ranami wouldn't have wanted that anyway. She seemed less desperate, less eager to throw herself into conflict. She'd settled, like a house shifting on the sands, finally nestling into a spot against bedrock. Maybe it was that she no longer felt she had to prove herself. Maybe it had been something Jovis had said to her before he'd killed Ragan. Either way, Ranami knew Ayesh would tell her in time. She could be patient until the girl was ready.

Below, the crowd parted, and the delegation began to climb the steps to the palace. They were from a smaller isle, remote, in the far north-eastern reaches. But they didn't appear humble. There were four of them, all dressed finely, all tall, with straight, broad shoulders and the sort of set to their mouths that told Ranami that they each had a stubborn streak.

Yes. More fuel for the fire. Just as Phalue had predicted.

Phalue leaned over again as the delegates grew closer. "Should we adopt again? I think I'm ready."

Ranami shot her a look. She was asking this *now*? Phalue

always did have the most ridiculous timing. But she looked out at the city, still in disrepair but slowly rebuilding. The people here within the palace walls. The air filled with hope and change. And the three of them here, together. Would there ever be a better time to ask? She hoped so, but she could never know for sure.

Why not, then?

She squeezed her wife's hand. "Phalue, I would adopt a thousand orphans with you. To the depths of the Endless Sea and back again."

"Just the one — that's enough for now," she responded with a grin. "No need to drown yourself in the process."

The delegates climbed the last step and she placed her hand over her heart, greeting them, welcoming them to the palace that was now her home.

Beginning the process to change the world.

62

Sand

Hualin Or

There were some who recognized her. Only a very few. Lin had done good work, the scars and pockmarks marring her face and skin gone. She'd not replaced the two last fingers of her left hand, and Sand was grateful for that. It would have been easier to have the hand whole again, but some changes were too much, too quickly.

And when people did recognize her, it was because of her hand. Perhaps Lin had intended it that way.

She leaned over the hole she'd been digging, taking a moment to breathe. The old shovel she was using had been worn smooth on the handle and her sweat-slicked hand slid down it as she used it to support her weight.

Lozhi sniffed the hole, his snout now as large as the opening. He'd gone through another hibernation period, and had shed his horns, which he'd given to her. The new ones had already begun spiraling out from his forehead. "Almost deep enough," he said.

"Oh, it's deep enough. You're not an expert on everything, no matter what you might think, my friend."

His ears pricked, enormous gray eyes fixed on hers. "But I'm good at digging holes. You told me so."

"Yes, you're good at digging pointless holes for no good purpose." She turned, searching for someone with free hands. "Can I get some help with a post?"

A few people glanced her way, but quickly looked away again. Others just ignored her, continuing their work in the nearby field, or methodically sawing away at wood. Damn her reputation. As soon as one person recognized her, they inevitably told others. Lozhi's presence didn't help, but she'd never leave him behind. And somehow, being recognized felt like fitting penance for the things she'd done.

They didn't have to like her. They didn't have to forgive her.

The sinking of Riya had created an innumerable number of refugees, piled into ships and forced to find new places to live. One of the first things the new Council had done – though it had taken them long enough – had been to set the remaining nearby islands to building housing for the displaced.

Three bland meals, a place to lie her head at night and a pittance of coin were her physical rewards for this project. But each new home she helped to build felt like a small way of healing the wounds she'd created. Coral would have wanted to return to Maila. Coral would have wanted to live out their lives on that isle, relying only on one another. But the world was so much bigger than that, and Sand was realizing she wanted to be a part of it. Not to rule it or to destroy it, but to *live* in it.

Sighing, she went to the pile of posts. She could manage it alone with a good deal of effort.

Lozhi followed, and the other workers gave way, giving him wide berth. She wasn't sure if it was because he was an ossalen or because he had been *Ragan's* ossalen. Sand was sure people whispered stories about him, none of which were true. The creature had been forced to be Ragan's companion; he hadn't enjoyed it.

She gave him a rub around the itchy nubs of his newly growing horns before reaching down and taking hold of the post at the top of the pile. The thing was heavy and unwieldy, and it took several grunting heaves for her to get the end of it onto her shoulder. And then she began to drag it off the pile and toward the post-hole she'd dug.

Lozhi, to her surprise, reached down and seized the other end with his teeth.

"That can't be comfortable," she called back to him. He was big, his jaws much wider than they'd once been, but it would still be work to get his teeth into it. He'd have a sore mouth if he succeeded.

But the load did indeed lighten, and she wasn't about to tell him to stop.

The distance to the hole she'd dug, which had seemed interminable, now seemed manageable. "Thank you," she managed.

"You're welcome," Lozhi said, trotting next to her, his face smug.

She nearly dropped the post. She glanced over her shoulder, expecting to see someone there, taking up the load. Hoping for it.

Her heart dropped a little when she realized: there was no one there. No one had come to her aid.

Yet the post still felt lighter.

That was when she felt it — a hum in her bones, as though someone had struck a tuning fork and was holding it against her skull. It filled her with strength, the vibration carrying through the soles of her feet and into the ground beneath her. She could *feel* it. And she knew, if she brought her foot down, she could make the earth tremble.

It wasn't possible.

And yet—

"It's you?"

Lozhi pressed his big head into her cheek. "Yes."

"Dione said—"

"I do not know everything? Well, Dione does not know everything either."

She let the post fall, cupping Lozhi's face in her hands. Sand was crying, her face red and puffy, tears falling freely. She didn't care. The Alanga powers – those were trivial.

What mattered was that Lozhi was hers. And she was his.

To others she might be fearsome, a woman who had destroyed islands on her quest for the palace. For the throne.

To Lozhi she was the one who had taken him away from a violent master and had given him a second chance at life. And he had chosen *her*. Of all the people, he had decided that she was worthy.

Hope flickered to life in her chest. Maybe she could prove to him – and to herself – that it was true.

63

Lin

Thrana

Seasons passed, one into the other. Wet into dry, into wet, and then again into dry. Everything changed, but I supposed that was the nature of passing time. Mephi grew and so did Thrana. Sometimes I missed the feel of her fur against my cheek, the way her breath would rise and fall as we both slept, curled into one another like mother and child. But children grow into adults, and ossalen grow into islands.

I still had the memories.

The sun baked the sand beneath me, and I shifted the book on my lap into a more comfortable position. It was old, the pages nearly crumbling. I shouldn't have brought it into the sun. At the same time, I'd tired of working in caves beneath the palace, hiding my work as though it were something I should be ashamed of.

My shifting disturbed the little spy construct at my feet. It let out a grumpy-sounding sigh before resettling next to me and falling back asleep. This one had found Ragan's stash of books for me and I was fond of it. Every construct I'd made had pieces of Thrana in them, after all.

There were mentions in this book of one of the swords. They were still out there, and though the Alanga and the mortals had been living in peace for these last several seasons, there would always be those who would seek out weapons like these. Who would use them for terrible purposes. If I could not protect the people of the Empire as Emperor, then I could protect them as an Alanga – one of the most powerful still alive.

I'd asked the Council for help once. I let out an annoyed huff of breath as I turned another page, searching for mentions of the blade. The *Council*. Bloated, inefficient, slow-moving. I'd once made decisions that turned the direction of an Empire writ on just a single piece of paper. Signed and delivered, just so. Clean. Quick. Everything in the Council was put up for debate, argued over, chipped away at until everyone agreed but no one was happy.

But I also understood that my decisions hadn't always sat easily with the people they'd affected. And I'd not been one of them. They *needed* to be ruled by their own. The role of a government wasn't to be ruthlessly effective; it was to reduce suffering. And there was too much suffering for me to ever fully open my eyes to. To ever fully understand.

They would make mistakes. And that was not a terrible thing.

I clapped the book shut, easing my feet into the sand. I could take a moment's break.

You can take more than a moment, Thrana said in my mind.

I patted the sand as though that were her fur. She didn't often speak to me these days, her mind consumed with other matters, but I could feel the beat of her beneath my feet. *I'll rest easier once I find all these swords.* I'd thrown mine into the Endless Sea, watching the glinting light of its white surface until it faded into the black. It was where they all belonged. If there was one thing

Dione had been right about, it had been that the shards should never be made into weapons to be used against the very creatures they were taken from. It *was* an abomination. But they could be used for other things.

That was the other work I'd set myself to: the artifacts.

We all needed faster travel between the islands, even the Alanga. Dione had explained to me what Ylan had finally figured out. Shards could not be used on living mortals, but they could be used on the flesh of ossalen, the flesh of Alanga and the flesh of the dead.

"What do these three have in common?" I'd asked.

He'd shrugged. "Ylan was the one who figured out that last one, and before he wiped out my kind, some of us hypothesized that the Alanga become like the ossalen when we bond with them, and the flesh of the dead returns to the ossalen, becomes part of them. So they are, in a way, similar."

Whatever the reason, I'd set to studying what might be done with this magic. Ylan had created artifacts of the bones themselves, but Dione had admitted to me that shards could be used in stone carvings taken from islands that had not yet gone brittle. Whose Alanga were still alive.

So we'd quarried some stone from Khalute and I'd begun my experiments. There were so many possibilities in this stone. I suspected some had been ground into paint for the mural in Imperial Palace. There had to be a way to distribute this power more fairly. But the thing I focused on first was a way to travel quickly between the islands.

Six commands per artifact. One to bring up the wind, one to calm it, four to control the direction. And then, with Dione's help, I'd begun to convince other Alanga to give up some of their shards for these artifacts, to watch over their own and to keep them from using their power unwisely.

It wasn't perfect, this loose network that we had. Someone always threatened to fall through the cracks. But it was all we had. I'd removed Ragan's shards from every Alanga who'd been coerced by him. I wouldn't repeat his tactics. Not unless a line was crossed.

I blinked against the sun, my gaze on the waves. Something moved out of the corner of my eye.

When I turned my head, I thought for a moment that I was mistaken. Someone was walking up my beach – Thrana's beach. I'd not given anyone leave to settle here. Not yet. That would come, in time, but for now the citizens of the Empire knew I was to be left alone.

But the closer he grew, the more I knew he wasn't some sun-baked mirage.

I think my heart stopped.

But then it was beating again, loud in my ears, and I was on my feet, both my book and my construct forgotten.

It was Jovis, striding up the beach, a slightly sheepish look on his face – as though we'd only parted yesterday and it hadn't been seasons.

He didn't look any older than the last time I'd seen him. I wondered if I did.

My throat felt like I'd swallowed a mouthful of sand. I tried to swallow. "Did you remember?"

He gave me a lopsided sort of grimace and then shook his head. "Not in the way you're probably hoping for."

I felt the last shred of hope within me wither and die. The Jovis I'd known was gone – truly gone. "Don't – don't feel sorry for me," I said quickly. "It's been . . . a very long time."

"I didn't come here to feel sorry for you. I came here to ask a favor of you."

My heart jumped. Why did he still have to have the same

mannerisms, the same tilt to his head, the same pattern of freckles across his face?

He opened his mouth to speak again, closed it, pursed his lips. "I should show you," he muttered, more to himself than to me. He lifted a hand.

Water drifted from the Endless Sea, droplets drifting through the air, glittering in the air like jewels before coalescing into a ball above his palm.

I felt my brow furrow, my lips part. "How——?"

"I know," Jovis said. "Mephi said that I'd died, that the bond was broken. And it was. We traveled together for a long time just as friends. I went back to my mother and father, and let them know – for the second time –" He shook his head ruefully. "– that I was still alive. Oh, you should have seen it. Barely knew the sky from the sea and there's an old woman flensing the skin from my flesh with her words. It took me a long time to get my bearings, but they were patient with me. Didn't treat me like Jovis, but like a long-lost son who had lost all his memories. But when I asked, they told me.

"After that, it was down to the Monkey's Tail to see an old friend. Maybe it's part of who I was before, the sort who needed to poke at old wounds, but I wanted to know what Kaphra had done to me. I still needed to know that part of myself. Or, well, my old self."

He seemed to realize he was still holding the ball of water above his hand. He let it drop to the sand, where it left a quickly-fading damp spot.

"The point is, Lin –" And this time I knew for sure there was something different in the way he said my name. "– bonds *can* be reforged if two parties work toward it. If they want it. Broken things can be pieced back together."

He took a step toward me, his lanky presence at once odd and familiar. "I found that I had a few memories left, and I worked to piece them together in that time between dreaming and waking. And in one of them, I was with you, and I was happy but also sad – because I was leaving you. I've had this dream, over and over, of promising you I'd come back. Of promising you I'd return. And every time I woke, all I wanted was to go back into that dream, because there was a moment where I knew exactly who I was and what I wanted.

"I wanted you. I think . . .I still might. But I need to get to know you over again, from the beginning. It's a lot to ask – of anyone. As you said, it's been a long time."

He was babbling, covering my silence with words. How very, very Jovis.

I reached out while he was still speaking and took his hand. "I woke with no memories once, and no one gave me the chance to discover what that meant for myself. I wouldn't do the same to you. But if this is what you want, I can help you. There are so many things I need to do for this Empire, for its people. But this – this I want to do for you. For myself."

The grin that split his face was the same one I remembered, the feel of his palm against mine the most natural thing in the world. It would be different, yes, but all things changed with the passing of the seasons. I felt his fingers curl around mine – hesitant, and then stronger.

And for the first time in a very long time, I felt whole.

ACKNOWLEDGEMENTS

WHAT. I wrote an entire TRILOGY. That's three books – two more than I thought I'd get to write in this world. When you're trying to get a debut book published, conventional wisdom says to write something new while you wait, because if your would-be debut dies on submission, any work you do on subsequent books will never see the light of day. So it feels like an enormous privilege to get to share the end of this story with you.

That said, in my embarrassingly long journey to publication, I'd written a lot of first books in a series, and not so many second or third ones (okay, zero third ones). This last book was a struggle and I couldn't have done it without a lot of help.

I was pregnant and we had a toddler during the writing of this, so my husband, John, who was already an amazing dad and subsequently vaulted into super-dad status, deserves a lot of credit. Thank you for fielding our excessively energetic daredevil toddler, and somehow also keeping her alive and without serious injury. And thank you for cooking all those dinners!

Thank you to my family, who are always encouraging me and offering to help. I am so, so lucky to have grown up with you.

To my editors, James Long and Brit Hvide, I appreciate your patience as I wrote the book, deleted the book, wrote the first third, deleted that, and then finally got it right on the last try.

It's been absolutely lovely working with both of you! To my copy-editor, Joanna Kramer – I swear I will stop using commas excessively. Someday. Thank you for being so thorough!

Many thanks also to my agent, Juliet Mushens, who believed in this series far before I ever did. Your support and enthusiasm are invaluable!

I will always be grateful to Lauren Panepinto and Sasha Vinogradova, the cover designer and cover artist for these books. Also Charis Loke, who created the map. Your work is just incredible, and I would never have had as many people picking up my books without it.

To everyone at Orbit who has had a hand in bringing these books to life and promoting them – thank you so, so much. You will never know how much this has meant to me.

I owe an enormous debt of gratitude to Tina Smith/Gower, Marina Lostetter, and Megan O'Keefe for jumping on a call with me after my second aborted attempt to write this book. Your suggestions and feedback finally got me on the right path and helped me to figure out what exactly in my plot was broken.

Thank you to my readers, who have made this entire endeavor possible in the first place. May you always encounter favorable winds and clear skies, and may you always have someone in your life who loves you as much as Mephi does Jovis.

And to my cats – thanks for nothing, you adorable ingrates.

About the author

Andrea Stewart is the Chinese American daughter of immigrants, and was raised in a number of places across the United States. When her (admittedly ambitious) dreams of becoming a dragon slayer didn't pan out, she instead turned to writing books. She now lives in sunny California.

Find out more about Andrea Stewart and other Orbit authors by registering for the free monthly newsletter at orbitbooks.net.